THE MANIFOLD DESTINY
OF EDDIE VEGAS

THE MANIFOLD DESTINY OF EDDIE VEGAS

BY

RICK HARSCH

ZEROGRAM
PRESS

Los Angeles, 2022

ZEROGRAM PRESS
1147 El Medio Ave.
Pacific Palisades, CA 90272
EMAIL: info@zerogrampress.com
WEBSITE: www.zerogrampress.com

Distributed by Small Press United / Independent Publishers Group
(800) 888-4741 / www.ipgbook.com

First Zerogram Press Edition 2022
Copyright © 2020 by Rick Harsch
Originally published in 2020 by corona/samizdat (Izola, Slovenia)
All rights reserved

Book design by Darinka Knapic

PUBLISHER'S CATALOGING-IN-PUBLICATION DATA

Names: Harsch, Rick, 1959- author.
Title: The manifold destiny of Eddie Vegas / Rick Harsch.
Description: First Zerogram Press edition. | Pacific Palisades, CA : Zerogram
    Press, 2022. | Originally published: Izola, Slovenia : corona/samizdat, 2020.
Identifiers: ISBN 9781953409072 (paperback)
Subjects: LCSH: Young men–United States–Fiction. | Political corruption–
    United States–Fiction. | Mafia–United States–Fiction. | Families–United
    States–History–Fiction. | Violence–United States–History–Fiction. |
    LCGFT: Historical fiction.
Classification: LCC PS3558.A67557 M36 2022 | DDC 813/.54–dc23

Printed in the United States of America

For Trent and Todd, and to Darinka,
whose dedication deserves a dedication

"If you'd permit me the luxury of seeing people falling in the street, dropping like locusts."

—THE ASTROLOGER, FROM ROBERTO
Arlt's *The Flamethrowers*

Table of Contents

1

FUCKING KENO

[Hole card: five of hearts]

He had been away from the States a mere four months and still the first cliché upon landing came as a gutsucking culture shock left hook beneath his guard, catching the sharp point of his lowest rib on the left side.

"If you don't like the heat, don't come to Los Angeles in the summer."

La nausée.

If you don't like clichés, don't return to the US. Seasons need not pertain.

And right outside the baggage claim, one step into the air, fresh fucking Mediterranean climate air, before his first cigarette in 19 years that seemed like 17 hours or vice versa, emphasis on versa.

Then it was Vegas. Not even a week later. The cab driver kept his mouth shut, spending seven minutes ripping across thoughts to the strip, where the welcome drive of the Luxor yielded seasonal palms and shockingly familiar terracotta Egyptiana.

The room was waiting. What else could a room do?

Eddie tossed his suitcase on the bed, sucked a vodka from the mini-bar, drank it in a fluidity of gesture derived from 19 years of not giving a shit for externae.

Then he walked to the World's Biggest Gift Shop at the far end of the strip, bought a deck of cards, some dice, and

a Vegas shirt with such paraphernalia scattered in a deci-
pherable yet black background design and walked back to
the hotel, where he plucked a vodka from the minibar and
drank it with a fluidity suggesting a smooth cool desert generated drink, before trying on the shirt, looking at the mirror
where he noticed himself, and pronouncing out of the muck
of mutter, "Fucking keno," with disgust.

2

FUCKING KENO

[Hole card: three of clubs]

Fucking kid was right about everything but one — he was dead fucking wrong the way he blamed Gravel. Gravel's fault? Sure, but had he not just blamed him, had he hit him in the head with something like a fresh tempered axe, it would have all been okay.

But no.

And there he was. Vegas.

Vegas and the clichés. First thing even before he picked his room, stepping into the fine feathers of the desert air outside the motel some shitbird in a Hawaiian shirt and the grease sweat of a bad eater was slinging the lowdown:

"If you don't like the heat, don't come to Vegas in the summer."

Worst of all, he said it with a lilt rising at the end, like a pimply ice skater coming to the beaten down beatific halt on the toes of the skates before the Rachmaninoff was ready to recede. Nobody's dreams were on the line.

Already in his distressed kidskin, tegu lizard inlay boots. Gravel was Eddie Vegas's reaction. And he didn't even have a gun.

Round up the goats and what? Imagine play waltzes.

Over and over again waltzes. Not the same one, but the same one seventeen times in a row and then cross them up with something heavy on the horn. Ship the lizards from some German in Paraguay, where it doesn't matter if they're legal or not. Stroessner goats. No doubt it could not be stranger than that. And somewhere between Nogales and Cuernavaca, Peedro is teaching his son the same trade. The easy part is keeping your mouth shut for years at a time.

The motel he had finally pulled into after going vacant of mind and cruising in enclosed geometries for a half or few hours was called The Electra Glide, no mention of gambling whores or wifery.

He slid his suitcase onto the narrow bed, slept the dark out, and went down to the front desk to ask after the nearest bar and the World's Biggest Gift Shop.

"Bar's out back, faces the parallel street. Gift shop even easier: That corner and the next, make a right and you're there."

You're there was seven city blocks in 107 degrees.

Gravel bought a Vegas shirt: he liked the black background.

The beer was well-deserved, but the heat had reduced his one need to a fucking Corona, with lemon inside and on the side. He stared at the shank while he ordered, he stared at the shank while he waited, and he stared at the shank while he slowly squeezed the lemon, that spurted nonetheless, into his glass, just two bucks for about a .33 glass. As he guzzled like a fucking cowboy he caught himself in the slant of light that made him electric in the mirror. Keno cards.

"Fucking keno," he said aloud.

3

THE HAND MADE VISIBLE

[East coast, whorey university town]

Donnie [Hole cards: five of diamonds, five of clubs] ten of spades
Drake [Hole cards: ace of diamonds, king of diamonds] five of diamonds

Others, high card showing: ace of spades. Bet: $15. Called all around.
Next card:

Donnie: five of spades
Drake: king of clubs

Others, high hand showing: ace of spades, ace of clubs, six of spades

Bets: $15 called by Drake, raised $5 by Donnie, called by double aces and Drake, others dropped.

Fifth card:

Donnie: king of spades
Drake: ace of hearts
Big hand: seven of hearts

Bh bets: $15, Donnie raises after Drake calls, Bh tosses in five, a look on his face as if yet again, yet again, a hedgehog had dashed across the table without upsetting the peanuts those who dropped are fracking at, their hands coon hands.

Sixth card:

Donnie: five of hearts
Drake: ten of diamonds
Bh: "Deuce, fucking deuce! Deuce of shit, deuce of my fucking asshole, deuce of the fucking Margrave of Malzovia, deuces of the long knives. Deuce deuce and deuce fucking attorneys at law. Deuces don't even have a suit, deuces don't fucking, deuces fucking, deuces are my balls, this fucking hand is a fucking scrotum…fuck it, I'm out."

Drake: "Guess it's my bet. Fifteen. You raise five… Enough of that shit. We start with $25."
"Raise five."
"Fuck?"
"Fuck? Raise five?"
"Raise five."
"Raise…Fuck you: raise twenty-five."
"Twenty limit."
"Right, forgot. Twe-"
"Sallright: twenty-five and five."
"Okay, so what's the limit now, smartass? Who let this fuck in the game?"
"You did."
"I know. Fine. Twenty-five limit. So there goes another trust fund. No fucking transmission of disease. They call it a disease, but ask anybody at this table, you rather have gonor-rhea or an empty bank account…Twenty-five."
"Raise five."
"Fuck you: twenty-five."
"Raise five."

"Twenty-five."
"Raise twenty-five."
"Call…fuck, did I say call?"

"Unfortunately."

"Let me bet once more? No limit?"

"Long as I can cover it."

"Hundred?"

"Covered. Call."

They could have been brothers, which is obviously not true. But if they were, Drake, who was older, would have been the older of the two. Donnie moved to deal the seventh card, Drake held up a halting hand, and Donnie set the deck on the table.

"Back and forth, back and forth. Inutile. Futile. I hate and I love it. Repetition, I mean. I have an…what is it, doll, ambiguous?"

"Ambivalent."

Doll: draped on Drake, knockneed riding his knee attending to his needs, loose slip, undie flashes, tightlipped, breast flips, bored hair sweeps, a real goatgetter.

"I have an ambivalent relationship with repetition, redundancy. Listen, kid. Whud you say your name was?"

"Is."

"Is?"

"It's redundant. Same again and again."

"Then say it three times so I can remember it."

"Donnie."

"Fine. I'll do it. Listen, Donnie Donnie Donnie, I got no problem with yesterday today tomorrow, even next day, day after. I got no problem with a three second shot of a head shot over and over and over ad infinitum if only that were possible. But when clear reason is cut by again and again, I get nausea. I got nausea now. You bet like you want me to stay in, to stay in and keep raising, as if I were bluffing and you knew it, even though by now you must know I'm not bluffing at all. So you think you have me beat…and I respect that…I might even respect you, even though I don't know you…But more to the point is that you don't know me, and therefore could not possibly know how nauseating your behavior is to me; so I'm going to tell you, tell you why this kind of thing is nauseating, and how despite the fact that such is rather cliché it has to do with an incident in my childhood, an instance involving my father, the kind of thing I would hope you have in your history—not that I wish you ill, just to say I believe it's cliché because it is universal, a fact of human nature, human and only human, though in this instance you could, and you would be right to, call it inhuman or not humane. Even if, yes it is actually, common—*in its way*—unique as it may be. Repetition. I repeat an old story, a story about repetition. Oh yes, it is, you will tell me it is, perverse. A boy, young, a young boy, maybe five years old, catches his first frog, I caught my first frog. And I had to have it, right? Leopard frog. We were up at Big Bear, not so far, a weekend trip from LA or wherever we lived around thereabouts. And I caught a frog, leopard frog, put it in my pocket, kept it with me when we went into the cabin to eat, and I forgot about it long enough, a few seconds really, because I was *thinking* about it, *intensely*. It hopped, it squeezed out of my pocket and then I snapped back to it, but then it hopped onto the table and my old man, a rough customer you might say, was about to bring a metal spoon down on it and I screamed—*screamed*—NO! And he caught it and there was a scene, me crying and him trying to get past my ma to fling it out the door, and jokes about eating its legs: not that it was a bullfrog, as I said, though leopard frogs can get big enough, and anyway if enough were cooked…So you see right where this is going. I get to keep it, and the next day I find a large box and perfect the technique of catching them—usually in the water, if not facing them and getting them after they angle on the hop away, confused. But usually in the water, jumping in and making back for the bank, and before anyone knew it I must have had fifty and one equals fifty in the mind of a little boy and I cried again when the old man said no, I couldn't keep them all. And here's the cruel part: he knows how the story will go, all of it from saying eventually yes to what I'm getting at, this problem with repetition. You know the line: fine, but you have to take care of them. We have to buy an aqua-terrarium and you have to catch insects, just grasshoppers will probably do, you have to feed them, you have to take responsibility for them.

I'll say yes, Mandrake, but they are now your responsibility. Well it's southern California so we all play baseball, and in fact I'm not a bad player, and the old man was already teaching me, playing catch with me every day when he wasn't gone and instructing me to throw against the cinder block backyard wall when he was. Meaning there was a quality Louisville Slugger in the house, probably half a dozen of them. But I bring that up, the baseball bat, prematurely, but by no means randomly, the fact of the bat, because you know, you know I am not going to walk a half hour to a vacant lot and catch grasshoppers every week. I did though, I really did, at least twice. And when you consider that by the time the old man brought the frogs up again, literally, they were down in the basement when he brought them up, I had forgotten they existed, so in fact I took quite good care of them while they were in my orbit so to speak. He set the thing right on the kitchen table and the situation was bad, couldn't have been any worse coming upon Auschwitz, being that the dead weren't what you'd see. Though one *was* dead. He held it about an inch from my nose and said see Mandrake, *that's* what they'd all be like if I left you responsible. *That's* why parents say no. Now I'm going to tell you why we say yes. If memory serves me right he already had the baseball bat in his hand and he cradled the, to me at the time, giant terrarium with his other arm, said, follow me, and led the way out the screen door to the backyard. He sets the thing on the ground, steps back a couple paces, bat on the shoulder, and says throw me that dead one here. Now I'm confused. I mean it's clear he means pitch it, toss it so's he can swing at it. But where is the dead one? I never saw him put it back in. Maybe only a second went by, then he goes, Oh, wait a minute, I got it right here. And he pulls it from his pocket, a frog about the size of my hand at the time. He tosses it and *splat!*, over the back fence. Now I'm relieved. We got that over with. Now I just have to go catch grasshoppers, right? Wrong. A kid your age, you see Drake, a kid your age could end up being anything. As you know my first choice for you is baseball pitcher. And you're off to a good start. Another is, let's say zookeeper. Not off to a good start. But you could still be one. But right here in the here and now we need to make the best of a bad situation, which I think calls for encouraging your strength, which is, as I suggested, pitching. Okay, I'm your batter. Reach in and get me a live frog. It's harder to hit a moving pitch—I like the challenge. I was frozen, wide-eyed. I'll tell you again and you will obey or you will eat the next frog out of that death chamber. I got it. Now I really got it. I reached in, grabbed one by the leg, tossed it a bit low, and the old man golfed the fucker way high and out of the yard into the kitty-corner yard, probably to their door step. You learn a lot about life from shit like that: it was gorgeous, of course, prodigious, and the horror quite specifically manifest in the way the frog stiffened in death even before it reached its apex. You could actually see that. Went stiff, kept the same arc it started on but sort of... you know, like cart- wheeling almost. I think I remember hearing it hit, which meant the cement stoop outside the neighbor's door. I can't say what state I was in at this point, but then the old man called for another, and then I knew, I knew him, and I knew we were going to go through the whole fucking squadron. And we did. And I was careful to pitch them all within range of his bat, one after the other, frog after frog, splat after splat. Can you begin to imagine how long that took if it was really fifty frogs, which is quite close to what it was. He took his time, watching each and every one to the end, the shrugging of his shoulders, adjusting his stance, like a real batter preparing for the next pitch. I'd have to say an average of half a minute per frog, which means more than twenty-five minutes, because they weren't all home runs. A few, a very few, were grounders or short low liners. A grounder he'd walk up to it, move it with his toe. Watch its state of death. One especially vicious liner hit near the top of the back wall and stuck, just stuck, but it was one of the bigger ones and had some lure for gravity, and it was maybe five or ten seconds before slowly, smearing like a paintbrush, swathing down. And of *course* there was gore, I remember the waves of simultaneous thought: a string of guts or something stuck to the old man's nose and fuck if I didn't know it would have been funny under different circumstances but currently *was not*, yet I was afraid that even though I didn't feel the least like laughing its very being funny was a laugh and I would get a batsmack to the calves. At some point, of course I wanted to cry, but he warned me that if I did I would eat the rest of the frogs. It was easy not to cry, for despite the slaughter and the never-ending nature of the event, I knew something of relatively rare significance was occurring. I don't remember getting blood or guts on me, but as we got near the end the bat was smeared, his face was smeared—though his expression was unchanged, he didn't get all demonic like you might think people do when they work through a situation with blood on their faces and aren't about to wipe it off because they aren't done with whatever it is they're up to. So it went. On and on. Until the last frog. And this is where divine fatherhood comes in. He couldn't have done it better. The last one was smaller than average, and he really ripped into it, and we both watched and saw nothing and realized at the same time that the fucking thing stuck—*stuck!*—to the bat. Would ya look at that, he said in wonderment, and he started laughing, showing it to me, the flattened frog stuck splayed to the bat belly outward, and I started to laugh. And he said, I'm glad you think that's funny, son, because otherwise you might have to think about how it was your irresponsibility that led to the suffering and eventual death of all these live beings. He dropped the bat, said, clean up the yard, and went inside and it was never spoken of again."

A silence grew like an embarrassment of an appendage from Drake's story, bristling with sharp hairs, and bubbling with warts, until Donnie spoke.

"You want me to tell you about my pappy or should we get on with the hand?"

"Well, I couldn't help but notice you were taking notes…"

"Nothing important."

"No, if you have something to say or ask…"

"All right. I liked 'swathy,' couldn't think of a better word there."

"Thanks. I like it, too: swathy."

"But I couldn't help but wonder about your father's dialogue. You seem to have it down too pat."

"Probably a combination of telling the story fifty times and living with him for seventeen years."

"Oh. I thought you would fall back on it being the truth."

"Maybe even word for word. He did take on a simple role."

"Right."

"Anything else?"

"Just the cards."

Donnie dealt:

Drake: king of hearts
Donnie: ten of clubs

"All right, kid. I think we've established that we aren't going to stand for anymore of this raise five shit. How much you got left?"

Donnie pulled a twenty, a ten, a five, and two ones from his right front pants pocket. His wallet, they both knew, was empty.

"Thirty-seven."

"Here's the deal. I hate sons a bitches who buy hands. I got plenty more than that left and it is my right to bet it—"

"But Drake, didn't we—"

"Shut up. What he was going to say is didn't we put a hundred limit on the game. Well that was before you turned up, so I figure it doesn't bind you or myself as related to you, leaving us with a nebulous circumstance. And normally, what with all the money in the pot, I would just bet what you have; but, see, I really fucking hate people trying to buy the pot, which is what you've been doing. You've obviously played before, know what you're doing, been winning pretty much since you sat down. But you took it a step too far. You've been getting good enough cards, maybe one hand you can just fold with the crap you're dealt. But no, with our losings, you try to bulldoze us right off the table with my least favorite bluff—I call it the accumulator. You have such a great fucking hand you want to keep us in with restrained raises. We know you got a great hand. Psychologically you got us by the nuts— we've been losing so regular to you that our first instinct is flight when you bet and raise. You got two aces up off and running—got him thinking even three aces can't beat you. Raise five, raise five, raise—"

"Why don't you cut the shit and make your bet. If you want to buy the pot buy it. I'm just a first-year student in a university spending a Friday night."

"You got money in the bank?"

"Probably less than most."

"You got a card, a bank card?"

Donnie kept quiet.

"What if I ease off a bit and just bet five hundred?"

"Call."

"We go get the money now?"

"I'm not leaving this room until the hand is settled."

"You swear you can cover it?"

"I can cover it."

Drake stood, pressing the woman to him so she wouldn't topple before getting her hooves right on the floor, walked to an enormous oaken desk, opened a drawer, pulled out a wad of hundreds, and peeled off five.

Sitting back down, he gestured for the woman to restore herself in her place.

"No need to get dramatic. Pot's light five hundred, to be collected immediately after the cards are shown."

"Unless I win."

"You want to raise?"

"Couldn't stand another childhood story."

"Fine."

Drake turned up his full house, looking straight at Donnie's face. Donnie looked down at the table, where he turned over his four fives.

The pot was about a thousand more than what Donnie had put into it.

4

OLD EPHRAIM

The mechanism that relayed the visual majesty of a still panorama of mountain and valley, river and tree line, snow and sun, shadows unseen yet known and darkness invisible where life ate life and thought not, or where desert yielded scrub cactus and range, the living seen still or as the disappearance following on rapid bursts of movement, what relayed these for indescribable sensory bloom inside a man as majesty, this is what Tom Garvin sought with his meditations and was awarded for delineating fecklessly in prose poems.

Garvin's specific and private precocity had always been intuiting and then knowing absolutely from his age of reason onwards that no single thought he managed to stitch independently was original to himself. His misfortune was that this awareness defeated all ability to derive pleasure from anything he wrote or material benefit from what he wrote that won him praise and easy employment. He wondered whether this insight or curse somehow was passed down to him as knowing an ancient landscape that relentlessly imposed its brute determinism on men, and knew that only bones remained of the others who had wondered the same.

Garvin knew and could never know that such a still, majestic landscape, witnessed by eagle, falcon, buzzard, hawk, and owl with like indifference removed by distance of time the sight of Old Ephraim near the Salmon River in what Garvin would know as southwestern Idaho awakening in early April back when mountain men outnumbered the traders they enriched, surviving in large part by knowing the natives and learning their techniques for survival, oblivious of the cataclysm they introduced and therefore largely under the delusion that they, also, were natives and so what came after was accretion of betrayal.

In some ways bears are like people; for instance, when they awaken some do so with a spark to immediate clarity of mind and sense, energy and high spirits, while others stumble about groggy for varying gropes of time. Old Ephraim, this particular Old Ephraim, was among the latter. In mid-April he woke, lay still for some hours before, moved by instinct, he rolled from his crevasse where the curve of erosion met the sharp of tectonic thrust onto the open verandah of the horizontal rock ledge, rolled further before his mind could strain for consequential thought, fell fifteen feet to a slope and rolled, tearing through saplings where a few years before a fire had briefly blown in geometrical spectacle burning a line of trees near where the slant of earth gave way to more monumental stone. His tumble was not unlike that of a funnel cloud's in its distinct resultant path to where he slowed and finally thudded against the trunk of a stout, high pine with yet enough force to bring heaps of snow down upon his head and the ground around. And there he sat and remained sitting—one could easily imagine him pulling a bottle of whiskey from a pocket in his dense coat with the muted glee of a boozer upon yet further survival of dumb luck. He had yet to feel hunger, and what pain from scratches and the concuss caused by the impact against the tree he was oblivious to. In fact, come late September he might choose to hibernate in the same crevasse should he find himself still in the area for all the comedy mattered to him.

If nothing else, it can be assumed that in the attenuate coming to senses his hunger was a relief if compared to the frenzy of the previous year's berry barren autumn hyperphagia. More than likely the hunger grew in stride with his mind, for he remained seated, back against the tree, to nap several hours, waking again to find night had blackened the scarcely recalled day. So he sat against the tree like a tavern regular undisturbed at his barstool hearing or not a soft humane Let

yourself out, Cyrus. Thus Old Ephraim slowly rose barely
ahead of the pace of the sun, instinct stumbling him generally downward and toward water. The biological and zoologi-
cal sciences have yet to yield definitive conclusions regarding
the legendary poor eyesight of bears after decades of study,
daring but to aver that they probably see somewhat better
than was previously thought. This is probably true, the previous native wisdom having been derived from the particular
indifference displayed by large, sated predators. Bears are not
much concerned with activities of live creatures within their
near vicinities (I refrain here from discussing mother bear
and her cubs) when hunger is not at issue — in fact, it is not
uncommon for a tired bear to drop to his side and sleep at
will, day or night, on trail, in grass tall or short, in woods or
on the plain.

By the time Old Ephraim's senses had focused on food he
had arrived to the bank of the middle fork of the Salmon River between the confluence with Big Creek and the Salmon
itself. The water was spring high overflowing grassy banks, a
good place for stranded fish to flop and flounder in blind-like
effort to re-immerse. So Old Ephraim slow-loped the riverine
for two or three miles, the focus and modest effort inducing
a more live quotidian hunger by the time he reached a slow
narrow feeder stream, barely fifteen feet across and so shallow
that rock rose humped high and dry and jagged and dry. Here
at this confluence, Old Ephraim stood erect on his hind feet,
stretching slowly to his full height of almost precisely thirteen
feet from pawsole to furred headcrown. Herenow the sun lit
his fur, the color of dry wheat, but for a split stripe of black,
a band down the center from head to something like a waist,
where it spread like the wings of a mythic bird to blacken his
ass and haunches. Old Ephraim's territory was harsh to mankind and thus he had been spied by human eyes but once,
just a few miles from where he now stood, nearer the Salmon, by a lucky mountain man name of Jenkins, who spread
the too oft disbelieved for legend word of the bear he called
Old Black Ass from camp to camp, trading post to trading
post: "I's a maybe a unner foot up hills down air win en I took

me a good long gander to pooter in me skulls afor I sneak away like air bobbercat quiet so to memmer nere come backen this are win two hunner mile." Only the size he claimed for Old Ephraim was subject to disbelief, and when called for by whiskey mockery, for Jenkins rightly "reckoner be thirteen foot ifn she stand, wich I yen no cline to wait fer." The listener was rare who had not seen a large grizzly himself, say an eight to ten-footer standing, so Jenkins was simply categorized a tall tale teller and generally let be to speak.

As he stood looking down, Old Ephraim saw the vague outline or the perfect detail of a two-foot fish flange off from the river into the calm of the stream and begin a slow advance, as if in the relief of an unanticipated safety evident upstream. The bear followed, first along similarly grassy banks, but soon enough into the waterwind through forest, until the stream had narrowed to a bare nine feet, where at a sharp bend the water both raced and pooled, the pool a still depth aloof the rush of stream. And precisely here Old Ephraim found his feast of fish: trout, salmon, carp, cat, and, to begin with, the fish he had followed, stabbing the shovel-nosed sturgeon as it hesitated between stones, fins out flanked to either side, wherefrom it was veritably torn from life, impaled by scimitars of bone, the claws raking in sudden strike, fierce as the surreal thrust of a viper, the fish to his maw before Jenkins could have dropped his jaw had he been there.

Had he been there, Jenkins would have learned a thing or two about the food chain. For Old Ephraim, having found something like a perpetual food source, remained within about 100 yards of his feed pool. There were berries, wild strawberries, cherries, something like an apple tree even, but these would be bearing beginning in July. For now it was a bounty of fish, water and, as it so happened, no niggling parasites. Two otters regularly balleted in the stream, sometimes making a meal of the smaller fish in the pool, as did raccoons, a large family of them, sometimes as many as seventeen moving in a good few hours after Old Ephraim moved off. Other animals—deer, elk, skunk, muskrat, even an odd pod of buffalo—dropped by or passed on or both, but no movement outside of his own did Old Ephraim intake with interest. An observation of his life those days would make a man ponder on the nature of human pursuit, for if that ain't what's called living, nothing so pleasing has grace of life; but one would be remiss not to think on Old Ephraim's satisfaction, physically evident yet as part of the natural scene itself perhaps not of access to the slanted rays of morning sun on the rippling stream, the gliding loops of the otters in the aflow, the delicacy of a raccoon's dining upon a trout, holding the flopper astab yet no more hurried in his repast than a vulture at yon morning's slaughterfield. What indeed did Ephraim make of the geometries of scarp, tree and endless space, asymmetries of slope, boulder, forest, illusion of order, illusion of nothingness, illusion of eternal content?

The cynic surely would grant this state paradisiacal, for soon its fall was arranged, born on an imprecise wind that didn't so much as rustle the leaves of the tree under which Old Ephraim had just awoken. A turbid odor, a death odor, a new odor, rank hide, matted unembodied fur, unnatural—chemical—emanations, aswirl in a scarce wind, katabatic, live and bare as a raven-picked bone, an ant-swarmed bone, dry and pregnant with intrusion; he looked over his shoulder, sniffed, his swollen damp nostrils contracting and expanding like valves freshly torn from within a body in a blind seek. Noises compounded: a rain drop and more drops, and then rain, but a foot step and then more footsteps, and the harsh physicality of human voices, a phenomenon without rhythm or sense. Old Ephraim was fifty yards up hill from the stream that the three men were walking astride.

Not hide nor hare:

Ripen and rot ripen and rot these two feet are all you got n if uncle Bob were here I curse your unborn may they be rabid badgers nibbling your rotting edges fierce fitzpacker ripen and rot uncle Bob and circulatory issues one dead doctor and that joke those jokes I got circulatory issues he says and I says tell me what's really wrong with me and he gets nervy and high talkin and circulatory issues you don't like it and I interrupt and says circulatory issues are them what keeps

moving around so you can't ketch em and I said your telling
me get a second opinion, well I'll tell you what to say, I said
doctor give me a second opinion, and here he gets nasty and
I took him by the throat and said when I ask you one last time
fer a second opinion you say, all right you smell bad too, and
I shakes him til he says all right you smell bad too and I put
a stop to his issues of circulation by squeezing his throat to
the cy-cumfrance of a raccoon's pinkie, ripen rot stop not,
foot rot til one day fitzpacker gets a snoot full a uncle bob
who shoulda comed with me but some folk got their furrows
dug and uncle bob had the two rivers said maybe we meet if
ye takes the overland back er a whale boat puts to in norlins
whin I's there, not that he figgered my idea fer a dead muskrat, no, he liked it, said I was the only smartn in the fambly
though I think it took only the sense of thinkin alone, cause
ya got yer couple a rich and million poor and why, cause
of failure but ifn you could make failure succeed you could
be a failure and a rich man or at least get yerself in clean
clothes on a bit a land lightning clarity claires kinby, o but
I see I know in the ripenenrot a blandness will erupt or the
Earth like an tempted sunrise and all white peeples ill long
fer nation-states and fierce, bibly no meanin battles which in
millions rush headlong to their sudden, caint be splained and
terrfying deaths o fuck I'm not right in the head no more...
no more of the ripe, the rot, the whatnot shitplot I summon
Uncle Robert Robitaille from his bungboat polacre Missouri
misry through my fancy fungals O Robert deliver me from
this Fitzpacker most foul fartsack smite—

THWACK! Fracked the fist of Fitzpacker backhand fast
against the fraught face of Hector Robitaille (surely that'll
bring a nearby bruin to bear!).

"Gyup, ya shatpup! Ain it yar graynmoodah gone fixn yar
ets issut?" THWAKK! "Gyon witya sloosecrappin bunghowsin
shatpup!", which though colorfully delivered lingo-wise was
yet delivered with restraint of homicidal, for, and only for, he
needed the body of the man sound enough to pull what he
called a tran-sumddie, a triangular, makeshift wooden drag-
sled of white man make from Injun design which would soon

be laden with inanimate, nay, hollow, beaver, and the soon meaning the better to be on the return through tribes of fisheaters and rootgrubbers, before the Blackfoot traipsed widely afield of winter's hydie hide to make menace upon what white men could be captured and slaughtered, robbed and rapined, and, for the sport of it merely, what rootgrubbers and fisheaters could be caught in small defenseless groups and tortured, raped and slapped about.

Robitaille duly dressed rapidly amongst the needless funs of further gruff kicks that served only to delay the departure from the camp, observed with fatalistic remove by the third hidebound human, mountain man extraordinaire Jeffers Phoebles, who reckoned little but what he deemed of pragmatic import, such as that one or two days grueling final stomp would bring them to the cache of beaver the winter come sudden and final to force his secreting down the Salmon and two hours up an unmapped tributary and the appearance of a bear of a height greater than most pines hereabouts, standing still yet peering with what could be taken for intense interest at Fitzpacker and Robitaille from the distance of one thin and shallow stream.

Battering about Robitaille being more avocational, habitual, not to say, certainly not, needless or arbitrary, Fitzpacker's peripherals were alert enough to take in the dark tree a mere seven feet distant registering its density of pine needle and anon the imposition of it where once it weren't, such that in due time, time enough, he looked up to see Black Ass, taking in stomach, chest, legs, chest, head, yet failing to pause long enough to attempt deciphering the gaze of the bear, or bar, as he would later call it in the telling ad infinitum when he would bear-beat his chest to emphasize his clarity of thought as he whispered to Phoebles "Grab his gun," meaning Robitaille's, slowly now—yet forgetting his most noble original wordthoughts to the effect of "what doomriding banjaxery be this?"—and the bear cocked its head an inch or two leftward, away from Phoebles, who obeyed with cunning, "Transumddie," Fitzpacker ordering/Phoebles obeying, Robitaille by now on hands and knees looking up at the bear, taking in the bear, wondering at the bear, his physiology a husk and there a bear, "Nah slewly tie the foodstuffs, jist slewly take yer start in whin ah siz git we git, jist whisper git it," "git it," and quicker than a gentleman can say, "So seein death's stalwart emplackabeel fetcher I kipt mah whets about me in panicky Phoebles I did calm," Fitzpacker lurched down to embrace Robitaille, whom he lifted over his head and flung full flight across the brook into the broadest beam of the bruin, who upon this assault reacted with simple pawscrapes to shoulder and thigh, and having become angered some, and Robitaille rolling about on the ground before him, clappering into the stream, halted said man with a scalp scraper that flipped him onto land, lunged forward and swiped again, this time slicing his throat. Even Black Ass would not recall what noises he made, but they were fearsome bear moans, for Phoebles, having a bit of the humane in him and confident of being unseen, had stopped, crept back and watched the dénouement, a word he figured the French Canadian would appreciate epitaphically, from distant cover, not creeping off to join Fitzpacker until he had seen the throat slice and final paw slicing back flipping dismissal of the man by the bear, who tossed Robitaille headwards over feet and atwist so that he came to rest upstream and head up against stream. "Dayed no question," was how he would put it.

Having vanquished his flying attacker, and being still of an inclination to devour fish rather than manmeat, Huge Ass, as one variant would later have it for the black mark extended beyond the rump in such a way as to emphasize those halves, followed, purely out of curiosity, the skittering, panicked duo a short ways, their tran-sumddie splintering to weightlessness as they clippered, until they were disappeared round a bend in the stream, the clanking clatter of their goods fading like a bird flying off and so of some degree of normalcy, whereupon he returned to his pool, clawed an eight pound trout and squatted to make his repast, likely not having forgotten the dying creature with blood gurgling and bubbling from his throat wound a mere five or six meters away on that opposite bank, his head anointed by serendipitous leaps of fresh water to bathe his torn scalp, which was attached like an unglued wig to the skull within which despair was delayed by delirium, and just above which an odd, let's say stray, branch of rootleberries hung low and nearly to the very lips of that natural wound, his mouth.

To which tale Garvin when in secure solitude would cast such thoughts as O great-great-great-grandfather, indeed your notions were noteworthy, yet not novel, and your bravery nought but the naïve, the optimism a dupe's, ye golden fool, your clearest longsight the mere premeditation borrowed from a distant age, the giftrickery of others and stronger, your true knowledge of currents of air and not the rootworks upon which so long so far you trod.

Of Uncle Bob, Garvin never heard, and what know bears not the worth of a fart post-lit.

5

AFTER THE DELUGE

The room, or suite perhaps, Donnie thought it, perhaps, was of people cleared but for the drowsing gamine on the bed with skirt hiked waistward thus the pulsing puff of pungent nether afro split by strand of undie properly, given the cultural norms, proposing, to Drake and Donnie, who had been firmly grasped by the host about the wrist in a clear invitation to remain behind to the last but for gamine, stood facing each other with exhaustion rebuffed by inquisition, the two of them could have been hatched from the same egg, the persons, I mean, for the qualities of cheekslope and the moustache-goatee oddscribble of undaunted youth as well as virtually mirrored glances of muted optimism, fairly wrought expectation, and old-fashioned interest—that is, untempered by the social back strain of self-consciousness.

Gesturing toward the sleeper, Drake asked, "You believe in types?"

"I believe in typing."

"You know what I mean. Scotch? A good one?"

"Sure. You mean as in she ain't my type? No, not really, they're too differentiated."

"Precisely, like good scotch. This here is a complicated affair from the Isle of Islay, spelled I ess ell a y. She's part Scotch, and a good one, not a type, loyal, ungrasping, available, smart, independent. You could probably fuck her if you want, but I don't think you want."

"Not at the moment. Not at the beginning of a beautiful friendship, not when you're so goddamn eager to know how I know when you're bluffing."

"You did, you *did* know, didn't you."

"You have a tell."

"Naw fuck off—I don't have a fucking tell. I've been at this too long to have a fucking tell."

"All right."

Donnie took in the room again, the tuft of hair, the amber of the complicated scotch, the class of the place reflected in the subjection of its disarray, the poker table with chips strewn and cards still spread to invisible hands, for the game never ends, the bottles of Gerbilshaven throughout, outposts of European class—even the full ashtrays contained themselves, all of them brass, and of many shapes: ships, turtles, a nun. He hadn't an eye for light fixtures, so he wasn't sure if the central chandelier was or not, nor if it was stained glass or beer sign pedigree, but that bed sure had a frame, Donnie guessed maybe six teak trees worth, if teak came in trees called teak. One thing he had no doubt of, the couch upon which he sat was of leather, Corinthian, meaning the buttons never obtruded the buttocks.

When he had the chance, he would count the number of lion heads carved into the woodworks, especially as he had noticed one on the baseboard he stared at in his default zone.

"Lagavulin," Drake remarked, handing Donnie a full four fingers of iced scotch.

"Something Finnish, then?"

"What? Oh no, the scotch, it's Lagavulin, a '79, double matured, finished, not Finnish, in Pedro Ximinez sherry."

"So it was still alive when they put it in there."

"Some say it lives to this day—a scotch that never kills nor dies."

A sip: was that an attack of pepper?, a smooth eggfarty transition up in smoke?, a lengthy pause of whiskey, salt—no! honey? The questions linger, linger as you long for another deep pull, in languid lazy love already addicted to Lagavulin.

They sipsupped together in silence, as intangibles accumulated and hovered in the attenuate vacuum of men with less money gone away. Probably I have even less money than most of them, Donnie reflected, as the gamine squirmed in the gamey cleft of sleep.

"You really can have her if you want, you know."

"I'd hate to wake her."

"Needn't worry, she wouldn't mind."

"Sir, Drake, I believe in most states that's considered rape."

"Prior consent. She would attest to it in court."

"A trap to get your money back, not doubt, you strike me not as a pimp, more a poser pimp."

"Fine then. I'll *tell*. The dame's a paid prop. A grand a night plus a percentage, which is none of your business. If we fucked it would spoil the play. That, and she's never shown interest."

"A bit of sunlight and you squirm humanish."

A momentary swell, a swill, and Donnie returned to his former state, like some awakened prehistoric seasloth, mid-sleep, lifting its overweighted cranium without a yawn, resting it again on its forefin/paws, a moment of movement without consciousness passed like an epoch or two, and so now, again, the two men were aligned in their comportment with the exoteric; a step had been skipped, leaving the recumbent, stunned, or nascent edentate rodent's burrow to its burrow, for the two were now lazing after the crepuscular moment each had allowed to pass, if for no other reason than that Drake without evident haste was in need of knowing of his tell.

"The tell. Do tell."

"You come from money, as they say, don't you?"

"Don't you?"

"Not at all—that air about me is the saccharine scent of literature. My parents are both writers of some note. Mom's a one-time laureate who hasn't seen a hair stylist since and Daddy's a highly regarded public recluse."

"Well, no matter—we're entirely new money...Now if you want another scotch, spill it about the tell."

"Her left nipple."

"Yes—I rub it often during the game. Just a slight edge, like serving the ninth best beer in Europe, second in the Netherlands, and drinking half what the others drink."

"Appreciate it. You managed to give me more than a slight edge."

"Bullshit."

"Then you don't want to know."

"Just fucking tell me what you think you know."

"All right: it's this: every single time you bluff, you rapidly wobble her nipple with your thumb until the opponent makes up his mind. That's it. And it's every single time. Back and forth rapidly over the nipple after you bet, precisely until the response, as if all the suspense you've engendered is concentrated in that meeting of extremities."

"But I play with her tits throughout the game…"

"Right, to the point where everyone is aware to the point of distraction of the distraction—all to the good for you, except I being new took a different view. Your left thumb lost you a lot of money tonight."

Drake gave great grave thought to this impinging grievance, for he was an honest man when not rigging the games, wriggling the gamine, innocently gamboling the gamble.

Donnie wondered only whether to advance his drinking speed in hopes a second was inevitable, for it was indeed a marvelous alcoholic drink, or, safely, to slow down and enjoy the last he was going to get.

Minutes passed without a snore; a breeze impelled a heavy burgundy curtain to suck inwards, a percussive enough event for Donnie to tumble the remainder of his drink without dismay of impertinence, as Drake was deep in thought.

But not so deep, really, for he noted the emptying of the fine glass, stripped himself of his stupor, and hopped to refill Donnie's glass as well as his own, which he emptied on the seven-step stroll to the bar that accompanies all older suites uncrowded with giant ornate wooden furnishings and their leather counterparts.

"I wonder, though, Don, is the word you're looking for actually 'wobble'?"

A laughspurt abrupt from his mouth, and Donnie admitted, "I can't say I'm comfortable with it, no, but, you know, just to get it out…perhaps 'fraggled'…or, better yet, toggled—that one may actually be accurate, mechanical as it sounds…"

"You're right, though, fucking absolutely fucking right. But I can't think of a time when anyone else might have caught on," and he proceeded in a near whisper, "cept one night maybe in the city…" and back to Donnie direct, "but no. Thank Christ. Thank you. You may have taken me to the proverbial…"

"Cleaners?"

"No…something else…public bath maybe…anyway, I owe you, my friend. I never would have believed it."

Donnie hunched with luxuriant satisfaction over the drink he had just reduced by a third, scanning the room for further evidence of the frippery of wealth. Above the bed, and how appropriate, two samurai swords were hung not crossed but one over the other, each with their dull glint from the low amber lighting, underneath which no sign was necessary to pronounce their authenticity and years of service. Yes, I have been burnished, they said, in perfect English. Oddly, as the subject had become weaponry, a rifle of what appeared World War One vintage, affixed with bayonet, was stood as if a walking stick between the back corner of the desk and the door frame of a room that likely led to a great deal more waterworld phantasmagore than the simple water closet Donnie had been directed to during the game, which was opposite this one, near the entrance. The desk, Donnie could see, would have more than one bottle within a left side drawer, and at least one gat on the right, for Drake was right-handed.

"So, nouveaux riche. Your father, probably. What was he, a paper clip executive? Rubberbands? Something everybody needs and forever will. Technology take that?"

"My father? No no, military man, submarines, intelligent seal, something along that line, maybe airborne invasion fleet, infantry, you know."

"Well, if I didn't I certainly wouldn't now."

"Sorry. It's just that we aren't speaking at the moment… not for about two years, in fact."

"I haven't talked to mine for two months."

"You mean when you got here."

"Right."

"You're what, junior, senior, the arts?"

"Freshman, undecided."

"Really! You look older."

"Every day. No, I missed a couple years of school—long story—I took the rap for a friend caught with a bomb in the trunk of his car."

"Why?"

"Why what?"

"The bomb."

"Kicks."

"Why take the rap?"

"At this point I wonder. The bastard wanted to take his own, rap I mean. But I wanted to get away, see the Wild West, the deserts, all that shit, didn't give a rat's ass for school. But hitch-hiking not being what it once was rumored to be I never got anywhere but the fuck out of the cab of a 300-pound night groper who smelled of a close orgy of leprous hyenas. Return home, technically a fugitive, which sounded nice, expelled, house arrest, leniency granted pleading parents."

"You?"

"Never hitched. It never occurred to me. Or I never had to."

"I mean school."

"I know. Freshman, 23 years old, fifth year. May still be studying history, but you'd have to ask one of a number of people who no longer allow me within their sight."

"So what's the story—the daddy one."

"First there's the name, which most assume I don't dig, though I quite do: Mandrake Winchester Fondling the Second. How many of those are you ever likely to come across? Then there's the military rich kid upbringing, confusing as hell, but a grand time all in all. But to get to the point, let me paint you a picture: Luxor Hotel, Vegas, floor 23, the room he always takes for himself. I took a break from school two—"

"A break from school? Two years ago? So in your third year—"

"I know, I know. But you see from tonight what I consider school, I mean one of its aspects…So we're leaning on the railing, having a chat, twenty-third floor, smoking cigars, Cuban of course, gazing into that famously suicide-inviting airspace of the Luxor inner pyramid, when I said, you know, reflexively, for such things happen in a different sort of time, See that, Pop? And pop was right, for a torpedo, the bald head of a man in a suit had just dropped at speed right before our eyes so that the See that, Pop, was spoken at perhaps the same split, I mean split, woodsplit sounding, a sort of muted wood-split sounding, moment of impact. Now the question I asked myself right away, and forever after, is Did it hurt? Shoot a man in the head he dies instantly, but the infinity of time runs both ways, doesn't it. So the best answer I come up with, though I am by no means thrilled with it, is Not for long.

"Don't laugh—that's exactly what my father did, uproariously, guffaws punctuated by hacking smoke signals, the kind of what some would call impropriety that was one of his specialties. I mean, if you asked, the best you'd get was, Fucker's dead ain't he? And to this I agree, and I even flatter myself he was laughing at my question. Not See that, Pop, rather Did it hurt? Except that I only asked that in my head..."

Now, perhaps Donnie didn't make the connection, odd as it may seem given that his parents each in their own way lamented the death of Senator Hafbreit (D-Iowa) by strangely sudden suicide in the Luxor two years previous, perhaps grieving over his inability to prevent US forces from forcing their way into the family meals of peasants Islamic from Iraq to Pakistan, flying freely fastidiously fatally fusillading (somebody f me a drone) five or six Yemeni per car—call The Hague—to the point, it was whispered, that Deia had a horn for the hairless head of the bravest of all senate holdouts, even Garvin hearing of her hot hosting hairshirting it for the sake of domestic peace if not of the volition of his own disinterest, or velleity, perhaps an acute disgust for the demagoguery of the greasy pig-gore of gossip. In any event, especially the death of Senator Hafbreit (D-Iowa), at which news the torrents of tears that tormented Donnie's nights for nights, bore a striking resemblance to the bald head bulleting the Luxor floor, yet Donnie kept his peace or poker face and simply lent an ear.

"Anyway, you see, Donnie, when you see something like that it's like finding a shiny new quarter on the sidewalk, you want to keep looking down til you find another one, and it's damn frustrating because even if there is another one it's not shiny like the first one, you become mad, obsessed, you want to go back to the Luxor, the twenty-third floor, and smoke a cigar waiting for it to happen again, which I hope explains my fury when my father flatly refused to obtain the footage of head meets floor, a simple request he could easily, given his position in life, his connections and power, have met, and yet he refused, and we haven't spoken since, or at least only briefly so I could tell him to fuck off over the phone. But—"

"What about dealing off the bottom of the deck? Where'd you learn that? You're damn good at it."

"You not—shit! That, too?"

"Every time, if I'm not mistaken."

"Fucking Christ!...Well never mind that. Anyway, my old man's booming laughter attracted the attention of some ac-ne-faced factotum who approached and commanded us to put out our cigars, which violated house rules, not to mention US customs. Not putting them out, smoking them in the first place. And you'd have to know my old man, but his Begone boy! was both aloof, resounding and indifferent, for he then turned back to the railing and looked out as we had been, at which point, or somewhere in there, having dismissed the acned manager, some linebacker security types turned up, you know the type, blown knees and no necks, at which point my old man's guard, four armed men with triceps that lurched their shirtsleeves from wrist to elbow, bigger than the linebackers, meaner and with perfect knees, appeared from the rooms on either side of the old man's armed with something shorter than AK47s and to make a story shorter father and son were left in peace to discuss the event and the footage of which that would, though I did not know it immediately, not then, would not be forthcoming for son."

"So you didn't get the what, the casino video of head smacking floor and for this you refuse to talk to your father?"

"That's right. The next day he sent his midget assistant, he didn't even tell me to my face, that there was no way he'd give me the footage. When I demanded to speak to him personally, the dwarf told me he was already back in LA. How's that for a father?"

"I'm really not sure. His midget assistant? That alone speaks volumes. Of what, I don't know, but definitely volumes."

"Not really, he always had a midget, or a little man, or dwarf—never a hunchback—because he was convinced they were utterly loyal. Two inches taller and you get the Napoleon complex, but jockey size or less and you get loyalty and obedience, no questions asked. Remember those Burt Lancaster films? He had that little guy who would die for him. My old man said that was as real as cinema gets. When he was in Nam he used the little guy, guy they called Tiny because they were always great with nicknames in the army—"

"Doesn't the army have a height requirement?" "Sure—this would have been as small as they allowed. Maybe they allowed one five sixer per unit or something. Anyway, Tiny was his snitch. And you know how they had some jobs no one wanted to do in Nam, right? Like send a guy down into a tunnel or take point or, I don't remember all the nasty shit, but my old man was gung ho, he wanted to kill more than anyone else, he wanted to set records—"

"Like with the frogs."

"What? Oh, right…I doubt that was the record…but yes, once into something he was driven. And he was a brave motherfucker, too. He couldn't send himself down into a tunnel, but he was often on point or first up the hill, first off the chopper. But he did so many tours and he was always in the shit if he could be—and who couldn't be if he wanted—so it was inevitable that sooner or later he would wind up with an outfit that hated him."

"This must be a fragging story."

"Yeah, only in reverse. But back to the bottom dealing."

"You're quite sure?"

"Sure as you."

"Meaning perhaps you, too…"

"Best thing my old man ever did for me was teach me poker fair and foul. But back to Nam."

Drake leaned forward, rubbing his hands eagerly. "Right, so his midget told him the men were planning to do it one day on patrol as soon as they kind of let him wander in front. I guess they figured he was in front so often because they were in combat so often. So they set up a simple frag.

They'd let him wander ahead and let him have it from all sides. But he was always ahead, I don't see why they had to even plan it. They should have kept their fucking mouths shut. So he maneuvered all day to be in the rear or middle and then all of a sudden in dense jungle he gave the order for the men to get down, like he'd seen something, and he called to Tiny, or whatever, Hey Tiny, you and me are going to scout ahead—I don't like the way this looks—they got maybe a hundred yards ahead, out of sight in dense brush, started shooting off their weapons and he had Tiny call in an airstrike, napalm and all, wiped out every last one of his men. His record was so good nobody ever called him on it. He said, Sure they questioned me: Where were the VC? I said, well since you bombed my boys, they all got away."

A silence ensued, worth noting—for silences are ensuing constantly and we but rarely need point them out—for the abrupt end of it. A red light flickered on in the kind of glass bulb in which red lights will flicker on Drake's desk next to a Bakelite telephone, he flicked a monitor on, examined the motion of a trio moving about in redundant light, for it was dawn by now, and gestured calmly for Donnie to rise.

"Look, man, it's getting late. Write down your address quick and I'll show you out the back stairway. The houses built in this era all have these terrific back stairways."

6

HECTOR GETS HIS ODYSSEY

What a lovely day! The sun over yonder and a blue and cloudless sky up there, and what with the sounds, morning birds, susurrations of surface water breeze bestirred, an Alpine breeze to be sure, yet counterpleading verst the sunhats—why, without the combination of intense variegated and vari-located pains with a good nine levels of death fear besides the very specific thought of a monstrous bear nearby having a good taste of him already and of a certainty preparing for more gristle, our man Hector would have felt positively hungry for bacon and eggs had he not been deeply a-fever when a display of streamflop unerring drenched his face.

This awakening wave came amid the third day of the throatslit blood bubbling convalescence, during which the dead man, who was still breathing, breathing albeit bubbles, who was still coursing in vein blood provided by pulse push, was still, incontrovertibly alive whether he liked it or not.

Slowly Hector Robitaille began surveying his circumstances, his milieu, his recent history as a man who had been flung into a bear, mauled appropriately, abandoned, and, if not worst of all, morally abhorrent, had his rifle stolen. He was not—and here comes the abstract—temporally of a mind to place the importance of a man's shoot-tube to a man in context of historicity, so that it is up to me to say that back then for the man of the West a man's gun was near important as a man's life, for without that gun he would be unable to dissuade Injun, slaughter game, assassinate the strong in drygulch manner. And he did know that, even if he could not sit up and gaze about, if he managed he would find no rifle, nor provisions of any kind, not even a spare scrap of clothing with which to bandage his wounds, them what he could reach, which did not include deep gashes down to his scapula, right side.

Can I say without irony that luck was on Hector's side? Certainly it had not been of late. Certainly his arrival at Fort Vancouver with the great notion of loading unsuccessful whalers with fur to cut transport costs at a moment when one debt-ridden mountain man and one shareholding furman of legendary malice, size and courage were looking to add one feller to their pelt retrieval troop was an unlucky infliction upon his life. Certainly the instant dislike Fitzpacker took to this river man reluctant to brave Injun territory, spring blizzards, and sixteen hour hikes through woods, up slopes, alongside death gorges, never mind the shanghai aspect of the venture, certainly the utter contempt, the merry contempt of the sadistic Fitzpacker was not a lucky prospect for Hector Robitaille. And close proximity to a thirteen-foot bear promises luck to no one, and the less so if one is transformed midair into provocation, treated thus as one might be, subsequently left for dead, and **having one's rifle stole**, this all a-might easily to add up to a fair summary of the worst of luck. Yet yes, I can say without irony that luck was on Hector's side, particularly on the back, nestled into a green medicinal bed of barley grass, as opposed to, say, a wind/whipped whipping willow, which more commonly than barley grass flanked the banks of waterways thereabouts. Thus no insects gnawed his worst wounds, but for the neck and scalp, the scalp particularly irritating in the way of say a hat not set aright on the head of an armless man, the throat being of particular threat to life. And lucky, too, for Hector Robitaille was the absence of the bear he had the odd notion in his hours now and to come of disability, absolute inability to move, the odd notion of wantin to have a word with, to tell this bear that far as he was concerned no hard feelings and if only Uncle Bob was here he could manage to explain matters to the bear and with Uncle Bob's vengeful determination n the big bear's natural sensory abilities track down that Fitzpacker and do him slow and dirty what he did deserve. Yet, and perhaps this is

lucky, the bear kept his snout from Hector's view, and in due
time Hector understood that this was to be the way of it, for
he would hear splashing nearby, the heavy indeterminate
sounds of beast on land, the teeth of beast rending fattened
fish, a sound as loud as the descent of a bee, the rustle of
leaves and grasses, the pitch of moving water regular, constant, oddly yet unpredictable, and the smells about his own
snout a festering of fresheties, spring and springs budding fecund flouting through dehiscence of burst-ripe the verdury
odor of long lies, sex rapid, opiate, a fiddles and whiskey barn
dance bereft of decadent scruple, birdsong, rackruttery deer
conking, squirrels, chipmunks, beavers, beetles: listen!

Five days and nights of fever dreams: in some of them he
was very cold. Those were at night. In some he was warm,
even hot (having fever after all). Those were during the day.
On the sixth day, Hector warmed to the notion that but for
some slashes about his physiognomy the world had actually been righting itself all along. Worrying himself over the
ravine slashed into his back, he rocked to his left and back,
wondering at the odd sensation of a cool painless message
sent from thar. One particularly deep scratch along his forearm gave him much pain, muscles having been parted. The
scalp felt as if he had cut it shaving—so should I live long
enough to fall victim to Black Footers at least it ont hurt so
dad much. But the throat was of much concern. The pain
was complicated, even indecipherable, inside and out,
alongside and hovering above, inflapped, outflapped, of its
own will and mind…will and mind, will and mind, oft em
separate you will find…in mind, Fitzpacker fartquakes saw
baby rabbit in the snow how it got that fucken how fracking
I would know I gets him come to me with bits of bread and
then smash his baby head and cackling a mouthfartquake…
pain…fading out, a slop of stream, stream of consciousness,
he wakes, wakes with wit, this grass, he buries his torn arm
in the grass, which is like a bed of velvet asparagus, it's the
grass n ifn taint I'b dead anyhow, nothing wrong with the
left arm, plucking a berry he can't swallow, reaching back
over his head, soaking it in the stream til it bloats and splits

and when he puts it past his lips it glides down past his gash like a golden marble midst a diarrheic storm, which follows on a diet strictly of rootleberries and water, rootleberries and water, soaked rootleberries and water, a race is what it is, hunger staved, satiation, aye it hurts to laugh, but hurts where?, in the neck, and why not drape that neck with barley grass, Hector figures, finally figures, and the flies bear off and away, two nights and a day the wound is...healing? Not hurting. Suppurating? Nay, and nor is the arm. How long has he been laying there? Ten days, surely, more like two weeks.

And the bear? Every morning he is there. There, yes but yon, ten yards, never closer.

Somewhere in what would one day be somewhere's in the wilds of Ideeho or Orgone a madcackling cannot be heard for the throatslit is still leaking sound, yet Hector laughs the laugh of life and love of laugh and life. Whosoever heard of a feller been mawled such by a 15 foot if it's a inch eepher n livin to tell the tall...And another day, full and long, of sleep for the energy to be drawn from the rootleberry race is a losing race.

Protein is what Hector needed and...Čćrhččrhččrhččrhččrhččrh: one of them sounds you never need have heard afore to know what tis, rattling, rapid rattling, so rapid, abrupt start abrupt stop so the air itself is mesmerized and behind the dry is the whirr: Čćrhččrhččrhččrhččrh. Again! Hector Jobed? On top of bear, rattler? Mights well git married so's wife kin fuck Fitz and kids die of the aygyoo. Acute ague. Narrative hands tied, I am as relieved as Hector to see that this rattler had just swallowed some critter and in nestling into the sweet barley grass had been disturbed by a nudge from his neighbor, Hector, who flexed his right arm, as the sluggish rattler was on his left, and for the first time since the mauling thought to check for his knife, a crude Cajun curved straight knife in a felt sheath, but sharp, sharp enough to slice the head off a rattler. But, of course, how to slice the head of a living rattler. Well, patience visits them that's near death for two weeks, and so Hector with great stealth lifted himself into position to strike, up on his right elbow so his trusted uninjured arm would make the move; the rattler, oblivious, actually stretched as if in offering, head facing away from Hector, and Hector struck, less lightning like than a rattler, but as this was a dull rattler, quick enough, quick enough even to adjust the grip that hadn't quite squeezed the neck—Ččrhččrhččrhččrhččrhččrh, was a rather feeble response as the snake by then was had and hadn't the energy to do more than a slow flop onto its back (though Hector had the head pinned, his whitened knuckles burying the head to the earth neath the grass), and as soon as Hector cleared the grass away to where he could see the head he'd buried, he did slice the head off the serpent.

Č!

And so he had protein. In his instant delirium he bit the snake and shook his head like a hyena tearing off a slab of the hindquarter of a wildebeest, but he was weak, and his teeth made for gentler dining, and he managed only to bring himself into a faint he woke up from after several hours, waking from horrific dreams of the sort to frighten off civilization once and for all. Happily, he soon remembered his food, remembered it calmly, and set about slicing small strips he would soak before eating. The first strip he did not soak long enough and would have choked on it had it not been long enough for him to snag and remove and fling in heedless disgust with constant absurd brushes with demise. The second strip, now that he knew meat must soak longer than berries, he lost when his hand became too cold and he lost his grip. The third strip was gored by a twig stripped from the rootleberry bush, which was green within the bark and bent like a fishing willow, a good three-foot long and a gratifying success, as the snakestrip fattened and resisted the rush of the stream and Hector thus swallowed his first meat for weeks. Despite the rumbling response of his belly, Hector did not rush to feast, rather dined at the rate of an inch or so long strip every half hour until night and sleep, and again at the same rate on sunrise and morn, waiting for his body to respond to the feeding, a wait that would last but one more night, for upon the next morn he felt something he recognized as energy, though he knew implicitly that it was the energy of the weak, the energy of but impending recovery, as opposed to the energy to rise and march back to fort and revenge.

In fact, Hector would not rise for many a day. Wisely, he remained one last day at the stream to finish off all but a breakfast of snake and sleep. And in the morning he soaked his shit-begorbed clothing in the stream, scrubbing as he could, and immersed himself, bearing it, revivifying, importing in a mind of paradise of calm about his near circumference, in which he built a fire for to roast the rest of the rattler, to warm himself and begin the drying of his clothes that would soon be dried anyway under the early May sun, moving about with a kind of stealth, lest he awaken the monsters that made long the odds of his survival. Maybe the time was noon when he set off for—he laughed—Fort Vancouver, west and north…think not about the chances of even finding the fort, nor of storms of Injun arrows…and he set off as he knew he must, hands and knees, slowly, hands and knees, an eye out for nourishment of any kind, any kind at all.

After half an hour of quadrupedal labors, he heard a heavy splash in the stream he figured he'd follow for sake of certain water; slowly he turned, and there, in his usual place, some thirty yards away, was the bear, sitting in the water, holding a large pitchforked trout before his eyes as if he never before beheld such life form. Hector slowly creaked his body forward to supine, laid his head on his hands and fell asleep. Awaking to the chill chattering clarity of enamel percussive echoes in a dark the color of cold, Hector nonetheless felt the next morning that he understood more than he had since perhaps even before he had naively approached Fort Vancouver with a bright idea. He now knew that something bad had happened to his Achilles tendon and that though it did not hurt it was a good half the reason he could not walk. Much of the other half had to do with the proximity of hunger—a wolfpack in the shadow at the edge of his dying campfire—to say nothing of exhaustion and trauma. He thought about his bearskin coat—maybe the bear was wearing it. He thought that was funny. For a moment or two he felt no cold whatsoever. When he tried to think of another bear joke he went on an Indian spirit ride inside some kind of raptor that could take his eyes up so high he could see himself disappear in bright daylight and then could see the contours of the land cut by gorges and extremely rapid rivers and finally a fort, Fort Vancouver, so far away he had to laugh. By now Hector was on his hands and knees again, and he said, chuckling, "Here I go."

Or was it buckskin?

The sun was in the sky and Hector was warming to fears.

What if Fitzpacker and Phoebles were to come upon him on their way back? (They had long since passed him, far enough to the north that they had no fear of running into the giant bear again.) Maybe they won't for fear of bear. I think my neck wound is squamming again. I have two short strips of rattler left. I have to go toward the ocean, that's for sure. The creek had bent and so he was out of sight of the bear, but he had gone a mere ninety yards so far since setting out in the pre-dawn.

Twice that day Hector had succumbed to exhaustion and napped; at darkfall he was energized and went on a crawl spurt that put the day's distance up near half a mile. When he had had enough he ate the last two strips of rattler, chewing so carefully, so slowly, savoring, feeling liquids coursing through his body, ebbing and rising like tides, taking so long that he feared falling asleep and choking on them, even the second one, despite the warning of the first. He thought that was funny and fell asleep with a smile on his face, and it was a happy night we know for his first words upon waking were, "Doggy's cocknoise."

Doggy's cocknoise, he repeated silently a few times, giggling and rolling about as if he were two people, coming slowly to stillness at the cramping of his stomach, when he realized he had slept until high enough sun for warmth, had slept through torture of cold. He had no idea how lucky he was that he had not yet died of what is called exposure, that the cold nights were but a few fahrenheital degrees from turning him from a sort of new reptilian into a plain dead

mammal. Yet he did not relish the cold and one night slept
well through it though it was not enough to shake fear of
more of it from his mind. He was a man, he knew, and men
built fires, maybe even invented them, though that hardly
holds up when you think of volcanos and all, and by garsh
dint Uncle Bob once build a fire on the Missippi shore one
night he didn't want to share his string of catfish one of them
a good fifty pounds, the thing a devil fish more wide than
long with a mouth Bob says like a twennywhore gaysh, this
here's a flint stone sayin and scratcht it on his knife and there
in his hand some funge-eye smoking and the grass lit, the
sticks lit, the twigs lit, the logs lit and the moon come up like
one a them eggs yaint sposed t eat. Suckyoulent, Uncle Bob
called that catfish oncet cooked to drippin greasies. Mooneye
sides up, Uncle Bob-ud say.

The land shapes a man's destiny, however appallingly
insignificant. A sheltered deepwater harbor invites a port,
a grand phantasmagorical history that arises grotesque and
jauntily squalid, degenerating into a carnival of murder and
fiscal cannibalism; a mountain range rises late and high to
prevent cultures from mingling before their perverse matur-
ities settle and set them upon each other once wonders at
the wonders of monolithic fervor have ceased and the cease-
less lust for attrition is born; a river runs wide runs deep runs
muddy a river runs long after you am gone, a bridge is a raft
of strapped bladders, a boat is a bowl of dry growth, a bridge
is a flat raft on a string, a boat is that raft with a sail and asses
for the return, a bridge is twine or wood and boats move upstream and down, a bridge is a strategic vortex of death and
a boat is aflood with the wretched to be drowned. A stream
winds along grassy bottoms and turns up as if in surprise and
the land away slopes gently down, miles and miles before
another rocky stream and miles and miles before the great
Salmon River, and Hector, yet on hands and knees and so
then unhurried in physicals, feels not the mentals to pine
at the loss of his last known natural guide back to Fort Vancouver, instead dutifully veers, in what he thinks should and

must be northwestern tilt though is and should be rather near true west.

Recovering, Hector cut strips of hide off his pantleg bottoms, which he tied about his knees to ease the scrape of knee travel, while his hands of their own accord turned hidely hard. Alert now, too, Hector had examined many a tree in a few copses he come across on the first day astray from the stream of his near doom, finding enough fungi to fill his pockets, choosing at least three kinds to better his chances at fire-starting. Flintrock was harder to come by, though in every meadow a sharp stone hid like landmines later would over most of the landmass of the globe — that is to say where children and the less maimed would find them, and Hector felt a degree of pride in his foresight, wrapping his knees like he done. Foodless, Hector rootgrubbed, for he knew Injuns thereabouts — meaning within something we now know to be thousands of square miles — oft lived solely on rootgrubbing, though these breeds were looked upon as lesser Injuns, a cause of some amazement to Hector, who grubbed not a root all day long: any Injun could live by the grubbing of root held Hector's admiration.

For a man of Hector's recent travails a long three mile traversed day without food was cause for discomfort yet neither panic or even fear, and he was dogtired from dogwalking while still pained enough and even slightly fevered that he slept where he halted and next morning knew not the difference between falling where he slept or the nightmares of dark, dense glacially moving masses and his own trek, and he simply rose up and went on as he figured he had, and he was right, too, for he continued more westerly than he figured, and his mind closed like some abnormally dehisced larvally substance singed by fire; a miraculous day of nought but the occasional thought apperceptual of thought thought not, a day that he did not apperceive in depth enough to realize it had been his most *comfortable* day since his arrival to Fort Vancouver many months afore, yet such that it was of no surprise to Hector when just before dusk he arrived to a wide, stony, shallow stream, the kind of stream one could trap a trout in, the kind of stream one could drink away one's hunger from, the kind of stream one could find a flintrock amidst.

The weather had held, as is said—though Hector did not recognize this flintrock of luck—for rare is the spring in this region that holds its rain aloft for suchlong as two weeks or so, and rare then the stream so near unspate as thisn, at the bank of which Hector eyegrubbed for edibles before spying a likely flint and figuring that would do for a night's hunger, a fire, that is, Hector asqueeze to such focus he watched the sandslide into the eggsize hole left by the removal of the stone from three inches of water, watched particulate, affording a thought and more for each slid granule as if in the flow of a dream in which significance was the void beneath the darksides of all, including thought and that such then was thought that meaning was as the afar lowering sun on distant mountains that stood firm in disappearance or sudden grandeur, all remote, pregnant with meaning, pregnant, a birth promised.

Two hours later, hunger cast forward, *content*, Hector lay by the dry grass collected, the cut fungals, drecklike, yet of promise, the steely bladed knife, and the flintstone. As we who write and read and laugh ourselves healthy in the fog of gregarial consumption oft do, waiting in the clutch of an intentional absurd, delay a drift toward liquor, so did Hector put off the moment of sparking his fire, his life-prolonging fire—for if *that* were prolonged...Even unto the onset of a nightchill, when he ceremoniously as could be considering struck flint to knife while thumbing fungus, struck flint to knife while thumbing fungus, struck flint to knife whilst thumbing fungus, the night remaining aglint only with stars, the fungus, dry enough yet un-sparked, the knife and flint met sharp and hard, and so on Hector frettled in this shoulder hunched controlled spasm, on Hector frettled, on Hector sped, sped the frettle to the freneticism of despair asparked by mania, reason shot from outside across the sensories and remaining outside, and no spark otherwise leapt; yet on did

Hector frettle, and faster, in less space, until the shoulders hunched up higher and lowered, high and low, regular, slowing like they were oars and his lungs the boat, and his weeping was of a source apart from despair, considerably similar to that of a beast come upon a slaughtered mate. And so the boat crossed in the night til it ran aground, chill but dry once the tears reconciled themselves to the failure they were heir to.

Sleep, even that beset by nightmare, is good, for without sleep one cannot awaken before recognition of any event past to find two Injuns settin by a fire on the banks of a shallow salubrious stream, whether they be still as their two dimensional future or giddy and giggly, as were these companayros who were pantomiming for each other Hector's fire-starting technique as if it were an act on a St. Louis stage, not that Hector minded once he sniffed out cooked trout and knew he need not guess at the intentions of these...well, who knew, Flatheads, he supposed. They laughed in what must be presumed the Flathead way, teeth clenched, breaths gusting out like a föhny wind, over the lower teeth, through the gap and down. And fine teeth they were, both sets, leading one to believe their eating and cleaning habits were superior to those of mountain men, who rarely had a full set and certainly bore no white enamels.

Hector snaked a couple feet around the fire to get an unobstructed view of his visitors, raising himself to prop his cheek on his hand. Both Injuns were entirely naked of clothing, though covered with some substance that befogged them, at once subcutaneous in appearance and as of a dry film, as if a powder emergent from bone. Most oddly, while they were of the same apparent height, they had two entirely different facial constructs, the one on Hector's right having an elongated face, a great rectangle with a bulbous crown and pointed chin, devoid of facial hair and with a mere black tuft atop. His companion had a round face with a great deal of flesh that was ribbled in symmetrical crescents outwards from his mouth as if a stone had been tossed into it. His hair style was the same but for a stick tied tightly into the top, holding a line parallel to front, ear to ear.

As Hector had come to life before them, the elongate face Injun reached across and snatched Hector's knife from under him. The flint was already in his hand. He mimicked Hector's late-night frenzy, and while his friend either laughed or exercised his cheek-flesh—for the motion was rather regular and his belly did not move—he merely struck repeatedly to no effect.

Point made, he lifted both items to emphasize their inutility to Hector, before tossing the knife back, reaching behind, and producing a metallic slab the size of his palm. This he held up for Hector's inspection before striking it with Hector's flintrock. Sparks shot out as of a comet's tail. He flicked this spun with the striker in two hyperbolae to Hector in offering, standing in the same motion, while the other tossed two footlong trout in the same spot, just beyond the fire's ash circle and inches from Hector's elbow pivot, seeming to stride along and away with the sparker in a rehearsed exit, the two of them taking exceedingly long, loping strides, crossing the river without looking back.

Hector watched them until they were enveloped by forest less than half a mile from the stream, thinking "bear," how badly he wanted to tell them about the bear, and in a collapse into funkle mouthed the words "Fort Vancouver," which produced an exhale but no sound related to speech. "Fort Vancouver," he tried again, and again speech would not come. Long into a day given over to recuperation, closely monitored for a sense of returning strength that proved elusive, Hector was still trying to speak, all the while thinking on Indians, what they were, why some were called Flatheads even though their heads were not flat, determining that the two he sort of met were nice—that was without question—yet had no desire for Hector's company, which raised questions. Everybody said Injuns stink, but all Hector'd smelled was the cooked fish, and he figured the Injuns couldn't smell worse than he did. Probably they found him repulsive, he decided, his hair lank and long, his beard untrimmed and here now he felt lumps in it, of the scum, and the mud and the burrs. It would be nice to have a farm, a clean plot of land and a

small clean house, and have them two Flatheads over for a
proper meal, by then having found a means to communicate,
and tell them all about the bear and how probably they didn't
know that he likely would have died without their help. He
could give them jobs and a place to stay so they wouldn't
have to walk around all the time, grubbing roots. If they wanted, they could grub his roots for free.

Hector awoke cold, boney cold, as Uncle Bob would say.
He dropped off before full sunset, and had yet to gather his
dry grass and sticks for his night fire. He sat up and briskly
rubbed his arms, and then he heard a canine call and another canine answer or pick up on the tune. Soon dozens
of canines were howling. He imagined them as a rear flank,
with fore-wolves snarling at the forest's edge. He stood quickly, forgetting his Achilles, but merely stumbled, some healing
had taken place, now it was stiff and weak, but utterly without
pain, and he hirpled quickly about gathering, feeling a sense
of optimism well up like the gut-rise of a strong whiskey. And
before long, working to the background sound of a pack or
two of wolves, he had his fire ready, struck his flint into Injun metal slab, watched with a revival of belief as his fungus
smoked, applied said fungus to a collar of grass, blowing but
briefly before it was aflame, slid this collar beneath a heap
of grass that flared strong and set about laying his kindling
atop. This is life now, he thought, and as the wolves kept up
their badjokery he ate the second trout, luxuriant enough to
be annoyed by the bones that passed inspection and found
themselves in his mouth. The thing is, he thought, whatever
a man's condition, tiny fishbones just ain't saloobrous. The
shovelnose sturgeon now, there's an eatin fish fer a feller don't
cotton to bonery in swimmer food: of the central cartilaginous variety, like a shark, the fish has a good strong bone-like
spine-like cartilage holding it all together, and once cooked,
the eating is simply a matter of grabbing off the meat. This
shared feed experience with Uncle Bob, Hector recalled with
near delight, warming his front to ward off the chill lapping
at his back, a full fed feller with a full-fledged fire. Only some
imaginary asshole would have tapped Hector on his shoulder
to remind him what hell lay yet before him.

This hell began with vast stretches of woodlands host to vermin of all manner, including preternaturally giant hirsutes suchlike as bears and wolves, and small aerial pests including bees, biting flies, mosquitoes, and flying stinging ants. The psychological hell would set upon him in the form of large docile creatures such as elk, deer, goats, and even fish that would all appear close and real and transmogrify into phantasms that vanish before the feckless hunting forays of a starving man. There would be berries aplenty and they would taste fresh and they would burst with elixir upon bite, juice dampening Hector's beard—but after a week they would come to resemble tree bark at first tongue touch, fierce with the redolence of possum piss. There would be possum piss but not sighting of possum and certain digitigrade carnivores as the ferocious sagonku (such a delicacy as would never be known back east and as far as Europe if you knew just how they roast) that would be difficult enough to elude when they drygulched you as they tended, the more so when the victim be a limper, and worst of all they et what they tore off of flesh and left with a sarcophery of stink spray that etched into the skin and remained to remind of the assault for weeks, all of which is to say that in beaver rich riverine forest why would not a man unfamiliar with said beaver find them to be the most nervewrasslin of all, the monstrous teeth, what they did to trees, the construction evidence of a great intelligence, especially once an Injun or two convinced ya that maybe Injuns are smarter than ye, in which case, and considering the implacable fleshungry sagonku, what did beavers eat and were them not bones crossed at the apex of them midstream huts where they could hide an entire search party. And of course there might or might not be Injuns, hostile scalpers, mocking forest dwellers that might or might not follow Hector just out of his sight, and though they not be cannibals, would be strangely detached, a superior species that lounged like apes in Indian jungles, spearing antelope at will, effortlessly, and they would wait for Hector to perish before they took his self-carved spear for a trophy to be displayed in their museum of the follies of white men. Probably they would display Hector's bones there after their pet vultures picked him clean; first, though, they would cut a strip of flesh from his buttocks and toss it to one of their wolves and the wolf would sniff it and look around at their eyes to let them know he got the joke and he, too, would laugh, and a vulture would lope over and retrieve the meat. Children would play at Hector builds a fire and laughter would rumble like a long heckling earthquake throughout the lands of the fur trade.

When the rains came, all aspects of Hector's hell would be refreshed, elusive, and incomprehensible.

7

A PAGAN FRIENDSHIP

Donnie's apartment was about half a basement of a two-story house no farther from the university than any other place more or less in town. He had his private entrance down six stairs descended from a backyard fenced in by a flecked and peeling white over gray rotwood fence that failed to contain a loneliness for children that was slowly killing a large maple, Donnie's least favorite type of tree, and all that rose above the grass in the yard, and spread its precise miasma to the more woodsome neighbors' yards, from which silence virtually screamed in horror during the days, leaving vast stretches for the peace of nights. There was no flower garden and no shed, not even a green hose wound up or basking on the grass. The leaves of the maple had mostly fallen by now, but Donnie could see they would remain where they fell, a circumstance of which he approved. The landlords were furtive, both husband and wife had something to do with the university, though neither had the heft required to bear their achievements well. Two children, both teenagers, one male and one female, controlled the second floor of the house, to which they had access via an external stairway and more often than not would say hello to Donnie if he said hello to one of them first. In two months at university these meetings had occurred but a few times. The parents he saw when he arranged to move in and twice upon paying his rent. He saw Datsuns in the driveway on occasion as he slipped past the front of the house, but he never saw them occupied and from his room he never heard their engines.

The thick wad of cash in his pocket did little to lift his

mood beyond the euphoria he felt as he always did after a fine night that kept him out past the dawn, such nights in the past having usually been spent engored in illicit sex, as on a particular night in a farmhouse with a colleague of his mother, her husband out of town, she thirty-five and flush with musk and curves, a woman as liquid and pulpy as a deep sea creature, whose scent seeped at him as he walked several miles into town past cornfields, walking on the highway on a Thursday morning in late spring, euphoric, he calculated, having no need to imagine a happier state of being, wondering only at the way pleasure attenuated itself as did a thirty-five- year-old luscious woman on a couch, lounging generously for him, for him to investigate and dwell in at his ease, the walk home not the least inferior to the hours of nightwrestling precedent. Which is not to say that this morning he felt the least bit ruttly, but it had been a surprising and fabulous night, and yet sodden with expensive scotch his first act upon descending to his basement apartment was to pour a glass of Gallo port and down it in one swallow. As the apartment was either lit by flickering tubes attached to the ceiling or the one or two small lamps he had picked up used, he was a bit speluncular in habit, seeking recess, crowding himself into the corner to his left as he entered, his mattress in a corner behind a kitchen stand on which a stove with two electric burners afforded him little encouragement gastronomically. A folding card table stood next to his bed, and there he took his meals and did what reading he did not manage in bed, a desk lamp wedged at the corner of the table where the head of the bead aligned with it. The bed was wider than necessary, and books ranged its length, for he had had his fill of bookcases, which he viewed as cemeteries for supernumerary editions of books with merit or cachet, sometimes both — one thinks of Gibbon — books that must rest with family, books that must, in most cases, be displayed for those best practiced in ignoring them.

Donnie clicked on the lamp and picked up *The Blind Owl*, nestled into the pillow resting against the slope of dirty clothes mushed against the wall for his propping, looked at his empty glass, the bottle of port, tossed the book gently into the wall, rocked up to click off the lamp, filled his glass with the port, and nestled back again, closing his eyes. His thoughts moved serpentine, following something like a Jacobsen's organ, somehow avoiding obstacles without focusing on anything in particular, though it is likely that at one point or another the snake would have found the little tufts of fur on the bed across town. More impressive, the wine remained in the glass as he followed the snake into ever-darkening recesses where eventually he found sleep without consciously acknowledging the belated lust unfurling in his loins. It's safe to call a measure of his character the calm with which he awoke, the wine not sloshing in the least, after less than a minute of sleep, when a knocking at his door, soft yet determined knuckles rapping on wood, sought to insinuate themselves into a dream he had yet to conjure. He downed about half a glass of the port, set it on the table, and wondered when he had stripped to his underwear, which is all he would be clothed in when out of what he would certainly, if he pondered the situation, condemn as otiose habit he moved to answer the door.

Standing before him, in a leather jacket, a tweed sporting cap, jeans, dock shoes, and an effectively insinuating smile, was Drake Fondling.

"You're the guy from last night," Donnie said.

"The very one—I believe we parted but little more than an hour ago."

"I guess you took it hard. Come in."

Drake crossed the threshold, immediately spotting the Gallo port, took the two long strides necessary to round the kitchenette and reach the bottle, lifted it, and gulped a quarter of the bottle.

Donnie shut the door and watched, waiting for the perfumitory expiration before politely offering words to make the moment easier for Drake.

"I gather your visit is a matter of some import in one way or another."

"Oh, very much so, very much so. Is this all the wine?"

"The store's probably open by now—I can get more."

"Oh, no need, no need."

"Do you repeat yourself when you're nervous?"

"Mind if I sit, if I sit? That was a joke. No, not nervous, just rather in a hurry. I have to get to the airport, Donald—"

"Donnie, or Don…"

"Yes, the very same, the very same. That wasn't a joke. I'll give this whole repetition business a great deal of thought… when I think the time is right."

Drake sat at the table, looking very much in control of a modest stupefaction for not yet having done what was an oversight amounting to a faux pas.

Donnie walked over to the bed and sat down, Drake handing him the bottle as if they had rehearsed the scene, and Donnie swigged, handed it back, and began rooting for a cigarette, and was still in root as Drake, having himself swigged, handed back the bottle.

"Have one of mine," Drake offered, a pack of Dunhill's opening as he flipped it too hard, so that Donnie had to react rapidly to snag the one that would have first hit the floor.

"Pass the ashtray."

Thus familiarly arrayed, seated on the bed with a bottle and an ashtray between his legs, an arrangement deeply familiar with his broodings and philosophizing, he sought clarity.

"So what's the deal?"

"Aptly put—the deal. Look, Donnie, I'm flying to Europe for a while, an indefinite while, flying today—you have a passport?"

"Yes."

"Good. I'd like your company, like you to join me. If you haven't gathered, I'm rich, really rich, and I'll pay for everything—and I've thought it over, what might make you uncomfortable, and the thing is this: I'll make sure you always have in hand enough to purchase a return ticket from anywhere at any time and plenty of cash besides—so you won't be dependent upon me or beholden at any time, right?"

Donnie suddenly felt as if worms had circled his eyes like creeping Injuns at night and were trying to squeeze them from their sockets.

"The cliché here is, isn't this rather sudden, but what I'm wondering is why me? We met last night. You're clearly a popular fellow. I can see why you might not want to take a woman given the complications if there were to be complications, but why me?"

"I like you. I liked you right away. I'm impulsive, but I find I'm usually right about people. You seem like someone I'd have a good time with, someone I wouldn't tire of, and wouldn't judge me in that strange way people habitually do."

Donnie muttered, "'I'll try a pagan friend, since Christian kindness has proved but hollow courtesy.'"

"What's that?"

"Just quoting Melville...See here, as they say in the movies. Say I agree, and I think I may, can we have a day to prepare, meaning mostly to sleep?"

"Not really. In fact, I'll need your answer in a few minutes or so."

"For how long? How long will we be there, and where?"

"Where starts in Brussels, it was what I could get, but if it doesn't appeal to you, think of it as a hub."

"It's a hub, all right. How long?"

"How long. God knows. We could contract scurvy on the flight over."

"There's that point. Yes... well, let's go then."

Drake arched his back, jerked his head to look directly into Donnie's eyes, and smiled widely. They both stood, Drake taking the step forward to initiate the required embrace.

"You have a suitcase? Don't forget your passport. Won't take you long to pack..." Donnie spoke as if auditing a grocery list.

"I *will* have to call home first."

"Can't you call from over there? We're in a hurry."

"We? You have a Hottentot in your pocket?"

"I don't know — how big are they? Look, I'll explain everything—no, that's a lie—the point is I impulsively purchased—another lie: reserved—two tickets for a flight that leaves before one and if it takes an hour to get to the airport and we have to be there an hour early—"

"Don't say 'have to,' none of this is compulsory. Breathe, relax, and think of what philosophy you know."

"Same river twice."

"Okay," Donnie began his packing by gathering what paired socks he could. "The river is going to change regardless: add that to 'same river twice' and you have a compound philosophy, one that requires reflection, which you have several minutes for before I'm ready if you still want me to come with you."

"Right, right. Look, I have a proper drink in the car to seal the pact. Good scotch. And like a river it reflects."

"Can't take it on the plane."

"Flask size—it'll never make it to the airport alive."

8

PHONING HOME

"What impertinence," Donnie smirked interior with consolate glee, considering of what little moment his news would be and thus how brief the call.

"Hello." It was his sister, full name Cleopatra, because, if you asked Donnie, that's the way his mother was.

The voice inflected just too much disinterest for manifest disgust, though Donnie knew the disgust was there, always. He felt physical disgust himself upon hearing the voice, but the call needed to be made.

"Cleo? It's Donnie."

"What do you want, no one's home." She never asked a question in her life—probably, he had decided, because it showed a level of interest that would challenge the supremacy of disgust.

Donnie resisted the urge to tell her either that if she was home indeed no one was home, or that in fact someone was home, if she were. If he did either she would hang up. So he didn't.

"Just tell mom and dad I'm going to be in Europe for a while, starting tonight."

"Fine," she said, and hung up.

For Donnie and his sister it was a fine telephone conversation.

9

MYSTERIES

Whether or not one devotes energies of thought to the question, and here are the shrugging narratorial shoulders in regard to measures of meaning, most if not all of what bears on a life is a mystery, most if not all of what life bears on is a mystery, and most certainly to the liver of life the life of that liver is a mystery. Do I cast thus an atheistic net over the accounts herein? Do I press on the reader a monologic, even monomaniacal perspective? Certainly not. Yet I do grant that this chapter arose from the coincidence of characters drinking cheap sweet wine and much reflection on the way in which such infected the narrator and narrative both with the strong desire to join them in finishing off the bottle, to sit with them for just a few moments and share the oddness of the scene, the brilliance of human souls alert within their exhausted corporeal, at the same time pondering the situation, not the meaning, no, the situation as regarded Donnie Garvin in comparison with his great-great-great-great-great-grandfather, Hector Robitaille, of whom Donnie had once heard when he was five years old, when his father said he had an ancestor who had been mauled by a grizzly and survived. Hector's most hellish days have yet to be described, days lived amidst the since decimated fauna of a paradise, during the early years of frenetic beaver slaughter when it seemed as if the beaver were hydralike in their tendency to meet slaughter with ribald reproductive frenzy (this was actually an incidence of the species concentrically migrating, a depressing paradox); days lived in pristine forests and extraordinary vistas little seen by eyes dulled by the triumph

of commerce over the beatific, when hills could advance toward mountains without being penned into trite repetitions
of the scenic without herd; days of prodigious populations of
pure fish, herbs, flintrocks, mushrooms, sap, pine nuts, fortunes of fungus, abundance, sacerdotal treats for creatures
in a world without the ease of flight from Philly to Brussels
taken by Donnie the great-great-great-great-great-grandson of
Hector, a young man whose travails may poorly be described
as ursine maulings of the mind and spirit—one mystery here
being the question of bloodlines: was there anything left of
Hector in Donnie? Would a transplanted Hector, replacing
Donnie, develop the same keen disgust with hypocrisy, the
same strength of opinions that guided him away from practical concerns of the life profane, the same inchoate will to live
as both mind and body urged with an honesty both preternatural and highly civilized (or is this mere fawning?). Nothing
of Hector's behavior thus far provides a hint as to the answer,
and admittedly the question might easily be tossed aside;
but we tend toward some degree of temporal linearity in our
quest, however earnest, with whatever demented tenacity, to
understand the events of the world, from the simplicity of
"he gets that from his father" (which is generally an argu-
able conclusion) to the complexity of the rollover of empires
which "carry within them the seeds of their own destruction"
(as was noted in the Muqadimmah, unless the interpretation
of the cyclical nature of kingdoms Khaldun describes stresses
the causality of the external corrective force, in which case
complexity multiplies complexity to the point where we may
no longer be discussing empires at all, rather the world that
seethes without its borders). So do Hector Robitaille and
Donnie Garvin find themselves in the same pages without
rubbing elbows, yet by the very nature of nature impenetrable seem to be the cause of our rubbing philosophical elbows
together, much like and much to the same effect as Hector's
first laughable attempt to spark a fire.

Some mysteries, fortuitously, are readily soluble. Why,
for instance, would Donnie up and fly to Europe with a

man he had just met, in the middle of his first semester at a
prestigious university with little or no regard to the thoughts
and feelings of his parents. Yes, the answer is easy, but this is
not the place to elaborate at length on Donnie's childhood,
though there is more than enough time to summarize his
views of his parents:

His mother was a phony and a tyrant who loved her luxury yet wrote pretentious poetry about historical tragedies,
yes even an entire volume on the Holocaust, part of which
happened in her backyard where radishes represented mass
graves, poetry with bombastic themes that earned her national acclaim and invitations to all the major universities
in the land including Harvard; in fact, a percipient reader
might guess at this point that Donnie's agreement to leave his
university has a subtext—that he was afraid Mommy would
invade (constituting a fraction of the greater mystery). His
father he regarded with something more adolescent than
pity. Donnie thought he was a good man ruined by love and
fear, too withdrawn to be a father and a friend, who made
decisions that went against Donnie's will as if he were being blackmailed by his wife, whose vision of Donnie's future
would prevail even if it meant the destruction of Donnie's
relationship with his father, even her, for if Donnie did not
become a leading academic or famous author then he might
as well be orphaned, for her offspring *would* succeed, as was
clear when Cleo published her first volume of poetry at age
14, a book of pentameter and precocious insights into rela-
tionships and the way they go sour, and which led to what
punishment the parents could muster, which wasn't much as
they attributed Donnie's outburst to jealousy—a radish could
be an entire quarter of Jews from Lvov, but Donnie's insight
could only be sibling rivalry—when he said, "But Cleo, pretty as it all is it collapses as soon as you have the pleasure of
getting fucked."

10

FORT VANCOUVER

There's no need to go hungry in the wilderness, even if you're a bumpkin, a citified riverbank crawler, the kind of guy who figures you ought to do what we all know we did when we advanced from whatever we did before to hunting with spears we made by ourselves and thrust or flung into large animals on the other side of the oceans, or maybe what the Injuns do, and so you carve a stout stick you cut off a live tree so it's got some grump to it—takes a long time if you want a good diameter—and sharpen one end to a point that can make your thumb bleed when you test it, but you have no stealth and never come close to any sizeable animal and suddenly, probably because you're on the hunt and the denizens of the forest know such things and convey it by forest means beyond your comprehension, you don't even come across a skunk or a coon, much less a beaver, those clever fucksacks. No, no need to go hungry at all, and so in the weeks Hector remained lost in the forest he ate all kinds of things, some even considered delicacies to this day, such as the champignon mushroom, which as the only mushroom he knew could be et without dying of nightmare visions was the only one he trusted to slip past his lips, and of which he found but few and only once, and some eatins he would probably never tell anyone about, like a freshly dead baby bird about half the size of a finch. But that's no indication of what nature has to offer the man dying of starvation: Hector also ate grasshoppers, grubs, flies, mosquitoes, ants, earwigs, butterflies, mouse bones, fish (one, small), grass, flowers, soft bark, several handfuls of ephemeropterae, worms, beetles of bewildering varieties and similar taste, bird

eggs, bird, a feather, dirt, dirt teeming with life forms smaller
than ants, squirrel (his greatest hunting triumph—he hit it
with a stone, stunning it, but it scampered away after falling
off the branch it had been on, mocking Hector, just asking
fer it, after which a chase involving much flailing, falling,
branch swinging, poking, and kicking before Hector finally
whipped it in an extended splenetic spasm, whipped it a good
fifteen minutes with a willow branch by the side of a stream,
whipped it long after it was dead, but did calmly roast it and
enjoy his first satisfying meal for days that numbered more
than he could any longer figure), millipedes, centipedes,
backswimmers, water boatmen, lacewings, the body of a rhinoceros beetle he decapitated himself, June bugs, three drag-
onflies, crickets, phasmids, (three times, as he was searching
for mouthwatering bark) frogs, bullfrogs (one speared and
roasted on the north bank of the Salmon along with several
leopard frogs, eaten guts and all so's it'd add up; this where
he finally crossed the Salmon near where these days you'll
find the Wind River packing bridge, almost far enough west
he might have avoided the last of the Salmon Mountains,
yet instead on a fog laden early morning followed the ravines
of least resistance, managing somehow to trudge northwards
to the east of Gospel Peak entirely unaware that he was in
the mountains and so on into a puzzle forest of valleys that
run every possible direction, sometimes five parallel roughly
north/south cut off by a run of east/wests [roughly], probably an indication of tectonic violence, the geometry of result
imposed by the human construct of order, a forest where he
wandered all too aware he was lost, for some three weeks remaining in a zone more or less bordered by the heights known
today as Baking Powder Mountain, Sourdough Peak, Nipple
Mountain, Bowl Butte, and Snowy Summit, an area which
if it were square would be something like 100 miles a side,
the whole time endeavoring to press on westwards and utterly
mystified that little westwards he did go), tree frogs, a shaven
toad, larvae, slugs, crawdads, a newt, a salamander (which led
to a wasted day of tearing apart rotted wood searching for another one), a handful of tadpoles, leeches, roots (a handful of

which were edible in the sense we consider edible), caterpil-
lars, inchworms, a not so freshly dead baby rabbit, and one
certain…well…it's really not necessary to mention it…

The result of this diet was, foremost, to prolong the process of starvation. The sign that it was not salutary was that
it brought on shitstorms such as no sphincter deserves to endure. Hector knew his time was running out. After nearly
three weeks he weakly walked up a ravine to what looked
like the highest point in the wild northwest and happened
to be what we call Sourdough Peak today. By the time he
reached the peak, feeling as if he could not manage more
than another few steps, he realized that his very purpose for
making this trek—to get a long view of the terrain and thereby find a means to get himself west where he hoped he might
find Injuns that would either feed him properly or finish him
off—would be defeated if he could not climb a tree at the
summit, a pine tree, a pine tree with trunk that failed to yield
branches until it reached a good ten feet or so, this simply
because the summit was rich in trees and not by virtue of its
height a lookout for human lostfolk.

Dispirited. Hector became dispirited. For all the brainy
feats he had accomplished—most noteworthy keeping the
squirrel hide for a water sack (empty? or was there a little
where the arms hung?)—and for all the sense it made to once
and for all get bearings, here he was, at the highest point he
could find, after a hike that was no easier all in all than his
several days of crawling wounded, shitting furiously on the
hour and too weak to stand without leaning against a trunk
that he forced to appear to mock his effort to survive.

Interestingly, Hector was well acquainted with the word
mock, while utterly ignorant of the term irony. Though of
course, at this point education was, as it was destined to become, academic. Yet man is not utterly defeated, at least as a
species, as long as he understands the power of the idea, and
the idea came to Hector that a tree, no matter how big, and
how high its limbs began sprouting, had not the ability to
mock. Local Injuns would beg to differ, but they had made
themselves scarce. Hector drained the squirrel sack to give

himself, consciously, the illusion of strength enough to go forward, to keep his mind working, and he thought, howm I knows this be the high point, all these tree around and such.

And indeed, but a short distance from where he stood the ground seemed to upslope, in fact, did so, for his lungs labored as he walked the seventeen steps to the tree that sprouted there; of course, this he did far more slowly than he thought in his condition of impending delirium—delirium did not lack for the talent to mock, nor did it lack that carnivore in the dark at the fire's edge ferocity, impatience, and gorelust—but in thinking he was moving rapidly he did so without much care and scraped his face on a branch, a branch head-high, and yes he did stumble and fall to the ground, and yes he did feel the creep of dispiritation, but he lay looking up at that branch as one would a mean and drunken father we know oncet meant well, and realized it was a branch from the tree from which he had suffered the blow of mockery, a very long branch, and one that as it would led all the way back to that tree for the root of all treeson is tautology.

Solitude maketh of man many an oddity, and this one, weak and, let's be frank, dying, stripped off his buckskins and smote the earth with shit such as that earth had never before been smote, wiped with a handful of pine needles, and began the swingclimb of the branch, which may not have held his weight a few months ago, but seemed more than hospitable now, even if his lack of weight and balance roughly put him at the break-even. Oh for the opposable toes, the prehensile tail, which would have allowed him to sloth his way upward, so he would not have to innovate under the constant duress of knowing failure meant death. Some way up, he slid round and was clinging legs and arms and hand to the underside of the branch that gave down and away and upswung to another branch, which Hector grabbed, finding that though the branches thus mounted sluggishly pressed to widen him, he was able to make rapid enough progress to enliven his spirit, to flood him with that physical manifestation of hope without blinders often mistaken for so many explanations where none exist (adrenaline, caffeine and the like), and in due time had scampered, albeit slothly, to a height that had, well, just gotten done mocking him, and he risked a turn to face the direction the sun called west and saw there paths of air through the trees, and far in the distance a high ridge, a peak that appeared much higher than this one, and so, knowing his next step toward survival aside from landing safely back on the ground was to find water, he climbed higher, and he climbed higher, and pushing branches from his view he saw a high ridge to the west running north/south as far as the eye could see, and beyond that a high point that seemed higher than the one he was on, and so he pondered, and he stepped to the north side of the tree branch by branch and gandered off thataway and saw a fold to the north, not all that far away, perhaps to be reached simply by retracing his route and may- be another half day, and he figured that fold for a river valley (let us not be coy, for he had spied the valley of what we call the South Fork of the Clearwater) that would run generally west, and he rested as he absorbed these thoughts, resting so that these thoughts could coalesce into enough of an idea that he could find the simulacrum of strength he would need to accomplish his plan of reaching water in time to survive (enough of happenstance and rivulet, I say), drawing a black curtain the meanwhile on the need to eat between now and the fetching up of what offerings the westerly had to offer. Maybe he'd find a dead baby bird on the way.

How horrible to report the return of Hector to the like- ly mortambulatories of the knuckle walker, a re-descent of a man, who, upon determining to descend straight to the river he knew was there and would both nourish him and lead him to westward succor, stepped north at too brisk a pace, gaining a false sense of strength of mind as well as speed, moving from step to stride to lope to leap to running loping leap from mound to rock to mound to rock to root to stone to mound to depression up root over ditch to mound, all in a dementium of glee as if the river were but a ghostflight off and not perhaps two dozen miles, so that when he slid on a mossy mound of stone, skidded through fern, side-loped a tree, now seeking without thought a leveling of ground, wheeling leftwards from the game trail into a stand of pine he danced about at still unfamiliar speed ticketicking branches until his foot hooked a yearning root and he flew to come crashing down hard to his shoulder, banged his head and flopped once, foot flying over head, foot following, to lay still awaiting the message from his body of catastrophic bone-break, his thoughts as vibrant with the ungainly as his terrible downrush, now recalling the laughter of Injuns, now dreaming a long slide on moss and fern to the river as if riding a bed of kelp, a louse on a giant bear knew not how he was separated from his family that lived on a sow, now stunned in incalculable pain such as one who has taken a fierce beating on a riverboat. Lost was the squirrel bag, torn were the knees of the buckskin, scraped were the hands, feet, knees, arms, chest, face, and ears, and bruised were the bones of the knees both cap and side, skull, particularly left side where first head bash occurred, ankles, which had been oblivious to the petty pummelings of obstacles, shoulders, particularly the left, and elbows. A man long alone but rarely looks at the spectacle of himself, nor did Hector recover to nought but thirst and need to quench, and such is the meaning of some endurance, for had he but lingered a moment over the stretched scaly skin that covered that of his bones what was not scraped through, scratched here and there through elsewhere and of the nature of dead leafage, he would have despaired not only of his life persevering, he would have thought it already finished, and this the afterlife, but a mental continuation of the final moments, likely for purposes of fully absorbing the folly that fells all. In fact, when he did begin to crawl, when like those innumerable species now lost in time, not knowing of the future knuckle walking that would usher in, unstoppable, unspeakable plagues of violence multiform to wash across the earth, he had yet to determine his next move, had crawled a good mile or two retaining the necessary unhingement of mind to gesture loco and motiveless at pursuit, finding the path the better to walk knuckly down, it be not as seen from on high, a riverine of green, rather an irregular tramping, with its obstacles, its ups and downs even if generally down, and Hector himself a spectre of autumnal colors, each move improbable as the last, the last never arriving but for sleep disturbed by thirst, thirst generating crawl, a spectre degrading wilds that so kindly mute disdain of his inchings.

Speak not of the mind of man now. Speak not of man. Speak not. The forest shall never fall silent. Big Ass heeds not the sojourn of the louse. Gravity shall ever pull, rivers never despair recurrents.

The sky was a phantasm, a phantasmagoria, a phrenetic phenomenon of phases in stasis, yet chimerical, kinetic chaos locked unloosed, the eye of a hurricane directly above, rippling as if reflecting on the wrapplings of the South Fork of the Clearwater that Hector awoke glancing rightward down upon like an expiring trout, his cheek feeling fused to the stone or the stone to the bone of his cheek, his facial skin tissue thin, thinner even, as to be near vaporous as the transience of the skyward mysteries projecting illusory distance even as it quivered in meet on the waters it would not enter nor disdain, waters flowing as if to depart, carrying not the sky even in mere image, flowing as if to depart yet staid in turgid agreement with riverine banks as in a dance unto death. Hector's head lolled, and his eyes defied gravity for a nonce, carrying his head beyond the capacity of his neck, and he looked at the sky as a simpleton, he looked at the sky in all its complexity. There was a hole through the lowering glowering layering swirls, ropes, rugs, canvasses, swells, drifts, aggressions, a detached eye from a wayward hurricane, and through the hole to the top of the sky Hector saw the zenith was white, the hole was a hole but the hole was white and ended in white. The sun had no place in this world. And so like an expiring trout Hector flopped head off rock to the grassmudbank and he drank—Hector drank and slept and slept and drank by the bank of the trembling stream, the dissembling stream neath the illusion of motionless sky, from whence in darkness came the trembling howls, and guttering growls of a pack of wolves, as if Hector so near the dead could no longer fall feverish to the blistering infernos of his own feary dreams, for to Hector these canine terrors did as the wolves themselves lap at his remains like tongues of flame, like wolves at prey, feinting forward side forward back side forward side back, five at once, feinting like tongues of flame in Hector's cooled and painstaking brain—for Hector's thinking soon was as spare and logical as a spine without discs. The thing was not to bend. There were five wolves, but counting wolves was not to his purpose, for he was a mere elk eater. Hector had pulled to a hide behind a bush, the other side of which was a spit of sand and grass, the arena for this blood spectacle, the elk backed tail to the river, beshitten and shitting anus to the river. The hole in the sky was in memory a moon, for the sky was not but moon and stars and the arena lit pale. The elk was on his forefeitlocks, in antler writhing prayer, unwilling to go to his god lambly. Both his front legs were more bloodwound than fur and a wolf was attached to a rear thigh, causing a spasm of defeat concentrate with power enough to fling the teeth from their hold. Hector's first assay was elegant in its economy. He must eat this elk to live, death dogs be damned. He leapt to the extent his slink from behind the bush could be abrupt and rose from a hunch to a hover, grootling with all his might, "Graway!", attracting the attention of three dogs, enough for a pause—two returned to the assault, one bounded a feint at Hector, baring teeth and sickly blackened gums, and returned to the assault so that all five were on the elk, who was agonizing in an elkatory, forewarned forlorn blast "Graway!" that was as feckless as Hector's. O mother of Rome, what humans brand thee! To you, Wolf, is granted much esteem we rob from each other—and for what! Coordinated attacks in teams of teeming canined canines, alternating attacks to overwhelm an overwhelmed foe combined with the curwit to retreat. Yet look here ye of higher houndry: such esteem and less I grant: a committee of hedgehogs with halfwit human brains could capably coordinate the demolition of nations and do provided the military might. What are you to Hector? Hector thinks none of this, nor did he then. Five idiot wolves could take down the most intelligent of medium-sized elk. No, Hector thought only this: five. Five wolves. And he was correct to refrain from exaggerating the prowess of the pack. For in the half hour or so that it took Hector to spark, flame, and fire, then burn to a torcher a stout stick, the wolves had only just begun their repast, the elk but minutes beyond the suspiring state. The spinal simile was hardly serendipitous, not for anyone. The skeletal spectre of Hector in the moonlight by the bank of the South Fork of the Clearwater, flame flaming afore him as a separate hellish agent frightened the beasts for far less than he was worth, for lack of reason, for a dog is a dog is a dog.

And Hector had his meat, and his meat was life, his life, for longer, the looks of it, and after being loosetoothed and weak, somehow gorge on the warm raw flesh, and sleep and drink and suck of meat and drink and sleep, Hector calculated larvae and fought sleep long to build a fire and a spit. And once the mighty carcass was cooked, Hector unwittingly initiated a rite of his own, making a circle of fire around his spit, diameter much in line with the mathematics of radius and circumference, inference enlightened by forest solitude, diameter fifteen feet, pie are not squared, keeping the fire aburnin two full days of slow dining and sipping from the horny skull of the vanquished, for that is what the rite details.

So that a man recognizable as of his subgeno now generated the git up in go of a circumstantial pilgrim, having, to what extent he was capable, wrapped cooked meat in a furry parcel, using flexible sapling bark for to tie, and knowing of the process of rot hoping, saltless as he were, to meet further meat or better, friendly folk, as he walked downstream toward the general west. His hair was still patchy, and his teeth loose but for one that he swallered after it stuck in the raw flank of the elk the first night, and which he picked out of his shit the next morning, washing it in the stream and placing it talismanlike in his knife pocket, which was by now a great portion of his clothing, as his shirt was lost between mountain and river in his delirious descent, while his pants had been repeatedly sliced for footwear, a process Hector had no practice in and indeed no related practice in and yet still more indeed no patience for so that he did in fact take to tearing at times and now his left pantleg was short enough in the crotch that when his balls swung that way they either swaggled free or caught on the fabric, causing discomfort and indeed bringing Hector to a genital adjusting stall. Hector was aware that these were better days and such was not to be downgormed by; in fact, Hector indeed brewed inward a spritely disposition, much as he was a filthy wraith with more beard, a heartier beard than that beard what grew timidly atop his pate, so's that in society he would be like men he had seen that scurried after trifles, spoke to themselves, sermonized strangers, dove into muddied streets after oddments their broken minds took for gewgaws or even baubles: he had often noted that these men scurried like fearful critters yet never seemed to have what Hector recognized as real fear in their eyes. Now he loped a lopier lope by the hour, gaining strength as he loped rather than losing it, and welcomed the return of that normalcy that may though it be each to his own a sanity underscored by either the hope or the evaporation of its lack, was not, nay and this for a sartin, the defective thinking of the damned, the dying, the deranged by dearth; perhaps, though Hector did not precisely formulate his mentals such, he had regained his previous self, the self that had suffered a slow denudation from the moment he set foot in Fort Vancouver and the remains of which were nearly torn from him as he himself gutted the rare fish he speared with a more carefully carved and longer spear, which, considering the year and globe placed him in the realm of tools in utter contradistinction to the Zulu subgeno with their assegai. Never mind. Hector's gutting was physically incomplete and mentally temporary, the scar tissue likely to engender greater magnitudes of frontal lobial capacities, not to mention the likelihood that the man who emerges from such travails has already surpassed the street scurrying spasmodics in potency and cannot but fail to re-enter the society of his fellows a finer specimen, provided further travails fail to, let us say, bring down lupinely, or if smaller and in greater numbers, wolverinely, this elk, and though Hector was in no mind to ponder his near future the fact was he was still far from halfway back to Fort Vancouver, quite possibly faced a more assiduously grievous starvation such as one in which food remains unavailable pre-corpse, numerous diseases, another bear attack, an arrow of a sudden piercing his neck through, a crippling fall, ague compounded by a merciless stretch of rain, countless sources of infection, revenge of the wolves, heat stroke, heart attack, an intensification of fungal assault on the crotch of such vehemence that life is no longer worth living or worse that madness returns in the midst of fungal scraping and he dies sometime in the midst of tearing at his own balls.

An emberizine bird flew into his head, how to explain across epochs, as if bunted, soft, verily, plopping to the ground, as if in sacrifice, righting itself to assume that natural dignity *Homo sapiens* bestows upon anything that looks as if it has shoulders and is wearing a suit or vest or both, and walked, stately yet not corvine, off into the pines. Days had passed loping the banks of the South Fork of the Clearwater, and the food was gone but for the tongue, which Hector fell to meditating on for long stretches, broken often enough by treacherous felled lumber, slippery rocks, boulders, even muck traps of nature, green atop, black as bloody mind below as far as the body could sink—these Hector came to spear afore trodding, so't that the worst of it was one scare where he was hip deep afore he had the idear to swift turnabout and use the spear as a paddle back to suckless land, making it yet knowing once again the tremolos of death nearing to the crepuscule of stillness, that last shade before passing over. The bird was rapidly out of sight, its color scheme matching the bark of the pines—it may have been flightless—and nor did Hector pause his lopestride, yet a distraction about a distraction brought his attention to a dense tuft of riverside grass, and there was the movement again and this time downward into the shallows, invoking the savagery of the huntsman Hector hoo hooted as he lurched as if powerful and speared the muskrat about the shoulder, lifted it high out of the water, and shouted, as a shout, "Fort Vancouver!" for that was all he had been practicing. Of time and the river as nexus, Hector had inchoate sense, if not wild eyed glee at the spectorale of the living furfish, speared, wet, spraying, gleaming in sun, not yet even having begun to die, and Hector feeling shoulders working for this purpose, the sun heating afore descent, trees shading, rustling, grass springing after underfoot, disease else-where, thirst dried desquamatories of memory, faint, hunger scant and to be appeased. Could such be life on the South Fork of the Clearwater? Not if a cut went septic or a winter arrived, no. And so it was all to the good that Hector went not foresty, but came upon folk, them what's always around a bend, for even the straightest stretch follers a bend, and the South Fork of the Clearwater bent and Hector went along with that bend and heard splashing before spying a woman in the bareness of birthright flapping textiles agin a rock. Near-ing her at a slowing lope, he began to see that she was of womanly age, fur below and wide sacks of tit bearing thum-bly nipples, hair black entire, body thin at ankle and neck, slightly bottom heavy less from rump than thigh, and nearer now, face shaped like a squat pear, narrow across the upper skull, beneath the level of the eyes billowing out at cheeks so much that the bones eponymous could scarcely be detected. Her nudity was not a surprise to Hector nor a concern.

Much as such sorts of subgeno meets be despicable to both sides so must they be carried out—one delights in imag-ining that each and every time instinct were illimitable repul-sion, action swift—oh! what a different world for the weary of today—and so Hector and the first of the Nimipoo to ad-mit setting eyes on him would make exchange of humanity, peaceable like, for neither had either a grievance against the other, and though Hector was not a legendary figure yet, he was a story, and it would be a matter of some surprise if this Nimipoo woman was not to some degree pleased.

She arranged her fabrics on a flat rock to be dried by the sun, and bade Hector sit where there was space while she squatted before him. He disburdened himself of his supplies and looked into the gaping vulva of the woman before awk-wardly noticing what he was up to and seeking her eyes.

To the white man the language of the Nimipoo was audible only in palindrome, though the language contained nothing of the kind. To the Nimipoo, the language of the white man was a mess, a disarray of words that ended without natural logic, which was why the Nimipoo always paused longer than was customary among humans before responding. To the Nimipoo, who would have, even through expert translation, understood nothing of the concept of tidiness, it was clear as the Clearwater that the mind of the white man was in complete disarray, like a bear in a bog, mucktrapped, a circumference of trackless infinities surrounding him—the closest to nature, the most generous interpretation the Nimipoo was capable of, the white man could be, must be, descended from, was the flightless bird.

"Nunpargrapnun bab tittlelttit magamanamagam furtuputruf, gemmeg tikapikipakit," the Nimipoo woman seemed to say.

"Fort Vancouver," Hector said, loud and clear. "I am, my name, is Hec-tor."

What the Nimipoo woman had said was, "You are the man who was attacked by the bear. We all thought you would die."

"Telflolflet ded naman gemmeg funfunufnuf lekrikriirkirkel."

"I sure's hell don't know as I kin say much to that," Hector replied, more astute than many a white man this Nimipoo had encountered, though she did not know it.

"You have come a long way and we must now feed you. The bear will not be angry."

"Finteketnif marnram fertigitref ded Rowor."

"Maybe I don look sagood, I uz attackitt by a bar n bin lost n near starved offenall."

"I will go find our tongue man, Rowor."

She motioned with a taut hand for Hector to remain seated, gathered her laundry, and walked into the pines.

She will be back, Hector thought with deliberation.

Naively, he had no fear of being attacked. He was indeed

in no danger of being attacked, we now know, but no tribe of Injun was immune to taking the life of the white man. (This aside from puma, bear, and snake.) The more pacific tribes, naturally, ended fewer caucasoid lives, but the everlasting horror of these events was in particular the utter impenetrability of them.

Often they were called arbitrary, and phrases like eruptions of bloodlust seem apt, though are far from so. Many was the mountain man who made merry with the Flathead, yet few were the white folk who suddenly found themselves facing unsubtle death doing so. Language being what it is, strides of tongue were made toward a common language, but the reason that one comes to hope underscores behavior was a long time in coming. Jeffers Phoebles would tell of the time a trapper he partnered with for a few seasons, a genial, capable man, not too talkative, by name of Howling Jake, shared their whiskey with three Flatheads at their own campfire, to which the Flatheads were invited for to be treated to venison—and whiskey—when, with a passive face, one of the Flatheads upsuddened and split Jake's skull with a contraption much like a tommyhawk. "Ne set back darn n went on wither repast like sif nut untord," Phoebles commented, a revisit of his original bafflement fully overtaking him with each rendering of the tale. Most of the Nimipoo men were gone west for bufflo, but given the opacity of eruptions of bloodlust Hector was none the safer nor none the more dangered. If he knew enough of all this business he would best mutter to himself, well, ull just have t see.

An hour or so'd passed when Hector heard a lope slightly off two leg human time heading towards him. Oddly enough this was the first time he thought "bar" since the attack, standing abruptly in preparation for a rush across the river. But he turned first and saw quite a different animal headed toward him. A mammal, it was, and hairy of head, but human, moving rapidly arachnoid, like a spider a scientist had removed five legs from in a grizzly experiment. It cradled a large salmon that seemed alive it was flung in such odd arcs and angles as required by the unusual manner of transport. The Injun locomoted his personal lope with one good leg, one good arm, and a second (or third) leg that was wobbly and bent 75 to 103 degrees as it worked and had a bone protruding from the thigh, up which skin had climbed near halfway to seal the wound caused when a compound fracture had snapped the femur that upthrust sliced through muscle and skin. Over time the upper portion of the bone had fused with the base of the bentstickbone, providing a solid enough limb, and flexible, if shorter than the other. The tip of the bone, about five inches from the skin patagial, petered up, looked like any other end of snapped bone; looked like it might be hollow as a flute. Maybe, probably, Rowor picked at it. But as a man must needs save one arm for transporting goods, such as this ere fish, yet this third limb was required for balance, as was a certain gallop speed. Hector had endured much and seen many an oddity of late, such anyway, that this phantasm, this spidermaninjun was as acceptable as any wilderness novelty; acceptable, too, as a tolerable sign of his own step back into civilization.

"Moyem bonhomie!", Rowor greeted the survivor with enthusiasm, though making no move to touch.

"Moi no belle sauvage, pero damn real grande. One tongue, many way. Ass felt. Beaverspelt."

This said, he appeared to pause for an appreciative gesture or word.

"Wall, I am name of Hector. I go to Fort Vancouver."

He motioned for Hector to sit, slapping the dead fish down next to him and choosing his own seat on the other side of the offering.

"Parlay." Here he played the fish's mouth to mimic speech.

"Let go, Rowor." he said in a child's high voice. "AAAAAAg-waaaaa."

"Hah." Rowor answered the fish.

Hector was amused, but still one layer of social skin away from spontaneity, so he simply smiled.

Rowor slit the belly of the salmon with a long and sharp nailed forefinger, reaching into the cavern to help along out the innards, which dropped to the ground at their feet, where three dogs appeared before the last thread of sangiunover-mury had drooled from the carcass.

"Sangfreud. Mangia."

He held the fish in both hands, apparently offering it to Hector, who mimed a full stomach.

Rowor laughed and fluttered a hand over the heads of the scrapping dogs.

"Tutto. Grimmeinshaft. Slurry…guts dropped, dog-swarm, hurry. Waste not no baby."

He scraped scales off with his fingers and held them up for scrutiny before shaking them onto the dogs.

"Dreck shine with all colors twixt sun and moon."

This was a moment for reflection. Rowor set the fish between himself and Hector, kicked at the dogs with his more typical leg, and tucked the other at some angles, foot beside his buttocks.

"Napolealaelopan bumub," he said softly, with apparent wonder. "Fort Vancouver. Water colo. Señor. Negro bootoob, nine say pa? Bridger speek this, parlay non, vaminos. How I go forth. Vous…beavermensch?"

Hector knew this comparatively long speech was over when Rowor looked at him. Not only that, his rather thin lips had met to go forth in what begins as an offer to kiss and ends as an expression of exaggerated wonder or thought, depending on the earnest demeanor of the eyes. The kind of look boys stop making late during adolescence if they have a mirror to look into. The deltas of wrinkle away from the eyes seemed no reflection of age, the ears were almost perfectly rounded and small like mushrooms after the stem's plucked out, and the body was exceptionally thin and looked to be rubbery—Hector refrained from looking at the wonders below the waist, except for maybe a passing glance.

"You mean am I a beaver hunter….I et un. But I ain't no beaver hunter."

"Porque beaver mensch tutto beaver morte? Tutto beaver. Mad banjax. Black Foot, Creecrow, nunnun like.

Make harmicide, tutto beavermensch. Is white king grande eefrum big beaver? Flekelf ded soroboros.

"Parlay now: think. Beavermensch make harmicide, nine say pa?"

Hector was unsure what all this meant, and it was spoken in that soothing way Injuns have just before they slice your throat, or when they're genuinely friendly and wind up not slitting your throat even for no reason, so if it hadn't been for the clear expectation that he respond he would have said what he wanted to, which was I don't understand you at all. Instead, he said, "I believe I agree with you mister," a phrase Uncle Bob had taught him for when he had to leave young Hector amongst strangers for a spell.

"Bien german. You go with river to Fort Vancouver. You martvich sienna tutto all time keep eye open back to wall. Bridger, borracho bad y tambien tutto beavermensch. Tak!"

"How's I t go by river, Mister Rowor?"

This was the best joke of the day so far and Rowor laughed about five minutes from the humor of it and another five out of customary politeness.

Sometimes an Injun'll laugh before killing with a tommy-hawk. Or even just a stone if you're laying down.

"Moi, ca va? I, Rowor, take you, one river, tutto. Half moon. Back, moon. I take you, nine say pa?"

That was unambiguous, but too good to be true.

"But Mister Rowor, I have no money and I can't grantee thell payap at the fort."

This was the second best joke of the day.

"I defenetre you near Fort. Rowor no try martvich sienna evil in fort. Bridger, borracho bad. Big Fixed Packer kneeyay-bezpyechknee—gefgarlick. Gonif grande. No meet on path. Viva leava."

"Fitzpacker! That's the cunnyass thew me innu the bar made me like, made me, why that there Fitzpacker's the shiteatin skunkcuntlickin…You knowm?"

"Muy merde cono, rompere balle schwein! Grande demon. Many arrows for beavermensch grande."

One can imagine the exhaustion brought on by Hector's good natured efforts to understand the polylingual freak, and he was grateful when, after, some English words nestled amongst a thick manger of others seemed to mean it was time to cook, and shortly after that, the words meant follow me, and he was led, refreshed by the spectacle before him that was Rowor leading the way in his scamper, let us say, to a short, roofed hut made from a frame of stout logs and draped with dear skins for a roof and most of four walls. Inside Rowor pointed to a woven mat, and on that mat Hector's travails came to an end during a night of dreamless sleep.

In the morning, Rowor had prepared for the trip while waiting for Hector to awaken. Their boat was something like a canoe, with less draught, though with a slash of a keel, and wider, made of lighter woods. Two benches, fore and aft, were available for the sailors; the midsection was rigged with a three foot pole (a young tree made branchless and scalped) and canvas that covered their supplies, which were limited largely to foodstuffs, though Rowor had included his bow and many arrows, perhaps enough to bring down a Fitzpacker. Both the front and rear of the vessel sloped visible downward and were separated from amidships by a tarred stick, a sort of midget bulkhead. A spongiform plug was affixed into a hole a few inches above the water line. From the looks of things, it would take a terrific downpour to soak their goods or sink their boat.

Hector rambled thataway on waking, coming upon three women and Rowor. The women looked him over at length, expending much curiosity on his wounds, especially at his neck, until finally one of them offered him summer buckskins and slippers. Some Nimipoo was spoken as he put them on, not the least shy of his nether parts and their nudity given the ghoulish aspect he figured he presented anyway, and one woman dashed off—like the one from the previous night and the other two she appeared to be about middle-aged and was only stout from the upper thigh to the ribcage or so. Yet she was back as fast as a deer, which would have had a hell of time hoofing the rope she brought for Hector to use as a belt.

For whatever reason, probably there was a mood of pre-voy-
age gravity coercing the moments, there was no mirth whatsoever, which Hector felt as the mild reproach of something
like an animist spectre betrayed by the sudden extinguishing
of a multitude of ignes fatui. Certainly he felt nothing but
gratitude towards the woman, and Rowor he was about to
spend the next two weeks with, if he had understood cor-
rectly—full moon back, so downstream there, about half the
time, and he thought he had heard the actual words "half
moon." In minutes, without even the ado of an embrace or
a look back at the women, Rowor sat hunched over in the
prow, all business until they reached a wide stretch, when he
turned around and said, "Yoom lucky, perche uno rio all way
to big salt water. Fegef ded rimipimir. Nine say pa?" "Nine
say pa," Hector answered, believing that what Rowor was telling him was that the river they were on went all the way to
the sea, which would mean it would have to pass Fort Vancouver, that there would be no navigational problems. He
thought repeating "nine say pa" would please Rowor, but it
seemed that Rowor expected him to say exactly that. Maybe
whenever Rowor spoke with white folk, whatever language,
and Hector did recognize some influence of French, though
wasn't sure Mexicans were white and rio was Mexican, maybe nine say pa was some sort of universal friendly agreement.

Maybe if someone said nine say pa and you said Non
you'd get yer gut slit by a big knife.

For reasons unclear even now, summer up northwest-
ernway bred far fewer mosquitos than the forests along the
Mississippi. After the first day of the comfort of travel while
seated, of the security of being among friend and local who
knowd how to do all that need be done, a cleanliness more
cleanly than before Hector had left the Mississippi delta, of
dining with the assurance that just as large and fine a meal
would be had when the need arose, of fearless ease midst the
static and erratic of nature wild, vast, inscrutable yet pacific
under sun and stars once they camped for the night, of water
cool as the heat demanded and warm enough to the balls,
of a night meal by a fire someone else made, eating a tasty

slab of meat someone else roasted, Hector fell asleep thinking about mosquitoes, the absence of mosquitoes, and, rare
moment, knew what he knew, knew what he felt and knew
that knowing, like a long slow comet Hector thus fell asleep,
a comet moving directly away from the eye to darkness, concentrically philoso- phizing; Hector fell asleep feeling more
content than he knew life offered.

For the next few days downriver Rowor rafted, speaking
sportively of such as the cliffs, the hills, the meadows, the
clouds, that other world in motion beneath the boat, the life
of a Rowor, the lives of fish and elk and bear and rabbit and
skunk and beaver, and many animals Hector could not make
out from his speech, but loved along with Rowor, for he had
come to love Rowor, even to the point he knew he would
miss him, wished they could be together for many years
somewhere that refused to make itself clear. There was no
stoic clarity of rational thought to Hector's vagaries regarding
Rowor, nor yet were there tears, nor would there be tears, for
something that does not quite change a man, something far
more subtle, profound, complex than that, something happened that would be more difficult to specify than a moment
in evolutionary time had occurred within andor without
Hector that would make his time on this land more pleasant
no matter what lifted and tossed him, no matter what sought
to rip out his heart and eat it raw. And so when on the fifth
day, Rowor stopped early, and together they bathed and gam-
boled, playing catch-it-by-hand-no-wrong-kind, and when after that idyllic afternoon and evening and soft night, Rowor
took him around one last bend to within sight of Fort Vancouver, Hector was unmoved by surprise, and merely said to
Rowor, pointing, "Leave me on that side."

11

BY AEROPLANE TO THE OLD WORLD

During the drive to the airport Donnie slept and never did remember to express his surprise that Drake was driving a 1985 Toyota Celica, one of those cars the cynical amongst the citizenry considered the classic example of an automobile built so well it quickly went out of production, and so it was a long time before he found that Drake had traded his own 2009 Volvo Tracer to his friend Red straight up for the Celica, destined to be abandoned at the Philadelphia airport.

Awakened with his mind immediately working like a perpetuum mobile, inflexible, inexorable, interminable, and built by someone else, Donnie went through the process of becoming a man on a jumbo jet from a man snoring in a taxi cab much in the manner of a mind-controlled terrorist, if such exist, deliberating on the exhibition of the human condition before him, the strange unbearable slowly pulsing contours that cradled context, the mind slipping ghostly to other worlds, the body contained, the self thus more body than mind, for the mind that roamed in simulacrum of freedom moved along with the body that took its shoes off and offered itself to the human touch of an airport frisker. Virtually sleepless, hungover, or stoned, Donnie was prey to such drifts of mind and subject to the torment of the giant context that mocked the humans that thought they had built it—perhaps they had—but the skin of the context was organic, he knew at such times, and felt he knew, that it was a living entity, it took pleasure in reading his thoughts when they most keenly tore at the absurdities dangling like shredding bunting all about him. Mantras developed: as Drake guided him through the logical progression from pedestrian to flyer the question What were the legs for? repeated itself, insisted that it be repeated and not be answered…Yes, it could all be managed without legs, of course, so what were the legs for. When, further, will they become vestigial? The enormous skin of the context never chuckled such that its movement altered its rhythm to the point it could be detected, yet a mocking storm of atmosphere accumulated about Donnie even as he boarded the giant winged vessel.

Thy bung
Hath flung
Some dung
On US, yes, but not on these two:
Donnie and Drake,
Fully fledgling, fetal near
Their fartings about fare far,
Fairly fly (as they are indeed about to)
Forth, fecund, and fainaiguely
Free and fearmounting
Fie! We else are nought but
Filthards!
Cackards!
Stinkards!

You should see what I did to my car, not in celebration of Hector's arrival at Fort Vancouver, no!, in thrilled thrall of my schemings, their schemings, that is, that interest me exceedingly—I did say fetal!—in that they have yet to fully form within even that which is known yet yet to be. Alack! nay, anon: never before have I had two protagonists so fit, both in mind and body, young men armed with wit, intelligence, without neurasthenic hiccups…that I feel as if anything is possible, perhaps as they subconsciously do, even that those aspects of doom I am aware are approaching them inevitably will not obliterate them, nay again, that there is even the chance of a sort of pre-death plane of super-contentment one or both may experience…that they might even outlive me as

I try to keep up with them drink for drink—the quest was not the thing, oh but rather the intensity of celebration, autochthonous, these two flying to Europe!, I quaffed a b'o-uh'l of Irish whiskey and Belgian beer and hopped slaphappily into the auto and raced narrow winding Slavic roads toward the mountain top:

Demented

Dented

Not rented

I returned, clutch burnt, tires flat, rims not round, a failure here to write of success there, and I will match them cigarette for cigarette still, for I embrace this common debilitating ailment that we perpetual yoafs with our aching backs and grotesque fungal toes adopt knowing we can't keep up, knowing that even if we could their pleasures are no longer ours, that liquor tastes better to them, cigarettes don't make them cough, and bedding women is managed without shame, regret, pathos, derision, and the intense pangs that accompany intangible loss. These youths both live with disdain of wisdom, comprehensive weltanschauunging awareness, the flexibility of physics's plattered offerings, without attenuate segments of angst, remorse, fear, trembling, rage—and neither are they oblivious feasters on zeitgeist, but rebel banqueteers: reveling sturdy amid the unraveled it is they who will upturn the table in their time, with aplomb or a bomb...perhaps I take this too far, but look there, in the aisle of the plane with tickets 22A and C, Drake leaning down toward a tall, slender balding man in his forties, already buckled up and stripped down to his suit vest, that is, having taken off his suit jacket, not everything but the vest, "Excuse me sir, but my friend and I are traveling together, and as such, we would like to sit next to each other. So can we offer you the window seat or the aisle seat?"

"No."

Not yet realizing what he was up against, Drake quickly asked, "No which."

"No I won't trade seats."

At this point plane-welcomed luggage had been stored above and both Drake and Donnie were standing as close as possible to the aisle seat, bent awkwardly forward, mid-mis-bent so that those still boarding and seated behind could pass, and their faces were as close to the bald guy's as they were to each other's. They exchanged puzzled looks.

Drake continued the negotiations.

"You won't trade seats? Everybody trades seats, unless it's a window or aisle thing. No one on a long flight wants to sit in the middle."

"They should."

"Should?" Donnie rhetorically reflected his puzzlement.

"This is the safest seat on the plane."

"How you reckon," Drake took up the oddly persistent topic.

"This is where I sit every flight. I fly often and I always sit in 22B and I have never crashed."

"Lucky seat phenomenon," Drake said to Donnie.

"Seems so."

"Well how about I offer you 100 dollars to exchange?"

"What good would an extra 100 dollars do me if the plane crashes?"

"The plane is not going to crash."

"I know, because I will be sitting in 22B."

"Christ's fucking sake, Donnie, we find the only man on the planet who prefers a middle seat and has that, what is it called, the logical fallacy where your preposterous notions are perpetually strengthened by the fact that they are nev-er unluckily disproven...Listen, mister, this is absurd, but you will only know that if you crash and then you will never learn. The only way to correct your error is to experiment."

"It's not worth my life. I have a family."

"My back is starting to hurt," Donnie told Drake.

Each had been politely bumped repeatedly by passersby, suitcases, humans and the like.

"All right—what if we force you to move?" "I'll cause a ruckus, I'll—Hey!—"

Drake had snatched the ticket from his shirt pocket.

"What now?"

"Ruckus: Help! These—"

Donnie clamped a hand over the guy's mouth. "Give it back—it's not worth it."

Drake gave it back. The man's face was nearly purple, and sweat was already beading his tawnsewer. In fact, he was so relieved by the return of his ticket he actually thanked Drake, who in climbing over his legs, said casually, "I once barely survived a crash—I was sitting in 22A."

There was no response, for the poor man had his head in his hands and was trembling.

"I'll take the aisle," Donnie said.

As a last dagger, Drake said to the almost broken man, "Just so you know, I'm no slouch when it comes to wrestling for the armrest."

In a peep through hands still clutched over his recovering facial pallor came, "You can have it."

Donnie buckled his seat belt and noticed his left hand was damp. He'd frothed, Donnie thought, wiping his palm on his jeans.

"Drake, he—"

Drake was already asleep, head forward left, against the window.

"You frothed," Donnie remarked.

"Terror," the balding guy said, having rapidly recovered his composure.

"Sorry—I guess we didn't know what we were up against."

"Who does?"

"Indeed," Donnie confirmed, then leaned back to the extent possible, stretching his legs to the extent possible, sliding his ass forward to the extent possible. He achieved the perfect balance between discomfort and stability that would keep him awake until the drinks came, when a scotch would pull his mind forward from the brink. He did not like to sleep on airplanes, for the simple reason that they went too fast and he was alive while they flew impossible distances in impossible times—impossible, yes, it was, and he brooked no argument nor spoke of this thought that would surely elicit one. To Donnie, the fact of 900 kilometers an hour was less likely than God, and as God was impossible as ever conceived, so then was this speed. The plane would accelerate rapidly to a humble enough height—not much higher than Everest, but then it would really get moving, fly in an arctic arc, and land in Europe in seven hours. He felt that if he slept the inevitable disorientation would be permanent.

Probably he had a point. There is no telling what aviation has done to the human animal. He felt sure that though countless factors of modernation were involved, madness was increasing among his species exponentially, and to lose one's symbiotic inner sense of time and space was to step into the psychotic realm. Drake would likely be unchanged on the surface once he was in Brussels, but the damage had already been done by countless previous flights. 22b was already insane, not because of his superstition, which was as rational a response to commercial aviation as any, but because of his determination not to die at the specifically designated moments of his flying, as if it would be no problem at all if he had his eyes scratched out and his heart eaten by a scrawny harpy armed with the power of genuine madness as he dragged his luggage behind him in the fast lane of concourse C once landed in Brussels.

Why, Donnie wondered, as thrustforce pinned him to his seat back in an upright position, does no one ever worry about the obesity of thought? So much fat to be trimmed. He imagined a desert, or a deserted scape such as that he saw once the plane sporkled through the clouds to where the sun held sway just to the extent that was fair. The mind needs to find some way to lose weight thoughts; it needs to speed up like the plane and the thoughts could desquamate at impossible speeds until the thought generator was bare, functioning without fat and repetition.

"Do you come here often?"

"What?"

"I asked," said 22b, "whether you fly often."

"No. No I don't fly often."

"I do."

"I suppose you're the type who doesn't like to talk to people you meet randomly, I mean just because you find yourself next to them on a plane."

Donnie looked at 22b. "Donnie Garvin," he said, offering an open hand like he were turning a hand-sized bluegill side-wise to the sun.

22b accepted and they shook short.

"Claude Robinson. You didn't answer my question."

"No."

"So I was right. I fly often, like I said—"

"Always in 22b."

"Right."

"So I can pretty much tell when someone isn't the talking or friendly type, either one."

"Or both."

"Or both."

"No, I can't say I have a consistent position on plane talk."

This came as a surprise.

"Oh! Oh I see. I thought—when you said no—reel it back...No you didn't answer my question. I got it."

"Well, it wasn't much of a question anyway. I'm not much of an airplane talker. If at all it's usually early on, then I sleep or enter a sort of mindless flight zone."

Donnie kept his face turned more or less toward 22b in case this needed to continue, but now the guy was just run-ning his tongue over his lips and Donnie had no interest in surveying that process. Besides, his mind was already in a sort of free-associating travel mode, and although he was merely making the rather mundane hop from North America to the sadder—to him—portion of Europe, his mind was conjuring galumphing lemurs, their knees bent as they run playfully, not all that fast, their arms over their heads and hands curled. A fleeting mind moment, to be sure, but an aspect of con-nection, a glue of sorts, ensuring the constancy of the time and space relationship, probably best understood by the douc langur, or tarsier, or some other creature that put a halt to things before the catastrophe of crossing the line to the to-ward human occurred.

Camels, of course, are a very different matter. In fact, with the exception of their speed, they are very much like airplanes, a vehicle that happens to be an animal, or an animal that happened to have the ill luck to be conceived of as a vehicle, for both people and goods, that changed the lives of people over vast areas when it was "introduced." This was on Donnie's mind, for he had brought along volume 1 of Marshall Hodgson's *The Venture of Islam* and was currently getting the lowdown on the environment, social and otherwise, into which The Prophet was born. Camels had a great role in this environment, to the extent that the very word Arab meant or implied people with camels, which was a very good thing in the Arabian peninsular region at that time. He underlined "The camel nomads called themselves *Arab*" because although it was mentioned earlier in the book in a long introduction on the Western intelligentsia and Islam he had not been stricken by it at the time. Probably he had been skimming. But now, with The Prophet due to arrive any moment, was not the time to skim, and that fact, that the camel nomads called themselves *Arab* seemed something interesting enough to remember. He doubted many people in his past circles, or his present and future circles, would know that and on occasion someone might be interested in hearing it.

"What are you reading?"

"Drake—you're awake."

"They serving drinks? Famous Grouse. Good enough, though it sounds like someone my old man used to…have engagements with."

22b was asleep, his body slouched vermicular, his ass actually slid off the chair yet supported by the proper bend of legs, though soon enough he would simply be on his knees with his head on the lucky chair.

"What are you reading?"

"About Islam. I just learned that the word Arab means something more or less like people with camels."

"Dromedaries."

"Huh?—press that button and a woman will appear with a pleasant demeanor and a remarkable willingness to grant you your grouse."

"The inferiority of the dromedary."

"Ahhhhh! Braudel! You read Braudel?"

"I said I was studying history."

"I thought you meant that's what you were supposed to be doing."

"I have a thing for nomads, so I attended all those lectures and read all the nomad shit. Braudel was the best. I took a seminar that was just Braudel's Mediterranean. Dromedaries— well, I guess you know."

"I do, and I wondered if we can really say that Iran owes its Shiitism to the camel."

"Appears so. They could thrive on the plateau, the Bactrian specials. Their folk 'Islamized,' and as enemies of the Arabians, to simplify, and so they were refuge to the Shiite. That's more or less how I recall it."

"I'm just reading it in more detail now, and I think, if you throw in Braudel, it makes a great deal of sense that way. But I forgot about the dromedary business."

"So what's with the Islam bullshit? Why the fat book?"

"It's actually three fat books—the others are in the suitcase. This is the grand scam of our times, the religious war of the early 21st century, and I want to know Islam in detail the better to tell scumbags to fuck off."

"I don't know…I may be one of those scumbags."

"I'm really barely into volume one, Muhammad is just coming on the scene, so it will be some time before you have to fuck off."

"Don't get me wrong, I'm not a knee-jerk jerkoff Muslim hater, but I'm getting sick of suicide bombs and such. I'm reaching the enough is enough stage, wherein the man says fuck history, this is now, and this is sick, and I no longer give a shit why it all came about."

"I don't care what you are, but to my mind the history makes a difference, and the more I read, the more I'm convinced. I'm not saying Muslims aren't insane, but they're insane in precisely the way Christians are, and Jews. Fanatics have merely torqued themselves to a finer point of insanity. Look, for instance, things I just found out: the Ka'ba preceded Muhammad, Allah preceded Muhammad—and there were Christians and Jews all over the place, for the most part accepted on their own terms as long as they weren't raiding and all that shit."

"That's a pretty speech, sweetheart, but when our hotel gets blown to shreds in Brussels…"

"We die. But what we think beforehand—that's who we are."

"Blah blah blah, my friend…explosions still kill children."

"But let's go back to the dromedary, Drake. I mean, that's what piqued your interest, no?"

"Right. Because I romanticize the wanderer. I was always interested in the nomad. Let's argue later. I mean, in Brussels we're sure to meet Algerians, no? My interest in Braudel, for instance, was in his sidetracks, particularly about the nomads. And that line about the inferiority of the dromedaries: what a fucking—well look here at 22b: is he camel or dromedary?"

"Camel, certainly. For he can take the high countries, the cold climates, the Balkans if need be."

"Right. But does that make us camels as well? Can we not take southern Italy? Spain?"

"Well, as we are going to Brussels first, perhaps we are mere pack mules."

"Good point. But my interest is in the nomad. Have you read the novel *Sleep of Aborigines*?"

"No."

"I'm not surprised. As far as I know the author is a nobody, as befits the writer of nomad literature. But listen, listen to this, my friend Donnie, I, Drake, who am I but a rich man's son, a fool, an intellectual beggar…"

"Oh please…"

"But the one subject I followed, the one I cared a little about, was the nomad. Do you know the novel?"

"No."

"I thought not. It's rather obscure—I don't remember the author's name. But I memorized one passage: listen, it's about what a guy thinks while he looks up a woman's dress, and it really captures the poetry and philosophy of the Bedouin."

"'*The Sleep of Aborigines*'?"

"Yes. I came across it and likely bought it because of the title. Anyway, it was worth it, one of the best novels I ever read, very perverse. Listen, this is just a Bedouin part, it's only one sentence, so be patient: and do listen because this may be the only thing I ever memorized that was longer than two lines —"

"But one sentence."

"One, but a songline. I quote: 'The skin of her thighs clove momentarily when they cleaved, making a sound more silent than an omen and creating a suction as nonchalant as gravity pinning the moon of his mi —'"

"Can I get you another?"

The stewardess had arrived. She tended to bend close enough to Donnie's face to bring about such discomfort as had to be disguised, for the silken tasseled hem of beauty had but brushed her, making her cheeks just a bit too pouched, so that her full and formly lips seemed set back too far, thus requiring dark and penetrating fresh blood lipstick, which then meant the eyes, brown, almost Asiatic, needs must be of blue overshade with heavy, virtually tarred lashes, and once this far into the project, and naturally made fragile with concern, a dementia of the lower order developed, and that required a layer of pancake makeup, which gave her face, on the close inspection she repeatedly forced Donnie to en-dure, the appearance of being masked, which wanted to be fine, and would have been, if she did not have black dots or holes, holes, yes, that's what they were, all over, so that the mask made no sense, was not, then, a mask, rather a face well smeared. Yet Donnie had a strict reluctance to offend on the basis of looks good or odd, and so for their brief exchanges it was he who swallowed her dementia for her — it went down easy enough considering.

"For me and a couple for my friend here who just woke up."

Off she went.

"How soon before she's back?"

"A minute or two — she's quick once she takes the order."

"Then I'll wait. Pretty good so far, though, eh?"

"I like nonchalant as gravity."

"Yes, but see this guy never quits, the sound continues, pinning the moon of his mind to the firmament descending on her oasis. And that's just the beginning."

"And you don't remember his name."

"No fucking idea."

Several silent swirls of thought connected their minds in ways they could not detect, until the stewardess returned with her face and their drinks.

It was all over quickly.

Once the drinks were poured into plastic cups filled with ice, an extra mini-bottle set aside for Drake, Drake continued about the passage:

"Let me start over. Ready?"

"Far as I can tell."

"Okay: 'The skin of her thighs clove momentarily when they cleaved, making a sound more silent than an omen and creating a suction as nonchalant as gravity pinning the moon of his mind to the firmament descending on her oasis, yet another oasis, where he arrived after a long journey over unshifting dunes of event repeated without ceremony, over sunhammered plains of desacralized thought, past the mounds of dead needles fallen from the cacti of deracinated, purposeless words, pausing at wells where a single drop of foul water cowered beneath stones hieroglyphed with an invitation to a quicker, less sordid, demise, passing nights unintercalated by the unwonted primality of dream, nights without moon cold from the deceitful indifference of a sun that would soon rise again in the full fury of its specific hatred of him, arrived finally at this oasis that tricked the sun with its mirror of water until night could descend again, the dromedaries sleep, the date palms find a repose unburdened by the most ancient traditions of hospitality, the pond replenish its secrets in subterranean denials of desert laws, men build boats in their dreams that will cross the ocean where no oar is dipped, women hold babies to their breasts where they hide their smuggled notions of home, and no wind carries off the silken tents that rise up silently, swaying in comportment to the soporific undulations of the dromedaries that correspond to the one unhostile meaning that sent these noble creatures, cloven skeletons of sand, among the people, all but one tent from which a single serpentine bangled one arm beckons the one man, Spleen, who remains outside the folds where night relishes its own multiplicity of oases, calls to him with the music of elemental chimes timed to the rhythm of footsteps and the dance of a charmed cobra tracing the infinite helixes of an hypnotic acquiescence, the very substance of the legs that carry Spleen to the labiate tent entrance beyond which he is encoiled by limbs comprised of the balance between water and sand, that defy the autocracies of sun and time and pursuit and division, that capture the uncapturable, calm the ineffable, derange the faith in absolutes imposed by the survivor by his journey, and he finds in the wine-damp fur darker than the night a nest for his slinking ecstasy, a harbor safe from the predations of mind, an empty quarter, unmapped by the false directions of names, an oasis inside an oasis inside an oasis unsullied by the identity shed in sands at the dehiscence of her tent, and he reaches to touch her face behind the burqa woven of the lacy fringes of the rarest desert clouds and his fingers caress the wind, and her fingers massage the features from his face like the simoom in mockery forming dunes of sand, and now he knows that home is the permanence of a wandering incorporeal secret at rest in the sleep of a mystery unconcerned with itself, swaying with the silken tent burqa, one of the many indistinguishable swaying tents around the desert pool, scattered amid the date palms and mounds of sand that will arise in the morning as dromedaries, swaying silently as the moon that watches throughout their inviolate night…'"

Silence, so much a part of the passage, ensued; miles passed in seconds, Donnie retained his grip on what he thought he needed to; Drake smiled.

Finally, Donnie responded: "Wow," he said.

"Great, huh?"

"Yes, but who is this Spleen?"

"I could say don't worry about it, but I actually do have an opinion. If the passage speaks to you, then you, you are this Spleen."

"All right, it does speak to me, so I am this Spleen, and clearly so are you, and there is of course Spleen one and Spleen two…"

"Between us that's all that matters."

"Then hopefully he didn't sell many books."

"Who?"

"The author, of course."

"Seems not."

"Sensual, philosophical, existentially determined…quite a piece."

"You left out poetic."

"Yes, poetic foremost, tied with philosophical. Plus, it would seem he had read his Braudel."

"Another drink?"

"Ahh!" Donnie subshrieked. "Did we press the button?"

"No, but I was passing by with my cart."

"Oh, how thoughtful, yes then, two more. He hasn't started because he's been reciting, but once he gets going, it will be full speed ahead."

She did her duty with efficient strokes of limb and went off, rolling her metallic pleasure cart.

"Too much make-up, no?" Drake offered.

"Far too much…but damn nice, and efficient, as you see."

Quietly, 22B, Claude, Claude Robinson, awoke, and climbed as slowly as a rachitic old cat onto the chair of life's perpetuation. This was a sign that it was time for this clip of row 22 to turn introspective. Donnie was surprised to be thinking that Drake was a great deal smarter than he thought, for Donnie rarely caught himself so far astray from his truly egalitarian center.

Down below, London had been rendered irrelevant, and land, begun again after a narrow, troubling stretch of water that history has condemned as interminably agitated, parceled with such conviction and precision over seemingly madcap deranged centuries of heave and upheaval, of precise plans undermined by surprises such as Vikings and carnivals, land on which one could rely no more on the constancy of a turnip as a Spaniard, much less a neighbor, who was as likely to deliver a bubonic louse as a common defense pact, parceled with such precision that forests were triangular and definitively brought to a tame halt wherever one looked.

There were a lot of people down there, one knew, but surprisingly few villages of them and much land, crossed by roads on which automobiles, mostly, made a seemingly thoughtful, deliberate journey between stations that could only be imagined from 37,000 feet and descending into a dark unaffected by the movements or clustering of lights.

"Donnie—hey Donnie," Drake said as the plane neared a space of many lights.

"Yeah."

"In Belgium they have two languages, right? French and Belgian."

"Walloon and Flemish, but yes, more or less French and Belgian."

"Do you speak either of them?"

"No."

"Neither do I."

"Donnie, how about you learn one and I learn the other?"

"Good idea," Donnie replied, wondering how long they were going to be in Belgium.

"But then how will we talk to each other?'"

12

RENDEZVOUS PLURAL

Hector's return to Fort Vancouver was not heralded by any sort of foofaraw. The fort was sparsely populated at the time, and while he was not challenged upon entry, nor was he particularly welcomed. Much was left unspoken. For instance, raw recruits looked at him and thought "Sure is rough out thar"; Douglas Stompett, Chief Factor and father figure for future factoti for a fee (Fie!) (foe of fumblers) and Friends of the Hudson's Bay Company, number one overall in charge at the fort, barely recalled sending him out against his will half a year before and entirely had forgotten what Hector was doing in the territory; and Stompett's factotum, Willard Gentile III, having once had to requisition Hector's needed supplies, now found irritating the need to procure sleeping space and food for this wraith out of place, not to mention seeing to it that his well-being was not only maintained, but ensured and, if possible, improved—and though Gentile could not contain his sense of having been born into a slender vacuum that only a tensile superiority such as his could fill, he was nonetheless a man of honor, making the minutes spent attending to Hector Robitaille all the more aggravating. He especially hated looking at Hector's face, where his few teeth presented the illusion of frenzied self-generate rotting.

Over the coming days, as Hector developed a hankerin for apple sauce and beefsteak, a meal that took him an hour or so to consume, he did notice the motley populace of the fort whispered wonderstruck often as he passed, less wraith-like by day, as if he were either disembalming gradually, or coming somehow to corporeal of a world something like that

what produces shadows, the common whispered word that
was as loud as any shriek *in effect* being "bar," for though man
had succumbed to bar bifar, and not so seldom neither, none
had survived such a mauling, none had died/been left for
sartin dead dying and returned, and from what maps as was
available the full grandeur of the journey had become clear
and the tributary sprung that was to lead to the great river
Legend by the time ten days had passed, ten peaceful days
for Hector, ten days of the beginning not of a recovery but
of a reconciling between what seemed two separate beings,
ten days, during which aside from eating well he found that
he was content to spend many an hour in the tavern within
the fort that was little more than a large room with a couple
round wood tables, supernumerary chairs, an actual bar or
šank lined with reglar barstools and behind the bar as much
whiskey as a man could serve for himself ifn he would just
sooner or later wash a glass or two, if not right when he was
done the next day after he'd slept off his philosophes from
the night before, ten days before he finished off a rasher predominant breakfast in about an hour and a half and found his
hankerin for whiskey strong and made his way to the in-fort
tavern, where he saw a man overbearing a stool, a shirtless
man who nonetheless damn near looked to be sportin a winter bearskin, him so big, back and shoulders, neck and arms
so hirsute if one didn't know better (and many who had not
were now dead) one might expect it best to train a rifle on
him to be sure the face attached to what turned around were
of the human sort. For Rory Fitzpacker was not a man to
overthink such a situation as a gun trained on im and nor was
an apology worth the waitin for. The guns that didn't break in
the process Fitzpacker kept or sold depending on the quality,
and he thus had a locked closet of his own at Fort Vancouver that, wouldn't you know it, also kept from the paws of
thievery the rifle of that famous bear surviving legend, Hector
Robitaille.

Approaching the bar, Hector knew immediately who the
man was, and though he expected no pleasantries, nor did he
concern himself with the man's murderous nature. He went

behind the bar, took his own bottle, poured a shot, slew it, and slapped the heavy glass down just hard enough it might make a man nearby think a man nearby was up to makin a point, about three feet off Fitzpacker's right. Fitzpacker looked up, heavy lids black with furabove and droop, recognizing and then narrowing to a fine slit of sheer and utter hatred.

If a bear had rabies...

"Want my rifle back."

Fire did not spit from Fitzpacker's eyes, but being on the other end of his glare was hardly more pleasant.

"I heerd bout ya shatpup gone on bout stolen rifles. Y mention it again, I'll kill ya wi my bare hands. Nifn ya don I'll bash yer skull in smother time."

"Yull give my rifle back," Hector replied, thinking the only way to kill this man might be with fire.

Fitzpacker rose slower than a centenarial skeleton; he had the chair over his head fast as a beetle popped out of a fire—

"Drop the char erall drop ya raht thar, ya English fartpig mother of devilswine!"

It was Jeffers Phoebles, and he carried two rifles, aiming both at Fitzpacker at the same time. Hector recognized one of the rifles as his own.

"Don make no bother," Fitzpacker said, setting the chair back down and his ass upon it. "Now just two more men t kill stead a one."

Phoebles here did something that shocked them what believed it for years to come. He shot the back left leg of the stool from under Fitzpacker, who crashed to the ground with such force, of his own in compliance with gravity plus a half ton of mean so's that it was much more than an hour before he was able to rise, and not one soul on the planet in Fort Vancouver to lend a hand, maybe a sort of microcosm of Hector's odyssey, though witnessed by none but the two new friends sharing a whiskey bottle and talking of other matters, for the other side of the beast was Jeffers Phoebles who would have given his life to make up for what he did to Hector Robitaille, and did his best from then on to do so, partnering up with Hector and teaching him the ways of the mountain

man, fine-tuning his already good enough shot such that the
only beast Hector, and for that matter, Phoebles, had to fear
was Fitzpacker, who from that cursed day on cursed them
both, Phoebles for his prank, and Hector for surviving for the
sole purpose of returning to Fort Vancouver to make Rory Fitzpacker look a bad man. Main thing is, Hector got his gun back.

For the next several years, Jeffers Phoebles taught Hector
Robitaille the finer life of a mountain man, and neither went
within a half moon of Fort Vancouver for many a half moon.
The closest they got was one summer on the way to the rendezvous when a good year trapping had the two men so loose of
foot and whiskeyed up they found themselves lost somewhere
between the Wind River and the Columbia, they figured after a weeklong bender that attenuated into a morning-long
question from a prostate Phoebles: "That thar a Flathead? If
that thar'sa Flathead, where in the Kingdom of our Lord the
Christ Almighty of Slaughter, Sluttery and Gooseflesh are
we?" Turns out that thar was a Shoshone, but in any case that
only meant they were further from where they thought they
needed to be, a situation that resolved itself by the coinciden-
tal miracle that Hector had been lost there before, at which
point he got it in his head to see if old Rowor, who was, was
still alive, as anyway that was the only way he knew out of that
maze of green mountains and greener valleys.
    So off the three went in a lighter boat, an upriver boat, a
portage boat, and before long came to the divide where they
camouflaged the boat and made merrily toward the rendezvous, and they did see a bear, and they did kill an elk, and
they did carelessly sing by the fire, and they did nearly fuck
up and end up dead, but for Rowor sniffing out the danger.
    "Nine—"
    "I know," Hector grinned, winking at Jeffers. "Nine say pa."
    "Non!" Rowor said with an urgency that brought Hector
and Jeffers to stiff.
    "Non!", Rowor repeated. "Rekkettekker, dedemed ded mi-
dim. Nine say die. Uomo blanc. Follow. Beastman big Fixed
Packer kneeyaybezpyechknee—gefgarlick. Gonif grande.

Harmicide they make. Vous et mois. Phoebles tudi. All padł.
Tiempo es muy nić."

This was enough for Hector to understand to osmote the
crisis to Phoebles. Fitzpacker and party of nine on their trail
with blood in their eyes.

"Ambuscado," said Rowor. "Hornswaggle, drygulch."
Clear enough.

Hector and Jeffers followed until they reached a sheer
rock that broke from a slope to about fifty yards from the
stream they followed.

"Aspetto," Rowor said, a hand up in the "wait" position.
They got it.

Then Rowor spiderscrabbled towards and across the
stream and into the woods beyond. Sweat pouring from their
brows, sweat of fear in spite of, sweat they were surprised was
not the color of blood, sweat they sweated until they heard
the eighteen footsteps of nine men converge on their ill-cho-
sen hide.

"SHATPUPS COWER IN FEAR OF VENGEANCE!"

Fitzpacker spoke loud enough thought Phoebles, who
genuinely feared this was the end of him, that maybe the
harangue would bring the rendezvous, yet another two hundred miles off at least, to their rescue.

A thin, bent young man with a thin suck-cheeked face
of bottomless amorality spoke up: "How should we do em,
boss?"

Another spoke, "Long, painfull, so's thar screams be heard
for lo, one hundred years or more."

A priest?

Yep.

Phoebles worked on himself to prevent the cowering that
came natural in such dire. Hector looked up at his and perhaps the world's nemesis, and said, "Oergrown shatpup, you
come here to live or die?"

And just then an arrow pierced Fitzpackers left bummup,
and he howled like a banshee, which, any way you put it is still
a she, and the spell was broke, the bluff was on, and the old
cliché of the cowardly numerous fleeing in the face of surprise

took hold and off all ran but Fitzpacker, who hopped, two hops
per stop to pull, two hops to stop to pull, and our three anti-hero
goodlads—though Hector did have the memory and pettiness
to shout off to Fitzpacker, "It's not tran-sumdee, it's TRAVOIS,
ya spawn of dimbrained mangemutts!" and that was the last
encounter direct they had with him until the rendezvous of
Pierre's Hole, Ideeho in 1832, a mere two years later.

Oh! And what a rendezvous that one was, despite the
absence of Rowor, who would never come on his own, and
Hector and Jeffers come from straight north of there, having
braved Blackfoot country, so Rowor was hunnerds and hunnerds of miles west.

Oh yes, the rendezvous of '32: they were right on time at
Pierre's Hole, now Idaho, the far side of the Tetons, where the
Chikisaw Crow held their annual trout twattery, and the balls
of gopher fried in whiskey, the bearkswillery cries of "Homch
fer that air bearskin" and the answer comic "Howmch fer
that bareskin," led to a dance ruckus laughfest of flapjawed
contestants for the folling days savvy parlay drum-timed
where-that-pig-get-to wrassle, and throughout the month the
backstabbing stabbing gargle of gargoyles of death dwarfs and
murder, and Scurvy Sam n his tales tall of wolves and rain-
muck-squabblery-frenly-like-oops-nuther drown-thas-losiana,
ya pale-face guzzlers, Jacques-knifed redskins, and Law? Hah?
Banjaxery ruleth the dog-tortured vomit bloodshittery, beaver fer bearskin fer hide fer hairscalp, and the backscuttling,
frontventing, anal twat cunny cockhole rectal labial nipple
ballsackery salted beefsides durnt saltedslabs hairdowntoth-
eass beard down to the knees and the shitting and pissing
and lakes and quicksand, and lookey here fren thatthereshee-
pyereatin, deerferall, axetraps, drygulching horseracing pon-
ytricking rifleshooting Blackass Creecrow, Crow Cree, Show-
showKnee. Pie-ute, Flathead, Blackhead Cheyenne Sioux,
Mandan my ass go-own git, ye pounding shrinking smearing
stinking beads-fer-suck-me-alls-slinking bowenarrah rattler
peddlin REDSKINS! How many redskins, if you just count
the Nimipoo, 1000 lodges, the Flatheads 800 lodges, the

mountain men, 4000, and if you needs to check particular they say there was 30,000 horses at the rendezvous that year, but there was more oh yes there was much more: oh yes, the atmosphere was festive, the dirt was festive, the women and men were festive, Indian, trader, mountain man, gambler, whore, all were festive, and their number in the thousands, and their thirst unquenchable, their hunger insatiable, their lust phallicimous vaginous, their mood ecstatic, their physiognomy boisterous, and such was there fooferraahh that one could not distinguish the dance from the game from the coupling from the trading from the stealing from the rapine from the camaraderie, so that the names of the dishes, the dances, the sexery, the so on and so off the et and the cetra were all, too, indistinguishable, for they were many and oft drunkenly accomplished, one acrostically, and that includes even

The itch and scratch	Harley, I can't break it
The itch and snitch	Ruxus and fluxus
The snatch and scrabble	Oh deer, I have shot you
Tendered is the bender	Ants in the hole!
Hogleg and whirligiggle	The grl and mer of life
Extravergeon and ropov	Whet the wistle
Yams for Gerty	Harlots heaven hellsup
Shame and Shone	Ingots in guts
Labial lectures	Leopard frog targets
Idjits fer midjits	Eviscerate the monk
The furbelow cuckold	Heads roll
Flick the nipples	Embed the lead
Ike makes haste late	Stringup the innocents
The priestly babble	Louis the rat
Zeno settles for half	Expectorate the worst
Pigpile on Vladimir	Precious my drool
Angles of Grind	Toesnails and bowties
Cram the lamb	The fledge and bardle
Kate, ye rewent me	The strake and dolp
Earwigs in the pie!	The stricken dolphin
Rumpus and bumpus	The beeswaxed dolphin
Sphincter, my lobe	The stem and stern
The wheat and the scroff	The storm in stem

Pierre the lippy
The crack and drown
The bishop and nun
The tangent and plangent
The termagents and pockets
The wharf and frizur
Woops-his-neck
The kolobokal train
The worn phrase
May hem mayhaw
The wolf and gristle
Liffey and Lucerne
The pig and throughle
Trottle the Irish
The suckpizzle and blowhard
Vultures and pickins
The blowhard and eagermites
The buzzard and pickaninnies
The maggoty robe
Backy tabacky
The frank con
The geese and spit
The scratch and flee
Johnnie longpipe
The pear and sight
The worlitz and turn
Friends and enemies
The welt and schlong
The lies and tongue tong
The rough and pitch
The stork and crotchet
The largesse and Smallesse
Gizzards, just plain
The crinkle of the squaw
The fig and fag
Shaggers at flog
The Fidgety marm
The geester and roux

The bane of chote
The chowblast and fixit
The genesis and extracyst
The jesus fucking christ
The greeks and albanians
Shark me swabbie
The plaphet and stawh
The ghain and cluck
Injuns make my jam
Tuck the rattler
The warm turd
Tickle the gringo
Tev, dee pie on
The slaver and meek
The stifflip and horkid
The limp and bole
The calipers and visor
Strike the night
Shoot the galoot
Pick off the beaver eye
Woops and suffritt
The clams are few
The fenster and deef
The dentist and mawl
The crimp and stave
The droop and clobber
Hand me the saw
Straight, no, droppit
Nine say pa
The poop and slobber
The feast of entrails
The yeast of archangels
Awaken the Hindoo
The prostate and Arky
The stink and vapors
The ink and poopers
The milk and runov
The fetch and saddle

The greef and aroma
The forgotten hottentot
Tamper me not
The gloss and selph
The lime and scurve
The east and goth
The lipth and thudder
The Paiute lute
The crapulous and klees
Slip and fall
The flap and continent
The cucumber and backup
The wattle in the wind, or,
Trade places, gentlemen
The fwap and rise
The pander and spew
The eternal cramp
The grampus and fahrtensund
The mount and pis
The new orlins stomp
The cheese of the chief
The puissant andiron
Whirlcat talismine
Symbiosis and rot
The vis and bratch
The drone and paws
The gusset and arbiter
Francine, your goiters
The ventral and whist
Lightning flush o'er my lucky
straight
Pour Judd his head
My old Kentucky ham
Secrete the blade
Fend the munch
The gape and winder
The grape asunder
The tripe of thunder

Tremble at speed
The loaf and worms
The rabies and flux
The vibe and jello
The myrtle and curlew
The whelp and baggy
Drag the hair
Drag the hare
Frag the fair
Frag the fare
Scare the pimply fair
Carve the pumpkin
Starve the bumpkin
Shuffle the stack
Lick my crack
The egg nates in sway
The slunk and shiptari
The dropov in duress
Mona's steer
The saloon icky
He dere, nay?
His tan bull
Can't stand on apples
The fragt and findit
The hind and flea
The gray pea and Kenneth
The sturl and feeb
The rank file
Squash the squaw
The snake and bile
Slanteye killarney
Starkweather come home
Vomitus rally us
Trench and gully
Snatch the pecker
Peckat the snatch
Chew the fat
Shane the pistle

Hide the salaam
Slamp the hyde
Snork and gaggle
Horn and swaggle
Bend and sniff
Wherever Hugo Igor
Ride the skiff
Torque the pork
The grind and feets
Befart the tart
Grief you may bed me
The slap and tangle
Who shaved me ass
The wrap and wrangle
Gracious be thou, who ye

Warp and warngull
The priest's revenge
The pack, yes, *THAT* pack
The Vancouver hustle
The beaver skin bustle
My cousin Russel
Hence the tussle
Sprout the brussel
Scout, a doomed hound
Uncle, thanks for the sack
Thumb the bumb
The staunch revanche
The stench and revenge
The wretch and fech
Squam the snide

might be the pissant scrum and the sadness that shades the pissed-out ecstasy.

And many a mountain man wondered as he wandered away in his own stride if the last good times had been had. But for of course them that stayed and fought the Gros Ventre, which Hector had learnt from Rowor meant the great fart, but twas not a battle but for the famous Sublette, who survived, and a few here and a few there, for the white man was at his fuse-lit best and bout to blow.

Jeffers Phoebles had that sense of it, and as a reglar old timer his sense was keen, and that was the end of the best of times. But for Hector Robitaille it was the beginning of good new times to which Jeffers Phoebles was always welcome to winter or summer, for early on in the squawsqueeze he found himself a woman he could not forgit, and who certainly remembered him when before the fires died, the wagons hauled off, the jugs emptied, she knew she had been well seeded by this strange white man who went at the grapple as if for the first time (it was about the fifth), with what she knew might not be tenderness or diffidence but could be both, for many a squaw had got her head shot through by just such an odd one—the olduns always said you can trust the ones that rough ya up a bit: beware the too boisterous and the too quiet. Well this angel of mercy named, shit Hector could never get it right but it went firefly or bird on fire or something like that, some Blackfoot name, for a Blackfoot she was, childless, griefstricken, her husband killed by a Fitzpacker raid along with their prepubescent warrior son whose name meant Eagle Wing (the husband was some other bird, maybe Falcon); and in the years they grew to understand each other just enough so as not to grate, she often spoke of them and knew that Hector did not mind, and sometimes late, late in life she would ask if he tired of her past and he would laugh and tell her, "Go on, lessn ya wan hear bout Black Ass agin."

They settled in Nimipoo land, within walking distance of the aging Rowor's clan, and they grew potatoes and roots and apples and shot hooved mammals, fished trout and cat, and never went want, and even had enough for the two quiet elderly loping Injuns they caught one day grubbing the south quarter and invited in, who Hector believed he had met one day and who had done him a good piscine turn, though there was no way after all these years he could say there was any resemblance, and firebird or flaming mosquito or whatever her name was bore them a strapping girl, who grew up on the land knowing the ways of white and red, and who had her comely side as well as a sharp enough tongue that when a man come through, a young lad, really, a boy, nothing more, an orphan, an individualist who listened to everything and obeyed little, a fellow by the name of Tom Gravel, brought by chance by Jeffers Phoebles offered to repair their roof, though it seldom leaked enough to make sleep a discomfort, Hector, seeing something in the eyes of Marie Fire in Flight Robitaille, took him on and in, and in season of work that varied from the needful to the trap the lad, the two were in love, and out of it Gravel became a sort of son, the sort who takes the daughter away to bigger notions in southernmore lands, who garners a grubstake and loads his optimism in his pistol and rifle and mounts his horse, the mare of her dreams a gift from Marie Fire in Flight Robitaille, and takes away, takes away himself and his youth and Hector's daughter and the tears of Hector's wife, leaving Hector his hectares and his

Injuns and his roots and fish and venison and memories and bottles of whiskey on the south facing porch he shared two or three times a year with Jeffers Phoebles and Rowor.

13

DIPLOMACY IN THE WHITE ROOM

The discussion would be held in the white room, where the females blended in like lemmings in winter snow, yet all the more so for the incensed or insensate blue eyes caught the mysteries of a sky that had no business boasting of a color. Garvin could never remember what in the room was llama, what was alligator, if anything, maybe the underside of the llama carpet, yet much as he quietly despised the room he was in awe of his wife's magical verbosity, which made plush sound like an exotic animal—it was the last one, but there you have it, what could I do, I fired my designer within five minutes but who better to assist than Cleo, it was her idea to use sheer silk for the drapes, not even in India can you find... The only redeeming feature of the room in Garvin's experience was the fact that no one was allowed in there—except, of course, when an emergency necessitated the white room's somnolent circumvallational effects. Yet on these occasions, Garvin was either a beast stomped in on ballet practice or a muskellunge panting in the undie drawer. His arguments, as all but his skin, were checked at the door; and the meetings became for him nothing more than an attempt to retain his ticket. Donnie had never entered the room, never, knowing it for what it was, knowing it was a museum for the defeat of antipodal spirits, and Garvin knew this that Donnie knew, yet he had always yielded to the summons without appeal, whatever accumulate distaste he was stuffing down the throat of his son.

For the women, the room was the manifestation of more than the yinyang fucktwine of their psyches, souls, cunts, geniuses, slaughters; it was the stream to their piscine elegance, the far off peaks to the lammergeyers of their incestuous epiphanies, the reversible womb of their virtuosities. Entrance must therefore be limited to moments chosen with the flair of nonchalant detumescent care, the emergencies dissipate upon entrance of these blondly impossible twins, Languideia (Deia, to friends) and Cleopatra (no friends necessary).

Garvin, much as he was disturbed, refused the provocation of wearing into the white room the trousers he had worn to work, which would have picked up forensic detritus that would forever spoil the sofa, sedan, ottoman, divan, tofu or whatever they call them that his ass alit upon. He had changed into jeans he had washed and his wife had ironed with controlled detestation, for in this there was no other way—even Garvin could not be pushed *that* far, despite his regretted temper, You want them ironed you fucking iron them, which had precipitated a short discussion in the white room.

This occasion was precipitated by a short phone call, recently recorded, in which Donnie had informed Cleo of his departure for Europe. Disconcerting as this news was, at least to some depth to Garvin if not mother and daughter, worse yet was that it took Cleo five days to inform Deia, and another several for Deia to inform Garvin. If you don't recall, I had my seminar on Hass, which was, though you no doubt didn't bother to listen, was recorded live on radio, and there was Cleo's dental, and a very important meeting with my best pupil, who I might remind you so that once she is a national phenomenon with no little help from myself, goes by the name of Kitty Kabuse, a naturalized, though I told you this you were yawning at the time, Hungarian, or granddaughter of Hungarian immigrants rediscovering her Magyar selves which she delivers in exquisitely complex multi-voiced near epic poems.

Garvin looked at the two of them, seated on a lambskin two-wench divan, twins of bizarre genesis, mother and daughter, Deia of a beauty not ageless rather enhanced by age: the feet of crows so delicate that they merely suggested an aging that was utterly denied by cheekbones that stretched and Diplomacy in the White Room released to exploit irregular dimpling; and the unfortunate, if but the male of the species registered the fact, Cleo, who had everything her mother had, including inspirational breasts of a size that brooked no ignorance without overwhelming anything but the habitually undersized bras, a Greco sinuosity of figure, an insouciance that boasted of an unlimited access to biscuits of any metaphorical shape and flavor, yet who had that inexplicable resemblance to a dog, the afghan in her specific case, given a nose elongate and upturned just enough that no man could for long keep his eyes from the delicately collapsing nostrils that quivered incessantly like twines of spaghetti perpetually dangling from a fork held in a nervous hand.

Quite to the contrary of rules long established by habit, buttressed by Garvin's studied passivity, which shielded a self-nurtured by the circumstance entire even if part by part his disgust had become first a mountain, then a Caucasus, though Cleo saw an endless basin, and by Cleopatra's birthright— which announced itself post-natally when she began rhyming at the age of one or so and quoting Wallace Stevens at seven, critiquing him at eleven, the age at which her breasts developed to enhance the buttocks unchanged that now turned the heads of uncles away so that they could bite their fingers in self-restraint and hips that ever so cautiously flared out from her narrow back, her birthright being that of what may be called queen of every instant she provided an other— yes contrary to the rule that in the white room Deia began the discussion— more usually a lecture Garvin took in in various percentages, a guilty stoic—Garvin began, and with an aggression beyond any his wife had ever known him to express.

"Why the fuck didn't either of you self-absorbed bitches tell me my son took off to Europe!"

A look of extreme guilt stole into the features of Cleopatra, only to be banished once and for all by the ferocity of Deia's instantaneous response, which consisted of two strides across the lambskin carpet or llama fur carpet or lemming... across to deliver a hate-driven slap of great force to each of Garvin's two cheeks.

The discussion was over. Garvin stood, having remained still long enough to be sure no further slaps would be administered, removed himself to his bedroom, still shared — if one dares to use such a word when Deia is involved — with his wife, thought for a few minutes about what he would need, gathered clothes and a few teaching essentials (a couple of folders), a few notebooks he was writing in, a pen with a pharmaceutical advertisement on it, leaving behind many expensive gift pens received through the years, retrieved two suitcases from the basement, packed them rapidly, and, one in each hand, walked out of the house without looking at the statuary that flanked the front door that was his wife and daughter, having to set one suitcase down to do so, put the luggage in the trunk of his three-year-old Toyota Corolla, and drove away from his wife and daughter for, what he mused was in two ways, good.

14

HE HORSE

[First card up: two of spades]
[One buck.]

There is nothing necessarily odd about a man sitting on a hotel room bed, Bushmills neat in a glass on the telephone table within reach and sweating like a shaven pig tied four limbs pegged to the ground stretched and lying in the desert sun, water or whatever bleeds from the bottom of a dry glass beginning to form a rivulet pressing out from the moat, about to drop onto the carpet, hefting a black steel switchblade, pressing the release mechanism, listening intently for the onomatopoeic value of that intestinally satisfying sound of the blade opening hard enough to knock itself out of a child's hand, pressing the round button that yields to the peace that allows one to tuck the blade back in with a solid, higher pitched sound much like klik, though upon opening again the sound surely enfolds subkliks on the order of m and mb, maybe mbh, though closing and opening again there is no denying the clichéd klik aspects of the noise, yet no klik could warm the belly as the slapopen of this knife did. More time passed by than would have if the event were not worth mentioning before Eddie Vegas licked his thumb and forefinger and rubbed what surely was a tiny speck of dried blood off the blade. The closing klik was not definitive enough, but he accepted the fact, stood, pocketed the knife, downed the drink, and left for the casino.

Death stalked the Luxor, he thought, what a title, and true enough, more suicides than the public would ever learn of, one of them more likely an assassination, of a senator from Iowa who opposed both US wars of the new century, apparently oblivious of time's need, when segmented, to justify itself by evolutions. And then, of course, a high-end hotel on the Las Vegas strip would by nature nurture intrigues that would outswirl into imbroglios, many of which would involve deaths. All this, true, and yet here he enters the casino itself, the tawdry, the seedy, the slummox, the dregs, the amoral, Satan's very playhouse, where the lights are dimmed to project a sort of Nordic twilight in which the all night light and all day dark are admixed, and no clocks to force anyone to figure it, and anyway the designers of the light seemed to have discovered the natural light quality of humankind.

He sat down at the blackjack table his legs seemed to choose, though he noticed the dealer was an Asian woman, and for whatever reason he always lost to Asian woman, yet was not the kind of man who would resolve thus never to play against Asian woman nor to bully up the tension and so pledge to play only against Asian woman until he whipped one's ass, which he recognized as the lost before starting approach to gambling. This table had a short, wizened Asian woman dealing, he chose it, he had ten bucks in chips in his pocket, it was a dollar table, play a hand. He would bet all ten dollars, and as there was no one else at the table, the event would be mercifully short.

"Good evening, sir."

"Madam."

He put the ten chips forward. He looked at her five and figure a three with it and could see how it would all fall apart, even after he stood pat on nineteen. She would get a lousy six, and top it off with a seven. Twenty-one. You lose Eddie.

But Eddie looked down and saw an ace along with his ten: blackjack! I'll be fucked. Pay fifteen.

Bet five.

Twenty tie. Lose five, still have twenty. Get up and walk away? No, this wasn't a hard luck story. Death stalks the He Horse Luxor, anyway, and unless he felt the desire to gamble was greater than the desire to walk about in the night warm, he was unlikely to run off for more dough. Bet five.

Queen/three: dealer has a deuce showing. About fifty/fifty take or hold. Hold. Dealer draws a jack that puts her at twenty for she had an eight, but the jack would have busted Eddie anyway. Down to $15.

Bet five.

Asian woman dealing: Eddie draws an ace and a five, she has a queen showing. Eddie draws a king then an eight. Back to where we started. Fuck it. Bet five.

Jack/four, dealer shows a seven. Another fifty/fifty. Stand.

Smart move. Dealer has fifteen. But she draws a four. Asian woman dealers.

Bet the last five.

Ten/nine, dealers shows four, has fourteen, draws ten, back to the ten he started with.

Bet five.

Nine/six, dealer has an eight. Draw. Deuce. Fuck. Stand. Dealer has eighteen, bet the last five.

Ace/nine, dealer shows two, has seven, draws king, back to ten. Would it be better if they could plug into the future, print the entire sequence in case he wants to see hand by hand how he lost ten dollars or won forty-five?

Believe it or not, Eddie did walk away with forty-five dollars, though that means he actually won only thirty-five, but considering how fucked he got three times, fucked in the way that often enough gets people thrown out for reprobate apoplexy, he had done well. He doubled the bet often, three times getting screwed, but if you walk away with that in mind you forget the time you settled for sixteen and the dealer's four had a seven with it and she drew a five and a six, and so on. Going up the elevator, he was more pleased with himself than he generally liked to be, thinking how wise he was never to have said anything to anyone anything about female Asian dealers. Problem with Vegas/problem with life: irrational focus leading to blown arteries of logic.

No, it wasn't the mbh subsound—it was a thump, this not an onomatopoeically accurate description, but what is known as a thump, so hard did the heavy blade swing before the click.

Onomatopoeically there were no vowels in the first part of the noise, it was more of a grunt. A grunt blade, that's what he had, that thump felt in the hand, sending a buzz through those parts of the flesh that receive little in the way of commands to labor.

15

HE HORSE

[First card up: eight of spades]
[Call.]

Mel was still around, believe it or not, so documents would be no problem, but Eddie had no idea how difficult it would be to find a 1916 Smith & Wesson .38, like the one he lost when...better not to think about that. Mel, now, after all these years he had aged so familiarly to Eddie it was as if they had both been in the penitentiary this whole time. Less hair, but it was always short and receding, now gray stubble on the cheeks, some gray up top, same short, curved nose that gave him the prospect of a multitude of ethnicities from Turk to Armenian, Palestinian to Jew, Albanian to Kosovar. Few besides Eddie ever knew he was Lebanese.

"Sorry—"
"Mr. Vegas."
"I like it. Sorry, I couldn't locate the pistol, but I got the rest, social security card, driver's license, passport, credit cards, even a concealed carry license. Matter of fact, I got you a background story. Seems there was an Eddie Vegas in Wichita, that's where you came from, Wichita. Almost the same age, too."
"He still alive?"
"Nope."
"Good. How much do I owe you?"
"A C note."
"That's very noir of you, Mel, but sort of cheap, don't you think?"

"I'm glad to see you, 'Eddie.'"

"That's right, Mel, keep to it."

"Intend to. Look, for the gun, I got the address of a dealer on Sahara, just about half a mile off the strip, east. Best shot, far as I know."

"Best shot."

"Like that?"

"When I get a place I'll have you over for steaks and whiskey."

"Look forward to it."

Sure enough, Justice Guns N Ammo had precisely the pistol Eddie Vegas was looking for, a 1916 Smith & Wesson .38, the exact same model as the gun he first shot when his granddad would take him out to the washes for "target" practice. Targets there were, though you had to know of them from somebody because they weren't private, not much of anything, really, a plywood board with concentric circles on it being high end. Sometimes it was just a piece of paper with the outline of a bad guy on it stapled to a stake and flapping in the wind. Wherever it was, it was a known place for no maply reason, thousands of casings cast in the sand and rocks. The best times were at the one wash where now and again someone would bring a dead farm animal, for there is nothing like the nearly silent sucking insinuation of sound the bullet entering the carcass made. Of utmost clarity in his mind was when they went with some guy, former army maybe, a guy with a lot of guns, and he handed Eddie a big handgun, a .357 Magnum or something, and when he squeezed the trigger the gun dipped and the bullet whizzed off the desert floor halfway to the bloated dead cow and before any time a human could count on could pass he heard that sound, a sort of fwup.

Or fwop/fwap. Eddie sat on the end of his motel room bed, pulling the trigger: klik klik klik klik klik klik. No, something was missing. Besides the bullets. That was precisely the point: it was not exactly fwap, and now it was not exactly-He Horse klik. And when his wife slapped him it was not

slap slap, or slap-slap, or slapslap. Splank splank? No—no n.
Splack splack? Definitely an ah sound; sp? That sp seemed
to have an inevitability about it that was cheaply gained, like
it used its uncle's membership card to get in. The only thing
that may have been inevitable was the slap and consequences, but not, no, not the sp. Why the non-percussive s? Those
were certainly not caresses. A p perhaps, as in kpark, or kpank.
Kpak! Close: kpak!kpak! Fuck it, close enough for a shit poet,
and who is not a shit poet? His son was right, the only Holocaust in their backyard occurred when he was forced to mow
the lawn. Cunt laureate: he could see her now, Circassian
chiffon sheer shift shaping her body as she bends over the
world's latest herb, some fucking visiting poet unsure how to
pretend not to see the cunt hair, the cling in the ass, where
somehow only the husband is dumb enough to envision the
shit-encrusted rectum: Zamzam, bitch!

Onomatopoetry: the only real poetry is dada…Nonsense:
Lorca: death laid eggs in the wound at five in the afternoon,
The Idea of Order at Key West—yet even that he could puke
to as his wife orgied it out in company as if Ramon was pale
from licking her twat then and there—Neruda: How much of
the darkness in my soul I would give to get you back. Funny.
Logic dictates that I reject such absolutes, yet I know what
death is.

16

PICASSO TITS

The sky was nimbostratular, spiteful, refusing to release the rain that would make sense of its oppressive blue of death and unheavenly proximity. There was no telling the damp from the cold, and even though the temperature was 11 degrees Celsius and a neighbor had just told them that this was warm for the season in Brussels both Drake and Donnie huddled as if against a brisk wind as they waited to cross the historic R20, both thinking of the morning's revelation, neither ready to talk about it until they had reached Santana, still several blocks away on the Avenue de Stalingrad. They got their walk sign, that little green man who is the gypsy's antipous, strode across with muted pleasure, and as soon as they reached the other side heard the crash of glass breaking, the humming pause that must follow on such a crash, and then a woman screaming something in Flem or Wally or both with such effect that it was obvious without looking back that some-one had smashed the window of a car waiting for the left turners to halt their perfervid dereliction, that a purse had been snatched and a victim meant to take it personal. Sure enough, there stopped, as traffic flowed again from the lanes they had left behind, a Ford Ferrari (apparently purchased before the injunction), driver's door winged open, driver on foot kicking into higher gear as the high heeled shoes went flying into the oncoming lane. The crime had nothing to do with them, of course, other than that they both instanta-neously realized they had been waiting for the same crossing as the victim, had been but a couple meters from the woman, who by now had disappeared around the first left turn back down the way they had come, in fact on the very street they had trod, the Rue de l'Argonne. But it was a long time before they could cross back, and they each spent that time wondering inutile why they had to return to something they had neither witnessed nor were affected by, other than that the intersection was the northeasternmost of their neighborhood, Saint-Gilles, and though news travels fast, it is much more efficient to reach the spot of an event before the newspaper comes out.

Unfortunately for their subconscious need for the monumentally histrionic to break in on their day, all they got was that initial frightful glance at a woman in high heels in hot pursuit, an image that brings to mind inevitably the attack of a persistent murderous flightless bird, the smaller the scarier. For when they finally had the chance to re-cross the boulevard the scene had been played out. The thief, an Arab, had been nabbed by some Africans—whose ancestors perhaps worshipped the giant ostrich—and who held him in their bistro, by which time the woman had given up, thinking the Arab disappeared into the maghreb of the city, gone back to the car, where police were already investigating, both men in the initial tightlipped gawk that is in advanced industrial countries the opening police meets crime scene feint, while the Arab's gang, notified by Arab phone, had invaded the African bistro and liberated their comrade, not forgetting to take along the booty.

Now they had to cross the street again. Both Donnie and Drake, despite all, despite every neutrino zipping through their groins, despite every bomb sending villages flying, despite the nuns the imams the devadasis, the trucks destroying the little Japanese cars, the fog of warts, the haze of fatties, the teachers...they were thinking about none other than 22b. The walk was a long three blocks along the wide, foresty avenue to the circle where the lady statue beckoned it narrow, and it was not unusual with such a prospect ahead, such a seven-minute talk-free spell ahead, that they would draw on a theme, but it was truly a coincidence in that it had been three days since they had last seen 22b.

That was the second time, as they sat drinking La Chouffe in the Grand-Place, 22b striding with a grace that provided counterpoint to his plane seat emittance. The first day in town, they had, quite naturally, left their hotel in search of a kiosk for to purchase cigarettes. Finding one, Drake took the lead, deciding against making this stop a language tussle, and simply said "Camels—that one."

"Seven euro fifty," the stout feller said. "No, just one pack."

"Seven euro fifty," the stout feller repeated.

"I see," Drake transitioned. "Okay, rolling tobacco…that one, Bali Shag."

"Sounds like the highlight of a British honeymoon in Indonesia."

They both turned to get a look at the wit behind them, forming a line unto himself, and what do you know, it was 22b.

"22b," said Drake.

"Robinson," Donnie explained, "Claude Robinson." "I'll be damned," Drake said, for lack of resolution, referring to the fact that Donnie had found out the man's name. "Good to see you boys, then," 22b said, as if *he* were leaving, and so they did leave, off to where such minor coincidences are so quickly forgotten, a shop about half a block further up the street, where Drake bought a steel Manneken Pis bottle opener that was magnetic. The midget pisser was of magnetic attraction to the sense of wonder aswirl in both young men. There was not a lot to say about the suave homunculus, yet they both found no need to walk away from him after giving him a tourist's going over, not even after a traveler's minute examination; so much like brothers they were that each without noticing the other went off to buy a beer, choosing La Chouffe, which has a dwarf on the label, to aid in the passing of time in rarefied streams of wordless wonder, though Donnie did think of Rabelais, who must have been about dead when the pisser was sculpted back in 1619 (he had been dead about 66 years, in fact). After perhaps an hour, as Japanese and Germans stopped, took photos, and made way for French and British, and so on, Drake remarked, "I wonder where he would have fit in Hieronymus Bosch's triptych." "I think he would have found a spot in each of the three." Another couple of beers, another hour, very little conversation, much absorption of the history of medieval comedy, of the lumbering gooseflight of meaning going north for the summer, perhaps to endure a Russian winter of the soul, and finally, as it was their first day in the city, the two returned to their hotel by hops, tavern to tavern, finding no beer to resoundingly defeat La Chouffe, so that a theme was born unbastardized.

"I already told you," Drake began, as they sat against the Broodhuis to revel in the asymmetries, the architectural jokes, of the Town Hall, a spot they had chosen for to assimilate in their way, with bottles of La Chouffe and time, "my father liked midgets, or when at war, the shortest men he could find. The last one he had, he was a guy named Rover, a loyal little bastard to the end, meaning a spy, perhaps an asslicker, but probably more a hero worshipper. I don't know the mission they were on, but it was secret, by then my old man was into some classified shit, probably some enhanced pacification of peasants or something. He was not all that far from Saigon, which was one of the worst places to be, who knows, maybe thirty miles off, but in a jungle village nonetheless, and they had been there the day before, found an ordinary village with ordinary villagers leading ordinary village lives, pretty fucking suspicious you know, and the next day they showed up and the place was abandoned, totally abandoned, probably because of the way the last such village was enhancedly pacified, and my old man knew right off they were fucked. To the jeep he told Rover, and before they got there the mortar hit, the old man was concussed, nothing worse, but Rover was up a tree without a tail, without opposable thumbs, without skin. My father says he couldn't move and he was right at the foot of the tree and looking up and what was there was like if Rover had been sent flying into the tree by a giant slingshot at tremendous speed, and my father seeing this gore, this boneless, liquid and strand, kept thinking or hearing the

word 'ganglia.' I didn't even know what it meant, he said, I
still don't, but the word ganglia seemed the only representative in all the languages on earth that could describe Rover,
who was dripping blood and some sort of white shit on my
father, on his face, my father couldn't even wipe his eyes,
some of the liquid gore got in one of his eyes, causing an infection, and he said it all proceeded slowly, very very slowly,
the gravitational effects of the Rover ganglia, like suddenly a
strand of muscle or flesh would slide down the trunk, or drop
a branch lower to leak a stream of the gore which would soon
slow to a trickle on or near my father, mostly his face. He gave
no thought to the inevitable enclosing of the enemy and the
torture that would follow, he was so entranced by the slimy
ganglionic former Rover—"

It was just then that 22b gangled past, moving quirkily
through the crowd as if the tourists were mines.

"There he is again, 22b, see him?"

"Yeah, I saw him, I didn't want to interrupt."

From what they could see, 22b did not spot them, rather
angled toward the Town Hall and took a left, perhaps on his
way to see the mini-pisser. Surely some of what fell to earth
in a small village in Vietnam the day that Rover died was piss
and shit.

"So what happened to your father?"

"Nothing. He was rescued within an hour. The village
was destroyed by helicopters and such a few minutes or so
after they were hit."

Three days later, on their way to Santana, the thought of
22b brought both of them to the ganglia. For when Donnie
awoke that morning, he found that Drake had connected his
computer to a new television—that is, it had not been in the
apartment last Donnie knew—and was playing a film, and
what he first saw were bodies in the long doomed flight of un-
fettered, unfeathered humans, body after body, leaping from
a burning building and then bodies, body after body, midair,
going down, Icarus morose, no one to pullastring, to rhealise
the danger, ratitic fits and calling it quits, the foreground blotting the blotting.

Drake sensed him, said, "Oh, here you are. Let me put it at the beginning," as if that were the polite gesture, or worse, that Donnie was the expected guest at this foodless banquet. Donnie said nothing, but sat on the couch next to Drake. The film began with a very tall building on fire, smoke winging up about the structure, a dry Neptunian wrath of deep boiling gray, the wings turning into paws into talons that curled back down upon the top of the structure, perhaps 100 stories high, and if so the black slanted wrathful maw issuing the smoke in one continual dragonian breath from rigid rictus was about 73 to 81 stories from left down to right up, the building's an-aesthetic aesthetic of endless cement ribbling bottom to top unornamented and hidden windows much the better for the grinning break in that cold architectural strategy that could only have meant one thing.

Naturally Donnie was not surprised that the next segment featured the magical appearance, or the dreamlike or surreal, the intrusion? of a passenger plane, possibly a Boeing 737, the kind that had that hydraulic problem with the rudder the company didn't want to tell anyone about until enough bodies were incinerated upon impact with mountainsides, some of stone, some forested, some volcanic, some rainfor-est, some taigal, many undulating, until a plane entered the screan (I typed scream, but why did I change it?, and why not screem?), banking towards a twin building, lower down by maybe thirty stories and just did make it into the skyscrap-er, nearly swinging wide, sliding into the right corner from the camera view, the plane going in, a double fire ball not exactly coming out, but perhaps, again the magic, flowering beside the building on the side the plane entered and the side it nearly wing-scraped, and a twin of even greater height from nadir to zenith diameter some, shit, forty or sixty sto-ries before the flames slunk and hid inside the building to send out their own roiling black smoke, while the twin was still sending out the same and up near the brains puffs and streams of white here and there like volcanic acne gathered to stream upwards. Incidental smoke of mixed grays swept off in air currents one way or another above the buildings, the dragon black smoke from the two buildings joining, lifting paws and moiling as one off to where no one was looking as the maw, the maws, several enormous maws with flaming gums seethed dragon smoke and the brains continued leaking, black, gray, and white smoke rising in columns of varied size, as one would yearn for, more alive, more artfully than the building itself had managed even at night when lights obscured the monolithic, arbitrarily as guano, the second swallowed airplane designed to offset the yawnful symmetry, coming in lower so that the black smoke would rise like a curtain to the top of the building with an effect much like that of the Hamm's beer sign with its eternal beerefreshing waterfalling. Now clearly was the gargantuan moment in the lives of these two buildings, 110 stories in height they were, and 35,000 offices they held, stout? nine square blocks each they were, 315,000 workers they employed, for lunch three tons of mashed potatoes they ate, 3 trillion dollars at afternoon tea they ate, enough water to refill Lake Erie they drank— but look! now the scene shifted to the leapers, the fallers, the pushed, the slipped, the toppled, overgawkers, assburnt, lungclogged, the unthinkable lone fallers, bodies twisting here and there, maybe one or two turns or topsides turveying on the descent, thinkable now that the cameras could not follow them all the way to splat, and so more of them, and the one who tried to climb down it seems, and the crowded windows with flame behind, and the woman who crossed herself and sunk, and the windows less crowded even if the cameras only captured the descent and not the push and shove. Suddenly one building elegantly sinks in upon itself, an affront to the gray boiling clouds of cement sent from the hell inherent in a known unknown, the boiling clouds roll agonistically down streets over buildings around corners, fat children that must tire quickly but are faster than they look and have teeth like barracudas; and then the second building collapses, and born of the elegance, finally taking shape is the thousand foot and more octopus pushing the hubris of mankind squidding and a-kraken all to the ground to smoketopus dust, octopining now over the scene of much Neronic fiddling before this current diddlefinery and who now is not, or who then was not wondering which pocket?

After those five discrete scenes of an average of ten minutes each or so, the screen showed the central event of each repeatedly, the first the rictus of the planehole, the second the plane banking in again and again from just two different angles, each played for a few seconds at least ten times, then the same three fallers, all the way until obscured, all three ten times each before the next, and then the first building collapsing colllapsing collllapsing, then the attack of the debris monster, and finally the octopus and debris as one, as one ten times over and over.

The first thing a foreigner notices walking into a bar in his new country is that somehow even if the brains don't at first register their othernesses, to put it neatly in an academic way fraught with solid signifiers that have endured the stretchmarks of modernism's attenuations, the eyes do, as if they had walked into a moonlit room inhabited by cats. Perhaps that was why Donnie and Drake felt so much at ease immediately upon entering Santana—the overwhelming presence in the tavern was a very large dog of the breed Dogue de Bordeaux named Rex, or wrecks—they never asked Fils, the proprietor and master, to write it down. Rex, probably, was tawny, with a prominent chin, enough skin to enfold a second skull and enough skull to swallow a baby with its nether half. Fils allowed Rex to slobber the customers, to stroll amongst the tables, secure in the training Rex had received, never a hand raised against him—Fils had used electric shock—and much society amongst humans. Fils, too, was an agreeable sort, though of contradictory nature, with an odd combination of strong jaw and narrow face, full lips, prematurely gray hair, and a churlish confidence that Drake and Donnie presumed was FlemBelgian, for despite the breed of the dog, Fils was Flem. Also of some matter was the number of tables outside on the broad avenue, with the extraordinary luck of being near the traffic circle where the statue of our lady of the narrows stood in the grass while cars with visible indecisiveness, aggression and predominantly bad temper adjusted to the change in width of their path. On rainy days an awning covered a full six four-chair tables. Already, after just a couple of weeks, the two young men had assimilated to the point of having a local, and a bartender who, though he never showed the slightest degree of fiscal generosity, tolerated their unkind humor directed at the mutt, whose breed they pretended to forget, making guesses ad infinitum, such as Argentine dogo, Arkansas razorback, Pittsbullh, Stratford-on-terror, something to do with grapes, or wine, ah, Shiraz devil horse, Kazakh bearhound, Istanbull, Zulu tosser, Pinscherbutt, Okhotsk polar hind, Tibetan yak shepherd, Dobermensch, Kurdish mastiff, Melancholy Dane, Bretagnan madstiff, Russian general, Presa carnival, Rottweiler, Protestant Irish wolfhound, Shanghai whippet, Beijing smokehound, Boerballs, Rhodesian ridgeback, Chow chowed/chowed chow, genetically modified Chihuahua, Silesian pugilist, Anatolian shepherd, Stafford's hired slave dog, Kraški ovčar, Brabantine wolfhound, Flemish schnauzer, Rotewailer, Maxbaer, Stark raving bull terrier, Welsh persecutor, to which each time Fils merely smiled and repeated Dogue de Bordeaux, and the two made great show of remembering it until the next occasion to give it a shot arose.

This day, however, would be their first without Rex and Fils, who had taken a rare day off and were replaced by a dirtyblonde-haired demi-wraith barwench of acrobalanced beauty—one false placement and the effect would have been ruined: for instance the nose had a bump but was small enough that the wide set eyes and pale prominent lips were of a combination that asked not for a straight nose, an upturned nose, a hawk nose, just a small little breather of some sort. Yet none of that was important enough for our men to have so rapidly become desperately satyric, no, it was a trick of the nipples, set wide, yet pointing forward stoutly on a wide set of breasts of billiard ball size and just a bit more oblate shape, so that at all times it was difficult to be sure the nipples were not lingering outside the body, orbiting the breasts, and if their eyes pinned one of them down with a hard enduring determined stare, which is what it took, the other was by nature the other, a thing apart, and seemingly actually so. At the first intermission it was Donnie who nicknamed her Picasso Tits, his crest suicidal upon realizing that his friend was demonstratively smitten before he, Donnie, could lay claim to the same, and so his sense of honor, which excluded angling for the same dame as a friend, called for his finer mating self to fade. In fact, Donnie was immensely sad, immensely, and quite brave of him was his endurance of spirit at the šank— they needn't have communicated to decide mutually not to drink outside as they normally would have.

Still, one universal rule in a tavern is never to make a straight- forward go at a bartendress, for we know she spends much of her tending fending, and so they merely took up positions on barstools naturally ordered and received La Chouffes in the bulbous glasses preferred by Belgian beermeisters, and made nothing but bon jour polite with Picasso Tits, even if it did not take long to find her an accommodating, curious, intelligent creature, woe unto Drake one expects.

"'The gringos are swilling again,'" Donnie commented as soon as they toasted and tippled.

"What?" Drake phlegmatically pursued.

"It's the opening of a Guatemalan novel."

"And who might that be?"

"Asturias. Read him?"

"No. I only asked to see if you were the kind of asshole who would say You wouldn't know him."

"I would." It was the bartendress, her nipples, a moment of erect nipple excitement that coursed like a message from the Tesla beyond through the three of them. "I read the English translation, *Ojos...Los Ojos* something..."

"Interred—*The Eyes of the Interred*, the last in the banana trilogy."

She leaned on the bar, keenly interested, and the nipples were gone with the slight billowing of her shirt, which was a long-sleeve thermal undershirt.

"You read it in English." Drake stated. "Were you a literature student, then?"

"No, not really. I am an art student, but I had a scholarship trip to Guatemala and found just that one book of Asturias translated in a book shop there. Nothing else was available. So I read it. The gringos are swilling again. Hah. And they never stop, it seems."

"Oh, don't confuse us with banana men. At the moment we are mere ramblers, in Brussels by chance, settling in for the winter before we move on."

"To where?"

They looked at each other and shrugged, almost synchronized.

"We haven't discussed it." Already Donnie noticed that her glances at Drake lasted longer, and now, in profile, he found Drake profoundly handsome, even sensual, with an ease of presence and promise of gentleness that offset the mustache and goatee. Christ! Donnie thought, he almost looks saintly.

Another aspect of Santana the fellows enjoyed was its mixed clientele, old folks from the neighbourhood, businessmen and ladies, local youth, very local it seemed, for Fils lived above the bar and was on intimate terms with most of the men between ages sixteen and forty, who were clearly regulars. Both of them, therefore, noticed the eight or nine young men in their early twenties who had shoved two tables together outside, and it appeared to be one of these who shouted none too politely what sounded like "le même chose," which Donnie thought meant another. Another round. And so the intimate moment came to an end for the nonce, clearing space for a more intimate moment, for both men knew that the morning's activity would linger like the memory of a man who was caught picking his nose and eating the angled hard snot nugget unaware that his friend, who probably did the same, was watching, and neither wanted such a banal psychodrama to enforce itself as their first moment of challenge in friendship.

Drake, being the victim in a sense, was the more devout in his stubborn pose, and Donnie knew it, and finally blurted out, "That's a pretty fucking strange habit you've got—you realize that."

"How'd you know it's a habit?"

"Has to be."

"Well insofar as a habit can be an obsession, I guess you're right. It is an obsession."

"I recall the reason for the split with your father..."

"Make of that what you will. It may well be a linear...It may well be...what you think it is."

"I don't decide such things. I don't leap to judgment, if you will. You can't very well spend hours drinking before the Manneken Pis and then think someone else odd for watching scene after scene of specific destruction."

"But you did make the connection."

"Without intent. I don't *think* anything."

"One thing I want you to know is that this habit of mine has nothing to do with the politics of it—I have no interest in the specific story vissie vee politics, Jews, Bush, mysterious flashes, Osama bin Client. I watch everything I can to add footage if something new comes out, but that's all."

"Then?"

"It's not even easy to explain to myself, but it has something to do with something like meditation on experience, having the feeling that somewhere in there is some explanation for something that matters in life, existentially, phenomenologically, something that lends meaning to the void, the reason the void, to me, has a faint suction."

"It seems to me quite the opposite, whatever you intend, or seek. Meditation is almost universally related to coming to grips with the transience of life, of moments, and here you are as if having captured a moment and studying it, having it repeat before your eyes, an artificial repetition...that I think can't but eat into the reality of the event, eroding its definition to the point where it has all the heft of fiction and none of the heart of myth. In other words, this artifice—cameras, film—renders the experience sterile."

"No, no: far from it. Look, Donnie, whether I saw anything or no, whether I view the film a thousand times or once, the event happened the same as the Battle of Actium, and what you're saying seems more applicable to Richard Burton and Liz Taylor fighting the battle than a real film study of the event, which played over and over, since it is real, since it is without artifice, actually enhances the quality of being of the event…"

"But—"

"No, to be precise, more precise, the enhancement is within the human engaging the event. The event of course remains the event, one time only, one series of instances."

"But what becomes, say, filmically iconic, what attracts more than its share of attention—think of Braudel and the quotidian—it's like Fallujah, with the Blackwater guys hanging from the bridge."

"Is that a random example?"

"What do you mean?"

"Why choose that?"

Drake displayed a look that could have been giving off a spark of paranoia.

"Strangely, because of my estrangement from my mother. I generally hate her poetry, mostly for the way that she absorbs praise and attentions and does nothing but spout global crisis phrases so that even if the literati are right that she is the queen of all poets, it's still bullshit. But when the US went full bore into Fallujah, she wrote a poem about it that actually had one good line in it, or one of the very few I ever liked. Remember it started with these Blackwater guys getting strung up, the image iconic of the event…"

Drake chuckled cryptically. "I remember."

"Then the hideous assault, taking the hospital first. And my old lady had this one line:

four burnt bats shine black through phosphor white
I loved that line."

A long silence ensued that became a wait for the return of Picasso Tits for the more mundane reason that they wanted another beer.

"You don't know it yet but you just took us way off topic. I want to continue about the film, but you just dropped into some twisted and significant terrain…wait til we get another beer."

Donnie felt the sort of welling inside that comes from knowing that you're about to finally find out who the murderer is in that rare film in which you both care about the matter and find yourself baffled by it.

Picasso Tits returned, they ordered, and when she had chopped off the heads of the beer and handed them over, Donnie did Drake the favor of asking what one of them would eventually have to.

"So are you predominantly Flemish or Walloon?"

She issued a laugh that conveyed a complete understanding of the situation.

"Mother Flem, father Walloon. I was raised equally. But everyone around here speaks both, or almost."

"You have no preference?"

"I prefer to practice my English."

"That's good," Drake said. "Cause on the way here we figured one of us would have to learn one and the other the other, but then we realized that if we did that we wouldn't be able to speak to each other."

Picasso Tits laughed without restraint, a belly laugh, turning from the šank to bend forward, her forehead nearly touching her knees.

When she recovered, she said, "That's the funniest joke I did ever hear."

"Speaking of jokes, where is that drooling Bavarian weisshundt?"

"It's a—"

"Dogue de Bordeaux, yes."

"Fils doesn't let him in here unless he is here…"

"You are both American, yes?"

"Well, Americans of the US persuasion. But we are innocent of significant evil."

"What do you mean?"

"Drake means that while perhaps many of our leaders belong in the Hague, we commit little crimes, like gambling where it is illegal."

"Drake. Does it mean anything?"

"It's short for Mandrake, but I'd rather not get into it. This is Donnie, from Donald, which is an awful name."

"I am Setif. From a political perspective unpopular."

"So your parents saddled you like a horse."

"Saddled me like a horse?"

Donnie found need to interject.

"I had a Russian friend in high school named Igor who repeatedly complained, 'Igor is a Scandinavian name. I am not proud of this.'"

Now the laughter was light, comradely and general, and this seemed to bring out the rudeness in the men from outside, who sent a different emissary this time.

Another round, predictably, and gone was the rebel angel, who was already about to be set upon by the after dinner crowd.

"Yes," Donnie said, "I want her, too, but I have already yielded to you."

"I noticed that. Gallantry?"

"Yes, I suppose it is."

"It's damned appreciated…been a long time since a woman made such an atomic mess of my physiology."

"In my case it's a simple matter of the rare hardon without intimacy."

"Don't let her notice. We must be as careful with her as the situation calls for."

"Back to situations: tell me about our new and twisted terrain."

"Your mother, my father. Fallujah was a great boon to him. Not many people know this, or if they do, they respect me and keep their mouths shut about it. But you know Blackwater obviously."

"Four burnt bats."

"Right, but more significantly, hundreds of dead Iraqis. Well through his experience in Vietnam, maybe some funny business during the Reagan years, and certainly the first Gulf War, he got it together, and through his connections received a lot of inside information about how things were shaping up, and he began a private security company, not much different from Blackwater, but initially much smaller. He gave jobs to lots of old military friends, that kind of thing. Some were having muscular, bloodthirsty children and he hired those, too. And he got his share of contracts. Probably no one was much bigger in the first Gulf War, but in the second the private money was significantly greater and Blackwater was really sucking it up. And my old man knew the Blackwater guy, the founder, Dane Frot, and they despised each other. So as soon as Blackwater fucked up, killing civilians in Baghdad, my old man, whose company was Blackguard, began a quiet ad campaign along the lines of As secure as Blackwater without the body count. You know, no dead civilians, no absurd and dangerous assignments, clear communication with the military, absolute discipline. He stole a lot of contracts from Blackwater. The problem was that though that picked up after the famous incident in Baghdad in which Blackwater killed and injured around, I don't know, thirty to fifty civilians and then the retribution you mention in Fallujah, the first contract they got was a direct replacement of Blackwater in Fallujah. Assignment: actually guard a bridge to prevent anyone, any male, over sixteen, from leaving the city, as they were potential insurgents and the bizarre idea the military had was to entirely evacuate this city of a quarter million and just fight real insurgents. Imagine: in this day and age. And can you imagine, it's asymmetrical warfare, so are all the insurgents going to say all right, we'll do this the Franco-Prussian way? It was fucking absurd. But nonetheless, my old man and his crew had the job of making sure no sixteen-year-old males crossed the bridge. That meant tearing some adolescent from his family, maybe carrying a victrola or something, determining that they couldn't determine and so sending him back into the city. Why give a shit? Because patrols on the other side of the bridge kept sending boys back, sometimes men, everyone wanted out of the city, probably insurgents more than others. And you know what happened, right? Of course. They bombed for several days, then the marines advanced, killed anything that moved because it had to be an insurgent, even though we know now that maybe only three-fourths of the civilians were able to escape the city—and to where? The suburbs? You should see a map. Desert all around. Where did they go? And snipers, and white phosphorus, and house to house fighting meaning the marines went into houses and shot whoever was in there. My dad told me all this and he was on the right side, the winning side, the American side. So when you talk about burnt bodies, this is what it really means, imperial revenge. Don't ask me for numbers, the city of mosques was flattened. And you know what, one of the flatteners was a vehicle, I remember this from a video, was something, something that pushed south through the desert in an amphibious assault vehicle, I mean in the Koran it famously says the desert is an ocean in which no oar is dipped, but the desert surrounding Fallujah fell prey to amphibious assault vehicles. It's bizarre. My father had no more contracts that involved himself in fighting, not that this was fighting, but it was an extension of combat, an umbilical cord had to be cut before he could get away, but that Fallujah business was enough to sour him. I mean sour him in the sense that he no longer wanted any part of operations, and he said that there was a lot more of that was going on than anyone realized, assassination teams, other shit. So after Fallujah the rest was simply his company doing what another could have done only in most cases with less chance of bloodshed, which was his selling point. We can protect the senator without killing or bullying or whatever. Each employee trained to keep his head, to fire absolutely only when fired upon, which they almost never were, even know some of the local lingo. But you know, that experience, knowing that those he let pass would survive and those he sent back would suffer bizarre injuries and deaths and bombs none of us know the likes of, that did not change him in the least—he merely stepped back from the fronts of war personally, and determined to make what profit he could being involved in the industry of war at the moment it was privatizing. He never expressed regrets, never told me about some boy sent back across the bridge, though there were many he said, boys he let go who were sent back or boys or men who escaped and were caught by the military and sent back, he never told any stories about them. But the implications were clear—he was like the receptionist at Auschwitz, choosing who to send to his doom."

"Do you have film of the Iraq business?"

"What, you mean like this morning?"

"Right."

"No, just what you saw and the one I told you about, the one I still hope to get."

"Another round, lads," Picasso Tits said, returning just to make that declaration, serve them their fresh beers before dancing off again.

"Agile," Drake commented.

"Lithe."

"And much pursued."

"That's your advantage."

Drake downed half his beer, as if to provide hops to his hope.

"You aren't watching those films to come to terms with the scope of terror, are you."

"No. If there is any relation to terror it is the banality of it that gets me, something about the way the multitude, rather than the small number of dead and injured, seem to have to exhort their, themselves, to feeling. To feel more than you would on an exhilarating ride at a carnival, say. But that's obvious. My idea is to use the available techniques to repeat the event, in my own head, to try to understand experience, which wouldn't work if the imagery were not exceptional, if I watched the same seven seconds of a man walking over and over, for instance. This kind of extravagant catastrophe is a heightened form of experience, but experience still. I think I can get at the nature of experience by immersing myself in it—"

"Which you can do because it's fun to watch."

"That's one way of putting it, yes. Where would my mind go if I were watching something ordinary?"

"That much I get, I just think the effect is bound to be the opposite of what you intend. If you either didn't see it, just had it described to you, or saw it only once, you would be engaged with it in a real way, with your natural imagination. But once you see it twice it's no longer the same event because you're prepared for it and can't possibly respond with genuine emotion, which includes, to say the least, surprise."

"No, you're wrong. Seeing it repeatedly really doesn't deaden my response, which is what you're basically suggesting. My inner response may be altered, but my thinking is that it will be altered in such a way as to move closer to the event, maybe without the interference of imagination and emotion."

"You contradict yourself. It doesn't deaden your response, but you hope to deflect the interference of the very lively parts of yourself, imagination and emotion. In other words, deaden yourself."

"Wrong again. I wish to isolate the event and enter it without the restraints of imagination and emotion. What happens in my brain will always be connected to imagination and emotion, but in this sort of case they are impediments between the event and my conscious understanding of it. I won't be having imagination and emotion surgically removed."

"You won't need to."

Drake paused and leaned back, his stool balanced on its hind legs like a rearing horse. He showed Donnie a wry grin that meant Donnie had won on the wrong level, that the argument would have to come to a halt but that Donnie had failed to find the proper arena of thought in the first place.

"The main thing, at least for now, is that we, hopefully, have established that I am not a psycho."

"Who is a psycho?"

The nipples were at what had to be full swell and as she arched her back, stretching away her servitude, we must imagine Drake focusing on her right nipple and Donnie on her left.

"Who isn't?" Drake replied.

The three searched together for a gently paven path to a near future.

"You are gamblers? That is how you make your job?"

They laughed.

"No," Donnie explained, "We met playing poker. We like poker. And in the interest of confession it must be said that we have played poker for money where such activities are prohibited."

"So you are outlaws." She said this with a combination of the rebel adolescent's love of the daring and a warmth of mockery such that both men felt as if a foetus were tumbling in their bellies.

"I want to learn poker. I see it played in cowboy movies and since I was a little girl I wanted to learn."

"Well you can come to our place and I'll get you drunk and teach you poker."

"You like cowboy movies?"

"My father loves cowboy movies and so I grew up watching them."

"Same here."

"Not me," said Drake. "I was always bored by westerns. And historical dramas. Must be a distaste for the past."

"But you will still teach me poker."

"Oh yes. I suppose tonight is out, but if you're free in the morning…"

"Which is your favorite?"

Drake was writing his phone number on a Jupiler coaster. *The Man Who Shot Liberty Valance.*

"That's good, that's good. I think my favorite though is *The Wild Bunch*, sometimes *One-Eyed Jacks.*"

"'I might go on up to Oregon.'"

"Excellent Brando."

As Setif took the coaster with a smile, down the šank a commanding voice barked her name. She appeared to delay deliberately, offering Drake a redundant acknowledgment before sidling slowly down the šank.

"That must be her pimp," Donnie said sotto voce. Fittingly, the sky had entirely routed the sun by now.

The guy was rugged about the face, taller than either of them, and more broad shouldered. His t-shirt left no doubt about his musculature. Both Donnie and Drake found wonted pleasure in a certain over-riding ugliness to his countenance.

With gritted teeth he seethed at Setif, the word "American" or some Brusselian-cursed version of it part of his admonishment. At first she bore it with an inexpressive demeanor, but he apparently belched out something offensive and she began to turn in disgust when the man grabbed her arm, holding her, whispering with a hatred that lacked only the sudden screeching leap of a cat to alter the entire feel of the bar.

Drake made to get up, but Donnie quickly held him down, his hand on his shoulder.

"Wait."

When the man had finished with her, Picasso Tits quickly filled two more glasses with La Chouffe. "That was ugly," Donnie said.

"Bit young to be your father," said Drake.

"He thinks he is my boyfriend."

"Or perhaps that he will be your last boyfriend."

At this she looked at Donnie, for a moment with her eyes too wet, but then laughed airily.

"Yes," Donnie said. "It's always worse in the movies."

"And the Ukraine."

"*Merde,*" she hissed.

They turned: a table of four had just seated themselves outside.

"When you get back we'll pay up and ease your burden. But promise you'll call me."

"Promise you will get me drunk and teach me poker."

When she had gone, Donnie consoled Drake, "The ones that are too good—and too quick—to be true usually turn out to be insane. It's much harder than dealing with a jealous ex."

"Right, hopefully I just have to take the one pounding."

And so they were jolly enough when Picasso Tits returned to take the money that they had to pay to drink in the drinking place. Each of the three felt some of the awkwardness of that arrangement, but given that this would be the easy part of the coming rigors of establishing their small tribe, she did not even say, But no, that is too much, when Drake tipped her five euros.

On a typical evening stroll from Santana to Rue de Suede above L'Empereur tavern, the crossing where the robbery had occurred would have been about halfway, but when the two foreigners had gone a mere third of the way to the crossing and discovered that they were being followed by nine citified locals, even arriving to that crossing seemed an unlikely prospect, and if reached, it was yet a true nine blocks from home.

No cars were passing, but it still seemed unlikely that a

brawl would ensue on this side of Saint-Gilles and the Midi Station.

Nonetheless, the threat was palpable. Drake was the first to speak it.

"I am really disgusted by a people who guard their women."

"From Americans—I think that gives them a special urgency, or at least a reason."

"Still disgusting."

Drake further knew that he was the target. He had been seen giving his phone number to Picasso Tits.

Would they surround Drake and keep Donnie from coming to his aid?

Before long the crossing was reached, the nine men maintaining half a block of intimidation between the groups. Drake and Donnie crossed against the light casually as traffic was light.

"Keep a steady pace, Drake."

"See, it would just be nice to know the extent of violence or threat they intended. Then I would be able to manage it better."

"You're managing fine, just keep a steady pace and we'll be fine."

A primordial anger was rumbling deep in Donnie, too deep for him to know that that was levering up his confidence, calming his demeanor.

They crossed where the woman had been window smashed purse snatched, remembering the stunning bloodless violence of it, as their pursuers were gaining on them. Naturally, like the window breaking purse thief, they took their first left. They had about eight blocks to home.

A third of the way down the block, Drake looked over his shoulder.

"They're down to five."

"We're still two."

"I haven't been in a fight since before high school."

"Leave it til we know what they intend."

Directly before the Africain, the intentions became plain. The other four had hustled ahead around the triangular block and were guarding the road; three of them had picked up iron rods.

"I think they intend bodily harm."

Donnie's anger was now a buzzing in his arms.

"Don't worry."

With four men in front of them, three armed, and five behind and closing, it became clear that this block, now devoid of Africans north and sub-Saharan, was deserted, an actual slice of the Sahara where caravans were raided to the delight of the history of everyday life.

Drake and Donnie had no choice but to pull up and wait for whatever announcement would precede the bloodbath. By now those behind were within a few meters, and those ahead were snickering, closing as well.

Drake and Donnie turned to face the followers.

Unsurprisingly, it was the boyfriend (ex) from the bar, who stepped forth from the five behind, a knife in his hand and in a language that was not French abused Drake and Donnie, who were rats in a trap that trapped rats.

The assailant then focused on Drake, and when he was within a meter, the knife held at waist level before him, the predetermined outcome, the fearful nature of it, aroused Donnie from any impending funk of fear into a combustion of rage that guided him, straight toward the ex, even as the other eight were forming a closer circle, and Donnie, frightful as the absence of his known expected fear strode directly to said ex and landed a viperine strike right cross directly to his nose, felling him, yet failing to remove the knife from his hand, so that Donnie's next move, fluidly made, was a stomp on the ex's wrist, surely shattering those little bones that connected hand and arm, freeing the knife, and he knelt, his own knife of a black tempered steel unknown even to Drake, slapping open hard, connecting to the ex's throat as he clutched the fellow's hair and bounced his head off the pavement.

The nine bystanders were stunned long enough that Donnie was able to check the ex's knife, find it dull, and toss it to Drake.

"Look at that," he said, his own knife at the ex's throat, blade against flesh. "Not even sharp."

Blood was pumping like liquid tusks from the nostrils, curling around his mouth.

Drake took up the knife, as the rest stood under the spell of Donnie's rapid action.

"Any of you assholes speak English?"

A small, feisty looking blonde replied, "I do."

"You want to see what a sharp knife can do to a man?"

"What you mean?"

"Watch," he said, and slowly sliced a surface smile into the ex's neck.

"See? Now, Drake, give that fucker that knife. You, give my friend your stick."

Dumbfounded, the two exchanged weapons.

Donnie lifted the ex's head and brought it down hard on the pavement, loud enough it echoed like a drum.

"The rest of you just drop your sticks."

They obeyed without translation; clearly English was spoken more than they would have liked, each of the eight taking a step back, unsure of the fate of their leader, whose neck was bleeding now, complementing the flood from his nose, his head held by Donnie's clench of his hair.

"See that knife? Run your finger over it. A good knife would at least give you pause. You couldn't commit suicide with that one. Now as you see, mine here is a different story. Right, shitbrain?" For emphasis Donnie gave his head a gentler bounce on the asphalt. Drake couldn't tell from the ex's eyes if he was fully conscious, but he was clearly beyond fright in the embrace of defeat.

"So this is how this ends, gentlemen. I'm going to let him go, and besides his wrist you'll find he won't require any medical attention—"

"You broke his fucking nose!"

"Right, good punch. Anyway, the neckslice is a surface wound that only a very sharp knife can inflict. To get this kind of effect with that knife you'd have to really jab it in and then turn it—it'd be a mess. Not expecting trouble tonight, this knife is all I brought. From here on, though, I will be moving about freely in your peaceable city with a gun they call a Smith & Wesson, so revenge is out of the question. You dumb asses followed a jealous child into battle and got lucky he was the only victim. But this kind of shit can get people killed and I won't tolerate it. Understand?"

What are generally known as mutters were heard as Donnie let go the hair and the head met the street one last time. He flicked his head toward Drake to indicate it was time to leave and they walked toward home without looking back.

Drake recovered his wit before they arrived home.
"Like a western."
"Cept Lee Marvin got out alive."

17

POKER

The young man in both love and heat is a poet: her pubic hair, he muses of his muse, the color of whey. And what is whey? And what is its hue. He does not know. (The colors of whey vary, so perhaps he is right.) Even if he has studied geography, it is poetry when he compares her slit to a graben floodspate.

Her body: prostrate, on the back, on Drake's bed.

Her skirt: short made shorter, hiked hem above navel. Her hand: three kings.

Her right big toe: in Drake's mouth as he kneels before the bed.

"So can I move up?"

"No."

"Right."

"The thing about poker," Drake had lectured, "is that it doesn't matter what game you're playing: the same hierarchy of hands applies."

He dealt her another hand.

"What do you have?"

"Two sevens."

"Can I move up?" he asked around her toe.

"Yes."

"Nope," he replied, spitting out her toe. "Quite often in five card hands especially, something less than a pair wins, like ace high. So we should at least include one example of a hand with nothing but something like ten high—"

Voila! He dealt her a hand with an ace and four loners.

"Move up!" she cried.

"Thank God, your toe was beginning to look like a large raisin," which she heard as reason but quickly calculated was wrong and the main thing was that he could now move up, as he did, with slow, short, soft kisses all about the tops of each of her feet as he shuffled the deck without looking before dealing five cards that rotored with class up to and landed upon her chest, between her breasts. As luck would have it, she had a pair of bullets and his lips were allowed to spend several dealt poker hands smooching her ankles.

The next hand he watched himself shuffle, which allowed him to arrange to give her the necessary two pair, allowing for a move to the lower calves.

Three of a kind was so slow in coming, he cheated again after a few hands. He rolled her onto her stomach when his lips and tongue reached her knees so he could explore the first found fold of her felicitous form, but she rolled again when he had proffered three kings, for the front of the thighs are the better path to the inner and up her.

By now she was unable to restrain her hips and was breathing irregularly. When Drake moved his lips upward and inward and his head hair touched her spated graben, she moaned breathily, sucking in, trying to capture what had already fled.

He was assembling the cards, preparing to shuffle when she gripped his ears. "Look at me," she said, "straight, flush, full house, four of a kind, straight flush, and this…" pulling Drake's mouth to her soaking vagina… "royal…straight… flush…"

Drake didn't know much about the anatomy of the penis, but he felt as if there were a tiny pirate inside his capo di capo who was about to bring a cutlass down on a tense rope.

Tail

Post-coital ease.
"I know you call me Picasso Tits."
"Does it bother you?"
"Not if I can call you Bosch Scrotum." "So seek a fine balance."
"Yes."

18

THE OREGON TRAIL

Standing washing himself in the south fork of what used to be called the Little Moose River, Jeffers Phoebles looked from Tom Gravel's vantage up on the bank to be made entirely of taut flesh; that is, other than the genitalia that hung like a dead bird, skinned, carried for times of bad faunal hunt luck. He was brown as an Injun, stretched and wrinkled both, his white hair down to the middle of his back. He washed himself like a woman, Gravel thought, taking his time, even though the water was freezing. Gravel's bath had consisted of little more than submersing himself before hopping out making whooping sounds. Summer was a lot warmer back in Ohio, where the water warmed along with the sky, but at least there were river otters gamboling about hereabouts.

Barefoot and all, Phoebles even sort of lady-hopped up the bank when he'd had enough, his beaner, as Gravel called such, putting up quite a horse show. And since the first thousand miles from Missouri to Oregon seemed focused on little more than the groin area, Gravel thought little of making a joke of the nude mountain man's outfit.

"Them three's looking like to conspire an escape the way they come with ya up the mound all going everwhich ways."

Phoebles looked him asquint, deciding.

"Spose yer pullpole's made a gold, then, is it, n yer balls is Chinee jade."

What a shame that history, that necessary inadvertence, that all-encompassing swarm of smarm and harm, that categorical march of breached boundaries, what a shame that history is, nasty paradox, hidden only from the historical. Young Tom Gravel, whom Spengler would have called a historyless peasant—but not yet, no, nearly a century: of history!: must first pass—was off to make history, was making history, was *being* history, his humility but an ignorance, the ignorance that Braudel would call a quotidian economic mulish path but simple taken, yet who is capable of determining that this young man, now partnered with mountain man extraordinaire Jeffers Phoebles, post-history, had not witnessed that advent of a particular type of murder to the west once wild. He did not actually see the murder take place, but he did indeed witness the hanging, and was central to the prevention of a second murder, that of Mr. Phoebles himself, enemy of darkness and evil in his direct simplicity, his taint right ifn isrong. Like others before him, Jeffers Phoebles used his skills learnt as a solitary man in the wildest of wildernesses to make a living guiding pilgrims, one might say, along the Oregon Trail, from Independence, Missouri, to the general region of that foul Fort Vancouver. One might make a distinction here, one might pause to consider that this in itself was not so much history as the slow dying of an idea, the slow spread of detritus in the shallow fetid dying of a mighty wave, on the surface a febricantic slapdash to Oregon for fruit, to California for elements, yet upon vaster distance of glance but the hopping of shrimplike weak creatures of the shallows now in the shallower uncertain whether to go up or down. Nonetheless aspects of the inevitable stand as footnotes, and such would be that specific premeditated, purely evil form of murder that speaks of the vacuity that remains in man once the thrust for gain has scraped such as gallantry and sunlight from his innards such that overactive brains sick with excess of psychomental backwash roiling from confinement direct bodies that function ungoverned by that which this final of creatures rejected in fear.

The wagon train consisted of seventeen separate farmer families and one pair, Bart and Pete Dodger, of river gamblers, among which included 23 firing weapons, three of which were pistols of Colt manufacture, Colt Patersons, five shot revolvers, not exactly rejects but sold off by deserters, one of which was a gift to Tom Gravel from his ma, who had so recently buried his pa, the other two of which were in the iniquitous hands of the Dodger boys. For trail guide Jeffers Phoebles this was weapon enough, for the Mandan had been quiet some time, the Blackfoot were sickly, and only the Cheyenne stood in their path before they reached possible Sioux raiders, but them had been said to have split north/south, so it was the Cheyenne before the Flatheads, who hadn't never attackit no one. Ah… fuck it, just fuck it. The story was best told by Phoebles to Gravel the day after the wagon train split up, rather was run off by Phoebles, or Phoebles and Gravel were abandoned by the wagon train, and we'll get to a cleaner version of that version by and by.

The first day out, the day they gathered after crossing the Missouri even though chances were they'd have to cross it again, and they set off in a near single file line of wagons, men on horses, cows and pigs on foot, chickens making their escapes from out covered wagons, holding up the whole train while little boys and girls made to fetch them, that day Tom Gravel approached Phoebles in order to insinuate himself into a sort of apprenticeship. He was a seventeen-year-old lad whose father had recently died, had three brothers to run the farm, none of whom seemed too sorry to see their dreamy brother who wandered the woods for long afternoons at a time while the rest worked the farm even though he was a willing and hard worker when he and work came together direct, decide to set off for adventures west. Gravel liked animals, all kinds, and though he wanted to learn to shoot the ones that allowed him to eat—he was without squeam—he derived a great deal more pleasure just watching them, particularly beavers and otters, because you could, I mean they didn't tear ass off like deer and the like, and opossums, which you could play with for hours they were so slow and perhaps dumb. In fact, the brothers were so satisfied with the arrangement, Tom's departure, they allowed ma to make him a present of pa's near new Colt Paterson.

Tom liked his pistol, but what he really wanted was a rifle, to go off hunting with the guide, that Jeffers Phoebles, and so he approached him the first day out and conversed as such.

"Sir, if you can use a hand I sure would like to be your shootin partner."

"Kinyunt?" Phoebles asked.

"What?"

"Kinyunt?"

"What?"

"Ase kinyunt?"

"I's sorry, I just don't unnerstan."

"Ye deef, boy? A say, kinya unt?"

"Can I hunt?"

Here Phoebles looked up to where God should have been. "What a sayd."

"I kin learn but I got no rifle, so if you can let me use yer spare…"

And the kindly Phoebles took him on then and there, even going so far as to buy the boy a nag.

Tom turned out not only to be a fine shot, but fearless as well, and a good all round hand who could fashion a new axle, attach a wheel, and was strong enough to lift the back end of a wagon out of a rut. He was quietly popular amongst the migrants, though he seldom spoke to anyone at length but Phoebles, to some degree for his shyness but more so in that folk tended to work hard and close, like as if being thrown together in this fashion and thus having to share 2000 miles of trek together did not weather the stubborn from them and they were used to being amongst folk who just weren't right, which is to say, not yet what the new nation had intended. They were right to suspect, but none could imagine the re-morseless and absurd meeting in such a fashion as it did near halfway through Wyoming when the events that broke up the group, divorced it from its guide and one of its best hands, occurred in their serpentine fatalism, events best described by Phoebles to Tom with the help of some more modern phraseology, which I turn to from frustration at the obscurity of some particularly difficult passages that I believe I have at least captured the essence of.

After dressing himself, Phoebles began to explain what he had just told Gravel would have to wait until after his bath, when they would tie up their horses and ambule about seeking antelope:

"Naturally, Tom, you being young and all, you didn't take no notice of the goings on in the camp, other than ye takin ta mooning over that Suzanna McGovern and maybe noticing she had eyes fer the boy Jacob Sorenson, son of the man Lars McGovern partnered up with, Paddy Sorenson, which I take for natural, though when you warnt looking she did give you the looksee now and then, but you hadn't much chance agin that strapping handsome lad as you got a bit too much clear enough wild in ya, and whilst a woman likes that, too, what she had for the taking, knowing she can play with it like a toy all the way to Orrygon, something you'll learn about in time which is called forebelaying the pleasure, which is sometimes as good as the pleasure itself with the right woman, damned cursed few have I found in my lonesome life of hard labor and travail, cold and hunger, pissass guns and damp powder, murderin Brittos and theevin Injuns...

"I knowed it, you knowed it near as much, but what you didn't know was that churchified wench be she but a teen is of the natural type can't help but put out the scent invites the men even them what repussles her. So that's whar in comes that Dodger boy, that Ross—"

"Ross? There's Bart and Pete, but ain't no Ross. There was that quiet feller with the sickly wife and all the kids, always bringin up the rear. Believe his name to be Ross, Ross Springboot."

"Well I don't give a raykoon's fart what the name was, it was the one with the black hair, the—"

"They both have black hair."

"Fuck my blind crack's squintineyeball, then—the one all crookbacked like a febral dog, a rabid retchet mongrel—"

"Well that's the younger one, Pete."

"Then it's Pete!"

"Bart's the older, bigger—"

"Kantrammit*sayd* it's Pete! Pete! Let me tell the story would you? Whucha never notice was Pete wants this darling

baddern anyone n e's a meanun, can see that right off, I know
you did, but what you ain't seed us his gutheavin lusters fer
the girl. Second day out, second day on the trail, camp at
night and Pete stepped on Jacob's hand by the fire pretendin
like he dint notice it, already the spite swelt in him like pus
in a rudgeboil. Ever day affer that I watchim cause I know
when trouble come down the trail aint but what we got fer
law an when a young girl is involved the law runs with the
rising blood ifn you are not careful, n ever day some way or
tuther Pete shown his hand, and I seen grizzlers, naysay I
seen wolves with less murder in the eye than Pete lookin it Jacob. We was notso far from them Dakoty hills when Pete saw
them two close together talkin back of the Sorenson wagon,
nobody lookin they thought, Pete stopped in tyin his horse
to a tree, n me watchin Pete, n they spoke with heads close
together like horses drinking at the trough and she let out a
hoot of laughter, threw her head back all carefreeless like n
Pete's ears was red, and that very same night after community
supper Jacob off n went to drop turd, Pete and Ross was—"
    "Bart."
    "Bart and Pete was off with they own whiskey by a tree n I
saw this: Pete saw Jacob off into the woods and made to falla
him when Bart grabbed his arm and there was a hard mutter-
ing dispute between them that ended with Bart giving Pete a
good hard slap across the back of the head and Pete just said
You didn't have to do that, but that was the end of it for that
night at least. (Maybe drop the vernacular entire? At least for
now?) Each night after that was more tense, only you, probably you were masturbating (he actually used the expression
"trying to yank the snake out the hole") away your despair
and you're too young to really understand the environment
around you. I don't mean to say you're selfish, but you just ar-
en't self-aware enough to be aware of other selves. Well I survive by knowing how to read a group and by god the second
day out I swore this would be my last time because I knew
not only that it was likely to end badly, but also I sensed my
own life was imperiled by the dynamics of the situation. And
you know just from one look at some men like this Dodger

varmint and you know the best thing to do there n then is to cut him a second smile neath the first, but ya jest caint, ya caint do it fer nothing for no prophet moves the hangman, n damded if I dint wait too long and make one mistake going off on that final hunt that now I know Pete got Bart to get that Lyle McCrayder to suggest, lyin about seein a herd a anteelope—they or Pete musta knowd how I would take the thing and maybe even that I was watching, and here's where I made my mistake: the night before I saw Jacob and Suzanna go off separately and knew right away where they went, which warnt far and they wasn't gone long, but I knew the thing was ready to burst like lava from a carbooncle, n shoulda bin on my guard better—fer whilst them two rabbits was gone, Pete was fidgeter than a blind cat on a skillet, Bart even oncet held him down with his hand on Pete's shoulder, and soon as they came back, about fifteen minutes apart, say, Pete calmed his body but looked like he was already watching a murder in his eyes. I saw him watching himself bangin Jacob's head on a rock, I swear to the truth of that.

"See here, the clever thing about them two pups disappearing was that Jacob come back first, which is less suspicious if you know what I mean. And therein lies the tragedy. Maybe the first time they just experiment with a kiss, and maybe they agree that they wait til they get to Orrygon afore marriage, and wait to marry before fornicating, but with younguns like them nature will force the issue, and one kiss if it be the first is one following day of thinking about nought but the next kiss which will last longer and will involve the rubbery of bodies and will certainly create a bloodswell in both parties that will not be bungholed up with a cork, so if you ask me that second night when they met they were steaming hotblooded and that Pete was himself bulge-eyed with lustbloodlust and crazy as a crosseyed coon with a thorn on his butthole, and we know where it happened, that they chose just the right place, just out of hearing should there be a moan or a yelp, and Pete like you saw went down early as trickery, and you dint have no idear what was going on til morning, or before sunrise and all the screaming, and we both know what happened and we both know if I'd been there either there woulda been no hanging or there woulda been a murder then a hanging, and if I coulda stalled some sense into them folk I coulda found a fragment of Pete's gun and maybe there woulda been a hanging of one brother and a shootout with the other, but what happened"—to which not even Pete as participant witnessed entire, much as Jeffers Phoebles imagined it, was one scene nature and one scene maybe nature, too, pity the living of every kind, a grassy clearing, a moonlit eve, a bank of raspberry bushes to conceal Pete, a half hour of love talk between Jacob and Suzanna, Jacob swollen full unsure what way to move because he sure as hell couldn't lay entirely still, and Suzanna like pulp squeezing out of herself, her nipples like grapes, her hips shifting like nervous to calm the lewd, before finally no more can she bear it, and she undid her blouse with her eyes hypnotizing Jacob who would only look at what she revealed when her own eyes led his down as they slowly did, and at a hint of an invite he as if sucked by maelstrom slapped softly into Suzanna and the kiss was animal, wild animal, what neither would have known and both knew would remain a kiss and breast-grabbing venture for some time and that only this time for another time and time after time this would be their life and how do you stop? Well you have that skirt and them things underneath it and that swollen pecker that would pop for now there was certainly a place for Jacob's restlessness, a ride on a thigh that knew by nature precisely what was riding and how to be ridden, and there were several minutes of catching of breath and no more kissing, a mutual sense of being maybe too loud or something wrong, maybe too much time had passed, for neither had the slightest idea how much time had passed, and even Pete had no idea for perhaps it was even longer for him, and knowing tomorrow night would bring all the same and more, a brief mutual deeply contented goodbye was said and Jacob went back to camp. Suzanna lay on her back chest heaving in a sort of remembrance of ecstasy, an oozing of desire that would require the time she anyway had to wait and Pete was on her, hand on her mouth and she bit his hand and her yelp was cut short by a blow that stunned her for he had punched her forehead but he saw she was going to let burst another yelp and quick as a riverboat deathscrape he had caved her skull in with his gun butt and only then did he tear her clothes down to skin and pull his own pants and such down and find her still lubricated by her moments with Jacob and so he spent perhaps a full half an hour inside her ejaculating twice before he saw the sense his kind sometimes sees and hated more than he had ever hated in his life, hated that bashed in skull and he went into a frenzy of gun butt bashing, ruining the gun butt and rendering the head of the sprightly Suzanna the wrong kind of pulp. Spent he stood. He picked the bits of gun he saw, went and found a rock, and without much more than a certain resentment at a chore unspoken for he bashed her a few times with the rock—"the unlucky fact that someone, who was it, that sickly feller, that Ross was up making tea for his sickly wife and saw Jacob sneak back into camp looking grateful he wernt caught and before long by that motherinstinct Mrs. McGovern woke up and worried after her daughter and a general todo like you sayd, the search directed by a quiet hint from that Ross feller and all goin everwhich way as it coulda bin Injuns, and by the luck yer youth and calm disposition waited it out, took a leak off in the BartPete direction, heard said they would have to gun me down if I came back and which is dam sure right, and off you go after me when what you should have done was stay there to tell everbody to wait for old Jeffers as I was the guide after all, and as you have seen was the only one with sense to look the locality of the murder over with some percepence, finding three wood bits could only come from a gun butt and woulda seed if Pete could produce his gun, but now you know what frenzy kin do in four hours, that poor boy hangin dead from that tree by first light face beat to burstin first, his own pa without a mark on his body, his own ma feelin more shame than instinct, and we both come on the scene gun drawn and I dam near outta disgust took a few shots, but who to kill? Bart and Pete, they aint tall there is to it, they caint do what was done what without the likes of any folks who be rusht to a hangin job, folks can be marniplated like beaver traps set by the beavers emselves."

The sun was high in the east, to their backs, and the gorge below ran nearly south-north, perfect conditions for a shot across with Phoebles' old buffler gun at the mountain goat Gravel had in his sights. Still the shot was more than two hundred yards, maybe five hundred, but the goat was standing erect and still, on a ledge that must have been but inches wide for it looked more like it was floating in the air. How did it get up there? Where was it going? Maybe shooting it was doing it a favor, because from where Gravel lay the goat seemed as if it would be standing there until it wasted away and must fall from lack of strength to stand and no place to lay down. No creature would be bringing it food. Down below was rock, all rock for most of the way across the valley floor, where a narrow stream lined with willows trickled a midsummer day's stream. Trout would be trapped in deeper pools. Gravel was naked to the waist, which seemed a good idea until he lay down and found that contact with each of the multifarious microscopic and big as weed earth yieldings produced its own particular itch. Yet he had to remain perfectly still to shoot true. The more he thought I've waited too long already the more he became convinced he had time to wait til the goat starved and fell.

Maybe the goat blinked—that would be movement.

Click/bang…Echo—about the time the beast heard the shot: and down about five hundred yards fell the goat bouncing once off the bare and barely sloping cliff, landing dead on a pile of boulders.

"Got him!"

"That you did, boy, that you did."

The swelling pride had no connection whatsoever with the life or death of the animal or the hunger or lack of hunger of Gravel and Phoebles. Had the target been the sphincter of a dead Blackfoot splayed in target he would have felt the same. And to Gravel's credit, even had he missed he would have remained buoyant enough; he was learning, learning from the best (as far as he knew, as far as anyone knew, as far as I know), and he was happy, happy enough to stand and face back beneath the sun at the vast basin/range and without tempting confusion admire, further swell with pride, empathetic pride for the land itself, perhaps largely admiring the landscape for what it could accomplish with such a limited range of color.

Only two days had elapsed since that horrific morning when he and Phoebles had ridden into camp prepared for them who were prepared for them, bringing about a quick stalemate allowing for the nausea brought on by absorbing the fact of the hanging, the dead boy hanging there in the tree, the innocent boy hanging there in the tree — for neither yet knew the specifics of the crime and neither would have believed Jacob guilty even had his own mother testified against him — the rest of the camp in a rough lasso formation about the tree, the hanging but minutes concluded, wet shit dripping from a bare dead foot. That nausea passed quickly replaced by the bizarre: aside from the most directly involved, parents of dead and dead, murderous brothers, maybe that Lyle McCrayder who seemed to have fallen in with them (he had not, and though he feared them enough to keep his peace, as soon as they reached civilized Orrygon he quietly left them with a great sense of relief), and then a bovine herd, fifteen or so adults looking expectantly at their guide as if they had no more than reached a clear fork in the road.

For the rest of his life Gravel would remember word for word, not to mention the style of it, the moral heft of it, the response of Jeffers Phoebles, dismounting his horse, gently grasping the reins (Gravel followed suit), said, "Best be movin on for mores dead. Sgo, Tom," and they led their horses back toward the way they had come, ignoring the butbutbuts and whatwhatwhats until it was clear to all that guide and migrants had come to a divining rod in the road.

Once well out of sight, Gravel and Phoebles made a fire and ate prime slices of the deer Phoebles had strapped over his horse, and after it was clear the train had pulled out they returned to retrieve their own supplies — which had been left untouched on the meanest chance Phoebles was out there just itchin for someone to touch them — and inspected the scene of the murder, finding three bits of gun butt wood.

The east side of the gorge had an easier slope, if not a trail, and the two men, after long looks back thataway, began moving down into the gorge, which Phoebles assured Gravel would curve northwesterly and after some miles they would be a short hump from the Snake River, which, if they like, could be their route into Orrygon and Phoebles's final stop now that his employment contract was up, which would be at the homestead of his one true friend, Gravel bein more like a nephew, Hector Robitaille, the man who had survived a bear attack—howeverso, if Tom wanted to divert some and have a look for Black Ass it was said he roamed much the same territry as that which was where Hector was near slain. Though Black Ass had yet to kill another human, by now he'd been seen any number of time plus the number of times he had not been seen but had been claimed to have been seen which was still plenty and verified for a certain his enormous size. For now, though, the main concern was easing down to the valley floor without a horse slipping, which Phoebles concentrated on more than Gravel would ever know, for he was daydreaming after flying grasshoppers, the big gray kind he and his brothers called Indiamen even though Indiamen could not fly, named after a photograph one of them had seen in a shred of newspaper that had entered their lives surreptitiously as packing material for a piece of fruit or some such that depicted a giant vessel that was off to India with a bulging load of civilization. The difference was back in Ohio where the ground was level you could catch these buggers by simply letting them tire themselves for the ground was flat and their flights short hops into which the grasshoppers in each harbored all their hopes only to be set upon and hop into flight again and again until caught in order in the case of Tom Gravel to be released again, in the case of Edward, Quill, and Festus Junior to be put in a sack with the others, brought home eventually to be tied with sewing thread very carefully about the waist *underwing* and used as playthings for the tough barn cats that seemed not to mind that so much energy was expended honing talents without catching anything they cared to eat. But here, going down the slope, it soon became apparent to Tom that capturing one of these In-diamen of the west was a matter of luck that did not occur, for he would have to scrabble upwards fifteen feet and suddenly downwards usually a step and a half before falling to cling to the earth in order not to fall as far as Phoebles was so carefully ensuring the horses did not.

One in a while, Tom would stop and scan the hill, the rockface, the stream, the distances, the sky, and wonder at the emptiness, the vast space that was alive with, as far as he could see, nought but the tiny creatures, darting lizards, ants of indubitable industry, beetles and their coevals under the occasional rock he turned, nothing even so large as a rattler, which was the one creature Phoebles told him he might want to watch, though thus far he had yet to spy one. Had it not been for that lone mountain goat, Tom might have imagined a world in which the Indiamen held sway. Down they went, following the trail topographed by nature, Gravel trailing behind, his mind entrailing his youth, enthralled and coil-ing about in a vermicularity of emotions, smells, thoughts, remembrances, atmospherics without nostalgia, without the rolling of entrails accompanied by loss, hopelessness, or dread, alive with purpose simple, clean, if indirect, and with-in purview, alive without grasshoppers' panic, alive bespoken by the acidic plaint of entrails invoked by fresh kill, and now, at the bottom of the long slope, in the narrow valley itself, by the splashing of a large rainbow trout impooled by evapora-tion, the pool pellucid, the trout engorged in colors, Gravel hopping off a tuft of grass into the pool to splash and wrassle and sport with the fish while Phoebles went off to inspect the dead billy goat, the valley silent but for the splashing and Gravel grunts, and soon, creating a symphony, barks and rip-ples of hilarity from the now dancing Phoebles, dancing as if about a fire that lapped at his gonads, the laughter only penetrating Gravel's sound sense once the fish was gillheld firm, and only then Gravel turning to inspect the surprise spectacle of Phoebles's laughdance.

"What? What is it?" Gravel was laughing now, too, caught up in it.

And finally, hardyharhar, Phoebles managed to mount to his mouth the words, "You missed!"

The billy goat had merely been *frightened* to a fall.

Tail: Tallit Taint Perty

Campfire talk overheard, voice of one Pete Dodger

... 's half brother was—not Ross, Pete, Burt—Louisville—Ross—Burt! Lewelville, a crustit sunburnt foreman a the ranch.

So the ranch owner's daughter come pregnant, and said it must a happened when she was sleep. All a the ranch hands was called into the ranch house and Rossburt he got him the dubbleass task of determint the crimnal. After a lot of questions, one guy stood out, dumbass galoot name a Willy Westlake. He kep on stumblin ansers wrong to question misturd and is on verge to git assrun out thar, when miss Bonnie Sue, hired girl, speaks up: "Twernt Willy—thwouda woke her."

Why, don't ya git it?

19

WAR COUNCIL

Excerpt from the novel
The Olive Tree

By Nathan Zimmer

Even in the dark of night Levi could make out the form of the olive tree on its side, its roots like fat, venomous snakes. He could hear the celebrations of the enemy from their village over the hill and it was as if a wound inside him flared with every shout, every rifle shot fired into the air. Yet this was the life he had chosen when he decided to migrate to Israel, to join the settlers in forging a new West Bank. He knew it would be dangerous.

"Levi," it was Deborah; he should have known she would not sleep without his muscular body beside her. "Are you still looking at the tree?"

"Yes, but it is very dark, and I can see so little." He had been thinking about peace last night, before the raid. Hah! Peace! Not for this unfortunate land.

They had come in the dark like bats, or panthers, (*or moths, Garvin chuckled*) and they had taken Yuri's tractor and pulled the tree from the ground and disappeared into the night. Just over the hill. Useless provocation, Levi scoffed: I could break any one of them in half over my knee. In high school he had been a Greco-Roman wrestler, but though he went undefeated, the sport was not for him. He despised the violence. How naïve I was back then, he mused.

"Come to bed my love. There is nothing to be gained sitting up all night." Did she not understand what it meant that it was under that tree that they had first kissed, first made love? It was as if the Arabs had violated the sanctity of their private life. "Anyway, what are you going to do about it?"

This was too much. What did she mean anyway? "What am I going to do? I'm going to build a fence around the tree and it will be a monument to treachery. Then I will go to their village unarmed and I will pick up their leaders and break their backs over my knee."

Yes, the people of Ber-Mit-Sabah would know the wrath of Levi Roth, would rue the day he arrived on their soil. Their soil! Hah! No longer. The history of the soil could be traced back three centuries and more. How could a wandering people claim a settlement as their own. It was absurd.

He knew that now he had spoken, Deborah would want him more than ever, for the righteous violence of a man is irresistible to his female partner. This is why the women thrived in the Israeli Defense Force. Deborah's nubile form was luring Levi to bed, shifting restlessly. Without thinking he was on top of her and her legs were around his ears. He was thinking about Spinoza, something he had written about love, and then, next thing he knew it was the olive tree again, and the word "desecration" was repeating itself in his head over and over with the rhythm of his pounding.

Spent, his body lay heavily upon Deborah, who knew him so well. "Where are you, Levi?" she asked.

Forward to the Past

A short story by Julie Orangeman

Medea had calmed herself, but she could not hide her rubicund face. The boy behind the counter looked at her as if he knew her secrets. Or was that just in her mind?

"Could you tell me where the tampons are?"

"Sure, down aisle C on the right, below the shampoo." (*Garvin wanted him to say, "Want me to show you how to use them."*)

There hadn't been much blood, not as much as she had prepared herself for. A lot of hair had sprouted, as red as the hair on her head. It started at her belly button and went down on either side of her labial parts, a sort of Fu Manchu.

"That it, just the Tampax and the Pepsi?"

"Yes, thank you." Was he looking at her flat chest? (*Why not an omnipresent narrator: He noticed her flat chest and was surprised that she was now technically a woman.*) Her nipples were still those of a child. Was this how it was for all women? If only her mother had not run off with her boss and she were not so shy and had someone to talk about it with. Suddenly she felt blood trickling along her inner thigh.

"Keep the change," she said, and scurried out of the store, her face red. Then she realized that the bathroom was inside the store. This could turn out to be a real mess. Her bus wasn't due for ten minutes. Of all the times not to have brought Kleenex in her purse. She could have ducked behind the store and cleaned the blood off. The very thought of even that brought a flush to her face, which was the color of shiraz.

Sitting on the bench at the bus stop she squeezed her legs together tightly so that the blood would be absorbed by the cotton fabric of her pants. Maybe no one would see the stain.

She wasn't just worried about the stain. Worse yet she had forgotten a bag and held the tampons in her hand. There was no room in her little purse. Maybe she could get on the bus quickly and spill the Pepsi on herself and all people would think was that there was Pepsi and they wouldn't think about the blood. It seemed like a good plan, but as always before she dared do something out of the ordinary her face turned crimson. Why did she care so much what other people thought? When did she start caring so much what other people thought? When her mother left, that's when. It was as if a lake of blood had formed inside her and her skin was translucent and everyone she looked at could see her mother drowned in that lake of blood even though she was really just in Omaha with her second husband, the one with all the money and so many kids that really there was no reason for her mother to remember her, Medea, here in Albany.

The Reluctant Recidivist

A short story by Hank Swellman

Steve's hand was so big it engulfed the coffee cup. It was a hard hand, and it could stand the heat of a fresh refill. He watched the waitress walk away and thought how long it had been since he had seen a waitress walk away. They walk differently from men. Men in prison. Later baby, he thought, and downed his coffee in one gulp before standing to his full height (*what other height would he tend to stand to?, Garvin was compelled to ask the story*) of six feet and five inches, with his broad shoulders spreading one end to the other (*as opposed to?*). He had a hard face, a rugged face, the kind of face men looked at once if they didn't want trouble and women were fascinated by the same way some people are by gorillas. (*Spell it out, kid, chicks dig gorillas.*)

A new start, that's what Steve needed. A new town where nobody knew him. He could kick back, play some pool, drink some whiskey, take a vacation (*eat a steak—let him eat a steak, kid!*). Maybe one day he would find a job. But not the kind of job where they pushed you around. That was Steve's problem—he pushed back, pushed back hard. Lands even a good man in trouble. But no more. Seven years in the slammer will cure you of that. No, Steve was not going to go back. He would learn to step aside before being pushed. After all, how many people actually do get hit by a bus? (*In class today, three*). (*What? Hit by a bus?*)

(*Suggest new title: The Gorilla That Got Hit by a Bus*)

Leaving town is the easiest thing in the world. You hop on a bus, a train, hell you can even take a taxi (*or a bicycle, or a plane, a unicycle, a long hike, a boat!*). Sometimes it's hard to leave your memories behind, but for Steve that was no problem. He had already left his memories. In prison. (*Where apparently they did not get time off for good behavior.*) Even Stella, every curve on her body, every blonde curl of her hair, the red, moist lips and heaving bosom, the thighs that had made Steve the envy of the neighborhood while it lasted, was locked in that cell.

He walked down the street oblivious to passersby. Steve

Portage had his mind on one thing and one thing only: the money Bernie owed him. Once he saw Bernie and had that money in his alligator skin wallet he would be on a bus to a life of decency. A life without crime. A life without lying whores and dirty cops. (*Go Hank go—finally a little life, a little emotion, cliché rides a hemi-cuda!*) (*Suggest alternate title*) (*Fate. Fate Drives a Hemi-Cuda!*) Even if the next town had crime and lying whores and dirty cops, they would not be his business. They would not know him.

A patrol car passed him, slowing down. Sweeney. That Irish pig. What does he want? Sweeney rolled down the window and scoffed once. Then he sped away. I guess he just wanted to welcome me back, Steve thought ironically. (A *cloud of doubt clouded his cloudy face: was Sweeney thinking how sore my asshole must be after all those years? What would he know about getting fucked in the ass. I could teach him a thing or two. With his own billy club, or that giant black man in the next cell. Stella was certainly different from that giant black man, I'll give her that much. But if it came to lending out small change…*)

Fuck. Got to go. Make it a double. Tullamore Dew. Jameson's had become a lady's drink and Bushmills was Protestant. Scotch was for assholes.

Garvin had made his peace with the war within; teaching writing was all bullshit, especially teaching fiction, but it was the price he paid for being in a small enough kingdom for his wife to rule with an absolutism such that even the rector of the university deferred to her in eager emasculation, for he must be male, the rector, a female would not be tolerated at such an elevated position. Even deans must be male; the last female dean had left with a black eye, literally, and a black stain, figuratively—she had never found another job, anywhere— simply for challenging the process of allotting financial aid to graduate students. Naturally it was a scandal, a genuine media scandal, the mortified dean finding the more she protested the version of events generated by Languideia's pretense of noble elision, that is to say the more she felt like a Vietnamese peasant shaking his

fist at a helicopter gunship, the closer she came to the insignificance of an incinerated Vietnamese peasant. No one
really knew what became of her, but Garvin imagined her
in some room, any kind of room, capable only of repeating
over and over "monolithic." So Garvin had to take charge of
both creative non-fiction and fiction, which he learned to
live with by establishing a set of rules that, followed, severely
curtailed the effect of these duties on his life and mind. He
had just violated a sacred rule of the writing teacher, who was
supposed to read the work once, straight through, no marks,
and then again, slowly, with a view to making the author a
better...What? What could Garvin possibly do to help any
of these academic errata? These avian soul-free pubescents,
these coddled, uncuddly, corngobbling, creepulous crap-
pers? Nothing. Quite obviously nothing. And so he did his
least. He read the three pieces per week once and then just
before class read the first page or two again and prepared to
enter class, orchestrate the nonsense of the apostolic twelve
supplicants of the week, and get out without having an experience he would have to remember, such as a fistfight or a
breakdown.

The classroom was arranged into a seminar-style rectangle of tables, surrounded by chairs, one empty one, Garvin
often thought, in honor of Socrates, who had fled the scene.
In one way or another, every time he entered a classroom
he thought, felt, or disgorged in silent gassetry the notion
that this was all very very wrong, that not only was this not
art, literature, writing, but that this was not education, that
anyone who did not have an intestinal level repulsion upon
entering was doomed to be nothing more than a clerk who in
one way or another counted money owned by others. Even
if they became "successful" writers. Yet, again, he knew his
thoughts were not novel. But, he mused today, at least he did
not write an un-novel novel about all this shit. Such thoughts
gave sluggardly impulsion towards completion of the duty
but did not prevent the scar tissue of pusillanimous acquiescence from accreting. Garvin did not hate himself for being

less than what others thought he was, but he was far from satisfied with his self, if indeed he had one. And, frankly, entering a classroom of credulous grasping lost privileged souls while contemplating the existence of one's own self boded ill for the coming session during which one's words were as potent as dynamite, as replete as a night's blanket of snow, as Mosesian as a bible in flames.

Donnie had been in Europe since October and now it was March. Two months had passed since the slapslap in the white room. He had not spoken to Languideia since. He had not spoken to that salamander, that was apparently what came from mating too often with Languideia. What he had done, what he had done right, was go directly to the bank and divide everything in quarters, pull out a quarter of their considerable savings and checking and deposit them in his own new account, as good a way of saying please divorce me as any. And he had rented an apartment above the pharmacy closest to the university despite the extra bedroom, not because he expected Donnie ever to return and occupy it. Yet he also knew that though he currently meant little or nothing to Donnie, what he meant to Donnie was his life's mission and should have been since Donnie's birth, particularly since he had been sleighted from all parentals Cleoward by his wife, who in that regard was Moreau and Frankenstein both guarded by all manner of three-headed canine. Garvin's persona was that of a strong man with great patience, and enough so he actually was that the search for Donnie and the revelations Donnie had long deserved would be forthcoming and there was no cause for panic. That did not mean anything in a practical sense but removing himself from the gravity of Languideia's increasingly erratic, if not hysterical, orbit. If he had slapped her it would have been different. If she had walked out if would have been different. But this was not like coldcocking an old cunt in the privacy of your office and getting away with it. In this case, Garvin was the silent one who attracted far too many adherents by simply going about his business while she struggled like an upended beetle to win a battle in which the opponent had declined to engage.

She snubbed him at the university as effectively as she could given that he never attended meetings and had always sedulously avoided his office. But she laughed louder and more often in the hallways, was almost comradely with colleagues, which mystified any who did not know about the break, yet only disgusted about a third enough for them to refuse to bask in her powerful heat. She did whatever she could to be seen with the handsome Dr. Francisco Franco, a Chilean teacher of Latin American literature, whose wife was both younger and more beautiful than Languideia and was not merely immune to her charms, but repelled by them. But when Languideia said, "You *must* tell me more about the writer Juan Rulfo," he was savvy enough to know that must mean two things when the queen of the university says them and so the two began sharing long walks down the hallways of the humanities building and back and down the stairs to hallways on different floors and up again and so on. Unfortunately, when a man like Garvin has had enough, he actually has; he was not employing strategy, rather approaching a new life with necessary stealth, and his reveling relief at getting away from Languideia was only limited by his lack of desire to think about her at all. Her only real weapon was her ability to destroy his career, which would have to wait at least a couple of years unless she could make up a brutal and believable story, which was unlikely to work in the case of a man with a reputation of quiet dignity, decency and diligence such as Tom Garvin, and, best of all, in two years he would be long gone. She could expose him as a fraud, but not without implicating herself.

Besides, walking into the classroom on this of all rude times he felt especially fraudulent, without the least vertigo, without the imbalance of a maladroit anchor, without so much as a fart of territorial fatigue: like a blue bottle fly blown off a swirl of cowshit into a world of strange furs and turns and terror returning landing gripping and sniffing and swelling with a harmony of emotions thinking Same goddamn shit. An involuntary smile arranged his facial muscles as he nestled his ass into the chair of sloping wood seat and back and metal legs, as fine a chair as a man could ask for.

He scanned the seated senate of softened sinister cynics and was pleased all were present, for it was Clay Strut he counted on to provide a physical edge to the criticism of the Zionist piece, as he titled it in his thoughts. He despised Nathan Zimmer, who had led a successful campaign to deny a reading by a Palestinian writer invited from a nearby university where she was resident author for a year. Nothing against her, or Palestinians, but without an Israeli author to balance the reading, well, you know, there was a danger of the peace process being disrupted to the point of actual success, success, yes, but for who? You see the danger. The counter-protest was led by none other than Clay Strut, who failed chiefly because he attacked Zimmer with his own imbecilic sign, which read **AWAY WITH TERRORIST LIES!** (*what?*), breaking it over Zimmer's back before campus security wrestled him off. In the next issue of the school paper, *The Peregrine*, Zimmer was provided a platform in a cozy interview during which he could, with a photo of an enraged, grotesquely gleeful Strut about to swing the sign he had just wrested from the skinny Zimmer placed next to his words, calmly explain that the problem was the inherently violent tactics of the Palestinians and their supporters that was precisely the reason it was necessary to be extra vigilant in academia and to prevent the least imbalance of publicity. In other words, thought Garvin, any number of terrorists could be hiding in that, after all Asian, Trojan horse of a book she was passing off as literature. And what is western Anatolia but a sort of proving ground for Levantiners. Not to get carried away, but perhaps a Greek Anatolia might be a future ally of an expanded Israel: imagine, standing on the Golan Heights the warm wet wind of the white sea (woops, that's an Ottoman term) whipping your face as you cast your whatever one casts in such cases 360 degrees over Judeo-Christian lands.

Today, Clay Strut had outdone himself. He had taken to wearing a kefiya to class since the successful banning of the Palestinian author, and so he had it affixed upon his brow today, along with either a genuine hand grenade or a very fine replica askew before a sign on which he rested his chin that read in blood red **THIS GRENADE ONLY KILLS HEBREW SPEAKING PISSANTS**. Garvin had long ago mastered the art of experiencing hilarity without expressing it, but his belly was beginning to heave and he was only saved by Nathan Zimmer, whose hand shot into the air as soon as Garvin had arranged his papers and was settled enough to look about the tables at the class.

He cured his guffaw into a wry smile and asked, "Nathan, why is your hand raised? We don't raise our hands in this class."

"I believe this is an exception. I would like to ask that that offensive sign be removed before we begin."

"Why?"

Nathan apparently had not expected to have to put the self-evident into words.

"Well, it's it's it's…it's…*offensive*."

"I'm not offended."

"What? Why?"

"Because we have only one Palestinian piece of fiction today and it is Israeli. Where's the balance required for real debate? Consider yourself lucky that I am allowing your excerpt to be discussed and the demonstration by Mr. Strut to be balance enough."

Nathan Zimmer straightened on his chair, looked around the room at the blank faces hiding the cathartine expectancy of aggrieved-by-nature white middle-class students, then stood with a purposeful, nay, Gandhian (as he regarded himself), solitary determination, saying, "Then I, myself, will remove it."

"SIT DOWN, you Zionist twerp," Garvin ordered. "I will not have the class abbreviated by the spectacle of Strut kicking your ass."

What did I just say?

Just following orders was floating phraseally in the atmosphere as a bewildered and injured Zimmer plopped hard back into his chair. Tears began to well in his eyes.

Clay Strut had the decency to cup his mouth with a hand, his cheeks ballooning in raggy time.

"For Christ's sake, Zimmer, get the tears out of your eyes, we already have Miss Orangeman crying today."

All eyes swung to Julie Orangeman, who in two previous critiques of her work had begun weeping after two people had criticized her stories and sobbed throughout the full hour of discussion. Would this be enough to break her?

"Oh my god, you don't like this one either..." Tears flew from her eyes as she blubbered: "I knew I shouldn't have written it..."

"Great," Garvin mediated. "Hank, would you like to begin whimpering? You're the only one left. No doubt your little tale will be emasculated as well."

Five feet tall, red-haired, and the son of the university rector, Hank Swellman looked as if he could not decide how his head should be arranged on his neck, an odd habit that made him seem as if he were following the flight of an insect, his eyes expressing the eternal conflict between stupidity and inherited grandeur.

"No, I am not afraid."

"Perhaps you should be." Where was this new Garvin coming from? And why had it been encaved so long—he could feel a yearning as from the works of lives unexamined massing, lowering.

"All right, as soon as Julie's sobbing allows, we will begin by discussing Nathan's Zionist superhero piece..."

Here it is necessary to interject an authorial abjection. The world has not developed in quite the way some of us hoped, what with commodities overtaking philosophy and emotion and the like. And so on occasion we are unable to avoid the murine—that doesn't sound as plague-ridden as it should— appearance in our tales of devices such as the cellular phone, which ultimately is as pregnant with destruction as a cluster bomb, and one of which, once it was clear that Garvin was going off the rails, as Zimmer saw it, or on the rails, as Garvin and Strut saw it, Nathan Zimmer had slipped from his backpack and was now holding beneath the table, activating the recording function, an action that Garvin picked up on when he followed the violent rays of Strut's gaze.

"**ZIMMER!**" Garvin shouted. "What the fuck are you doing, you fucking subMossad weasel! You're going to *record* me without my consent? This isn't the fucking Gaza, nor a tenement in Haifa. This is a classroom in the United States of America, where only secret government programs can secretly record people."

"I would like it on record that you are an anti-Semitic fraud."

"Fine. Hand me the phone."

"What?"

"You want it on record that I am an anti-Semitic fraud? Hand me your phone."

With a look of redressed injury, Zimmer set the phone on the table, still recording, and slid it to Garvin, who snatched it, said "Tricked ya," and tossed it out a window, where it fell two stories, landing on the cement of a strategic study circle, coming apart dismally, piece by piece, not, that is to say, *exploding*.

Zimmer just did manage to remain attached to his seat, his mouth open, waiting for the insect that had been pestering Hank Swellman to visit in the form of a plague of locusts, while Garvin turned to Patricia Mull and Cord Ferndock, a couple who Garvin knew despised him, if less than he despised them for their twin attitude of appearing as if there were a plate on which sat a well and finely arranged turd deposited beneath their chins. "All right, Mull, you have my permission to record this session. Happy, Zimmer?"

"I would very much *like* to record this session, sir." Mull agreed.

"Ferndork, maybe—"

"Fern*dock*."

"Yes. Perhaps you could also record, to guard against, what, fate I suppose."

"Already begun, sir."

"Good." He looked to Julie Orangeman, who had her hand over her mouth and nose, but was no longer sobbing, her shoulders still now, the tears in her eyes holding fast.

Mark Grbac, a ratface, always looked as if he had just slunk around a corner and would soon be retreating. His most significant moment in Garvin's class occurred while the group was discussing a raving piece by Strut that had apparently intimidated most of the class—Garvin had no idea what Strut was saying, but the use of language was energetic and musical, and it went on for over forty pages. The first five students to speak had nothing but vague superlatives to offer, and then the discussion reached the corner where Grbac kept his snout. In a slightly nasal voice he began, "I guess I wasn't as impressed as everyone else. I had to stop reading after 20 pages, but—" And Strut, outraged, berated him violently, actually hounding him from the room. "What?" he had yelped, "You didn't even read the whole thing? And you have the sleazy balls to offer an opinion?" And so on until he had risen from his chair, was standing over a cowering Grbac, who rapidly removed his effects from the table, grabbed his jacket and exited swiftly with Strut beside him continuing to, as one might say, tear him a new asshole.

Garvin decided he would be the first to discuss the Jew piece.

"Grbac, why don't you begin the discussion of *The Olive Tree*."

Grbac stretched his neck, made to clear his throat, which was already clear, making the prelude to speech look like a lizard's preening before a mirror.

"Of course, ten pages of a novel is not much to go on, but as these appear to be the first ten pages, I think we can draw some conclusions. Given the lack of character detail, I chose to read this as a rough sketch, in which case the author has begun to set up a duality of various dimensions, from the broad Israeli versus Palestinian to the individual or personal with the coarse active American versus the nuanced, perhaps inert Israeli, which, one hopes, will evolve into a sort of formula of personalities, testing themselves against the broader conflict in order to refine and for lack of a better word *complete* themselves."

Normally Garvin would remain silent, waiting to be sure the first speaker was done and letting the next take up where he left off or whatever. Next would be Melanie Gaston, to Grbac's right, probably his second favorite student, a woman in her mid-twenties, always as remote as she seemed to think safe, not condescending, though Garvin guessed more than capable of it, one of the two students Garvin considered writers—along with Strut—who was, as a writer should be, in her own world working on her own characters in her own book, politely oblivious to suggestions and critiques of others, likely having arrived at the writing program that gave her the easiest two years during which to write freely, avoiding the working world, which, if her novel was anything to judge by, had recently involved the seedy alcoves of the beluga trade.

Instead, Garvin responded to the rat. "Why?"

"I'm sorry," Grbac had to come back from around the corner, which although metaphorical was more recessive than any ratnook in a squalid tenement.

"Why what?"

"Why would one hope that?"

"Well," now the throat was not clear, the word filling a lizard's neck sac, "to me that seems the obvious direction for the novel to take."

"In other words, you did your homework, you wrote a couple nice sounding sentences, memorized them, and despite the fact that they mean nothing, brought them in here hoping no one would be tortured enough to think them through."

Are ye rat or lizard? Lizard.

Grbac retreated a few centimeters without moving his shoulders, then froze, like a lizard, knowing it was seen yet somehow suspecting that it could blend in yet, before the strike, perhaps sensing that the current peril in no way discounted worse peril elsewhere and near.

"I think the best we can take from the comments of our colleague Grbac is that with luck these first ten pages are not at all what they appear to be, rather the prelude to a comedy of manners with the romantic backdrop of eternal conflict. Nice. I like it. Melanie, do you think that's what we have in store?"

Melanie's disinterest was disguised by an economy of movement guided by a natural tendency toward elegance that she made just enough use of to endure the charade of a class filled with avid talentless fiction perpetrators. Her legs were crossed, her arms resting on her lap; she had only to lift her head to look around the room to include all, before settling onto Garvin.

"No, although I'm not sure exactly what he means. The first paragraph is so full of, well, rather typical action movie writing, and much is made of the breaking of Palestinian backs on Levi's leg, so that it comes as a surprise that ten whole pages elapse and no one is hurt yet. In fact breakfast has yet to be served. So I guess my thought is that as this is a novel, the heavy-handed symbolism and sketchy characters will be fixed while the real story, whatever it is, emerges."

"So you don't think the novel is going to be a simple story of Jewish settlers feeling insulted that the Palestinians don't approve their trespass and fight back in order that the settlers can achieve a rousing victory led by the chiseled and idealistic wrath of Levi Roth?"

Melanie, your husband or boyfriend waiting for you elsewhere is a lucky man, Garvin mused without emote when she suppressed a smile so suavely that it appeared to be quite the other way round, that the traces left by a smile were the far reach of her person at the moment.

"I suppose that given such an opening, my contribution is best limited to...well, expressing what might lead the author to...reconsider..."

The ensuing silence involved more than the entire class looking over at the Zionist after receiving the first actual harsh criticism that Melanie Gaston had yet delivered in recent memory. He had a handkerchief, luckily, and had been dabbing at his nose and eyes throughout, so it was unclear whether he had been rendered meek by Garvin's outburst or the suggestion that the extension of his being that was ten pages of a novel was being appreciated more for what it could and would be than what it was. There was also the enlivening presence of Clay Strut, who was next up and looking like a giant caged vulture watching the little edible man gently laying down carcass, in no hurry, oblivious...

Strange to think that vultures don't drool.

"All right, then, Strut, you may have your say. I do agree that your political statement is apt in view of relatively recent events, but can you say something about Mr. Zimmer's, uh, work, something of a literary vein?"

A man whose looks are shaped by his persona, Clay Strut was a dark-haired, burly fellow, whose face was never without expression, setting him off from the predominantly immotile-faced norm, and thus, whether he was warm or not, radiating a humanity that, for lack of other places to turn was accepted as warmth, and therefore attractive. Now his eyes were less savage than a moment before, wide open, his lips compressed and his cheeks consequently expanded and of what Julie Orangeman might consider a rubicund hue. He was like a man who may or may not vomit in the car, the others compelled to take part in the prelude by the sheer drama of it, a sort of physical manifestation of Hamlet, or Arjuna, except that what he clearly could at any moment spew was a very corporeal laughter, a veritable storm of it was brewed in him; yet he wanted to speak as well, and so he stopped short of snorting the excess of burgeoning humor through his nostrils and actually did begin to speak.

"First of all," he leaned forward to look past Gaston at Grbac, "I must apologize to my colleague Mark, who I chastised for presuming to criticize my work without having finished it. And while I hold that it is true that we learners of the writing trade are a blessed lot, earning an advanced degree by reading about fifty pages a week on average, actually if that, and therefore generally should make the effort, and so despite my apology I can't say I find Mark's behavior acceptable without some sort of an explanation, I have at the same time to admit that for the first time in my nearly two years in this program, I did not read all of a work up for discussion."

The class was riveted. Something fun was going to happen.

Already Nathan Zimmer looked simultaneously defeated and miserable and resentful. This was not how literature was meant to be discussed. It was not civilized. It was, in fact, *Bedouin*.

Mull and Ferndock were in a bind, suspended as they were in their expectations between the need to despise the despicable Strut and the despicable literature that was written by others. Garvin imagined Ferndock with a steak knife turning to Mull and saying, cotton napkin bibbed, let's give it a go, shall we, and the look on her face expressing that very rare love one reserves for the lover who grants permission to, yes, cross that border. Just before the knife touched the loaf, Garvin's attention returned fully to Clay Strut.

"I'm sure we all have our favorite novel openings, and we all know the famous ones. Call me Ishmael, which of course would have worked here had it not been taken. Probably most of you share with me as one of the most unforgettable, from *Coin Locker Babies*: 'The woman pushed on the baby's stomach and sucked its penis into her mouth; it was thinner than the American menthols she smoked and a bit slimy, like raw fish'"—that was the end of the meal for Mull and Ferndock, who were back to their normal expressions of repulsion tempered by disdain—"and *The Olive Tree* actually begins with that epic quality that if carried to the end, the end of the sentence I mean, could make for a memorable opening line. See? Look here: 'Even in the dark of night Levi could make out the form of the olive tree on its side, its roots like,' so far so good, but then: 'fat, venomous snakes.' Fat venomous snakes? Roots of trees don't look like any kind of snake. But that's okay, they kind of have the shape of fat lightning bolts, but really, you're setting yourself an impossible task trying to find a simile here. But you have other options, like, '... the olive tree on its side, the roots so many dying Auschwitz survivors waiting for the Red Cross to reach their row,' or, another direction, 'roots as tangled and feckless as an Oslo peace luncheon.' Anyway, what I'm saying is that the novel is off to a good start, needing only a little adjustment.

"Okay, then: ...enemy over the hill...wound inside... flares out and in, symbolic symmetry in an asymmetrical warfare setting, good...life he had chosen, cliché maybe but then the big ideal—forging a new West Bank, not my line, but lets you know this is a book not to be trifled with…description of body: muscular—not really the work of a real writer, but one imagines the author in a hurry to get the grand tome underway…good… woman calling for him, mentions tree to make sure we get that it is of some significance, perhaps even a symbol of some kind, good…cynicism, history, bats or panthers, sooner or later you have to choose but rough draft, let's not nitpick…and here…" Strut was now in the grip of the laughter, perhaps one of its venomous, snakelike roots, for he held his sternum and rocked back and forth, his face as if it had no choice but to weep if not soon let free… "and here…" More rocking, air puffed up into his cheeks, and the laughter itself began escaping in gusts…

"O Nate…you fucking slay me… Yuri's…Yuri's…**YU-RI'S TRACTOR**…oh god…"

By now Garvin's upper teeth were biting into his lower lip, his arms crossed over his chest, himself rocking, a couple laughs spurted out tentatively here and there in the room, Strut was entirely lost to the force of the comedy, howling, Mull and Ferndock were looking about like storks of great wealth and position blown to the lost island of ravenous crabs, just about to comprehend, exhausted, wings soaked and heavy, heads held as bred to be held, that despite all this indeed is how it ends, and more spurts escaped, some trotting into gallops of laughter, Garvin now with his head in his hands, his shoulders expressing his mirth for the rest of his body, and then finally Melanie Gaston virtually shouted in long suppressed glee, "**YURI'S FUCKING TRACTOR!**" and then there was no stopping it, at least it would take a bold act, but for the time an underground nuclear test couldn't have better expressed the berserkeree effect of humans come together beneath the accumulate layers of history and invention and inexpressible stupidity all ruined all dead all for nought with yet just enough guano left if shared to form one last shit pool in which to riot, feathers filling the room falling flying feathering, time faltering, pure yogic loss of mind to union and euphoria, ah, how good it feels, even if you weren't there, recalling those few times without the specificity that corrupts the memory, oh happy *people!*, no one noticing Nathan's face leading his reluctant soul into righteous anger, flinging feathers, foul feathers of false fate!, making its way, at first, sure, a bit unsteady, and finally, unseen, to Clay Strut's long wild hair, digging his hands deep into Strut's hair, and pulling like a banshee, howling like a Central American monkey, silencing the room that had thought itself human alone now filled with an eerie intrusion, perhaps a cousin of some lost emotion, and Strut reached up to grab wrists of the offending claws, stood, bent over with the clinging Zimmer now draped over his back, stumbled into some momentum, and just before reaching the wall, turned to mash Zimmer into the cement block, and for good measure, as Zimmer slumped like snot sliding down a wall grabbed *Zimmer's* hair in order to cut the distance his knee had to travel to bust Zimmer's nose, which, wouldn't you know, with all the spattered, spurting and splattered blood brought the mood to a skidding bewilderment, required the calling of a doctor and the cancellation of the class, which would be Garvin's last.

That weekend Clay Strut dropped by the apartment and the two downed a bottle of Tullamore Dew, generally made like professor and student, told stories, laughed a few more times over Yuri's tractor, and, Garvin remembered as Strut left sometime after midnight to hand him two envelopes, tying up his loose teaching ends.

Dear Julie,

You'll cry again, and they'll tear you apart and all the female blood will surely upset both Mull and Void, but I'll tell you one thing: the idea of the vanishing tampon and the refusal of adulthood is the most ingenious idea I have come across in years.

Yours,
Garvin

Dear Henry,

There's no point in lying to you. You're among the worst writers I have ever taught—or sought to. You're a master at accidental humor (Men walk different from women, etc.). I don't know why you want to be a writer, but we both know how you got into the program. That's fine. And I've seen you bravely endure nearly two full years of pretty abusive criticism. So maybe you've got one thing being a writer takes, that ineffable desire to be one in the face of all reason, against whatever odds. So in that light I'll tell you one thing. In this story I saw Steve as Sterling Hayden in The Asphalt Jungle. It occurs to me that you have a cinematic touch—not that you should be writing for the movies but that the way you see, if not overly dicked around with by you trying to be a writer, is delivered in an easily visible manner. So perhaps this is your calling: crime fiction. If so, forget Chandler, read Simenon, not Maigret, but his straight crime stuff, watch 40s and 50s noir, and keep at it. Pay close attention to the close readings. Don't put a lady's legs around a guy's ears like Zimmer did. Describe it simple and keep at it. Learn French.

Yours,
Garvin

Dear Nathan,

I know that nothing I say is going to prevent you from bringing the nations of Israel and the United States down on my head, nor am I interested in tempting you toward a measure of life-enhancing tolerance or flexibility. So let us stick to fiction. Given what you brought to class, my suggestion is that you entitle the piece Yuri's Tractor and critics be damned. Run with it!

Yours,
Garvin

20

LIEFDE IN BRUSSEL

"Are you in love with me?"

I want you now…if this is not hate

"I suppose of course…incurable, but I can still live a full life."

The components of Setif's smile were engaging in a resacralizing carnival while her body on the couch lay ambivalent as a translucent sea phenomenon emitting steam.

Donnie had been taking it all in, naturally, the tits Picasso made, the nipples seeming to anchor them to the air, the sheer lavender nighty—as Donnie spelled it in his thoughts—covering her pubic herbs (he thought of a satin sash windblown catching and catching on a fragrant plant in a Mediterranean land), leaving her thighs exposed, covering nothing—tensile thighs and Donnie's disguised sighs, and Picasso Tits's teasing smile, her mothering smile, her mocking, seducing, taunting, innocent, temporizing smile…

I hate you now…if this is not love

"I don't understand, Donnie. Does he love her or not?"

"Do I love you or not?"

"You don't hate me."

"Right, I don't hate you, nor do I not not like you if this is not love."

"But I want you now, I hate you now…Why so extreme, this man?"

"*Here on Earth…with the bends and the rust…*" Donnie sang along, laughing after from the wormy nethers at his favorite line in the song.

"The music is beautiful, even if the man makes no sense."

"You want to accuse him of making no sense? I mean, making sense…What if we examined you? But I don't agree with this line of thought."

"This I suppose is good for me?"

"No. No, it doesn't matter in the slightest."

…with the gray I've earned…and my heart now fully formed

here on Earth…with the wind and rain they love to erode what you love to sustain here on Earth…these things remain

"The orgasm."

the crackling water

the crackling light

from the crackling clouds

in the crackling night

Fluid nexus: Picasso Tits rolled to stub out her cigarette, Donnie watching her form, his awe subdued as a rebel angel retired, both given over to the song, Picasso Tits on her back again, head propped, smiling with Donnie, hearing the orgasm of the song and saying "The orgasm," arching her back in a genuine stretch, listlessly lifting her left leg the while and luring Donnie's eyes, Donnie smiling, maybe his penis pulsing to an appreciative ease of growth, and Drake finally having woken entering the room.

"Great song," Drake remarked. "Great pussy, too, eh Donnie?"

Picasso Tits's body invited Drake to fully frontally hug her, and his descent was as the glidely landing of a paper plane in an origami wind.

"Donnie is in love with me," she said. "Of course he is, Jesus!"

I hate you now…I want you now

Donnie, warmly ensconced in a wattly daubly wintry heated haven in a land that felt just now barely here on Earth felt as deep a contentedness as possible for one of his species intending yet to live on.

21

NIMIPOOOOPIMIN

What with the light slant geometries, the globie nature of the nates of Smoking Heron, one half in the outdoor lightshine the hijinking Phoebles and Gravel had at first no idea of the nature of their intrusion, snuffling with laughter enough at the grandeur of their inspired undertaking to sneak up on and surprise Hector, and so as also Hector had by now balded and bore semblance to ballpeen, and the fact that his head was side- ways and far lower than the head of a standing feller normally is, and the snuffling was insucked silently where it was kept temporary like a bird caught by a whelp and put in a bag from which it would as a phrenetic phoenix and more burst free, and like heavenly bodies the globie nates shaded left and the baldy head shaded right and by now Gravel and Phoebles were frozen in the ambivalence unbalancing glory and woops, they watched on as Hector thicklipped the left nate and gave it a powerful suck like a thumb plopping from a cheek, and before Smoking Heron could giggle her private ambiguities both Phoebles and Gravel snorted the winged god of laughter from their snouts and Hector strained his stiff back, nearly straightening, with a "Guh-ga, guh-ga, guh-goddam ye!" and like a wraith Smoking Heron slid to the elsewheres.

A quick study, Hector figured on Phoebles, and the back pain, and outlingered the surprise, and he was too old for embarrassment.

"I guess Marie Fire must be off somewheres, lessn ya giver the same treatment." Hector wore now a grin like a mask— though he shaved more or less regularly he hadn't seen his face clearly in years.

Phoebles stood in the doorway, Gravel half a step behind. "This here boy is Tom Gravel, whom I took up with when the wagon train went to murderin-like. Saved my life, this boy, and I sorter hope ye could put him to wark or some-en."

"See mah rockin char on the way in? Built it mahself, and Marie Fire, she rigged the hand strap when she saw it didn't rock straight—firs time I sat down and did a full fast fallin circle like a conked weasel n come up with a sliver the size a yer Phoeble peckers. Good with her hands that girl."

Phoebles turned to Gravel, "That's his girl, Marie Fire." "Gart dam, you fellers bring out chars, Jeffers, didn't spect ya fer another two months. And ya bring me this here snipe fer a new partner."

Marie Fire had overseen the construction of the chairs and so they were all level both for the ass and on their woodfeet.

The three formed an arc with Hector in his rocker held in place by holding a strap that dangled from the porchscarp. The sun was 45 degrees off left and still on the rise.

"What with the lightnall, ah couldn't see Smokin Hairn, aintat so, Tom?"

"The Injun woman? No, we did not see her,"

"She here?"

Hector called to the logs behind: "Tall Bird! Bring at one with the X on it."

Before further could be explained Smoking Heron stood in the doorway with a two-liter jug of Hector's homemade remedy, something none ever saw need to tell him ought be either fruit or pine but not both. She had dressed herself in a plain deer shift, straight-hemmed fallen to just above the knee. Her face, while youthful, was of chisel type feature, as if crafted by a diligent child, everything precisely placed and slanted so that, when all was said and done, her chin was at the bottom, perfectly centered, her eyes at ear level, her nose straight and symmetrical, nostrils near perfectly round, the tip of the nose the forefeature of her face not exceeding in downslope the return attachment, her forehead perpendicular to the ground, her black hair sliced in the middle and falling at equal lengths either side—and as if by some panic of inspiration the child had added a wispy moustache above straight lips that nonetheless were lips so her mouth was not a mere hole in her face.

"That's my best yet, why I put the X on it. Thank you, Tall Bird—maybe you want to pull out a chair and join us? And where's Hellfire?"

"You talk and drink. I will begin to cook." As she spoke she looked at all three men in the eyes, maybe moreso at Tom Gravel.

"Little Fire is in the horse barn reading."

She retreated and the men turned immediately to the jug left at Gravel's feet. He hefted it, pulled the plug, and swug, righting the jug before shaking his head like a man up from a near drown.

"Smooth! And I can still taste it, like it's turning about in my mouth."

Hector was mighty pleased at that. "Ain't that so? I been doin this over ten years and last year I finally think I got as good as it gets."

"Yayayayayaya!" rumbly exclaimed Phoeble, who threw his head backwards, eyes open wide, as if to let flames escape the damnation of his duodenum.

Hector took his turn and smiled with simple self-satisfaction, passing the jug after back to Gravel.

A few minutes passed thusly before Phoebles unpacked the tabacky he'd brought back for Hector and then it was both an Injun type pipe and a jug passed around, and before long finally Gravel could hold it in no longer and asked Hector to describe his legendary tussle with the giant bear, which mild-mannered Hector was happy to oblige.

Strange to consider these comrades in drink and previous trial as their United States was sucking Mexico's northern to its giant pig teat, for though they were not yet within the bounds of the United States thar in Orgon, no one truly believed another war with the British would be necessary before the continent tilted ever so slightly enough for the northwest to slide to fill its Pacific limits, but them Mexicans had some

fight in them and none on either side had the visionary soul
that would have seen a Texas best left lonesome with star.

In Europe, too, ferment seized the urbanites, and perhaps
a remainder of piquancy bloodied the Vendée, neither with
effect on Oregon east, nor the seas high shipped with colonial runners, forerunners, gun runners, slave runners, opium runners, not to mention the bumfuckery hijinks aboard,
which doth maketh history quotidianally smacking of rollick-
ing interest.

How many mules for that there gal? and so on.

So that, in desertified land, alone with jug, tabacky, talk,
and woman cooking inside, when from out the mythstory
of shadows came a girl of fourteen one posits a manmind
ranging with the stallionosity of youth, purblindly eager, and
a womanmind of radiant conscious burden of species precociously prescient of folly of man in prime mating time, hefting a tome called *The Last of the Mohicans*, skeering over
Jeffers Phoebles and Papa to the man who would be hers, a
pact natural was knitknotted ethereal and in her other hand
the tail of a rattler held just above the rattles emerging mirth-
storily from shade to sun, the snake a rope like a lasso swirled
overhead and finally flung misshitstorily scattering males,
slapping against the logwall stunned, and both Hector and
Phoebles grounded by age, Gravel, intuitively entering mr-
shitstory, leaping back to the porch, taking the rattler by the
tail and flinging it back at the laughing girl, who ducked it
aplombly, completing the rite of marriage naturale, indigenous to the precise longitude/latitude, phrenoHector-topog-
raphy, Blackfoot/white feet, extant in time of August, year
1847.

Was she a beauty, Marie Fire? Not fair. No, darker than
her mother, as if there was color in Hector's geneticals, but
full of hip, lip, and nip, she was voluptile and nubulous,
fully formed in a full form at fourteen, stretching her leath-
ers to fit caressing tight, her cottons constantly tearing. For
Tom Gravel there was no interval between sight and smite,
in such instance was he smitten; for Marie Fire there was a
scent sent sniffed and accepted, which is aside from ques-

tions of interval, a fluidity in denial of time, unborn, riverine without source or cease, and banked low to oft oerflow,
something she thought of as a sort of eternal river in flight,
with fishbirds, opacities of gulping wonders never defined so
not defiled, clarities in freshets, and I think it would be fair
to say that no two young lovers ever thought less about their
own union howsoever the wild of it appeared in dream and
daze, though also fair to say that neither of them ever felt that
whatever they described or could not describe was a thing of
the dirt, the earth, the ground.

What might be called a honeymoon occurred the following morning, and we are too eager to describe primus coitus
that we skip beyond the poetry of parental wordless consent
and gorging of travelers and the open lusty leers of a lady
whose mother asked of her only to learn to read and write in
obeisance to some evil that might thus be warded off when the
fall came but otherwise to be as strong and wild as a puma, to
respect her own instincts above all, above even those of her
mother, even those of the silently sly Hector, to develop her
body for the wilderness, for what could not be endured in the
city of the white man with a body that could live free and happy in the wilds of the lands of the Nimipoo. And soon Gravel
was to find that this girl indeed was a wild one, thighs as strong
as his, arms and shoulders near so. On the way to her reading
barn, where the marriage ceremony would be held in sacred
secret duo, Gravel spotted an opossum and immediately gave
chase, a few seconds worth, for these marsupials were slow,
confused creatures—he hadn't seen one since Ohio and gave
himself over entirely to the gambol, delighting Marie Fire
with this evidence of the kindred spirit that, though she had
no doubt of it, was eager to share. She watched him cut off
the opossum's escape, so that it had as cover a sapling about
as big around as the pecker she would soon take in, and the
opossum climbed a foot off the ground, cocking its head so its
eyes could not be seen by Gravel and so he no longer could
know the opossum existed, which, sportingly, Gravel accepted as logic, making as if to continue his search for the critter
before throwing up his hands in defeat.

"Listen Hawkeye, and your ear shall drink no lie."

Gravel had allowed himself to be wrestled into a corner where Marie Fire had several blankets woven by her mother arranged atop hay bales for a reading bed, though presently she had wrapped her thighs about Tom Gravel and was quoting James Fenimore Cooper. An oil lamp hung from a slanting rafter to the height of Marie Fire on her knees, as she now was, naked, having flung off her soft leather shift. She turned up the lamp while arching her back, presenting herself to Gravel, who was allured into the act of a practiced lover, slowly undressing without taking his eyes from his betrothed. The breasts were heavy, and large, and her stomach, though firm, was also plentiful, as were her hips and upper thighs, leaving only the incongruously thin area above the knee, the graceful knees themselves, the skinny calves, with their sparse hair. Elsewhere the hair was abundant, in her armpits and her pubic mound, where it reminded Gravel of the hair of a wet beaver, thick and straight, and damp in essence. When he was naked he sat up and she held him to her belly. Her hand felt for his penis. "Not tall enough for a opossum," she said, "but I think a perfect fit for me."

"Will it hurt you?" Tom asked, for he knew of the thing called hymen.

"No. We Nimipoo, or half Nimipoo, we take care of that before so that the first time there is pleasure for us both." Gravel wasn't prepared to ask how they took care of that, but he was glad, for much as this moment meant to him, he was sure that they would both be better off without blood and pain.

But the engagement was not to be without blood and pain, for Gravel was a forceful, durable driller, who enjoyed the obvious pleasure Marie Fire screeched into the wilds, and Marie Fire found the pleasure of such enormous, uncontainable emotion, she tore into Gravel's back so that in this way he came to resemble his new father, though his father had to fight the bear but once, while Gravel would be wrasslin this bear thousands of times in years to come.

"This is the battle no one loses, Natty Bumppo," she said after about two hours of natty bumping had passed and they lay on their sides with their eyeballs less than a foot apart from each other's.

Getting into the spirit of this demimonde, Gravel declared, "These wounds I will carry with pride into the world."

As the laws of this land called lawless were therefore specific to human clans of varying sizes, so by the laws of the Hector/Heron clan Gravel and Marie Fire were now wed, and after another hour of barnjaxery Gravel emerged and looked ahead as a newly married man is wont to, Marie Fire testing his endurance and a different aspect of his stallionosity by riding him, Gravel could not have expected to see anything but a different angle of the oddbuilt house of Hector/ Heron coming into view and was therefore amazed to see a human spider moving toward him with speed, while behind in the posture of recent arrival dozens of Indians were gathered about the house.

"Uncle Rowor!" Marie Fire exclaimed, leaping over Gravel's head and running like a deer from forest fire towards this seemingly dangerous highly unique creature, who, had he but slowed a hair, would have revealed to Tom the features of a human man mangled so mangly locomoting. Surely as if having executed this operation before, Marie met him just enough askew that they rolled perpendicular, frenziedly from their collision line, whooping "Galemelag! Galemelag!"

My wife speaks Injun, Gravel thought...That must be Nimipoo! For of course Phoebles had described each tribe whose range they passed on through, and Nimipoo had been last. But wait—Smoking Heron was Blackfoot...and Phoebles said it seemed like each tribe had their own separate language. How would Marie Fire know Nimipoo living with Hector and a Blackfoot? Was this her natural father, maybe? Phoebles knew of some beliefs regarding the spirit world, how Injuns entered the bodies of hawks and snakes and wolves and who knew, Phoebles had said one night neither could sleep for Phoebles's chatter, even ants or grasshoppers—when you think about it, if any of this spirit travel garfoosh is true, you could be surrounded by Injuns at all times. But most tribes were peaceable, Phoebles averred, and all Injuns were shocked by the strange thoughts the white men had about land. Whenever he mentioned Fort Vancouver to an Injun the Injun would laugh—any Injun, from whatever tribe he happened to be from. Why, at the great rendezvous of '32 he must have talked beaver with men from fifteen different tribes. From what he could make out, they seemed to think white folk even like Phoebles were fools to work out of a static station, that is to say to do the work for people who lived as cripples or old woman behind high walls. It was one thing to have a sort of settlement with your own people, though all settlements were really just half settlements, the men such as the Nimipoo off to hunt buffler during the warmer months— but that was the end of the business. You bring back your kills and sometimes you moved your settlement, maybe more aptly called a resting place. One time, Phoebles said, not so long ago in fact, he had tried to explain to an Injun who spoke pretty good English that where them Injuns were living was being fought over by the English who were across not the nearer sea but another one a long ways from here, and who owned Fort Vancouver, and the United States, only each side was doing it quiet like, the United States sneaking folk up the Siskiyou and across the Oregon, while the English were bringing them by sea and from somewhere else they settled, way up in the coldest north and east. Naturally, his interlocutor knew all the tribes in the entire Oregon and knew they had been roaming these parts for countless moons before white men appeared. It was laughable—which the Injun proved by laughing heartily—that these two tribes of white men thought they were fighting over something that was not theirs, that in fact could not even belong to the Injuns. "It does get a fella ta thinkin'," Phoebles had said, looking over the embers to see that Tom Gravel had fallen asleep propped on his elbow.

Grassy dirtstreak disheveled, Marie Fire and the barely clad dangly Rowor spidered up to Tom rubbery of limb and spirit life, wabbling his rawhide riveroon face, "Silver plate, mon amica! Jesuit circumference, is it not, da to, royt flank,

Io nueve uncle, und yet, ye be like as bambini son to me," proceeding to hug Tom as Tom had not ever been hugged before, at an impossible angle with limbs all acling with strength one succumbs to by a law of nature involving spirit pace and a novel despair that threatens storms of glee set flight as oxygen puffs from the body. Upon disengagement, it was difficult to locate Rowor for his head moved to a rocking or rolling body as he stood, if not still, intending to remain for conversation.

"Heaps of monkeygrubbing this night, per tu non bacilli no mas hombre, glocken der spiel all night indaba for man of Marie Fire, finest of the finery in locus parental."

Back at the house, more of which later, the house that is, scrums of Nimipoo drank of Hector's finest, appeared to laugh out of proportion to speaker, though it was a night of much malayalam and elbaable babblelbbab, dancing, fornicating—it seemed as if the Nimipoo resembled much the bonobo when in their horns, more whooping from Phoebles than jibberoo, and as sweet a porch scene as ever was seen, Gravel thought his last remembered thought, his new ma with a jug in one hand and the strap in the other, Hector on her lap as she succored the both of them with facility of juggery, the dark of her face just lighter than the night, a penetrating serenity in mystic pacific mastery of the banjaxery.

22

GARVIN INTERMEZZO

"Eight ball in the corner."

"Which?"

"Back here, three bank."

"Double the bet on this shot."

"Triple it or keep the bet."

"Well fuckin fine. Triplit."

Garvin had made such shots in his sleep. He often dreamt of pool, never of the circumstances that necessitated the long and intensive practice of it. He had the gift that separates the best players from those who simply could not believe they could so easily be beaten given how good they were compared to their friends and hostile neighbors. He saw the outcome before he saw the shot and every shot was true. So the eight hit three rails solid, slid between two stripes and dropped straight into the corner predestined and proclaimed.

A small Midwestern bar on the edge of town was a good place for an eruption of ugly fencing with inappropriate equipment, but the opponent was no younger than Garvin, had entered the bar alone, and admitted immediately he hadn't the money.

"How much do you have?"

The chastened billiardiere emptied his wallet and pockets on the table.

$13.37.

"At least you had the original bet covered. Makes a difference. I'll take the ten and we'll forget all about it."

"What are you drinking, buddy? I got enough for two beers."

"Whiskey and beer. Buy yourself two."

They walked more or less together back to the shank and took up stools side by side.

"Name's Roger. I run a roofing company."

Roger had raw roofer's hands, oddknobs like stony desert in an up-close satellite shot, a lank body going slack with overwork and age, patches of unfortunate white-ruffed red on his neck and face, maybe eczema, and a habit of jerking his head as if to toss the itching off onto the bar like a roach. Garvin never saw him scratch. Roaches, it is hardly known, do not cling to people, having a preternatural understanding that their machinations are in opposition to the more likely daylight funglings of humans, and so are quite easily removed from the neck if found or finding themselves there. They don't like it any better than you do. Fungal conditions and the like are a different matter, parasitical rather than piratical.

"Tom Garvin, in limbo."

"Ah, I see," though he didn't, of course.

Garvin wished he'd scratch. Either scratch or stop that fucking head jerking. He thought this not unkindly. Roger seemed all right and Garvin wished his condition gone. But lacking Lourdes at least a halt to the, well, maybe just a tic. A guy can certainly have a tic, that's fair enough.

Roaches are too ferocious for ticks, though the two rarely meet—rarely, but it is not without precedent: think of a big dog in the woods, coming home to the trailer with the fur-couch and the frantic, skinny chainsmoking alcoholic wife brushing the dog that was shedding the fur anyway, and the tics now and again flying toward the kitchen where the roaches ruled at night, the ticks by their nature seeking to cling and the roaches by their nature tearing them to bits with those legs so rarely seen by the human eye that in their world are as cutlasses in the world of the pirate—again the false fencing.

By an incontrovertibly well directed fate-quirk, only of semi-limp mockery, this bar was called **THE JARGON**. Garvin had been here before the separation, though if his wife had known she likely would have contracted hysterical gonorrhea at the notion. Rightly so: the place was known for its lowlife and fistfights, sluts, skanks, large bufotenine buffoons in their thirties with jean shirts torn off about the shoulder, pimply, carbuncled and mean, tufts of wild prairie grass on their triceps they picked at like landscapers. Once in a while some Mexicans would come in nasty, wearing tight leather pants that forced their complete genitalia to choose sides, packages better off delivered elsewhere that they usually left **THE JARGON** grasping, the natural choice when bleeding from the face and suffering indignities to the reproductives.

Garvin visited the tavern in flannel shirts, blue jeans, Texas cowhair belt with Mexican gravesidescene buckle the size of a small omelet and genuine alligator boots, pointy-toed, making an impression that had to be pounded down to size, the faggot, and which Garvin knew no amount or knowledge of lingo could prevent and so when it came to it he was up against said three hundred pound toadman-type and a more dangerous, tall, strong lifetime fighter, this one a legend name of Andy Malvasio, who once knocked the shit out of four cops who tried to remove him from a chain pancake restaurant over the spillery of some, as one dimwitness put it, maple surple. The big feller had no gonad protection and was on the floor truly damaged and in need of surgery while Garvin had an egglump already, had used a stool and a broken bottle and was still looking to get stomped like a rebel turd in a cowpen, when in waltzed of all people, though better said, the only person, Clay Strut, who could have kept Garvin from that scary range that cannot be choreographed from hospitalization to imbecilic demise while prone and crawling prior to or in choreographed preparation for fatal headstomping, who in lacertine lashings speed close enough to that of light, flickering light, in the kitchen of the trailer, impatient roaches cursing, ticks having evolved lurking in desperation about the dog's bowl, dislocated Malvasio's knee and left him to writhe as such and with his hands to a neck that could have been lethally stuck had Clay Strut been so inclined.

"Rather not say," Clay said to the question Garvin didn't really want to ask anyway. They were able to stay at the bar and drink off the fight, friends of the insulted and injured carting them to the hospital, no police involved (and no guns—the place had a code of honor: Strut and Garvin were now welcome denizens of the dive, and whether they liked it or not would now and again have to guzzle whatever swill Malvasio and, as it turned out, a fat dude named Craven, honored them).

The bartender was a heartattack called Fox, who stationed himself on a reinforced stool that accommodated his 400 to 450 pounds, not just by refusing to collapse but by being within reach of anything Fox would serve, which was limited only to what he could reach given the unlikelihood of a customer provoking him into standing and taking steps for mankind. No one who first entered the tavern and encountered Fox could have been declaimed pusillanimous for turning and leaving upon first look at his bloat cetacean—and indeed he was pale, likely the result of having the normal ration of blood and only the normal ration—aspect, his biker costume—another sleeveless sartor—long greasy gray hair and beard, and by way of habit subconsciously calculating the likelihood of him reaching both vessel and bottle and walking straight out to any tavern that at least did not seem to persist in the latter days of a long plague. Yet for those who stayed for a drink they found his voice was almost tender, and his every utterance combined aggrievement, long endured and unlikely to persist other than but by the putrid airs of tortuous time exacerbated, with avuncular toleration, if not affection.

But that was, of course, another tic being discussed. "Can't believe that last shot. You a hustler?"

"Did I take your money?"

"Stupid question…My ex, she was constantly telling me I asked stupid questions. One of them was Where were you last night?, but that was only stupid cause I knew the guy. Best friend if you know what I mean."

"Cliché."

"How?"

"I mean the situation, not anything you said."

"Anyway, great shot. If we were playing for higher stakes

and you *did* take my money, I got a knife in my pocket that would have argued the point. Dangerous shot in a bar like this."

"In a bar like this," Garvin quietly repeated—a happier man would have sung it.

Natural tavern mates, the two allowed each other now time to mingle with their own simple drinks and complex organisms, their histories and the toxic fragments of phraseology that flitted in and out of their inutile thinking fungosities.

No mirror was affixed behind the bar in which to notice the quiet approach of Clay Strut, who mounted the stool to the left of Garvin.

Fox said nothing, for it was obvious, wasn't it?

"Whatever you got that's strong within reach, on the rocks if they are near, and a beer."

"Clay."

"Professor."

"Professor? You from out to the college?"

Many from out to the college took offense to this diminution of their institute and inherent status; or, if you're of a mind to think that way, this reminder of their lack of status in a world of ticks and roaches that outnumbered those of the academy.

"He was my writing professor."

"Roger, Clay—"

"—be damned."

"Clay, Roger. He's got a knife on him, so's you know."

"Aww," Roger shuxed, cute as a scrofulous weasel.

Clay's drinks were set on the bar and passed down to him. The whiskey went in one cataract, which he followed by draining half his beer. A boy wise beyond his years...Garvin found himself curious. Strut kept his eyes ahead and kept his mouth shut. Fox was looking at pictures in a motorcycle magazine. A couple toughs were playing pool and there was a stringy biker harpy cloaking her drink in dangling blonde hair. She may have been asleep. Garvin had spoken with Dr. Franklin Swellman about the complaints, most from Zimmer and his father, though a surprise from a parent of this or that muddled student who thought Jews were a race apart and thus were appalled at the sudden and fierce racism of their admired professor, agreeing that the stress of his separation had become too much for him, thus guaranteeing a paid leave of absence without consequences, both a shield against Languideia and fodder for her spite. Such a stroke of genius guaranteed him his freedom to brood over his son, which he found could be managed as well alone in an apartment or amongst human types in a tavern. Before the epic barfight he had been alone here, too, though he relished, to the extent his nature could now relish, the freedom of drinking unsupervised, the retrieval of memories, the pool table, the ex temporae of tavern drama, the comfort of the giant Fox, the occasional niente of a woman's advances. The circumstances of Donnie's sonship were horrific in hindsight, the barrier imposed by the context, the satanic imposition of Languideia's conditions for pursuing a life together that had not at the time foreseen a child who would live as a repudiation of the very notion of a life together, the utter failure of reconciling the Garvin poet husband character with the fading intimations of a disastrous fathership. The worst of it was that they *liked* each other, yet by the time Garvin was prepared to shuffle the cards, Donnie had fled the table. The last three years of Donnie's high school years, along with his year under house arrest, were the most painful of Garvin's life, and Donnie had no idea, there having been no longer any way to tell him. This could not stand. The correction of this horror was all there was now for Garvin, but he simply had no idea where Donnie was. That purufestering cunt of a daughter had neglected to ask. Calls to airlines had produced no record of his name, depriving Garvin the opportunity to fly to somewhere more appropriately estranged, where he could make a list of hotels, carry a picture of his son, cross items off lists, move on to the next cities, operating in a radial pattern. (He was perversely grateful for what he perceived as the impotence of computers, as long as failure remained the likely outcome). Worst of all was that Donnie would not call because Donnie would be convinced that no one gave a shit whether he called or not. And if for some reason he did call, that vindictive bitch would never tell Garvin. Strangely, idle fixation on futile purpose proved to be a more salubrious loneliness than marriage had been, and these tavern visits were becoming what every faculty gathering failed to be. Now he seemed prepared to count an emissary from that depraved collectivity something of a friend.

"Professor," Clay had intuited the moment, "You got something up your ass."

"Watch the way you talk to the professor," Roger warned with a rickett of violence.

"Sallright, Roger. In fact, I need to talk to the boy. Let's take a booth. Fox, the bottle, new bottle. Pitcher of beer. Go sit down, Strut, I'll serve."

A primary benefit of Fox's oversight was his impatience with loud music, he himself controlling the volume. But the blonde had got up, put on something vaguely familiar from a time when musicians required antibiotics to prevent fowl bacteria from shortening their schedules, most of whom died of benign if not jocular visitant illnesses that wouldn't have killed an infant, and now she was crawling in a sort of copulatory hallucination about the machine looking to turn up the volume. Each time she fell she lost ardor, not uncommon in drunken love, yet each time she did rise, again not uncommon in drunken love, so that Garvin had filled a booth with drinks and she was still yet to collapse for good. Garvin noticed while Fox was not exerting himself that Roger was furtively assessing the woman, most likely concluding that the gentlemanly act of buying her a drink, taking her home to where the music could repel angels would result in his eventual brutalization by someone who this very moment was pounding away on a truant high school minx.

Hence even the act of a man with a measure of sobriety as a sort of remaining profit simply rising from his stool to walk out of a bar exuded the dramatic. Garvin and Strut watched as Roger paused, having reached the lady just as she had slid for the last time from the machine, stepped around her, lifted his chin at Fox, then Garvin and Strut, and made exuno.

The floor was sticky from beer on wood, and Garvin could

not help but imagine her eventually having to be peeled off, bits of her shirt remaining like Mexican painted roaches squashed.

"I've got something up my ass."

Garvin poured a shot each, lifted his to Strut's and the drinking began in earnest.

"And more than one thing, Clay, more than one thing. Like you happening in here the moment I needed help and having the means to actually save my ass."

"Lucky, eh?"

"Well?"

"You mean what, was I following you?"

"I don't know precisely, but it was more coincidence than I can usually accept face value."

"There's a lot more coincidence to it than you would believe."

"But not all of it."

"No."

Creedence Clearwater Revival was emanating from Fox's jukebox, and presently seemed virtually all that ever did.

Garvin had more than once spent money solely to prevent Fox from playing it. An emotional man, Fox, perhaps the type of man who truly should not age, entirely without pursuit, utterly content in attenuate stages of nostalgia.

"You know from that one story, I suppose…I suppose you reckon I hate my father."

"*Operatic Asides*? I thought probably, didn't assume." "That was straight from the spleen. When they divorced, I went with my mother. I don't figure he gave a shit. That was early high school, sophomore year. He kept tabs on me, but only looking for a chance to exert whatever control he might. He came to our house one night drunk. Beat the shit outta both of us. I have no siblings. He was raving about some missing money — we had no idea what the fuck he was talking about. He broke her nose. Me, just a bloody lip or two. After—"

"Cops involved?"

A sardonic laugh spewed from Strut's nostrils.

"Yeah. *He* was a cop. At least at the time. Not for long after. So to answer half of one of your questions, after that I got deeply involved in martial arts. And I was growing and I lifted some weights, but mostly I learned how to hurt people fast. Came in handy in high school. We had blacks and whites. I had one fight with each. Then people left me alone. Except for friends. I did have friends. There were regular guys, even regular girls. Not like here where if they're worth a shit they're here on business. I only fuck undergrads here…"

A glutton of a fly, black with lace wings, alit on their table on a wet ring where Garvin's beer glass had spent a few minutes. They both watched it as if it were a fawn in their backyard.

"He must have been feeding on Fox's nose fungus. Of the many things that make him a great bartender one is that the flies generally stick to him and leave the customers alone. Then again maybe it just made a break from her twat," indicating the passed out broad at the base of the juke box.

Garvin was smiling, a flash of apperception chiding him for enjoying the amusing company of another of his species.

"You really want to be a writer, Clay?"

"I am a writer."

"That's what I was getting at. You can do better than a fly from a poor barwench's pussy."

"Lingering adolescent need to impress."

Proud Mary keep on burnin…Could there really be anything wrong with that, with a man loving a song that brings him back to days that could hardly not have been better? Fox was 48 and would not make 53. Still, Garvin had to will the bile to rest, like a yogin preventing a rakshastik eructation.

"So your father."

"Next victim. A couple years later his bitter, sodden brain recalled our address…and this time the police did come. For him. He had quit the force, become a private investigator. I broke his knee cap, his jaw, and, with steady deliberation, a keen memory, and a biblical sense of justice, straddled him, straightened his senseless face, held it in place with one hand, and splattered his nose."

At the stall of conversation brought about by a violence spoken as with hammer blows, they two looked down. The fly rolled over, dead.

"If words could kill," Clay touchéed.

"But they haven't killed him. No one has. It's hard to understand. A bastard to the core, a cop in Vegas—"

"Vegas?"

"Yeah, I'm from Vegas."

"Hm."

"You been there?"

"Yes. So you and your dad…"

"After that he tried to help me. I knew I wanted to be a writer and figured it didn't matter where I went to university, so I chose to stay home, stay with my mom, go to UNLV. But I studied history and wrote on my own. I took one literature class and had no idea what the fuck the guy was talking about. Hemingway, Faulkner and Sherwood Anderson. I was the youngest student in the class and it seemed the rest had learned a code I would have to learn if I wanted to study literature, but there was something…epicene…not sure I like the word, but I think it fits. Something *epicene* about the community, but worst, it was to me clearly alien to fiction. It was good, though, in that otherwise I probably never would have read *Winesburg, Ohio*.

"While I was there, my old man sent money, tuition money, sometimes extra. My last year he was sending my mom about a thousand a month, which was good because she was not trained for the workforce, hadn't gone to college, and had a job at a drugstore overseeing a row of slot machines. She loved the job—it was a sort of neighborhood place, at least as much as such a place can be in Vegas, and she enjoyed banter with the gamblers. But the important thing was that though I saw little of him, the old man had, hadn't changed at all, was still a mean, petty, resentful prick, but had some sort of fatherly thing for me and wanted time together. That was a real pain in the ass. We met at bars now and then, but usually I walked out on him after the conversation reached a few minutes into the political. Sometimes I was convinced that *he* had brought the towers down out of sheer need to expand and deepen his hatred and objects of hate. You know Vegas is filled with Mexicans. If a Mexican walked into a bar we were in, he'd go off like the guy was al Qaeda. When you're a kid you remember certain things like they came from the burning bush, and one thing I remembered when I was real young was how he told me he solved a domestic killing. You got to look to see who benefits the most. The attacks on New York and Washington seemed to benefit him even more than the Cheney cabal."

"Where was I?"

"I'd say dad's money."

"He got a job working for one of these security companies, called Blackguard."

"Blackguard."

"Blackguard. Seedy characters. Tawdry and global both, as far as I could tell. He wouldn't tell me a thing about it. Probably some was secret, but I think it was more that he wanted to be seen as a big shot. Not just by me, but definitely he wanted to impress me. He got me into one of their hand to hand combat training sessions. I did that last summer."

"So actually you went easy on Nathan."

"Very."

"You know, I didn't ask you about that. Sorry, I'm guilty of self-absorption—"

"Clearly. Something up your ass. I got expelled. I lost my campus housing."

"You don't seem the type for campus housing."

"Cheaper. My scholarship wasn't full."

"Since then?"

"Motel."

"Motel? What the fuck. You can't afford an apartment… now you're paying, shit, you must be paying twice as much."

"I got a job."

"That won't do. Look, I have two bedrooms. You can stay at my place free."

Clay guffawed extensively, loud enough the billiard balls quit their colliding. Even Fox looked up. Only the harpy remained still, stuck to the floor.

Who'll stop the rain?

The only one Garvin liked.

Garvin set his palms against the table and leaned back

to watch the laughter subside, resume, and finally come to rest like a sputtering heart giving out. Luckily, Fox's interest proved to be brief.

"Sorry. You mean it?"

"Why not. I'm not a fucking hermit. And I'm sure you have the sense to manage the...to, not to be a pain in the ass."

"I'll take you up on it, sure—if the offer remains after full disclosure."

"I think we're arriving to the pertinent point, or points."

"We are. Coincidence that I had the wherewithal to disable your adversary. Not coincidence that I was there. Coincidence that I came here—the best overall aid package, though I was fucked out of the work I was supposed to get."

"What? Why—"

"No, leave it, please...I was supposed to have seminars with undergrads that paid enough to cover 'rent,' if not more. These never materialized. I'm grateful. No offense, sir, but I have no desire to do what you do, if you still do. Anyway, this year this job came up."

He paused. Garvin deserved the opportunity to ask. "All right. What's the job?"

Clay leaned back and looked casually and frankly into Garvin's eyes.

"I get two grand a month to keep my eye on you."

Another fly should have landed, supped and died, but all that happened was billiard balls clicked and Fox started the disc over.

Garvin was a notably unflappable man. There were many reasons, or causes, for that. And as a true artist, at least in the sense that he didn't mind thoughts gamboling about comportly with his aesthetic diversions, he had a healthy interest in the absurd, the bizarre, even the perverse. But as always he had a slender Sardinian fishing knife in his pocket that was sharp and would be a deadly surprise to its target. His jeans tight enough, he took his hand from the table and rested them on his thighs, comforted by the knife.

"Want to hear more or withdraw your offer and I quit my job?"

"How long have you been doing your job?"

"November. Five months now."

"Go on."

"The head of my father's...firm...he's a rich guy, that's all I know about him, except these guys who run security firms are generally fucking fascists, mercenaries, completely nuts and outside the law. He's got a son. Apparently he went to Europe with your son. Apparent-"

"Donnie? My son Donnie? They know where he is? *You* know where he is?"

"So *that's* what's up your ass."

"That's right," Garvin growled in a slow, tiger warning.

"Sorry. I don't mean anything, don't mean to be flip. No, I don't know. Europe, yes. I know he is in Europe and the two must be together or they would have no interest in you. This is a sideshow. Cover all angles. I'm pretty sure of that. This kid is worth a lot of money, I think, and the business they are in is more dangerous than the kid knows; again, I think. I was going to tell you—"

"Who knows where they are in Europe?"

"I have no idea, but I promise I will do my best to get my old man to either tell me, or find out if he doesn't know."

"Tonight. Keep your job. Move into my place. But start making calls tonight."

"Look, professor—"

"Tom."

"I'm sure as can be the only interest in you is going the extra mile to keep up with what the kid is doing, who he's with. And one slip my old man made was he used the word suddenly, like suddenly your kid was in the picture."

"Donnie."

"Donnie."

"Let's go. We'll take the bottle. You can pay. Apparently."

As Garvin arranged the money and a generous tip (five dollars, which Fox received with all the glee as if Garvin had dropped two manic twirling quarters on the bar), Garvin said with an authority unusual in **THE JARGON**, "Too cold to roll her outside tonight, Fox. Might just leave her lying there if she's still out when you close. If you're nervous about the prospect, take something out of her purse."

Tail 1: Life Eternal

Beneath the shank where the roaches sharpened their legs on slivers of broken glass, the ticks gorged on the nether leg parts of unfeeling Fox, the flies were fanged, ants and termites hollowed a cave for the bats that followed the last patrons home, dancing macabre in the air about their besotted heads, signaling compact armageddons that in their stealthy accumulation would one day have extinguished all.

Tail 2: A Spent Bullet in a Broken Whiskey Bottle

Outside the bar, Clay Strut and Tom Garvin were met by Andy Malvasio, held up by crutches and flanked by seven brute friends.

"Today's your day of reckoning," Malvasio said without affect.

A fully recovered fat Craven had his hands behind his back, his pigvicious eyes looking small as BBs.

The rest of the gang consisted of tavern familiars with whom Garvin had had little intercourse, maybe a drink bought here and there, a passing nod. He figured most had grown up with Malvasio. Apparently this wasn't a case of the common fearful folk pleased to see the big shot taken down. Malvasio was too much the legend. Chasing some innocents one night—one of a bunch of guys had apparently looked too long at his girl-friend—Malvasio was on back of a motorcycle doing seventy to keep up with the frightened driver, who happened to be the one who had stared, and as it was a summer evening the driver's window was down, and while doing seventy, Malvasio had coldcocked the driver—that is, he really knocked him cold, connecting flush with the temple, causing the car to veer off into a cornfield that brought the car to a halt with such tenderness that the three other occupants were uninjured and able to climb out of the car to be set upon by Malvasio and the driver, who pounded on them until all four were out cold.

A click cleared behind Craven's back, and then another behind a man directly in front of the two, a rawboned type, with long hair in a ponytail and irregularly arranged black facial hair streaking down his cheeks. One hand twisted his goatee as his other pulled back the trigger.

"To the corn!" Clay shouted as he and Garvin both got the same idea: run for your life and figure these fuckheads ain't experts with giant handguns. As men with guns they had no notion that the situation was not in their control, and were shocked when Garvin and Strut ran right through their lines, across the street, and into a cornfield, which they had already entered when the first shots were finally fired, striking ears and stalks and whizzing high while the rough physical intrusion of two strong enough men with pumping arms and heedless torsos and driving legs made sounds of the crackle and rustle sort.

Long after the last bullet sounded, after the two had angled unpredictably, finally making a horseshoe shape, beginning away from town and curving back to the highway closer to town than where the bar was, they sat to rest. Garvin noticed he still had the whiskey bottle in his hand, but the top was busted off and it was less than a quarter filled with liquor. On further examination he spied a bullet at the bottom of the bottle.

"We're in a fucking cartoon," Garvin said.

23

THE BRUSSELS STRUT

"Look: there goes 22b."

Sure enough, 22b, in a long gray wool overcoat, a blue and white striped stocking cap pulled down an inch past his ear lobes and a rapid short-stepping stride, unhindered by the tight grip of his crossed arms clamping their opposites as if to keep them from winging south to warmth, was heading in the direction of the Grand-Place. This was the coldest winter in Brussels in many centuries, or less, yet the young expatriates had not broached the topic of moving as of yet. After the brawl, they had gone on a celebratory spree of purchasing, Drake choosing a black borsalino that cost more than 200 euros and he had bought Donnie a burnt orange porkpie, which had grafted the two with personae to near the degree that they were now *of* Brussels, even Donnie, who had no steady local mistress other than the two taverns he frequented, the home L'Empereur and Setif's Santana, where 22b could pass a hundred times this cold winter without that they bid him join them for reasons both obscure and precise. 22b had his place, that is to say, as a creature encountered variably, to remain in his seat whether figuratively or in flight, the chance meeting outside a locked toilet not of moment for thought nor a true variance on the principle. Besides, cold as the winter may be, winters in Iowa were colder and winters on the northeast coast of the US just as damp. While it was true that after several months in Brussels neither Donnie nor Drake were inclined to ponder the impulses and impellings that brought them to the capital of conspiratorial Europe, it was also true that the ingravid circumstances of their arrival to this particular city were not of sufficient clarity of purpose to generate with speed the necessity of a next step. It goes without saying that they both thought occasionally of Spain and Italy, and Donnie of Monte Carlo, Monaco and San Marino, the latter of which he could not locate on a map, but which seemed like the third ace in a winning hand. Yet the two had an abundance of curiosity and experiential alertness to defray the creps of apperception. They had made themselves at home more or less in the way that a dog does when it is driven a few hundred miles from home and left in farmland as the station wagon speeds away, distracted by a superpungency of new and alluring smells.

22b would have been a particular nuisance on this of all days, when Drake had arranged for a watching of his tape on the tavern's television. The television was not inevitable, in fact was hidden in the storeroom and brought out only for football matches deemed significant—which meant international. This was an elegant signature of Santana. To bring it out for a showing of the tower falling tape and play the tape repeatedly throughout the day, Setif had had to tell her boss that Drake was conducting an experiment, studying the reactions of customers in the bar. For Drake himself it was a significant matter and what promised to be a felicitous convergence of obsession and desires. He loved drinking excellent beer in public, loved being in the proximity of Setif, loved talking with his friends while drinking, loved sharing experience. Yet, as Donnie noticed, within half an hour the obsession certainly had dulled Drake's pleasures. At first, he had something to say here and there. Watch this guy, look, they say he jumped—I think it was a press of people behind, pushing him. Pretend you didn't know this was going to happen…Stunning! And again (and again and again, Donnie more than agreed); but before long even when Drake spoke he was mesmerized by the repetitive visions of the horror, and Donnie was much like the ashtray he could locate without looking, though preferred to look at as a way of removing himself from any undetectable suction vector twixt Drake and the television. Or was it mesmerization?

He responded to all questions—nother beer?—without evident distraction; generated the requisite intimacy with Picasso Tits—have time to sit with us?; acknowledged the comments of strangers—Vat's dis den? America propaganda hour? Depends on the viewer, sir; what are you, not Flem or Wally...Czech?

Who told you dat. I fuck dare mowder. A fusing, that's what it was, an absorption of the event and/or the abstractions winged off the event into his being. He was Drake plus event/film/? equals Drake. So not actually dulled. Certainly it should not have mattered to Donnie, who felt no need to question his own reaction to the lengthy tape. Like he imagined was the case for most people, he was less bored than overfamiliar: it was all very interesting, but a piss was still a powerful occasion for diversion and there was no hurry to return. He would scan for Setif, and if she was at the bar he would ask her if she was missing her period yet, or if she knew that Drake had secretly gone to see a doctor, whatever popped into his mind. If she was moving about with glasses full of cherry beer for the cluster of elderlies in the corner to the right as you enter he would stop and take in the street or look about to see if anyone else was watching the film. Returning, Drake would physically acknowledge him in one way or another, shifting needlessly in his chair, or ensuring there was space for Donnie's drink. Then a sequence of bodies would fall eighty or ninety stories into the eclipse of the shot, from too far away to catch the actual meeting of human and cement, tree, car, or whatever no one ever discussed because the United States government was a fearful mother who had read just enough psychology to be unsure whether her children could endure the worst the human body had perhaps coming to it and so chose to play it safe, or perhaps, more generously, knowing that enough young folk would always be witnessing such that they sought to limit exposure of horror to a minimum. Donnie heard her, the United States, speaking in the voice of his mother, saying, If I want you to know what it looks like I'll send you to Iraq. But from all the stories Drake had related, nothing had been too horrific for

his father to describe to him. And his father was the United
States, this notion bringing to Donnie's mind an image of a
small living room with plain furniture in it, his mother in the
corner with her skirt over her head and Drake's father pounding into her so that her head banged against the corner while
he yelped Two bald spots! Two bald spots! His mother's legs
were nearly skeletal in this vision, the ass of Drake's father
full and nearly hairless, bald where the sides of the buttocks
barely yielded a concavity, the ass of a man impervious to the
depredations of other men, so to speak.

The volume was low, enhancing the effect of a growing
disparity between the professionalism, as it would be called,
of the newscasters and the generous self-perpetuation of the
cataclysm that continued to offer more of itself as the first
hour turned into a second (in Manhatto time) (in Brussels
time it would be impossible to say, perhaps five or six hours
to every Manhatto hour). Donnie knew that the announcers
were as pleased as he had been when he had watched footage
of the recent tsunami roil into Japan, and that that would
make it easier for them to hold back their tears, to maintain their composure—a monolith of eerie composure that
had spread from channel to channel, for inside each talker
was a rat gnawing at the wiring that they called the choleric
child within, just as adorably naughty as supposed. And he
surmised that that one house hilariously aflame, surrounded by water, no doubt covered by flood insurance and not
fire (borrocks! went the punchline) was no more titillating
than a good bombing or plane flown into a building, but that
if there were an easier command of the self on such occasions as nature dictated it was precisely because the inability
to blame nature for doing exciting things made pleasurable
confluence with the inability to hack through the lianas and
all those other fecund thorny plants that crowd the mind and
for which the human has been given but a dull machete for
the job of hacking through towards determining the cause
and effect of the cannibalism daily reported to us.

"Watch this again."

"And…"

"Briefly a new camera angle—you never see this angle again. They just catch that one body falling, from just the right distance, see: again: the guy, I think it's a man, had to have jumped, and did so as with probably a natural elegance that came from practice jumping from heights into water. At quarries and the like—"

"Or he simply wanted his last willed act to be performed as well as could be..."

"Maybe the concentration it took, maintaining that form, toes down, arms out, look again—perfectly straight—maybe that concentration took his mind off the horror."

"He starts like Christ on the cross, that might have been—""

"No, his arms are actually a bit over his head, it's clearly a plunge, see how slowly he brings his arms to his sides."

"And vanishes behind the foreground...Is that why you want that tape from the Luxor so badly?"

"What."

"You said you and your father were at odds because he wouldn't get you the tape of the bald suicide."

"I never said it was a suicide."

"I don't specifically remember, but you know what I mean. You want a tape of a body hitting the ground..."

"Because of...no, no, entirely unrelated. I mean in that sense."

Donnie just looked at him.

Dark had gnawed right up to the windows and he looked at himself in his hat. He loved the hat and wore it every day. Sometimes in the morning he was quicker out of bed just so he could get the hat on his head and look at them in the mirror.

Drake was different. He wore the hat more days than not, but he took it off when indoors and he never seemed to be aware of himself as Drake in the hat.

"These don't—I was *there*, that's what it was. These films don't make you want to see more, they don't make you want to see the poor fuckers hit the pavement."

"You were in New York when this happened? What, you were—"

"No, I wasn't there—I mean the Luxor—but I saw most of it live like most people. My old man woke me up. We were living in LA so it was pretty fucking early, but my old man waking me up to watch something, you don't forget that."

"Before six? Your father was in the habit of watching news at six in the morning?"

"You're awful curious today. No, he got a call from a friend. And if you must know, the call came within minutes because I remember it was before six when I was in front of the TV. My mom was already making coffee for us…"

"What'd your old man say about it? How'd he react, being a military guy?"

Drake finally took his eyes from the screen and looked Donnie in the eyes.

"First thing I remember him saying was 'Drake, now your grandchildren will be rich.' He had it figured from the start." Donnie looked back in time to see the second tower fall for the first time, the one that got hit by a plane first. "He and some military pals had started up a security company. He saw this meant big overseas money, military, government money. He's got a shitload of stories as you probably guessed—I think you'd enjoy talking to him. Maybe when we move on we can get him to fly out and see us."

"Why not here?"

"Look at that. I have no interest in the figures, the amount of cement, the forces that pulverize, all that shit, but look at the way it moves…"

"Same way every time."

"What was the question?… Oh. Sure, I didn't think of that. We could invite him here, I'm sure he knows the place well enough."

"I thought you were going to say Don't mock me."

"What is your mockery to me," Drake replied, Shakespeareanly.

At which point they were forced to attend to a gaunt, bow-legged English-speaking Flem who had been standing with his hands on his hips, his bulgy eyes and long, bumped snout gathering the screen, who had crossed from the corner farthest from the set, a barstool just around the final curve of the šank, his demeanor that of an aged bird of prey regarding a limping desperate mouse, glancing in detestation of genetic fate over its shoulder, craving deflation of hope. Finally he had turned to the men and spoken: "Sicular. I read history. It's not before was sicular. World War One, I fancy you Americans know a bit less about it than I. Nay. I had a grandfather died in that one. We Belgians did not like that war one bit. You might think we did, but WE DID NOT"—here Drake and Donnie glanced at each other with raised eyebrows—"and who did? Nobody. So we slapped the Versailles on the bastards. Lost our tempers. Forgetting it could be sicular if yer not careful. So what. We get the Germans again. You Americans think you know. Hitler, we got Hitler—NO. We got Germans. Hitler was a furzhal [so it sounded—guessing something along the order of pissant]. We did not want Germans again, did we? And you didn't either. Every time we get Germans, you have to come to France and we know you hate France. Least them got balls hate France. So this time the Marshall Plan, not the Versailles, the guudam red carpet. We Danke not to repeat. Now you got yer own problems and what? Learn anything? Apparently you did not. Look up there. Is that not the same thing what happened nine years ago? You slapped two Versailles on them. And you plan more. And you build them up and look: down they come again…Well, boys, I am saying I pity you."

With that he tottered back to his stool displaying what dignity his physiognomy could muster. On full look at his face he seemed surprisingly young, maybe mid-thirties, and it was difficult to restrain a curiosity about his mode of living. Not more than a week had passed since a bald obstreperous Flem had bullied their conversation, finding reason after reason to expose a tattoo of a very ugly woman he had had etched into his extravagantly-veined left shoulder. Turned out he was a retired jockey. Now this guy, with his bow legs and cowboy stance. A stable hand? A stable hand. Donnie wondered whether there was any more to the pulse of aggression hereabouts than it being a tavern where they most

intimately encountered folk, or whether it had to do with
their mid-range foreignness. They could not be dismissed as
wogs, kaffirs, or whatever names Africans went by in Europe
these days—sandniggers!—yet at the same time they were
dandies, and more accessible than wogs and kaffirs—rag-
heads!—which, paradoxically, made their utter strangeness,
their posturing alienality, all the more repulsive, their meaning and their doings more intimately opaque. He could hear
the two horse-folk, as he thought of them, telling Drake and
he to go be inexplicable in their own fucking territory. And
if the tribal protectivism of women be primal, worse is it yet
when the woman shows signs of adaptability, not only speaking the foreign tongue but suckling it. And what is worse than
the elasticity of your feminine ideal, she who betrays your
tribe, betrays your tribe yet demonstrates its fundamental in-
terweaving with the tribe of the other? In betraying your tribe
glibly denigrates the very notion of tribe, genocidal hips swaying impossible innocence, nipples replicating like tearing
firmamentals, somewhere in there that palindromic endless
cave, eternity, that is the first and last tool of the tribe.

Fuck it. He went and sat alone at the bar, five stools from
the cowboy and three from someone he refused to look at.
Should he be considering the untenable nature of his current situation? Fuck it. Who says it's untenable. Any unease
at all that was at least as real as a worm could be explained by
the feeling he needed to fuck with someone who liked him.
Or was it the sense that the cowboy was intent to grovel his
way into a conversation?

"You may not like what I said," the cowboy called across
the bar.

Donnie downed half his beer.

"Americans don't like the criticism."

Donnie rolled a cigarette and lit it.

"I don't mean it is your fault."

Donnie looked to the customer on his left, a skinny young
black man in an expensive suit.

Meanwhile the cowboy had the gall to approach and take
the stool next to Donnie's.

"I think the Mooslims should be slaughtered. All I mean

to say is that the United States failed to learn from the secular of history."

Donnie finally looked at his interlocutor. He had green eyes that seemed to have just stopped rolling about on a slick surface and a short snout too close to the eyes, the bump of it less obvious head on. His face had not been shaven for a couple days and he smelled strongly of tobacco.

"You got a job?"

"Of course I do. I work out at the race track, taking care of the horses."

"No races today?"

"Are you kidding? Look outside."

Donnie obeyed and saw that now a fine snow was pelting down at a 45-degree angle.

"It's not the best winter sport."

"Well, I'll tell you what. I'd like you to return to your stool because I am a Muslim American of Circassian stock and I take a great deal of exception to what you just said about Moooslims. I will keep in mind your Viconian-style thoughts on history, but for now, bugger off, as the English say."

"I didn't mean—"

"Just go," Donnie said curtly, as Picasso Tits returned behind the bar. The cowboy returned to his stool, dropped money on the bar and made haste away into the slanting snow and the increasingly gusting winds.

"What was that about?"

"Not wanting to take up conversation with a man whose mind is overfilled with colliding facts and too much…obscure need."

"How about with a bar hussy too long on her feet?" She sat on a stool behind the bar.

"And with a boyfriend absorbed in an old disaster."

"Tell me what does stochastic mean?"

"What? Why?"

"Drake looked over at that guy that gave the speech, looked back at the television and said, 'stochastic inertia.' So what is stochastic?"

"He said that?"

"I'm certain."

"Interesting…maybe through the arbitrary yet necessary mad intrusion we finally found the last monkey needed for Dostoevsky to bomb Manhattan."

"I don't understand."

"I don't understand it any better than you will when I tell you. Stochastic suggests randomness in time, but also repetition, I think. For it to mean anything you have to apply it to a system or process. In this case it might be that Drake has had a moment of prophetic autism or something of the sort. You know, he's got to be up to something with those fucking tapes. He can't explain it as you know, but he's got the dedication of a Chinese violinist."

"You don't understand the meaning at all do you?"

"No less than before you asked. But as far as that goes we really have to admit we've been pretty gullible when it comes to presuming to understand meanings at all. We manage by refusing gravidity of meaning to mystifying objects."

"I have no idea what the fuck you are talking about."

"See: just what I mean. You say that when as far as we know you have a much better grasp of my meaning than I do. But if you want an example, take this empty glass. Not yet, but consider it. More meaning may be contained in this glass than in the entire works of Kant, or Enrico Fermi. We simply don't know. If you ask me, Drake is onto something that he'll never be able to express. One day he will be smiling like a congenital idiot, like a man who has finally shit after three weeks, and he'll be so happy he won't even feel the need to express what he can't. Which is nirvana probably.

"And now you can fill the glass, so that I, a lesser hominid, may proceed toward my artificial and rather seedy nirvanistic moments."

Picasso Tits bent about 43 degrees—she was one of those elastic-torsoed women who cannot ever truly be sized up, one of her nipples boring a hole in Donnie's forehead—to fill the order.

She didn't bother to shave the head off the beer. "Thanks."

"It's on the house. You'll talk less."

"Ironic, isn't it. Precisely when I should be talking more."

Though the volume was down, a veteran friend of Drake could tell that giant clouds of pulverized capitalism were chasing multi-fascinated people down lower Manhattan streets.

Time passed, but the event did not.

Picasso Tits, drinking a cherry beer, was obviously either in the midst of deep thought, or chiseling at opacity.

Donnie had the fleeting thought that he was in Brussels for some reason.

Picasso Tits spoke first, "We are all the time saying There are two types of people, those who do this when that and those who do *this* when that. I think I understand Drake with his beer glass very well. And I understand that for myself the beer glass can only be one type of hole through time, and down that hole you find Breughel and Rabelais and Petronius and Charlie Chaplin and Andre Breton...But I have no idea about you, none whatsoever."

One street light was available for the downsweeping display of tiny frigid snow pellets. Somewhere out there 22b is trying to survive, Donnie thought. He's trying to survive a wind that could freeze piss midair and drive a brain through rocksolid turf down into the sewers.

With spring came a month of further winter and dilatory winds that swept away all the unasked questions of thoughtful men, rains that drowned regrets squirreled off in places easily forgotten in gangly pursuit, deceitful mornings that excused men their failures and their failures to recognize the otiose and dank failures inherent in languid redundancy.

As events rotted and ripened it appeared as if the weather required an equally stochastic process to move it along, for it took a crime wave to bring sunny skies and warmth to Brussels that year. And no, such causal is not to be scoffed at considering the oddly neglected at the time widely renowned meeting in Brussels in November of 1851 following on more than a year in which the sun never shone for a full day in the city, at which met climatologists, cosmologists, astronomers, navigators, poets, novelists, playwrights, philosophers, philatelists, philanthropists, and politicians, gathered under the auspices

of the Municipal Crisis Committee led by a certain Captain
DuBois and his coeval Professor Rankin, and which after five
scrummeling full day and night meetings determined that
the Atlantic, the North Sea, and the Arctic had their effective
atmospheric confluence precisely in the skies above Brussels,
which was thus then the unfortunate most of locations for
urban civilization, not to mention a permanent condition,
and a vote was held to move en masse to either Ghent, Antwerp or Bruges, but such was the confluence of exhaustion,
lassitude and neurasthenia no decision was possible and the
affair gradually forgotten over the years, especially as it was
no more than three months before a winter high pressure
zone squatted over the northeast of Europe, providing Brussels with several full days of sun.

To be fair, a crime wave may be a mere coincidence of
diverse criminal acts finding their way into the same space
near enough in time to alarm or ignite an observer or observation. When a stolen helicopter landed in a prison yard
in Bruges and plucked several murderous types away to safety no one at the time thought to declare the beginning of a
crime wave, and even when a mass riot in another prison led
to both a strike among prison personnel and the renting of
prison space in neighboring Holland, the most anyone could
say was that there seemed to be a sort of prison difficulty aris-
ing. Indeed, in the coldest of this cold winter, three reputed
drug kingpins were kidnaped by masked gunmen right in the
Brussels courthouse, kidnaped, that is, by reputed members
of their own gang. Carrying Kalashnikovs, to all appearances they seemed to strike the Belgians as a bit off the beaten
path, perhaps lost Londoners having had a trip to Paris and
missed the tunnel on the way back. Certainly these were no
Belgians, or Brusselians. But come a rainy late April day, a
rain-soaked jewelry heist turned into a highspeed chase under a glaring sun, the car theft killing a child and the ensuing
crash coming off rather badly itself, killing the perpetrator, an
immigrant from Morocco, a policeman, and three bystanders (bystanders…or something: gawkers, layabouts, tourists,
the unemployed, the disenchanted…no one really knew).

And within the next glorious, sunny, budding, breezy, week three more armed robberies resulted in two more deaths and a great deal of loot successfully swiped.

Other than the effect on the dead and presumed beloved of the dead, the worst of the spree was the disconnected collective handwringing expressed in newspapers, speeches recorded in newspapers, and subsequent editorials in newspapers. Drake and Donnie recognized this phenomenon from, primarily, the recurrent practice of school shootings in the United States, all of which were about the same: one or two—how can we not assume—disaffected teens would haul modern military hardware into school and in squeezing (or whatever) off hundreds of rounds exterminate six to twenty or so of their erstwhile colleagues. And the handwringing would begin as if afresh; and though no one knows what handwringing really is anymore, the word holds inherent all the grotesque charade of forced pretense of remorse, the smarm of the strange members of the governing class willing to take to podiums, sometimes even when it was not their turn, the sickly inverse of the absolute need to stare the bloody intestines of devastation into a knot of otherness upon passing, say, an auto accident. Now it was Brussels. The two had never felt safer in their lives, free to roam at will, even into what police were now admitting were "no go" areas, like the largely Moroccan slum Molenbeek, which made the television news one fortuitous night when the machine was out and turned on in the tavern. We've been there, one of the two said. Right, Picasso Tits told them, I took you to one of my favorite chicken joints. Little did she know that the English she was learning could lead her down the path to a misunderstanding with the law. Not in Brussels, though. She was a local, and as such fit in well enough to avoid the extravagant scrutiny every male in the Saint-Gilles district was now attracting.

By day the cops gathered at street corners throughout the district as if in preparation for a parade, and by night after circling the Hungry Girl Fountain waiting for the fezzes to turn up had dispersed in dilatory demeanor, to street corners and the like. Drake and Donnie joked that the strategy was an utter sham, for the more violent and profitable enterprises engaged in by the Saint-Gilles outlaws were perpetrated else-where, elsewhere unpatrolled, for all the police seemed to be here, guarding the homes and families of the criminals while they were away at work. Of course, two happy young fops, albeit of neither sub- nor sur-Saharan appearance, in their fancy hats and evident expansiveness of mood combined with lack of want, were bound to attract the attention of said law at some point—if nothing else curiosity would prevail when an international town of millions suddenly had shrunk-en to a police state the size of a neighborhood. And so it was that across from the Africain of earlier drama, on their way to make obeisance to the Manneken Pis late one Thursday morning with the temperature, having no clouds to suppress it, already approaching 20 degrees, a white van jumped the curb, and triangled them in, the bumper of the vehicle com-ing to rest without rancor against the stone wall enclosing the Af-Hair beauty salon. Before they could so much as say, let's go get some Hebrew guns and fight this one out, they were hemmed further in by the simian hands of a plainclothes de-tective of medium stature, sturdy frame, and Pigalle face— strong nose turned down prematurely against the blows in store for a man with a strong chin with an actual flat bottom to it. He greeted the bemused pair in French, a hand squeez-ing the outer arm of each, bringing them into a virtual scrum of sudden intimacy. Quickly noting that French was not their language he skipped without surmise of Flem straight to En-glish, which he spoke with a slight accent that seemed to be for their benefit alone.

"Papers, gentlemen."

The gentlemen looked each other over for signs of experi-ential recognition. This was not a matter they had considered.

"Papers," Drake said. The detective had yet to identify himself.

"Would you prefer that I go first?" the detective asked, a detectable increase in aggressive energy lifting his heels a centimeter or so.

Donnie was visibly irritated, so Drake continued to parley.

"Oh…no…You have very much the demeanor and carriage of a lawman. You have the whole of my public trust."

Donnie found it necessary to glare over the detective's head, past the ass of the van, where several sub-Saharans were bestowing on the scene the grandeur of spectacle as they gathered. His grievance was intensifying at calculable speed, for he had never in his brief adult life been able to tolerate the assumption of authority that flamed like trick napalm from any man who could interrupt him without his consent and without inevitably miserable consequences adhering to his defiance.

"...But, you see, sir, we are not in the habit of carrying our passports with us. You do mean passports, am I correct?"

"Passports, identification cards..."

"Funny that you still say papers, like in an old film."

He smiled without opening his lips. In fact, his lips retreated into his food hole when he smiled. It was not at all an unpleasant facial maneuver. One must imagine he was well liked.

"Yes. It is very amusing. I like very much to be considered like an actor in a, how would you say, *quaint* old film. Allow me, then, to introduce myself: I am Inspector Alenus. And now let me explain to you that this is of course very much like such a film, especially when you have not *papers*. For then we are the law, the *lawmen*, who take you to prison and interrogate you at our pleasure. In the quaint old film, we would call you our guests, with a bit of a smirking, or would you say subtle mocking? Perhaps we would hold you overnight. You sit smoking cigarettes in a foreign cell, uncertain of your future. This could be an existential film, no? Will you be prosecuted? Deported? Yes, very much a gray scene in a black and white film."

As if to bring cinema back up to date, Donnie lost his temper.

"Cut the fucking bullshit and show us your iden-" SLAPT!

"That is my identification. I am *the one who can do that.*"

Donnie's porkpie flew to land on the ledge of the boutique window, which had thus far had the perspicacity to remain aloof, where one mistakenly imagines Donnie wished he had remained. Instead, Donnie, who had received enough slap to sting his eyes wet and enough smack to bruise his cheekbone, looked through the tears that could have been a miasma further off destroying none but the suicidal. As the shock of the blow ran its two second course, Donnie registered it as a blow in such a way that it would remain as both a moment and a torment, much like a baldachin of fury carved to live in eternal suspense of action over a marble coffin.

"My mistake," Donnie said quietly, "we aren't accustomed to being braced on the street by fascists."

"*Braced on the street,*" Inspector Alenus repeated. "This is certainly a term to remember. Tell, me, does that include the slap, or is the slap after the brace on the street?"

Donnie now looked through one clear and one yet blurred eye at the detective and he was right enough that only the circumstances of authority conferred upon this man the right to be free from the terror of the incipient victim. Yet Donnie knew the incident would attenuate into a night of mere discomfort and chances were that he would never see the man again after this day.

"You enjoy your work too much," Donnie said, almost lovingly, "and for that one day you may die too young."

Drake fancied he could see the shifting of potential responses on the still and still smiling lipless face of Inspector Alenus. He angled his torso between the two, gently turning the detective away from Donnie.

"Please, sir, never mind all that. My friend is simply not used to the ways of Europe. The fact is that we live a few blocks from here, an apartment above L'Empereur. If you would be so nice as to accompany us there I am sure we can convince you that we are no more than two harmless tourists who have come to enjoy your city—"

"Tourists living in an apartment. In the worst part of Saint-Gilles. An apartment...so you have residency permits, of course...and work permits..."

The relinquishing smile returned the lips to the facial fore and Alenus's eyelids lifted in evident pleasure at the look of bare estrangement from circumstance that passed between

Drake and Donnie, who were clearly no longer free and happy young men in a foreign land, but that worst of all live, un-
wounded creatures, illegal aliens—as if, and it was of course
Donnie who put clear thought to this, the planet on which
they were truly nature's bounty had been swindled from beneath them.

Donnie thought all too deliberately—My gorge is rising.
"I have a rising gorge," he said with a natural menace that yet
could be subdued. "Perhaps you can put that in your fucking
phrase book. Slap me again if you like, but—"

Alenus lifted his hand, and Donnie was mortified at the
irretrievability of his flinch—but the gesture was merely calling his underling, a manchild on the order of one of Drake's
father's bodyguards, who appeared with rapid agility and had
Donnie in the back of the van in handcuffs so gently and
swiftly, where he was bid sit on the floor while the New Simian took a bench, like a man, as if he had nothing to do with
the obfuscation of both the conceptual linear and irrational
thought itself.

Alenus directed Drake to the passenger seat of the van
and said simply, "Direct us to your apartment, I don't know
this tavern."

And so our boys obtained work and residency permits.
In the apartment, while Donnie kept his expressionless eyes
on the giant, striving in mighty futility to manufacture a fart,
Drake collected the two passports, spoke quietly in the kitch-
en with Inspector Alenus, a reasonable man after all, who
set an appointment at the Manneken Pis for the same hour
in two days' time, when he would return the passports along
with the necessary permits, Drake trusting that his 3000 euros
were not being swindled from him, as of course they would
not be.

Perhaps this was a day for drinking indoors anyway, and
the refrigerator was currently stocked with a good supply of
Leffe, the La Chouffes having been frenetically removed
during a rare spat between Picasso Tits and Drake that had
been generated by her innocuous mention of the money she

could save by moving in and Drake's self-defeating impolitic remark that implied intent of encroachment. In any one
shared mother tongue the argument would have lasted an
hour, as it did in this case, more or less, though it required
many rough twists of caps and sailorly swigs on both parts.
That left Leffe, for Donnie, rather importunate himself,
nabbed the last two bottles of La Chouffe when he saw the
way things were going.

Three cigarettes into the silence Drake knew was not his
to break, Donnie asked him straight, as if intentionally revealing an accusatory, how he had come to learn how to handle
officials so smoothly.

"Why my father, of course!" he guffawed. "Thought you
would have known that by now. Haven't I told you enough?"

"I suppose...he was in Vietnam for some time, and, I
don't know, some other stories—I'm a bit befogged by this
brush with..." he trailed off before the magnitude of the
forced confluence of very bad indications he faced.

"Iraq? I told you he was in Iraq?"

"Maybe, I think so..."

"He runs a private security company, and he made much
of the Blackwater scandals, in fact took a lot of their business
away. His company is called Blackguard. They—"

"You told me about wanting to get a film of the bald guy
in the Luxor, the suicide, the one that happened about the
time the senator from Iowa died there in an apparent suicide."

"I don't know about this senator—and I'm sure I never
called it a suicide—but yes, we had a falling out because he
wouldn't give me the tapes of the impact. But we still spoke
by phone, always a payphone, for whatever reason. I mean
I used a payphone, not him. He seemed to believe he had
a secure line. But the thing is he dealt with a lot of...shady
people, important people, and he was quite highly regarded
so he was allowed to bring me along to many meetings, usually in bars. From an early age. See, he had one longstanding
rift with my mother over his being away when I was born. He
was in Honduras—"

"You were born in..."

"'86."

"Honduras. So he was involved in running guns to the Contras, right?"

"Never repeat any of this. Yes, he was. He was involved in an acronym, SCROTUM: Special Corps Recruited to Operate Totally Under Me, Me being the president—"

"Quite ballsy."

"The boys loved it.

"They were a predecessor of today's assassination teams. Their job was to go into countries and ensure that the gov- ern- ment was going our way, the US way, and, you know, convince them that any other way would lead directly to the death of leading business and military interests, meaning people, if not the executives themselves. They knocked off one in Panama and one in Ecuador...at least. Anyway, my mother, a gentle, conciliatory soul, could not forgive him for missing the birth of their only son. The thing festered until I was about ten and they had the one argument between them I ever witnessed and it was ferocious. She was the violent one, breaking china and so on. I was pretty upset, so he took me to a bar and told me a lot of classified things. I was rather mature for my age, I suppose, and I could take everything in stride but the parental fighting. So he told me about...I'll give you an example, my favorite.

From before I was born. See, he was recruited straight out of Vietnam and was already a veteran Scrote, that's what they called themselves, when things started to really go to shit in Guatemala. One of their roles was also to tame the beasts they worked with and this guy, you heard of Rios Montt?"

"Yes."

"As swine as porcine can be. My father was very persua- sive, and so he was sent to meet with Rios Montt, but before he could meet him he found an itinerary had been set up for him. Why not, he thought, see a bit of the country again—he knew the whole region intimately. So intimately, he told me that once in Belize he and some locals gambled on highway fatalities. There was this section of road, this curve, on a fast highway, and it was banked the wrong way, and cars would just

fly off into the jungle if they were going fast enough. He spent
a night getting smashed and betting on which cars they heard,
judging by the engines, would end up smashed in the jungle
as well. So you see, he knew the region. So he gets to Guatemala and finds he's being put in the care of a general who is
going into the country on some mission or other. What the
fuck does he care—he'll see Rios Montt the next day. They
spend half a day mostly zipping through jungle in a convoy
of jeeps and such until they reach this squalid, poor Indian
camp—the rulers are all 'Spanish descent' whether they are
or not. The general tells him this village had given succor
to the enemy, so they arrive, gather the populace, which is
suspiciously minus young men, and they march them to a
ravine and gun down every last one of them, children, wom-
en included. Old people, male and female. My old man sees
enough, says nothing. That night he surprises Rios Montt by
insisting on an interview. They had to go find him in a whore
house or something. Anyway, Rios Montt is in his office now,
surrounded by guards. My old man is placid, composed. He
dismissed the guard, for this is private US government business. Rios Montt can hardly refuse—he knew enough what
my father represented. So the guard leaves the room, my father approaches Rios Montt, lifts him by his lapels and as he
begins lecturing him on the various very bad reasons for sending my father on this mission of slaughter he starts banging
his head into the wall of his office, repeating over and over
'Never do that to me again.' He said he must have banged the
back of his head into the wall twenty times. Rios Montt collapsed to the floor, trying to restrain his weeping. He wanted
my father dead but hadn't the balls to have it done. But my
father had a larger point as well—that was no way to pacify a
country. And if by any chance a witness survived and my father was identified...well, Rios Montt must have understood
on some level that he was lucky to be alive. My father left
him with the assurance that no decision had yet been made
on his retaining power, and the clear message was that not
maintaining power was tantamount to death. From what I
gather, in all my father's involvement in historical events that

was the most satisfying. He wasn't a bad man, you know. I believe he thought this—all this secret government shit, all this imperialistic shit—was going to be done regardless, and he felt he could inject a dose of humanity into the procedure. Of course, many times he could do little but go along with the government's decision, like to take down the Sandinistas. But all in all he did have his ideals. Like he really despised Blackwater, a bunch of mercenaries on steroids with no real…what do you call—rules of engagement. No honor. They hated the foreigner and enjoyed killing them. First of all my father was against the privatization of the military. He only got into it because of friends who felt as he did that a counter was needed to these fucking killers Blackwater and such hired. A disciplined body that would protect diplomats, keep roads open, even work checkpoints—but checkpoints at which you ask questions before shooting, risk your own life over those of civilians instead of the other way around…"

"Okay okay okay…let's get the resume straight. Your old man went from Vietnam into this ballsack of killers and arrangers of governments—"

"Right."

"Guatemala, Honduras, Nicaragua, probably El Salvador—"

"Most definitely, a tough nut to crack he told me—his cliché not mine."

"And…Grenada?"

"Coincidence. It happened while he was there on a fishing trip."

"Panama?"

"He was against the assassination of Noriega's predecessor, I don't recall his name, always hated Noriega. He used to say that when his face was on fire the soccer team that put it out should have let him burn."

"Nasty joke, perhaps apt. What did your old man think of imprisoning Noriega in the US?"

"He thought it was utterly stupid. The US pulls enough clearly illegal—I mean in world terms—he thought it was stupid to do something so high profile."

"Not to mention setting a precedent that could backfire."

"Oh no, not that. He didn't worry about that. I was young when we discussed it, so naturally I asked, Daddy, what if they come to arrest Clinton? Not much chance of that, son. No, he felt that some things the US did need not be so obviously repugnant to others. Do the dirty work quietly—that's probably part of the ethos that kept him so long in Scrote."

"What about the Balkans?"

"As far as I know, that was the turning point for him. He saw that as an insoluble mess that the US should stay as far away from as possible. When Scrote was sent in he resigned. Who the fuck are they supposed to go after! He would shout. My mother would quiet him for my sake. Later he explained it to me, pretty well I believe from what I've subsequently read. Far too complicated and far too embedded in Europe for the US to become involved. What did they have to gain?"

"A base in Kosovo, their very own country, as it turned out."

"Maybe, maybe."

"What about other stuff, other cold war shit? East Germany? Africa?"

"Hah! Good shot. Yes, one assassination in East Germany. Don't ask me the target. It was I think the combination of the most daring thing he ever did and the most secretive. And it was late 80s, so it had to have something to do with the wall coming down, with Gorbachev, I'm not sure. But from his demeanor when he refuses to talk about it, I know it was pretty big, and he is so proud of it I know he wants to tell me about it, but he never has."

An exhaustion suffused the room and they both leaned forward to light smokes. Their beers were empty, but for the moment the atmosphere required freedom. Donnie had the sensation if he closed his eyes he would be in a snowstorm of moths, fighting for breath by wielding a badminton racket. "Beer," he said decisively, setting his cigarette on a Manneken Pis ashtray, for nothing any longer really hung in the air that could not be banished by resolve.

Donnie returned, set a beer on the center table before

Drake and leaned back on the couch with his own, both more eager to resume conversation than drink:

"And the Islamic" colliding with "Did your fath-"

They drank, both taking long pulls, ceding to the other the next choice of topic.

"Your father have any military?"

"He's younger than yours—just missed Vietnam. Anyway, I think he would have gone to Canada. But it was never much of a topic. I know that if he was married and drafted, my mother would have barked him up to Canada, nipping at his Achilles', then remained behind to seek peace awards. What does your old man think of all this modern crusading?"

"Nothing patriotic, I can assure you. He thinks every single move made so far has been utterly stupid—that everything will create a worse reaction in the long run...much worse. He spoke to me once about the drones and he was scathing.

The problem is you can see the fucking things—we have stealth technology and they send hovering wasps to fire missiles at peasants and the occasional terrorist. So it isn't only obvious and ugly, it's not deniable. He thinks it's incredibly stupid, that it goes against all instinctive understandings of war, that it'll turn the entire world against us even before our elites benefit enough financially to balance it..."

"But he went to Iraq."

"The country went to Iraq. And it's his kind of business. He can do it right, so better that he go and make his money off it, and prevent a few dozen civilian deaths. He won't get any medals, but I am certain the presence of his company there in place of any other saved some number of lives. Nothing gallant or anything..."

"Clearly," Donnie said, chuckling a percussive transition to a light knock on the old wooden door.

"He didn't forget his truncheon," Donnie remarked.

"We'll see," Drake said, rising, crossing the room, opening the door to a chest that met his eyes even as the feet below met as equals in height.

He looked up at about 45, degrees of course. A very black black man stood there.

Drake made his face invitationally inquisitive. But looking up only allowed a view of a chin that was like a place for him to stand in the rain.

"Bobeaux would like to see you."

"Bobo?"

"Yes."

"I don't know any Bobo."

"Bobeaux would like to see you," the yeti repeated, the effect being rather more than the sum of its utterance.

"Okay."

"He will be here in five minutes."

"Here? You mean here? In our apartment?"

"Yes."

"Good. That's very easy. If you get the chance to thank Bobo before we…"

The yeti was already walking away. Drake returned to his seat.

"Bobo would like to see us. I was informed by a giant African, if I am not mistaken."

Donnie smiled, his body finally relaxing utterly after the two hours of interruptus irritatus.

"So now we have Bobo."

"It would appear."

"We haven't actually broken any major laws have we?"

"Not really, just over-stayed. I somehow don't think Bobo is the law, but beyond that—"

The door opened and in slid sinuously a slight black man who had triple streak scars on each cheek that appeared older than himself, who could have been in his late teens.

"Don't get up, gentlemen." He said. "My name is Bobeaux. I believe you were expecting me."

"Need a beer?" Donnie said, rising. He was amazed at how truly dark the man was, though the color wasn't true black. Clearly the races did not spend enough time mixing, not in any sense of the word. He could not but imagine that Bobo himself saw himself and Drake as somewhat sickly of pallor.

"Thank you."

Bobeaux took Donnie's seat in the center of the couch and when Donnie returned with three Leffes, Donnie sat close to him.

A Manneken Pis lighter was passed around, bottles were raised, drink was downed.

"Cigarette," Drake offered.

"Don't smoke. The occasional beer is all. No other bad habits."

"Well," Donnie said, lighting Drake and himself a cigarette rolled earlier, "you don't mind, as this is our apartment."

"Yes. Your apartment. My building. My neighborhood, in fact."

Silence wedged into the room, unwelcome.

"You really don't know who I am, do you?"

Donnie looked for diplomat Drake to field that one. "Nope," Drake replied.

"Well, then,' Bobeaux leaned forward extending a hand to Drake. "Drake, I'm Bobeaux." After they shook, Bobeaux turned to Donnie. "Donnie, Bobeaux."

"Pleased, I'm sure," Donnie felt necessary to respond.

"I know you two," Bobeaux began what the two knew to be a soliloquy, "from the night you were assaulted in my neighborhood. I often thought of you since then, but as you had already…deflected the disturbance, I felt it was not my place to disturb you. But now that I am here I would like to congratulate you on a difficult…disturbance, so well deflected, and in my station at that. I thank you. But now, and I am sorry for this, I must ask you to be very forthright in answering this the following: what precisely did Inspector Alenus require from your services?"

Donnie gave no thought to any hypothetical reservoir, of patience, of fortitude, of irritation even. Instead he put his hand in his pocket and caressed his knife.

The day had taught Drake the warning signs.

"Bobo, —"

"No, Bobeaux."

"Uh huh: Bobo. We Americans are so poor at pronunciation. You I take it are from Africa, Western Africa no doubt."

"My parents are from Congo and Gabon. I am that odd thing white people cannot grasp, a black mongrel."

"Well, Monsieur Bobo, we will grasp it if you like, but I want you to know that this has been a very irritating day for us and we would very much appreciate your coming to the point and leaving us in peace."

Did Bo*beaux* look dangerous? Perhaps.

"But I have come to the point. I have asked you the purpose of your soirée with Inspector Alenus."

Donnie's determination to remain mute seemed to require reflection, and what loomed half-hidden was the face of Picasso Tits's ex-boyfriend, before he had damaged it, a face that now, upon first conscious reflection seemed to be intentional impetus to phrenological inquest, the forehead just slightly larger than what would have made sense with eyes that as if in conspiracy then were too small for the forehead, and a chin that served to frame the face without exhibiting any character of its own, perhaps deprived by a defective lack of structural curvature beneath the eyebrows, beneath the eyebrows and all the way to the chin.

This Bobo was without phrenological interest. But his manner, which, paradoxically, on any other day would have been a provocation, was, in the exhausted mind of his observer a sort of coda to the day. His presence made enough sense after the scurvitude of the police encounter.

"Because," wondered Drake, "you are perhaps one of our local criminal masterminds, is that it?"

Bobeaux smiled patiently.

"Please. I ask that you respond to my inquiry."

"Right, fuck it. What a fucking day. Alenus braced us over—"

"*Braced you?*"

"He stopped us on the street and asked for papers. We had none. We came back here and settled the matter."

"Settled the matter? That is to say you arrived at an arrangement."

"There were no questions about anyone besides us—I think that's what you need to know and all you need to know."

Bo*beaux* looked like a man considering whether to confront the conundrum: best way to say I will decide what I
need to know without taint of self-mockery.

"Very fine, very fine. As I have relayed to you we are not
unaware of your presence here and of the favor you proffered
our ingenuity on the basis of volunteerism—"

[What?]

"and indeed without so much as a to do. We had discussed, my Algerian counterpart, Moussaka, and myself, at
a convention of strategic planning, whether there was any
cause to brace you—Moussaka was particularly interested in
your poker games at your tavern of first choice, and it out-
came of nature the posit regarding the perchance gambling
in our territory, a violation of neighborhood decorum which
we would have to correct. But then there was the event in the
street and after much browbeating I was able to extract from
Moussaka the promise to leave you two alone unless and until such time as you barged in upon our gruntlement. Per se."

Drake stood, perhaps having suddenly recalled Picasso
Tits, who would certainly be wondering at their failure to
arrive as yet.

"Good then," extending his hand toward the immobile
backleaning Bo*beaux*, who ignored it. "I believe the interview has been satisfactorily concluded."

Standing with his arm now back where one would have
wished him a loaded holster he fought with fortitude to defray the awkwardness thrust toward him.

"All right, what the fuck is it?" Drake asked. "What do
you want."

"Not myself. For myself the matter has been no matter
whatsoever, and a blank slate remains mopped by the cleaning lady and dried in the salt-free winds under the sun far
from the shoreline. I hope with sincere feeling that you
found that poetic. Now to the point. Moussaka is a gambler
and he is in ardent desire to sit at a table with your prestigious
persons. Although, as he is a man of insight, he is aware that
should you two play together, you could quite easily work in
a sort of devil's tandem against him, and so he would like you
to choose the better of you two and challenge you to a game

at which also would play persons of import from neighboring communal activity. I am guarantor of his fair gamesmanship that he not bring to the table a cohort with which he could play the devil tandem game.

"We shall close the bar at darkness fall tomorrow night and commence upon an hour's socialization and society."

With that, Bobeaux, stood, rather economically shook both hands, walked to the door where he stopped, turned to each with a pleasant smile and nodded before disappearing as if it was simply his turn.

Mezzanine

For the dirty jobs they called in Rod Strut, former PI, former cop. Quit the force because of the corruption. He was left out of it, figured on his own he could extort money before it was laundered through the precinct. He was wrong. His contacts dried up and he no longer had any idea what was going on at all other than what his clients told him, which was usually true: the spouses really were cheating and the children stealing and buying drugs instead of going to high school.

He was vetted by Blackguard's best and designated perfect for a job, any job, any job no one else wanted, any job that might require a fall guy. His internal security clearance at his new high-paying security job was too low for a number to be assigned to it.

Strut had an acne-scarred face that was difficult to look at without thinking Wife Beater, or the kind of cop who stops blondes to trade tickets for blowjobs, who can't make a taillight violation stick. He was aware of all of this and it made him mean. He had no use for hookers, pimps, gamblers, blackjack dealers, pit bosses, bankers, barbers, bank clerks, record store owners, food stamp recipients, tax dodgers, golfers, motel owners, pawn shop flunkies, opera singers, housewives, children, high school teachers, jaywalkers, speeders, slow crosswalk walkers, drivers who used their safety flashers, nurses, vandals, lifeguards, people who pram their goiters in public, loafers, loungers, peepers, hustlers, guttersnipes, sharpies, vultures, parasites, moles, lackeys, junkies, typists, flunkies, turncoats, liars, snitches, ass kissers, moral authorities, priests, pastors, nuns, Mormons, Jews, Christians, Mexicans, foreigners, negroes, sots, cryptologists, Italians, ethnic restaurants, joggers, alcoholics, smokers, potheads, coke sniffers, boxers, copy cats, slackers, vagrants, bellhops, clerks at sporting goods stores, bums, hobos, bartenders, delinquents, tramps, circumforanean types, somnambulists, basiphobes, stalkers, delivery boys, drifters, grifters, beggars, loiterers, hikers, men of the cloth, environmentalists, bicyclists, motorists, motorcyclists, hypocrites, packrats, muggers, muckers, dealers, cops, security guards, big shots, midgets, stevedores, penny pinchers, schizophrenics, neurasthenics, psychotics, sociopaths, straight arrows, maids, gays, lesbians, butches, transvestites, pole dancers, lap dancers, tap dancers, ballet dancers, trumpet players, girls with guitars, cowboys, politicians, epileptics, shrinks, ballpark vendors, anyone who worked closely with the elderly, yackers, yeggs, yoafs, scout masters, university students, university teachers, janitors, grubs, cons, ex-cons, peroxide blondes, pickpockets, captains, workaholics, deadbeats, commies, fascists, liberals, conservatives, moderates, libertarians, voters, abstainers, volunteers, Californians, anorexics, the obese, bulimics, paraplegics, tarot card readers, protestors, union members, strikers, scabs, crabs, corporate bullies, pregnant women in public, pregnant women who answer the doorbell, gigolos, pretty boys, smartasses, panderers, tricksters, insurance fraudsters, insurance agents, animals that ate their own shit, people who let dogs lick their faces, the lice-ridden, the bedbugged, gandy dancers—whatever they were, tormented souls, preppies, yuppies, hippies, touts, vultures, dingos, badgers, wolves, sheep, dingbats, lounge lizards, scabs, feminists, night owls, weightlifters, glue sniffers, typists, fingerprinters, leeches, mutts, weasels, skunks, assHOLES, petty tyrants, brides, grooms, buzzards, scavengers, the cadaverine and putrescine, jackals, disc jockeys, infernal bores, infernal boors, goofballs, volunteer firefighters, wife cheaters, wife beaters, child molesters, prigs, children,

athletes, junior high school students, jazz aficionados, jazz
musicians, drummers, gold diggers, tippers, tipplers, bad tippers, bald tipplers, tippers and bad tippers, large men with
small heads, bums, hobos, grifters, loan sharks, loan officers,
bank clerks, tobacconists, greeters, wops, guineas, goom-
bahs, krautmicks, Swedes, economists, journalists, clients,
bodyguards, feral women, outliers, the manchild, pygmies,
aborigines, Paiutes, Greyhound bus drivers, family, garbage
men, junk dealers, craftsmen, hardware store managers, high
school employees, traitors, patriots, motorcyclists, bicyclists,
tricyclists, unicyclists, trapeze artists, swimmers, water tread-
ers, chlorine manufacturers, pharmacists, Turks, funny guys,
mobsters, gangsters, greasers, locksmiths, pinsetters, bowlers,
cactus dealers, electricians, plumbers, roofers, pilots, veter-
ans, flower delivery boys, farmers, lumberjacks, carjackers,
stockers, stackers, sticklers, sergeants, privates, sipahis, bashi
bazouks, crooks, borzois, bourgeois, ice cream vendors, ramblers, clochards, existentialists, Frenchmen, whores, ladies
in waiting, midwives, and more and if some are mentioned
more than once, as the Greek chorus sings:

A man of spite
Has no respite
Unless he can defeat us
So we multiply
As our reply
An infinite repeatus

And the man is never the sum of what he hates: what he
did like were condors.

Now, unbeknownst to the poker players and observers
down in the tavern he sat waiting for Drake, and where he
sat a veinglorious boulderage of hemorrhoids assembled that
made the passing of excrement much like the mad, senseless
passing of an insensate human through a narrow defile of
hypersensitive cacti, a condition not an illness, and so of permanent groyne to his personality.

Back to the tavern, where a baize cloth had been found
and spread upon a round table seating five ardent gamblers

whose game, on the insistence of Drake, was stud, five card
or seven depending on the dealer. Donnie sat at the bar with
Fuad, Moussaka's body guard, discussing the least fine of
points regarding the history of Islam.

"I'm just going on what I read recently by a scholar of
Islam."

"What do you mean 'scholar of Islam?' Is he Moslem?"

"No."

"Then he cannot be a scholar of Islam."

"Does that mean he's wrong?"

"If he denies that the rapid spread of Islam had to do with
anything but the word of the prophet, then he is wrong."

"Would you say then that history does not exist when the
topic is religion?"

"No. I would say that history is spoken by the one true
religion."

"Good. For in the *Muqadimmah*, Ibn Khaldun, a fine
Moslem, posits the formula that Islamic society over centuries had the tendency to stagnate as cities or city-states, at
which point wild true believers from the steppes, as it were,
would descend and right the ship. He was a historian."

"What he wrote is quite true, that the corruption of Islam
by external forces often led to the righteous rebellion of those
of the true faith who overthrew corrupt rulers. In fact, my
infidel friend, that is the story of the Ottoman Empire."

"And now?"

"Yes, again."

"And you are the lieutenant of a gambling sheikh, or
what?"

"Do not be clever with me, English."

Donnie laughed at the reference and threw back his per-
nod, produced at the pleasure of Fuad.

On the baize, the currents of natural predilection had
washed up increasing stacks before Drake and Moussaka,
while the other three, dilettantes for an evening, withered
like unlucky herons. Behind the bar, Drogba the yeti, now
known by the boys to be a lieutenant of Bobo, kept sleepy
eyes on events at the table; armed with a sawed off, Wunto,

a more active lieutenant, rested against the wall with a line on the front door, which said "open"; while Bo*beaux* himself had a stool slid near the wall that he might oversee the game. No one really expected trouble, but both Fuad and Donnie were aware of the location of each other's knives.

Having had a run of lesser luck at seven card, Moussaka dealt a hand of five. Three inept players looked at cards that remained turned down like people who cannot understand pedestrian traffic suggestions and are forever dodging lorries. Each was waiting for one of the others to withdraw first. Drake was given a five of hearts, while Moussaka managed to obtain the king of the same suit. When a queen of spades was turned up for Drake and the two of hearts for Moussaka, and Drake bet two hundred euros, all dropped but Moussaka. The bet remained the same when Drake paired his five with a diamond of that number and Moussaka dropped himself a six of spades. The seven of spades was added to Drake's motley assemblage, an eight of spades to Moussaka.

Drake paused before betting. "Donnie, should I fuck him?"

"Explain."

"I have him beat but he is a gangster and it may be safer to let him win."

"Situation?"

"Paired queen. He has a king or ace and a slight chance of pairing. I am allowed to raise up to a grand."

"Fuck him. This is poker, not a territorial strongarm."

"Thousand."

The seconds passed like longer seconds. Finally Moussaka threw in his cards, but as Donnie reached for the money, Moussaka suddenly gripped his wrist with one hand and inspected the cards with the other, finding Drake would have received a four and himself paired his eight.

Drake yanked his arm free.

Donnie absorbed Fuad's tension, calculating the outcome of the worst.

"Game's over!" Drake pronounced furiously. "You should be fucking shot for a pissant move like that. You're not a gambler, you're a spoiled child. I don't play poker with cheaters!"

Moussaka, no larger than Bo*beaux*, yet had a ferocity of face not even his smiles could render to pleasantry. His thin moustache and trimmed beard, pointed goatee, though rather trite, failed to disguise an innate menace. Fuad, similarly barbered, was rather more handsome, smooth, ophidian.

"Wuntu!" Bo*beaux* indicated that the sawed off cover the table.

"Now, please if you would deign to describe the offense." Obviously he was speaking to Drake.

"You drop out you have no right to see the cards of your opponent. Simple as that. Like a fucking retarded child he simply must know if he made the right decision to drop his hand like an unlicked ice cream cone—"

Bo*beaux* merely lifted his hand to abruptly silence Drake. "This is true?" he asked Moussaka.

Humbled and deadly, Moussaka merely nodded, then spoke Arabic to Fuad in a low, threatening, dagger of voice.

Bo*beaux* shocked Moussaka, interpreting for Drake. "He has said that you are not to leave this establishment, which is owned and operated in all legality by myself, that you, who have gravely insulted his womanly figure of a cowardly neophyte at the grand table of studly poker, will not leave L'Empereur with his money. He has therefore failed perhaps without opportunity of retrieval to uphold his honor on neutral territory under no other auspices than myself.

"My dear colleague Moussaka, is there perchance some mitigation for mediation in the innate human shared bond with which we all have the potentential for the rash words and bespoken yet unfelt betrayal of both friend and honor? If so, contrition is the best position."

A slow, yet inevitable deflation resulted from the baroque details of Bo*beaux's* elegance. Before long Fuad was clearly repressing a grin, and his boss was extending a hand to Drake.

"I beg you to accept my apologies and to continue the game, to, as they say, give me the chance to recoup. You three, I fear," his head swiveling to indicate the others, "would very much like to leave with your honor intact. Well, as it is I who dishonored myself, now would be the time to withdraw. Let the game resume in ten minutes."

This last was a statement but a lift of kohl-drawn eye-brows politely questioned Drake, who merely nodded.

"It's not the money, you know, it's—"

Drake waved him quiet as he stood to look to loo to let leave of his urine.

The winds and currents calmed, a slight seasonal tilt almost imperceptibly leaving the detritus of mediocre hands more on the side of Drake, who had taken leave of seven card, the bet-ter to protect his advantage. At this rate he could continue the entire night and leave several grand to the good in the morn-ing. He caught Moussaka bluffing once, which was enough to prevent a run at his winnings. After three straight hands in which Moussaka's last card paired him a win, he proposed unleashing the stakes.

"Only if it is one last hand," Drake said. "I have no wish to bankrupt you."

"Spoken like a viper to a mongoose, my friend."

"Nevertheless…"

"One hand? Then I will deal seven card stud. And we bet on each card, beginning with the first down."

That's fucking asinine, both Donnie and Drake thought to themselves, though the word assassin was certainly in the air for the stabbing.

"Five hundred," Donnie bet after each his king and queen down.

"Thousand," bet Moussaka, receiving a queen up to go along with a hidden king and ten.

"Two thousand," Moussaka raised when the queen was followed by a jack, though Drake received a queen.

"Fine…Should I fuck him, Donnie?"

"Absolutely."

Receiving an ace, Drake bet five grand, matched with a hint of petulance by Moussaka who was disappointed by a six, yet delighted to see a second jack land next, delighted to a splenetic cry of ten thousand, for Drake had but a two.

"Raise five," Drake said.

Both cards and odds apparently in his favor, Moussaka, in his pride, raised five more.

"Should I really fuck him, Donnie?"

"Most definitely."

"Raise ten."

Sevens followed for each, along with cagey check check.

Impatient to destroy his opponent, Moussaka merely called.

On the final card, down, Drake paired his King and Moussaka his queen.

Drake had won, but on the strength of three hidden cards. As Moussaka began to open his mouth, Drake said, "Call.

Whatever you bet I call. Let's just get it over with." "Fifty grand? You have fifty grand?"

"Yes, since you are impolitic enough to ask, yes I do."

Bo*beaux* could not resist, apparently immune to the tension in the room. "Impolitic enough to ask. I very much like that and will use it often."

"Thank you."

Hands remained still at the table.

"I called *you*," Drake reminded Moussaka, who responded by slapping his queen to the table and suppressing the triumph in his declamation: "Two pair, queens and jacks."

"I fucked you," Drake replied almost somberly, flipping his hole cards, "Kings over queens."

Later, after all had been made good in what Bo*beaux* called the social emotial, Moussaka, not such a bad sort after all, asked Drake, "But how did you know I did not have a straight, for instance?"

Drake replied, "Meaning no insult all I can honestly tell you is this, people like you never do."

And soon the two, Donnie and Drake that is, mounted the stairs, strung out on the durable fatigue of noctambular pariahs, prepared to drink themselves to sleep if it be possible, entered their apartment to find the pugnoxious face of lucifer's triumph glowing in a dull lamp's simmering, diseased light.

"Mandrake Winchester Fondling the Second?" Rod Strut asked, dangling a pistol from his fingers.

Amused, but too exhausted to enjoy it, Drake simply replied, "Yes."

"Your parents have been murdered. I am here to bring you back to Los Angeles."

24

LIKE A TURD FROM A TALL STALLION

Wang diddle ang diddle ang dang doodie
Wang diddle ang diddle ang diddloo

Wang diddle ang diddle ang dang doodie
Wang diddle ang diddle ang diddloo

Wang diddle ang diddle ang diddle long
Wang diddle ang diddle diddle diddle loo
Wang diddle ang diddle ang diddle long
Wang diddle ang diddle diddle long loo

A gotta gal her name is Susie
A gotta horse her name is Sal
A gotta gal her name is Susie
A gotta horse her name is Sal

I'm gonna wang dang my gal Susie
I'm gonna wang diddle my horse Sal
I'm gonna wang dang my gal Susie
I'm gonna wang diddle my horse Sal

I'm gone home wang dang with Susie
Less I go home diddle my horse Sal
I'm gone home wang dang with Susie
Less I go home diddle my horse Sal
Wang diddle ang dang wang diddle doodie
Hey diddle hay wang dang my Saaaaaaaal
                —Anonymous, accompanied by Jew's harp

On an early sunny morning on January 13, 1848, a long walk from Drexler, California, a man name Frank Sod, snake hunter, was out looking for a rattlesnake den in the hills, a process that involved much turning over of rocks, seeking a cavernous retreat. Upon lifting one particular rock he found a large mineral clump that looked like it might be gold, something he knew nothing about. He dropped his original intent and began turning rocks, as often as not finding nuggets. He climbed into a dry riverbed and noticed veins of gold streaking the rocky sides. Smaller nuggets were scattered about above ground in the riverbed. Before long his burlap sack was laden—gold nuggets in the sack meant for sluggish wintering serpents—so that his walk back to his humble shack on the very edge of Drexler was virtually a struggle for survival. After a week of such easy pluckings, Sod was a very rich man, though for some time he kept most of his gold well hidden, off his property, in the hollow of an oak tree that stood next to the narrow Rio de la Vaca. Though history books say different, this was how the gold rush actually started.

"Reach for the sky, pilgrim."

Truer words were never spoken, we know, for the letter to this day remains a family treasure, kept safe in some locker in some Las Vegas detective bureau store room, and dated April 23, 1850, sent from Tom Gravel in California to his wife in Oregon, the first letter he sent after he was held up on the Siskiyou trail.

I said, sir, I ain't no pilgrim an I don know why you suppose that, but looks to me like yor intention is to rob a pilgrim or jist anybod you kan find so you better make yor intention more clear afore you gone round givin orders to strangers.

An he said I says reach for the sky an shut yer jabberhole.

I said I never done surrender yet to no man on this earth and I make out I kan shoot a gun quick and straight like and if he want he kan take the chance a killin me on his first shot and soon as he got that look a constipation I drew and shot the fore arm of his gun carryin limb.

That man was who you will come to know as uncle Rance,

Rance Hardupp, former mayhaps outlaw by trade, badluck roostabout by naycher.

Anyways you kin see all that gun exercise payd off quicker than I hoped it need to. Leastwise I shot a man with a gun at me and not Hector or you or Rowor or Feeble Jeff or even me! Aint sure what I ment by that cept I wernt the feller got shot.

Funny think is this was after the first easy day on the trail after all the trubbles at first to find the north and south trail, getting lost twixt thar and the trail head and then. I mean whenceupon finding the trail head sort of just south of Fort Vancoover the trail from theyr is might hard on man beast and wheel. Hardly do you go one hour without finding some poor souls reck, the skin tayrd off the skeleton still a skeleton unless the wood was no good in the bilding of it. I fine myself happy not to no the circumstances of the hundred or more badluck cases leaving theyr lifes behind them not fit for scavengers.

Which brings to my mind beasts like bears. They say the bear is all over round here and the big cats too, but the safest place is the trail I think because I hardle but saw a few deer and occasional critters off the trail up some crick I went to for peace now and again betimes. Long lonesome night afore Rance and me met up I got to thinkin maybe too much, but what I see is them animals is smarter than us in the forest way in the naycher way, and see this is what that makes me think that if we are critters of naycher too maybe we are long gone about it the wrong way round, for the critters, and I mean the grizzlys and the ly lions they no sumthing we do not nor ever can no so they stay clear or the trail. If Big Ass lived here and hector was on this trail he would niver have been clawd up like that because they knows the trail is, well sumthing like poyson to them. Do not think I am changing my mind or changing at all, you are my love and I am always yor Tom but did we not study philosophy together under the stars and I am jest doin the same only by myself without yer gydance. Which I miss with all my blood and bones, for I am ever yor Tom and love you more than my own blood and bone and I will male this letter from the town of Portugal where they tol me at Digginz there was steady male runs.

Sorry no date I don no the date. It is summer by now maybe but snow all like a giant head of hare on the mountain Rowor told me I would see and was he ever right it takes a month to see the back of it once and for all. He called Astikelekitsa I had to member it, think I mighta seen it once yesterday and today…

The bullet went clean through the little flesh of Rance Hardupp's forearm, barely missing the bone, barely missing the epidermics, so leaving a genuine hole.

"Fuck my granny's bullcow!" Rance exclaimed, waving his arm about, spraying blood about the greens. "Look what ya done!"

Gravel dismounted and searched his saddlebag for ad hoc medical supplies finding only whiskey and a greasy gun rag. That would have to do.

"Mover here and set down," he said to Rance. "This is goneta hurt."

"It already hurts."

"Then you'll be fine." He offered the bottle to Rance, who slugged down a quarter of it and nodded stoically. Gravel poured the whiskey through the wound, Rance screamed and passed out backwards, falling off the rock he was sitting on, his head pounding the turf behind. Gravel got to the arm, turned it over and poured from the other side, then wrapped it neatly with the dirty rag. Maybe there was a doctor in Portugal.

When Rance woke in the middle of the night, the embers of the fire Gravel had built were still glowing, the smoke rising straight into the trees. They were on a rise above a stream. What manner of fool is this? Rance wondered, whom I hold up, who shoots me, administers to my arm hole, drags me to his camp, and falls asleep like he's safe as a baby. These thoughts were not undermined by the throbbing pain in his arm, but by hunger. He smelled game, but saw none. Maybe the guy wrapped some for him somewhere. He stood and took a couple unbidden steps for balance, looking around for some place meat might be stowed. All he saw was Gravel's horse and the saddle bags. If he put the meat in there wouldn't it attract pumas?

Then again maybe the plan was that the horse would be a puma alarm. Anyway, it seemed Hardupp's only chance for a meal, without which he was assured a long, throbbing night of pain. He didn't even see the whiskey bottle, so maybe that was in there, too. So he walked softly over to the horse, which inevitably had a rifle slung against its side and as he touched it to get at the flap of the saddle bag open, he heard a throb-halting click.

"Move an inch," Gravel said.

"I's just lookin fer food."

"I hope so." Gravel turned from him, reached forward, shifted a trio of rocks set against each other on another, larger flat rock and flung a roasted squirrel to Hardupp. He pulled the whiskey from beneath his blanket.

Rance returned to his seat, braving the throbbing arm, and ate like a Paiute at a buffalo steak festival. Gravel watched, waiting for him to finish before offering the whiskey.

"Tom Gravel," he said, extending the bottle.

"Rance, Rance Hardupp. And I sure thank ya fer overlookin the manner of our meetin and treatin me like a Merican."

"Don't know about that, maybe a Nimipoo, but I know plenny of Merkins would have shot twice and lifted what ye had to lift."

"A waste that woulda bin, considerin. I ain't got coin and ain't et fer two days."

"Ya really got a granny with a bullcow?"

"Back in Kansas once. They's all dead now. Some disease carried off ma, pa, and all four my granfolk, along with my little brother Lerkis. That's when I come west, just when the gold fever hit. At this moment I sure don know if gold can buy off bad memories cause I ain't found none.

"Fact is, it is a hard business. You slave fer summon fer nothing or ya stake yer own claim and fight off croachers if yer lucky to find anything. I been back n forth over the Sierras three times tryin to figger it all and I tell you, mister, I been places I never intend to return to. On this side of the Sierras they's a place they call Hangtown and I got out at night afore they woulda hung me for a unpaid whiskey. I come direct from there to this trail robbin."

"Any luck, besides bad?"

"Scorched a bunch a religion folk, enough to live a week in Digginz three meals a day. Left there owin a barber three days ago. Yer the first I choosed. Maybe not so bad a choice all in all."

"So what yer sayin is this side there's vigilanny law and that side there's claim jumpers."

"Both sides both. That side, Mormon country, I see there the most promise as you have trade before the mountain, desperate folk comin out of the desert like they lost Moses on the way or he maybe turnd back. But they got a lawman there now, big mean bastard name of Fitzpacker, was a Texas Ranger fought Messicans, run with some Messican bandits some say, which don make no sense, come up and can shoot and by god he is the law. And that means no claim jumpin but that he does the claimin. Some say he even was the law in Whorelock down in Apache territoree."

Timely Narrative Confession

Boozers, I know you'll grasp this quick. Since I was a kid I lamented the lack of fascinating ancestors in my line, which included no one of any note whatsoever but a certain deputy sheriff of Cheyenne, Wyoming, who also happened to have driven a stage between Cheyenne and Deadwood during the mean days of the 1870s. His name: Hector Robitaille. A little envious of folk like Tom Garvin, whose ancestors include a mountain man and a gunslinger both—though as time marches on the landscape expands at the same time as the population grows into something nearer and nearer to indistinguishable, less romantic figures arrived on the western scene (and so this rather lengthy chapter, maybe an ode of sorts)—I thought if I re-named one of his ancestors Hector Robitaille, replacing the actual Jacques Bertrand (sorry if you spent time looking it up), maybe I could infuse some of that historic romance into my own life. But meanwhile I came to understand, as I wrote and felt nothing, that my own kin did just fine—we had alcoholics, wanton women, bible thumpers, a quiet killer, and from Hector a line of transport pioneers, not to mention a guy killed in a car crash. Hell, one of my uncles even fought in Vietnam. Another was a Mexican who died from working with asbestos in the LA shipyards. His son even lost some fingers in an industrial accident. So what you boozers ought to understand is that what makes for romance is a šank and a beer and a bottle of whiskey and stories unblemished by censor. So get yourself said booze and sit back and read about lucky Tom Garvin's gunslinging ancestor Tom Gravel, and enjoy it as you slowly besot yourself to the point where you start to rave about how his folk ain't no bettern yourn.

Wet horse shit blocked a narrow isthmus of the osteopath in the driving rain where two wagon bones canted parallel wedged like rails uphill blocked at the bottom by an apparently recent stage, debacled. The shit, surely from at least fifty to one hundred horses for whatever geoequine reason concecatentrated there, was a meter deep near the middle of the isthmus running to two meters below where it had not the force to dislodge a wall of well-constructed stage, door unfortuitously locked against external demonry. Fanning out from the shitsink cauldron was oer head high and higher hedgery of spinescence on every side thick to the hornrizen. Narrowing to this same stretch of trail had been more and more bones of horses and cows and dogs and people and cats, rusted metal of pistols and rifles and implements, worn wood of wagon wheels, cart wheels, stage wheels, boards, posts, breaks, strips and straps and flaps and knouts of leather, standpiles of fine bones, hollows of rib bones, bones in fall position, bones arranged, bones strewn or spewn, skulls in rictus, skulls in agon, skulls in crush, skulls in twine, skulls in maggotry, all suggesting perhaps this was recently and maybe might yet be a bushwhack bottleneck.

"Maybe we ought not pass today!" Rance shouted through the false sharps of rain.

"Reckon we best ought to go while none else would!' Gravel replied.

"How?!"

Enough of the downed of the deluge spread through the thornage not near nough was left to shove the shit down up and over.

"Easy!"

Rance tried to cast his eyeballs at the feet of the fool. "Tie—shit. Goddamn, Tie! Tie a length a rope to my horse. Shit!" Lightning hit somewhere beyond the thorns. "I walk the side and hop down past and lead my horse through the shit."

"*I* cain't do that!"

"Right, better: Tie…Tie! Goddamn—Tie the line back agin to yer horse and you foller ridin. Ifn the horse lives so will you. Got an axe don't ya?"

"What!"

"Gimme yor axe!"

"What for!"

"So's y kin ask me what for!"

So the rain without let up, Gravel scrabbled atop the planks, thorns shoving toward his exposed face, hat tipped sardonically against, his shoulder picked at as if a starving lunatic by starving crows in an old country barn trick, the axe in both hands balancing for a dash ahead, a knotted end of a long stretch of rope in his teeth. His first few steps were slow, more sure than Rance expected in the wet, before Gravel saw in clarity the madness of afore him and broke into a dragging dash that curved his upward half ever inward before a last leap that pre-empted a fall allowed him to step and leap once more, from the top of the stage door and fall into the emptiness the other side.

Gravel looked up with the wind knocked out of him as the Indian rope trick took the knot flapping up the stage coach door and was on his feet leaping to grab it before he knew what he was doing, having no time to wonder at the sudden shrinking of his will in the universe to the knot at the end of a rope.

He got hold of it just before it slipped shitside, stepped over to the lower side wall of the odd deadend, and pulled his horse toward him about three inches before the beast yanked back in disgust, nearly pulling Gravel back over the wall. He let go of the knot and went for the axe. A couple mighty blows toward the bottom of the stage door had the desired effect of opening a hole through which the horse shit reluctantly globbed at a rate that would have kept Rance waiting on the other side for some hours. Gravel took another futile whack, stood in the relentless rain to regain his rights within his climate, walked over to where the coach door was higher than the wagon wall and delivered a mighty overhead blow that knocked the door flat, releasing a torrent of shit in which the significant lumps of his horse and Rance and Rance's horse oozed through in graceless clumpery in no mood to applaud Gravel's efforts.

Because good and bad oft intermix, the rain remained intense, loosening plooms of shit from the horses and Hardupp, whose face reappeared with a look of insult suffered without option of dignity.

"My hat!" he said loud through the rain. "I lost my hat!" And he started back toward the bushwhack bottleneck. Already the streaming ground was less than all shit—quickmuck, sticks and freshets of the stew of it all skimming toward Hardupp.

"You'll never find it!" Gravel said as they both laid eyes on a shitclump tumbling like a hat full of and covered with horse shit that finally wheeled off the petering runnel and stuck on a bush. Sure enough, Rance Hardupp had recovered his hat and the rain remained to wash it clean of shit. The rain continued torrential through dark fall when the two stumbled upon the river they had followed from Portugee Flat and lost in a confusion of trail narrowings and unmarked expanses that led finally to the ambush of horse shit, the river which was now a torrent overflowing its banks, giant dark trees closing in the river's future despite the aggression of the water into the woods. Hardupp and Gravel wound a path through the forest, maintaining sound contact with the roar of the river, determined to move through the night to remain warm, hoping the day would dawn dry and the river be their

trail. They knew somewhere near enough ahead lay the settlement of Poverty Flat, said to be on this very river.

Half-awakening to shouts, whoops, gunshots, galloping
hooves, curses multiplied by three, for the horsemen were in
triplicate, Rance and Tom at first had no memory of having
lain themselves to rest. The duration of the spectacle, brief
though it was, prevented the casting back of thought and certainly placed the present in precarious mode. But a hundred
yards up the trail and the river bent and the sounds were de-
voured by the geometries and acoustical geniuses of nature.
Thus after five minutes awake, they recalled the sudden halt
of rain and the first light of morning, the recession of trees
from the calming—for it was broadening into its flood plain—
river, and the rapidity of sun shooting high into the sky to cast
blocks of heavy heat straight down upon the wet men.

"You still stink of shit, Rance."

"I know…you sleep away off if you like."

And Gravel did choose a spot several trees off to tie his
horse, strip his clothes, lay his blanket, and fall asleep directly
upon recumbence. At the same time Hardupp, having also
conspired to lie down, felt as if the earth were sucking his
head inexorably centerward, and looked up without terror,
without regret, without acrimony, without stinginess, without
the urge to flail, at an enormous sky no bigger than usual shot
with shades of sundown reds and purples, a night sky for his
morning of exhausted insomnia.

But now the second dawn commenced with the high sun
sucking the rancid vapors from the two travelers, stirring a
steaming stew of stench over their camp from tree to tree.
Their horses strained as outposts away for shade beyond, snuffling and distorting the musculature of their necks as if bereaved and unwilling under a crush of impending extinction.
Hardupp and Gravel rose and stretched in ape of equine, no
pains of travail accessible to self-ministration yet ineffable life
generation a physical yearning slowly surpassing thought as
determinant of motion until smoked and salted fish were eat-
en, coffee boiled and slupped, horses mounted, and a step
about to trot when Gravel said, "Get the mule, Zeke!"

Rance looked quixotically at Gravel, wondered at the Zeke, and rapidly calculated that some number of days, maybe one, had passed since their mule had trackled off with the bulk of their supplies.

"Mule's gone, Tom."

"Right," was all Gravel said, turning eastward to follow the river.

They rode quiet and outward gruff turning south with the river, keeping distant from the mud left by the retreat of the lazier waters, reaching a rise, a hump of dry that promised little but further mystery of traveling, for as far as they knew it was a foothill of the Sierras that shunted the river norther, where a precipitous ravine would be required to allow the south flow they would somehow have to find a way to follow if they were to engage peril and not relinquish their opaque destinies to geographical quirk. Yet the hump was only that, a mound, perhaps a horst, and from that they saw through strange trees how the river easted again and ran on toward and round a settlement that must be Poverty Flat.

The river modern at the time was carving an abrupt turn from east-northeast to south where Poverty Flat had clearly having been hastily constructed or expanded to meet the rush of gold-fevered influxers on the north side of the Sacramento during a time of low water that was now high—not, of course the same water but water of the same course—so high that from the distance of their lookout Tom and Rance seemed to be viewing a lake pocked by slanted roofs without beneaths on which dots that were families perched huddled in insignificance, surrounded by loose slivers that were up closer swirling or basking planks of crocodilian aspect, menacing in comportment with nature these proto-Okies who very likely were cursing that concretion gold, burning its hole in the blue above.

On the south bank the river had come up against sterner rock, first having carved a hill, an Aztec step upon which the town corporeally prospered, after which it had relinquished, leaving a cliff, the sheer some thirty feet from high water level. Someday, if the far bank unfortunates survived, someone would build a bridge across the river here; for now an inoperable ferry was berthed fast to the south bank about a mile upstream, where the town road began its upslope.

At least we're on the right side of the river, the travelers thought as they began their serpentine descent toward Poverty Flat.

From a distance, but not so far they could not see a dwelling beyond, Rance and Tom spied two giant trees apart from forest, redwoods or sequoias or something now extinct from excess of logging or diligent parasites that appeared as a gateway to the town above and beyond (the swamped town across here obscured by scarp and gentle riverbend); and it was up there where the trail began its rise that the ferry was tied to a clipped dock, a stump of man-made humbled to new and practical proportion, nary longer than the ferry itself. As long distance horsemen do, the men corralled their senses inward, marking their progress by sporadic assessments of ocular illusion such as the breadthly expansion of the two extraordinary trees on which they failed to focus until so close that the bizarre apparition of two hands gripping the nearer, on their right, just two hands that would have had to belong to a youngster with a wingspan of some 15 to 30 feet, startled them to a halt, while at the same time they noticed nailed to the tree just left beyond a wood sign nailed at man on horse eye level burned the words PORTUGUESE FLAT, not so unexpected that it held gaze from a closer examination of the bizarre: the two hands of the hypersuperannuated youngun holding by a foreleg each a giant bullfrog, belly forward, hind legs defeated downwards having found nothing to leap of purchase.

Let the reader here suffer the same exasperpentorigors as the riders, while from behind a sudden second sign, four feet high reading "THE AMAZING JIMMY AND THE FURTHER FAMILY BLADE…one gold piece bet," emerged two little girls in identical bluebell dresses moving entrancedly to tree, each gripping a frog leg at what would in the human be termed an ankle, redundantly restraining the resigned am-phib who was looking to the sky and gasping orisons of after-storm fresh air followed by an overalled braggart with a face that sneered in need of a hammerblow who held a hand on the hilt of a throwing knife sluffed in a makeshift holster who began his barkery, "Witness the amazing Jimmy Blade, the amazing Jimmy Blade, witness the amazing Jimmy Blade pin a bullfrog to a tree, a bullfrog to a tree, with a knife at ten paces, ten paces pin a bullfrog to a tree, one gold piece bet one gold piece bet, the amazing Jimmy Blade, for one gold piece watch the amazing Jimmy Blade pin a bullfrog to a tree, lose the bet tell your friends you saw it, your friends won't believe you were there to see the amazing Jimmy Blade when he was just a fresh youngun pin a bullfrog to a tree. Gentlemen?"

Late morning sun warmed the scene, the river wide and swirling lazy like a sated beast, not bringing to mind the catastrophe beyond sight, for up close what is crocodilian but clearly cut wood makes of high water nought but fluid obstacle? A sense of sense spread into the scene, a house up yonder a minute's walk surely that of the ferryman and these his kids, whippersnappers precociously creating scenarios for the earning of cash.

The horsemen dismounted, Tom Gravel stepping forward and extending his hand, asking, "You the one they call Jimmy Blade?"

"That's me mister," the runt replied, guiding Tom away from the tree with hermetic huckster gestures, touching his elbow, establishing an alliance of momentum, "that's me all right and my deed's as good as my word. You willing to risk a gold piece to make me prove it? See that frog. It's a mighty bigun but let me—you too mister" (Rance obediently trailing) "—let me show you the view from ten paces and tell me YOU could split that frog's belly."

True enough, from ten paces the frog was smaller, and certainly seemed an impossible target for this imp with his knife, which he had slickly produced and now was flipping blade to handle to blade to handle to blade, but the tree was so enormous, so wide, that the effect of a mere ten loped paces of a ten-year-old was not such that the event in question

was much imbibliorated; the hard parts remained: getting
the knife to hit blade first, and being accurate enough to hit
the frog, the latter challenge being the leaster. Nonetheless,
Gravel produced a gold piece and held it before Mister Jimmy Blade. He could see that the grass from where they stood
was beaten to a trail leading to the tree and surmised that
this young feller might just be able to live up to his boast,
but there again was the true fact that if indeed he pinned
the bullfrog to the tree that would be a gold piece's worth of
storytelling in the long run.

"Mister Blade, I believe I will take that bet."

Rance sidled up to Tom and whispered, "What if he don't
have no gold piece, Tom?"

Having already bent his left leg at the ten-pace line drawn
by his boots, Jimmy Blade backed to straight, glared at Rance
with contempt, and withdrew a gold piece from his pocket.

"Here, cowhand, you hole em."

Rance was forced to take hold of both gold pieces, his
gaunt cheeks sucking redward from brief, intense regret.

And again Jimmy Blade stepped to the line, birds remained without apprehension, the river was muted in bari-
tone, the people stood still — until in a surge of energy Jimmy
flung the blade into the hand of the bluebell dressed girl on
their left.

The knife stuck the hand to the tree momentarily, all
paused in awe, then the knife dropped, the hand came free
spurting blood, and the girl twirled, lifting her dress to wrap
her hand and screamed, "I'm never gonna be your sister
again, Jimmy Blade," as she ran up toward the town.

The other girl remained still as everyone else yet was the
first to break the spell, her thoughts pulsing waves of fraught
energy until she let go of her frog-ankle and ran as fast as she
could after the other little girl. The two hands holding the
frog did not move at all, Tom and Rance now looked at each
other with brows lifted, Jimmy Blade mined for the two gold
pieces that weren't there in his pocket, and shrugged. Rance
slipped the prize to Gravel.

"Bad luck is all that was," he said, handing the purse to

Gravel; "bit of wind come up and sawed at it. You saw how close it come."

Tom may have felt kindlier, even considering the knife slice in the hand of a little girl, but Rance was fed up. "What happened, you runt, was you missed and lost yerself a gold piece and likely ruint yet sister's hand fer life."

Jimmy Blade rounded on the tall horseman and working foam to his lips so as to effect a spittle to underscore his venom, or venom to engorge his spittle: "I could split yer mammy's twat fer ya only summon done it fer ya already, ye pissdrinking scumsack! An if ya dint hear, the little slut aint my sister, peabrain!"

What's a man to do in such a situation? Rance had a vision of Jimmy Blade with the same face and the body of an infant and all the men he'd known the past few years surrounding him in a ceremony meant to defeat the force of evil by slicing off the kid's head and burning his body.

"Now, Jimmy, son," said Gravel, "talk like that just won't do, not even from a little feller as yerself. You do best to apologize right quick afore I let the gentleman rip yer clothes off n spank yer feisty little ass."

"He won't be wantin to try that. Clem! Jem!"

Out from the trees slouched two tall teens, each wielding a long bear knife, advancing in their own slow inexorable lopes like beasts soon to depart the globe for inheriting a bad, if at times deadly, idea. Gravel drew quick and marked their stopping points with a bullet in the earth afore each.

The twins—for they were, *and* Jimmy Blade's blood— halted postures near forefall, aproterodontal mouths slacked open, eyes apopply, as if having witnessed something altogether new, appalling, and curiously aptotic, projecting a uniquely magnificent frugality of thought.

"You knock them teeth out with yer knife, Jimmy Blade?" Gravel teased. "Now I think things've got out of hand here. Tell them boys to drop them there blades and we'll be on our way, no harm done."

Gravel saw grievance subdawn in Rance and added quickly: "Still just a kid, Rance. Let's leave it."

"Leave it? Leave it?" Jimmy looked to be mocking his own disturbance as he turned and—"Shit! Clem! Jem! git the frog, git the goddam-ned frog!", for in those few moments of menace the frog had been dropped, likely taken a few seconds to snap from stupor, then begun to hop away in near six foot bounds. The twins sheathed their blades and hopped too to it, the two loping as the frog leaped, six foot bounds, surrounding it in practiced fashion—that's how them creatures once thrived on these here plains, a man might've thought— that would have failed rapidly had the frog had the wit toward water, but having in fright gone forestward was no match for the Blade twins, one of whom caught it midair (both), clutching the enormous representative of its species to his upper chest and neck.

"Ya done good, Clem," Jimmy called. "You two git back to holdin it to the tree." The natural depression that wafts in after spectacle was repulsed by Jimmy Blade, who touched Gravel's forearm with familiarity, the warmth of the barker returned. "Mister, you got my money. I done made a fool a myself. I ask you one chance to get that gold piece back."

Rance snorted as any sane man would.

"You can get in on it, too, mister—and I hope there's no hard feelins: I embarrassed myself, is what I guess. I do apologize."

"You really want to try again, son?"

"I'll take some a that bet—can you cover five gold pieces, boy?"

"Let me git my knife."

"Sure Rance? You got five to spare easy?" Gravel asked betimes, eliciting a disquieting look from Hardupp, as if suggesting Gravel were an imposter.

Jimmy Blade returned, his lips tight pursed, hand upward thrust before Rance's belt.

"Where's yern?"

"Right here," Jimmy Blade replied with inarrogant pride, unsheathing to reveal, held in both hands the way one offers not a gift, rather a recognition, the rustic grandeur of his singular knife. The blade itself was fresh polished, sharpened evenly from hilt to tip and back the other side to hilt. The handle was wrapped tight in crimson leather, forming a tubular grip of such apparent mass it was difficult to conceive a substance beneath, as if it were a cylinder of nought but dense, taut hide. This effected a stylish contrast with the surprise wood of the hilt and butt, which were painted in checks of black and white.

"Get this fer a bet a five yer getting a thievy bounty. No pirate ever flunged a finer dagger."

Rance, entranced, needed no Bladely boast, gazing rapt at the knife all the while he counted five gold pieces from the purse sack tied to his belt and handing then to Gravel, the implicit arbiter, whose own allurement was coaxed aside by prophetic vision of a con unfolding. The first throw missed, to be sure, but by mere inches, the illusion of catastrophic ineptitude created by the slice of blade into eftesque feminine paw—yes, the point a mere handspan from the frog's belly, which would remain a relatively massive target from the, come to reflect, relatively short distance of these ten paces: the next throw would be precise, the sawed off confidence man taking away four gold pieces rather than a mere one.

And so it occurred, from the explosion of energy that projected the blade ten feet in a second, this fling flung more brisk and violent, compact, splunk and thwang, splitting the belly centrally, sticking the bullfrog to the tree, Clem and Jem instantly releasing the two legs each they'd held, fore and aft frogwise, up and down that is to say, one each side of the target, lifting their now free hands aloft as they slunk away from the display, the spectacle of a giant bullfrog pinned to a giant tree, the three others abruptly approaching, effervescence sparkling their aspect, even the soothseer Gravel disimmuned by awesome of nature and artifice convergent to glamorous effect.

Jimmy Blade tugged the knife from the guts and tree, the victim jerking in its dying physios from cling-to-steel to back-barked before yielding to gravity in league with fate of fucked frog floppery. Blade wiped the blade on his pants.

"Always keep it clean...looky there at the balance...

handle's a iron rod, see, looky there neath…can't see here but they's welded together, what the smith told me 'welded' swhat he said…on yer finger jes like that…" The bullfrog came to rest belly up, hitting back flat and bouncing but little, his head a-rest on a tiny clump of earth so that in his gutspiring final minutes he may have observed the underjoints that worked out sounds he could not comprehend—let there be no doubt: the dying bullfrog understood nothing of the discussion regarding the unique tool that was the guarantor of the day of his demise, the way the iron and leather brought to balance the blade of slim sharp steel, a knife of such handiwork the likes of which Gravel and Hardupp had never seen, accustomed as they were to handbound country knives for close-up killing and so new to both aerodynamic design and its inherent avial aesthetic attraction, less serendipitous than even Jimmy Blade would have guessed. And so, rapt, the men and boy conversed excitedly above the frog in clustery oblivion not unmerciful, for when Rance shifted such that his bootheel crushed his head as if it were a ripefallen plum thus bringing the absolute of death to that amphibian's life lengthy ordeal all that was lost was an eternal already misplaced by an apprehension proscribed by protean providence, a gust or a huff or a gasp without scorn, without charity, without taint of coursing blood or mirror clean of breathmist.

"Hellfire, Tom, a feller has an itch a feller has ta git it scratched, that's alls I'm sayin,"
he says, so I figure I partnered him for good or ill, we ken stay one more night n payd for him as we agreed to share what I had til his experience payd off and so I give him five dollars and upstairs he went with Miss Hastie Bundles while I did have fer myself some sippin whiskey that probly cures ague n kills weeker men. While many in the town did go about there busyness, we were surprised that on the far side of town many were laboring to reach the afflicted across the river and bring them back across to higher ground. There was even a place where they could eat and sleep, the Silver Lode Hotel, which

is now full and therefore there is no place for Rance and me to put up but for a stable run by a german fellow named Horsebane if I heard right. He does not speak English clear. I do not suppose you kan imagine a town with so many people thoe I cannot say how many and we have heard of bigger towns it is not possible that any more ken make much differing if you caint move without that yer elbow ketches some busy lady in the jaw, it may as well have been Saint Louis though I know Saint Louis to be much bigger I swear it can't be seen. What I mean is when a town is full it is full. And fer another thing theres more whores here than horses here too. In Saint Louis the horses had a small lead. Yet Rance told this is nothing compared to Hangtown, which is our destination next and which name I will ask you not to fear but will explain by and by. Well I drank my whisky in a saloon called the Diggers Paradise and counted myself lucky to find a seat at the bar before darkness and the last gold pickers come in, singin and fightin and losin at a card game they call pharaoh which I did watched late still waitin fer Rance and seems a game of luck entire, luck you guess right and luck the dealer aint cheatin and other games of chance one of them played so fast I could not understand it. It is a kind of poker I believe but not like your pa and Jeffers tawt me. There was much merriment for here there is much money or enough money to make up for not enough money if you take what I mean, and stompin and a fiddle player who survived many glasses broken on or about himself in good spirit, although before the night was over he had back so far up the stares he was still playing but we could not see him for where the stairs bent. I don't know if he gets payd but he should. There were only two fights or maybe three and two seemed to be one. Althow I kan not say if 100 fights happened outside my per view. This one I saw in which a small man was throwd over the bar, I do not perfess to now why. The barman was a large feller and throwd him back. Which is when I saw the original antagonist throw him back over the bar for that is apparently where he wanted him but the bartender felt better off alone back thar and throwd him back this time following him whenceupon he barenukked the brute who first throwd the little man nokking him cold out on the floor with one right hand to the forehead. Something broke if I judge the sound right. Maybe the forhead split in two. He was carried out and Harlee, that is the name of the barman, returned to his side of the bar and no one was throwd over agin that night. Sad to say the other fight may have costed a man one of his eyeballs for price of enterey. I had the good fortune to see it up close for the instigator was in my emediate proximity of me at the bar. For some time the feller and his I hesitate to say lady had bin crossjabberin when of a sudden the feller hawled off and smacked her, I mean the lady, a backhand so hard a tooth flew out of her mouth, which is true for I saw it come to land next to a bottle of whisky on the ledge behind the bar where such are kept. It was a moller like the one yer pa pulled out last spring. The noise in there was mighty high and there was nawt but confusion at all times but yet one gentleman saw the intsident and stept gallantlee forth to express his objection with a blow to the very jaw of the first feller who dropped to the floor next to my stool, a sturdy wooden conjunction with a solid back. They say you don't never get to understand woman and I am not goin to say I don't understand you for I do love you and that is understanding enough for me, my Marie Fire, but that only makes me happy I don't have to understand no other woman, for this harpee minus one tooth bloody mouthed bitch seeing her attacker git claboozzled right front of her and the gallant feller turn away did jump upon his back and screeching like a owl on fire tare at his eyes and must of got them claws in good for he screemed too asudden, and tried to nok her off by backin into the bar all as while he was atemptin to remove her claws from his face. His misfortune was to what I said in temtpin to back into the bar collided with the man he did fell who was in the process of as he recoverd from the amboosh, and who seein the fooferaw occurring now rammed his showlder into the feller nokking both backwards and that is when I saw much blood dripping from the eye of the very man who intended to do this same woman a faver. Now presently he was on the flor which is much like ourn if you add blood and peeyuke and horseshit and a little more hay. He had the look of the strikken man which arrived to his face which was very white against the blood as he fell backways to the floor ontop the harpee who still had one claw in his bloodgushy eye while now her manfriend pounded blows to his jaws and teeth. And now here my view was blocked as friends come to his aid and much dancing ensued and I do not think either harpee or mate come out too good, but if you have ever thought much about what it would be like to step on a egg that run out of its shell that is the horrible thing I saw as folks come apart in very slow gatherin towards peaceful conclusion, the feller screamin suddenly stopt screamin an took his hand away from his face fer but a second and first I saw the emptee space where the eye should be, dark bloody cave, and then his poor eyebrow hangin down all tore up, and the eye was crushed by a boot just then when I saw it on the flor beside his hand in fact the boot stept on both his hand and his eye for he yelpt like a kayote and I hope that spared him the knowin of what become of his eye.

Well Marie Fire love of my life you told me to stay out of trouble and so I done so that night though you kan can see that it will not always be easy. Having nowheres to go but the stable I thought to wait for Rance of maybe I would have been spared the awfulness of the great and happy life of celebrating in a mining town, but he did not come back down for so long I did go to the stable without him and slept very good for you know I am careful with my likker at least when I am away from home, maybe you do not know that, Marie Fire, but I am saying so now that you know. Although I could have slept longer, but for the german who woke me such that I said good morning to a barrel on the busyness end of a rifle. Far as I can understand he did not like me bein thar and so last evenin we must have had a misunderstandin. Back at the tavern I waited for Rance some more, so long I had to go to the hotel and eat a meal of some kind of meat and fine fresh bread. When I went back to the tavern late in the afternoon he was settin at the bar drinking a beer with a smile like as your pa would say a skunk eatin a plate full a coon shit. I do believe he had the best night of his life. I could not feel bad for his smile was so wide he looked like a monkey in one of them pitcher books you have.

Well that day we started on down river and from Poverty
Flat the road is less perilous and more folk are along it, so
it was not unpleasant, though I must say for two days I had
to listen to everthing Rance got up to that night with Hastie
Bundles and othern though I will spare you the details of what
they played at (though I have no reason to spare my readers, among you: copulites, connoisseurs, parasites, voyeurs,
hoplites and men of the church, boozers, thirsty truth seek-
ers, avid readers if still with us, and thus I provide a random
selection; Rance and his lady and ladies and men of mining
did play at

Fetch the grapplette
Gulp the freshet
Frig the gob
Grasp the fletcher
Flash the groper
Grippe the fever
French the gaper
Groak the fleshpot
Flooze the grackle
Gamble the fudge
Flap the gaffer
Grieve the fallen
Flog the griper
Greet the flogger
Filch the gweef
Glomp the feffer
Flay the gormless
Grow the fife
Fly the goose
Gyp the fagend
Form the group
Griffin the fair
Finch the gorgeous
Gimp the farmhorse
Fry the grouper
Glork the flooche
Forge the grampus

Greed the fallback
Frappe the gills
Grill the flamer
Frisk the grampa
Grind the floozie
Flank the geegaw
Guess the feeler
Fluff the growler
Gird the falcon
Fake the gasp
Give the fee
Fudge the gravy
Green the farter
Find the girl
Gaffe the fatty
Frame the gonif
Grope the feeble
Feed the grapes
Guppy the famous
Force the goat
Gouge the furrow
Ford the gully
Gander the folly
Fester the goad
Gam the forlorn
Flake the grotto
Guano the fate

Fasten the garter
Guard the fort
Force the gates
Glib the female
Flem the gruel
Gather the feet
Feather the goon
Gas the fawn
Fortissimo the groove
Gather the feckless
Fickle the gander
Garner the forte
Frottage the gillygooser
Gallup the foal
Free the gavel
Gravel the fool
Fillip the gonfalon
Gravid the fowlmouth
Flail the gonorrheal
Gamble the fey
Fetid the granny
Gait the fanny
Fence the goods
Garrote the fiend
Frack the garbage
Gropius the foul
Fork the ginger
Glide the fire
Fret the geton
Guide the finger
Fie the gaspipe
Gash the fruit

Fathom the grater
Gert the frigid
Fend the gent
Gonad the farmed
Foil the gambler
Germ the fairy
Flummox the galoot
Gobble the fern
Frighten the geezer
Giffle the flaccid
Forget the guy
Gnome the florid
Festive the guinea
Gestalt der fräulein
Frag the grosbeak
Gerundive the frangent
Fling the gabbro
Gyrate the furbelow
Fumigate the groin
Grog the flotsam
Flouncing the geriatric
Gainstrive the fledgeling
Flood the gripy
Gyre the fistuca
Flout the gluteus
Grout the façade
Fiddle the gorcock
Ghain the fffflutterer
Fanchow the gadget
Gainsay the furseal
Floche the gingham…

25

FLYING THE GRIEFSTRICKEN

"Gesticulate the halberd," Drake said with oddly designed foresight that roused Donnie, who withdrew an umbrella from its metallic wastebasket and brought it swiftly and firmly down on the wrist attached to Strut's gun hand, whereupon Drake snatched the gat from the rug and pointed it at the intruder.

(Rod Strut was not without his street smarts — it was other smarts he lacked — for within hours of landing in Brussels he had procured a gun — but why did he think he needed it? He was to fetch a young man whose parents had been murdered. Nonetheless he had merely found an African and told him he needed a gat, you know, a gun, pistol, pistola, you know bang bang and within an hour had paid 500 euros — he knew about euros — for an Ivers Johnson .22 that was poorly aligned and likely would have blown up in his hand had he the opportunity to pull the trigger.)

"My parents are dead and you're pointing a gun at me so you can take me back to Los Angeles? Pardon if I ask what crock is this. Who the fuck are you."

"I'm Rod Strut. I worked for your father. Look, don't pull the trigger, it'll probably blow up in your hand. I was told little but that your parents were assassinated —"

Drake's mouth opened to let a process of equilibration begin. He licked his lips. The gun was light, the light beyond Strut inconsequential. Strut was hideously ugly.

"Why not call. Why didn't someone simply call?"

"They were afraid you wouldn't come — you were estranged from your father."

"I wasn't estranged from my father."

Donnie looked on, alert to minute alterations in Drake's facial comportment.

"Assassinated."

"That's what I was told."

"Was it that Blackwater guy?"

"Who, was who—"

"The killer."

"I have no idea. I handle mostly Vegas jobs. I never even met your father."

"When?"

"Night before last. They got them outside their house. Snipers, high-powered rifles. One shot each in the head."

"And you bring a gun to break it to me."

A tear could have been lapping into view—his right eye squinted and Drake rubbed it shut with his gun hand. He cocked the gun and pointed it at Rod Strut, whose face seemed to recede into the nostalgia of a familiar, more profound desolation.

"Don't shoot," he said laconically, like a private eye, his resignation having defeated his wit. "The cylinder doesn't line up properly—it could blow up in your hand."

Donnie had since replaced the umbrella, and now leaned against the corner of the wall, casting an opaque presence over the sadsack interloper, who now looked as if he were trying to fall asleep to a television.

He would comport himself according to Drake's wishes. His parents were dead, apparently. He was in a pause, alert to the still, toadlike figure of Strut, but apparently reviewing the news, two parents, both dead, violently dead, a fact he seemed to accept despite the oddity of the means of bearing the news, violently dead and Drake immediately formed a guess regarding the perpetrator, perhaps committing an indiscretion—for who was this Strut? A cheap, inutile gun in his hand that yet had more heft than the dead parents, who would likely be in a funeral parlor, embalmed so that not even the blood of his life with them could be retrieved, bathed in, drunk. Dead, and by now as good as vanished, yet his presence would be required for the funeral. And perhaps he was the only heir. He had never mentioned a sibling. Parents vanished, creating the absolute need to prevent the vacuum that was inevitable, the need for their touch that was already a grotesquerie. Bullet holes in the heads. Morticians hiding wounds, artists of denial. He would fly to Los Angeles tomorrow, adding dislocation to the new bizarre of his life.

"You have to come with me," Drake addressed Donnie without pleading, asking as if perhaps the imperative had escaped Donnie, who, in fact, had figured he would return to the university.

"What about Setif?"

We meander through life, Donnie thought, yes: meander, meander but with certainty, crepitations of certainty, but rarely pausing to absorb, pay homage to, merely recognize enigma, which is what life really is, we skate with certainty on enigmatic ice without concerning ourselves with its properties, and we do get to the other side, but still we skate, still we ignore the essential properties, injecting into nothingness what we take to be our substance which is naught but illusion, for there is no other, so that when parents die we are as we were, without them, as we were, and if we weep we weep for what was already lost, we weep, bereft, for the mistake we made from the beginning, for the inherent misunderstanding that is forward movement, meandering though it may be...

What about Setif was all he could say, yet she, too, was nothing but a false certainty.

"Maybe she will come, too," Drake replied feebly. Maybe she will come, too.

No, no she will not come. Setif will not come.

Setif remained behind in Brussels, without shedding tears, without eliciting tears. The future was clear enough: Drake and Donnie would fly to Los Angeles and see to the funeral and whatever else one sees to when one's parents die, or when one's parents are assassinated.

Strut was easily taken care of, told to meet Drake and Donnie next day at Manneken Pis at four in the afternoon. They boarded a plane at 11 a.m., first stop New York City.

Donnie gave the Ivers Johnson to Fuad. "Don't pull the trigger less you have to."

Yet another taxi ride to an airport on little sleep, Donnie's thoughts were frisky as heated electrons, here he was unrefreshed, fresh from his rarefied oddment of freedom that followed on the phlegmatism of his American academic period, now sucked vortextually into a compression of worldly violence such as he figured most Americans have no intimate swirl with, violence of an order duly exceeded by that of the universe or space of Drake's father where tables were occupied by poker types who as easily lay a word like semtex as an eight of spades, who knew what B-52 bombers looked like as well as their load capacities, who could drop a two-ton bomb onto a conversation like an eight of clubs on worn felt, waterproof felt if need be like subaquatic fuses and the fuseless napalm and white phosphorous for if there is a difference it is they who would know, they who torch infants as suavely as they swirl an ace of clubs to the pot, not Pol Pot, not Peenom Pen, nor the hoi polloi of Hanoi, ah ye rent females fatal with yer foetid foetueses , ah fractured families cracking like femurs, oh heat-sensored cruise missile of imperium, what more, drone me a drone, the blind onset of a new century, redolent of vicey victry than that helicoptering ace of spades?

"How do you feel, Drake?"

The plane had taxied in an apparent geometric pattern, a zig-zag. The engine wasn't all that loud.

"Bereft."

"Bereft."

"It's absurd, but I really counted on him being here. Not just hoped, not just expected, but really counted on it."

"You don't mean—"

"Yes: 22b."

"I'm sorry—I took it as the whim of a rich guy. I didn't think it mattered…and under the circumstances I didn't want to tell you you were crazy anyway."

"You should. You should have. If I learned anything from my old man—what a cliché, let me rephrase: one of many things I learned from my old man was not to hold back your words if you have confidence in them. You're a better friend if you tell me I'm crazy for buying seats to allow for his presence."

"Maybe he tried to book—"

"No, I described him and said if he wanted it, it was his. I specifically said a guy who asked for 22b."

"I don't think it's crazy. Quirky. Moderately eccentric. Not crazy. Besides, one way or another you are bereaved…"

"So normal behavior is not to be expected."

"Not *necessarily*."

"Three planes ahead of us."

"So there's still time: he could come running across the tarmac. Wouldn't that be great?"

"In its way."

"Do you think I'm too enamored of him?"

"Are you enamored of him?"

"No."

"Why did your old man's company send that washed up pugilist to get us?"

"I don't know, but one thing about the way my old man ran things he kept you off guard. Everything was unpredictable…Rod Strut. From Vegas. What use could they possibly have for him?"

"Combat vet?"

"If so, that ain't it—my old man was surrounded by combat vets. I met—more or less met hundreds of them. None of them was feckless like Strut."

"Feckless. Odd word for such a thuggish sort, but apt. Maybe he's much smarter than he looks."

"No. Whatever his purpose was, he was used because he was exactly as dumb as he looked. I don't know enough about the old man's company to get it, but I'm absolutely sure of that."

Now they were the second plane in line. "What about your mom?"

"What about her?"

"Why was she killed along with your old man? I realize you don't—"

"Terror. Terror first off. Maybe second because she could

know as much as he did. She didn't—I'm sure of that, but how would they know?'

"Who?"

"The assassins, who else?"

"I get that, but it seems you know who they are."

"Blackwater. Nothing else makes sense. Unless I find otherwise from his dwarf, the only guy who really knows everything. He's like an uncle to me."

"His dwarf—like a pet monkey."

"Not so far off. Nordgaard is his name. Remember that story I told you about Vietnam and the little guy who tipped off my old man?"

"Yes."

"Nordgaard."

"I suppose he's a wizened dwarf by now."

"And wizened, too. A survivor. Brilliant guy. Brilliant advisor. And stealthy. He would have made a good target, but there's a chance Blackwater doesn't even know he exists. I'm not supposed to."

"That seems unlikely—I mean that Blackwater."

Next to take off.

"Your parents getting themselves assassinated is unlikely."

"Just so you don't think it's a matter of luck."

"Luck."

"22b. It's not like that, lucky seat 22b occupied by lucky ass 22b. Something—"

"Ethereal, mysterious. I think if I had the dough I might've done the same thing."

"I just hope Nordgaard talks to me. I mean honestly."

"Doesn't he have to?"

"Not at all."

"He will. Your old man obviously kept his eye on you, obviously didn't take the rift too seriously. You're an only child. Nordgaard is your dwarf now. Count on it."

Hundred years' war, German onslaughts, plague after plague…and no bones. The plane was up and rising into a cloudless sky, the little forests were sharp in relief, the roads maintained their deliberate cars, fields without serfs yielded their intentions plainly, but no bones.

Donnie watched the altitude put Drake to sleep.

He had to have been thinking about Picasso Tits, that sultry, sly siren who took the news of death and imminent departure as if she were herself part of the weft of such unsurprising events. She didn't laugh, to her credit. She didn't laugh when Drake asked her to accompany them. And her maybe in response to a future reunion was of a rubbery adamance that likely as well comprises Truth.

Donnie fell asleep thinking about Picasso Tits, a book called *Hell in a Very Small Place* on his lap.

When he awoke, Drake was leafing through his book, a tray full of empty Famous Grouses before him. "What about the Muslims?"

Donnie had yet to open his eyes.

"The Muslims?"

"You were reading about Muslims."

"I decided they were all right. The Shiites weren't such a big deal after all and Mohammed was just another rabble rouser gone godly rogue."

"So what's this?"

"I found it in a sale bin. The rest of the English books were new…or standard literary classics."

"My old man used to tell me about Dien Bien Phu a lot. He told me he suspected Nordgaard was behind the whole thing, a spy for Ho Chi Minh advising the French."

"Dastardly. Brilliant."

"I would say so."

"Get any sleep?"

"How would I know…I miss Picasso Tits. I should be thinking about my parents and I'm thinking about Picasso Tits."

"Me too."

"Why should you be thinking about her?"

"She's the best thing that came close to ever happening to me."

"You tell me this now?"

"We're gone. Why not?"

"She never told me, but I think she loved you as much as

me. I'm not saying that to get back at you."

"Get back at me?"

"For wanting my girl."

"I didn't. I do now, but I didn't then, not in Brussels. It wouldn't have been right."

"What if she visits?"

"Or we go back."

"Or we go back."

"I'll probably become decent again, turn gray, fade into the arras."

"The arras."

"Land!"

Donnie made haste to 22b—without necessarily throwing caution anywhere—to watch the descent into New York, face parallel to Drake's, wondering what Drake made, if anything, of the towers that failed to rise and fall in perpetuity, though before long he was reflecting on the grid pattern, the composition of grid patterns that formed the abiding notion of the grid pattern, how much had been made of it, yet how little had been, as far as Donnie knew, pondered regarding the rice paddies they could well have been, especially on Manhattan, the skyscrapers perfectly disguising the rice paddies, for who would tame wonder to investigate? Yet if they were flying over the Mekong Delta right now, gliding down to Saigon or whatever they changed the name to, would Donnie not be in a state of similar wonder at the way man parceled in grid pattern to make abundance?

Ho Chi Minh City, that's what they changed it to.

When you're looking for something you divide space into grids, right?

The same principle seemed to apply to the airport security check in gridland Newark, where the young men were thoroughly examined for contraband and mussulmanic redolence before being bewildered to a sector of the building where the illusion of freedom was available in shops that sold luxury items in concentration.

Drake bought a popular history of the Allied bombing of Hamburg, opened it, examined the table of contents, turned to the introduction, set it on his lap, and slept until the plane to LA was boarding. He dropped the book in the trash before he reached the line.

The terrain from the plane in the main was plane before the drainage basin of the Mississippi, which was reached long after the youngsters, occupying seats 22a and c, fell asleep again. By now Picasso Tits was a dream of young men fallen into dreamless, falling sleep. Drake remained deeply unconscious until the landing, while Donnie awoke just in time to observe the Los Angeles sprawl, ungridded in pattern as if the force of an idea had been trampled underhoof by the product of the idea, or the idea had exhausted itself, dying in agonizing spurts of implacability.

26

A SIX-SHOOTER SHOT SIX TIMES

Well Billy Fitzpacker he warnt no packer
Lessn ya mean packin a gun
As the law of the land
He held one in each hand
To shoot down an outlaw on the run

This lawman Fitzpacker came across a dirty bushwhacker
Name of Tommy Gravel
Bad move by Gravel for thar warnt no judgin gavel
I bet he wisht he never touched Fitzpacker's gun

Oh the day it was fare
The contest the same
Just shooting down targets Is a harmless game
And Fitzpacker he won him the game
Fitzpacker won him the game

When behind him came Gravel
Who picked Fitzpacker's pistol
Shot him six times in his frame
Shot him six times in his frame

Off Gravel did run to the Californy sun
That coward ran like a outlaw
But Billy Fitzpacker so hated a bushwhacker
He survived and pursued after the thaw

It war pretty goddamn soon in a Califomee saloon
Fitzpacker ran his man to the ground
He let Gravel draw then shot him in the jaw
N mounted horse and rode home neath the moon
He mounted his horse and rode home neath the mountain
      mooooooon
              —Traditional western song

William Festus Fitzpacker was no more middle-named
Festus than he had been a Texas Ranger, but more than one
passing stranger would tell he heard tell of how it was none
other than Bill Fitzpacker, that's aright—William Festus
Fitzpacker—who killed more than thirty Messicans, more
than fifty Tonkawa, more than a hundred Comanche, some
two dozen Apaches and a good eleven bounty criminals for
pay which is why they call him or used to a bounty hunter.
Bounty.

But that ain't nothing because you can't count all them
what he shot during the war itself and after on raids rooting
out raiders intent on wreaking havoc cross the border some
say, believe it or not, warnt legitimate. The border.

I guess it would have been the rambler in him, the boredom of life without danger, that set him on west, they say,
some say, through Mexico, along the border, the Apaches
maintaining a wide berth—though it goes without saying
you could add a couple dozen to his total just by happenstance (was he really known as the Raging Puma of the Sonora?)—and it ain't true he robbed a bank here and there to
pay his way, for no federales were ever reported on his trail
as they would have been sure were he up to criminal ways,
which anyway don't comport with what we already know of
this legendary larger than life figger, not to mention which
Mexsican authorities were known to employ him to bring in
the scalps of recalcitruant Apaches.

"Three men in this camp are named Festus, so why not
just add a middle name? Plenty a folks have middle names?"

But, really, though it be said with certainty how likely is it
he befriended the legendary outlaw Joaquin Murriata down in

Sonora? Sure, plenty people spotted the two and sure enough both are the type you see once and never mistake, what with Fitzpacker's size and dark Murriata with that scar from eye to ear. And don't get all het up, it's just like I'm sayin it's, what, improbable, unlikely, but then again that's what these fellers is is unlikely and that's what makes them legends, but when you think about the odds of them meetin up again, and, you know, given all that happened—and try crossin them mountains and go on down into that valley and say it didn't happen. What if Murriata was seen again? There's plenty outlaws and plenty Messican outlaws, plenty more Messican outlaws than other Messicans, and I don't figger like some it makes no sense does it that Murriata was from Chile, what'd he do, swim up here? no, Fitzpacker broke the gang, shot Murriata through the forehead in Death Valley like they says and then retired havin avenged himself on that miner scumsucking pig and pacifying to the Pacific and nothing left but the quiet life in the city and that, what was it? Gout?

Late morning of a Mexican summer day with the sun hung so low cactus burst one after another like gunshots, a dry, rancid pilgrim rode up to the lone cantina in the shadeless arroyo village Muertefeliz on a dead horse or a horse that died before he could have though he wouldn't have bothered tethering it to the post that wasn't there. He stood six foot and five and wore two heavy pistols in a holster slung low enough to mince his gait a mite. He carried a sheathed Bowie knife attached to his belt. Inside the bar, silence wafted, not truly concentric, from a round wood table where sat the fearsome bandit Joaquin Murriata, his table strewn with an autumnal premonition of buzzard feathers that drifted in through the holes in the walls. Anyone knew it was Murriata from the scar that ran from the corner of his left eye to the missing tip of his left ear, but no one was in there to know—they had left and taken their fear with them—until the tall rank stranger strode in, his natural force of primate belying his dehydration, his proximity to death that incidentally did not change upon entering a tavern in Muertefeliz in which the only occupant was Joaquin Murriata, as fierce a bandido as ever shot holes through the lore of the south and west and up into the valleys of California and the foothills of the Sierras. He once shot a priest between the eyes point blank, bullet real. In those days the region was so poor it was said the only way to survive was to die and eat the buzzards that picked at your corpse, so it is with some surprise we note a fat worm in the bottle, half empty, standing before Murriata the bottle standing, the worm standing in the liquid in the bottle that was mostly alcohol though no thicker than the shadows for that fact. All trepidation had been annihilated by heat and the fear that had fled pushing smaller things before it as if a wild wind that dare not pause for gust. Outside the tavern where the cemetery would have been had there been a hill with soil and hope two skeletons beneath their respectless piles of stones discussed the way incident bore down on circumstance.

"Why did he come to Comala?"

"Did he come to Comala?"

"You felt the earth tremble as did I."

"Yes…This is not Comala."

"Nonetheless…he came."

"Yes…yes, and the other also came…eventually."

"We exchange them as if they were no more than corpses."

"What are they?"

Inside sat two men at one table with one bottle and one worm. One of them emerged alive and he had a scar that ran from the corner of his left eye to the missing tip of his left ear.

I have it on good authority the two ran together for two years before the federales forced them up through California where Murriata formed his gang and continued his lawless ways and Fitzpacker crossed the Sierras with a new story, a clean slate as it were, and better ability with a six-shooter than anybody else at just the time when some law was of need around here. And declare right here and now I am in agreement with the authorities of the time, and I expect that like many of you I spoke with the man in Virginia City or somewhere else and found him well-spoken and in fact would dispute the very tale I tell in that in my opinion I believe he was working as an operative of a higher authority with writ to bring the scourge Murriata represented down entire as he did later accomplish.

So I went down to that village in Mexico and found the ceiling a mere seven feet tall, with a cement roof, or adobe, which may or may not be cement and if it is consists of ground up bones to make the good stuff stretch, and interviewed a witness who said neither was a hunchback, said they was gonna shoot it out in the bar over a cultural insult having to do with a local variety of alcohol but neither could enter the saloon in shooting position, so, like they say as the worm turns, the two was last seen galloping off in search of a saloon with higher ceilings. Having thus given up on collecting a worthy story, I slept that night in the rib bones of Fitzpacker's dead horse, covered by a blanket bigger than a teepee, and was joined upon my own request by a pretty young thing called Juanita, whose grandfather asked for fewer pesos than I had and with whom I spent the entire night before exhaustion befell me chasing without success of capture that Mexican filly inside the confines of our osteoparadisiacal bedroom.

We seen him up in Hangtown with Bob Carson and Pegleg Smith, gambling at the Pan and Rocker, where he shot Big Bill Pemberton for calling him a cheat and they fell to wrasslin for Big Bill was like a bear and afore they was done Big Bill got some chewin in on Fitzpacker's ear. Took three growed men to roll Pemberton off, strong as Fitzpacker was, for the man was like a musken ox of the Himalayan mountain heights, and in all that wrasslin none was tending to the wound in his neck which spouted like a geezer the whole time, not a one of us didn't leave there without what we had some of the blood of Big Bill Pemberton on us, and like they say about the lucky rattler and the horny toad it was of course Big Bill who was the hangin judge, saving Fitzpacker a lynching because it was next day Injuns came, Injuns came first and then whilst Fitzpacker organized the defense of the town in from the other side come Murriata and his gang and cleaned out the bank and emptied the jail which was only holdin a couple drifters had insulted Big Bill Grampus over to the Gold Mine. You remember that kind of thing in detail if you make a home of a place, for it was that and only that—remember Grampus and Big Bill Overdew both stuck their heads up over the basin at the wrong time and got arrows right through the skull, I saw the one got Grampus come straight out the back of his head—so the town goverment right there lost sixty percent of its legislature body plus one in the live form of Bill Hyde who was not to be found hair of after the goldless dust had settled and so the damn fool idea of changing the name from Hangtown to Billtown died with it, and the meetin was next day and you know how it is when you have to think of a word right then and there, that paralysizing struck the whole town meetin, which is why we ended up with Placerville, which ain't so bad if it weren't such a bad joke so quick, n not one to go about myself I got rifleshot while I was tending to Big Bill and felt it in my leg like a ramming antler (I say leg, but rather up where the whole thing begins to crack like a bloody waterfall I was never afraid of the dark but in the rapid bloody rapids in a shoe a pinniped in a shoe I don't know how to use flippers it was all I could do to keep in the shoe was good Injun leather but good thing is flippers is attached you don't have em pult by waterdevils and sit thar watching them Harbinger away yer life, though the shoe was well sewed and I don't know if I'd got past the worst of it when I fall asleep but somehow I knew I was goin u make it.)

William Festus Fitzpacker returned from his recent venture into California this week, our sources have revealed. Sheriff Fitzpacker again would not reveal the nature of his mission, which some had speculated before his departure involved the dissolution of a certain San Francisco bank into which he had the misfortune of having deposited the fruits of many years of labor. As you recall, our intrepid reporter, Lancet Mudhen, who left behind a sister who remains among us, Miss Florrie Mudhen, now returned to the cities of the Eastern shores, was set upon by the good Mister Fitzpacker on the main street of Virginia City during that interview, emerging with two eyes entirely shut by swelling, and several broken ribs, apologizing profusely for the indelicacy of his

assertive questioning right up to the moment his ribs had
healed stageworthy. Fortunately, our correspondents did on
this the occasion of the lawman's return manage to interview
his confidant, town farrier, plover, and blacksmith Frank Hall,
who when he chanced to speak with Mr. Fitzpacker in the
Truckee Tavern did have the opportunity to ask after his quest
for equalizing matters re the coward Tom Gravel, at which,
we quote the quote of Sheriff Fitzpacker, "I am satisfied,"
which we invite our readers to understand as they will.

William Fortsworth Fitzpacker, son of Rory Fitzpacker,
later come to fame as William Festus Fitzpacker, first lawman of the territory of Nevada, Indian fighter, veteran of the
war with Mexico, survivor of 32 wounds, killer of the dread
outlaw Joaquin Murriata, is of interest primarily—at the moment—for his counter-migration: that is to say that he was
a man of the west who went east to come west, first leaving
the Oregon territory in 1845 in the company of the famed
horsefilcher, miner, Indian killer, bounty hunter, botanist,
and scout Pegleg Smith, whom he met up with in Idaho territory for to travel south where the English did, to join the
Taos beaver annihilators, though Fitzpacker's time amongst
the least of the mountain men was short as a New Mexico
beaver, for he soon set out to learn the martial ways of those
wild new white men who went by the name Texans. From
Galveston Island to the Staked Plains, from the Rio Rojo to
the Great River, a breed of no nonsense settlers, among them
homesteaders, ranchers, murderers, thieves, bowie-knifers,
antisocials, Protestants, rickety short-lived infants, hairtrig-
gers, frontiersmen, cuckolds, deliriots, alcoholics, wanderers,
antsypantsers, lawmen, sawed-off backshooters, men with fingers like potatoes (Winchesters were their gun), hydrocepha-
loids, merchants, horsemen, evangelists, cyclopean ruffians,
ruffians, barfighters, Romans, bufflers, riverboat renegades,
diplomats, the goitered, noctambular misanthropes, Czechs,
rapists, booklearned cardsharps, hangmen, opportunists,
pregnant teens, negroes, tired Indians, homespun philosophers, kids with no more sense than a fence post, runaway

sailors, sawboners, the lymes diseased, hags, dwarves, pros-
titutes, wagoneers, settlers, sheepmen, cowboys, dogfuckers,
coonkillers, warmongers all, you could see it even in the dying infant, the lust for landgrab, the succubi of hate in need
of host, eyes vacant as distance, alive as bushwhackers in the
landfolds. History relates which and what survived, though
little is elaborated vis a vis the Texas joke, the vast territories
of Mexico they never wanted that became the provinces of
pisspots full of perverts, not to elaborate further than to clarify
that a native Texan—not to say a Mexican, not at all, not to
say, worse yet, a Comanche, not at all—would prefer a New
Mexico and Arizona of Apaches raiding cross borders than
a grand canyon in the shadow of Mormons and spineless,
louche assgrabbers, a bad joke at that as time grinded, grind-
ing, ground and grinded on, and the same grunting country
became more and more of the same groaning country until
the air got closer than a tiny shed full of pork and bean farting
ranch hands, and the native Texan came to prefer the Mexican and Vietnamese to the them what they was told were *like*
them, like *them*, and the shootings have never stopped, never
will stop, and so there is hope, so there is a winged future to
convey to a dying infant, vague visions of dead moths neath
a streetlight at dawn, O! hope be not squandered lonesome!

Gold is what I mean to say. Fitzpacker did indeed fight
Mexicans and Apaches, but it was gold that brought him west
again, for he was young and did not like the smell of dust, the
taste of cactus juice, the arrows slung and the horsey dung,
and the mites and the bees and the scorpions, and the miles
without cunt, and the smell of men, and the sound of fear,
and the bold charge into fate fecund and fat with punctures
unplanned and pregnant with verisimilitude of dread and
drear daydream of man all alike and wrought with reason, and
the blonde boy gutshot Shut yer fuckin shatpup noisehole of
course yer fuckin cold yer gutshot and worst than the whimpering the screaming and the crack of the gun butt caving in
the blonde boy's skull and the lieutenant from what he referred to as an academy who used the phrase military bon-
ton and martial courts and yet that shatpup too whimpered,

too screamed from his facehole, and he too needed his skull caved in by a gun butt, and neither dead soldier had a scrah of tabacky, so he took their water and horses and guns and made for Santa Fe, the war as good as won anyway, and found in Santa Fe a trace of Pegleg, a sniff of old Bob Carson, the two gone west for gold was struck, and it was a well-worn trail he followed, grubstuck selling the horses and one of the guns and a few horses from wandering Paiutes who weren't supposed to have them anyway and if he hadn't shot the lot of them it would have been more whimpering and screaming, and all that could be sold up by the Truckee for passage and stake, but before he knew it that giant Bill in Hangtown made of him a legend and as a military man, a big man who knew how to handle a pistol and lead men against savages, for over on the other side of the Sierras men were needed to guard the desert trail from the Injuns, William Festus Fitzpacker was a Nevada legend, first elected territorial lawman of Nevada and owner of piece of land by a stream that yielded twenty dollars a day if a man worked it. You think Fitzpacker worked it?

While the condition cold is not subjective, while temperature is so connivingly measurable that mankind continues to express this factor of the air in two different ways, yet an oddity that nears the stature of paradox persists regarding the suffering of extremes, particularly the extreme of cold. Bear witness:

I swear to you tho it make no sense that night in jail in Hangtown was the coldest I ever been and it bein midsummer and you and me having been and I thought this many a time through the long waking night in that igloo we made, the thought of whichall made me colder still I hope you can understand that without you take offense.

Our young Donnie Garvin would recall Fernand Braudel discussing just such a near paradox in regard to the Mediterranean regions, where, for instance, inner and upper Spain in winter feels to its denizen as cold as a tundra's wolf woofing winter night.

I knew it would be harder for Rance to bear up under the circumstances, as he is given to volatile (see? I remember some

things you taught me) emotions at times and he was mighty
scary to be jailed in a town known for hangin. And if that were
not all the blanket was about as heavy as a chicken feather by
which I mean light, maybe I should say lighter than a floating
turd, he was near sterical come morn. I hugged and rubbed
and warmed Rance no one give us coffee nor grub and he shook
an cried and tho I myself thought we were soon to be hung I
give him comfort of lies til he fell asleep agin like a babe in my
arms and not at that moment but now I think of our baby by
now come out to see us when you bring him which I hope will
be soon, tomorrow Rance take me to our claim. As I was tellin,
he was a sleep like a babe in my arms and with no reckoning
the cold or night was the high heat of day and gunshots rung
out ever which direction. This maybe gone on for a half hour
before I hear yelling they robbed the bank, which was right
cross the street from our hotel into which come like a devil from
heaven a very dark of skin Mexican fierce lookin like a grieved
wolf with a scar that run from his eyes to his ear which was
part missin and he ask which is my guns an I pointed to the
old hoggyleg he give it to me his men taking the rest of what
was in supply, and he unlocked the door and they went out
but before he left as if he forget something of great import he
turned back stepped to me and I am not joking he bowed kind
of stiff, give me his hand to shake and said, I mean not to be
rude but as you may see we are in a mite hurry, I am Wakeen, I
said, Tom Gravel and he was gone and for some fifteen minutes
more there was shootin, and Rance was alivened up by then,
we found two horses with no one tached to them retrieved what
was left of our gear including the last of my money which the
law of Hangtown did not find and made haste the other way
from the shootin and found a trail that went up into the Sierra
mountains.

Upon reaching Gold Canyon, Rance Hardupp and Tom
Gravel staked their claim, or Hardupp's claim, which was a
couple weeks from running out as it had not been worked
for more than five months; they staked their claim literally,
pounding sharpened cottonwood saplings into the ground ev-

ery ten feet and tying rope from post to post, from the stream back into the mature cottonwoods, a good quarter mile, and then again upstream the same, and behind enclosing a copse of their own. Hardupp's scant supplies had been locked into a rudimentary shed that had been broken into and robbed of every last nail and pan, and what Rance said was anyway a near useless rocker he had made himself, and which was why Gravel was required to buy another one at the trading station down toward Carson Valley at Mormon Station, a brand new one Rance insisted on testing to a point beyond the exasperation of a red-haired vendor of such who worked out of a tent alongside the trail, which was empty as far either way as a man could see yet sold his wares in the brisk manner of a an up and comer and spoke with the cadence of a slow starting engine: "Yer... yer...yer...yer...yer...gonnabreakthatthingnthenallavetapayfrit." Rance pronounced the mechanism fit and more than fit, later confiding to Tom that it was as well put together as any he had ever seen.

As far as Tom could see, this crude yokel Rance Hardupp had concocted a plan that verged on genius. They were stationed on the east side of the Carson, which they would work for gold, but he had also and primarily staked a claim to a mile-long length of the intermittent feeder stream known as the Dry Muddy, which was where the more spectacular finds had been. Ah, but gold is a fiendish bedrockfellow, and a man can't pan a dry stream. Some years spring runoff doesn't fill the Dry Muddy. But you had to figure wherever the Carson flowed it gathered some of the same minerals as the Dry Muddy when wet, and further, if a feller had a claim on the Carson and the Dry Muddy both, when the Dry Muddy was dry, or muddy, he could load up a wagon with a hand-shoveled load or lode and rocker it back at the Carson, a mere three miles away, and if one had a partner, the work could pert near go on perpetual like, in cycles or whatnot or whatever.

Thus did the partners proceed after constructing a small wood sleeping shed back in the cottonwoods on the east and near barren of folk side of the Carson, this one with a secure metal lock as big as a fist, though in truth a big enough fist could probably have pounded through the wood of the door, and as we know today them was lawless times, yet Tom had his hogleg and curiosity was some ways yet from shedding the shards of its peril. Furthermore, the Carson heaved hard east thereabouts, which tended to rile more silt on their side of it, while at the same time, Hardupp had found a stretch of the Dry Muddy that was a virtual mini-canyon, awkward to work for a stretch of a hundred yards or so, having no bank to speak of and narrow enough to prevent two men walking side to side within its confines.

All in all, a fine plan effected, efficiency the watchword, a clumsy pioneering efficiency of fugatory efficacy, if not prophetic of funge, neither feeble. Yet the nights are chill— in the morning they take unthinking comfort in proximity, not only to the cookfire that boils their coffee, refries their beans, but even more to each human other, so that more often than not they set off together up the Dry Muddy, the horse with its wagon, working, and they, after arriving to their claim, take up surveyance, engaging in rudimentary geologic discussion, determining that spot, random despite, taking turns with the shovel. Rest is taken in the relative boscosity of sparse undergrowth between two cottonwoods that split the sunshine, bread and water passed back and forth. No birds sound. Snakes sleep in their hollows, within the drythorned fraggus plants. Lizards dash out silent inscrutable spurts of lives unexamined.

"Reckon we keep loadin or go back and run through what we got?"

"Don't know, Tom. Ain't too eager to larn what we got is a wagon full a dirt, which I already know."

"What's gold but a shiny spak a dirt?"

A pause for thought as prurient doubt hung along the time lull of the long bright day.

"Them Mormons sayin we bein on the wrong side…"

"Jis tryin to run us heathen off with that what the red face one said…"

"'They's fekkin goldconder yonder!'"

"Pointin as if over the range…"

Hush.

Hoof aclop desert rock cancels silence, for here one hears fer near a mile yon such, and there did approach astride horse sheriff lawman William F. Fitzpacker, no Mormon he, though like as Mormon in lust fer mammon, specially now that slaves worked his claim, as he saw it, even if the workmen themselves, Hardupp and Gravel spied neither mammon nor master, were masters in thought of their own leechy seekings, much more mundane than mammon, beans being their manna.

"'Tis some visitor," Rance muttered.

Attenuate anticipatory silence ensued, desertified, draftless, dry as the sun.

Perhaps one hoof was three miles off. Gravel and Hardupp lounged attentive.

Four hooves sounded like two, one betimes precipitate, slapping odd like a wingshot bird.

Closer now, the hooves hesitated between hypnotic clops.

Twin apparitions preceded the horseman, such is mind in desert time.

The horseman appeared black, back to the sun, on a black horse, black through, it seemed, and he from equestrian statue grandeur gazed down at the two men, naked to the waste, dried dust on dried sweat thick as shirts above the waist, a superior position for one who would grant himself hierarchy, as this man of greed and violence did.

"Boys," he greeted them. They nodded.

"I's thank ye fer working my claim, but looks to me like you're shoveling dry dirt into a wagon and I don't right see how that brings me benefit."

Rance looked at Tom, then sprang to his feet. "This here's *my* claim, mister."

"Yes, son, settle yerself, I heard down at the Station how two upstarts had encroached upon my investment. That's why I took the trouble to make me some inquired about you two. I stopped in at your homestead first, of course, and finding the door poorly locked took a look around, but as you

know you were not there to receive me, so I took it upon myself to ride all the way out here in this heat. You can see what
the sweat's done to my shirt."

Tom slowly got to his feet. "What is it you want?"

"Like everybody else around here. Gold. Silver. The
spoils of the earth."

"I hope you ain't suggesting you tramped into our abode."

"Abode. Abode? Is that what ye call it. Yer abode? Why
anyone can see it's but a shack badly shackled. One shot and
the look unlocked. It's a way we have of knocking on the door
of claim jumpers hereabouts."

The first marshal of Nevada territory did not wear a badge,
or Rance would not have made the mistake of telling Fitzpacker he would have the law on him.

"Why, son, I am the law. Marshal William Festus Fitzpacker by name. Hired out to keep order, and that order bein to
tend to claim jumpers and other such of the lawless breed."

"My claim's good, mister—both a them."

"I got six months logged without presence here."

"That's a outright lie, marshal or no marshal. I was gone but
a week over four months. I was off raisin capital as you call it."

"Each to his own calendar, son, but my calendar happens to be law. And worse for you, the next claim up is my
own, meaning this one as well, for what you have here is the
wind-blown, and torrent tossed of my own whilst I awaited
spring run."

"You lie mister!" Rance shouted, and began forward,
whereat Gravel gripped his pants top to hold him back.
"We'll take this to the law hereabouts and beyond if need be."

Fitzpacker laughed heartily, part genuine.

"Truer word never did I speak, fool. I *am* the law! Yet I
am not unfamiliar with the calculus of slavery, and find it not
to my fiscal advantage. You shall continue to work my land,
and as we are three so shall we divide the unspoilt, in thirds.
One third to you, for labor, and two of those thirds to me for
investment, right neath the umbrella of law."

"You will get not so much as a nugget from my claim!"

"You, son. A calmer sort, where be ye from?" observing

Gravel's quieter response and fiercened eyes.

Silence: squeezed, pulsing, nothing of the desert. Silence of civilization away off on the march.

"Speak now, boy, for I will have all knowledge in due time."

"Orgon."

"Best you go back there...But you will not. You take your own counsel, that is your type. You will soon have cause to remember my words: Go...back...there! For you have a half brain, unlike your colleague in scampery, this befuddled, blinded by—"

"Why you scumsuckin pig, git down off yer horse an see who's what!"

Gravel, almost in a whisper: "Settle down for now, Rance."

"Dismount of my horse would be the mount of your death-horse, trespassing claim jumper. Be thankful to whichever your ill-conceived deity I not dismount, rather come with kind warning."

One sees the rattler in disguise in retrospect after the strike: thus did the pistol uncoil from Fitzpacker's side holster and discharge between the feet of Tom Gravel, a statue next to Hardupp, an alit marionette.

"I take not kindly to insult, Rancid Hardupp, the second I happen to know [deliberate ambiguity, this man of careful speech]. Now you got right on the edge. Make mention like again and I shall tear thy arms from thy torso. But it is you, half-brain"—turning now to Gravel, as he returned his pistol to its rest pouch—"who most must heed"—the same hand reaching further down, unflapping saddle bag, retrieving a Colt Peterson, long travelled—"if this be the cause for your quietude, take extra heed, for now tis mine, an insult tax, a land tax, a claim jumper tax, and, of no minor incident, a pistol I have long coveted..."

Nothing altered in the outer mien of Tom Gravel, though the universe he sensed to convulse.

"...and shall now be one with my living legend. My excitement is such that I am near to the point of thanking you, though it be clear you had better remained in your Ore-egon."

The worst of men are as good as their word. Some of the best of the men remain at variance with the world of words.

Thus did Fitzpacker in some weeks make good and be successful on his claim to claim, visiting Rance and Tom at their many locked abode after first enquiring of witnesses to the effect of their successes, rumor and testimony determining a rate of near ten dollar a day. And near seven dollar a day did Fitzpacker extract from the humiliated, behumbled soil toilers, for fiery Rance and becalmed temperate Tom were but biding their time, for reasons obvious enough and further, for recent handbills had been tree-posted announcing a spectacle at the trading post of Neverworth Rodney Haskill and Washington Loomis, not half a mile from their abode at what might seem the mouth of Gold Canyon, or afore where the Dry Muddy wetted its desert tongue in the Carson. Seems the famed gunsman lawman William Festus Fitzpacker would be displaying his pistolarian dexterity for the public at one quarter per head, later to offer lessons as well for a dollar only.

Twas a Sunday. More than 19 workers of prospect, including one female, arrived. Haskell and Loomis had erected a lean-to for shade, and on neath table served cool drinks of fresh Carson River water and various eatables. Rance Hardupp and Tom Gravel were among the spectators as Marshal Fitzpacker drew up at high noon, precisely on time, atop his black horse, sporting a vest backed in red satin with elaborate silk stitched on cotton design up front, painted nacre buttons, along with pin striped pants and a collarless white cotton shirt. He did look sharp. Haskell and Loomis had taken great pains to entertain, fashioning a life-size man of wood, painted red once and white over that red, so that a bullet would appear to bleed (this did not entirely succeed, as the bullets mostly spat interior, unpainted wood debris). The white wood man was nailed to a mature cottonwood tree, the nail heads twice painted as well.

Fitzpacker wasted no time getting started—cutting short the incipient barkering of Haskell, he dismounted and seemingly in flight shot two eyeholes in the wood man. One showed a trace of red if you looked close. He appeared to have drawn a Colt Walker, an awkward piece that brings to mind a homestead afterthought to keep granny at bay, though the aberrational eyesore is between the cylinder and the barrel. Perhaps only Tom Gravel gave that much thought, for Fitzpacker commenced to approach the unarmed wood feller, come face to face with him, walk away from insult, and turn rapidly, withdrawing with his same right hand cross to his left holster, from which he pulled Gravel's Colt Paterson and with five shots drew a straight mouthline beneath the eyes.

Much clapping ensued. Rance Hardupp yippeed and jumped up and down. Gravel clapped politely.

Gravel noticed that as now Haskell was allowed to speak—"How's that ladies and gentleminers? Ready for a more impressive display?—Yeehaw!"—they were—Fitzpacker reloaded both pistols, before firing from about twenty paces, carving a perfect heart on the upper left breast of the white woody man, a heart true, a heart yielding fragments of wood framed by a trace of red and a heart-frame of white.

Who knew what was next?

"Hows bout a pecker shot!" one enthusiast suggested, for example.

Gravel decided not to wait. As Fitzpacker reached into his saddlebag to find reload for the Colt Walker, he come up behind, drew his own Colt Paterson, and before he could stand Fitzpacker down saw that Fitzpacker intended to dispatch him with whatever rounds had been established in the cylinder of the Walker. Gravel's first shot hit Fitzpacker's right shoulder, turning him around, and when Fitzpacker showed sign to turn back emptied the four remaining shots into the lawman's upper torso, took quickly to flight, hopped his horse, tied to a sapling but ten feet or so from the site of the shooting, and, well, went to Mexico, or what was now not so Mexico anymore, but California, though he sought there the famous Mexican, though some said Chilean, Joaquin Murriata, and the trip was not without exhaustion, hunger, cold nights, and sleepless moments visited by gutwrenching longing for Marie Fire and the child that was surely by now borned.

Gravel found Murriata while drinking from a stream outside French Camp, where inquiries had led him to look for the legendary outlaw. Better said, of course, Murriata found him, an anticipated stranger with this danger, scar-faced outlaw in his sights. Gravel recognized the reflection in the water to be one of the men shootin up Hangtown not so long back. The wappling scar on the water surface suggested the man standing over him was Joaquin Murriata himself.

Gravel rolled to his back.

"Tobacco," he said, and Murriata reached into a pocket and tossed a small cotton pack tied by a string near the top to Gravel.

"Papers."

Murriata obliged.

Matches.

These too were forthcoming.

Once he had rolled and lit the cigarette, Gravel was ready to talk.

"Ever hear of a lawman name of Fitzpacker?"

"Might be."

"I killed him."

"No, you did not."

"Yes, yes I did, señor Murriata, I surely did, shot him five times."

"Didn't kill the bastard, boy. Heard all about it. Don't know why you done it, but I sure as hell liked to hear of the effort. But he is still alive, on the mend at Mormon Station, and will be riding this way sooner or later come looking for you."

Gravel couldn't speak for shock, nor could he look with focus, nor raise his eyes above the level of Murriata's knee beyond where he saw approach two black clad legs hip-holstered high up, legs horselike in height, and hair fallen either side down past holsters, for it was a woman he saw, raising his eyes slowly, a woman with a stunningly cropped torso, a thin lipped, weathered face, with black animate eyes, flat or absent of aspect but archesporialtype, reductive, absolute in undisclosed purpose.

"Señor," Gravel began, looking back up to Murriata, "though it were not yer intention, you and your gang sprung me and my pal from the hoosegow in Hangtown, and when I shot Fitzpacker figuring I'd be strung up I fled cross the mountains seeking to find you and join up. I can shoot pretty fair."

"Five shots without killing a man. Is that shooting pretty fair?"

"Not a one missed the shitpig."

"What do you think, Louisa?"

"Let me kill the bastard."

The voice was like lead skimming off zinc, definitive. Gravel was sure his death was imminent, and that the bullet would be in the very center of his forehead.

"Finish your cigarette," Murriata instructed Gravel, confirming the verdict.

Well, thought Gravel, nonetheless bemused, it was an idear.

"I like that: Not one missed. And got off quick, too, is that right?"

"Didn't think about it. I just wanted my gun back, but he turned to fire and I got his right shoulder, and he was about to turn agin n I emptied the cylinder, got on my horse n left."

"What do you think, Louisa?"

"Let me kill the bastard."

"Which one?"

"Both."

Murriata thought that was funny. Gravel hoped so.

"Louisa, if we take in this young man, you may just get your chance at that lawman. But we don't turn away a man who shot a lawman, especially one who has come so far to find us."

"Obliged, señor."

"I will only warn you once about Louisa—never approach her or attempt to speak with her. Got it?"

"Anything else?"

"Use your gun when I expect you to."

And the following Spring, Fitzpacker, reconstituted, did come looking for Tom Gravel. He was not hard to find. Murriata and his gang hit mining town after mining town, robbing banks, big claim-holders, and lawmen, Gravel taking part as any hired gunman would, never firing a shot other than to send a bullet skyward to announce the intimidation of their arrival and the futility of resistance. Of course this scourge was not overlooked by the larger interests of the nascent state of California, whose legislature hired a band of California Rangers (you won't read much about this motley, nefarious crew) to hunt them down. They got Murriata and Three-Fingered Jack in a tussle at an arroyo near Coalinga down south, chopping off Jack's hand and Murriata's head, news of which reached Murriata—and Jack—at French Camp, where they were taking ease between raids, when the jars were placed on exhibit in Stockton. Fitzpacker was said to be among the law gang, which was composed of former Texas Rangers. Of course, Fitzpacker knew a scam when he was in on it, and, after a brief return to the Nevada side returned in pursuit of Gravel, whom he found in a Stockton tavern in mid-August that year.

In the morning, Gravel noticed that Louisa wore her hair gathered into a horse tail, which always meant gunplay forthcoming, though he was not informed of the incipient showdown until the three—Jack was at the bar for distraction, amusement, and, if need be, an unlikely need, back up.

In the midst of a game of five card stud, Tom holding a pair of sevens and intent on taking the pot, Murriata said quietly, "Here comes your man"; in strode Fitzpacker, gun already drawn. Gravel turned, assessed the moment, pulled his Colt, eyes met, Fitzpacker's intent on murder, Gravel pulled, shot the gun out of Fitzpacker's hand, the bullet creasing the thumb, bade him stand still, put two more bullets into the planking at his feet, told him he would live if he quit Nevada and Hardupp remained unharmed, to which Fitzpacker readily agreed, making to hasten away before being ordered still by Murriata, who extracted a more solemn promise, made to hasten away before Louisa bade him stop, rose from her chair, strode to him—Gravel was not surprised, though considered the vision likely illusory, that she stood taller than the lawman—and coldcocked him. Fitzpacker came to in the dirt street under the summer sun not far from his horse. A month later Tom Gravel was back at the claims with Rance Hardupp, who had built from their earnings a two-story wood home with a circumambulate balcony on the ground floor, and sent for Marie Fire and child, instructing them to set out in the spring to join him.

Legend has it that Fitzpacker, though he steered clear of Gold Canyon, did come and go between the general area of San Francisco and the ore banks of Nevada, alternating between gun work and mining, never making a fortune, but engaging in battle with Paitues and courtrooms, surviving to the year 1873 when he died in an asylum in Stockton, his head still attached to his neck, though it is said he survived 31 bullet wounds during his lifetime.

Tom Gravel was taken by influenza the winter after his return to Nevada. Marie Fire and Tom Junior arrived the following July oblivious, took up residence in the house of Rance Hardupp, and remained in Nevada.

TAIL
The Vexing Vicissitudes of Realism

A stroke of good fortune for our account is the disappearance of the Fitzpacker line, for William Festus Fitzpacker left no heir, no bastard, no fortune to be fraudulently claimed by the mulatto child of a white mistress, and thus the reader—and writer!—may drop guard, may cease anticipating with that peculiar combination of dread and glee the return of family intertwined conflict, may no longer need envision a Gravel generations hence in the shit ditches of Verdun, say, without knowing, just knowing, that Colonel Fitzpacker will appear to order Gravel out of the turdous trench into the sheer wall of German bullets, that his son, Judge Fitzpacker, will not plant papers in a pumpkin on the property of the playwright Gravel, call the gendarmes, who will find the secret papers, proof enough of treason, the communist Gravel condemned thus to the gallows, after giving birth to yet another Gravel who will, in full furious fit of fate come face to face with the evil murderer Colin Fitzpacker in Elko, Nevada, on the night of a rare and ferocious hailstorm to waylay him on his way to check the gate of the sheep pen, returning to the homestead to slaughter the rest of the family, he is sure, while the eldest child inexplicably overlooked, the quiet one, little Tom who didn't say his first word until he was nine years old, though he would have been but four at the time of the gruesome events described herein — but now only, not later — so that it could never be determined whether witnessing the bloodletting contributed to his condition, his slowness, such quadriver of event contriving to deprive the townfolk of gusto for gossip, nay, responsible for the letting down of *their* guard, and so the rape, the pregnancy, the hanging of, say it, *they* would: a *retard*, all this prevented by the joie de vivre lacking in the spermatozoa of William Festus Fitzpacker.

27

THE FICTILE AND THE FINGENT

The nipple placement was not all that was illusionary or anti-corporealist about Picasso Tits. As Donnie remembered her now, he could almost imagine her in one of her near sheer dresses that fit her as if she were a pulsing ghostwoman, almost see her gliding over the Pacific waves in the dark that was neither black nor blue, approaching in a sort of drift of foggy flight, approaching, fading, somehow rapid like a gust of wind—and why not? Are there not those for whom the strict logic and lines of transport are far too mundane? Are there not those ethereal ones for whom enclosure violates truths glimpsed in ephemeral mockeries? If so, Picasso Tits, here now on the California sands so intensely desired by the one who was not her lover, is of these mythicals.

Back in Brussels, Picasso Tits was not surprised that she missed Donnie more than she missed Drake. Though not of narcissistic kind, she was wholly aware of herself in the world of desirous men, and though she was too slender to be voluptuous at first sight, she was fully formed and tensile, voluptuous—after the fact, the fact of wide ranging breasts and nipples out where yonder ought be, after the fact of face, fingent, never twice the same, full enough of lip, small enough of nose, and subtle enough of eye that a man once entrapped by tit, could become lost and later in lustry lunging lunglessly in love, for the vivacity of her lissome animacy.

Many of these men, most in fact, would be of a type classifiable only as wanting, perpetually wanting, and would be unable to resist sexuality of greater immediacy. They often returned to her in tears, which she never grew to scorn, for she understood.

Then there were men like Donnie, who saw it all and contented himself to seeing. If ever there were a man to last out her lifetime it would be such a one, she thought, but for the paradox that he would eventually have to break through the zone of separation and would then have to remain, say, Donnie, and she had no idea if that would happen.

She was not surprised that Drake had not actually asked her to flee with them to the United States. He knew it would be a selfish request, and she knew he knew she would understand everything and that including his own understanding of everything. Yet missing them, she felt pain that it was not Donnie's place to ask her to join them, to ask anything about her future, their future, the possibility of a return to Europe even. Donnie would have, or would have been unable to keep the question from his eyes, and he would be recalling her with more tenderness than Drake, who, after all, was a fine man and perhaps the best she had ever been with.

Donnie's thoughts turned, too, to his father, for there was no mistaking his return to his father's land. His father did not fly gossamerly from the black, feet above the waves. His father's feet were always on the ground, stomping, no—pressing, pressing down on a carpet that tended to curl up at the corners, for beneath this carpet were secrets, the truth Donnie was never told. Donnie did indeed despise his dilettante double-doucher dipshit mother, for he knew her deeply, and like his miner ancestors he had found the scoured out gaseous scarred innards to be bare of yield—nothing to proffer, nowhere to go but deeper into despicable depths. But his father was different. Did his father really believe that Donnie hated him for his diffidence, his distance, his desquamatory daddy clichés? Seems so. But Donnie did not hate his father—he resented him, resented him for never revealing the secret that impelled a decent man, and a man of depth and originality, to live in the near death of a demi-lackey to that bitch of a mother, and further, to allow Donnie to reach the age of leaving without realizing that he could have revealed all to Donnie, that as far as his father was concerned that was all that Donnie lived for, the day when they went to the tavern in Nevada, the Green Jockey, on a Saturday afternoon in spring, shot a few games of pool, during which a few hints would be dropped, before the bellied up to the šank, sit down, son, two beers, I know you've been waiting for this day for a long time, but once I tell you everything you'll understand why I had to wait, of course your mother must never know… But his father kept his feet on the ground only to prevent the carpet corners from curling.

Inside the bungalow burned many candles, disguising matter, bestowing an illusion of substance on their mario- nettes of shadow, yet so many candles that the two faces alive with conversation remained undisturbed by the trickeries of light, retaining their opacities, contours, emoting aspects. Across a common plate of victuals from Drake sat Nordgaard, a man of indifferent age, if definitively old, bald, the head perhaps deformed: high and narrow, elongate, without eye- brows to break the wrinkling stretch from eye to apex. He had damp, motile lips, an extravagance, black deep nostrils that glared like the cave mouths they were, betraying no illusion of an accompanying or enabling nose.

His voice was flauty, as of wind given voice by sudden compression, a force of unkempt yearning.

Nordgaard had been with Drake's father since the early days in Vietnam, indeed it was Nordgaard who saved the se- nior Fondling from his coming frag, when Captain Fondling had called in an airstrike on his own men. Now he was telling a story about a battle that occurred before Drake's father had even been in Vietnam, back in '62 or '63, when Nordgaard was a sniper for the ARVN.

What matter if the wee man indulge himself, Drake figured.

"This was a turning point I'm telling of, lo, even if we were the mighty ones yet again visiting on the rebels, the VC of course in this battle, a new instrument of death deliverance.

The M113 armored personnel carrier—ten fucking tons! This was particularly effective because most of our surprises up until then, lo, had come from the air—napalm nearly won us the war, us then being the French. I should point out that not many share my point view, nor am I offering a tactical opinion vis a vis more napalm. But this was Greek fire from the air, and we all know that Greek fire speaks its fear in the pages of innumerable books of history and memoire. Perhaps, lo, it is the atomic age, the beast, beast*most* of bombs, that overshadow napalm as a weapon. Or perhaps among the Vietnamese napalm is still recalled, written of, *memoired,* in the same way as we of Europe recall Greek fire. Hot tar, too, though, ought have its place. Yet it does not. Why? Simply because from the first day a man stormed a high wall, something nasty was dropped on him. So strike that about the hot tar. Nonsense. Anything at hand, not just hot tar, entrails of oxen, yesterday's soup, donkey shit, corpses, scorpions…Therefore here, lo, was a machine all the more frightening for the fact that it crawled amongst them—*and over their hidey-holes in the embankments! Uprooting trees!* Not very big ones, but saplings and the like. And as they conquered their fright enough to maintain a shooting crouch to pepper the beast with bullets that zinged off harmlessly, lo, up from a hatch popped a sniper…or in most cases an ordinary soldier made bold by his newly safe method of attacking the VC. The embankments, they were for dikes, you've seen rice paddies. Dikes everywhere, and the VC hiding in holes in the dikes, or in the jungle vegetation along the dikes. And our 113s could surmount the dikes—they had nowhere to run, nowhere to hide but where they hid. Clever devils. They hid in holes on the dikes, in the side of the dikes, everywhere. Imagine the first VC to hold his position on the far side of the dike, in his perfectly camouflaged hole, holding still, crouched with his automatic, in his mind, lo, the machine will begin its crawl up the embankment and flip over backward—imagine his horror when the machine rumbled over his hole in perfect balance. Of course, imagine that in the 113 ARVN is chasing horrified VC across the rice paddy, and popping up out of hatches to take pot shots at runners, now imagine the little son of a bitch with his hidey hole picking off ARVN unfortunates one by one until they realize they're getting hit *from behind*. He's probably alive to this day, that runt VC, telling the story to his best friend's son, in a bungalow, on the waterfront. But he had a cousin, lo, and this is where I come in, being the top sniper in ARVN. When the 113s scattered the enemy, they would often run mad into the paddies, where they must have endured nightmare horrors of making absolutely no progress while running for their lives, the water up to their waists, before they get slaughtered by raking fire. But the VC were a well-trained bunch, cool headed, and some of them would break off reeds, crouch under the water, breathing through the reeds. Sometimes it was easy to figure: five ran off that direction and we only shot three, where'd the others go? Under the water. And we'd have our drivers rock the big car — they could do that, rock it back and forth, and create waves and the rising falling water would expose these poor little fuckers who now looked so ridiculous, at war and all crouching with a tube in their mouth, heads bent back, and I'd drill them in the temple. They were some of my favorite kills.

I've written a poem about it, lo:
Hollow is the reed of the head above water
Naked is the wearer of wave cloth
Enemy. I shoot you in the temple
You laugh in your eternity
as laughter echoes in my mobile chamber
I have written thousands of poems about war..."

"Each in its time, I suppose."

"Meaning you fear me reading them all to you now."

Drake smiled. "True enough."

"No, not now, not ever. I am old enough to know how easy it is, lo, to be an old fool. I have a poem about that, too, if you would like to hear it."

"Please no."

"Right, about your father, where were we?'

"Donnie! Glad you're back. Nordgaard is just going to tell me what happened."

What happened? Time and distance appeared to have

over-reacted to event, and now after having been met at the airport by the Suave Facilitator, Drake and Donnie were being driven through the disorienting expanses of Los Angeles, when the Suave Facilitator explained that for reasons of safety they were taking a circuitous route (to where?) and would change vehicles twice. At some point after landing, probably before clearing customs, Donnie had already realized, Drake's parents having been assassinated, that safety would require much reason, reason applied to executing his, reason for the executioners of safety to apply to his safety the same standards that would be applied to Drake's. Drake, just as he spoke no explanation for absconding with Donnie months ago on bare notice, spoke nothing of the current situation vis a vis dead parents, dangerous business, next moves, a future requiring the absorption of parents dead by head shots. All he said was that he wanted Donnie with him.

Nordgaard would tell them what happened.

When they arrived at the bungalow, an old man with smooth facial and skull skin standing between three and four feet opened the door; he was barefoot, wore a t-shirt and grey shorts so that his spindly build and enormous limb veins were plain to observe.

"Do you prefer dwarf or midget?" (Drake)

"Call me Lew Alcindor, it won't make me any taller." This was Drake senior's executor, right-hand man, compañero, Rasputin, Sokollu.

Amazingly, Drake had never met him, never even knew his name, though more than vaguely knew of his existence. He was certainly the little man in all the stories.

Not absurdly, Donnie, stepping into the bungalow, flashed on the suspicion that Nordgaard was "behind it all."

"I have their ashes inside," Nordgaard said, putting very little to rest.

Exhausted, charged with renegade momentum, Donnie flashed on Senator Hafbreit. Drake Senior had arranged his murder, he was sure of it.

In the moments of human reaction to oddities, the Suave Facilitator had disappeared and the three appeared to be

alone in the bungalow. Would there be giant vehicles filled
with modernist goons parked a hundred yards down the
street, another outside the guardbox outside the gated beach
community? Would the guardbox be hit by the VC? Or did
he wonder that later...

"Good, I'd like to hear it. Can I have something to drink?"
"Tullamore Dew?"
"I guess you know something about me."
"Yes, lo, of necessity not malice. And I apologize for the
intrusion."
Donnie looked to Drake.
"If I had thought about it, I guess...but I didn't."
Drinks. Low chairs, attentive bodies leaning forward,
three men slanting toward each other.
"There's little doubt who was behind it, Drake: Dane
Frot.
Your father encroached on his business every chance he got.
They knew each other from Nam, hated each other
there."
"I know who he is."
The two looked to Donnie, who shook his head.
"Ran Blackwater."
"Right."
"Did he ever tell you the Frot Nam story?"
"No."
"Better you hear it. This was '69, when your father was
special forces. Frot was special forces, same rank. What they
called Vietnamization had begun, though it was more an im-
minence at the time. For it to succeed, the architects knew
two things: the north would have to understand that the time
of reason, such as it was, was over. They were dealing with an
utter madman who valued his own life and none other and as
such would bomb anywhere and everywhere at an intensity
greater than ever until the enemy brought acceptable peace
proposals to the table. On the ground, lo, the terror would
both have to increase and appear to be relentlessly closing in
on higher ranking Congminhs. That was your father's job, to

conceive of and carry out operations that would strike terror, reverberating terror, into the fiber of the enemy. In a way, it wasn't a hard job. The horrific had long been a fact of that war. The hard part was ratcheting up the horrific. This would require creativity. No cock and balls stuck in the mouths of the dead would do. No tits carved off mothers, no bamboo staves shoved up the cunts of virgins. That stuff was old. The solution was rather obvious. Surprise. They had to get close, closer than the enemy thought possible. This would require action in the north, since security in the south was always lax, duplicity the norm. By the north I don't mean Haiphong, either—too easy.

Escape by boat is always comparatively easy.

"I don't tell this story to aggrandize myself, but because the action was in the north, I, who could appear as Vietnamese as Ho Chi Minh and know the languages, was able to move relatively freely throughout the country and was expert at intelligence gathering. I will tell you how this all came about some other time, lo. But suffice to say that north or south, Hanoi or Saigon, the typical Vietnamese looked at me and saw, lo, a hick, a sad, poor peasant of the hills. My height? Given my slender build, my height was generally overlooked. I am no hunchback, nor seized by dwarfism. Allow me to interject one poem, lo:

You think you know what is an eye
Your eyes, you think, see
But you think, you think
Do not think, and your navel sees
We look eye to eye
And it is I who does the thinking
It is I who sees

"I trust you understand. What I wish to emphasize is my necessary role in these northern conspiracies of terror. Your father, Drake, was a very intelligent warrior. Unlike almost all warriors who fought the Congminh wars, he never, never, lo, underestimated his opponent. As such, in this context, he paid special attention to the best fighters on the enemy side. One of these was a northerner who was one of those who rejected the Hanoi line in the mid-fifties or so, and went south to continue the resistance. He was a master strategist. Ngu Cao. From a village near Hai Duong, a city in the delta halfway between Haiphong and Hanoi. First you must understand that this entire region was red and had been since before the war against the French, probably before World War Two. Almost any enemy activity would be conspicuous, but as your father pointed out, at the same time any personal enemy activity would be entirely unexpected. Security precautions would be taken, but the human element of inadvertent, unconscious laxity would also avail. This we could not factor into our plan per se, lo, but we could expect a greater chance of success. Most important of all was intelligence. Periodically, main leaders from the south would be called to Hanoi for general strategy meetings, as before Tet. These we always knew about. More important, we knew that Ngu Cao would send an underling to Hanoi and he himself would visit family in his village near Hai Duong. Our plan, therefore, was to strike a fearsome blow at Ngu Cao and particularly his family when we learned of a great strategy meeting being held in Hanoi in the spring of '69. Special forces had operatives who could pass for northerners, or were northerners, trained as well as any American. Both your father and Frot would infiltrate the delta with a cadre of five, not including me. As a sniper and intelligence agent, it was important that I never be seen on a mission. But I would be there.

"When Ngu Cao had the opportunity to visit his extended family, it was a festive occasion that had to remain quiet, of course. But it was important to him, for in perhaps fourteen years he had been home fewer than five times by my calculation. He did not return to the north personally for the planning of Tet. The family gathering would not be held in the village itself for fear of bombing, though I very much doubt that Cao feared that his movements were known. For the most part they were not. We were just lucky that there were certain nodes attaching to him. In the south he was as elusive as a jungle snake. Half a mile from his village, there was a Confucian school just big enough to host his family gathering. The school was in an area of rice paddies, but for a kilometer or so in every direction was surrounded by foliage, a sort of thought environment for the students that was sacred. A dirt path went in and then out of this little jungle. Both entrances or exits would be well guarded. How would we get in? How would we get out?

"Suicide missions are really not so frightening, after all. Guards would also be placed outside the school. The only way was to enter the jungle, making our way through rice paddies, enter the jungle, find the clearing, and exit the other side, without alarming the soldiers guarding the road. Once we assessed the guard situation at the clearing and quietly eliminated them, we would probably cause a great deal of screaming that we could not be sure would be heard but had to assume would be at the entrances to the jungle. We determined that we would have fifteen minutes to carry out our mission before we would have to flee. Your father would lead the mission into the jungle. Frot would lead the covering mission on the other side of the jungle. If we managed to succeed with our mission, we had only a forced march through rice paddy terrain of between 20 and 30 kilometers to reach forested mountains to the northeast, from where we would make our way to the coast to a secluded spot between Ha Long and Quang Ninh, a journey for which we allotted ourselves a week, given the terrain and need for utter invisibility.

"So Frot really had the easy job. He and his men would choose a spot halfway along the line where jungle met rice paddy and simply wait. If all went well, lo, our team would meet them and we would quietly scamper off, mission accomplished. Frot fucked up. First, he was careless of his position, making toward the jungle not 100 meters from where one end of the road entered, an area swarming with soldiers. Second, he gave us away by tripping onto a dugout on a dike. One of the men shot the soldier inside who had a radio in his hand. At that point, he fled with his men, figuring the entire mission was fucked. His third mistake saved us. He was about ten minutes late.

"So our group reached the Confucian forest. We made our

way to the clearing. Five guards were in front, two in back. Your father and I shot the five in front while two of his men knifed the two in back. No one inside heard a thing. Your father entered alone. In the school were perhaps fifty people. One of them was Ngu Cao, of course. This is terror. Deep, deep, deep inside your home territory, at ease with your family, a white man strolls into your sanctum, and, lo, the end is at hand. Your father walked in alone for effect, but his men soon came in from all sides. Two of them grabbed Ngu Cao. Your father ordered his eyelids sliced off. Then he took a pistol and went from frightened woman and child and whatever range of men, and, lo, he yanked them by the hair and shot them in the brains in front of Ngu Cao. After something between ten and twenty of such executions, which included the wife of Cao, lo, your father ordered the slaughter of the rest, followed by the slaughter of both of Cao's legs below the knee. He personally put at least ten bullets in each leg. Then we took off into the jungle. As we neared the paddy we could hear much shouting, a few rounds fired. Peering through the foliage, we could only see a swarm that was about to turn its fury back toward us. We saw no sign of our comrades. There was nothing to do but work our way back through the jungle, try to avoid the clearing, come out the other side and hope we could leave the way we came. Whichever end of the road these soldiers came from, it was certain those at the other end would be heading toward the school. Remember, lo, we didn't know if they would hear our automatic fire. They may have already been alerted.

"Your father and I stuck together, one of our men was hit and dropped beside me as he ran. The others we lost track of. Presumed dead. We encountered no one, slipped into the paddies, quietly made our way away.

"Before dawn I found a village I was familiar with, where I was known as a traveler and trader. I was given shelter. Your father hid during the day, spending miserable days in the heat, beset by insects, in bushes where he could never be sure he would not be seen or pissed on. No patrols came through. We hoped and assumed that the enemy was on the trail of chickenshit Frot and his squad. Of course, that settled one matter for us, lo—no escape route. We would have to improvise. We did. We travelled by night, slept by day, stayed in a few villages, and in a couple weeks made the jungle mountains south of Ha Nam.

"Much later, in Da Nang, your father came across Dane Frot. Frot didn't know he was at the base and his first involuntary start told your father all he needed to know. He heard Frot out, heard a story not unlike the real one—they were fired on, who knows what happened, figured we heard the firefight, no choice but to hightail it out of there, flanking movements both sides, not a second to lose. How many dead? Lucky group. All survived. None wounded. Frot twisted his ankle and made the forced march on that the whole way, using a bamboo staff for support. Behind a dispensary your father nearly beat him to death. I wasn't there, and your father sometimes doesn't tell much detail, but I could well enough imagine. And his profile is known for the broken nose. At some point, he tired and the notion entered his mind that Frot need not die then and there. He often told me himself he regrets not finishing him off with his fists. A poem, lo:

Left to die
Why inflict this redundancy on me?
I who have slain boredom
I who have slain your demons
I left to die have become your demon

"That is one of my favorites. I hope you like it, as well. At any rate, now you know the origin of the conflict between Dane Frot and your father. Surely you know much about the competition between the two in recent years, particularly in Iraq and Afghanistan."

"Yes, quite a lot."

Slowly Nordgaard turned his head toward Donnie, his eyes steady in their bloody white globules, as if incapable of independent movement.

"Does any of this make you uncomfortable?"

"Not that I know of. Not to any extent that I know of. Perhaps after I catch up on my sleep. I take it that soon I will be made aware of the extent, if any, of danger Drake and I are in."

"Yes, lo, that is a question we need to assess. First I would like to describe what I can about the circumstances of the deaths of Drake's parents."

"Please."

"Refill."

Refilled.

"Drake, they were shot once each in the head from about five hundred yards, from a tree up the hill. It was a high-powered sniper rifle, no point going into the details, but the kind of rifle you don't miss with, don't have to be an expert. However, lo, we believe they were marksmen—experts—hired by Frot. Much remains to be understood. The view from the location the shots came from is obscured, by design, by a row of cypress trees. A very narrow gap between two of them from that angle would allow an open view that would allow such shots if the car stopped exactly where it did, so that as each head rose from the car both would barely be within the range of sight. It was as if your father was in cahoots, lo, with his assassins. What is remarkable most of all is that he stopped the car at all, I mean outside the gates, which is something he never did as an elementary security precaution. Guards posted saw the bodies fall. No one heard the bullets. These guards have been questioned and have no idea why your father stopped the car when and where he did. As far as they could determine, there was no reason to do so. There was nothing wrong with the car, with the gate mechanism, which anyway can be controlled from a manned sentry box within the gate if something went wrong with the mechanism in the car. The car is fully bullet proof, so at that point the only thing that could have killed your father was a bomb...unless he stopped the car and got out. If you care to, I can take you there and walk you through it—"

"No."

"Well, what—"

"Maybe..."

"Lo, it is something to think about. There is very little else to tell you. The assassins escaped. A car waiting nearby no doubt. That isn't the kind of neighborhood you can easily move through on foot. Virtually every house has security. The property the assassins were on was vacant and the alarm system disarmed. An elementary job, simple security system. The chance of the killers being identified, captured, etcetera, is very slim. A detective, Schneider, has been assigned the case and we are in touch. He knew your father and liked him. He is good enough, but this is simply an impossible case to solve. The killers were not local. Likely they trained in Carolina at Frot's facilities. They probably spent time in Iraq and various other countries. Their resumes would read like many of those of our own people and like dozens of Frot's. In any case, lo, it is Frot we want, for there is no doubt in my mind that he ordered the assassination. Without a secret tape turning up or something along those lines, a disgruntled employee close to Frot approaching us, say, we have no chance of proving that it was Frot. Therefore, ipso facto, this is really not a matter for the law, but a matter of revenge or revenge foregone."

"You asking me a question?"

"Not right now, but that is the question, and you, as his heir, will be the one to decide. I am prepared to execute your will. And speaking of wills, executing them and such, lo, it is I who have been named executor of your father's will. Well, lo, and your mother's will as it turns out, for in this event what he left her he left you. I won't complicate. Various provision are made in the will for his employees, for their pensions should you decide to dismantle the company, something he foresaw as a possibility given that it was not your line of work and was not likely to be. It is set up to run itself—I would be CEO until a re-placement could be decided upon—but he wanted you to feel free to leave it all behind as well. Much of what I have to tell you is not the kind of thing that is found in a will. For instance, he wanted you to know that despite appearances, he was not emotionally attached to the business. Furthermore, as you will see, he did not need the business to earn a living. Your father, your father, lo, formed the company to provide employment for some very difficult to employ friends, comrades in arms... The world became the kind of place in which such companies thrived. When Blackwater became big, your father did all he could to damage it, though with Dane Frot at the helm the company did quite well damaging itself. But, again, the world is the kind of place where such men thrive. Your father delighted in being a thorn in Frot's ballsack, as he would put it, but he knew that that was *all* he was, lo, a thorn in a ballsack."

"I can certainly hear him saying it."

"Lo—Mister Garvin—"

"Donnie."

"Feel free to stay or leave, drink as much as you like. Please feel free and comfortable. You may also ask any questions that arise. Drake has already informed me that you are to be trusted and nothing is to be kept from you."

"Does that do me any good?"

"Comes down to it, Donnie, I think if you're fucked at all by this you're already fucked. If you know what I mean."

"I do. I'm not concerned. But I do wonder…it's an obvious thing, but…pardon the cliché, but is this not, this assassination, possibly an inside job?"

"Long story short, lo, absolutely not. I can explain in detail if you would like."

"No no, good enough. Go on."

"Your father, having engaged in this business, found delight mostly in getting Frot riled. He often pointed out that it wasn't fair in that Frot could not in the least disturb your father while at the same time your father was virtually a daily nightmare to Frot. Frot sued when Blackguard was formed, but your father had anticipated that and had the legal question completely locked in before the suit. Not enough colors to go around, and, of course, a blackguard is a blackguard, a thing, a person, it has meaning—how can it reasonably be equated with Blackwater? In fact, as your father had his lawyer point out in court, the very name Blackwater was rather senseless in comparison, for as much of the work of the company was in fact guarding…And, surely you know a great deal about the Iraq years. 90% of the contracts Blackwater lost went to Blackguard. Remember the slogans? 'Blackguard: Our Business is Security, not Publicity.' 'Blackguard: Protection is More Economical than Killing.'"

"No, that one was mine: 'Blackguard: At the Intersection of Safety and Savings.'"

"Right, he chose yours over mine. I remember."

"But there were others, several along the lines of yours: 'Going About Our Business Quietly So You Can Go About Yours' type of thing…"

"'Criminals Fear Us, They Don't Work for Us.'"

"Good one."

Enough candles had burned out that the light was much the same as the color of Tullamore Dew.

"I can feel it now," Drake said. "Can you hold on a bit longer?"

"Why?"

"Best to get the financial aspects out of the way. Not in detail, but enough so you can begin to give it all some thought."

Drake's face reflected the oddity of the request, but amiably so.

Donnie felt now as if his physiology were dependent upon Drake's.

"Sure, Nordgaard, go ahead, then."

"Where I was headed, lo, was toward stressing that your father did not need the Blackguard business. He was already making a fortune from the military. This is a secret of the state variety, so probably Donnie should leave the room, but I will settle for a sworn…"

"I promise."

"Yes, lo, call it what you may."

"Don't tell anybody. Anyway, Nordgaard, you, sitting here, you've casually testified to the fact that my friend's father is a war criminal many counts over. I have a lot to keep quiet about. And I don't think I'll feel morally compelled to disclose any of it. What's a single state secret to me?"

"Precisely."

"Precisely?"

The quiet imbuing the room was turning the color of Tullamore Dew.

"Well," Drake prodded. "I got the war criminal part and I'm still listening, so while we can endure, please get on with the rest."

"Yes. Where to start…Why not. Area 51."

Both young men laughed.

"Yes, Area 51. Why not. It does exist, you know."

"So it is said."

"And so it does. Your father has been there more than once. He had a good friend stationed there. I won't say which branch of the government, but a close friend I also happen to know from Vietnam. He had become a very important, a very powerful person. He was in on the drone project from the very beginning. Your father was up there with him, drinking at Sam's Bar, lo, and they were going over the drone idea, back in the earliest days, and your father, shooting from the hip, happened to mention that this thing, which as far as anyone had yet conceived would look much like an airplane, ought to be blind, that it would be all the more fearsome were it to be blind—that is, windowless. His friend had made a sketch on a bar napkin and it had windows, and your father quite naturally asked why it needed windows if there was no pilot. And he imagined how it would appear to its victims, the extra bit of terror it would inspire by appearing…further removed from humanity, I suppose you could say, he conceived of a monstrous insect face, which is not so far off what ensued. It was a brilliant idea, lo, and he was credited with the patent, the patent for the windows, or lack of windows. A funny way to make money, really, getting paid, in effect, for something that does not exist: the windows of the drone. I don't know the math off the top of my head, lo, but you can imagine—the expense of those weapons, and a percentage of each one made. Your father, Drake, was a billionaire. You, Drake, are now a billionaire."

"Well," Drake drew out his response thoughtfully, "I figured I'd have enough to get by."

28

A FACE FULLY IMPOSED

Maybe love is a viper with a head on each end, no tail, and so when it, meaning love, dies, what actually happens is one head detaches, and leaves behind love with a viper's head and a tail, a head fully envenomed, a tail blunt and void of signal, love lone remaining, facing the world alone, fanged, vicious, demi-dulled to days gone by. Surely if love is indeed a two-headed viper, it is other snakes in other cases as well, with two heads—we know of love as a two-headed anaconda, of course, being probably the most common of loves.

Yet if Languideia fancied herself a viper, fanged, venomous, unloving—though she did of course still love—Garvin fancied her a different beast no less deadly: a large-mouth bass with vast and motile lips that could unhinge its jaws and take in his head entire. She was not an anaconda, for he was absolutely certain he was a different species of creature, from a different central era, one of them a vestigial the other a precursor, having in common only their inability to be what they were supposed to be.

She's underwater, therefore I must be...bubbleless words she swallows to my earless fishhead, windblown tresses sea swarmed and swirled, blue eyes she fancied hazel for fathomless...fathomless?...fathom this: a bass aswim across the room with a human-type nose, nostrilly, pert, and pert too her breasts still, once never still, nipples now larger yet never not large, waist mermaidenly slim, leverages of labia, long lobsterial laughs of labia, loosely, lobely lubber's labia, labottom cracked as they do, swell again, not yet shrunk, skirts yet flowing and swinging both, legs of lore poetic, fins unfinished, fanning as if to propel lips that yet perpetuate their proprietary tropeees, this trophy trollop making mirth if she but knew, a swell swept her hair past earfins therefins far-from fairfins, terrafins Mesozoic which would explain much of over the years the lack of hear in ear, not gray hair in ear, no, tis optically illusive, she being much mirrored not one to miss a sprout of age asproutinear, nearing now in full flap of lip, basslip not slipping teeth agape not yet gripping, Garvin sees in the seas the fishmist in shark-mouthed blood frenzy, fuck she's going at it, ain't she?

"Let me get that," Garvin interrupted.

"Hello."

"Mister Garvin — a miracle!"

"What! Strut?"

"Yeah, it's me: Clay Strut. My old man found your son. He's here!"

"What? Where here?"

"Vegas."

"Vegas? Donnie's in Vegas?"

"Yes, your son Donnie's in Vegas."

"Where in Vegas?"

"I don't know, but he is, he's here. Look, Mister Garvin, I'll be back day after tomorrow and I'll tell you all I know."

"Tell me now."

"He was in Brussels, then LA, and now he's somewhere here. That's all I know aside from the details."

"What details?"

"Look — I'll be there day after tomorrow."

"I'm leaving tonight. What details?"

"He's been travelling with a guy named Drake Fon-dling — Fondling's parents were killed he came back to LA with Fondling and now he's here."

"In Vegas."

"Yes."

"But you don't know where — give me your old man's number and address."

"You have to go."

"I'm not going anywhere until you answer me." Garvin leapt to his feet and gripped her upper arm. "The answer is fucking sue me if you want. You make more money than I do, you got the house, you got custody of the sweet little girl we made until she comes to her senses and seeks to regain her sanity, so fucking sue me but you gotta get the hell out of here now. I gotta go."

And so was shut the door between them.

29

FARO

[Second card up: two of diamonds, paired his two]
[Five bucks.]

Casanova dealt faro. Maybe it was different then.

Certainly the dealer did not always win. Eddie Vegas liked five card stud.

The first midget he found working in a casino was dealing five card stud to a table of four, before Eddie made it five.

His first hand he got an eight down. The two men to his immediate left both wore straw cowboy hats, had fat bellies and turquoise belt buckles. A mother and daughter, both in orange sweat pants and shirts, made up the rest of the quintet. The ante was five dollars.

A seven came up next.

The midget was dwarfist, with the pudgy finger and forearms that implies, and he stood on a small platform that likely was not designed for that purpose; he had to helicopter the cards a long ways and did so expertly, which, Eddie figured was why he had gotten the job. He imagined a midget, the same size, years younger, eleven years old maybe, flinging cards for hours on end.

The midget flung an ace and a six to the ladies, and a two each to the cowboys.

Ace bet five, all followed. Someone probably paired a deuce.

On a ten with no pairs showing Eddie raised the five five and the first cowboy to his left dropped. The rest kicked in.

Soon an ace, nine, and five was up next to a six, king, jack, Eddie's seven, ten, eight.

The cowboy showed his deuce and a pair of fours. He raised Eddie's raise and all called.

Eddie's next card was a nine, the older broad's was a three, the younger paired her six, and the cowboy received a jack. He didn't have a two, or if he did, was not confident with two pairs. Eddie raised the fours ten bucks, the idiot folded, the ladies folded, and Eddie had the pot. Now he could play for half an hour without losing.

The simplicity of Faro, the, not to be unkind, lack of *intricacy*, of the game, along with its extreme popularity in days gone by, suggests an innate *need* on the part of the human species to gamble.

30

FARO

[Second card up: jack of hearts]
[Kick a buck. First hand kicks four. Called.]

Given the vagaries and all, deaths from faro probably exceeded deaths from poker. As the west tamed to profitry, so ordered lawlessness, and by then faro was near extinct. And as for the old world, duelism was long the rage for raging losers at faro, a game designed, it seemed, for cheating dealers.

Eddie Vegas had other reasons for being armed. The first was that he was in Vegas, where it was good to be armed if you were roaming the streets of the downtown and strip zone in a particular or predictable pattern, as when looking for someone. Another was that he would be driving an automobile in Vegas, where the size of the vehicles was as large as the bloated deranged masculinity of the imbecilic drivers who bored through stoplights and blamed others for the very miseries brought about by their own deranged bloat of imbecilic masculinity. People got shot for no good reason in Vegas on virtually a weekly basis.

The third reason, the main reason, was history, a past, a shady past, a violent past, though in essence Eddie Vegas was a peaceable man. But then again so was Mel, and look where that had gotten him. Look: Mel, gunning down an undercover cop in a parking lot over a dispute between, in effect, shopping carts. Witnesses saw the cop go for his gun for no good reason, and Mel therefore did time for other crimes, petty raps set up for him by a corrupt law enforcement clique, imbecilic, bloated, deranged.

The first place to look for someone in Vegas was in the popular casinos, meaning first the strip. That meant a lot of walking, a lot of encounters with lives that pressed on a lone man their otiosity, their perfumes and bermuda shorts and little white socks, and paternal duck parades, along with silk shirts and short dresses, not to mention the uniformity of dress donned by employees who managed to arrange their faces into looks of dignified indifference, schadenfreude withheld.

But worst was the lighting, the rank amber of false timelessness in places where time was more necessary than elsewhere. He soon found that his eyes were good for three or four casinos at a shot before they began seeing the same people again and again, losing the ability to distinguish features to such an extent he could imagine all, male and female, becoming one multiplied by something that probably had to do with the key to a winning keno card.

Then he would have to find a place to drink, preferably outside a casino.

The Mirage was the fourth casino he entered on the second night of his search, and he knew he was pushing it. The rule of three had yet to be established, even as he knew it would have to be. Yet if he were intent, seriously intent, in his search, an extra ration of fortitude would be required on top of the requisite patience.

There was that tall guy in black again, for the fifth time, playing blackjack, his lank and long hair and sideburns down to his shoulders. A midget dealt to him and—Christ!— there's a guy with the same fucking shirt Eddie was wearing. He wheeled about, feeling faint, disgusted, hating himself hard so he would not hit somebody on the way out. The shirt would be in the trash as soon as he hit the motel.

31

THE RAT OF THE NAM YUM

Mixed drinks, bars of languid light, lackluster, anti-lambent, located on boulevards, bartenders with pimples or sleeveless motorcycle jackets, lone women in green dresses that cover the knee.

Men without suits failing for lack of suit, longing for manly-hattans that would, they are sure, drive away the wrong impression reflected in the coverd knees of the women drinking their cosmopolitans, the men drinking their manlyhattans slowly, grimaces outfeigned into veritably ugly facial contortions that depress the women's thighs that would rather remain crossed and still, but are signaled that they must move on, perhaps to Arthur's, five blocks away and virtually identical.

A week in LA and Donnie says, "This can't go on."

And Drake knows precisely what he means. "I know, I know…it just isn't the same."

"Of course not, everybody speaks English—which diminishes our own, if you know what I mean."

"Know what you mean? I hear us, of course I know. Look, I could go back to Brussels tomorrow, but…"

"Yes, of course, but I have to say it, especially here, and now."

"What do *you* think I should do?"

"Like you said, if it was only your father it would make sense, but your mother, what was the need? And I add, as you know, was there a reason? Any reason at all. And of course, if not, how can that simply be accepted. I won't say unavenged, but accepted without action? That's why we use the word quandary."

"My mom."

"Yes, your mother."

"My mom was…tolerant—I mean towards my dad. To-wards everyone else she was just plain good. Nothing up her sleeves, you know? She had good friends, normal friends, card playing friends, bridge and the like, and she knew enough that she thought it wise to quietly give to charities. She *paid taxes*. What kind of woman is that? Not one that gets a fucking bullet in the head. I mean, politicians can get murdered and 90% deserve it, but you don't fucking assassinate my mom. My mother. A woman without a job, without an enemy, without a crime, without malice, without…*She never carried a gun!*"

"It's only been a week, but, all that about your mom included, something has to change. I can listen to Nordgaard for nineteen hours a day only so long—"

"You don't like Nordgaard?"

"I like Nordgaard. You *need* Nordgaard. But this has yet to evolve into an acceptable change from Brussels and I don't think it will without planning."

"No insult intended, but it's not that you're a target, is it?"

"No. I think Norgaard is right. This Frot is certainly psychotic, but there's no need for a prophylactic reaction to something he already knew was likely to happen."

"*What?*"

"I mean, I doubt Frot's long term intention was to destroy the company—he just had an intense need to kill your old man. Maybe he killed your ma because he couldn't tell them apart— wait: what I mean is that he could never be sure to what degree she was behind things or facets of things and they were so close from what Nordgaard said, no secrets of much import, Frot couldn't imagine just killing your old man would suffice. That's badly said, I know, but I hope you see what I mean. Anyway, I really don't think that Frot wants to kill the ex-king's offspring and all that Greco-grandiosity bullshit. At this point he likely doesn't give a shit about Blackguard anymore. Of course, that's likely to change with any further successes at his expense and then you, maybe me if

I'm around, could be in danger. But right now, no, I don't feel unsafe at all. Except for my innards. I feel my innards are in danger. Only a week and I already feel I'm being gnawed on by bacteria with giant teeth—and splenetic jaws."

"Finefinefine, but what was that prophylactic bullshit?"

"Ah, it's the beer talking."

"No, really."

"Just that he, this fucking Frot fuck, fraught Frot, would only need to kill you to prevent you taking the company over, unless of course he's psychotic enough to want to kill every last gene your father left behind, and that's pretty unlikely."

"I think."

"I hope."

"See? Talking about it makes it worse. Just when you think it's safe to inherit a billion bucks or so..."

"The bright side, then. A veritable mercenary army fully committed emotionally, physically and technically to killing Dane Frot."

"I guess."

The sunset into the Pacific must have been spectacular on this cloudlessmost of crepuscules, the crowd on the balcony, three making them that, all watching its progress as conversation formulated subintestinal; all watched the sun with glancing flickers at the waves in their insistent irregularity, their magic trick of sound grown trite yet not irritating—but neither soothing—not much different, Drake reflected as the sun continued its reflection, from cars passing on a busy street down below an apartment in a city on the east coast. A mood was formulating like the gathering of storm clouds they were lacking, a mood that shrank from light, that would remain on a wood floor as dawn forced the doors, would shrink in the light like a planked cephalopod, perceptibly but not enough to deny its nocturnal shenanigans. Before long dark would be replete with a midst-wave silence that would be broken by the cetaceatic sonors of giant ships, pushing their heavy opacities north towards frigider waters. Then a voice would find itself besieged by night-triggers, brought on by whisky and a whiff of misanthropy if it not be homophobia in its original skirts, and the words would begin slowly to find unseen currents, like pipesmoke, that could not escape the ears of the two listeners, whose need for these words would come as a surprise similar to that of sudden slumber, and a sort of slumbering it would be, a monoformission defiant of will.

"I love watching the sun set into the Pacific, lo," Nordgaard remarked. "The worst days of my life were spent watching the sun set over jungle mountains."

"In Vietnam?"

"Mostly."

A rogue wave brought water up the sand to where it fringed into the light.

"The worst was in '54."

"You were there in '54?"

"Of course."

"Not at…"

"Yes, Dien Bien Phu."

"You were at Dien Bien Phu?"

"Of course—I led a unit of Montagnards…they were my size…more or less, mostly more, but not so much so."

"You fought for the French?"

"Yes, though I hated the fucking French. They were the worst bastards I ever came across. But, yes, lo, I wound up on their side."

Several waves met the sand without interdicting the silence formed by the last words.

"Bastards, I tell you. During the worst of it, not that every day wasn't the worst of it, they decided to charge an Algerian unit with cowardice. Well, I'll tell you, those 'cowards' stood up to the French. Their platoon leader said, "Then you'll have to shoot every one of us, because each man is as brave as the rest." The French backed straight down. Worse yet, if you read about the battle—"

"I have."

"—it's the Algerians who get the worst of it time after time."

"Fucking maggots!"

"Maggots...there's your story of Dien Bien Phu—maggots. There were maggots everywhere. Maggots are worse than lice, for they are bred on death—even if you could for a moment forget that you were absurdly trapped in a valley of death you would see a maggot waving up from some unexpected spot, directly out of the Nam Yum even, breaking the surface next to your foot, to be sure, to *insist*, lo, that you know where you are, that you are living utterly without reason and solely of maggoty providence, that before long you, too, would be sprouting maggots. Every trench was filled with body parts, I don't care what you read about the crowded, unsanitary hospital—there was no way to collect all the corpses, all the pieces of corpses, all the enemy corpses, all the pieces of enemy corpses. A hand to hand fight, and there were dozens of them, corpses everywhere, you think the French cleared the hills of every corpse? Soon as they beat off an attack they were under artillery fire again, or white phosphorous *and* artillery, recoilless rifle fire...human flesh and organs rotted everywhere, and the maggots multiplied in biblical proportions. And the maggots were on the side of the locals. They never went crawling up the hills after the Viet Minh, they went after us. You could clear an area five feet in diameter before you slept, when you could sleep, and you'd wake up crawling with maggots who couldn't wait til you were dead. There were in your ears, your mouth, your nostrils, your asshole, trying to burrow into your cockhole, lo. Day after fucking day, night after fucking night. Every other trench war, and this *was* trench warfare—the French had no fortress, lo, they conducted the battle underground and on the bare hills—you read about rats and lice. In this case it was maggots. Maggots running the battle, and maggots thriving on the dead and stupidity of the French. As for rats, I became one of them: that's what they called us—the rats of the Nam Yum. "You have to understand. We knew war, jungle war.

"And we began to know modern war, disproportionate war, in which one side, in this case our side, had all the technological advantages, the airplanes, the splinter bombs, the napalm, the white phosphorus—we, or they, the French, used it first. They terrorized the enemy at every turn. And we mopped up. Or we marched into deadly jungle battles. But we risked our lives in ways we understood. We knew the jungle, the Viet Minh knew the jungle. It was a fair fight. An honest fight. Dien Bien Phu was a colossal idiocy that made of us a mockery. A mockery of maggots for the maggots to send to their deaths. I was a sniper. And my side in the battle of Dien Bien Phu was no side for a sniper. The enemy was in the jungle and we were on the open ground. Our landing field was in range of their artillery. It was like a game for them, blowing up our planes. And they had artillery they weren't supposed to have — that's what everybody knows about the battle — but, lo, what they also had was excellent air defense, flak and whatnot. The French could do nothing with their planes but drop supplies, and they had to drop a lot of supplies, too, because half of what they dropped went to the Viet Minh. The dropped men, too, and I watched some of the paratrooper drops: man after man floating like a clown, a target for gunners of every kind, riddled with bullets on the way down, landing dead in the branches of trees that had yet to be chopped down and used for firewood. The Viet Minh were invisible; their artillery was invisible. What use, lo, was I in such a case. I had virtually nowhere to hide and was supposed to shoot at an enemy that was perfectly camouflaged. On occasion I could shoot at flashes. But flashes are flashes and by definition they are extinguished before you can shoot them. I got a few. And that was always a pleasure. Picking out a spot a mile away, a hint of unnatural movement of foliage, sometimes hours of stillness, watching, and then the unmistakable appearance of skin, facial skin, between two leaves, skin that has no idea it has suddenly become exposed. And wasting no time I squeeze off a shot and I have another silent personal victory.

"No one on my side knows, and no noise carries the distance even should the enemy cry out — which would be rare, for near every shot meant instant death.

"Instant death...but no maggots. They had the high ground. They had the jungle for hundreds of miles all around.

Maybe they had a leech problem. We had those too. Especially when we became the rats. But leeches were a pleasure
in comparison to the maggots; in fact, for me leeches were a
pleasure of their own accord. I enjoyed pealing them off my
body. I liked them, lo, for what they were trying to do to survive. They were honest bloodsuckers. Compare them to the
French, notorious wasters of blood. Flinging man after man
into pointless, hopeless battle, blood wasted. Blood and body
for maggots, not leeches.

"Of course 'flinging man after man' was a tactic of the
Viet Minh, the 'human wave' assaults, which failed again
and again by body count, yet succeeded again and again
to terrify the French and if more Viet Minh were killed, a
greater percentage, lo, of the French whole were killed, and
the Viet dead did not take their maggots with them. The war
of the maggots was a slaughter, a complete victory, lo. The
French were brave, and so they sent their men to the hills
for slaughter again and again, and every time the maggots
were victorious. "It was perhaps a month before the final Viet
Minh victory that I became a traitor. My men, the Montagnards, the Tai people of nearby mountains, they could have
been on either side for all it mattered to them, they understood little of what was happening and they turned to me
for explanation. Rational explanation was called for, lo. And
what rational explanation was available to me. Who were the
French? Why were they here? Begin there, lo, and see how
far you get with mountain tribals. Airplanes were astonishing
enough, veritable miracles. Why then did they drop hideous
death bombs? Why did they, if they were French, drop so
much materiel to the Viet Minh?

"Why were they left on the airstrip in plain sight so the
Viet Minh could destroy them? Did they come all the way
from France? They came from near Hanoi. We have heard of
Hanoi, what are the French doing there? What is this white
air? From where these bombs? These bullets? You want us to
do *what*? *That* hill, and what is her name? We cannot even
pronounce that name. A woman's name? *Huguette*? That is
not the name of that hill? When men go to that hill, the Viet

Minh attack them in droves—leaving maggots ten-thousand-fold for each body, lo.

"When they go to that hill they are hit by bombs that blow them apart, spreading the maggots far and wide, lo. Why would we go to that hill. We will *not* go to that hill. How was I to explain that they must go to that hill? By that time I was not inclined to. I was inclined to admit: we are stuck here, lads. What are we to do? We will not go to that hill. My boss became impatient with us and I slit his neck as he slept, careful to leave the maggots a wet, dank, inviting environment, lest we be followed. I slit his throat in his sleep and I led my men to join the rest of what are called *interior deserters*—and what the French were calling the rats of the Nam Yum. Most of us were on the banks of the Nam Yum as far north and very near to the air field, which initially provided us protection from the west because useless as the airfield was it was at least an open space and all eyes were on it. Up the hill on the other side were the VietMinh, but they soon learned we were no longer meaningful targets, we were noncombatants, and in addition they could use us, for we were expert at obtaining supplies. With great courage, the disgusted French thought, we who had not the courage to draw maggots had the courage to venture into dangerous areas where supplies were dropped. But of course there was no danger, for the Viet Minh knew of every move we made. And we bartered materiel for food, by their mercy, or if it were food we ate it. We had everything a human sacrifice could want—food, relative safety from maggots—oh the maggots did come, lo, but found little on which to feast and few reproductive zones, no mountains of flesh for their orgies. They appeared, as I said, anywhere and everywhere, but only to remind us of what the humans were up to and how these follies made for them a paradise. And the rats—lo, those we ate. *We* were the rats of the Nam Yum! We had everything, yes, but of course, little shelter from the constant damp, the rain, but little, balled up in holes in the banks, heat—for it is cold, lo, in the high jungle when there is much rain, when the mud never dries. We even had fish. Why the fish had not high-finned it out of there I will never know. Perhaps they were victims of over-crowding, but it is a wonder, lo, to see what a hand grenade in a river pool will bring to the surface, and the taste of a giant catfish grilled in a carefully sheltered fire, perhaps the whiff of grilled delicacy advancing in drifts and coils like white phosphorus towards the nostrils of the starving besieged…And they *were* starving, towards the end they had nothing left, little ammunition, nothing but French courage, which I would define as akin to an automaton walking off a cliff. While all the time, we ate, well enough, slept… slept in discomfort, in fits, some in lunatic spasms, some to wake up dead—it was after all only a *relative* holiday…You are wondering if they were mountain people why did they not escape through enemy lines. Many did, many did. But to uncertainty. Our Viet Minh friends nearest may happily allow us to pass, but from there through dense hilly jungle and cordon after cordon of Viet Minh, what were the chances of gaining freedom? What were the chances of capture, torture, death? Better to wait to the end—it could not be far off and it was *not* far off. Though neither was death. I was burrowed in with a Moroccan one night, we had eaten, we were happy— considering, considering. We went to bed huddled together for warmth and I awoke in the morning to find him dead.

"Seemingly healthy the night before, he was now a corpse. A corpse will not keep a man warm for long. I took him across the Nam Yum and carried him up the bank and left him in the ditch that ran along the airfield. The day after, a rare sunny day, I sat on the bank, contemplating…*what?* Did I philosophize on the condition of man vis a vis hierarchy, animosity, murderous nature, the weak, the strong, the stupid? Perhaps, for long, lo, were the hours and many a time long were the days, the Viet Minh entrenching a strangulating circle about the French posi- tions—if you could call them that. The French on the radios all day pleading, planning, for salvation from the air. More troops! More supplies! Such faith in technology that surely to the very end they believed their technology would save them. And as we now know, and believe me I suspected it then, the salvation was to take the form, some hoped, of nuclear weapons supplied by the Americans. This I feared and so put out of my mind.

"Already it was absurd. Not only Korea, but also the Second World War had demonstrated the futility of air power against masses on the ground, yet for the French that was the key: air power versus masses on the ground. How could they lose? The same way the Americans had in Korea. By not winning, first, and at Dien Bien Phu, by humiliation they would lose, by elimination they would lose, *by the triumph of maggots they would lose!* What innumerable thoughts were available to me as I sat on the bank that sunny day, gazing at the paradox of the ever-flowing river, which the Greek said could not be stepped into twice and be the same. Go tell that Spartan that if it is not the same, it is not much different. I sat on the bank and the sun glinting on the river and I looked just upstream and a glint caught something, a white patch far off, heading downriver, and I was lost in thought, and, lo, after some time I chanced to glance again, and what, lo, did I see, but a great white mass closer, approaching *me*, as I felt it then so that I now grew apprehensive. Understand, lo, that we were all insane in our own ways to our own degrees, or equally so, with but different means of persevering as if not completely out of our minds, perhaps because the environment itself was commensurately insane—and so the mass was come for me! Now when I looked away it was a deliberate act and I was immediately drawn back to the white mass, closer now, close enough I could see now that it was a thing alive, that it was writhing, and as I could see it writhing it had drawn much nearer and I could soon see it was writhing as a population of maggots writhe, and indeed it was a mass of swimming maggots, as I calculated come from the direction of that very, and very dead, Moroccan who had found his death in my proximity, and now was coming to take me back to his maggoty ditch, had sent his army of maggots for me! A hand grenade, lo! I scrambled up the bank in panic and snatched a grenade from an Algerian gangster, ran to the bank and tossed into the middle of the mass while it was yet fifteen meters off, and blew them apart, into the sky, which therefore became our nightmare, a rain of maggots, at the fringe of which was the fire where sat the Algerian gangster and within which was I, I with maggoty guts, and maggots enduring on my helmet on my clothes. I ran mad into the river, up river of the rain, and I stripped and clawed and scrubbed and wiped, and awoke some day or days later, that same Algerian gangster mopping my head in the rain.

"'It's over,' he said, 'let's head for the hills.'"

The waves had risen and by now all three were underwater, contemplating the vast distances and close proximity of events attenuate and immediate that sank neath these same waters.

They conferred on that self-same balcony days later, Donnie and Drake, resisting the fluidity of immersive and cumulate circumstance. A hinterland sun burned into the cool humidity of the sea fringe.

"Of course I haven't forgotten her. I think of her every day. I long for her at night. What did you think?"

"It's just that we haven't spoken about her once."

"Donnie, I know how you feel about her, and that's not an easy thing for me. And besides, none of us have the faintest idea what will happen in a week, a year. For now, though, I need to bring her here and I need to be alone with her. And what I have in mind for you you may find ridiculous, but I have to have some idea what to do with my future."

"I'm not mocking you, Drake. I have no idea what I would do in your position. Probably buy a baseball team and live a happy life. You like to gamble. You want the house odds. You have to do something with your life. Everything in Vegas is absurd, so why not The Brussels—"

"Not *The* Brussels, just Brussels."

"Right, that's better, and all I'm saying is that I don't think Americans know about the Manneken Pis, not enough of them—"

"But they will when we get through."

"Maybe. And maybe you can call a casino The Pissoir and build a giant urinal in front and it would succeed. Probably it would. But you have to think it all through. Midgets working everything but security?—"

"Maybe security, too."

"Sure, up in front of the screens, why not. But what I'm trying to get through to you is that you have to find hundreds, probably, that's a rough guess, hundreds of midgets. Do you think there are that many midgets in Vegas?"

"That's exactly why I'm asking you to go and find out."

"I canvass the streets of Vegas counting midgets."

"Yes. Something like that. Just scout the situation. See if you can talk to anybody about properties. Scout locations. Get some estimates. This will probably be the hardest job you'll have for the rest of your life if that's what you want. Once we build the place, you and me are the bosses and we delegate and do what we like."

"So let me summarize. The Dane Frot situation takes care of itself, you just give the word. Our hands are clean. You have the money to pay off all the pensions. We dismantle Blackguard or, if someone is interested, farm it out, give it away, whatever. As simply as possible we get that out of our way. Then you invest in a casino—"

"We."

"You. It's your life and your money and I'm grateful that you treat me like a brother, but however much I may feel like your brother, I am not, and it was not my parents murdered. So let's at least be clear on this one thing. I'm not talking about keeping a ledger, just being clear that this is your money. Your life. Into which I am invited."

"And you will earn your share by doing simple favors, or in this case, you scram, a more difficult favor, but while scrammed you begin laying the ground work for a pretty grand venture."

"It's all probably a lot harder than you think."

"That's why we hire people—to make things smooth."

"So I go to Vegas and count midgets."

32

NEVER MINED or
THE ORGY OF ORR'S ORE

For the rest of her life Marie Fire wore nothing but soft, light, leather shifts without frills, without adornment, for all that was to her was in her, and a fire indeed remained raging.

But it was as a wild fire in remote wilderness that raged for itself, for its own reasons, raged privately, but for those witnesses who were of necessity warned to flee—those who attempted to get too close, those who did not heed the menemenetekeluparshin of her tribe were scorched. They were but few.

Late spring near about two years after her arrival a mysterious flood wiped out the homestead she shared with Little Tom and Rance Hardupp. They lost everything and nothing, for they had and needed little but the treasure Hardupp was saving, which they retained entire. Good fortune was represented by the need to find a location that would prevent such loss in future, so they chose a spot half a mile downstream on the west side, smack in the middle of the Old Emigrant Trail, where a few others had also got the idea that a might bit higher ground would serve better, and where along there was always need for bed and supply, which was how Marie Fire established the Nevada Overnight and Supply Emporium, the NOSE as it came to be called, and which served always both the best liquor available and the freshest meat, more often than not shot by the Injun or Halfbreed madame herself and later her son too and cooked to outdoor campfire Injun perfection everytime by that same madame or Mister Hardupp himself, who learned as labor lumbagoed him to settle for a different means of livelihood.

From the moment Marie Fire arrived mid-tragedy, which ended an enduring nightmare Rance suffered pitilessly every waking hour after Tom Gravel's death, Hardupp had helped the widow and child with their every need, beginning with home and food and family, rapidly establishing his good intentions unthreatening, becoming a brother to Marie Fire and an uncle to Little Tom. He never for a moment forgot Tom's easy generosity and loyalty, and once only mentioned his debt to Marie Fire, following on which was repayment as need required, including the investment in supplies for the establishment of the NOSE, and Marie Fire in her turn returned the favor seeing that Rance Hardupp was an uncomplaining fool who would otherwise work himself to death from a momentum of origin long forgotten.

Soon the collection of abodes and endeavors grew to be a town known as Nevada, oft thought to be the original name, though travelers had long referred to the spot as Ponderer's Rest, given what there at the mouth of Gold Canyon and by the Carson the choice was whether to continue following the river south or hie it oer the mountains for Californee gold. Other names are in the books, even Chinatown, for at some point there were upwards of eleven Chinee in the area, but more often Mineral Rapids, on account less of rapids au Carson that appeared a mite slower than the moniker would suggest than of the rapid influx, not to say torrent of vermicular sprout, of miners upon discovery that the ore John Orr carved from neath a foot of snow back in 1850 up by American Fork as they waited for opportunity to cross the Sierras represented or was said to, geologists and mineralogists for reasons only they can—or perhaps cannot—fathom, dispute to this day, that that ore of Orr's was a fragment of the Comstock Lode. Suffice that enough traversing through in and over the huddlement about the NOSE was made that a need for naming the town arose in the minds of the less argenaurically febrile, them what took the notion of settling serious, and quickly decided on Dayton after a shifty, lowdown, conman/surveyor name of John Day, who might just as well have been a kindly man of poor lifeluck.

Naturally, this sudden second embellishment of the lo-
cale of the NOSE led Marie Fire and Rance Hardupp to rapidly add to their supplies the fuller array of the mining trade
from arrastra to Geordie lamp. And so they did prosper in
a modest western way, and despite the common knowledge
that Marie Fire was the wife of that scoundrel Tom Gravel, the coward who shot Marshal Fitzpacker six times in the
back, not only did they pragmatically take her for the great
deal she was worth in retaining travelers, the mythology was
tempered by the bizarre common agreement that Gravel had
returned only to die where his hopes were held, that, in fact,
it was perhaps he who prophetized the voluminous veinage
of Comstock ore, for he had gone from ore, ha ha. Of primary concern to Marie Fire this land and life appeared to be salubrious enough environ to raise Little Tom, even if the general community of simple striving folk was oft enough torn
asunder by violence, especially when the growth of the town
necessitated a true tavern, the Grumbler, which attracted its
share of brawls and gunfights, though the violence extended
outwards as at last year's wake for Baldy Johnson, where Gor-
man Brewster met his end at the pistols of Sing-Sing Johnny.
But Marie Fire would have had Little Tommy, schooled at
home, of course, on an intense course of gunslinging anywhere on the globe where guns happened to be slung, and
rifle-trained wherever game was to be found. It wasn't what
happened to her, the death of her husband, and her stranded
far from home—it was home itself, what home had become
in two generations, it was the foreboding everpresent of an-
nihilation, the divisive element at the root of all community,
for even one such has that which burned her roots had it not
that element, had it a core adamance, would yet remain a
community, here or there, one way or another.

Naturally she blamed the white man, despicable breed,
yet she had also seen avarice, cowardice, duplicity and delusion cause disturbance within her tribe, and make not of
it what she would not, a world of the human prevailed, and
she would make sure her Little Tommy had as good a shot—
literally—as anyone, to survive, which she was teaching him

was a very different affair from merely thriving. How many miners thrived in the fifties, especially in Californee, before what was called an economic collapse (the Placerville *Semi-Weekly Observer*) not only broke men by the thousands but prevented the fabled rich of San Francisco from responding in a timely fashion to the good news emanating from the Washoe? She had brought books enough to provide Little Tommy an excellent education within the home to buttress the talents he was developing in the wild. She knew all the main subjects, particularly English and mathematics, better than any man or marm within hundreds of miles, but she did have cause to worry about his general vocabulary in mine-mad country, for the Ophir was soon followed by

The Osiris
The Sphinx
The Pharaoh
The Tantamount
The Catamite
The Dig-and-Die
The Humbug
The Come-beg
The Gould and Curry
The Best and Belcher
The Belcher
The Fast Fading
The Savage
The Übermensch
The Grampus is Fey
The Fudge is Gambled
The Boomerang
The Traipse-and-Tickle
The Mexican
The Graph and Fight Her
The Frightful Gaffer
The Old Gasper
The Try-And-Grasp-Her
The White and Murphy
The Con. Virginia

The Old Virginny
The Sneaky Pete
The Peter's Out
The Chollar
The Gray Eagle
The Columbiana
The Grand Mogul
The Great Republic
The Liberty-Equality-Fraternity
The Sultana
The Golconda
The Silver Slipper
The Samson and Delilah
The Root-Hog-Or-Die
The Treasure Trove
The Universe
The Cosmos The Galaxy
The World-As-We-Know-It
The Back Forty
The Grand Poobah
The Clue-Crux-Crammed
The Maria-Jane
The Branch Mint The Gazilly
The Galore
The Bank-It-Fast

The Kossuth
The Buckeye
The Cattle Might
The Shatpup
The Mighty K-C
The Doublenight
The Doubleday
The Napoleon
The Murriata
The Prussian War
The Pacific Rim
The Paradise
The Hound's Retreat
The Crassmeyer and Floop
The Sydney Stock Exchange
The Fyodor
The Mickey Finn
The Rape-To-The-Finnish
The Occidental
The Succor
The Monsoon
The Sucker's Success
The Swindler Granny
The Croesus's Fanny
The Alta
The Basso
The Dig-Rock-And-Lasso
The Exchequer
The Fereday
The Big Al's Bane
The Utah Straight
The Grimly-Bare-It
The Fiesta
The Sierra Nevada
The Sierra Nevada
The Sacramento and Meredith
The Potosi
The Seven Cities of Cibola

The Onion Soup
The Dayton
The Trojan
The Hardupp
The Hardupp and Liev
The Lady Bryan
The Ninety-Ninth Hole
The Arabian Nights
The Knights of Malta
The Pit
The Stink Pit
The Viper Pit
The Innocent Broad
The Sublime
The Whale-Of-A-Mine
The Scripture
The By-Your-Leave
The Honest Injun
The Washoe Washout
The Hog's Wash
The Justice
The Knickerbocker
The Barren Vixen
The Frigid Trixie
The Niggerboxer
The Hale and Norcross
The Hail Mary
The Overman
The Overland
The Inland
The Underground
The Prosaic
The Mosaic
The Savage
The Blue Marble
The Dakota Jack
The Minnetonka Shuffle
The Bowers

The Plato
The Gold Hill Consolidated
The Piute
The Paiute
The Pharoah II
The Rice
The Eclipse
The Bacon
The Tricolor
The Trench
The Chicago
The Baltimore
The Alamo
The New York
The New London
The New Idea
The Woodville
The Daney
The Trojan
The Trojan Horse
The Sisyphus
The Kant
The Silver Hill
The Seg. Belcher
The Julia
The Union
The Confederate
The Ulysses
The Union Jack
The Jack-Strapped
The Travail
The Draining Vein
The Mademoiselle
The Caledonia
The Socrates
The Zanzibar
The Crown Point
The Crack Pot

The Belsing Inc.
The Kentuck
The Imperial
The Empire
The Innocents-Abroad-And-
Every-Man-Jack-Within
The Statesman
The Cliff-Hang Shebang
The Conquistadore
The Benefactory
The Bullion
The Silver Ducat
The Drake's Revenge
The Andes
The Shaft
The Mein Shaft
The Provisional Irish Argent
Minery
The Speculatory Scottish
Investment Opportunity
The Manchester
The Winchester
The Colt
The Central The Stud
The Golding
The Mary Anne
The Merrytime
The Horseshoe
The Mirage
The Geyser
The Geezer
The Paris
The Constantinople
The Chollar-Potosi
The Gem Mine Shaft
The Mexican
The Bellagio
The New Rome

The Alpha
Los Tres Amigos
The Happenstance
The Neva Mine
The Gold Nugget
The Pygmy
The Padre
The Pope
The Chinaman
The Mandalay
The Caesar
The Nun
The Pyramid

The Square Deal
The Sam Banger
The Grumbler's Folly
The Utah
The Cons. Imperial
The Winnemucca
The Humble Humboldt
The Rock Island
The Confidence
The Guess
The Revenge of Zeno
The Flirting Gusher
The Courteous Usher

The Count, and The Justice, not to mention many more unrecorded or faded from the ledgers prehistoric, some burnt to evade the feds, others to outwit progeny when not death, enough of them anyway to supply a full vocabulary so that if Marie Fire never taught Little Tom a word of English he could have spoken fluent *Nevada Mine* and lived a full, perhaps prosperous life. As it was, by the time Little Tom was eighteen and full grown to a height of five foot ten and a sturdy build much like that of his father, he was despite being rather wild and excessive fond of the out of doors and the horses one rode thereabouts, a voracious reader of any and all books having to do with nature. When he was thirteen he had from a trotting horse drawn a six-shooter and picked off a rattler most would not even have seen, but he had "winged" it, had by instinct gone for the head but picked off a portion just below where the wings had been burned off in an Era pre-Holocene, and he watched the snake writhe in agony — a rattler writhing in agony, flopping about the desert floor, and the felt paradox of these paroxysms stayed with him long and affected him greatly. He squeezed off another shot, the bullet boring through the snake's head and ending its life and death throes, but it was a day that marked him for good. He had no enemies in the wild after that day, and he sought to learn as much of all the creatures as books available would teach. He knew the story of Black Ass and Hector and he even saw bear up in the mountains now and then, and he knew the danger posed by the puma that roamed forest and mountain in their region and he came upon them occasionally, but the only death he caused was to the leporine and cervine, which he did mostly for his mother, though a part of him remained that understood the man with the gun as part of a natural cycle. Still and all, he would not let anyone in the NOSE kill a scorpeen.

And by the time Little Tom reached the age of eighteen Marie Fire's breasts had dropped several inches, her shifts had shrunk, and her hips had added heft enough to press on the material, presenting a voluptuosity naturale that shamed many a bashful eye that caught itself in a state of disrepute that required no external punishment, for this iconotrix of Dayton deserved better than their feckless transgressions and they damn well knew it. Naturally, on occasion a stranger would drift in for a few days, long enough to discover the fact of her widowhood, and such could be forgiven their lust and most of them their advances; still, for the most part these types were warned off before they walked head first into the slammed concrete door of her absolute rejection.

Marie Fire was a contented woman and more, having a philosophical bent that laid the ground for her intensity of patience, for her wisdom sustained between human contacts, that diluted what maternal anxiety is lain bare by raising a single child. She did not particularly dislike people, but for her Tom Gravel still lived in a way she could never describe, that did not resemble anything having to do with animism or souls, and therefore she had no interest in pursuing romance, in restoring sexual experience to her life. The wild west was wilder for women like her—most of them were raped more than once, of course, and Marie Fire was not necessarily safe, despite her position in the town as a known, sensible, helpful and generous citizen. Nor was she standoffish. She had a good eye for a man: no matter his getup, she could detect in any man his circumstances vis a vis work, from cowhand to bookkeeper to miner she knew on first glance whether a man worked for a living or was willing to, as opposed to those, who whatever their pretense, dress, hair tonic, moustache or pearl handles had others do their work for them. Naturally it was one of these latter who after a decade of peace and prosperity enough for most sane mothers and sons invited himself to disturb these gentle people.

Jack Boot was, Marie Fire saw in that brief first glance, a man who no longer did a thing and very much enjoyed that and the concomitant fact of power over others whom he commanded. A wealthy man in his thirties just like Marie Fire, who was a woman, he dressed in the finest San Francisco suits, favoring black and leather from boot to hat, including a fine vest that was cause for much shedding of suit jacket, even in a cold room in dead of winter. Marie Fire also saw he fancied himself an honest man, fooled himself into thinking as much, and that he had arrived at his position through the hard work of brute force. Jack Boot owned The Savage, a mine that from 1859 to the end of 1881 yielded $15,664,162 in ores. He settled on Dayton precisely because it was a growing town yet small enough for the richmost ruthless citizen to run it. He had an immense hacienda constructed a mere half mile from the Carson and quickly became a regular customer and visitor as well as an aggressive purchaser of going concerns. He owned The Grumbler within five months of his arrival, before the hacienda was completed, through an inchoate sequence of events that involved at the very least rumors that were rapidly forbidden speech in the town, following Carl Steel, who sold his tavern, out of town for good.

Boot was personable enough, even telling, albeit ad nauseam, the same semi-joke on himself—that he'd hire a man soon as look at him, which quietly perceptive witnesses took to be a play on a truth of his past he had worked hard, moved far, and learned to act suchlike to put it behind him. Never was it said aloud that he never left a live partner behind, yet twas a sure thing Jack Boot never did. Fear can be bought by a rich man, fear that can shut even the mouths of the drunkest of bitterine men, but it can't snip fibres of fact that flay the very air of lives such as is lore, and his resemblance to a certain Black Jonny McCall, an early 49er, as they say, out of

Chicago, next on record in Sacramento, where mining made money, faro led to fighting, partners died, and posses rode, on up to Oregon and more posses, dead miners, into Canada, faro and fighting and posses of dead miners, back to Californee and posse long left behind a run in with none other than Joaquin Murrieta, who shot him dead in Death Valley in a fair gun duel, so it was said, and if otherwise pondered or knowed it was not sayable lesn ya figgerd to git yer eyeballs shot out by Sing Sing Johnny or Rattlesnake Pete, a couple of hacienda hands oft seen leaning on posts pickin at their teeth with twigs or framgrass looking for someone to look askance at or gunbelt up to the shank in the Grumbler, berth about them a wide one.

Jack Boot called these two men his aides de camp, for he was a more educated man than most, though no one knew where he received his learning. He fancied himself suave, and by comparison in the region probably was. When he arrived to Dayton, he intended to settle down, a gentleman mine owner, who, at the age of 37 was young enough to start a family.

During his initial frenzy of purchasing he met Marie Fire, and the attraction was immediate and possessive. He recognized in her a woman of depth and intelligence, a woman who could rule over a hacienda, a more fit fit for her than a mere roadhouse inn. He was as smooth as the few seconds Marie Fire had for him allowed after she definitively spurned his offer to sell her place, and she was kind as she knew how, if direct, in spurning his offer to visit for dinner some fine summer's eve. But Jack Boot was not one to quit, not one to be spurned, not one to accept inward he was being denied what he wanted, and so his offers and invitations continued, each abruptly spurned, but as he was a gentleman he never left the NOSE without a smile on his face and light of boot, so that it was on the ride home that Marie Fire's talons shredded his innards to the point that when he reached his enormous hacienda he hastened to find offense with the first underling who crossed his path, whom he would accuse of miscreancy of various sort and then beat to within an inch of his life, or, if not, an inch further.

What few knew the tale kept their mouths shut about the time he returned from yet another refusal to accuse a Chinaman who had a hut on his land of stealing a chicken for his family, a man Jack Boot horsewhipped some 200 times *after* the man had died, the orgus of murderous frenzy entire lasting more than two hours.

After a number of years had passed it had become inevitable that Jack Boot would begin to despise Marie Fire, and so he took to dropping in to stand at the NOSE shank flanked by Sing Sing Johnny and Rattlesnake Pete, intimidating customers and making off color remarks near enough to direct insults but elusive enough that Marie Fire could but hold her peace and bear the circumstance, though it did begin to make her miserable, and though she never said a word to Rance or Little Tom, it became evident that the situation was gradually descending into a hellish conflux that would need exceeding violent nourishment.

Not only was Tom full grown he was muscled well as he worked hard about town on constructions and was building himself a corral some miles out of town towards the mountains, for he determined his life's work would be raising horse. Thus it was without fear—thus, and perhaps fear was alien of his nature as well—that one evening when Jack Boot visited the NOSE alone one evening, behaved with a bare relict of civility, Tom followed him out the doors when he left and accosted him before he could mount his horse.

"Mr. Boot?"

Boot turned.

"I don wan you comin back her n botherin my ma no more. You unnerstan?"

Twas the addendum that truly infuriated Jack Boot.

"You little upstartin lump of horseshit. Who do you think yer talkin to?"

"A fool don know when t quit. My ma don like ye, never will."

At that, Boot pulled a pistol for to knock Little Tom about the head. He swiped, Tom ducked, and the gun swept the air above his head.

Tom responded with alacrity, throwing a right as he came up from his crouch, driving his fist square and proper into Jack Boot's nose, which cartilaginous spackled, atomized, one bit about like a toothpick driving up into his brain, the doctor—Doc Toomis—who performed the autopsy guessed, though he had never taken a gander at a man dead from a single punch before.

Word rapidly spread around town—"knocked him so cold he never warmed up"—so that naturally a deadly scuffle was to brew, for Sing Sing Johnny and Rattlesnake Pete would be out for revenge. This did not disturb Tom Gravel, for he was a good shot and he had two friends his equal, the Doc's son Lew and the blacksmith's kid Tim Loomis.

The ensuing encounter would not become grist for western lore, whether fortunately or unfortunately. Even in such violent times, most men did not want to die, and both Johnny and Pete, on coming to know of the skill and temperament of the three young bucks agreed to leave for Californee.

That left but the murder trial, for there must be one in a town designed by such a dead man, the offices therein having been cynosurely filled by cravens of bought cronies. Still, back then law and lawless did oft exchange offices and apparitions, and the folk of Dayton had had their fill of the rein of Jack Boot, so that when Judge Reston Fitzgalloughs began the trial, pronouncing articulately, "Like father, like son", he was interrupted first by Rance Hardupp's "Like hell!", and then by a good fifty more men who took apart the courthouse by hands, leaving just enough space for the next judge—literally a bench and a desk under a twelve square foot shelter—whom a committee of their own would hire.

Little Tom Gravel was found innocent by means of popular approval of said verdict, or, more technically, guilty of nought but ridding the region of rascality.

33

PHANTASMAGORIA

The cyclical venting of surplus or superfluous blood, the cosmologically directed temporizing of her rage in ensanguined torrent, began precisely as Picasso Tits hefted the envelope that held no surprises and that she knew immediately she had expected to arrive just when it did, whenever that would be. Her first impulse was to tear it in half, but she thought maybe even though Drake had left her a great deal of money already there might be some bills in there. This was not cynical.

And there were three thousand dollars in the envelope, not a lengthy love letter; or, perhaps a love letter from a man of taste to a woman of gesture, a cynical woman who yet immersed herself in humangrind. There was also a plane ticket with an open-ended return and a departure date but a week hence. A phone number and a modest greeting were part of the package. If he didn't hear from her, Drake would be at the airport in Los Angeles when her flight arrived.

Her periods ranged from about four days of relative pleasantry, for we all love to bleed, to eleven in times of dark thoughts, and no thought could be more darkling than those that immediately beset her now. She smiled at the thought of a romantic reunion bloodflooded out. That was not cynical.

The word "caesarian" insinuated itself into her consciousness. She knew nothing certain of its etymology, but certainly didn't like it. Never having been pregnant, and so unlikely to be so in the near future she never thought about being pregnant, there seemed to her no reason to have that word in her mind, much less to be indignant about it, other than that she was suffering the onset of an extended periodical misery. Still, a caesarian? Why not a mussolinian? A stalinian? A bushian?

What could be worse than a bushian? Perhaps an attilian, which would probably be done Filipino style, by hand. They say, she thought she recalled, you—or he, the Filipino doctor—can tear the foetus out with his hands and the wound closes right up as if nothing happened. A leopoldian. A mobutuvian? Who was that guy? Lumumbian. Donnie would call it a lumumbler. This could hardly be cynical given its utter lack of connection to her current life. She was not left pregnant. But she was left. And not so unhappily. So why go to the Evil Empire, as Donnie called it? She knew little of politics and history, being but a lass of 21 or 23, a student of art, not a frequenter of cafés that raged with debate, though she had heard of raging debates and did work in a café of sorts.

She thought about history. Vietnam. The United States. Iraq—the United States again. Israel—the United States. Nuclear bombs in Japan? Yep, the United States. She knew who Che Guevara was, an Argentine doctor, revolutionary in Cuba, fighting, guess who? The United States. Apartheid… South Africa. Maybe the United States did business there. Oh—Afghanistan! The United States. The Drake tapes of New York—where but the United States, though that was someone else attacking it. Donnie spoke often of his parents protesting United States involvement in Central America. Central America: Nicaragua, El Salvador, Panama…shit… Honduras, the Iran/Contra scandal! Panama, the canal. Costa Rica. That other one, Belize, the safe one one of the two called it. But what of the rest of the world and its history? Was she ignorant? There was the French Revolution and industrialization. There was Karl Marx. There was East Germany now not East Germany. There was the Soviet Union, now Russia and Ukraine and—were the three Baltic countries former USSR or colonies like Poland and Czechoslovakia? What about the Caucasus, of which Donnie made such a ruckus having to do with the highest mountain in Europe. El Bruce. New countries down there. Georgia, and the horrific one—Chechnya. And speaking of Afghanistan, there were a lot of new stans: Kazakhstan, Uzbekistan where the US approved of the state apparatus boiling people alive. There were other stans…three others…Turkistan, Tajikistan! Fuck it, that's probably more than most people know. But to get back to the point, did she not know a bit too much history of the United States to happily go there? Wouldn't, if she had been asked abruptly, have answered the question where would you, would she not have said India or Morocco? Madagascar or Greece? Indonesia, New Zealand, Borneo? Dear Drake, I have decided to take you up on your offer, with one slight alteration. I would like the destination to be Nepal, anywhere in Nepal, to wherever you can get a reasonably priced ticket.

You might say that it sounds like she knew immediately she would accept the invitation, and you would be right. She did—but not without a gumbo of disgust, disdain, discombobulation, divergent derision, dread, even distemper.

Causation, of course, is quietly cacophonous, and her decision may have been made by that of the jet stream to bolt southward toward Barcelona in this early August, causing temperatures in Brusselian Europe and surrounds to dip into the 40s Fahrenheit, the 8s and 9s of Celsius, while the frigid waters of the northern Atlantic and North Sea had rushed to form massive clouds before the winds made landfall, confused winds of westerly, northerly and even easterly direction, so that a Decembrist misery befell the summer and low pressure weighed heavily on the sensitive, who included among their number serious painters in Brussels. And of course, Europeans had long been conditioned to, when offered up images of California, select mostly those of a sunny paradise first, a violent, highway blighted sprawl second. Picasso Tits, for one, had never read Raymond Chandler. (She often read Simenon, especially after meeting Drake and Donnie, but never located him outside her current region of heavy, wet summer days.)

Nagging, which despite her eloquent English, Setif—we shall name her, as her parents had—misrendered as "naffing" (once, a cute blunder so retained—shouldn't have spoken with her mouth full and a little drunk, or her skull full and her little mouth), is not necessarily disturbance, like say

when swimming a little fish with rubbery nubberies of teeth
has your toe and though is a mere handsizer is trying to pull
you under, perhaps on a dare, one never finds such out, und
zo, for our Setif the darkness that surrounded the crepeti-
tions of Drake's taped plane/building event was a bobbing
blanking burp of doubt draped as dawn darkening darker,
something that seemed to be waving her off, like as if that
fish were gazed down upon in the act caught, finning off the
swimmer with a sort of seedy nothing, nothing, never mind
me, in hopes the affair escapes your cluttered mind, your
gragasping lungs. Yet, and oddly this was never brought up
among the three, there was more to it than that, far more, for
Setif was in the prime buddance of her fingility, when youth
is most yieldy to the raw power of the convergence of dark
truth and great art, a moment in her life perhaps captured
at but one instancing, the viewing and immediate reviewing
and reviewing—seven times in two days—of *The Battle of Algiers*. She semi-consciously fetishized Gillo Pontecorvo, and
I may add as well this at the very moment of surging surcur-
rents of paintery and the like, of daring drawings deftly done,
periodless paintings parsing the pulses of life stroke by stroke,
pushing parameters, purpling parti-prose presciently—that
too convergent. Thus a very specific historicity, not phenom-
enal for a youthful student of the arts, yet brittle of phenom-
enology, was an unsharded part of her being, her participa-
tion, though not clandestine, unspoken, unknown but to her,
fleeting thoughts of Algiers bombs while buildings blew and
fell, blew and fell, planes blew without yielding their eggs,
their napalm eggs, julk!, all over the Kabylia, blew and fell,
desertific, dry, pulverized concrete saharazide, which war
wonderance worried at her with the magi versatility of quiet
anxiety without loci.

What would, ultimately, if not sooner, be relevant in re-
gards to Drake's sole detectable neurasthenia? When he held
the night of fallen towers—Betonnacht—at the bar, it was an
event, if an odd one, and his hours at their apartment viewing
same always ended upon her return—though she knew from
Donnie's occasional remarks that Drake indeed indulged

his obsession significantly (significantly? Well, *now* the word seems to work. It didn't then.) The thought now, and it was of itself without emotional pull, was born of her natural sense of flux: would he quit watching or would he be sucked entirely into the event? Donnie had once made reference to another tape, to Drake's irritance, apparently a tape Drake lost. Yet this was but the bas-relief of her apprehended torment, for there was Algeria, *her* war, and she had just picked up a book about the war in order to practice her English. This was a war forty and more years earlier than the Drake-tape events, Christians and Muslims of her own, atrocities of her own, and if it was not an event to shake the universe as the pounding of Manhattan, it was yet more significant given its time, the minds involved in the struggle, The Frog, de Beauvoir, Fanon in of and around the struggle. The first thing she did when she returned home with the book was to check its veracity. Sure enough: a picture of the obliterated apartment of Ali la Pointe. What she means to think here is that everyone has their own everything, of course, obviously, and speech is translation, obviously, and intercourse is estrangement, obviously, and farts are an exchange of an acknowledged acceptance of mutual suppression of futility, fine, and more than she can or needs to thinkulate, but can a man be, what?, de-speciesfied, or the woman…can mind, miracle human monster, unmastered ever, can mind withdraw the self into separation from species? How odious, how fungal, what a rash if a man and woman share intensely physicals emotionals and mentals only to find themselves of differentiated evolutional fate! A sea urchin crawling into a fortified, virginal vagina. Fie, imagery! A period. Horrific, for it is anything but. What chimerical savageries the agitated mind is eager to fulminate!

Before long, as the bloodtide of thought continued to rise, Setif, without giving the action much thought was packing a small suitcase. She packed her passport in a handbag. She placed her history of the Algerian war in her bag. Paints and brushes? All to be had at destination. But no need to buy new underwear. So underwear it was, two pairs of pants, loose shirts, a sweater, two dresses, socks, sandals. Bloody fucking Americans and their napalm. Soon drones would be in Algeria. Drones *were* in Algeria. She had no question. Drifting from Yemen, or perhaps they were now buzzing, silently, buzzing nonetheless, imploring. Her parents, in the suburb of Hoeilaart, would have to be notified, but not visited. Though, come to think of it a visit might take her mind off bloody fucking Americans. When was the last time the old man drove into a relict of nature, a tree, a pond, a forest, an embankment—demi-relict? Who was mother fucking? Younger? Older? Nice guy? Probably a feckless, gentle dolt. Why would she not return to the city and re-establish social ties, a vivacious intellectual pub-crawling life? Because of *him?* That made no sense, for he was not just an alcoholic, he was mad. He invented stories, delegating himself grandiose roles that bored his rapidly diminishing group of drinking pals. The best thing for him would be to let her sell the house so he could afford friends again, but in one version of one story he was a prideful man on the brink of a technological breakthrough that would make him a sought after computer engineer (again?). Once, according to mother, he had claimed to have invented a refinement of the drone so that finally they were capable of operating at high speeds delivering deadly weapons, fully cameraized and the size of a large bee. The patent was stolen by partners of course. Dutch. German. Walloons. Flems. Even a Dane was once implicated. They met at a bar in Antwerp, a fortuitous meeting between a military man, well connected, who overheard something of technical brilliance daddy said that zipped like a bee-size drone over the heads of his pals. The Dane, or Norwegian, maneuvered him aside. Setif actually remembered that period, at least the trips to Antwerp. The funny thing is that *something* was certainly transpiring in Antwerp—and knowing him, it wasn't even something that made sense like a whore or a jewelry scam.

Perhaps Setif knew that some of her allure derived from composure, a maturity that belied her years, which began developing side by side with her first menstruation, when she

first found herself embarrassed in a tavern by her father's inca-
pacity to grasp the reception of his drinking companions, who,
for an example, despite being able to see as well as anyone
that he was a short man knew that, especially as they lived in a
community frequented by retired jockeys, he was hardly short
enough to have been a jockey himself, and therefore had never
ridden a horse to victory, taking to the rail going into the last
turn, taking the jockey of the heavily favored horse by surprise,
leading both rider and horse to hesitate enough so that soon he
was ahead by a head, a lead that given the momentum of the
underhorse and preternaturally skilled jockey rapidly length-
ened to a lead of five lengths, bringing a thirty-five to one shot
to victory, leading to some rough stuff in the stables when the
gangster owner of the losing stud threatened Setif's father, who
pulled a knife and despite being outnumbered three to one,
two goons and one notorious racketeer, managed to turn them
out, his parting words being to the effect that if he was jockeying
the race they ought to consult him before they place their bets.
Looks were exchanged, laughter muffled exuberantly, and forever recorded in Setif's brain an Irishman calling the race over
and over: "…Dusseldorf taking to the outside, and it's Birdshit
on the rail…" Birdshit on the rail, as good a summation of her
old man's sickness as any, his alcoholism combined with his
subfusc invented reminiscences of preposterous derrings done.
She recalled one other jockey recollection relayed in one of
his taverns—why did she have to be there? Why did mother send such an unfortunate combination on simple errands?
She would rather have walked kilometers on end by herself to
buy cheese—when he failed to notice one of the retired jockeys further along the bar, who, having heard what was coming
drank up and left quietly, unseen. Never a sculptress by volition, in one university course a bust was required of her, and it
was the lumpy backpate of that gentleman jockey she molded,
a planet of decency without eyes, ears, nose, mouth, forehead,
a poxy penetration into the essence of symmetry, an impenetrable, ever-receding decency, as ugly as a carbuncled ape tes-
ticle, as the sleaze of divergent sensory receptors trapped in the
false cahoots of a tavern.

No, she was not disturbed, perhaps a result of a 21st century malaise, she was not disturbed, in those moments when
she wondered whether her lover had similar gonfalonic ir-
ruptions or galloping internal diatribes that were as horse
races in the intestines, brain-called, illegitimate or malleable at least. For fuck's sake, for duck's Drake, Drake's old
man—malhomme, mallethard—was an actor on the stage
of world violence, and he had been shot, along with his wife,
and killed. Setif's father had no enemies whatsoever, just a
barfield of acquaintances that wondered at his luck or endurance. None of them wished him dead any more than anyone
wished someone dead when they heard about a potentially
fatal accident. Moranus again?

And he survived. Like a cat, the bastard. More like two
or three cats. Why don't they take his license away? Ain't the
same as taking a car away, is it? Lock him up? Been locked
up a dozen times. It ain't like he's a rapist or a strangler.
He drinks and drives. He drinks and walks. He drinks and
hits people with pool cues. But that was just the once and
he got the worst of it. Did he? I assumed not—that was his
version, they set upon him and he defended himself to no
avail. No, he started it, and over ten euros, too, a clear case of
bad sportsmanship, though understandable as he had been
fighting to the finishing of the tale of his getting jobbed out
of the Irish championship billiards tournament some years
back. Mockery is one thing, not letting a man finish a sentence, that's quite another. But he could still tell a tale tall
and sure, like wait'll you here this one kid, so I was on the
phone with my boss, I shouldn't say boss, I'm just a consul-
tant though he calls me every day practically, minimum a
hundred euros per call, and he knows me a long time, so,
you know I drop the phone, simply drop it on the carpet,
kicked it under the couch, accidentally, before reaching for
it, but when he called I was on my way out for cigarettes, so
it wasn't long before I forgot the call, I had pretty much given
him a grand's worth by then anyway, answered his questions
and more, free advice, that kind of thing, so I, I don't mean I
forgot the call, just that I figured no need to call back, but I

did anyway, got down on my hands and knees, got the phone out, by then his line's busy, I put the phone back under the couch, good a place as any, and so I'm out the door for cigarettes, but he knows about my "situations," my "blackouts," he was actually there with me in Salzburg, or his boss I think it was, he gets worried, suddenly the call breaks off, he thinks its Mack, could maybe he have blacked out? And so he kept calling and no answer, what did I need the phone for going for cigarettes, but you know me, Margarette's is next door to the shop, I stop in for a beer, it was already past breakfast time, already past breakfast time, so I stop in to Margarette's, some other couple is in there eating toast, to be polite I step outside to smoke, and maybe the third cigarette, going in and out, not counting, standing smoking a cigarette there on the street corner, sirens you know you never hear them but then you hear them after you hear them, then they're right on you, I look around for a fire, two goddamn fire trucks, three ambulances, cops, Christ at least five cars, two guys hop out of an ambulance and grab me, schlup me in, and take off, won't listen to a word I say, won't tell me anything but it's an emergency, I can see that, though of course I *can't* see that, not from flat strapped on my back in the ambulance, not from a *gurney*, they take me to some hospital I don't even know the town, some other suburb, they run tests, I never find out what happened, not never but not for hours, they won't listen to me, finally the boss, not the boss, I consult for him, he calls and asks after me and that's when I find out what happens, but there's papers to sign, three doctors have to certify my condition vis a vis need to stay, release me from the hospital, clause 37© European Medical Code, EU/EC/WHO, which I have had cause to consult previously and so I knew quite thoroughly but figured under these circumstances, a mistake having been made, they could simply forego, and legally of course they had to, and I could sue them for false imprisonment if I had a mean streak, and I may if I don't get my forty euros back, which because the third doctor arrived at four in the morning they shoved me on the street without further ado I had to call a taxi, cost me forty euros to get back home. Can you imagine a day like *that*. And Setif, though of course daddy didn't like laughter while he was telling a story, given the array of suggestives, Setif laughed or started to half-way through, and he was in one hell of a mood because he laughed too, yes that was the last time she saw him. And the last time she saw her mom she made casually reference, to which a lady who had wasted her capacity for astonishment on what in the end turned out to be, ectoplasmically…no, well, he wasn't worth it, that's enough to say, her mother serenely corrected Setif, No, what happened was he was at the bar and he had a dizzy spell or thought he did, and he called the ambulance himself. That's all there was to it. He turned out to be all right so they didn't keep him.

Floundering. I'm floundering, she said aloud, without bitterness. Was there a better word? She learned it first, flatly, as a fish, flatly as a fish, unable to find a copy of Grass in her own language. Then she learned another meaning from Drake. Then yet another from Donnie: phalse phloundering, he told her he spelled it, phake, phony, a survival tactic. The difference between strategy and tactics? None, don't phall for that phallic bullshit. So she was floundering when she should have been phloundering. Minutes had gone by that would have been better used simply deciding to leave a message on her mother's phone. Phinnished. Finnished faffling, finished faffling about like a skidding balloon asphalting, assfaulting (thanks for the new habit, Donnie), floundering but not phalling on her ass.

Donnie's best was "He faffled in his flannel naffage, a failed fluffer, to his offal finale." As far as she was concerned, that is, Donnie's best, but he was a simpler man who said the best was "The smell was offal." Probably someone else has thought that one up, but phuck it, my decision is flannel. And you can quote Amplibilius Negrophilia on that one.

Did you see the tomb to Amplibilius Negrophilia?
No…or yes, I mean we saw so many things…
That's the most famous one in Rome.
Oh really, then I'm sure we saw it.
Good. I believe you call such a thing a "must see," no?

That's right.

We have some must sees right here in Brussels.

You name it, we saw it.

Oh honey, let her tell us her favorite

I'm not stopping her. Why is that line moving?

Oh no, I know you can see all there is here in half a day—

Our tour was five hours.

If you skip the cemetery of Amplibilius Negrophilia.

We saw a cemetery, didn't we, hon?

Have you *ever* chosen the right line?

He gets nervous when we travel.

Men are like that.

We saw at least one hundred cemeteries in two weeks. Who is that you mentioned?

Just the tomb, the...what do you call it...*mausoleum*, of Amplibilius Negrophilia, gothic, marble, Romanesque, in-the classic style, nearly two thousand years old, right here in Belgium, in a small cemetery, by the train station. It's rather hidden away.

Oh *that*, of course. We saw the station, and we saw a lot of gothics.

What can they be *discussing* up there. Either you have a ticket or you don't.

Honey, just be a little—

Don't tell me to be patient. Why do they tell us to get here three hours early and then make us stand in line.

Imagine the line if you were late.

What's that young lady?

I came with but an hour to spare one time and the line was out the door. In the rain.

That must have been awful. Did you see the Manneken Pis?

The Manneken...Yes, but I, well, I don't mean to be im-polite, but honestly I would hate to be from a city known for its naked, you know...

It's not easy. Everywhere I go, you know what I mean?

He liked it, of course. Had to have his picture taken with it.

He! Right, last city on the tour you'd think a couple

breweries would suffice, but my intrepid wife must see every gothic brick in this dump.

Honey!

No, he's right. If it weren't for Amplibilius Negrophilia I would have left long ago. City of perverts worshipping a urinating midget.

Oh, it's a *midget*, I thought it was a little boy. Not much difference. *Finally.*

Well I liked Brussels very much. It's—

Christ! What now? Look, look at this: he's coming back.

They aren't going to leave without us.

It's always the goddamn Indians, too, family of nine, grandmother never—

Keep it down.

No, he's right. I once went to India—to see the statue of Amplibilius Negrophilia in Ladakh, of course—and you wouldn't believe it but every delay was caused by Indians. The whole trip. Except for one stoplight in the taxi after I got back.

Never mind him, I found Brussels utterly charming. Not my favorite city, of course, but really quite charming.

What was your favorite city? Oh that's easy—Trier! Trier!

Christ! Can't you leave that alone? I knew I'd be hearing about it all—there, looks like they've finally gone.

Trier was simply beautiful.

Only to be followed by a clan of more Indians.

We wanted to do something a little different, and we found out there was a little river boat cruise—

Something different like go to Rome. Well we *had* to see Rome!

So you went on the Moselle.

You *know* the river?

Of course. When Amplibilius Negrophilia visited the north he lived a few years in a castle on its banks. Not far from Trier, actually.

The trip started in Metz—which I had never even heard of…Have you?

Of course.

The boat travels the most gorgeous wine country, from Metz to Koblenz, which I had never heard of—we were quite bold, come to think of it, all these places no one ever heard of.

These people will be as long as the others. Go on, get it over with, tell her about the incident at Trier.

What happened at Trier?

Tell her. Get it off your chest...Again.

Honestly, I don't know why you're making such a fuss.

The man was downright rude, that's why. And you took his side.

I did not take his side. I merely followed protocol and tipped him.

Which was as much as an apology for *my* behavior. That's not how I meant it. Anyway, it wasn't really his fault.

Not his fault? Not his fault? So you admit you think it was my fault.

It was no one's fault, dear. These things happen when you travel.

Not to me they don't. And not when people who are supposed to serve you do so properly.

But he *did* serve us properly.

You call sarcasm, you call *laughing* at me, proper service?

Honey, you might have laughed, too, if it were the other way around.

Really? Well you know why it's not the other way around? Because I am an executive in an aeronautics firm and he is a goddamn tour guide on a goddamn pissant river in France.

Not France, it only started in France. Trier is in Germany.

Great. Glad you got my point.

What *is* your point?

That I will not be mistreated on my vacation by some scumbag arrogant French boy.

It wasn't *that* bad.

He...laughed...at...me.

He couldn't help it. I might have laughed had you not lost your temper so quickly.

You might've—

Excuse me. I know it's not my business, but I'm curious.

These people really must be polite so people like you come back. What did he do? What happened?

You tell her. I want to hear your version.

Honey, I—Look, it can't be true, they're moving off already. Tell her. I can't wait to hear what a rude asshole I am.

Move it, fat ass. There, reached the counter in under 25 seconds. Go on, tell her.

I will, then.

We're all ears.

Well, you see, when you're on a riverboat trip you stop at all these towns and they have tours suggested for you. The stop before Trier, not a real town, but anyway a really great wine growing region, we took a bus tour to all of these marvelous wineries.

Get to the point.

I'm getting to the point.

I'm sure the young lady knows what a boat tour consists of.

Actually, I've never been on a boat tour. I always wondered what people did. Like whether they could get off the boat or not or just went fishing the whole time.

I wouldn't eat the fish in these rivers.

Oh honey, they aren't so polluted.

I didn't see you drinking it. Anyway get to the point. At this rate it's the tortoise against the tortoise—can you finish the story before we get to the counter.

You don't have to be nasty to me.

I'm sorry, Please go on.

Where was I?

Wine tour.

Yes, well, at Trier, there were several tours. It's not a very big city, you know. And just off the boat there was a big sign announcing a walking tour. It said simply "WALKING TOUR." I guess that was where you were supposed to gather if you were taking the walking tour.

You suppose?

Will you let me tell the story?

Sorry. Look, fat ass has gone back for his wife. Unfuckingbelievable! Why…fuck it.

I apologize for my husband—

Yes, you're coming to that.

He really does get irritable when he travels. Anyway, so we disembark, which is what they call it when you get off the boat, and Glenn here sees the sign, and the tour organizer is standing right there, so Glenn asks him, about the walking tour, if there is a bus.

I meant did we have to take a bus to the walking tour. Not such an unreasonable question if you ask me.

Except that all tours were divided into walking and bus tours.

Good god, what I wouldn't give for a good scotch right fucking now.

Well. The tour organizer does a sort of comic double take, you know, looks at Glenn, looks at the sign, and you can see he's trying not to laugh. But Glenn sees this, doesn't get it—

How do you know I didn't get it? Maybe I didn't get the rude little bastard laughing at a perfectly reasonable question.

Glenn asks "Is something amusing you?" and this just tears it, the tour organizer—

I don't know why you insist on giving him that grandiose title.

Because that's what he was called. The tour organizer bursts out laughing, but quickly composes himself rapidly, and with a straight face replies, "No sir, that would be the bus tour." And that was it.

That was not *it*.

Right, honey, That was not it. Because you had to lose your temper and he had to threaten to have you removed from the boat for the rest of the trip because you were physically threatening him even though he was half your age and fit and could easily—

Enough!

Ladies and gentlemen, we are about to begin our descent into Los Angeles. The blue you see beneath you is the Pacific Ocean. We are over the ocean because the plane is on fire and we do not wish to put the lives of civilians in danger. If you are having your period, you might just as well bleed out entirely. The estimated speed of the plane as it noses into the water will be 573 miles per hour, or 900 kilometers per hour, or, if you have a calculator simply multiply the miles by 1.6. Whatever the result, it's pretty goddamn fast—I'd hate to be a fish swimming along in the way of *that*, or this—so buckle your seat belts lest you smash heads with those about you and hit the water already dead. If you need to use the bathroom, now is the time. Sorry we forgot to feed you, but it's a long flight and we are all a bit tired. Hold on—what's that? Oh, that *was* your meal, calorically sufficient by industry standards, industrially sufficient by caloric standards. We trust you enjoyed it, and I personally feel you should be damn grateful you had a choice because when I was growing up, *my* mother never gave me a choice. And there are plenty of people in Arkansas who would love to have *either* of those meals. Yet we are required by industry standard and the laws of the air to throw all leftover food in the garbage. Makes one wonder, though, whether as we are crashing into the sea if our food regulations must needs be in accordance with maritime industry standards. Perhaps some fish from Arkansas will get themselves a free meal. I am not trying to be amusing when I remind you that there is a flotation device underneath your seat—joking. We have never actually had those, and it's pretty fucking hilarious how whenever we tell people they are there they believe us even if they check and can't feel anything. *No one ever asks.* It's no wonder we treat you all with barely disguised contempt. Nonetheless, be assured that the oxygen masks do exist and are fully operable and one of the funniest things you'll ever see is when the system malfunctions and they all plop down like a puppet climax of Mahagonny and people are screaming and shoving their kids to the floor so they can get them on first like they're told, while others are smothering their kids trying to get them to fit like the masks of mimes while they themselves are turning purple from the mere imagination of lack of oxygen and we're standing up here like conductors pointing: look at that guy!

Hahahahahahaha. It's fucking hilarious. Come to think of it, as we are all on our way to flaming death, I'll ask the captain if we can activate the masks, it's such a riot. And you know what, while I'm on the subject of special occasions, if you want a second dinner? Fuck it. Why not? We all eat at least two. Call it a bennie. Not that we don't have plenty of those. You know we only work nine days a month? And of course no lines, no customs, sexsexsex, all for surviving the safest form of travel ever invented by mankind. Of course, here we are having this conversation, I mean me delivering your death monologue, but I'm the one who signed up for it, eh? But I wouldn't call it ironic, I'd call it that one in ten hundred thousand we aren't supposed to think will ever happen to us, but apparently in our cases will. Of course, oddly, you are all fully prepared since 79% of all air passengers expect on one level or another every flight they are on to crash. This is like hitting the jackpot in Vegas—everyone has to give it a shot, even though they know they have no fucking chance, yet 79% fully believe they will win it. Can you believe your luck? If any of you were going to survive I would suggest you get right on the next flight to Vegas because never again in this life are you going to hit such long odds. Hold it, okay, I think by now it is ironic. Getting hot back there? What's it feel like to be on fire?

The plane slammed to the tarmac a great deal harder than Setif expected, bounced, shook the altitude off its wings, and began its powermad braking. All this without feathers. Why had they decided not to garb the aeroplane with feathers? Would make people a lot more comfortable with the entire notion. Her skull tingled. She felt her body in its repose as those around her jostled in place preparing but not daring to disobey their orders to remain seated until the plane had come to its final resting position on the apron. Her arms felt lighter than her legs. Her crotch felt as if it had been glued to the seat, for during the entirety of a bad period she was more alive, preternaturally was not really the word for it, but she was vagina-blood centered throughout, and now what blood had clawed its way out of its stoppered cavern seemed to be making a rather humorous effort to keep her seated. It needn't have worried, for of all people on the plane it appeared that

Setif had the most balanced notion of time—having been unable to hurry while speeding above a large swath of the globe, blundering through its atmosphere—the other passengers seemed to feel the need to hurry intensely. Setif was probably not a superior sort of human. Perhaps she was in no hurry to confront what she had not been in a hurry to confront in the first place.

Though, in that light, she would hardly be unique; certainly, for instance a number of her co-sojourners were returning to miserable families, slowly, like a sun-magnified victim, returning to a form that had been patiently adopted through countless minutes of restraint, of disguised intolerance, of restraint from what must have felt a native, a natural violence, been freed if daresome a long ways off, in distance, and if so perhaps now in panic to reshape.

She was not the last off the plane, and she smiled with genuine warmth at the outushering stewardess, whose practiced grin was horsey-tooth, thicklipped and maternal. The air in the removal tunnel was, if anything, more stale than that in the plane, and after the downramp, the upramp was depressing near to disorientation, for now she was among them tip of the continent or no. Everyone in front of her wore shorts unless they were in a wheelchair—and then it didn't matter, for these were not, in her mind, strictly denizens of this country she had never wanted to visit. In fact, she had a particular distant fondness for people on wheels in general. Pastels and plaids were the predominant match and mismatch, and baseball caps closed the heads of both genders, though older women generally did without, either wearing white visor caps or hair they seemed to fear would slide off now that they were walking, one hand always catching it just in time. Lone men walked faster than anyone else; men in groups appeared to want to walk faster, but held back gracelessly. Perhaps these were the tragicmost of air-delivered lives. Their primal-forged fornications had wrought inane complexities that worked against the few impulses of nature that had the fortitude to urge them to motive. Somewhere ahead Drake was waiting and he was not yet one of them, that at least was comfort, if not for her. Of more immediate comfort was the division of native and foreign once she had endured the wait for luggage among the same people, all of whom seemed to have the habit of impressing facial features on her unguarded memory, which was reduced to the rather pathetic defense of compressing them into one androgynous, bird-legged family leader aged fifty or so, whose luggage, naturally came with unexpected rapidity for everything about the creature suggested the expectation that it would arrive last if it wasn't lost.

The brute force of United States gates was manned by a surprisingly scrawny specimen with a brown moustache a couple shades darker than his hair, aiming to encroach down to his mouth, which had lower teeth tiny as desiccated adolescent corn on the cob, far more facial topography than normal, though symmetrical, and, thankfully, a small nose. His short-sleeve shirt seemed necessary to air the thick veins that plumped profusely from lower bicep to fingertips. But his job was in his eyes, the eyes of an arboreal rodent with the vigilance of both incipient savagery and fear.

He regarded her passport, scanned the visa, and returned to her photo.

"Setif Moranus. That's you?"

"No. Setif Moranus is me. Not set if more anus. Setif Moranus."

"That's a Muslim name?"

"Which?"

"Yours. Is it a Muslim name?"

Her eyes flitted to his name tag. Initials of some kind of rank and "Tom Bleeth."

(Hindoo?)

"Which?"

The eyes locked in indecisive menace. "What do you mean which?"

"Which. First or last."

People in his position cannot afford to be made to look ridiculous. He comprehended.

"Well...either."

"My first name is presumably Algerian, for it is the name of a village in Algeria. As for its religious affiliation I have no idea. Did the village pre-date the Islamic invasion, or—"

"Sounds Moslim to me."

"Could be Maasleem sounds developed from those of their new surroundings."

"What about that last name?"

"Which?"

(Pause. Composure.) "Your last name."

"My last name, to put it simply, is Belgian, probably derived from the Latin."

"And you are Belgian?"

"Yes."

"All right, so not Mooslim."

"No."

"No what."

"No I am not Mislim because I am Belgian. I am not of the Islamic faith and I also happen to be Belgian."

"So you are Belgian."

"Still, yes."

"Your mother and father?"

"Both Belgian, if that's what you mean."

"And your purpose for entering the United States?"

"Good question."

"Can you answer it, please."

"Not with much conviction." (Impatience.)

(Loss of tonal differentiation.)

"Can you answer the question?"

"Visit."

"Then you're a tourerist," he stuttered, releasing an ampule of frustration.

"No."

"Are you here on business?"

"No."

"Ma'am, these are simple questions. I am asking you to please co-operate."

"Which simple question are you referring to?"

"Look, lady, are you a tourist or are you here on business, are you a student…"

"None of those. But you're right, that was a simple question."

(Breathing amply for patience.)

"What is the purpose of your visit to the United States?"

"At this point I really cannot say."

(Rapid response.)

"Would you like to have this conversation in a private
room?"

"No, really, this is fine here."

"Then simply co-operate. Where are you intending to
stay?"

"I really have no idea, perhaps you should be having this
conversation with my boyfriend."

(Compressed extravagant enlightenment.)

"Is your boyfriend a US citizen?"

"Yes."

"Are you here to see him."

"Yes."

"Is he picking you up here at the airport?"

"Yes."

"Thank you. You may go."

Surprisingly few turns and stretches of walking beside horizontal machines that carried people past here, some walking
as they were conveyed, Setif came to a slung rope on the other side of which stood Drake, whose face broke violently into
happiness on sight of her. He waited for her to choose a direction, then broke to that side, his left, to meet her, gripping
her tightly—more muscular than she recalled—seeking her
lips, which were gurling about in evasion, attempting to ask
the question that had expressed what had stiffened her with
dread, for she already knew enough of the answer.

"Where's Donnie?" she finally huffed, freezing Drake's
lips like snails in their tracks.

34

THE BENDS AND THE RUST

Proviso

Boozers, pederasts, housewives, costermongers, flashers and thieves, I ask you all and others, that if you are going to read this chapter, for *whatever* reason, you drop all pre-conceptions about prison life, life behind bars, hijinks and low in correctional facilities. Do not even begin to imagine one of my characters face down flat on the floor pants around his ankles with a giant penis-head forcing through his reluctant rectum while he is screaming, weeping, whimpering, swearing, struggling, unconscious, subdued epileptic, drugged, rhythmic, catatonic, stoic, philosophical, gritty, down for a count, a spelling error or elision, a forgotten man, a loner, a man whose father drank or died young of cancer or whose mother was a whore whose old man left her with the kid, skittish, patriotic, repentant, recalcitrant, truant, getting what he deserves, like-minded, Zionist, foreshadowing, graceful, grateful, incorrigible, unshaven, virginal, dutiful, wishing he were elsewhere, cursing fate in a Jungian manner—just don't think about it, don't think anything about it. What do you really know about life in prison anyway? Unless you're in prison. If so, yeah right, innocent. Tell it to Eddie the Hacksaw, Injun guy in Cell Block D. All I'll tell you is you meet criminals there, in prison, you make some good connections that come in handy on the outside.

Driving to Vegas

Only when the Maverick reached 70 on the highway west of Ames did Gravel tooth the cap off a beer and know the feeling of relief and uber-liberty of a man waking from an interminable nightmare of sphacelatic parasitical death by succubus. In fairness he knew that the succubus was also himself, for it is an awful, an attenuate and thence all the more horrific circumstance to voluntarily secede from one's own being, as he had some twenty years back, and to remain that rebel with its fading flag on a fat ass for the entire two decades. To be falsely labeled a murderer pains not the being, no, it is the theft of liberty that scalds—but the surface, yes, an entirely surface terror at its onset that has in the being its final, eventual, target. In no way did Tom Gravel repudiate any of his actions impelled by the need for freedom, nor the need to remain free. In no way did he expect himself or any man to know how a wise man exercises his freedom. But he had been a fool—and for that he would die badly, already acutely and without letup a metaphysical polycrotic decrescendo timed to his failure as a father. Certainly his wife was a mad egotistical bitch (but how could he have seen that back then when she was the best poet on campus and a lithe serpentine slathering lustlowering slavering lover?), who accumulated wicked powers as she ascended into orbits he disdained—but disdained fecklessly, privately, like a man alone in a rude one room house in country of basin and range writing prose poems who imagined forceful interactions between clouds and ridges, writing as no man had ever written metaphorical visions that transmogrified into metaphysical lies that conned readers including the estranging literati of extra-orbital nobility into believing that a man alone in a rude house in basin and range expanses was a finer being than a father at home playing baseball with his son, who developed in solitude the strength inherited from his father to disdain without rancor the very communications that bind father and son.

The rain disregards any agenda of the stars

This now was Tom Gravel as Tom Gravel, driving 77 west, the Tom Gravel that expanded boundaries within his own sense of delimitation, and who no longer mocked or refuted the self-commiserations of coerced serendipities such as feeling his own sense of rejection of what he *could* reject by choosing a four-door Maverick forty years old, older than the battle of Nicopolis by an injudicious reckoning that factored in Iowa and the rest of the United States, finely tuned, and settling into the pleasure that finds him the way rainwater that gathers on the surface of a karstal sinkhole and seeps slowly to the depths of unvisited caverns to succor those amphibious albinos in their primal utopia finds them, the pleasure of self-selected music, the song "Four Door Maverick" from Howe Gelb's *Hisser*, which he had listened to for more than a decade driving to and from a job that provided him a precise dosage of misery to offset his comfort, music made by a man of the deserts of Pennsylvania and Arizona no different from a man who maintained his life in basin and range rather than visiting for a year to extract for a crowd selective symbols to please an Externae of self-congratulatory inconsequence, while at home he professed without moving his lips not to tire of Schubert, Chopin, Beethoven, Brahms, Tchaikovsky, before the guests arrived, and Bach, Bartók, or Górecki (never Schnittke, who found his way into Gravel's car) once the hoi oligoi had gathered their ears for asparagus Marseilles and New Brunswick mussels, and that rarest of sauvignons from the bloodiest patch of the Vendée.

And now he found the car was nearing 90 as an eidetical vision of the idiot eidolon, in fact her bare ass, skinnier than the limitless lusters would have liked had they but known, shogged sexlessly to her walk-in closet to choose an identity retrieval costume for the night that would begin with a plate of glazed carrots and some grandiose form of fungus graduating to a botched Ethiopian stew, the guests gorefully gleaning the docile, dour drammage of Bach, unprepared for the shift to Bartók, whom they would nonetheless profess to find as tantalizing as tango, leaving one by one or in twos to Górecki's Third, which of course found its voice in the verse of their Languideia, inevitably one would remark.

when the lightning can't touch you and you can't go wrong
in a four door Maverick
four door

"How you've kept your figure!" Gravel thoughtscreamed out the window, slowing down, releasing her like cigarette smoke, rolling down the window.

He had yet to determine his route to Vegas, through Wyoming, where he would best pass at night through basin and range he had held as if enraptured once, through Denver, where he once thought he would spend his life after the, you know, we'll get to it…or down to I40 and the panhandles. The choice was due rather soon, so soon in fact he had no choice but to take it, take the exit and head toward Kansas City, for among the worst symptoms of his crime against life was the development of patience and care to such excess as to make of them not only diseases, but contagious, such was the regard with which he was held, such was the esteem that so steamed his ass, his fartless flattening forfeiture of an ass, now, too fucking late now, now that his escape contained condensed an unaccountable violence, a violence that he would not hold to account, a violence he would not turn on himself, a violence volcanic unvulgar! even if it turned out the volcano was his own skull, his brain gone magmatic with the disgust that smothers despair, and if only metaphoric the skull was open at the top in the form of an all-seeing eye that would not blink at his own putrid beings over time yet neither the rot to the core of all he had lived with and known for the past twenty years but for a son who had no fucking idea of anything true about his father, who every five years found new cause to delay the soteriological necessity of delivering the gift of truth to a son who at five was too young, said Languideia, and at ten was too fragile, Languideia convinced him, too fragile and could that bitch mouth the words that need not be? ever? yes, she could do anything to preserve her self as she imagined it must be, so yes, she could, though he had already agreed to delay the confession, she could say Anyway he could never keep the secret, he's too young, she could say it and he cracked the window with thoughtscream,

"She could fucking say it to my fucking face!" and when a gas station loomed he veered in wild and bought a carton and six more beers, ruminating on the thought of how a border was not something you could lift your wife over so to bring her down hard on it and break her fucking back and these fields, corn mostly, trees and fields of Midwest green, these were inutile to intellect, infertile for the formation of thought, and all thought that grew from them was necessarily worse than a lie, stillborn, its movement no more alive than that of a branch riding a river to a scumcatch. Missouri or Iowa, misery or stuttering tensely in the past like a moron caught red-handed violating an inane and arbitrary oath.

Gravel sat in the parking lot, his Maverick like a brick ghetto among the gortation of trucks which he knew were driven by people who would without a ruffle of contradiction in this universe both enjoy engaging in billiards, banter and beer with him the same as running him down as he dashed naked across a vast plain, with any luck him catching good on some under pipe-clasp so he could be drug some. He drank a beer in too few swallers and quick to light a cigarette first, but when he did light one he again watched eidolonian Languideia, this time in white swish dress that he knew was georgette fabric because she insisted everyone who compli-mented her on it know it was georgette fabric, he watched her cross leg spread the slit when she sat, and her nipples perp to sight as she arched her back, and he watched Tom Gravel approach her from behind and break her neck, and he knew the meeting continued as she drifted out the win-dow and drifted high and thinner, and as he flicked the butt to a fleck of the asphalt and as he lit another, cracked another beer, started up the car and headed out of Iowa or further into Missouri, the meeting droned and cacaphoned and he drove on away and knew he had long been gone as Donnie had long been gone when he was fifteen and again the time was wrong, this time Gravel aware that it was entirely too late and that his own suggestion that the secret must be would be all things worse than pathetic, all things crawling til smashed and dead.

There's nothing wrong with Simon and Garfunkel! once said the Imperiatrix and only once and thus was Gravel's brain implanted with their parasitical lyrics and melodies. There's nothing wrong with Simon and Garfunkel, he rolled down the window and in thoughtscream to Missouri that an arroyo, a scarp, an arête, a broken bottle, a car crash, a fucking atom bomb! a fucking drown in the blood of their own bloody flux! wouldn't fix. Fucking lecture in the car, analyzing "America" for Cleo: the window rolled down again: I vomit in your faces! Bloody vomit! In your faces on your whitest dresses before your most precious and fragile events you fucking cunts!

An Imperiatrix requires a docile subject class. Gravel's peasantry contained multitudes. He rolled the window up, lit a cigarette, cracked the window, cracked another beer, looked in the rearview mirror at himself, but he wasn't there and he wasn't about to lean into self-view.

eyes that stare and don't turn away

Back to the beginning of the song, settle the fuck down, back to Donnie, back to Donnie, absinthe, your absinthe, your pathetic absinthe, how abscene that in your own absence you pacified yourself with such private musical rebellions...

you poor old fucked up load
crippled up on some crumpled road
you don't show up with out some flack
here in the core of the crust
when your thrust turns to dust
here in the core of the crust
store front display
eyes that stare and don't turn away
wearing the same clothes for weeks
feeling the same way for days
new way to harbor the day

But you never really found a new way to harbor the day... Reberth! Hah! Gravel suddenly surged with optimism (had it been more than a decade, really?): Donnie could be found and told everything and that was the future in itself, that was the circle circled (Gravel suppressed an image from Meyrink, "a cat with half his brain damaged walking in circles"), that was the luck of a life unlinear. Can you succeed only to the degree that you fuck up? Can you soar to mediocrity? Can you deliver unto yourself context for martyry? Can you climb a tall building and stand on a ledge, checking your watch with uncalculated regularity like the ticking of an alien clock, wait for the police to wait for the police psychologist to try to talk you down before jumping?

Que pasa, hombre? This is not you/me Tom Gravel neither before nor after, tis just the vex of the sphex, the fauxnious of the unharmonius, the sputria of the phoneutria — roll down window, spit — a momentary, yes, just that — a momentary, a momentarium, a museum of spite, scorn, febrile white fabrics, fabrications, languid patter, bring your own disgust — you can leave it behind!

Where was it? 13? 16? Calm yourself. In a four-door Maverick, down to 60, "Halifax in a Hurricane," no, not so fast — there: that salubricious opening, those first notes, long long before the storm

with the grey I've earned

Indeed if not earned. Nor the heart full, nor formed. A grotesque, puppeting himself through a transition, that's all, a momentary, that's all, for never before nor after was there a Tom Gravel who whooted and/nor hawlered out a window of a fastmoving vehicle — that was him and we won't say it weren't, but he was seeing how it wasn't him as he eased as the song eased into

the cracklin water
and the crackling light
and the crackling clouds
here in the crackling night
I want you now
if this is not hate
I don't know how
I ever over underrate

here on Earth

Where the wind and the rain prevail
Bends what you build

and rusts what you nail
here on Earth

I hate you now
if this is not love
I don't know what
I've been a party of

Here on Earth

with the bends and the rust
you hide from the rain
and the winds you mistrust

air turns warm

and the cool rains return
and the winds finally form
and the storm we finally earn
yeah, I return
with the weather its warm

with the grey I've earned
and my heart now fully formed

Here on Earth
with the wind and rain
they love to erode
what you love to sustain
Here on Earth
these things remain

The cracklin water (the cracklin water)
The cracklin lights (the cracklin lights)
From the cracklin clouds (cracklin clouds)
In the cracklin nights (in the cracklin nights)

I want you now (I want you now)
if this is not hate (if this is not hate)

I hate you now (I hate you now)
if this is not love (if this is not love)
if this is not love (if this is not love)
I don't know what (if this is not love)
I've been a party of (if this is not love)
I hate you now (if this is not love)
I want you now (if this is not love)
          want you now

Here in Missouri, with the bends and the rust, the bends from coming up too quickly, the rust from twenty years without the moist illumination of self on self. Yet a self of some sort had been, a Garvin self now repaved to Gravel, and if nothing else Gravel knew that this name change meant leaving his literary life behind and he was grateful to end it knowing that his prize winning was limited enough that his works would not have to withstand eternal accretions of scrutiny, that his two books would not be colonized by the winged conflagrant myrmidons of academia, that he would not be hearing of that self, that self that he had disappeared, that had disappeared without so much as a slough of sound, externally a mystery without detectivity. The same mystery of self persevered lonesome back in writing days, when he could sit for hours at any designated writing spot, in a cabin at a desk of dusky wood redolence, in his school office after dark or in the morning, or between students, between classes, or at a diner, a coffee shop, at home even, in his study with the window that looked out on generation after generation of inconsiderate cervine attitudes, and opossum that a younger Gravel would have run to have sport with but lately for twenty years lately would deflect his mind toward something inconsequential and unrelated, and he was never lonesome, for he cared nothing for the mystery of his own marsupulated words, and he eructed for the posture, the same way he had mechanically erected the events that brought about his successful gathering of an impeccable shell to slug into.

His trip to Chicago had been eventful. He went to the art museum to see the guitarist with the broken neck and the untermenschen dripping with the cold sea their invitation from Böcklin. Oscar was easy to find as he had, as he had said he would, retained the same phone number after all this time, though he had been gentrified from Wicker Park to the neighborhood of North and California, the humbler Humboldt Park, a prosaic bullet-ridden neighborhood where mornings brought the sunrise of taco stands and evenings the crepuscule of blood feuds and the worst musics of the world mixed to avoid identification and ensure the tension that neighborliness and tasty food had been endangering for centuries, if not always in that particular area.

Immediately after the phone call from Clay Strut, Gravel had gone over to THE JARGON, changed paper money for coin, went to the phone booth—"Delta Dawn" was on the juke box, not loud, Fox volume, Fox's quarter (slid down the bar with two partners to what would be called a biker skank reglar)—with that number he had found in his wallet despite twenty years of wifely inspection—redundant given a memory that faithful in distrust—for he had glued the edges of two defunct laminated bank money machine rectangles together with the number inside twice, once in lemon juice, oh yes. As far as he knew Malvasio was still in jail on a statutory rape charge unlikely to hold him much longer, and since the flight to the cornfields he had returned often enough to the bar anyway to find that he and Clay Strut had, as he soon came to suspect, merely been toyed with. At any rate, he wasn't of a mind to be concerned with a vengeful psychopath. He was more in fact of a mind to mold his own mind that he was riding like a juvy mustang toward his own very particular vengeful psychopathy.

Strut had not returned to Vegas for Gravel's sake, and for all he knew Gravel was still Garvin. "I have to subsume all this perversity," Clay had said on announcing his imminent departure, "and besides, if a man can't write in and of Vegas, a man from Vegas, then he can't write."

"Garvin?" Portento answered. "Sure I remember. Of course I remember. Sure I'm still in business. Of course I'm still in business. Come as soon as—"

"Tonight."

"Sure tonight. Of course tonight. I'm on the ground floor now, I'll leave the porch light on for you. Tom Garvin. I'll be—I moved, though, Tommy. Had to. They gentrified Wicker. Tell you what. Park at the old place, your car will be safe there you can find a spot. Walk to North Avenue, take a left, soon as you see a hooker look for the first big street, take an immediate left, stay on that side of the street if you ain't carrying. Walk down half mile to the next big street turn right, stay on the right side, cross two blocks brownstone on your right I'll be looking for you in…You leaving now?"

"Yes."

"I'll have an eye out then."

… "Tommy?"

"What."

"Hear any gunplay hightail it back to North and give it til sunrise."

Gravel hung up, marveling at the comforting onset, as of a fog, of an incorporeal immediacy akin to that of coming to whole mind from a chaotic dream, almost as if he had been at a bar in the film *The Asphalt Jungle* for the first half of his life and had just, after twenty in the pen, walked in to find the same gimp bartender still there.

Gravel, of course, had heard about Oscar Portento in the slammer. He had no idea how Portento had been alerted that he was on his way, no idea how he knew precisely when Gravel pulled up to the house on Wood Street near North Avenue.

Portento hustled him in and up the stairs—the two-bedroom apartment was on the second floor. Portento shared it with a man called Red who never spoke, a short man with black hair on the back of his arms, balding, rarely seen, now and then in the kitchen, barefoot, dress pants, bunion, menace steaming from his every pore. Gravel was told not to ask questions, not to address him. "Think of it like two horses in a stable, both of you got blinders on. Neither knows why. We work in my bedroom. I got everything in there. See, yes, I'm Oscar Portento:

How'd you get out? Don't tell me, the bends and the rust. Them old prisons with the bars those molecules moving for all them years the bars bend and they rust and you don't have to be Hercules to, but you look strong enough, natural forearm strength. Yeah, never ask, what you're in for I mean."

"Beat a man to death."

"Everyone innocent, cept you and you got out."

"Two others, they got caught."

"Like you planned."

"Hoped, yes."

"They's moving everybody to a new prison, am I right? Out in Ely."

"Made it easier."

"You'd think they'd be looking all the closer a time like that."

"They were, but not in the right place."

"They created the heat *for* ya, the dumb bastards. Yeah, see molecules are always moving, I read a lot to keep my eyes sharp for my work, got started as a favor for a friend sprung me in Kansas City save ya from asking, he's in Canton now, wife and kids, salesman, got him a little degree, new social, birth, made my first batch of twenties back then, give him a few stacks, no one ever bothered me since. Haven't seen a copper in 20 years, cept on the beat chases whores off North Avenue, or driving by. They don't see me. No one does. They think they're protected in their cars so they don't see. See, the molecules are always moving—watching corn grow ain't as stupid as it sounds. It all changes, molecules defeat *every* effort, especially efforts to contain, which most of what them with money is driven to attempt. The bars *all* bend, the bars *all* rust. Cops are meremaidens of doom. Crime will out, mister. Crime is on the side of the molecules. Crime is always on the move. Crime is…*molecular*. Every time they think they got it down, predicted into predictable, they miss the neutrinos, they overlook the reactions, the transitions, they think structure exists where you and I we know it don't. It's heat see, they got heat all wrong, the heat do, think they're the heat, but the heat is indectable and it's on the side of crime,

change, life, evolution, dwarfed by the neutrino, the smallest
particle in an infinitely giant world that contains multitudes
of Bastilles if you know what I mean— bending Bastilles, rust-
ing in vacant stretches of dematerialized ruins. Look: when
a dame is in heat feel her forehead it's colder than a welldig-
ger's tonsillectomy, that's because she's sweating it out, but
she's movin her ass you bet! So the molecules are bending,
just a little heat to get it going in and there's always a little
heat because we can generate heat, and we have to because
the structure is so goddamned cold! And ain't nothing like
a little rust added to the fire, the rusted coffee can left aside
the charred railroad ties, tarred like that hot ladies thighs,
which int get all self-dynamo-like but by the molecular necessitated by the heat—them legs doesn't *want* to be in them
smothering nylons, and silk heats the legs they get a little
thinner and slip right off. Think of it like this: like the Inquisition: they got themselves all torqued a hundred thousand
Muslims and Jews, say ladies, lined up Bastille to Bastille all
in their iron neckties, and in the blink of an icicle you got
yer Shepherdism and Hashkings, not to mention yer Hassidi-
mists, more Jews to begin with, hell times near a billion, got
a little heated up by the fires tickling them ready for hell they
slipped their collars. Now with Hitler there's probably in ten
twenty years eleven more tribes discovered and Jews in New
Zealand and Antarctica. You know was Jews that taught the
Russians prison slang, all started in Odessa? Factual truth,
that one. I read it. The rest is hypothetical science, which
I also read and worked out to fit the history, given my spare
time and interest in the being and the done, and the why and
this what I believe to be not an obsession but an innate not
even need, but innate ability that perpetrates *itself* against the
law in order, like I wouldn't feel no pain from stopping but
just from doin the other thing, whatever it might be, but the
proof is in my utter inability to identify that other thing. You
can't dream you are dead, same you can't dream you're in
prison once you been there. I was born just that slight degree
higher temperature and if I were not I would have cooked
myself up to it. I am free even in my loathing for the law for

it is but my nature and nature in accordance with the laws of the particule universe. And you, my friend Tom — innocent or guilty of self-defense, the accusation if not the incident provided the heat, the accusation got yore molecules moving at a fever pitch, fever pitch in comparison with the run of the mill, the workaday, the structures made for the working man, the lawabidingcitizenry, you've caught the heat, like a long slow brush fire from con to con, I imagine a slowmotion film of a match to saranwrap revealing the meat unpackaged and raw, what's under the skin and the fur, the real thing, the steak, the bloody steak of life…Do I talk too much?… You seem the quiet type is what I want to say but maybe I int give you a chance to speak. In my experience a man comes to me he's lost, a little warm talk provides comfort, matching temperatures, going from in the can out into the cold, I talk to keep your ashes from going out entirely, see."

Chickens began barking from the neighbors' back porch.

Gravel went to the window, pulled the shade aside and scanned for natural light. Bullets sounded in the not so distant. Street lights or their jaundice were visibly sharing in the tarry amber of the Chicago early morning.

"Barely three o'clock. Could be just city roosters are different from country roosters."

"Mexicans next door. Never have to buy eggs."

Gravel wondered if it was just the Mexicans who didn't have to buy eggs or if that included Oscar Portento.

"Warm."

"What's that?"

"Eggs. They're warm, warmer than our hands."

"That's right, I get your implication."

Gravel was sweating in the heated room, the smoke from Portento's cigarettes was beginning to crowd him, the glazure of travel had been constricting over the past few hours. Though Portento spoke a great deal, the work was clearly delicate, so it was impossible to know what he was supposed to do, if he was expected to speak, to sleep, to observe, to listen acutely and respond intelligently, to listen as Portento spoke, with distance, nebulous, non-committal. In his increasing

discomfort he grew thoughtful. He was a killer. For all practical purposes, he thought, for all practical purposes, I am a
killer. People will say, Tom Gravel is a killer. Yet he only killed
that once. Throughout his life he farted simianly, he had no
idea how frequently compared to others, but he farted what
he took to be a verisimianitiudinous norm in number and nature, in nurturing also normally, mostly as a teen. But no one
would say Tom Gravel is a farter. Or a *breather*. Though if
he moved into the neighborhood and they knew he was a
killer and someone started calling people at night breathing
heavily into the phone. An eater. A biped. A biped so a killer.
In the big house you didn't reflect on yourself the same way,
you only suffered and wanted out. You wished it wouldn't
have happened or you hadn't got caught, but that gave you
White Heat migraines. So you reflected like a man in prison.
You yearned for fresh air, for sparrows to train. Various foods
came to mind, came to mind but not to the cafeteria. Tom
Gravel was a killer. Always a rather quiet man, a quiet boy
then a quiet man, Gravel was now thinking he was a man
of few words. Thinking back on the last few days, especially
after the intense concentration preceding the fact of escape,
of getting away, getting away *with it*, he realized he was a
man of very few words, nearly to the point of impolite. But
quite apart from Gravel, this señor Portento was quite the gre-
garious man, talking throughout even the most demanding,
finely wrought machinations required to produce convincing documents—I hesitate to call them fakes, for they served
their purposes as well as those produced ex-artisanally. Gravel tuned in again just as Portento began relating a story—bent
over like the desklamp he worked to—about his first and last
visit to the state of Arkansas. "Can you imagine that, visiting
an old pal, first off dropping in, like you said all along you
would though such fidelity exhausts itself once the bars open
to ya most cases, as you bring yer dog along, nothing special,
mangy five-breed mongrel, best friend like they say, faithful
and all that, bastard—let him out to shit, five minutes later
this ungodly screeching, banshees like, like owls pecking out
the eyes of Dante's suffering dead in apocalyptic conflict, not

a good sound, and turns out its wild pigs tearing yer dog to pieces. The horror...the horror, never go back to Arkansas. Couldn't sleep that night, got in the car and drove back up to here to Chitown in one go. Never looked back...Never looked back—what the fuck does that mean, tsnot true anyway, I look back all the time. I just told you the story, didn't I? Wild fucking pigs. Can you beat that?"

"Hot pigs, cold dog."

"Bet yer ass, tsall molecules. Knowing it though sometimes don't make it prettier."

Never seen a wild pig. That's what Gravel would have said had he been talkative, or had he not become a man of few words. He even thought it the way one speaks. Yet he said nothing more, nor waited for Portento to speak; he receded. Portento spoke anyway. "Not that dogs can't be all heated up and I am not ready to get into the infernal vortex of the hot hound versus the fiery pig. Wolves and wild pigs. Probably the best you can say is they generally don't mix. False question. False opposites, or whatever. Just pure happenstance my dog and them pigs. Night before the pigs were probably three miles away rootin...whatever pigs root, vegetables or moles, whatever."

Admirable philosophy: people like Oscar Portento survived, became old, pacific, even wise. Now he was relating a story about his own face, which only now Gravel noticed was clustered about the cheeks with scores of blackheads that he had apparently never noticed because of the general grey and fade of pallor that encouraged an impressionist chiaroscuro, the streak of black among the bush of grey eyebrows, the grey tufts and the black of the listening holes, the teeth, all of them gray, short as if overused for gnaw and filled with black, even the eyes, near grey and the pupils black pins of focal—Gravel had never noticed the blackheads, but now he was fascinated by them. They were distributed rather evenly about the nose, if clustered more heavily in the nostril vaults, but were pointillist shading under the eyes. "Big Irish guy, good references, big mouth, Ever consider fracking your face, he cracked. You know what fracking is?"

"I do."

"New way of fucking, limitless oil and gas, though obviously limited, if you see my point. What's left after the seas are all on fire, and the smell of burning plastic's moved the population hinter, then all out fracking. That crack set badly with me. I'm no sensitive soul, but you have a condition for so many decades you forget about it, long as it doesn't make the bartender vomit, long as people look in your eyes, long as most people don't really even see it. I know, you get cooped up in here til I finish my job, and here I'm alone, and the rule is never go outside til I'm done, so sure you get cabin fever, but that remark, that remark didn't set well with me. I do a good job, I ask no questions, I forget what I'm supposed to forget and remember when I ought. Won't tolerate some displays of rude, though. Nobody ever laid a hand on me, threatened me, turned me in, returned with a complaint. I make a living I can live with. I am easy of mind. But funny as it was, Ever consider fracking your face was intolerable. Big Irish thug, bald near, maybe 45 years old. Never asked what he was in for. Like I says, good references. A crack like that though, gotta make him pay. I know a cop or two, could have used em, but you either take the one side or the other. I couldn't use a cop. Had to do it with documents so he wouldn't suspect me. Loaded him up with good money, too, nothing counterfeit. Worked quiet like, didn't talk to him like I like usually to talk while I work, easier to concentrate, though that be counterintuitive, though with him there was nothing wrong with my concentration—"

"You still think about the heat and the molecules?" "You remember that. I'll be damned. I figure most folk are just being polite, so I'm sort of working it out outloud, working it out for myself see. Sure I got lots more on that. But for this Irish feller, I think what you got is something like a brush fire got out a control, I mean to keep it simple not to get sidetracked…You remember that."

"I do. Made a great deal of sense to me."

"Never said a word."

"You said enough."

...

...

"Well...this Irish feller. Frack your face. Fucking funny. Spose that's what rips it is it uz truly funny. You can see the fool's got a big mouth or may be he's oblivious is all. He told me where he was headed, which when you're leaving the country may not be such a...Well there's no point. But he can't stop talking about it. Belize. Get himself a ranch on the beach. 'Like back in Ireland,' I'm thinking to say to him, irony you know...A ranch on the fucking beach. No wonder sometimes a guy's on the lam, giant imbecile, killed a lady with his bare hands, an accident he said like I asked. Told him, Didn't know the dame, put his mind at ease. Got a record, he's identified.

Logical solution, a ranch on the beach in Belize. Real wise guy, too. Passport's all worn, he wants me to make a passport all worn. I make a passport all worn. He's going straight from here to O'Hare, wouldn't know one passport from the other, I hand him his documents, go over them. Each one a work of art. What he doesn't know is his old passport's in his jacket pocket. He'll think he accidentally reached for it, slipped it in there. They nabbed him, he's doing life. I were him I'd have fought it all the way, get the chair—happened in Dallas—put myself out of my misery. Fracked that fucker good."

Gravel chose the name Eddie Vegas, which he figured would leave an impression that would trail off into netherworlds where the law disappears, and registered as such at The Pandle, a motel just off the highway in Guyman, Oklahoma, when he was finally too tired to proceed at about three in the morning. At the counter he encountered a short, entirely bald man the color of sand wearing an uncreased three-piece suit, who welcomed him in a South Asian accent.

"Good evening, sir. You would like a room?"

"Yes, please."

"We have very many empty rooms presently, do you have a preference of any kind: first floor/second floor, front side/back side, king size/queen size/that little one, television multiple stations/with pornography/television local stations only/even we have no television at all. Top of the line for one person, as I see you are without passenger, is first floor/back side/king size/ multiple station with porno, lowest price second floor/ front side/that little bed/no television. All rooms equipped with telephone service, check-out time for you late arrivals we make exception and call it two o'clock in the afternoon. What is your pleasure?"

"Thank you for the explanations. I will have the low cost and a wake up call for ten a.m."

"That is thirty-nine ninety-nine, which you may round up to forty dollars. You see, we do not own this motel and we must charge what the ownership requests even if it is an awkward or perhaps misleading figure."

"One gets used to it."

"That too is true, I also am *used to it*. My family has only been here for seven years and we are all used to it."

"From India, right?"

"Yes, that is correct, sir. We are from India."

"Where, where in India, the north I would guess."

"The north. You may say if you wish it is in the north because it is indeed not in the south. However, landforms do not conform to form. Ha. We are from Gujarat. I would consider that the west."

"I think that's reasonable."

"Reasonable yet ironic. For if we are the west, Bengal is the east, yet our Bengal is West Bengal, even though it borders Bangladesh, which was not so long ago called East Pakistan. Where is east and where is west, we must ask ourselves."

"Well, we're west of west Texas right now, are we not?"

"I am sorry to contradict, sir. See this map behind me…"

"Right right, *right*. I guess one tends to forget that the panhandle is not the westernmost part of Texas."

"Indeed, there is extensive extension of Texas westward into what one might call no longer Mexico and not yet New Mexico north/speaking so to speak."

"Interesting. I'm fifty-one years old and I never once realized how much of Texas, in fact that any of Texas, is south of New Mexico."

"We must hope that the denizens of that part of Texas at least are aware of the fact. Ha."

"Indeed...So where in Gujarat? Seaside?"

"No, sir. We are from the inland city called Rajkot."

"The capital, no?"

"No, I am sorry to say you are not in the right on that one. Gandhinagar only is the state capital."

"Never even heard of it. Was it renamed?"

"Yes and no. It was not a significant city, and it was not called Gandhinagar until it was planned as the capital of Gujarat because it is near Ahmedabad on the Sabarmati River. But I am impressed that you knew of Rajkot. No one else in your country I have met has ever heard of Rajkot."

"That's odd—didn't Gandhi spend a significant period of his life there?"

"He certainly did do so, that is an absolute fact."

"And it's got to be pretty big, right? A couple million?"

"Very big indeed, yes, more than one million, of that I am certain, but not so big as Ahmedabad, not as big as Surat."

"How far is it from the Gir Forest?"

"Ha. Now you want to know about lions. At three o'clock a.m. in the morning you want to know about lions in the Gir Forest. You are a very interesting customer, I must say. We are very far from the Gir Forest in Rajkot as a matter of fact. I would say it would be like driving from here to Lubbock, Texas, that is to say farther than from here to Amarillo, but not all the way to the southern part that stretches here into the underbelly of New Mexico. In India that is farther than it is here because of constraints of traffic, multivarious vehicles on roads, including camels and buffalo and cows.

"I see you have registered with the name of Eddie Vegas. Your real name is Eddie Vegas? Please do not mind this as intrusion, for it is mere middle of the night curiosity."

"My real name is Eddie Vegas."

"You are from Las Vegas then?"

"Never been there. It's pure coincidence. My grandfather was Mexican. I got the name Vegas. I am actually from Pennsylvania."

"Then I must attempt to be of help to you. Just last week a man of some prominence in Las Vegas stayed at this self-same motel. He is a promoter with 'hands in various pies,' he told me. He offered me a place to stay until I became settled should I want to upend my family's less than splendid existence in this hellhole is what he called it. If such a man of business acumen as myself wished to make his way in Vegas I could do worse than be in cahoots with Mister Harry Vetch. These are the matters he discussed with me. He seemed a very knowledgeable man with connections all over the strip and downtown. Here in this drawer, let me see, here, yes, in this hellhole some time longer."

"Says here he is a lawyer. A lawyer and a promoter."

"Could be a valuable contact should trouble befall you."

"Indeed."

. . .

"Well, Mister Harsh Rupareliya, it was a pleasure meeting and talking to you, but I think it is time for me to turn in."

"Turn in indeed, my good sir. It is our pleasure to host you. I wish you a fine sleep and I myself will personally call you promptly at ten o'clock a.m. in the morning."

Gravel awoke abruptly to see the curtains sucked out the window, and a chill of lonely night earth pulling at his bare skin. He did not recall having opened the window. He recalled Mr. Rupareliya—he hadn't had so long a conversation since Clay Strut had left town. Even the soliloquys of Oscar Portento were of a different order—while in Chicago Gravel resembled a dog, a mute beseeching listener who received far less than what his ears earned, without regret.

Nine hundred miles to Vegas, be there to see the lights in the valley. The last thing he wanted was to see the innkeeper again, and he knew with inutile prophesy that the man would be there at the desk fresh as ever. He peeled off three Portentos, sixty spendable dollars, and left them on the bed with his room key, walked rapidly to his car, pulled out and was onto I40 and well into the Texas panhandle before he relaxed out of his automatonomous frailty.

The mystifying crane and pump sculpts of this enormous zone of land were leaden under a leaden sky that did not relent even unto Tucumcari, nor Albuquerque, and even descent of night was a metallic blue going to black, and then the mocking signs: elks, watch for fucking elks, Christ the thing to watch for is you don't drift offroad and fly into the canyon, fucking elks. Gravel had no idea he'd forgotten to eat and was averaging 77 miles per hour until around eight o'clock he saw a sign suggesting an easy two hours to Vegas. He'd passed Flagstaff without noticing—he'd stop at Kingman for a hamburger. Looked like the stars were out, no crackling light. He'd even forgotten about music. He had become a tunnel.

35

DEPRESSION

Tom Gravel died in childbirth at the age of 61.

Wouldn't it be nice to relay the joke Marie Fire in Flight repeated to the crowd at her baby Tom's funeral, Tom's favorite
joke, about the little Injun boy who asks his ma how they get
their names, and she says, well, after we give birth we have
to stay and recuperate in the teepee for a while, sometimes a
few days, and so when we finally get to go outside first thing
we see we name our child after, what makes you ask this
question, Two-Dogs-Fucking?, and some would laugh, some
weep, Marie Fire in Flight, her voice a whisper beseeching
the mountains for breeze, they would all understand, they
would all understand what this meant to mother and son,
who lived as much apart from folk as they decently could
while still hoping to sell them horses long after they had sold
the joint in town, lived so far apart it was a rare event for Tom
to meet a single woman, rarer still for the thought of her being single and he, too, and so they could, that rare was the sex
act once he had reached his thirties and old were his horse
breaking bones when the shy, slender, barren some would
say, Ethel Rothgerte fell for him before the menopause that
overtook her features at age 19 but not her body until after
the birth her husband had tragically attended of her son, fell
so hard she asked him to marry her, upon which shocking
moment of event Tom asked, what's your name missus, I
ought to know that if I'm going to marry you, for Marie Fire
in Flight was not the least concerned with extending a family
line or coddling a grandson, enough of life having signaled

smokey to her from what all she knew and all what beyond related, an apocalypse, a world dying fast and if another world
were rising it was no concern of hers, for hers was but her life
and hern such as Tom even if she did have what from the outside seemed to some a family way sort of feeling for Rance,
who bought the joint, further distancing her from the worlds
that were tectonically migrating different directions, or rather
distancing her from the puppet show of commerce and quotidian pretense of purpose, she would rather not observe as
long as she could sit on her porch like old Hector and would
have like to have with her man Tom long into evenings una-
feared of high mountains, mountains above the clouds, snow
atop the mountains, vast vistas from cold foothill ranch country all the way to fiery morning desert, horses naysaying, the
few daily scratches signifying Tom at work, limbent cries of
tree in bluster of long gust, rushing of stream or brushings of
windwrenched forest in distances cold as dark or frozen as
lambence of magical northery skies, the hottest of day cold
with lack of odor or odor of cold imagined distance natural meanings of mystifying presences unquick with life, if in
movement movement unseen, time to Marie Fire in Flight
untied of fear, for if ever she awoke inside a teepee, young
and vibrant and exultant expecting an exalting day she had
emerged to see one dog fucking, not two, one dog fucking
another dog, fucking and fucking and fucking, its great dog
cock locked in concupiscence of death, fucking as natural as
a bear fucking a beaver fucking the coyote fucking the jack-
rabbit, fucking the dog to its death? But you can't just make
things up and say they happened if they didn't. Which don't
mean you can't joke, especially as we do about the alienating,
clashing, whiskey swilling othern with their names like

Black Cloud	Young Beaver
Still Deer	Flapping Ear Of A Coyote
Sitting Bull	Bird
Buffalo Limp	Condor of the Sun
Shacopay	He Interrupts
Louise	Mink
Pinus Strobus	Witch

Lean Bear
Snake Maiden
Dawn
Not Yet Dawn
Spider Woman At Middle
Age
Mud Mound
Porcupine
Bear
Crazy Horse
Horse
Lone Horn
Young Man Afraid Of His
Horses
Owl
I Love You
There Goes The Coyote
Low Dog
Black Knife
Running Dog
Eskimo John Walkara
Blackhawk
Black Hawk
Blue Jay
Brown Bear
Blue Eye
Green Eagle
Yellow Snake
White Buffalo
White Hawk
Blue Balls
Bull Balls
Bear Balls
Blue Horse
White Bull
Black Moon
Maroon Molly
Old Chief Smoke

Flumulf
Fast Salmon Swimming Up
A Rippling Stream
Osceola
Tumult
Alpacapla
Green Turd
Feather Weeping
Tree
Savage Son Of A Bitch
Heart
Moose Horn
Killed Many
Roman Nose
Wovoka
Little Raven
Great Sparrow
Fart Dragger
Gray Owl
Luckless Neophyte
Antonio Garra
Pouncing Wolf
Black Kettle
Screaming Scorpion
Cornstock
Snarling Wolf
Sly Snake
Heavy Feather
Light Feather
Rainbow Warrior
Otter Eyes
Many Treaties
Little Wound
Mirthless
Ambush Snake
Night Snake
Snake In Tree
Bury My Heart

Dagger In My Heart
Little Crow
Teal Eye
Amber Snake
Gator Snout
Crazy Horse
Wild Horse
Horse With High Ass
Little Turtle Deer In The
Woods
Flying Deer
Eagle
Spread Eagle
Eye Of Hawk
Soaring Eagle
Soaring Hawk
Song Of Owl
Talon Of Owl
Dog Eyes
Cat Eyes
Night Jaguar
Puma
Bear Belly
Conquering Bear
Salmon Leaping
Condor Of The Moon
Star Blanket
Charging Thunder
Lightning Bolt
Burning Teepee
Jump Like Frog
Climb Like Squirrel
Tommy Graywolf
One Woman For Every Moon
Man Lover
Eel Fingers
Beaver Tooth
Crazy Son Crazy Sun

Neck In a Noose
Nose In Soup
Forgegrof
Tenet
Rowor
Rumbling Innards
Cochise
Chases Butterfly
He Who Talks Too Much
Peace
Black Fox
Grey Fox
Black Wolf
Gray Wolf
Mountain Lion
Gray Puma
Magpie
She Brings Happiness
Black Mountain Lion
Sparrow Chaser
Swift Arrow
Wind
Soft Wind
Moon Shining
Moon
Half
Moon
Moon On Water
Moon On Leaping Water
Leaping Water
Strong Hunter
Strong Like Bear
Strong Like Woman
Strong Like Man
Present For Chief
Someone
No One
Black Foot

Child
Oglala Girl
Digger
Sky Runner
White Man
Invisible Hands
Forest Water
Peace
War
Hair Cut
Crow
Mother Spirit Hawk
Mother Spirit
Laughing Maiden
Coughing Fish
Green Raven
Raven
Brown Dog
Poke-Her-Highness
Billy Two Moons
Jim Thorpe Professional
Nathaniel Canak Henderson
Abelewasi
Eareye
Sawelba
Bear Feet
Twicsttwn
Beaver Fart
Tender Wolverine
Gray Squirrel
Runner
Dinty Havesuminjuninum
Hippocrates
Darwin
Tell No Lies
Burn Forest
Strong As Tree
Dancing Bear

Dancing Otter
Dancing Wolf
Dancing Dirt Devil
Dancing Arrowhead
Dancing Madam
Dancing Wolfpup
Dancing Magpie
Dancing Trout
Dancing Vision
Dancing Dog
Dancing Cat
Dancing Puma
Dancing Tracker
Dancing Left Behind
Dancing Jack McPhee
Dancing Moon
Pas de Deus
Folie A Un Grapple
Senator Wind
Dancer
Zipping Zendel
Red Cloud
White Cloud
Keokuk
Red Grizzly Bear
Black Ass
Grizzly Paw
Bear Cub
Wife Of Grizzly
Grizzly Wife
White Bear
Many Names
Atwin
Whiskey Joe
Irish Whiskey
Joe Kentucky
Whisky Joe Canadienne
Whiskey Jacques

Firewater Joe	Wequash
Hoppone	Sassafrass
Hop Like Rabbit	Sassacuss
Hasay-Bay-Nay-Ntayl	Sass Mouth
Apache Kid	Jefferson
Jack Ass	Measly Pikkins
Whiskey Jack	Skunk Ass

No Longer Deer, even Young Tom Gravel, why not, and the infinite rest in their sacred volcanic mausoleum dreaming in the fumaroles of massacre, risen smoke signals the Battle of Bad Axe, Marie Fire in Flight looking down at the river splitting the coulees, the cuts of the driftless zone, and on that river a giant ship gassing the sky like a lofty predilection, and on that ship white folk with guns, and along the eastern bank white soldiers with guns pursuing a peaceable assembly of mostly Sauk and Fox, whole chunks of Winnebago having wandered back to villages in ingenuous warpminds of peace they had declared to lively ignorant ears, a moist, heated summer day begins early in the morning as the white soldiers rise early to fall upon the Injuns, whose scout leads them astray, but the riverside is a trap, the bluffs steep, the tribes cohere too well, so well that as the men are bayoneted, the women and children flee into the Mississippi to drown, hundreds of Injuns are killed, and look now down and see women and children Sauk and Fox too clever to flee spilling their blood with the men, that countless years of negotiations might cease, the many aggravations the Injun brought to the tables of budding statehoodery might cease, and Marie looks there, up a bluff, three soldiers piling nine dead Injuns when a shriek rends the ploppery, a timber rattler has appeared, and see there: a brave soldier bludgeons it with his gun butt and it goes the way of all combatants; risen smoke signals a stone wall Marie Fire in Flight flies fearlessly above to witness a camp of Chehaws or Muscogees, the neon signs are cursive, confusing, the taverns are closed, the neon blinking intermittently, but there: there is someone, an adolescent Chehaw, hopping with adamantine purpose that unnerves the heartiest of anthros, entering a village of Chehaws or

Muscogees before he stops, animated now only from the bent
waste up, his slopy shoulders flapping out arms, fear shuddering of flaying arms in restrained flight, birds laugh, cruel
crows cackle, and old men laugh for they are not at war, they
have just sent two canoes to Cuba on a tribal trade mission, a
skinned eastern diamondback a good ten feet before chop-
page cooks in the fire they tend like the crops they tend to
tend to, they have bullets for eye holes and frantic women,
entirely out of control as if blood were not of the quotidian, as
the man who neither dismounts nor draws a firearm wonders
at this display of foreign custom, this grating cacophony, this
mock shock, the wide eyeholes, that one hopping as if a cricket with its ass on fire; risen smoke signals reveal to flying Marie Fire in Flight a dry sky burned blue, desert terrain below
of mountains, ravines, arêtes, arroyos, rattlesnakes in crannies of sharp stone or husks of saguaros, men scattered, striving, alert, familiarly execrating the horrific terrain in this year
when all the cacti and the mesquite died of winter heat, yet
the men do not melt despite temperatures above 110 in
spring, temperatures that put humans on edge, discombobu-
late their minds, Marie flies to witness this phenomenon,
which is much worse where people are gathered close as they
were near a dry creek bed, Apache refugees on one side, on
the other the white Americans and those who did their bidding, in strokes of heat, the Apaches invited the white Americans and those who did their bidding to cross the crackling
creek bed and end their sorrow, cool them into the celestial
drifts, or at least in some cloud somewhere for none were
here about, even the children begged—29 were not so lucky
for they were forced to live, sold into slavery—for mercy, for
death, vivid death, violent and sure, and further for the scalp-
ing which should always follow directly upon death that the
skull might cool should there be any delay in postmort take
off, which can certainly be the case when women and children stricken by heat and already prone to feckless thought
having been raised dependent upon savage men number
nearly one hundred and fifty, lamented one sergeant that
day: it is so much easier to organize the kill than the after-

math; risen smoke signals strolls up and down the Siskiyou,
Tom Gravel shaggy on shaggy plug, Tom Gravel held up,
Tom Gravel and Rance Hardupp partnered passing through
Old Shasta, Tom Gravel pissing into the, Tom Gravel passing
into mist, for such is the rigamarole of the fumarole, wherein
Pakistan elders convene, drone blown, a casserole of flesh
and bone ashed—a mist mistake—for no, now Wintu elders
are convened, for there's troubles fuming from furnicularos,
white men in the morning are black men at night, seeking
something sacred within ancestral earth, a substance one
Wintu, Walleye, claimed to have held in its pure form, which
he found too soft as to doubt it would retain its form piercing
a fawn hide, no magical qualities would confine themselves
in such inutile fragments, so council it be, these white to
black men were lunatics, certainly, but lunatics en masse, so
it would take more than the rope around the waist like with
that half-Flathead juvenile, Woeboy, or Woe Be-Guile, let
him wander the woods and take turns winding towards him
at dusk, yes, these white to blacks were a ferverous febrile
fulmination, a fixed idée demon, a demon of fire, fire everywhere in the council house, Wintu elders fleeing to the crepuscular guns of miners, who had already slaughtered even
the Rattlerman and as well his pulsing blue Pacific rattlesnake necklace, which anyway meant doom for a doomed
tribe; risen smoke signals weird alewifes aplenty if mystic in
the stakepole fortress village of Pequot remainers, lazy wom-
enfolk and lackluster lusterless chuffy adolescents refusing to
watch over angstbawling young'uns, that one there screeching tears even as clung teethy to a wide bloated breast, while
finer men went off in seek of salvation as if they believed it
were thereabouts within the protoconurbatory expanse of
grasses and woods and short stubbed, inconstant rivers, for
life were getting measly and promising meagerlier both here
and wherever the proffered there might be if the land
stretched beyond the Mos, hawk or hegan, well, if it even
existed as other birdly ethereals, and thorny saplings backslap
to scratch thighs—did the white man drive all the deer and
rabbit into the Mo lands? Can we convince Sassacus that as

the copperhead is not so deadly and is plentiful and we haven't seen hooved creatures for three days that one hundred copperhead will do sometimes?—while the white coalition creeps to the stakepoles not even bothering to keep their voices down, for their spies have let it be known the men-folk are off hunting, you know, looking for white female flesh, the idiot Injuns and their stickpole circumscribance with its mere two door places, and the fires started at opposite corners, meeting in the middle, all who didn't burn shot, all who were not shot, swordsliced, all dead, five hundred?, six hundred?—they knew; risen smoke signals infundibular, so lies: upturned teepees, where the gas will go once the tin is finetinned, reflective Marie Fire in Flight casts her eyes about first taking in the birds in their millions, casts her eyes about for the moles in their millions, for irresolution prevented their apocalyptic armageddon, *their* redundancies, yet even maggots in their teethy billions stalk not the moles, even the most carnophagous among them are as the sarcophagous-most among them, having as they do a *thing* for the dead likely indescribable, impervious to research, beyond reason, as beyond reason reasons Marie Fire in Flight as what she has seen in her century more or less of human, too much of it white human, shades of failure to reason that perhaps Baby Kelly warnt no baby no more, and Jimmy Footlong of the farm down mile away long Red River was up to some funnin that got them thinkin bout Saint Louis or Natchez, the problem being to gain time, the easiest way being to bloody up a doll, break and bloody an arrow, a note I'm a gone to see Baby Kelly home for she hath gathered much a whatever needs gatherin, a Comanche arrow being most effective as they's still feared near abouts though they be gone and the longer the gone the finer tuned the tale like the cottonmouth venom tipped arrowheads, though them Cheyenne the federals say give up their weapons cept for hunting arrows and them bow things, but there being still near three hundred should they get their asses lit afire could wipe out a family or two before they could hear about it at the fort, and look now the Baby Kelly Massacre on the banks of the river Redder than before, three hundred fourteen with precision in this case, for reasons that escape the historian, for the reason that none escaped, not one, Marie Fire in Flight knows not the relation between her will and her visions, only that the wheel-barrows are dreamlike gigantic overflowing European apocalypse painting type and the shadowy drooling hirsute Böcklin giant employed to infant toss the corpses into the volcano emanates a certain sense of placid damnation, a dumb feint towards delight, an endurance almost human, a mole badly in need of sunlight buried miles deep and magma hot on its ass digging toward the light that will be off in its brain before it comes anywhere near the surface; risen smoke signals, fumaroles and roles within fumaroles, holes and hole, dying moles, the scourge of assholes...

Tom Gravel, dead of heart attack in childbirth, age 61.

36

STANDING TO REASON

How to express my bamboozlement without giving way to the soporifics of unsavory affection for my two boys, Drake and Donnie? Is what I take to be their preternatural *naturalness* a knavery of life mocking a mere author? No fancy schematic diatribes awkwardly awarding the two some djinny freedom— rather an earned study, detachment as vacation. Little has been written of Donnie's homunculaden noctambulatory episodes thus far, though we know, or feel we know, enough to be unclear as to his motive for persisting, dwarf by dwarf, drinking enough alcohol and eating enough tacos to instill a subsistence level sense of place or a detachment of his own, more of a supra-patience, really, than anything else. Yet it would be demeaning, in my opinion, to write this...*juncture*...off as his youthful "why not" response to a sequence of surprising and happy events planing down into a phase of imperturbable if bizarre ordinary. Besides, we know from having lived past the apex of confluencing science and social research that there is little or nothing the human will not happily engage when properly funded.

As for Drake, I have the same optimism, though beshaded, or shadowed, as if my following thoughts of him were themselves being followed and formed to form, followed by a fear that a reluctance will shapen like a sudden, gigantic facial fumarole, form rapidly, just at the last moment, a moment—I call it last, but one often misuses the word—when I am least disposed to testify in regard to his various contempts and malevolence. Of the two, only Drake could survive a Victor Hugo novel with a semblance of pulsing apeman to

behold at the end, whether on the brink of demise or ensconced in an Irish bungalow. That alone should be clear
enough. Yet for now Drake is the likelier of the two to please
a discerning reader, one who has not made the gross error of
dismissing the two for the many and petty reasons one does,
though I never have.

Yes, it does stand to reason, and as friends grow closer,
all the more so, each step stands to reason…and next thing
you know each step steps to reason, and reason may be rather
quick, like—again—an ape in the canopy, and a mad dash,
leaps and bounds, gymnastic maneuvers!, all may be required
to follow wherever, say, dwarf or bald missile man may lead,
let us not shrink from the very possibility that it may be a sinu-
ous speed of light death race to reason, and, too, let us not be
disappointed that much of the race may be as redundandull
as a marathon, that reason require a few hours in a lonesome
tavern, or a long, steady drive on a desert highway through
strange landscapes made stranger by oddities referred to just
seconds ago.

I repeat: it stands to reason. Let it stand.

37

YOUR FATHER LEFT YOU A PRESENT

The bald senator, lo.

Over and over it played in Drake's ear recorders: The bald senator, lo. The bald senator, lo.

This was certainly not the reunion he had expected—and he understood it vaguely, perhaps as something he should have expected—but the timing could not have been better. Picasso Tits would be fine in a day or two, and maybe he would ask Donnie to return, or they could go to Vegas...in a day or two.

He figured he knew her well enough: she wouldn't want to argue about it immediately, and Nordgaard would be around to keep her company. The bald senator, lo. Nordgaard would absolutely fascinate her. The bald senator, lo.

Your father left you a present. Fucking unbelievable!

The towers could multiply into dominoes as far as Drake was concerned (in one reconstruction, they actually were virtually arranged like dominos, though it was collapsing dominoes, you had to use your imagination, or want the physics of domino fall causation to change): the head meeting the tile in the Luxor!

"I looked on the map. I suppose we're on a highway that takes us to the coast where it curves into the sea—that's Malibu, right? And we're going to Malibu?"

"Not exactly, but you get the right enough idea."

"We'll be on the water."

"Yes."

"High security..."

"The highest, but rather unseen."

"So if they fuck off, you'll never know."

"Uh, theoretically—"

"Just fucking with you. I'm not worried about anything yet outside myself."

"I assume [The bald senator, lo] you would rather we speak about it tomorrow, rest, spend a little time with our small man, Nordgaard."

"Will he call me Picasso Tits or Setif?"

"If he gets it wrong, he'll only do it once...but..."

They were off the highway and the road was winding up a forested hill, only that it might wind down again to approach the sea.

"...I'm thinking Picasso Tits, and no doubt Donnie is, too, so—"

"That will be fine just now, after all the travel formalities...the lingering amply bilious...necrophilia, brought on by time changes and the force of false certitudes. Identification, the utter falsity of what has been mastered. I'm tired, yes, and I can't believe you have cleared Donnie out of the way. So yes, please, treat me to this Nordgaard, some good food and drink, and fuck off til tomorrow."

She mustn't see him smile, but she knew he was smiling and did not care why. He was like an adolescent on the threshold of the third date after his first fuck (in her mom's car), this being the first night they would have the snuck luxury of a bedfuck, his first, another first, another threshold that of the sexpsyche with its awareness of lurking anuses and neckties, the entire physiology made giddy beyond capturable reason. But all that was in the past for Mandrake Fondling, though this present giddery not be mystery. The only mystery was the timing of Nordgaard's revelation: why just before he had to leave for the airport to pick up the woman he probably loved? In here, in your father's office—Nordgaard in his father's chair. Drake bemused: what's this little guy up to this time? Sure, upon close inspection Nordgaard showed at least seventy of his years, but he was so spry and impish, it was difficult for Drake to treat other than as a squirrel monkey with capacities of thought and voice.

"Your father left you a present. Something apart from the will."

Nordgaard swiveled to a safe that had already been cracked and pulled a manila envelope from it.

"This is everything from the Luxor," he said, raising the envelope to the height of his head and passing it over the desk to Drake.

"You mean…"

"The bald senator, lo."

"Impact?"

"Everything."

Drake gawped, dust motes dared not fuss; neutrinos apprehended, sought corners of the room.

"You must go. While you are gone, lo, I will prepare the viewing room."

The patio facing the sea had been prepared for Setif, who was escorted there by the little man while Drake scooted to the viewing room. A wooden table resembling cedar was lined with seafood snacks, octopus salad, escargot (a sea food that made good on land), sea bass with cilantro, garlic and lime, grilled shark fillets, mussels, cuttlefish stew, fish soup, salads, olives, mushrooms, a chilled chardonnay, and a portable refrigerator filled with Leffe.

"I'll start with a Leffe," she said, and, though certainly quite tired in one manner or another, finished it off in three long drafts, immediately helping herself to another.

Nordgaard regarded her with secretive and sage scrutiny, lest she find him an oriental of type.

"Would you mind if I opened the wine? I would prefer wine just now."

"You're just being polite, right, there must be a good many bottles of wine about."

"Of course."

She stood and looked out to sea. Her denims been last yanked and buttoned 24 hours earlier, her torso was covered by a mere wisp of sheer shirt by now, her bare hips artless fully in disarray of display.

Nordgaard saw no reason to avoid viewing her as a sexual creature. One Picasso tit was highlighted by sun.

She spun abruptly: "How many languages do you speak, Mr. Nordgaard?"

"Just Nordgaard...I haven't really considered for some time...lo, by some counts it could be more than thirty."

"Tell me then, is the air just now pellucid? I find that the most apt description, but I fear it is only because I want to be in pellucid air."

"Most likely you have already spent much time in pellucid air. As far as this moment, I would not hesitate to aver that you are, we are now in a not unpellucid atmosphere. The cool sea giveth rise to clarity rather than haze, and the sun is yet high enough to, without trickery of any kind, shine through to each separate object unconcealed. Yes, my dear, you have arrived at a pellucid atmosphere, to a pellucid...a pellucidly embellished state of affairs."

Setif stretched a downward grin in satisfaction, looked off at Catalina Island, the sky above, the waters before, the jungle of foliage near enough to giraffe, turned to the table, and sat, eyes now widely confronting Nordgaard.

"Good, let's eat some of this. You *will* eat with me."

"Of course."

Dripping besodden blood of Christ, he's short, she thought—but he has presence...probably could have beaten Gandhi in an armwrestle...out-veined him, mountain gristle.

An amber persistence of light without source sleemed the room...with a subtle quadratic pulse. Drake sat in a leather reclining chair. He was about to start the video when the thought struck—when the thought *struck*, that's what it did, it *struck*, rare behavior for a thought. Your father left you a present. Left me a present. That's pretty fucking eerie. In his will? In his private will? Impossible, right? It had to be something like, Look, Nordgaard, next time you see the kid, give him this. Right, simple explanation, except why would Nordgaard see him before *he* did? And the way Nordgaard said it, just as you would a thing left in a will or if something happens to me make sure the kid gets this damn thing he wanted so bad.

The force of this unusual moment of perception, with energy that was moving it like a wind scraping a steel bin across an asphalt parking lot toward apperception, was strong enough to delay the beginning of the film, to stay Drake, to prevent Drake from slipping the disc from its case after he had prepared the machine, hunched forward like an un-thinking primate, something that drools with neither aplomb nor regard, and he had then splashed back into the chair, holding the disc case with both hands at the nexus of offering and acceptance, sat still in that posture, locked out of the loop of thought that brought him to pause, conscious now of nothing but a discomfort in his diaphragm, the expression of a need withheld.

Meanwhile, on that back porch, saturated with the pel-lucidity of the Pacific perhaps, Setif was peeling a mélange, perhaps inordinately tuned to the melancholy of Nordgaard's woodwind of a voice, lo. His questions seemed very much like a jungle path must be, indecipherably directive to the outsider, perfectly intent to the native. What, she wondered, no—why, did this odd little man want to speak to her at all? He was not so awkward as to come right out and declare that considering her position (*vis a vis* Drake) she should know more about the deceased, but perhaps she had fears that needed to be allayed, and if she did not, perhaps she should have had, for the sake of the future.

"You see, the security is my design, with, of course, input from Drake's father, but my design, and I have great faith in it still. The single failure does not at all indicate that we, lo, are in any danger, even—"

"Especially if no one is after us. Or you. Or Drake."

"This we cannot know, nor must we assume."

"What if we assume otherwise? Were you not involved in security for Drake's parents?"

What if dolphins began to leap into the picture? Setif thought the entire landscape would take on a phony hue, that this hueless meet of sky and sea and sand and palm and impenetrable bush, thorny bush—lantana?—to prevent as-sassin-crawlage, this would all be overwhelmed by the intru-sion of non-human life.

Or whales, what about whales. She knew these were cool Pacific waters.

"What, lo, but it is true. And security we provided. We own the houses on both sides of this, the beach is blocked two hundred meters in each direction. The location itself was as secret as can be. And in each house on either side, lo, we have five of our men living and working only at protection. Further, we have devices that prove that none of our men was complicit in the assassination. Yet I did fail, if that is your implication. Ah, lo lo lo, I did not mention, nor will I elaborate upon, our ability to detect and monitor traffic up and down this entire street."

"Yet Drake's parents, I am sorry to persist, are dead. Murdered."

A thin arm rose to wave falsehood away and embrace the miasma of truth, an arm with veins like muscle and muscle like vein, an arm as of a supra-ophidian inception. Such an arm could scare a woman from Belgium, a woman of limited experience in that it had never encountered murder's remaining limbs and their powers.

"And I am quite sure that we who remain, lo, are entirely safe for that very fact. The killers have accomplished, for now, what they set out to accomplish."

A near imperceptible drop in temperature riding an imperceptible breeze raised mini-nougats on Setif's bare arms, and she fancied the blond hairs above them waved as frondage to form an atmosphere of her very own. The sudden What the fuck am I doing here? came, weirdly, as a surprise.

#######

Most bizarre in real time was the moment, an embraceable moment, actual, at impact, when nothing at all happened, so that the retort delayed by space was timed precisely, or so it seemed with the crack and then shatter of the skull, the pause, the crack, the shatter of the skull, the pause, the crack, the shatter of the skull, the pause, the pause the pause, the crack—assumed?, assumed, the crack and shatter, the pause, the crack, the shatter, the pause the crack shattering, pause crackandshatter, the pause, the crack, the shatter, high (high?) resolution, pause crack and shatter (suicide dance), pause, crack, shatter—the pause, the crack, the shatter, the question of impact, impact itself, the *process* of impact, why missiles don't have shoulders!: black pant legs dancing, slow dancing, still dancing, a line of ten legs one two with the right, swivel on the left, white speckled redspray—what resolution!, resolution, back to impact, pause, crack, shatter, pause— crackshatter—back: pause, crackshattersplatter, crackshattersplattercracksplattershatter, (back) i m p a c t crackshat—ter, splatter pants long pause pants turning, impact, the process of impact, that pause, the crack, the shatter, the splatter, the dance, the impact, crack after pause, shatter and splatter, back: crash, dancing, mayhem, splatter, falling not bouncing, falling, not the head, falling, the body somehow falling front first: back, undeniably a pause, pause, re—undeniably a pause, a crack, a shatter, pause/resumption, splatter, dance— short pants, white socks spotted fever legs dashing, crisscross dashing legs, black pants, more spotted barelegs—fuck it— back, lobby, tile floor, milling, standing, which is, after all, what one does when milling, whoa! splat and splatter! Lobby space, milling—seeing more bare legs now—air-conditioning…Bang! Pop! Splatcrack! Splatter. Imagined shock. Imagined heads. Back, space, Splack! Back space Sprack! Splat and splatter, splat and splatter splat and splatter splat and splatter splat and splatter (good times with dad) splat and splatter splat and splattersplat ##################################### ########### #################################

and yet the being here, in a healthy exocarapace, supple of mind and with leave to summons youthful curiosity, hardly cause for panic (gin and tonic), sun downing, and the homunculus like an altarboy lighting the candles supported by four tall bamboo staves at the patio corners, flames to add nexus to the orbal quackeries of the sun, the salubrious temperature shifts of the breeze, the blue deepening of the sea, the cubist effronteries of the greens and their quickenings of tones, here and not belonging here yet why not here since here, gin and tonic and the epicene glabrous gibbonian Montagnard Nordgaard what do you call them acolyte maybe, not altarboy, candlemonger, see how eagerly he recedes from his eagerness to speak, to relate a story he designs me for, Drake's lady arrived, a mood descending as arranged, Delphic for him, Delfinic for her, his eyeballs esurient, gluten liquefying in ghoulosity, hers Mona Lisa–like, those of dolphins, hidden wariness, alert; and she knew another cigarette, another drink, when the cigarette glowed brighter than his eyes, and it would begin, so she thought please just don't start with As you are Drake's mistress...

"This I will not tell you," he began when he was supposed to, "Lo, this I tell you for no other reason that he has passed, and as he was my lord, I his servant, no night is short, and memories of nightmares shared that were not nightmares now begin to haunt me, to instill in me a heretofore unknown fear. To you, who will vanish, in whom I may be sure my words will vanish, I safely speak the whole of the truth, that he was fallible, that it was I who made him strong, that it was I who preserved his mythic...his mythic *bearing*— for, lo, he was a man whom once broken could not be fixed, and it was I who prevented the cracks from spreading, I who sealed the fissures of fallibility. The place was called Ban Ho, more accurately the jungle hills above Ban Ho, near the sacred Thac Nuoc (over the ban ho near sacred thac nuoc, she repeated melodically, not yet there), and, lo, did we both not know that we would have done well to have been elsewhere, anywhere but there, for we were without support, without communication, on punitive raid deep in enemy territory, though, lo it be much as the jungle hills of my home. But it was not my home. And we there on a punitive raid, a revenge raid, a retaliatory terror raid, the one and only aim to murder any man, woman or child we came upon near the small base camp, or supply depot, one of hundreds of its kind, a small, barely fortified but well-hidden enemy depot, manned by women more than men, from where supplies would be carried to the Ho trail, a logistically brilliant conception,

arrangement, that we had no means of countering, just as
no amount of bombs dropped generally near the trail could
much disrupt the movement of supplies, not enough to, no
never, never enough to relieve the south of its bold effect.
Yet tons of bombs were dropped nonetheless, expensive sor-
ties these, and why. Why: terror. The nature of our work, lo,
took us incognito into targeted areas, at times targeted areas
included more than half of the whole of the Vietnam, Laos
and Cambodia—just don't hit these cities, these bases. You
cannot by imaginative effort alone grasp the terrifying nature
of these tremendous bombings…and so it continued. And so
was the nature of our campaign. To spread terror. The most
remote depot could be under attack and all there would be
horrifically slaughtered. Within a short time, lo, our enemies
would be aware that *no* place was remote or insignificant
enough to be safe. In point of fact, we—our group consisted
of a classified number of personnel, I would guess between
twenty and thirty, only three whites—began by determining
where it would seem most pointless to attack, destroy, burn,
murder, dismember—do not blanche, for this is war.

"Not that you appear to blanche, for night falls, but again,
do not blanche, for this is war. We made a game of imagining
the traveling of words about us. We would hit three straight
depots where a fourth and a fifth would clearly be next in
line. We would establish the logic of that line, and the fourth
would be terrified. At night we would race like apes through
the jungle and strike forty kilometers the other side. Word
would reach the fourth of which I spoke, and lo, they would
be relieved and they would be next.

"The unspeakable was our unspoken motto. Who could
possibly torture and burn a three-year-old child? And so we
would torture and burn a three-year-old child."

Nordgaard's eyes slid from the face of Setif, looking off
to the cleave of sea and sky that was scumbling itself toward
unity of night.

"The hunter alas and lo becomes the hunted. We knew
that would be the case. Careful as we were to avoid harm to
any of the Montagnards, undoubtedly there had been those

pressed into service at the depots, or carrying supplies to the depots, and who were, unlucky, present when we attacked. I have no doubt that we eventually lost the tacit support of my own people by killing them grotesquely, grotesque though they already were in service of the enemy. Drake Senior, I will call him, had few favorites in life and in war. I was his little brother from the beginning, though perhaps I am ten years older. Yet on this duty he had become attached to one of our finest guerrillas, known only by the nom de guerre Pham. He was perhaps nineteen years old, a crack shot with anything that delivered projectiles, a jungle man, fleet of foot in forest in flank, flight or fight, the man we sent in to silently slice the jugulars of the guards, a handsome youth, not to say pretty, nor, lo, to imply that the Colonel had feelings for him that went beyond the soldierly familial. I, too, adored Pham. I owe my life first to Mandrake Winchester Fondling, lo, but second to the late Pham"—here a twine of arm serped aside for a bottle of whiskey, which much of was swilled immediately. "For this I do need the strength of firewater, for fate fucked us that f—no, it was a different day, early in the week, Tuesday, or a Wednesday. We had been operating in a semi-predictable pattern within perhaps a seventy-kilometer radius of Ban Ho, hitting two in one night, or in successive nights, travelling long distances, hitting two more, like that. When we felt it was unsafe we hit a relatively large depot called Ho Shat, guarded by no less than seventeen fighters, as if they had some inkling that was their night. Nonetheless, Drake and Pham, together, went ahead in the dark, returning to where we awaited an attack signal, each carrying two heads, blood, well—lo, my dear young lady, it is all bloody, is it not. Thirteen left we were told, but no warning, some sleeping. Be aware, kill soldiers first, but be on the lookout lest a civilian reach for a weapon. We moved off in a whoosh of near silence, the business lasted less than five minutes, and in an hour we were safely away—not in the direction of the nearest depot, but to Ban Ho.

"Lo, it is impossible ever to know whether one of our number gave us over to the enemy or whether the enemy

out-monkeyed us, but awaiting us at Ban Ho was the cleverest
of ambush. We expected but few at the tiny Ban Ho depot,
well-hidden up in the jungly, we expected few—and found
none. *None*. Yet somehow we had obtained the unfortunate
habit of sending two, Mandrake and Pham, ahead to scout
the depot, and so it was they who suffered the blow. The
blow: Pham tripped a mine that flung him up a tree never to
descend but in parts—parts thrown by me, thrown by me—
while Sir Mandrake, to say this to a lady, lo, but one who
does not blanche, for she knows war, somehow, perhaps the
very birthright of the Belgique, if not, my pardons, and, lady,
lo, it is all bloody, is it not, the mine tore the manhood from
our leader (temporal calculations, Vietnam, latest early 70s,
Drake born...nope, adopted for sure, doesn't seem to know,
fuck it go on little hairless fellow), who at dawn was still in
shock, looking up into the tree [down there beneath the lower canopy up which Pham draped and leaked, thinking that's
mighty heavy-handed those hanging hands—orisons obscur-
ing horizons, tendrils of tendons twined shoulder-free freeing
from shoulders onto *his* shoulders, *his* face, branching off a
branched body a body branching out, to tender drips and ten-
dril drops and exotics of bluebottle cousins of green and gold
and such amber as blood would maroon like 1001 vultures
on a pinch of pinschershit, carnadine, crimson blackning,
the startle of white, white strips unstrapped, stropping! And
strapping!, like fluid bonery, utterly so, utterly seen, utterly
felt, e'en in eye, on lip, mouthed, drunk—such is gore, such
is gore in its liquid aspect, fancy I spy an eye, a Phameye
more likely a shameye, typical jungle phantasmagoriflage,
mocking my hide in plain sight motto, parasite, yet another
parasite, no, not a parasite a carrion eater merely carrying on
scavenging, jungly supermoth tearing into Phamcorpse, even
though to name us Phamcorpse how do you like it, winking,
see!, winking your next white man, juiciest of corpses, exotic
jungle death meal, what creature be that carrying off my eye?
Carrying off my eye! Ahhhhhhhhh! Shit! Shitrain of Pham-
strains, god! Nooooooooooo!—] twitching and weeping and
nightmarescreaming, eyes wide open as always but this time

not seeing what was there to be seen, not as before seeing
what no one else saw but was there to be seen, no whatever
he saw was not there to be seen, I could have shot him—I
climbed the tree and I too knew my hysteria, for, lo, I suffered a fit of screaming "This isn't you! This isn't you!" Until
I could stand it no longer and though most of what gravity
could bring of Pham down had come down, some sap perhaps slowly descending, I peeled and stripped what I could,
and I was up in that tree, tossing intestines down, skin flecks
down, I held bits torn—well, cut with my knife, so bleeding
fresh—I held them over his face so the drops would land on
his eyes, in his mouth, anything to shock him back to himself, the last, I am sorry, but not so, I had but two tries, the
head you see had been hung by lucky twist of twine, awful
if Drake were conscious to see this largest chunk of Pham
staring down at him, and Drake's mouth was wide open as he
was now screaming more or less continuously—I could hardly bear it, but, lo, someone must keep his head in such…I
gouged, not spooned or knived, though I did use my knife, I
severed and plucked and took careful aim, but one has little
practice at this game, and the first bounced off his cheekbone
(what an odd sound it made, a jungle sound), but the second,
directly in the mouth, almost too good a shot, for it nearly
went to tonsil, such a shot that it disgusted Mandrake, so disgusted Mandrake it brought him back to his senses, for he sat
upright, abruptly sat upright, legs sprawl, crotch bloodied to
a delta of blood between the legs, shook his head, rolled the
eyeball just so, as one would an olive, and spat it out, looked
up at me and, himself again, I shall never forget his words,
lo, 'All right, Nordgaard, that's enough, let's get me out of
here…'"

Far from Hollywood, the colors of a misplaced Mediterranean flickered with the bamboo candle lamps, the breeze
huffed and quietly outsucked, like some pleasantry bestowed
upon a sleeping feline, a lion, the largest of his pride, the
proudest of his humble, the humblest of his size. Setif, of
course, visualized all she was told, yet without taking her eyes
off the sea, or the sky, whichever was, tremulous, levering the

darkness with its pulsing implacability, the unavailability of it to reticence. She still felt misplaced, orphaned, still like a drugged socialite in a car trunk, the thing to do refuse to shake off the sensation, to delay the moment of clarity one expects to arrive as a hammerblow. Yet a good story was a good story, and she had learned much of war, from stories of war—it was no difficulty crossing the Empty Quarter from desert rock to sweating jungle. Being a good listener she had been drinking little, just the one glass, and now reached for a bottle of wine and began drinking from it.

"He must have lost a great deal of blood. It's a wonder he survived."

"Partly true, yes—at the same time, we had done our contingency planning well. The bleeding was stopped or, yes, he would have died. I will not describe his injuries in more detail, but to say we were able to stop the bleeding, or enough so that he survived a bit of a trek and a helicopter flight— out of country to a nearby field hospital secreted in northern Laos, among friendly mountain folk like me.

"Lo, you have made your simple calculations and have determined your mate is a bastard, orphan, or whatever, that he is not the son of Drake Winchester Fondling and that is true, no matter the advances in prosthetics and refrigeration. He was never told, for reasons that are beyond my reckoning, for in my culture it is most important for a man to know what he is. But it was not for me to question, nor was I wont to think about it, for, lo, think: this event occurred something like forty years ago. The war did not end for either of us. Mandrake was already a legend, but not the legend he would be when he returned to face the rumors, returned to lead again, returned to strike fear throughout Vietnam, amongst both his enemies and his own men—but, lo, I know not what the young Fondling has already told you of his father."

"Actually I was told, Nordgaard, years ago, when I was thirteen, I believe."

Drake stood recessed in shadow off behind the right flank of Setif, facing Nordgaard, his face on occasion flicking to lit.

"The idea seemed to be that if I were told at the right

time I would find it of no issue, and of course as you don't even know that I know, I would say the psychology behind the decision was sound. Of course, I don't know how it feels to be the blood son of a magnate or whatever rich man my father was, but I know how it feels to be me, and my guess is the oddities are rather plebeian."

"Glad to hear it lad, glad to hear it."

"I thought you were—"

"I was. But then I changed direction, did a little research, made some calculations...Nordgaard, you can tell me how accurate this is, right?"

"Certainly. But, lo, my own accuracy depends to some degree upon acquaintance with topic."

"I think my old man received, for his design input, more than half a million dollars per drone. Is that right?"

"Good round number, half a million. Initially a bit higher, perhaps by now a bit lower. Good to have friends in dark places."

"So in drones alone he has probably earned...let's multiply by two thousand, so—"

"Rather conservative figure, but keeps things in bounds, perspective..."

"So a billion...is that right? So many fucking zeros and yet none if you just say it, a fucking billion off drones alone, am I right? Setif?"

"Half a million times two is a million, a thousand million is indeed a billion."

"See there, Nordgaard, and that's the minimum, am I right?"

"Where are you going with all this, boy?"

"Nowhere. To bed. Soon. We'll be visiting Donnie in Vegas tomorrow, I suppose."

Setif watched Drake's still face, candles flickering profile, and, the subterranean trickle of disgust ate deeper into the rocks, slowed to pool in a darker place, and for the first time in nearly two weeks, more—since she had received his invitation—she felt affection for him and the calm through which her lust might safely return.

38

OF DOLPHINS AND NEUTRINOS

[Third up card: four of diamonds] [Bet five.]

On the twenty-third floor of the Luxor, maybe he was drunk, in his room the lamp beside his bed on, he was asleep, probably he was drunk, the door was open, the book lying beside him, open to the photo of the painting in which the mandrill and the dwarf—Perkeo, from Heidelberg—leered sinister: so then, if the baboon leers over Perkeo's shoulder, Perkeo leers over yours, Donald. (If you keep up this paranoia they will kill you, Donald.) I'm heralding all you spankers…a hot breath on my neck like you would expect me to smell, like the way they say I smell. Good night, Donald. Good morning, Donald.

You virus.

(And a snickering like the hideous quababbling of mandrills.) What he means, Donald, is what's carried from rat to lice to you isn't alive or dead nor light nor dark. They want you to compromise, Donald. We all recommend against it. We're all on your side.

(Donald.)

Everybody heard you, anybody could have heard you, the door was still open, he might have been drunk, I wasn't quite asleep…it was a half-dream…Somebody came in and snickered. I thought it was you. (Laugh bluesnout! Laugh redass!)

It helps to know what staff the mandrill holds/what's black and shines unlit and sterile, cold, ungleaming, gripped by hands a lot like yours, Donald. What do you suppose that little handle's for? And glancing manic cross homuncule eyes you know it's there, he know's you're there, you know he knows and so you know

how far up it goes.

(Bugging eyes are never wise)

O hideous dwarf o me On Heidelberg I take a pee On Heidelberg I take a pee, me and my monkey, my monkey and me: you have two nipples, I might have three—My fat monkey cock looks just like me

On Heidelberg I take a pee.

(Fastknuckled monkey darkscurrying—alley)

Blink, Donald—relax, man. Remember Melissa Mounds, whose tits were lighter than air? Maybe that's what they're looking at, Monkey and Man: Ah, pink and bulbous oriflamme; ah, rosy infinitum cheeked and fat thighed garter Tramp of the Trampoline, rise, rise delicious weightless wench: O how neverloved and doublehumped, what wicked things we did and do: he quababbled me, I quababbled you all over Heidelberg, the world and you.

(Maybe we'll kill you anyway.)

For love of life we nibbled you in dark, distaffic sanguine fissures. O Triumph of Mockery, you cried (all hail the bats and all)…Did you say honor, false humblarian? Did you say dignity, modest didactician? Were you afraid of your own boast? Do you regret those baubles now? (Tonight, Donald, we march!)

"Wattloofhuhlf," tremoloed, shuddering…wake up with the absolute need to fling off something sticky, necrocoprophragous, splenetic like doused cellophane: "flulblahfa..faa. Shit!" Sitting up, drowsy more than drunk, the door is shut, the lamp is on, morning light, shirt undone, sweating. Melissa Mounds, the fuck did that come from…Everybody did bad things in their childhood and if maybe the most spooky result was burning all his sister's dolls when he was young he never dreamed about it, even if he recalled the frightening aspect of the shadows of the fire and the resistance to night and the eyes of the dolls and the one doll the next morning when the crime was discovered, the one with one good eye that she insisted on throwing away, somehow making it worse, haunting him to this day, though sporadically, never like this fucking nightmare. This midget shit is insane. Three nights playing blackjack with midget dealers, getting a feel for things. They each confided that you aren't supposed to call them midgets, but it was okay to call them dwarves, because they were victims of dwarfism, unless they weren't in which case they were short, but midget had become unacceptable. Though they used midget themselves and knew of none who minded. "Don't you think *Little people* is quite a bit more demeaning. Hah! Demeaning. Fuck it. Belittling?" Worse, he had seen dozens of advertisements, dwarves and midgets tossing their wares at the presumably bizarre, market researched bizarre:

Beacher's Madhouse in the MGM, owned by midgets, run by midgets

Rent a Midget Stripper
Rent a Midget Gambler
Rent a Midget Gigolo
Midget Firebreather
Midget Hockey
Midget Guide
Midget Host
Midget Racing
Midget Wrestling
Dwarf Tossing
Midget Elvis
Midget Stag Party
Midget Magician
Midget Balloon Man
Midget Balloon Woman
Midget Pole Dancer
Midget Lap Dancer
Midget Cops
Midget Elvis Wedding
Midget comics
Leprechauns Gone Wild! Fremont Street
Midget Strippers

Midget Rock Band
Extreme Midget Wrestling
Midget Minister
Cambodian Midget Fighting League
Midgets Date Club
Midget Fart Contests
Midget Dart Leagues, with Midget Lady Daredevils
Smoking, standing on chairs, the ashes knocked off by
midget aces
Midget Fire Fighters (also for midget fire breathers who
caught fire)
Midget Gang Fights
Midget Secretaries
Midget lawyers, lawyers for midgets, bar ready
Midget beer bottle tossers
British midget tossers, for stag parties
Midget brides and grooms
Midget witnesses
Midget evangelists outside the Bellagio
Midget Geography contests
Famous Midget Trivia (Perkeo of Heidelberg!)
Midget bowling league
Midget Circus at Ex Calibur
Midget clowns
Chinese midget buffets
Blind Midget Ice Skating
Midget wheelchair racing
Midget cancer drive
Midget hairdressers and laddermen
Midget nylon saleswomen were probably the straw that
thucked the thwat, as the saying went before the grute fell
from the rafters. He opened the midget refrigerator, poured a
midget whiskey into an adult—no—full-size glass of ice and
mixed in a midget whiskey, drank half it off, lit a smoke and
sat at the desk looking himself in the mirror, or in the eyes,
however it would work. Knowing the task was over meant no
such thing as momentum going a different direction, like a
step onto a different escalator or escapalator, whatever they

were when they went across ground instead of up or down. It was a stupid idea and he had been a sap, he tried to think, but at this point in his, again fictile, again fingent, life, none of that hardly mattered. Surely the thing to do was call Drake and let him know, but when? Last night wouldn't be possible, and it would be fair to say he knew it already then. Now would be as if it existed and that if it did it also had a measure of meaning, that it was enough like a container that he could define it as the time to call Drake, which was not something possible to arrive at from any logical direction. So he would call Drake, tell him it was a sham project, a deal for a dope. Or, fuck that, it could simply mean an alteration in the deal, and if that were the case, would there be any sense in calling Drake at all? Drake shows up, give him the dirt, take it from there. Meanwhile, or, meanwhile… out by the pool reading copious Procopius, or whatever one finds where books gather in Las Vegas. Midget Books…Midget Books—magnifying glasses fifty percent off. Or a dame. I could use a dame. The dames had been in and out of his periphery—there's a lot of gam in Vegas—sinuously slipping and sliding, probably sloshing their drinks, bimbos, hookers, the avant riche, the nouveau aristocrats, the narrow-faced bored. He had not kept his eyes peeled at all. There had to be some place where a young man—look at him: look at you: unshaven no more than usual, not bad looking, not musclebound, neither lacking in shoulders, wiry…insouciant, too. He hadn't had trouble finding someone to fuck since he had reached his current height. Probably, now, yes, it feels good to think about it, now that he was having it in for a drink, this thought, he could make of it an objet d'noir. That or the desert—he's had plenty of thoughts about the desert since you could see it every day in every direction, a magnificent valley this, and the exotica of fauna out there blending in making the mistakes of movement. He'd actually been wanting to take a drive out there for a few days now, come to think of it. The desert and a broad. A broad and the desert. Maybe that means Palm Springs to most folks. Maybe that meant Palm Springs to Donnie. How would he know. Fucking change of pace, is what I need. He snubbed the butt and quaffed the drink, repeated—looked back. He was hungry. He would shower, get the fuck out of this joint, head north on the Boulevard and choose a spot, start looking for where there might be dames, dames he could pick up. The best time was probably before dusk, the best time to start. Not so long after that it's too many couples. Midwestern broads wearing dresses up to their netherspokes they'd never wear at home, their dorky husbands looking at them more in one night than they would the rest of their lives. Maybe he should beat someone up in a parking lot. Put himself in neutral. Better to avoid them, what's easier. Find a pleasant place where the music isn't too bad, where you could both think and talk, a place with a little traffic. Before long he'd certainly have someone to take home—which he liked to think of his hotel room as for precisely its unsuitability. Home is not where the thing is, that home cliché thing; home is where home is and when that no longer is, then there isn't home. Donnie was quite comfortable with that notion, for he had come unglued and he watched himself shrinking as his stomach roiled the last unloosed months of emotions he refused to vomit like as he figured he should not though one must or one lands like a hard cliché in Vegas talking dames. How long could he watch himself watching himself watch himself when he wasn't refusing to watch himself, waxing riverine angling away from shore, angling away from shore. Fuck it. Home was long gone and would not be returning, nor be waiting, nor be on a path. Home was finished. Home was midgetsville, man. Home was dwarfstown, baby.

The music was so low Donnie, bellied to the šank, could follow the televised news. Jirga, they called it, a meeting of tribal elders. And just as he was thinking Now there's democracy in action, a subtitled interviewee of Tajikryghindoafghuzbek descent was calling it democracy in action. Cut to scenes of terror and mayhem. Viewer discretion is advised. A weeping man who looked too young for his beard and more fit for a beanie than a pakol, or should at least have had heliblades affixed to his pakol (any resemblance to the historical

Greek mathematician and philosopher Heliblades is either
real or imagined), was being interviewed—his father, a local
tribal leader had been decimated ("...and the next second
he was gone. I don't know why Allah spared me."). What he
meant was that no body parts were available. Yet plainly visible over his left shoulder, in the dirt, as what seemed to be
villagers ran frantically back, across, and forth, loading the
wounded—not a euphemism if effectively so, guilelessly, unnatural it would be to refer to the innumerable bloody messes
with hearts pumping at rates variable—somehow not dodged
but in the chaos in a circle or gross amoebagon of safe space
untrodden, lay visible a twitching severed arm. (How did this
get on television?) Endurance and focus were required for
Donnie to determine that the news was no more than two
weeks old, that the film was from a Pakistani professional team
covering the "Tribal Areas," that the station was a local public station affiliate. He looked again at the bartender, a middle-aged man, a man of the Middle Ages, sneaky Renaissance
prophet fellow, with a Vegas moustache, ordinary brown hair
ordinarily styled, doing what a bartender must do in such a
scene, toweling beer glasses and shelving them. Was he listening? Down the bar two women in casual attire, shorts and
blouses of no particular breed, and two Asian men in suits
with unloosened ties and jackets over barstool backs were in
conference separately. To his left, a brunette he gauged at
thirty-seven, at least younger than his mother, was sipping a
gin and tonic through a straw, head angled eyeward toward
the screen. Her maroon, velvet dress was Vegas, her thighs
were Vegas tanned and gamly gamine enough to draw Donnie's interest, heavy—his interest and her thighs—and half-
bared. She wore rather more lipstick than the gals down the
other way, but precisely so, carefully chosen and applied—as
if Donnie were an expert (but one must use one's brain as one
must a bow and arrow, in lightness and dark). Any black used
for the brows was indetectable. From two stools down—she
sat just shy of the curve of the bar to the wall—Donnie could
make out the side-bowing of her right breast (the neckline was
not, but nor was it low enough for cleavage to be visible). She

could be anything from a classy dame to a freelance hooker to a happy housewife, a harpy halfwit, a hippy whorebag, a humping Hermione, heavy with experience and years, not to suggest he was herm-happy, but he rather liked her squat indeterminacy. She could be thinking anything at all about what was on the television, as could be the bartender. Or nothing about it. Nothing was what was usually displayed about drone strikes, a particular bane of Donnie's since the first one his father told him about when he was about twelve years old. He still remembered it clearly, his father emphasizing the distinct nature of the weapon—a child's toy, remote controlled (though he was not sure he knew then that the children were playing just north of Las Vegas while the poor folk were getting bombed in Asia—swooping—no! not even swooping, cruising, no, more like aerambling about beneath the clouds, they were said to be rather too loud to be spy planes, at least so the early models—crossing borders as if they did not exist and they did not, and this one, this one back in it must have been 2002 early that, as pops had made clear, had been said to have killed an important al Qaeda leader, blowing up the car he was in, *in Yemen*, no attempt to hide the extraterritorial, nor the presumed innocent clause, nor the too bad about them other folk, you run with the wolves (presumably), that kind of thing. To Garvin it had been of unprecedented appalling nature, this death strike. And to Donnie it had indeed made an impact. Yet it was difficult to discuss. He had written since a couple of papers on drones at school, received with high marks and higher indifference; it was not something easy to discuss with his one or two friends he had at various points in time, only Brian, but Brian was beyond the need to talk about it, Brian was building his own bombs. You simply did not need to say that a pilotless plane was simply not cricket—and that wasn't said in his country anyway. And now look: a new president, same war as that one they started after the towers came down ten years ago, an improved war, effervescing in Pakistan, where previously it was only gratuitously delivered in the manner one disposes of by-product. Though he knew the arc of the weapon was simply on a standard rise, that of course the attacks would increase, the range would increase, the suppressed joy of being in any way on the side of the weapon would *not* effervesce, but piss out in sprees of express ecstasy. Yet here he was, and what was he doing in Vietnam town, as it seems it may have been known, anyway?, Las Vegas's Vietnam town, surely the least of Vietnam towns, here he was with Hermione and Sal—surely Italian twice removed, Uncle Sal in Vegas—in still orbits round the screen, round the dronescreed of the screen, in orbit to the gore, the blaring glaring screeching V2 at high speed symbol of democracy disintegrated by a single blow (actually there had been four missiles) or blowup. He knew outrage was outmoded, yet he was uncertain what replaced outrage as response. Surely sitting sipping a gin tonic through a translucent green straw, virtually immobile even with no back support, surely that was response; surely, white-toweling beer glasses and reaching across and up a shelf to fill up for some imagined impending night crowd, surely that was response. Clearly his own thoughts were response.

Viaggio: the first several blocks up the Boulevard, the long long blocks of Boulevard, were taken at high walk speed, express centrifugality, before he began to look about for a means of navigation, apt metaphor, phor he was much like a sailor in uncharted vast water, the fucking thing he was looking for was obvious, land, he knew he would know when he saw it, but the one thing that became rapidly apparent was that the bar he needed was not going to be inside a Casino, and he decided this upon nearing a major eastwest intersection, which insinuated like a breeze or a cricket whisper to a sailor a left turn, a turn west, fuck, grandiosemost of insinuated navigationals, he turned west and it was several blocks of casino trappings to the interstate highway and after that the landscape that can come to seem the underbelly and spinal of Vegas itself, the square fenced lots, never entirely empty of something, palleted usually, tires, or machines more alien than drones that have to be corralled somewhere do they not, the giraffes of the construction world, the tapirs of urban infrastructural upkeep, and a

couple halfblocks of vacance with corner establishments, a first
outpost of Vietnamese writing like a skull on the long road,
then two more, then this bar and simply no choice.

"Hermione," Donnie spoke.
No corporeal fluidity was interrupted. He tried again.
"Excuse me, Hermione."
Hermione contracted her brows and nearly swiveled her head.

This might be hard to believe, but as people do come and go from bars—look the Asian business fellows have gone and we hadn't even noticed—it is likely enough that something familiar...to say it plainly, at the very end of the šank, a stool down from the second lady, sat 22b, whom Donnie just now noticed or wondered if he had. 22b looked anything but absorbed, though nor was he looking about. He had a drink in front of him, a mixed drink, and was looking desultorily from the drink to the spaces before him framed by a periphery he seemed not inclined to expand. At some time the bartender must have lay down his towel, gone and conducted bar business and set back to his prop.

The light in the bar was pre-dusk, slanting in through the open door, having no luck at the curtained windows. The room constrained the temperature to a pleasant lower nineties, unimposing and eunuch-subtle fans shaking their heads in solemn, shared and in one case sciatic cross-sympathies.

"Hermione?"
She finally looked. Donnie immediately liked her face, its structure, its green eyed, fullcheeked, full lipped, sardonic expressioned face.
"You are talking to me."
"Yes, hi, I'm Donnie, and we're both watching this news program, well now it seems suddenly to have shifted to some sort of two man delivery, a form of news doubles, but as I was saying, we were both watching, you seemed to be, and I was both watching and listening intently, and so I simply wanted to ask if you were having any thoughts on the event."
Her laugh came as a bark would from a waking dog, one syllable, genuine and vague.

"Grizzly. It's a grizzly affair…Donnie."

"Yes it is, isn't it."

"sa fuckin shitmire," the bartender added rather too loudly, a bit of anger resident, a bit risen.

"Yes, it's a grizzly shitmire."

"Bach," the bartender said, dismissing the topic. Hermione and Donnie look round about each other.

"So? So what were you thinking, Donnie?"

"Oh, shit, lots of things. I was surprised to see it on a television in a tavern, first off. But then, primarily—well this goes back a way with me. Drones are a particular evildoing with me. I won't shrink from saying it. I think they are internationally criminal weapons, there's no less stilted way of saying it. I know people generally don't like to think about such matters, much less discuss them. But they get me worked up."

"I don't mind."

What a thing to say.

"Don't mind…"

"I don't mind discussing *such matters*. Fact, one of my particular irritations is people who bluntly announce their desire to refrain from discussing politics, or issues." She lifted her drink to Donnie in what would anyway have been an indefinable gesture, and he reacted automatically by lifting his own, and they both noticed both were empty.

The bartender knew his business, his mating calls.

"Two more?"

"Another whiskey soda and that looks like a gin tonic."

"Is that your way of announcing you're buying me a drink?"

"No—I mean, no it is not that, not that I wouldn't buy you a drink or offer, no, I mean yes to buying you a drink or having you buy me one and *but* I merely reacted with accustomed speed to solve the problem of an empty glass."

Before Hermione could respond they had fresh drinks and saluted each other, each with a personal version of immordant sardon riding an undercurrent of pleasure.

"What I'm saying, if I recall," Hermione recalled, "is that if it's interesting I'll take my gossip straight up as well as my politics or anything else, and I'm irritated by, especially women I know, who get all cutesy bimbo and, with what normally would be taken as abject rudeness, cut off discussion."

She is smart, this one, Donnie reflected.

Probably she was preparing to believe the same was true of Donnie.

"That's rather refreshing. Though where I escaped from—"

"Escaped?"

"Escaped. Where I escaped from we had sort of the opposite problem. Academic community. The thing there was quite often to bend to the rude by never shutting the fuck up. And worse, by saying shit you don't mean."

"What about this then?" she asked gesturing languidly toward the television.

"I don't know. For one thing, don't you think they, they meaning government as well as media, have become rather blasé about war crime?"

"Is it a war crime? Grizzly, what was it, shit…"

"Mire, grizzly shitmire."

"Right, grizzly shitmire no doubt. But what makes this one in particular a war crime?"

"Oh no, no, not this one in particular. This is just this one. The one here and now on television. Frankly, nothing particular about it. This isn't in a country the country's at war with, but if they kill forty civilians in Afghanistan I would call that, too, a war crime."

"I quite agree. How can you look at that and not?"

"Indeed. As you were saying, more or less, about the indecency of mentioning politics on certain occasions, in certain contexts, like here in life, definitely the wrong context there, what I find tedious is suffering through conversations with people with whom I more or less agree but would like to make distinctions that strike me as useless."

"Such as?"

Donnie regretted making a grimace of disgust, but persevered, "Hard to think of the right example…Well, this is a bit weaker than what galls me severely, but just such a distinction as might be made between droning an ally and a named enemy."

"Probably you'll think I'm silly mentioning that perhaps all this…this international slaughter, this, all this *shit*"—veritably spat out—"is a war crime."

"Oh, of course it is. The problem is that's a discussion ending observation…"

She arched her eyes at him. Clearly she had been enjoying herself.

"I don't mean here and now, I don't know you—that's a discussion opportunity in any case—I mean generally. I've known, sorry if I let slip a personal, I've known my father to use it just to shut my mother up. And he knows what he's doing, and she knows he knows, and all the way up it goes, upstairs, after the dinner party, where she's a banshee and he is utterly silent, I used to think hopefully he's asleep…"

"In confessional mode, tonight, Donnie? Did something just happen?"

"Astute observation, but wrong. Just picking scabs."

"Lovely image. This leads me of course to speculation: he's a student, quite young—I'm thirty-seven, if you're interested—angry—"

"Unformed, searching, living one cliché whilst groping for another. No, none of that. I am young, not yet twenty-two, but I'm a man, I'm not a student, and any residual family anger is of the moment, not some temporary thing I need to get over. And besides that the anger, such as it is, spreads outwards from the entirely completed family shit."

"Are you being touchy?"

"No," he smiled, "not at all…I haven't had a good conversation for a bit too long, more than a week."

"You in town on business, then?"

Now he fully laughed.

"Are we turning this into a cliché?"

Hermione smiled, finally crossed her legs the other way, left over right, while turning at a stooltop canter toward Donnie. "Are you in town on business?" she repeated, with an element of scold.

"Sorry. Yes and no. Yes, I am, no I am not simply so. There's some chance I'll be moving here. That I'll stay here for the time being and even for some years."

"Mysterious answer. I am resident."

"I thought so."

"What else did you think? Did you make any occupational guesses?"

"Nothing with conviction. Vegas is a strange place for that. You should see what your midgets are getting involved in here. They're into everything. What's a lady sitting alone in a bar in Vietnamese town compared to that? They even got a place in the MGM—"

"'Owned and operated by midgets.'"

She let out a genuine guffaw that Donnie joined.

"Of course, you would be up on your midgets."

"That one just struck me, that's all."

"You can also hire a midget to strike you, if that's your pleasure."

"It most certainly is not. But back to my occupation."

"Shit, that's a bit unfair. What would be a good guess? Do I flatter you with something false or inane, or do I insult you with something more base than I had reckoned?"

"Realtor. I have an office not all that far from here. I'm in the neighborhood for the food and I happened to have a free afternoon. And as I am childless and divorced—you didn't seem to check my finger, but the ring signifies nothing—and sometimes prefer my own company with alcohol to my apartment and friends."

"That's a mouthful. Just when I was going to guess you ran a stable of midget jockeys."

She smiled, but was determined to press on. "So you, then. Enlighten me."

"Someone needs to enlighten me, first. The midgets being on my mind is no accident. I am here scouting the situation vis a vis midgetry. Really. I have a wealthy friend, perhaps partner, who would like to establish a casino with a Brussels theme, and you know they have a tourist attraction called Manneken Pis, a midget fountain—"

"Oh stop it."

"It's true. If you've never been to Brussels there's no reason you should have heard of it."

"And you've been to Brussels."

"Recently. I was in a card game, which I won by a rather

spectacular margin—I was a student at the time, technically. Well, it turned out I was playing at the home of a very rich young man who took a liking to me and abruptly took me to Belgium for reasons I never investigated. Then after some months his parents were murdered in LA, he inherited a great deal of money, and a great deal more than he expected, and came up with this casino idea. And he sent me on ahead to look into it. In short."

"You're either a pathological liar or greatly in need of slowing life down to manageable speed."

"It's not only all true, but it gets even more bizarre here and now." He lowered his voice a degree.

"This is going to tip you over to the pathological liar side, but see that guy at the end of the bar?" he glanced back to be sure 22b—and it was definitely him—"we, my pal—Drake— and I, we call him 22b…it has to do with his seat number on the flight from Philly to Brussels, he was adamant about not exchanging so we could sit together…we saw him afterwards several times in Brussels, and it was rather unnatural because we weren't tourists, we were staying there, and we saw him…I don't know, but it was, let me downplay it a little, it wasn't a topic of long conversation, Guess what, I saw 22b again today, that kind of thing, until now, right now, his showing up here beyond coincidence, truly bizarre—"

"You're right, pathological liar it is."

"But it's true."

"Then go talk to him."

"I'd rather not. Anyway, what if he simply denies it? No, I'm content to have you think I'm a pathological liar."

"You don't seem like one, I'll give you that."

"Probably few do, not the well-practiced ones."

"Good thing you're not a defense lawyer."

"A spade."

"What?"

"Sorry, cliché, calling a spade a spade."

Hermione returned to her drink, switching on an action switch in our man Donnie.

"I'm staying at the Luxor, we could have dinner, I mean

I would like to invite you to dinner. And, well, whatever that might or might not lead to. We can go now."

"See if 23b follows?"

"22b, and no, I just had the thought cross my mind one too many times and didn't want to wait until you committed to excusing yourself. I don't have a car, but if you are too unnerved by my tall tales I could meet you somewhere, take a cab."

"A cab would be easier anyway if we head toward the strip."

"Then it's yes?"

"Oh absolutely. I haven't had such a good conversation in years."

What a pleasure, and even at Donnie's roughtreated tender years he knew to recognize it, to see a woman after the coupling exit the shower in a hotel bathrobe—yours!—wringing her wet hair, intent on settling in for the night, *that* happy with you, with you and her, as if your own contentedness was conclusion foregone fore foreplay!

"I know I'm on the young side, Madame Hermione, but this promises to be perhaps the finest night of my life."

"We're in the Luxor, shall we leap the railing together?"

"The pathological liar and the psychotic femme fatale."

The two shared their self-satisfaction a moment.

"As the elder might I ask you to fix me a drink, I mean without sounding like Martha in—"

"*Who's Afraid of Virginia Woolf!* Could this night get even more better?"

"'More better?'"

"Yes, I guess it could. Yes, I will fix us drinks—from the bar of the dwarves, who run this hotel, this strip, this city…"

Hermione settled on the settee, wrapped her hair in a towel, and odalisqued to comfort, her legs dehiscing the robe up to her lush boscage. Donnie marveled at the way the being contorts and combines its inner responses as performing circus feats, his sense of well-being ratcheting up to fearsome lust tempered by a gathering apperceptual within that could have as easily smoked opium and watched the night as in a play performed for his highness.

Her highness spread her legs with his hands on her thighs, her liquid coming forth in the rhythm of waves unrecedent, his tongue slopping from plumping clitoris side to side lips to nether hole sliding side to side up to plumping clitoris, all setting her atremble, he recalled the last one, a shaven Brusselian like a fucking manikin, the hair here damp from both mouths, her trembling arrhythmic accelerating in frequency and force, her orgasm arriving in a spasm of strength, holding his head to her gaping lowdownmaw, shuddering and shuddering and shuddering, and his a surprise blasting response, the two of them becalmed now, the thought that this is the only reason for a man to kneel, maintaining the position in stillness longer than in tongueing and gyrating and trembling and shuddering.

"About that drink," she said, releasing him.

"Yes, and then the leap," he replied.

"I think we just took a leap."

"I know *I* did."

"It's better this way."

"This way."

"Yes."

"I feel heavy."

"I feel weightless."

"I was joking about the leap."

"Are they still?"

"Leaping? I don't know. I think maybe they hush it up when they have to. The last one I remember was a few years ago, that senator."

"Senator Hafbreit. My mother knew him. He was from our state. She campaigned for him, antiwar as he was. Not the kind to jump, if you ask me."

She adjusted herself to prone, the robe wide open, one leg drawn up.

"Were there suspicions of foul play, is that what you're saying?"

"No, that's not what I'm saying. I haven't thought much about it. My mother mentioned such suspicions, but by then

I listened to what she had to say as little as possible. Anyway these days I wonder if it's necessary, assassinating senators. They show their war crimes on television with oblivion and serenity prevailing. Why spoil the thing by creating a ruckus. It's not like Hafbreit was going to become president."

"I suppose no one knows."

"Or they do, *they* do but **they** don't, whoever would look into it."

Donnie brought her a drink, sat beside her breast, took a long draught of his own drink and leaned over her, kissing her as if he were long her lover.

"Is it too early to speak of tomorrow?"

He shook his head.

"I mean tomorrow the day all my appointments are cancelled."

"In fact, it's high time to talk about that, or to skip past talk about that. It may be time to ask for your father's hand. Or yours, whichever one one asks for. Is your ex a killer type?"

"My ex is the never seen again in these parts if he knows what's good for him type."

"Any inclination to talk about him?"

"None."

"And I'm quite single, by the way, if I haven't made that clear."

"I would hope I was able to."

"Oh yes," Donnie replied and the night grew more still as if to usher in the fury at the door, a fury as of gorillas pounding on that inanimate and docile divider of scenes.

ABCD, in that weary rectangle, stood in the doorway after midnight on the twenty-third floor of the Luxor Hotel in Las Vegas. A, wearing a thin dress, no undergarments, was all goosefleshed in the chill of the artificial cool, her nipples taut and swollen, or just bigger than one might expect, motile or seeming so, never quite where the eyes of BCD expected upon glancing. B, in an undershirt shirt, or what Indians, and probably Brits, too, called a bunion, a sleeveless black t-shirt, that, with the jeans, gave him the appearance of a greaser from the sixties. C, towel wrapped around his torso, hair

mussed up into an eraserhead, after having fiercely hugged A
and B, stood back and gazed from eyes to nipples to eyes. D,
in her terrycloth robe, leaned against the wall, refusing to be
intimidated by her lack of familiarity with A and B.

A was the cornerstone of this geometric configuration,
the most surprising reference point. Drake knew she would
be there, but Donnie had not known she was on the continent, and Hermione had not imagined a women who meant
something, whatever it was, to Donnie could possibly turn
up so soon. Setif was absorbing her feelings like an alcoholic
testing her return to the hard stuff after a long enforced absence, finding it good: she had finally, that morning, made
love with Drake, with extreme abandon and physical energy,
riding the blessed state of unconcern to a sequence of orgasms
unmatched in her relatively short decade or so of fuckry. Yet
what she had set aside, mysterious even to herself, her love of
peculiar sort for Donnie, remained a lump that roamed her
like a nomadic nipple, like a tumor, a benignant lovelump,
a djinnipple that could take form in emotion or intestine, on
the tongue or up high within the skull. Looking at C now, she
recalled the warmth, she felt again the warmth, that she had
felt engaging Donnie since their first meeting, the warmth
that counterpoised that other kind of love, the one people
were so goddamn stupid about that she shared with Drake.
Seeing Donnie, seeing his poise perhaps more than anything,
having been interrupted during a night of lovemaking and
still loving her the same without hesitation or expectation,
seeing Donnie as she loved him eased her feelings for Drake
back where they were no longer threatening her, nightbeasts
with fangs though they were, nightbeasts howling outside a
campfire, howling for her death and her abdication.

B was never as dense as people roughly his own age
thought, his sophistication graced by nature, even but half-
glimpsed by himself. Knowing Setif needed Donnie, he did
not—much as he wanted her as a lover does want a Setif—
he had no inclination to interfere with her desires, allowed
his uncertainties to snarl in a kennel of subconscious, conveyed toward happiness by instinct. And he also was pleased

to see, had missed, Donnie, short as the time had been. He had loosed one beast from the kennel in the morning, but it had returned upon one sharp commanding whistle. This D, well, he was pleased to see her if only because, without his own knowledge, Donnie had been rummaging his psyche in what could have been, but apparently was not, a search for a more intense fealty. Yes, it does seem a bit awkward: seeing that C is fucking D, B feels good for C. But it was more than that, for B wanted very much to find C in good condition in every way, and so it appeared, largely—sure—because of D, but what D had insinuated into Donnie was more than what little that B could have known she may have. And B was relieved that D was not insurance against A, that his longing for A was unchanged by the knowledge of matters with D, a fair assumption.

C, for his part, was not one to be overly concerned with the reaction of any type of A towards an unexpected D (he had room in fact to wonder how B found his room) yet he could sense immediately that A was indeed surprised to see a D and underwent a barely perceptible, speed of lightswitch adjustment, and he could not fail to respond with a rising snake of regret that required a foot on its neck, a venomous snake, and so a carefully, assuredly placed foot, but a foot and a snake put down nonetheless, for despite the clamor the simple fact was that he had been quite happy with D and hadn't the least actualized regret. He would not have been surprised if neither he nor Drake, B, had never seen Setif again, but if she were to be here, A to his C, he could not but be suffused with surfeit of well-being, a post-coital false sense of superfluity made real with the infusion of his people. He smiled with a joy he would have denied having felt before as he introduced Hermione, the lucky D, the unexpected without which the faults in the structure would have remained and collapse inevitable.

Little is known about D, but D will do. Her languidity was if not a force a presence, a gravid desiderata of persona. She had separated from her husband over two years previous and had sex seldom, never with gusto, never with passion—

certainly never tempted to dare a look toward a future, even of a following morning. She was struck by the resemblance of the two men, who surely she would have taken for brothers had she not known otherwise. Drake's hair was a little darker, his beard less wispy, his arms shorter and more muscular; yet there was about him something softer than what she could see now in Donnie as he was framed by his life again, not hard, but raw and tough, as she saw it. The Wench, A, was a rare creature, far from beautiful yet exuding oblivious sensuality, fremescent with sexual potency—which she could control.

From D one could see that either B or C could have been with A, that the odds were even, that she made her choice for love of life and love of both and therefore could only have done so as one would choose a card from a deck. One may be forgiven for taking one more step back and observing two very similar yet distinct two-eyed jacks, and likewise two queens, albeit one from a fresher deck. D heard coyotes, faint and distant, slim customers, the kind that never go away, that return every night.

Of mad dogs and rhomboids, of slavering packs of predators and strict formations floating lost, of the sad and strange esteem of simple selves and horrors in spate concurrent, cachinnatory, cursed and kitched. Context concave context convex, contextual slaves contextually vexed. Or oversexed. Drone strikes brought Donnie and Hermione together, four Hellfire II homed laserly air-to-surface, high explosive anti-tanked warheads and of course there were no tanks, so it was an apt choice, but for insurance was added a metal augmented charge and, why not?, about a fifth shape charged for better blast fragmentation. Drone strikes brought Donnie and Hermione together, drone strikes shall tear them apart, shall they? Why not. Nah, drone strikes brought them together, only the drone of the death dearth of day after day can pull them apart, or sink them down to the desert floor, the high desert floor, then off drifting in downpull to lower deserts, through ancient passes, sunward and down, into the sunken near desert and down into the valley of death, death valley, below sea level, unsuitable clime for mammalians and there they will perish.

Round about hotel hearth they lounged, sated, satyrs and hussies, studs and strumpets, sipping champagne, chewing cheesy crackers, slooping olives and spitting seeds, all now in whites of hotel, towels and bathrobes. Drake, cigarlipping, arms around Picasso undertits, her robe open to navel, thus... "ya sure I was here, what was that three years ago, right here, saw the thing happen right in the middle of a morning conversation, bullet head, thwap! Dead, deathdive dead. Fuck, I asked my old man—I told you this, Donnie"—he was directing his conversation toward Hermione with some vigor—"I asked my old man to get the security tapes cause I knew he could, and sad to say I had a tantrum when he refused, we barely spoke for two years, then he gets murdered..."

Hermione glanced toward Donnie to recognize that his bizarre story was indeed bizarre, as she had already recognized that it was true.

"Drake, though—you know who that was, don't you?"

"Who."

"Your suicide."

"No idea."

"Senator Hafbreit—you know, the Iowa senator, the most vocal opposition to the war, the one who actually used the phrase *war crimes* in public. Probably the only suicide in government three years ago who could've had people thinking assassination."

"Well, *I* certainly didn't do it, he came from above me."

"Odd your father being there, though, eh?"

"And a good thing—I got the tapes now, watched them all yesterday—What! Odd? What the fuck is that supposed to mean?"

At some point after a rapid skull descent, a delay before the retort, the crack, the shatter, at some point an utter silence ensues somewhere insucked within impact zone, and so too, here, on the twenty-third floor of the Luxor, a silence of palpable force, a silence of menace, ensued, a silence as of windblast, as of a rapid concentrate cataclysm of time.

39

OF DOLPHINS AND NEUTRINOS

[Third up card: four of hearts]
[Call.]

Watching television at The Electra Glide, cleaning and oiling his newly purchased Smith & Wesson .38, a replica of the gun he would have inherited had his life proceeded without violence and jail time as it should have, Eddie Vegas, as Gravel was beginning to feel himself, was acutely aware that every hair on his forearms was stout with loneliness, limp with emptiness, lank with redundancy. Why not call this the quintessential American experience, this leaning forward on a green plastic cushioned chair with wood legs and armrests, in an undershirt, cleaning a gun with a vague sense of purpose looming before a backscape of utter and indifferent unknowability, a soundless television casting changeable aspects of light, dolphins breaking the surface of some sea somewhere, somewhere else, a mammal that knew enough to stay in the sea, to remain hairless, a sleek, sociable, scintilla-less scintillating blue bullet of beauty. I have never seen a dolphin, he thought: how fucking ridiculous. The world has dolphins and I have never seen one. Fifty years old, and the most sane thing I could ever have done was one year arrange to go and see dolphins. A crime against the self.

Because this is not the quintessential American experience, for that is too grand a theme. This perhaps is the quintessential endangered American experience. Canada, Mexico, the entire south — that will define the American experience over time. This will all be seen as excrescence, rude corruption of being hyper-aware, vapid, utterly disconnected from enduring life. This America, this United States of, has been making last stands from the beginning, practicing the last stand until they get it right and finally can indeed stand for the last time. No, this scene here, this man in his undershirt oiling his gun before a silent television, this scene has nearly been perfected to extinction.

His great-grandmother had owned a Smith & Wesson .38, and it had to be out there somewhere, wherever that was. His mother died while he was in prison and there were cousins in California he had seen little of, but who would have attended the funeral as a sort of last of the Gravel line. They would have kept what they figured was worth anything, so the gun could be tracked down to one of them. But as a writer of written scenes, Gravel knew the value of an original. The gun was worth nothing and the less so for its material illusion of sameness, for its having retained some molecules that had once been part of great-grandma's hand. Or perhaps not—he was no physicist, or molecular biologist, of whoever would know—he was a thinker, though, thinker enough to know meaning where it was absent. Nonetheless, he'd liked that gun and having such a one back in his hand felt good.

Eddie found Rod Strut at 37 Pair-a-Dice Court Apartments, just off Rancho almost beneath the interstate, an old-fashioned affordable once rather upscale cluster of housing that had come to look more like a motel.

On first sight of the man's face, Eddie thought of Scottish bridge-hidden monstrosities, toadlike demons that meant no harm in eating children. For all of his experience describing landscapes, the face of Rod Strut presented him with a spacious lumpenterrain of potholes, pitfalls, pitted stretches, a nose the size of a giant champignon like a field of tiny disassorted fungi, a corrugation of basin and range squeezed stalagtight, a carbuncular conurbation, seething fracular with pus, fairly bursting with sickly sauces unseen, one man's béchamel The rest of Strut was the body of a creature to be wary of, with a low center of balance, like an ape with rickets a creature with unpredictable agilities and limitations, furry, his lair dark and close with must and an ironic velleity, a man whose smell had become so familiar to his own nose he had lost sense of the self-odoriferous as betwixt the external world. Beer cans were strewn about, giant glass ashtrays mounded with cigarette debris, the sink predictably full, clothes with crests and stiff reaches forming a patchy carpet. From this is Clay made, Vegas thought—it's as if several generations of evolutionary necessity were lopped in one leap.

A man who once beat another human being to death, Eddie Vegas was nonetheless wary of the protohuman in this imbecile, for what made him suffer most was akin to what gave him brute strength—his very ignorance was lethal, and it was obvious.

"Garvin! Sit down, I've been waiting for you!"

This already was a surprise. The grufftroll speaks.

"Where's your gun, tucked behind your back? You won't need it. I know why you're here and you get no problems from me."

Eddie looked about the dark, close living room. He wiped clothes from a chair to the floor and sat. Strut sat on the clothes on the chair that flanked with this one a glass table grimed with solidified liquid rings and dunes of ash, citified with bottles and cans.

"So you taught my boy."

"Yes, I taught your boy."

"And you've lost yours."

"Yes. I've lost mine."

"Well, I don't know where he is. Somewhere in Vegas last I knew but that's all."

"When was that?"

"Few days ago."

"Where?"

"Don't know. Try the strip hotels. He's on Drake Fondling's dough."

Eddie Vegas started up from his chair.

"Sit down. Get you a beer."

"No thanks—"

"Sit down!...Look, I knew you were coming. I know my kid hates me. I know you think I'm a piece of shit. Mexican beer okay?"

Vegas nodded. Maybe this was going to be more interesting than he thought.

The golden liquid in the clear bottle came clean to Vegas like a comet burst across the sky. It was a visitation.

"You're place is a fucking mess, Strut. You live like a pig."

Strut's smile was like a gash in a hoofed mammal's hide.

"Yeah, I'm not a real likeable guy...You know your son hit me with an umbrella? Yeah, in Brussels. Was my job to bring his pal back cause his old man got himself murdered. I had a gat on them, fucking Ivers Johnson .22 that didn't align. Was all I could get on short notice. Kid's got balls. Plus I'm stupid. I knew it was a, what?, a prop, yeah. Just in case. When Fondling sent you on a job, you fuck up you pay for it. Know what I mean? And I don't know these two fuckin kids. Weird story. They're in Brussels, think the old man doesn't know. Guess in your case that was true."

"So he hit you with an umbrella? Did it work?"

"Sad to say. They took off ahead of me. But it was considered I got the job done. Message delivered, kid returned."

"But Fondling was dead, what did you have to worry about?"

"His outfit. He's got people, people still running shit for him. I don't know much, cause these people they don't like to talk. I once heard his right-hand man is a midget, deadly fucker but a midget. They were in Nam together, Iraq twice. You know that Gulf War Syndrome bullshit? True. Fondling apparently had a real thing about it because see what they did, what our side did, was they gassed, presumably by accident, like maybe a hundred, two hundred thousand of our own. No fucking mysterious illness, basic sarin gas and shit like that. Lot of people on his payroll suffer from it is what I hear."

"But you don't hear much."

"Wise ass, eh. Low level people always talk and you figure some of it's got to be true. Or you figure out how to tell what's true. I may be a fuckup, but I'm never as stupid as you think, as they think. Know how much money I got in the bank? Know what inheritance my estranged son has coming to him? He don't know but I got half a mil. Live in this dump, but I got half a mil."

"Rod, I think I want to call you Rod: this wouldn't be so much a dump if you cleaned it—or, given your wealth, hired someone to."

"Fuck's it to you, I clean it. When I need to."

"No you don't. You need to clean it when you have a visitor. I'm a visitor. I don't want to visit a dump that doesn't have to be a dump."

"Sensitive guy, huh?"

"Sensitive? It smells like carcasses and farts, with a smear of ceiling shit. Why live like this?"

"I drink too much. I suppose you don't smoke."

"No, I don't smoke. But if it was just smoke I could live with it."

"Christ, maybe I should shoot you."

"Don't even think about it, I'd just grab an umbrella…"

"Fuck it. Nother beer?"

Vegas looked at his beer. It was about half full.

"Sure."

"I got something hard if you want."

"Beer's fine."

When they were settled again, Strut started in.

"None a my business, but I gotta ask, since my kid likes you so much. What the fuck is your kid doing mixed up with Fondling?"

"Is he? Mixed up with Fondling?"

"He's been with his kid in Belgium, came back here with him, back to L.A., now he's come here to look into the casino business or something. That's all I heard and even that may not be true, but he's definitely *in* it, yes. Does he have the money from you to go to Europe?"

"No, just to university. I didn't even know he left the country."

"Not on the best of terms, eh? Well, I know what that's like. And don't give me that look. I don't give a rat's fucking ass what you done or what his problem is. Yeah, I drank too much, I beat his mother—never laid a hand on him far as I recall. But you ain't no better than me right here and now, not here. Fuck, or if you are so what? I ain't a happy guy and I don't think you are either. But I expect you love your kid like I love mine. We don't fuck up because we don't love our kids, we fuck up because we're fuckups or we aren't careful enough or don't stop to see what selfish is or whatever. So I figure you love your kid, you need to know whatever he's up to it ain't something you want him up to."

"So tell me what he's up to."

"I think I told you I don't really know. I know I got half a mil in the bank and most of it is dirty, and I mean as dirty as money can be. Fondling got assassinated. His *wife* got assassinated. That don't happen to good clean businessmen."

"Who does it happen to?"

"You mean besides assassins?"

"What's that mean?"

"Wasn't Hafbreit from your state?"

"Hafbreit?"

"You think that was suicide? I happen to know Fondling was here in Vegas when that happened. I seen his picture in the paper. I know what he looks like. I get a job that day, odd job, big pay, little work. I won't tell you what it was cause even though you seem like the kind of guy who can keep his mouth shut it don't matter. Anyone finds out I talked about any of my jobs outside this once with your kid I'm a dead man. Least I think so. I don't even think that would go down so good. Point is I get a job seems a little thing but it involves my former employers, the Clark County coppers who I like to avoid as much as I can, just talk to a certain couple people at a certain time. I got a prior engagement down on the strip, pure coincidence I'm in the parking lot of the Luxor and who do I see but a couple of Fondling's men and then I see the great man himself. Only time I ever saw him."

"So he was at the Luxor. Is that where it happened?"

"Not half an hour later."

"Wait, if he's such a big shot, whatever the fuck he is,

what?, a security guy, right, Blackguard?"

"Blackguard, not Blackwater."

"Why would he be here in person?"

"How the fuck would I know? He was some kind of operations guy or something, had a hand in everything after Nam. Filthy fucking rich. Knows everybody in the military. There's a rumor he was even in on the design of some fighter, AWACS maybe. Spy plane. A regular over here in desert spy land, Area 51. There's so much shit said and so little known, you know a lot of it's got to be true."

"Tell me what you *know* is true."

"He pays me to do shitty jobs like fetch his boy when he's dead. Like I said, other things I don't talk about."

"Okay, I get it, but what…what do you know he's done, not you, but him."

"With absolute certainty? Kill people in foreign countries under the guise of security firm head. Sell weapons to the same people he kills. That part I got on good authority. A lot of military people wind up here. Some in security on small scale, casino staff. I know people like that. Shit gets around. That guy at Blackwater, Dane Frot, he hated Fondling. Probably was him who killed him. Fondling took a lot of business from him and virtually destroyed him, purveying lies, or maybe truths but the kind of shit he did even better himself, like keep the right people safe and safely kill the right people to make sure they're safe. In Iraq at least some of the people Blackwater was supposed to have killed were killed by Blackguard. Remember Fallujah?"

"The four Blackwater guys?"

"Right."

"They were killed because of shit that Fondling's guys pulled. This much I know. And this was early enough in the whole shitstorm no one knew his ass from a hole in the ground, so while Blackguard is killing left and right they're also selling off RPGs and such. Everywhere that guy went, rebels got armed and got dead. And I can't tell you more for certain, but stories from there go to torture, how good he was at it, how much he liked it. Ask me, the guy was a fucking psychopath who woulda looked good in Nazi black, einsatz-gruppen gray, whatever."

Eddie slugged the second beer as Strut began to rise. "I guess you'll take another."

Vegas nodded as he swilled.

"I have no reason to disbelieve you, Rod, but I know my boy, and this isn't along his lines. He hates the military. He hates all authority."

"Like yours, huh?"

"No. Oddly, in my case it was more a lack of authority if I'm right. He doesn't hate me, not as far as I know, he just doesn't think much of me. That's my guess. And don't you dare fucking ask."

Strut held his hands in surrender.

"I could give two shits. Life is ugly any way you look at it. People are ugly and they do ugly things. You may be a professor but I guarantee I think as much about this fucking swamp of feces we live in as much as you do. Drinking makes it bearable. Cleaning the fucking apartment does not. Everything I've done wrong to my wife I remember—bullshit: enough of what I did I remember. I think about it but I ain't gonna slit my wrists over it. It's an ugly world, I did ugly things, I'm an ugly man. I've hurt people. I've hurt people bad. You probably know I was a cop. When you're a cop you get a lot of chances to hurt people and you take them too goddamn often. There's niggers in this town that'd kill me if they caught me alone at night. Fuck, it's a miracle none of them have looked me up and come for me as it is. Maybe it's because there's worse cops even than me. Maybe I was one of the nicer ones. I wouldn't fuckin know because being out there in this shitswamp makes you want to hurt people and then people come along that hurt people and it's your job to hurt them, or arrest them and when you do that too often they just beg you to hurt them. Sure, you fucked up, that's all I need to know and I know that because you're sitting here, and even if you weren't you're still in the swamp with the rest of us subneanderthals. I tell you, Mister Garvin, it's been a long goddamn time since I gauged life by anything to do with happiness or any crap like that. And by the same token I can't remember the last time I felt unhappy or depressed. And I ain't gonna cry about how I wanted to be a good guy and they wouldn't let me, the bad cops, the bad guys, how you can't be a good cop in this city, cause I don't give a shit about that. I never thought about that. I was never no idealist. But guys like Drake Fucking Fondling are a whole nother level of bad and as long as shitheels like that are runnin things, Jesus Fucking Christ couldn't make anybody's day worth a shit down here at swamp level…"

Eddie went through the breach of pause like a sipahi:

"More beer, Strut! Pull up, and get us another beer." In fact, Strut had a gulp of his left and Vegas had been dry for a couple minutes.

"Right, right," he said, pushing up with effort, but maintaining a unity of expression that spoke of more clarity than Vegas would have credited him just ten minutes before.

The flow of pity and concern had ebbed, was neaping toward tide of spring, towards Donnie. It had not occurred to Vegas that his son was "mixed up in" something, that he was not himself the center of a drama of his own configuration, the only bad ending he had envisioned, in attenuate nightmares of evenings long, never finding Donnie, never seeing him again, wandering the world in search of his son. Now he knew he would find him, and was coming to know that finding him would be its own trouble.

"Get me two, Rod."

Somehow Rod kept his peace until Eddie had twisted off the cap and slain half the bottle.

"Something wrong, Garvin?"

"Vegas. Eddie Vegas. That's my name here. Please use it."

A smirk on that face was but a rehiscent gash.

"Eddie Vegas."

"You comfortable calling Blackguard or you want me to?"

"Call Blackguard?"

"Ask where my son is."

"You don't *call* Blackguard…Christ!…You can't even find their number."

Vegas mocked that fact with wide eyes.

"Occurs to me—did anyone mention his name? Of course they did or Clay wouldn't have known. So he's going by Donnie Garvin."

"Apparently."

"So we call all the hotels and motels. That's our first step."

"We?"

"You have a phone, right? I'll run for some beer and you can get started. Start at the Luxor, makes the most sense."

40

THE SICK MAN OF EUROPE

The Sick Man of Europe was such a healthy metaphor, diseased body parts still being sold off a century later, the mori-
bund fellow fascinating in his decrepitude, shrinking as they
do like healthy verdure under a too intense dry sun, the regi-
men of the new model of health was ignored until it was too
late, the doctors all gone psychotic like any Freudian subject
over-thrilled with the death of the other. Tom Gravel's grandfather was born during the Second Balkan War, after which
the Ottoman Empire was on a respirator, an immense area
totaling about one million square miles having been ampu-
tated from its European body, while the empire of the United States, during about the same period, had grown from
healthy pre-pubescence to a manchildhood of nearly 12 million square miles. Tom Gravel's mother, Ethel Gravel, was re-
juvenated by the death of her husband and his grandmother,
Marie Fire in Flight, who expired the following day without
a word, Ethel finding her in the morning, sitting cross-legged
facing the mountains, her soul gone away with the setting
moon. Only her grandson, Tom Gravel, Tom Garvin, Eddie
Vegas, would ever consider her, consider her place in space,
her displacement in time, a woman bereft, though her bar-
renness he would not know of, alone, more so than he would
know, but a woman sure, a woman with perhaps a grubstake,
raised in a small desert town befuddled by the shadows of
mountains, a desert town besnaked and bescorpioned by day,
stalked by wolves and cougars at night, coyote cacophony
from crepuscule to cock call of early rising, empty rising, an
esurient atrophy of Christ-stricken ages past, an emaciating

habit, broke by her life giving love, Tom Gravel, who died for her, she sometimes thought, that she might awaken to life, alone, to life, moving from horse ranch to town, from riding to driving, emerging a speck in empire, the first female owner of a taxi company in the state of Nevada for she was the first owner of a taxi company in the state of Nevada. And she bought herself in 1916 a Smith & Wesson .38 pistol she was known to wear and wave when wild with menwariness, menweariness, mannerkinder shadyfreud.

She read newspapers delivered from Carson City twice a week a whole batch of them, read them with her feet hanging out the door of her Scripps-Booth Rocket, her head out the driver's side window, and thereby came to know more of the relatively current world events than any man in Virginia City.

Rusty Forthwith, a widower banker, her only suitor, was about to rap her softly on the head, thinking he had snuck up on her, when she said, "Where you want to go today, Rusty?" He was angular, polite, and a man of some humor, but she would only be companionable with him. She thought now and then of his penis resting on her passenger seat as they drove, usually somewhere that required traverse of some desert, how it must lie there resembling a recently dead salamander, legless, back half still on the rock where it gave out living, drying but not desiccated. It was an absurd thing to have hanging there, but she saw no reason to call his attention to the fact, as long as some fabric kept it from touching the actual seat. She wasn't cruel in the least, hard as she had become since Gravel died.

"North," Rusty said.

"True or magnetic?"

"Which one is Carson City?"

"Neither."

"I reckon neither, then."

"Long fare, won't make it back before dark."

"I invite you to dine with me in the capital, then Miss Gravel."

"Long as you don't propose again."

"Can't promise that."

They set off on the sand track south at a pace that would
get them down to Carson in an hour if they were lucky. There
was the succor of ritual in this weekly trip; more importantly
there was the assurance of solvency. She had invested in a
Packard truck because it seemed goods were moving more
than people and there was a niche market for freight that
was too much for a man to handle and too little to hire a
rail car for. Her most trusted driver, Chester Hardupp, took
most of those jobs on, even crossing the Sierras, once going
so far as San Francisco—which he gabbed about for a good
month upon return: he has seen seals, hundred, nay, thousands, of seals, among many other wonders, including more
free negroes than likely existed in the entire state of Nevada,
especially on the wharves. About now, Chester's runs paid his
salary and covered the payments for the truck, the rest of the
business up to Ethel to bring in, and in 1914 in Virginia City,
Nevada, a gal could sit in her taxi lot for days at a time waiting for someone willing to pay to go somewhere. Emergency
runs odd times to Reno and the regular fare of the bachelor
banker Forthwith supported the company, kept Ethel eating
and reading. Yet such thin margin made no mark on Ethel,
who had of accident like a dry and light wood figure buffeted
by wind and wave and brute hands landed in new circumstance, bizarre in both appearance and scape, yes *her* and
the earth, oddly, almost unconsciously live and free, began
to act upon her freedom before she recognized what it was—
her mind, it turned out, was like robust ivy unwatered upon
first renewed wettage clinging, crawling, stretching, filling,
fluttering, flinging forth fructiferous, and her body, thin and
hard, once but faintly feminine now furtively fulsome, not
hungry, rather more in a state of permanent sate. She *felt*
herself a woman in a distinctly different way than she had
before, even when she had been sexually active—that had
never ceased to be a separate event, like going to a show; not
like, say, eating or drinking—perhaps, on the rare occasion
she bothered herself with apperceptual examination, it was
the mere acknowledgement she granted herself that she was
no more nor less than that other gender, that the design of

her life had been washed out and in the act of re-designing it herself she became...*vivid*. Tom had been a fine old man, but he was indeed much older than she, and though of gentle humor, rather on the dull side, as she had been taught to be, though now knew had wished not to be, had like all folk the wish to be entertained.

About a mile out of town, the stale wooing would begin, and one of the human comforts that she enjoyed, for though the banker may be forever serious, he no longer held out hope, and thereby was friendship evolved.

"I just don't see, Miss Ethel, I just don't see why a woman like you must take upon herself such a rough and tumble profession, which is not offense to your capabilities, rather complentary to your mind and extraordinary sense."

"Why Mister Forthwith, I believe I have told you before that I do what I do *otiosaque diligentia ut vitarem torporem feriandi*, and there is no better illustration of such than one of our leisurely drives to Reno or Carson wouldn't you say?"

"I'll say again, if you would only spare a moment to write that down for me, there is a Catholic Preacher in Reno who speaks that Latin and would he translate your words for me our conversation might fruitfully commence."

"Aw, shitfire, Rusty, and gulp the coon fart, what's fruit is already full and if were to commence further we would but find our world a cul-de-sac, which is not, sir, an Indian tribe but a blind gulch, a self ambush."

"You talk more learned than any man in Virginia City— you are a marvel."

"I talk more learned than any man in Nevada and you know it. Do not be insulting me."

Soon she would have to navigate deadman's hook, a turn and a dip so sharp and ill-fortuned in design that long before the engine combusted internally and seemingly for good horsemen were known to die taking it too fast going southways.

She slowed a mite.

"Tell me again, now, Miss Ethel, what is this thing in... Austria?"

"It has much to do with the last two wars, Rusty, and please as we are now in the desert be free of constraint in using my name less formalawkwardly."

"Which two wars?"

"I explained them last time we were together, Rusty. Have you no memory whatsoever?"

"I reckon if I had a map I might remember better."

"Whether or not you have a map, the places remain where they are. As do events that take place therein. But let us not argue. I mean the wars of the shriveling Turk. Two years in a row. As the Turks lose their European empire, the peoples who live in those lands fight, after throwing off the Turk, each other, for there are no strictly drawn borders to speak of where there has been no sovereign nation. Now it is mainly the Greek and Bulgarian who fought last. This time it will be many nations. For the Bosniak peoples, unlike the Servs, have not thrown off an empire and are not free. The Austro-Hungarian Empire has the Bosniaks. And within those borders are many Servs as well. The Austrian Archduke, on a visit to the Bosniak capital of Sarajevo, was assassinated by a Bosniak Serv and in order to make the event worthwhile of war, the Austrians are blaming the act on the Servs of Servia. Now, the Russians are bounden to protect the Servians, the Germans to protect the Austro-Hungarians, the French the Russians, the English the French, the Italians the Austrians, the Turks god knows, and so soon there will be what is called a conflagration, a war like no war we have ever seen."

"My, but Ethel you do get yourself in a state!"

"Give the matter some thought, Mister Forthwith. This is not the Crimean War, which with such a name must be fought on the Crimean Peninsula. Nor is this the Franco-Prussian War, which must be fought somewhere convenient to the French and the Prussian. This war will be fought all over the world, for the different parties fancy themselves present on various continents other than Europe. They will fight in Africa where the German endeavors to establish its empire, where the Italians have been so actively engaged. They will fight on Polish lands, for though Poland disappeared, to the inconvenience of Germans and Russians the Polish people stayed where they were. The Germans will attack France, and if you do find yourself a map you must ask yourself where they will attack? Will they attack at a mutual border, or rudely violate the lands of Belgium and Luxembourg. The Italians will have to figure out where to fight, or their masters will tell them where. But now with this damnable engine that drinks oil, desert lands such as Arabia and Persia that are suspected to be rich in oil will become prized properties and battles will also be fought in those places. Britain is a small island but it has a large army already in Asia and I believe you will see brown troops in English uniforms in Africa and Arabia. Then of course you have us, the United States of America..."

"What's it to do with us?"

"Whatever we wish it to. The point is that we *will* wish it to in order that we have our excuse to expand our business in the world—careful here, lean hard to your right...there... and straight up...my but your knuckles are *white*..."

"Ooh...never quite get used to it..."

Rusty Forthwith showed no fear, though the skin about his cheeks and eyes contracted as if in effort to control by muscled mind the outcome of wheely events.

"You were saying, Ethel..."

"Yes, what was I? Us, we, why this war will include us, you know. We only have to determine which side, which is of course with the English and French, but we must wait until we can provide a proper reason, which might take some time, but must not take too long for we must not miss the war."

"Why must we not miss the war?"

"Don't you see where we are now in history, Rusty? Why you are in banking and from a family of mining fortune, surely you see how the world is changing. We cannot acquire more and more land, and so we will acquire more and more business. Can you not see what is happening, the change with China? A mere half century ago, a little more, they were entirely at the mercy of the British Empire. The British were the operators of perhaps the most ingenious business operation man has ever known. They had their coolies grow opium in India, and forced their coolies in China to buy it. Business was so profitable they fought two wars to maintain it. But our very brilliant policy makers have undone the British with a very slick policy in China called the policy of the open door, which means Let us not fight over trade in China, nor even fight with China, rather let us all trade fairly with China. Who could argue but that such is fair? With our resources, eventually we will colonize China simply by virtue of our superior trading mechanism. But if there is a war, the winners of the war emerge most powerful and the United States cannot afford to watch such a war pass us by, perhaps only to rejuvenate the British Empire, setting us back fifty years..."

"That's an earful, Ethel, it sure is. When is all this going to happen, then?"

"Next week, that's my guess. My newspapers come a bit late, you know, but it seems to me such things usually are best started before the summer is gone. I would say August first is as good a guess as any. Right now the Austrians, the Austro-Hungarians, are insulting the Servians, making one request after another, balancing between maintaining the appearance of some reason, as the injured party, but desirous of war, careful not to provide the Servians a reasonable alternative to war."

From the straight stretch they drove now, with the sun perhaps forty minutes above shelter, they saw the tear of the range across the sky, the roll of high desert—though you wouldn't know it—to the left, and though it was not flat, the infinite of desert nature was plain enough, plain enough it was not a stretch to be trifled with. If either wanted, they could have then and there chosen to comprehend the world and their places in it, the need established by restless animus, the break where desert crossed meets range to cross next and vice versa, an accident of locus, serendipity of locus, a place where some hundred thousand or so white folk could settle even if the mines one day were thorough in their unyielding—but of course that would never happen, such was the fervor of the myrmidons of the new empire; no, the tunneling would never stop, the bulldozing would begin, inutile soulless pyramids would rise throughout the desert landscape—men had remade themselves in new chimeras that, gravelike their cuts may oft be, were solely of this world. They drove past Gold Hill, through Silver City, past abandoned mines and mines shafted with hope, past solitary men who planted their legs wide apart, placed their hands on their hips, and shifted their eyes from the horizon to gape at the taxi rolling by, men in transition, from pioneer to guardian of evanescent ways of life, men who would be striking the same posture a century hence.

And the coyotes, already accustomed to, undisturbed by, the internal combustion engine, merely loped ten yard into the desert and looked with vulturine sagacity over their shoulders back at the odd locomotors. Ethel drove slowly enough that now and again they would see just near their path a giant desert scorpion rock back and forelow to raise its stinger two or three inches off the ground. Snakes were too clever to be observed, but jackrabbits panicked every few minutes or so, bounding toward the calm of their predators. Even bears could be seen at higher elevations—the Sierras were bustling with ursine goings on. And of course the hawks, eagles, vultures, yielding the sky to enormous owls at night, and occasionally a condor, mocking the biplanes men were flinging skyward, sputtering graceless sky intruders, such sheer sorry spectacles they seemed harbingers of nothing but sacrifice to gravity, mankind giving science and technology its due.

Such thoughts as these gurgled within Ethel Gravel inchoate, throwing up details trailing tendons, tails in the prime ordeal of thought soup, such that philosophizing was just beyond her grasp. What meaning to make of mankind? For women it seemed easy enough, grim though the turnout be (Ethel Gravel was the only woman in Virginia City with a young child left behind to family while mama worked), and she was yet philosopher enough to think If there were two or three of me they would gun me down in the street. Nonetheless her free ranging thoughts with their thousands of facts compelled her to restless efforts at historiography, resulting in a private macaronicon.

Bulgaria—defeated by Greece, well, and the Servs, yet slain a millennium before by Byzantine Basil (II), called thus the Bulgar-Slayer, blinded 40,000 Bulgars in one day—*one day*, imagine that, 80,000 eyes! How many knives, or swords or arrows, knives or they'd miss too often, imagine if we had to blind a hundred here, at least an hour, depending on how many, figure 10,000? Two per Bulgar?...Was it raining, windy...

Albania—Skanderbeg, the Eggnoggian Way, surely there's no better way...

Indochina—French plantations, the inverse of slavery, a better idea because the slaves don't have to be transported, they're already there and happy to be there, though one must imagine at some point they will make the French unhappy to be there...What do they have besides rice?...

India—The British version, the classic colonials, indigo and opium, forest philosophers and red dots on foreheads, elephants and tigers, princes and generals hunting tigers, cobras, fakirs sleeping underground for years (waiting for the British to leave?), Cochin!, jungles rice and madwomen rebel... yes, the Ranee of Jhansee...*Bengal* tigers, Clive of India!, Mutiny and then the queen steps in, a queer thing...

China—the other half of Indochina, how did they lose Indochina to the French, maybe it fell off of its own accord, maybe in an opium hallucination, they—giant treasure ships in a picture book, a wall that could enclose the whole of Mexico, maybe one day we'll do it, pony tails, Boxers!, dynasties, Ming and Tang, tong wars in San Francisco, what really were those... haven't heard much since the earthquake, could be it takes a while to get one started, keep an eye on the laundry, they may not be what they seem, secretive people, the center of the world, forbidden city, yet Sun Yat Sen, Empress Dowager, times are changing?, times are always changing, but the vases remain...meanwhile our sailors get shanghaied...

Portugal—and the Lisbon earthquake, worse than San Francisco, the Chicago Fire, strange how they're stuck to Spain, no *vases* survived *that* earthquake I bet, set their mind on spices, rounded the Cape, took India but couldn't keep it, mean and incompetent like the Dutch, maybe better for it in the long run, think how many people hate the British and French, oh but not to forget this New World, yes, they got a lot of this place, but not as much as Spain, which for the main went the easy route, why round the horn when by such a short hop, and Cortes and cheap captain labor from Italy, Vespucci, Columbus, what all of a sudden? while for all that the great Spanish Armada in 1588 was a sunken flop, still they got an entire continent between the two of them and Mexico besides...wonder why they kept the Portuguese and got rid of the Jews, the Moslems, the half- breeds, strange land, Loyola and Catholics...

Italy—there's a funny one, the Catholics and Savoy, heel and toe, Sardinia yes, Corsica no, Sicily, all in a few Garibaldian years, the Alps even, the Alps—odd, is Italy really Alpine, too? Guess it was up to Garibaldi...Oh and don't forget Venice, I suppose after Napoleon they're glad to cling to land, so to speak, like Pompeii in a way, a living—wrong word—a museum, anyway, where it stands, all the writers go there and fall in love, who wrote that about poets loving death?, funny how now Genoa and Venice are together the armpits of Italy, though mustn't think too poorly of the Genoans, not compared to the Venetians, with their Methuselah doge sacking Constantinople for a lark, for a crusade, crusades but larks, religious larks, what good did they ever do? None then, certainly not that time, now the Pope is Venetian, right? And what of Rome, where did it go? Spalato, Constantinople, England, limes, Roman limes, aqueducts leaking like the udder of a scattershot cow...

Japan—the most mysterious place of all, rejecting all, then taking all, changing nothing, selling samurai swords to sailors while they copy the designs of the ships, the cannons, silk kimonos and wooden shoes, defeating the Russians! a busy people, quietly, mysteriously busy people and only four islands...pearl divers?...

Ceylon—pearl divers...

Siam—Chang and Eng, princes and kings and elephants and snakes, jewels...what's happening there now, must look into that, try to find something...must belong to somebody...

Burma—*Not Siam*...

Dutch East Indies—spice islands, pirates, malaise, mal-
aisia, mosquitos in Batavia, languor in Batavia, jungle fever
in Batavia, gross white men in white linen jackets in Batavia,
Joseph Conrad in Batavia, Lord Jim in Batavia, native assassins in Batavia, Bligh in Batavia, blight in Batavia, berserk
in Batavia, barmy in Batavia, Batty in Batavia, giant bats in
tiny belfries in Batavia, bloated pink blotched sweaty silly rul-
ing faces in Batavia, dead wives sent home from Batavia, sly
mistresses in Batavia, shrunken head stalls in Batavia, crook-
ed daggers in Batavia, jetties of ghost ships in Batavia, Roman gift to the Dutch mythic Batavia berserkers?, look up,
mythical Dutch withers in Batavia, malaria in Batavia, the
cemetery of Europeans in Batavia, kept Sultans in Batavia,
celibes, celibates in Batavia, Soerabaja, cloves, cinnamon,
cardamom, peppers...

Australia—cantankering Kangaroos, transported Irish
and criminals and Irish criminals, welcomed by aborigines,
or not?, vast deserts, crocodiles, sharks on the beaches, other way around, cold in the south, Tasmania, more at home
there?, must be, they did in the last aboriginal sixty years ago
if I recall... how do you know something like that?...Sydney
Harbor and New Zealand—fierce tattooed tribals...Mow-
ry...snows there...

Philippines! War! Our colony, or one of them, but of
course we don't have colonies, do we, just destiny manifested
after the Europeans went home, leaving their color behind
to rule the darker ones, who are luckier than Mama Marie's
folk, who get corrals they can stay in as long as they want
unless something gets dug up there, when even then they
are generously allowed land elsewhere, and when you think
about it since they say our Injuns didn't look at land like we
do, the only land they owned or like owned was the land they
stood on, if you think about that in a mathematical way, all of
them got a great deal more land than they had coming, so it
seems odd they would complain, though seems most stopped
complaining after one or two massacres, which is not to say
the Philippines are a real colony for we freed them from
Spain and remain there as friends, advisors and I suppose
dissuasion from further meddling by Europeans...

Spain—Neighbor of Africa, so Spain in Africa, visible from Gibraltar so they can see the folk they kicked out every day, and be seen by them! Must be cause for some strange feelings...

Africa—the source of the Nile, what romance, worth a sword in the cheek, first there was that comic book with just the first few pages, so he gets the sword in his cheek, the ship lands, he gets the sword in his cheek, and that's the end of the book, kind of funny, all that trouble, 500 people or so for a safari and one foot on the sand and the natives attacked and he gets a sword in his face, unspeakable misery, don't recall the other guy's name, just second time I had a whole book and funny thing this time was it wasn't like I imagined, fearless safari people crossing penetrating, making way inland where no maps are known, no, they know people, have guides, everybody in Africa seems to know where they need to go, just they don't know or care it's the source of the Nile, hilarious, I was so red with embarrassment, Uncle Trevor come into my room wondering something was wrong with me...the Nile... so much about the Greeks, but think about the Sphinx and the Pyramids and the language and the tombs: Pharaohs!...put the bible to shame, god forgive me, wish I could read the Egyptian bible...cats, beautiful cats, rare jewels...did some of them come from India? Can I find that out?...but then the Moslems came like a wildfire down the Sierras, same place, left the pyramids alone at least, but how *fast* they moved! across Africa above the Sahara mostly, all the way to Spain, into Spain! Martel, how I first imagined ten million Moslems and Charles Martel standing there saying No, that'll do, far enough, but then who was El Cid, I don't remember, afterwards, four hundred years maybe? and Cervantes—I never found that book, someday maybe in San Francisco, he was in the battle of Lepanto, why I remember that I don't know, even the year, 1571, *after* the great siege of Malta, this next war won't end in September, this next war won't end when the weather turns foul...people live in the Sahara, nomads, maybe our people will go *there* someday and put them in corrals so they can rest, maybe we will take their oases away, finding gold under the water, but there were trade routes, too, across the Sahara, all this fuss and seven hundred years ago they were going from the coast below the Niger all the way to Egypt, crossing the whole Sahara, I guess they used to take slaves from the other side, though, from the Ethiopia side, Greeks and Romans both I think, Romans for sure had elephants and—yes, Hannibal, and lions to eat the Christians, and probably the Jews, too, and now everyone in Europe seems to get part of Africa, or try to, from West to East if they can, even little Belgium, how many Belgiums fit inside a Congo?, enough to make the Germans angry since it gets in between their Cameroons and East Africa, and the French have more than anybody but it's almost all desert, a giant chunk of Africa but then at halfway nothing until— Madagascar!, which they probably won in a poker game, the one where the British won Kenya and Capetown, *after* the pesky Hottentots were tamed but not before the Zulu, and worst of all, wildest, berserker Boers!, nasty business as the British papers say, but good sport, good fun, good practice for the coming conflagration! And it seems like it was two re-gimes fighting each other for the right to run a regime keep-ing coloreds apart from whites, sending the colored into the mines that the whites sell all over the world, just like with the Injuns when they found gold on their land here…I wonder what they'll find underneath the gorilla lands…maybe our ancestors…

—England, or Great Britain—funny if Rusty asked, I'm not sure I'd get it straight where England is, what's Great Brit-ain, if there's an Ireland separate of if it's part of Great Britain, maybe eventually Australia will be great Ireland, Scotland, Wales, whiskey, scotch, bourbon, Bourbon, which takes us to France, when I want to think about England, and Napoleon and the Napoleonic wars, very confusing, there was that book by Thomas Carlyle I read about and my uncle Trevor brought it to me he said he got it off a sailor from England or Ireland or Wales or Scotland and I thought here's where I start to understand everything that will lead me up to today and here and now but I didn't understand a word, I felt like I needed to read one hundred books just to understand that single one, I never finished it I still have it, but maybe I read two hundred pages, and if I can't understand the French Revolution how can I understand the Napoleonic Wars, I remember John Paul Jones was in it, or some other American hero, with the French, helping with their revolution, but I still don't know how they got to Napoleon who got to Austerlitz, and somehow when it was all going so well — he got to Venice, he was said to *end* Venice, he somehow had to go to Moscow, where no one should ever go, and that was it, and somebody said the problem is that he was no faster than Caesar, only as fast as his slowest, which makes a great deal of sense, but then he lost and he lost, he was exiled and he came back and had Waterloo, which I have checked is actually in Brussels, so maybe he was fighting for the Congo, maybe to keep the Germans from crossing Africa, who knows, but the thing is that it becomes a story of British naval might, and that brings us back to Africa but mostly India and China, and opium and indigo and transportation and prison hulks, those ships off the coast I try to picture them, in the Thames, the Thames estuary, giant dead ships filled with prisoners, who surely tried on a daily or better nightly basis to try to swim to shore, transported, Jesus forgive me but those were some cruel bastards and yet they speak so upright, as one should or as one ought?, I can't rightly say…Dickens: I prefer Mark Twain, but sometimes he gives you the sooty truth of it and though Mark Twain made fun of us folk here he makes sure you understand why you might want to be here where things are a little wilder… maybe you start out low and end up lower, like might could happen over in London, but you might breathe good and in that crisper air suffer loneliness, yes that's what it is, the loneliness, which is the silence made by the coyote's pause that gets to you that maybe you don't have in London where you probably would give your last pence for a good night's sleep in Virginia City, though from what I gather of back east it's but New England stole from the Manhattoes and them other uns, Uncas and his tribe, Mohicans and Shawnee or, well, must be fifteen tribes in Cooper alone, never could abide

his books, but Dickens, sometimes yes sometimes no, don't
think his opinion will change anything, but at least he warns
me I won't like that gloomy clime, that business capital of
the world, those superior mariners, those redgarmented slave
drivers making a virtue of opium trading, makes you wonder
a little about the Moghuls, for were they not a bit of the live
and let live with the Hindoos?

You get the impression they wanted to kind of live it up
in their palaces and the rest of you just go about your business, we'll make some merry and culture, you do whatever
a Hindoo does…and whatever gave them Ireland I'll never
understand as opposed to Ireland getting them, is it something in the people like Irish could live eat potatoes and let
live, while the English were the type who wanted other peoples' potatoes? England's island is surely a little bigger, but if
you lop off Wales and Scotland, maybe not so much, so how
come the English got the rule—I ain't asking them for they
would ascribe a superior nature which I have come not to
believe much in seeing what I seen in my forty maybe some
more years of life here, with lowdown scoundrel white men
and the finest Injun woman I ever knowd just for the simpler
example…so what, by virtue of factories, soot and ships, the
more soot the more factories the more ships? Is that all there
is to it? Mustn't make too much of the language—that's a
trap, just because they speak the same language don't make
them no better than the French, though the French may for
all I know be worse yet, though I doubt it. Napoleonic wars!
What about France versus English here? What was the Injun
to do. They should have banded together against them all,
burnt the pilgrim ships and bibles and sent them all back, but
instead they allowed inroads, roads into the land and once
that man gets past the lance through the cheek on the beach
you've had it, for there will be an onslaught of goodwill ill,
and you have to choose sides and neither side is on yours,
you are on theirs, until of course, they win and then you are
the enemy, that's the way I understand it and even if Cooper
be a bore and a fantasist I believe that is also the way he saw
it, but I did not read enough, maybe he liked the French, or

was in love with a native woman. I heard tell we get much of our law from the British, but as I understand our law out here it seems no nevermind, for when the papers and the satchelmen speak the fire of righteousness there is always someone with a gun to sway their mind, and might thereby surely maketh right, which seems from the limits of my understanding more like the transportated Irish than the civilized colonized children of Cromwell or them others like what was his name, some English fellow of great repute who if I have forgotten surely most will never have heard of in these parts, and eventually too be forgotten. Come to think of it, who do we know from the Great Britain? Napoleon and the only English guy is the seaman Nelson, and he died ten years before Napoleon, did he not... then the Welsh, who speak little, but the Scots who mingle with the English and get their chip of Ireland, tinder for a mini-conflagration when you get two stout religions going at it like they do. You see what the English are up to don't you? Long as there be Protestants on the island, Ireland must not be free for free must be free to squash the Protestants. Clever weasels. I can only imagine how they survived the Mutiny, because surely the queen only arrived after it was over, for it is unlikely those numberless Hindoos said, Oh, sorry, did not mean to offend your queen, we shall now lay down our arms. Rusty pretends interest in this part but I wonder if it is an elaborate mating ploy, oft as I disabuse him of the possibility; yet there are times he is like an eager child, as if he really wants to know something and does not mind a woman teaching him. If he were truly eager to marry me, perhaps he would not succumb to this teacher/child relationship, though again if I feel no lustings for him I will not succumb myself.

Ireland—for it *is* there, when they come here they are not called English subjects, but the Irish, and they are a distinctive bunch at times, McFeeney down at the saloon to name one, twenty years and no one yet killed there, fistfights nightly but never a killing, calls himself a "publican," not in a highfalootin way, came from New York because he says they didn't like him there, swine, he calls them idiot swine cause they call Irish potato eaters when we came here precisely because there were no potatoes to eat, funny man, longs for not the green they talk about just the whiskey and the beer and the way his gramma played the fiddle died on the boat on the way over so they tell him…

Norway—seems like a bit like Ireland, famine driving plain folk to the sea, more Norwegians than Swedes or Finns, though everywhere you go there's a Swede and every second place a Finn, probably because there's more Norwegians so they start their own settlements, and Swedes and Finns maybe they aren't so welcome or would rather not continue their neighborly ways over on this side of the sea…

Danish—like the Germans tired themselves out getting to the Baltic east of there, that one last peninsula oversaxed them…

Netherlands—Spanish energy, or they would have been just another lowland little country, now embarrassed by their Boers, emboerassed by their beers…

Belgium—How long can they have a Congo? Probably they'll lose it this year, probably the Germans will use their little country as a road to France, them and Luxembourg…

Germans—are they not just Austrians elsewhere or are the Austrians but Germans? All through history we read of the Germanic tribes, manic tribes of the forest, fearsome, unconquerable, yet they have only been a country as long as Italy, as if the Prussians are a superior breed of German… everybody is afraid of giant Germany, but how much of it is Poland and how much do the Poles hate the Germans, there is no Poland but what war has been without Poles, even we had our Kosciuszko and others under him—one day both the Russians and the Germans will regret the disappearance of Poland, you can't subdue what doesn't exist, the Poles will have their day… though come to think of it, will there ever be a time when they are not squashed between German and Russian like a sausage? Why a sausage? Funny how silly the idea of a German empire sounds, German East Africa, German Camaroon sounds like an expensive dessert, seems odd that it seems odd til you think about how they have so little outlet to the sea, how they have never been a sea people, so how do they expect to compete with the British and French?, I suppose they would have to take their territories and their ships, maybe they want this war so they can get to the Mediterranean and Black Seas...will they go for the Pacific? repeat Napoleon's mistake and make a success of it, what's to stop them other than ten thousand miles of earth, the Russians retreating north, imagine a German meeting a Chinaman, what are you? Hello, where is the Pacific, this way? Danzig. Something always disturbs me when I pause to make that sound. Hanseatic, another disturbing sound, vaguely secretive, which I guess secretive must be, yet also highly suggestive of a lost—or hidden—continent...black forests...Rhine...Oder... Grimm people, Hansels and Gretels, cannibalism as it must be, with lots of sugar, old cold universities with crazy preachers throwing inkpots at devils, spiked cathedrals, fragile castles to God against—what are they built against? Gotterdammerung? Where did I get that?

France—Liberty, equality, fraternity and a Napoleonic dynasty forgive my confusion. What do the Algerians think about that liberty, equality, fraternity? What does a Frenchman do on Saturday night in Madagascar? Maybe that's why they gave us the statue of liberty, having no use for it themselves... Germans have philosophers and the French have painters—that could mean trouble in the war. But the French had a navy, again and again they had a navy, but the British sunk them by Egypt all around India...Surely I am forgetting something...they even lost Canada, though why they wanted it is beyond me, you can't grow sugar cane there...or tobacco. They have some islands, but even the Dutch have that...Why is it so hard to like anybody? I mean by their country? Mexico is all right, but we took half their country, a humbling experience for them—for us, something that will one day come back to haunt us...it's not like they were Injuns, and so we treated them like real folk, attacked them, took their land, leaving them a country not just corrals. What restraint. Now a revolution. Everyone's wife wants Pancho Villa for a lover, that moustache! That Sombrero! Those tremendous balls! I shall not blush at history...look at Rusty, pale from wheels on sand...if he only knew...Cortes, Seven Cities of Gold, Potosi, slaves, slaves and more slaves, silver and gold, fountain of youth, dreary desert days, dreadful diaries, Aguirre the only sane one left to history, who said, if we can take, I take—indeed, why not he? Incas...the Atacama... the Andes...Garibaldi, red shirts, Venezuela: Aguirre the compass, the wrath of order, Simon Bolivar—destiny, destiny manifest: Panama sliced, Forget the Maine! rough riders come home...Carson City.

"Wake up, Rusty."

"I'm wake. When did you say that war was starting?"

41

A SHORT—HA HA—BUSINESS MEETING

Daydreaming, driving, dementia without dolor, a fare without an affair, a frolic, oh the calm creep of crepuscule, safe on the sunny side of the Sierras, the sunnier side of the century, great-grandmother Gravel, of whom our Donnie knew nought but of Nevada nativity and a taxi trade, while now Donnie, nude, feet on the patio table, coffee near, Hermione head nearer, nuzzling about his nethers, late morning of the third day of mating, reading the *Review-Journal*, "Christ, listen to this, after the usual drone strike kills militants in Pakistan, war crime enough, listen to this: US soldiers accused of hunting Afghan civilians, um, they made a game of it, picking out—it says at random—victims, taking turns, just killing whoever they felt like, shot kids in the head, old men, ladies, quote 'There were few men of military age,' so the game was a sort of psycho roulette, as perverse as it gets, as if the least deserving, the most innocent"—now she lifted her head, "You're serious?" "If it makes the newspaper you can bet it was ten times worse. Normally this kind of shit gets hushed up...wait, here: for the last half year at least...reported by British, suspicious sequence of deaths...Ah: someone's talking. That's the thing. Unnamed. In protective custody. I wonder where that could be, the guy's got more guns aimed at him now than the entire Taliban..."

Of course, Donnie had no way of knowing what went through his great-grandmother's mind when she drove a regular from Virginia City to Carson City, the prescience wasted traveling from brain to mouth, but how utterly fulfilling it would have been to *have* known...*and* been able to fill her in on what happened since, perhaps even pick her brain for more thoughts. Did she know of the Maginot line? Did she intuit the Schlieffen plan or was she just vaguely correct in assuming a sort of Berlin to Paris route? Had she any notion at all, gathered from the practice wars leading up to the big one, that war itself had changed, that material technique had surpassed mental technique, that the war would be won by the rats and viruses? Her man was the last in the line to have foreskin: what would she have made of that? Maybe her son had foreskin, too, we can't be sure. Donnie didn't and he knew why and how ridiculous the procedure was. He was not a man for the trenches, not at all. Did she know how long it was all going to last, and did she know that the interment in trenches was unsustainable, so that the next big war—there would *have* to be two, anyone could see *that*—would of necessity be both bigger and necessitate the slaughter of civilians to end it. And that the extraordinary advances in civilian slaughtering techniques—accelerant bombing from the sky, factory gassings, nuclear bombings—would necessitate the fragmentation of wars, would have a multiplier effect on war itself, so that the civilian killing devices (there would be so many more—so many types of mines and ingenious combinations of cunning culling creations of new and ancient like cluster bombs and napalm) might be used more discretely, and more often, that areas of the globe previously of little concern outside colonial offices run by gin and quinine quaffing clubmen would of necessity require extraordinary concentrations of weaponry, that finally all these *casus belli casuistree* would castrulminate in a perfect symmetry of killing by drone whereby the machines flown by men at desks killed people who knew nothing of war—into the valley of death rode nobody anymore, and such had never made any sense anyway: when you're at war with a country, what good does it to fight a fragment of that country called its military? That was never war at all. War, true war, is one side against the other, nation versus nation, and in that war one must recognize the nation as its people, and it is they one must defeat, not some mullah-picked army, not some upstart tribal chief's soldiers, not some ideologue's converts; what you want is the family of the enemy people at table, preferably an extended family, a family compound, twenty or thirty of them, round dinner time, and you unloose your typewriters on them and five or six or three Hellfire missiles interrupt the meal, deal the *people* a blow; or you wait for a wedding, then you get fifty to a hundred, and you hit them where it hurts, right in the procreation, right in the virginity; and then you'll have a funeral, attended at times by up to two hundred if you've done your job right, at which point your typists can strike at the very heart of meaning, the death ritual, which of course means nothing if it is accompanied by more dead than the dead, multiplies the dead, making of the funereal epic of tribe and nation a farce.

But tell me: would great-grandmother want to know? Would she consent to die as she subsequently did, self-some-what-satisfied, disappointed as she was that her son was a drunk and yet poor roustabout, that is to say not one to come out on top in a brawl lest it occurred between he and his wife, and even then not so likely? The Great War's surprises were now known to her, yes, but she certainly had no idea what they really meant, that such extravagant dementia was but a catalyst for suffering even trenchrats and gassed and shellshocked could not prepare one for the factories, the flames, the evaporations, the one hundred civilians for the single Kraut, the famine of victors, the thousands eaten by sharks and crocodiles, the hydracockery of mass war rape, the six hundred in a valley narrowing to ravine and foibe yet increasing their catch to one hundred, one thousand times that number, a garish eldritchery of exponential executionism.

Never mind, odd sentiment, Donnie minded, for he was recalling the guignolery of the tale of Drake's very father concocting the window of the drone, the fright of the blind allseeing eye; but whose idea was it to shape the thing like a locust, like a viciously fearless biting insect like the preying mantis? For that, too, added to terror of the machine, and the name applying to both operative sense and sound sense, for the tribals in Pakistan were driven mad by the constant

droning presence of the slow-flying menace. He had seen
enough film of the Pakistani tribal areas and Afghanistan to
note the startling resemblance to the desert in which this
flower of splenetic artifice, this laboratorial ectopicon *Famil-
ia gammlenia,* this bizarre combination of *Americanus exter-
nicus* and *Americanus internicus* thrived strangely languorous
as if in tropical heat and not in separation of sere August 110s
outdoors and sere luxuriant 71.7 indoors. Silenced by his halt
in conversation, the city was called by no bird, nor did any
engine dopple by, there was the breathing of an odalisque
who rose at the insistence of a distant phone ringing, a rolling
supplicity of buttocks, stomach and thighs the color of the
landscape, yet in common with the cacti the absolute refusal
to disguise the fact of pulp and liquids beneath the skin, this
creature quiet as a lizard in an arroyo. Even the black flower
of her pubic hair, he thought, resembled the tufted areolae
at cacti crotches. But the drones and the assassinations, and
he wondered if he had bidden the anger he felt that was dis-
solute in the tsunami of the insipidity of the politics of his
childhood. A line by Victor Serge had long clung dankly to
his skull: "On the walls of our humble and makeshift lodg-
ings, there were always the portraits of men who had been
hanged." On the walls of the spaces where the politics of his
parents and their friends were diminished by upright plas-
tered scorn were thematic reproductions, a Chinese room,
a surrealist room, an impressionist room—What of a childhood that renders Dalí trite? a Dalit rite? a trolley ride, a trollop's rights, a flop all right, a polite oversight, a maggot white,
a dollop bright, a scallop of shite, a palette of, a mallet of...
on the fucking head...

"It was Drake—he needs you at the office as soon as
possible."

The phone call that preceded the establishment of an office was made to the secret Nordgaard number, for purposes of
determining how much money could be blown weekly without
causing the least concern. The answer was surprisingly high.
Not surprisingly, the office was across the suicide airspace from
Donnie's room on the twenty-third floor of the Luxor.

"So, Donnie, when I was back at the bungalow, Nord-gaard gave me the lowdown—"

"The lo-down…"

"Funny, eh?"

"Very. So what's the lo? I haven't given this much thought, but this lark has to extend itself in some interesting way or I return to a life of academic crime."

"No no—never. I mean, somehow—look see what you enjoy in this casino business and you can go your own direction, whatever makes you happy. You don't think I'm mad that you wasted a week or two?"

"What do you mean?"

"You know, you said pretty much all you came up with was that there are already midgets everywhere. You could have found that out in one day…"

"I didn't. I didn't because I took an interesting idea seriously, seeing no reason to do otherwise. So I spent some time in the casinos, long hours with a few midget dealers, got comfortable, began to take note of my surroundings, and quickly realized that an interesting idea was also one that would fail, that made absolutely no sense, particularly because midgets already make this city their paradise."

"That's not exactly how you put it to me the other night."

"I thought it was. Was I too casual?"

"Too casual? If you mean that you discovered that making a casino by and for and about midgets is a bad idea, an idea to be scratched, yes you were too fucking casual. It's a brilliant fucking idea. Your midgets will give up their current jobs to be part of it. No, hear me out. I've been reading up on dwarves—Nordgaard has a library devoted to them, not just dwarves, but homunculi, little humans alchemists created in jars, gargoyles, the smaller ones…and, well, Remy de Gourmont midgets…This is a real segment of the human race, these people are real and together they are a *horde*, a fucking *horde*—"

"Any studies on minnie-folk and gambling?"

"Wh—fuckoff. These aren't, these are deeper than that, I mean they aren't modern social science studies. The point is, or one of the points, is that they are human, only smaller.

So gambling? Intuit. Of course they gamble. Look at Napoleon—"

"Not a midget."

"Precisely, but short even then, so close enough. Which
brings me to another point. We don't need studies, we need
common sense. We don't get just midgets, dwarves, we get—"

"Gawkers. Unfortunately that part is actually true."

"Not what I was thinking, but yes. Collateral benefit. No,
think, this is deeper. In the land of the short the least short
is king, right? You'd have tall midgets coming to throw their
height around. And no midget is tallest, right? There's always
someone taller—"

"Call me Lew Alcindor. Eventually we have normal
heights and the jig is up."

"Mock me, that's good. I have to admit part of our success comes from pandering to the darker side, those who
would mock, but that too is part of the success: some people
pay to swim with sharks, some to look at the colorful fishes,
some... others..."

"To gaff the losers."

"Excellent! Gaff the losers. Besides, let's not forget one
essential ingredient: gambling. We're all appealing to the,
not worst in people, to the, not really even necessarily a dark
side—"

"Then we are talking about something else."

"No! No, not at all, it all adds up to the tawdry, the cock-
tail of it if you'll pardon the expression. We live in a modern
egalitarian society in which the rights of just about everyone
are guaranteed yet it's still sexy broads that sell, right? If you
want a dark side, there you have it. Because they're part of
the mix. This town *destroys* women—it takes money from
men but it *destroys* women. Perfectly nice, intelligent women
come here to sell their bodies a little bit, just a little bit, and
then what happens?"

"What happens?"

"How would I know, but they're...well, they're bent
from then on, once they've compromised their ethics,
their... intellects. Meanwhile, hundreds of thousands of

fat women, or ugly women, or just not sexy enough wom-
en, who would love to run cocktails at the Bellagio haven't
got a chance. I tell you it is a very ugly phenomenon. We'll
fit right in, only we won't be exploiting nearly as much
as we'll be offering opportunities. Midgets can't all get the
occasional movie part, not even one percent of them. This
could even develop into their Mecca, their San Francisco.
They'll have it better than the gays!"

It had gone on long enough. Donnie knew Drake would
have to have his say, but it was said, and, sadly, he would have
to re-report on his research. Drake took Donnie at his final
mocking word. Las Vegas could be the *San Francisco* of the
shorties. The town was already their Mecca; they already did
have it better than the gays, but in Drake's mind they could
rule the town. Note to self: Donnie, read up on the midget
mafia.

Donnie's desk was an enormous and blond maple inscribed with ghostly scenes of Chinese poet haunts, forests
that faded into invisible skies, cataracts swallowed by bamboo, lone fisherman and poets on mountain tops surrounded by fey woodlands and soft serrations of hills suggestive of
infinity.

In a porcelain bowl, also Chinese, were what looked like
fried grasshoppers. Drake had been popping them into his
mouth at medium intervals, crunching them with dental delicacy.

"What *are* those things?"

"These?" Drake replied, pinching one from the bowl and
holding it up to look at its underside. "A gift from Nordgaard,
as was the desk and the rest of the office. Good idea this Chinese motif. I love it."

"But what are those?"

"'Driedgroszenhopper,' a relic of Tanganyika, quite rare.
Apparently, these particular locusts are extinct."

"He couldn't have sent caviar?"

"Wouldn't fit the motif. He did though. Want some? I
have a bunch in the fridge."

"Yet another mysterious Sino-African connection."

"Nordgaard, though, is hardly Chinese."

"How would you know?"

"I suppose you're right."

"The word beluga mean anything to you?"

"It's passé, if I know my elite water beasts."

"Perhaps not for the Hottentot and tots of Hottentots."

"Lots."

"Draw lots for the tots of Hottentots, if you've got lots of Hottentots—"

"With spots. Draw lots for the spots of the spotted Hottentots's tots, lots available, lots with leopard spots—"

"The leopard-spotted Hottentot—"

"Left to rot on the Boer drift."

"A Hottentot tot with a spot drew a lot, was left to rot, deserved what he got—or not?—"

"He was shot by Frot so certaintly Hottentottently not!"

"Which brings up Frot."

"Or not."

"Let's."

"So say Frot assassinated my dad and mom…where does that leave me? What am I supposed to do? I asked Nordgaard if we could find out for sure and he said though probably not we could certainly deliver a shot to Frot."

"On the spot."

"Hottentot, no?"

"I'm beginning to see the dilemma. So the law is most definitely finished with their part?"

"Nordgaard said it will remain an open investigation, but will get nowhere because there is no probable cause, evident probable cause, to properly investigate Blackwater."

"Leaving you with the option of revenge, but not 'justice.'"

"Exactly. The problem is that I was not part of the feud, so all of my hatred and disgust and revenge lust is second hand, if you know what I mean. So while doing nothing seems impossible, I have no idea what meaningful 'thing' would be an option."

"Blackguard couldn't stage an investigative operation to make certain of events? Kidnap and torture a Blackwater insider, that kind of thing…"

"According to Nordgaard, if Blackwater was indeed behind it, the only satisfaction would be to kill Frot. Whoever did the actual shooting would have been an ignorant soldier. And getting to Frot would require a long, intensive operation that he would in fact be prepared to oversee."

"How do you feel about it?"

"That's the thing—I don't. I don't feel. I don't feel about it. My only feelings are a sort of sorrow, or rather more accurately an indication of sorrow to come. That, and joy at the possibilities before me. The Manneken Pis Casino!"

"But you know that…Look, Drake, you did listen to me, right? It still may, conceptually, have some value, but your… your vision of a midget kingdom simply isn't going to work."

"Bullshit. The midgets shall come to me. And you know what? You told me all the little things they do? One thing, one obvious thing, well besides the fact they don't have a museum yet, while the mob has two and the hookers got one, besides that: consider this: midget coffins! We could set up a guy in our own space, novelty coffins, little coffins, we could probably even get one of the famous ones, pay his family to dig him up and put his remains on one of ours, I mean one of our midget morticians."

Donnie forged a neutral look, thinking of how he used to look at his mother after she read him a new poem and had exhausted herself emotionally in the reading of it so that the best response, the only safe response, was this neutral look, from which he could say whatever need be said and be believed, for she would think he was stunned by her magnificence.

"Oh yes, we create the right combination of circumstances and they will come."

"No, no they won't—but forget that, forget it for now. We have a long way to go, we don't know anything yet, how to buy property, get a license, all the practical shit. Maybe in the end you'll have fifty dwarf specialty shops right on site…So, changing the subject, how is Picasso Tits?"

"We're calling her Setif now."

"Okay, how is Setif? *Where* is Setif?"

"She's been driving out into the desert and drawing. I only see her at night."

"She happy? I mean, how does she feel here?"

"Right now that's a little too personal, meaning mostly something complicated is happening and I can't fathom it, nor want to yet. This is obviously not the place for her, but I don't know what is outside of Brussels. But she is beginning to show signs of feeling for me like she did back there, and I'm positively lunar over her, so it's a lot going on and a little to report. You?"

"I'd like to see more of her."

"No, I mean you and woman, you and your love, you and Hermione."

"Sorry...But I do want to spend some time with Setif. Ask her tonight if I can go out in the desert with her tomorrow. Yes, Hermione. Strangely I feel more at home than I ever have in my life. Three days and that's the report. I felt at home at home, of course, but it was the involuntary home and a daily trial in my memory. Since leaving I've felt comfortable being away, but never had a sense of settlement. I had that the first moment I woke up with her, even here in the hotel. Same at her home. So it's her, not the place. Strange thing. It keeps my mind from digging into existential matters."

"So you don't need to fuck Setif."

"Ah...Now that's a different story. I never will and always will want to. Need? Same, but I'm not sure which. I do miss looking at her every day, that's one thing I can say. But look, Drake, this is like a natural disaster: our lives are still unsettled since the sudden news. We ought not to think too much. Don't worry about Setif, about me and Setif, if that's it. I represent no threat to you and Setif. Setif is the threat. She may simply not want you enough to overcome the geographics. She may not want to be involved in a Brussels theme casino. She may—fuck, you know, she's got to be thoroughly unsettled right now."

"She's in the desert right now, for fuck's sake, it's not a major philosophical situation."

"Defense. I get it. Anyway, you know I checked out of here to stay with Hermione, right? So be a little less, you know, whatever it is, and try, if you can, to think more linearly about starting a casino—one that is not a midget mecca."

42

HELMAND PROVINCE...WELL, THIS TIME

Nine soldiers crept down an alley or a dirt track or at least something that cars didn't drive on, a path, let's say, between baked mud dwellings two stories high, leading to the main street, also unpaved, but with a shaded fruit and vegetable market. The sun would be down in one or two hours and the count for the day was zero, largely because of a seminar on homosexuality and sensitivity toward the "other." But the other was a US Marine, not a fucking Taliban or other raghead or flophathead with a nose like a bird of prey and a scroff of beard that grew in at age 5 and never fully fleeced.

Carmine, who was from Vegas, couldn't get over the similarity of the mountains that defined the valley to the ones he knew from home, that though the same defined a far shinier valley, also a valley chiefly of targets. What kind of idiots could make nothing of such a valley, much less one with a river that ran through it. Vegas had springs. These fuckups had a goddamn river. What were they thinking? They were thinking hide the daughters, hide the wives, live like Muhammed. Fucking idiots. This place could be a riot of strip clubs and casinos for rich Pakistanis and Russians.

Lieutenant Fromwell had said at least five today, but had he reckoned on the seminar? It is not a soldier's to ask. Five is five. All nine could hear it mathed out to them in the morning. The thing was: five at once, or one here and one there like usual. Except that new guy, the private one, the ex-SEAL or whatever, Borm, had set the pace, had acted from the beginning like he knew what he was after. "We go this way to the main street, we get there when they're closing up shops, we look left there's the madrassa, right? A tall guy, one tall guy. That would look fucking great in a picture. We get the tall guy. The tall guy and four more and we're off the hook."

"Why only four?" Mancuso asked.

"Because," Borm said, "you little fucking wop, four plus one is five."

"Oh, a precision mission," Mancuso responded with sarcasm. "We weren't trained for those."

"Fine," said Borm, "One tall guy and four or seven or nine, but not enough to make the wrong papers, get it Napoli?"

"Right!" Mancuso said with a savage glee, or at least what abruptly became a still and sharp-toothed hyenic rictus.

Drippen, who had begun in ROTC, was wondering at all the talk, as if they weren't on a mission at all, or as if the enemy were presumed to be either elsewhere or deaf. He checked his helmet, for what he did not know, but found that it was a helmet, and that there was comfort in that. He had begun to think that this reconnaissance mission was oddly shaping into something more, that he hadn't been informed, that there was a great deal more danger than he had been informed.

Suddenly, to Drippen's left, a face appeared at a window and he fired. She was dead, probably hit by at least five rounds, knocked fore and back and rocking fore, finally falling out the window to the dust beside their line of sneak. Physics, what the fuck do we know.

In this place, a sudden burst of rounds meant virtually nothing, not to soldiers, not to civilians. Certainly not to the woman hanging her children's underwear out to dry. And that was when the breeze picked up and sand, dirt and dust clouded the whole scene, just when they reached the corner of the main street, and Borm turned to his left, fired one shot through the head of a tall Islamic academic, a mullah or whatever, and it was Firpo who cried, "Media!", and Drippen got one, but the other raced off in his jeep, somehow understanding his life was in danger despite the obvious protections in place vis a vis the sanctity of the press.

Mancuso sighted a teenager, probably a thirteen-year-old, who was sauntering despite the firefight, and got him just as he reached his home, spotting him from ass to head with a rosette burst. Firpo took off right, past the dead teen, and all he had before him was a wailing wench, god knows where she was going, but he mowed her down, rather, tripped her up, one shot in the foot, she flew, ass fore/head back and just as she landed one in the skull. Did they count the bitch in the alley? No one knew. Did they count the journalists? Probably not. So that meant three of five. But the fucking sandfleas were in their homes, to dinner and bed. Oh, and prayer. What to do?

House raid, Mancuso shouted. Beliveau motioned to a house that had been quiet the whole time. That could mean a heightened sense of war awareness, battlehardenedness; in short, mujahedeen or Taliban, or just plain Mohammedan Christian haters. Drippen was first to the door. Mancuso took the other side. But it was Beliveau's call. A tear gas canister upstairs, he decided, and then they burst into the front room and slaughtered three teenage girls, a mother and a male of indeterminate pre-pubescent age.

Certainly that would do.

As usual Davenport cleared the street for the photos. Drippen arranged the girls in the house like dolls, one in his lap, his arm around the other two. The important thing was he remain unbloodied and you not see the little carpet on his lap and the lace tablecloth—these must have been rich funders of terrorists. Mancuso posed with one leg on his boy, an outside shot, fresh kill, rhinoceros stance they called it. Firpo got a great shot, his foot on the neck of the bitch he'd killed. Sandusky found himself in five photos overall, though he hadn't fired a shot, protesting that he was more deliberate than the others, that he was after a virgin. He had proven his mettle in plenty of battles and so they indulged him. Thomas, with the camera, did not forget Borm and the tall guy, but they apparently forgot him. By the time he found Borm the tall guy had been born away.

Carmine Draper was confused by the whole escapade. He had shot off plenty of rounds but could not state honestly

that any of the kills were his, and he had a sense of hon-
or about such things. No trophy photos unless he was sure.
Drippen tried to persuade him to pose with the woman in the
alley but he refused. "There will be other days," he said. And
indeed there had been plenty, but for this group there would
be no more. For cowering in a kebab joint between the death
steps of teen and Firpo's wailing wench was a journalist left
behind, a photographer, an angry photographer, one who
would under different circumstances have played along—but
the death of a colleague was too much. He got photos of several action killings, killings in action. But, more damaging,
he had gotten dozens of trophy photos, and even photographers of trophy photos, large scene, showing all. And he had
the resources to determine that this reconnaissance mission
had absolutely no concern with the real enemy, that this was
a trophy hunt and nothing more. The very reason his crew
were there was because they wanted three days in cleared
territory, three days away from combat, and they had sought
a region from where the Taliban had retreated, where the
elders from a dozen villages had gathered and forged a cease-
fire, declared a stalemate, divided territory between Taliban
and the enemy. But not their enemy, their friends, who had so
often arranged their copy, alerted them to drone strikes, told
them when unless they wanted to be real war photographers
to clear the fuck out. AP (angry photographer, his identity
forever a secret) enjoyed the fourth kill—he missed the first
two, the third was his best friend, but the fourth, that fucking
kid who earlier in the day had seemed to be mocking him
when all he wanted was a shot of a poor Afghan kid or two.
Clearly the little fuck wanted to be the next bin Laden. He
certainly wasn't the next Jesse Owens. The way he ran, panic
over-energizing his knees so that they pumped up to tit level,
and the five hits, spotted ass up, or head down, so rapid, so
artistic—and then disgust and fright caught up with him. He
was next if they stopped to eat, and Lenny was a goner, Lenny
who had taught him the difference between a cartoon war
with real blood and whatever else it was that used to happen,
Lenny who had taken him under his wing and explained why

he needed to delete the best footage he had ever taken, up at Bagram, an outdoor ritual interrogation, a female GI shitting on the face of a skinny naked Afghan man whose hands and feet were bound such that he was stretched as if about to be quartered, or halved, and a german shepherd was licking gravy off his groin area and every time he screamed and thereafter every time he opened his mouth, another female GI wearing nothing but high high high heeled boots, kicked him in the head, or heeled him in the head. And AP had snuck some shots, moved closer, smiled like one of the guys, cozied up to some onlaughers, snapped a few more, got up to some soldier cameramen, joined them, eventually snapping well over a hundred photos in the thirty-five minutes the torture lasted, the only one he missed was when some guy in fatigues and gloves—ordinary yellow kitchen gloves—brought a large scorpion out after they had finally begun working on his back and shoved it in his ass, the scream leading to a kick that knocked him out and ended the ritual. Lenny made very clear why he couldn't use the photos, why they were not really great war pics—impeccable logic: if they gave a shit, if they were the least concerned about what they were doing, you would have had to work very hard to get a shot, see what I mean? Christ, I'm beginning to think you're hopeless. Can you at least tell me what happened to the guy? What guy? The guy they were torturing. Don't say that word. Torture? That's right, that one. Never again. Fine but what happened to him. What do you care. Uh, curiosity? I'll find out. And that was the thing about Lenny, if he said he would then he would. The slightest promise, however fleeting. Insane now they think. Can't tell if it's permanent. Test: (AP), I'm going to tell you something. The woman who shit on him—not the one in the boots, the one you might think—the one who shit on him, she's got a canvas rucksack with more than fifty cocks in it. What do you think of that? Amazing. What else. Gruesome. Test. Right, of course, gossip, interesting thing, not news, certainly not news. You'll be all right. That Lenny. Now he heard the drone, flying low. He always heard the drone and imagined a fleet of helicopters, for the sound to

him was like a stealth copter, the blades so fast and near silent it could be a sort of medley of choppers. Odd, rather
over-intricate thought, but still, what didn't bugger the imagination out here? He looked up with the same fear: it was
so fucking brilliant to design them without windows—even
AP got the impression it could strike any second, anywhere,
whenever he heard one and saw it, it was looking at him. A
thinking caryatid or whatever, thinking freakishly, wanting
to kill, needing to kill, looking at him the way eyes in paintings do, just as effectively. And if you duck behind a wall you
know it sees you and is all the more likely to zip a Hellfire at
you. Only this time it signaled the end of the mission, the so
to speak mission. This means they called in a firefight. A doz-
en militants killed. Let them. Give them a week or so, then
make goddamn sure the photos get out.

43

A FRIENDSHIP FORGED

Is not the recognition of friendship between two humans in each case an elogium to a species to all appearances miscreant, ill-fated, not playing along with the evolution game, fratricidal, sororicidal, infanticidal, matricidal, parricidal, cannibalistic, misanthropistic, derangedly mystic, yet humorous for its especially corybantic will to outlive life as it sciurinically tears about seeking novel grotesqueries of greater and less apparently revocable destruction, laboring to gather and store balls of destruction of power previously limited to such as comets, poisons previously limited to individuals of unthinking commitment breaking tooth and ingesting a fine mist, those same sadists now mass murderers capable of delivering said poison (at least in their collective imagination) to an area the size of Mexico? Or more prosaically said, creatures capable of at the same time bombing Europe Ural to Eire to Oblivion and gassing the entirety of Asia, tundra, taiga, Taiwan, Thailand, Timor…yet preferring to visit upon each other rather tiny explosives clustered that they might yield a near infinity of little cuts, we shall call them, or rain precision Hellfire from desks half a world apart? Yes, yet, believe it or not, any two of these animals may at any time, against odds we would assume insurmountable, may become friends, comrades, tovariši, amigos, pals.

So it is, that at a wooden table in an old time Vegas bar less than a mile from the strip called Lonnies Two-Step as it had been for seventy years or more, a bar with a busty peroxidal bartender, a poker game of housewives, three of six slot-machines in action, a bar that smelled like beer and desert air at peace with one another, Eddie Vegas and Rod Strut sat simmering the sadness of their lack of success, toasting each other, for failure was not for lack of effort on either part, particularly Rod's, for it was not his boy they sought, but Eddie's, and Rod had volunteered, made hundreds of phone calls so far, and had even used his scarce but not feeble influence on the police force to have a proper missing persons type effort used to locate the lad…that did not locate the lad but did definitively slam a door—the cops were out of it.

Perhaps now, this mid-afternoon, was the time for Rod to fess up.

"I know who you are," he said, but too soon after the glasses touched and so Eddie rather affectionately responded in kind, "I know who you are, too, Rod."

"No, I mean I know who you really are."

Vegas narrowed his eyes unconsciously, unafraid but attentive.

"Don't worry, I don't mean to make too much of it. But I don't feel right knowing and you not knowing I know…"

Vegas thought that the sculptor of Strut's face must have started with a cantaloupe, and like the Injun with the buffalo had left virtually nothing to waste.

"…but I figured it out once I saw you. And I had my suspicions before."

He gave a casual turn of conspiratorial eye about the bar. He couldn't be heard. The juke box was playing something that had apparently not been buried deep enough.

"I mean Tom Garvin, Tom Gravel. First time Clay mentioned you I thought of, well, I thought of you, the other you, the real you. You."

Vegas continued to leave space for Strut to talk, his face betraying no emotion.

"You won't recall, but you did me a good turn once. I'm three years younger than you, I was in the same school a couple years, we lived only a few blocks apart. Last year of elementary school, you stopped a bully, a known bully, from kicking my ass. He overheard me bragging to a friend that if he tried pushing me around I'd teach him a lesson, with a knife if necessary. He turned me around with one paw, grabbed my shirt and lifted me, banging me into a locker and it was just then you arrived and told him I wasn't small enough for his nature, and it took me and it took him a moment to get it. But he dropped me, took a swing at you, and you decked him."

"Danny Fitzmire."

"Never forget it. Or him. Or you."

"And?"

"Well, a few years later you killed him. With your bare hands…and you went to jail and you escaped."

"What do you want to know?"

"I want you to know that I know, that's all."

They both turned toward an ancient, in United States terms, Drewery's beer sign, that showed water running through a mill, a mill at the foot of a factory, a brewery, that dropped filled bottles of Drewery's into crates.

"He was my neighbor. Did you know that? His house shared backyards with mine. He was, it was as if he was born to be my nemesis. Where I couldn't have cared less who lived there, where he did, it was as if he was born to hate me, me and my family. Did you know my father died of cancer?"

"No."

"He was a kind of geologist, and he worked north of here. You know what that means?"

"Where the tests were?"

"Where the tests were. And after my father died my mother was always in poor health. Fitzmire plagued us. He threw rocks through our windows. Sometimes I think half of my father's pension went toward glass…."

One wintry windy day, when grit from the high desert was swirling in the low valley, Gravel's mother was in the backyard when a rock the size of a baseball hit her in the head. Tommy was in the house when she came in, blood streaming from her scalp, bright and streaming, masking her face as if she were an Amazon tribal ritually brought to adulthood. She fainted, frightening Tommy, who at 21 years of age yet had no experience of trauma. Thirty-three stitches were required to close the wound—there was no concussion, and she soon recovered full aching health and was allowed to go home directly after an X-ray showed nothing and she proved she could touch her toes without collapsing. Gravel held her hand throughout the stitching, determined to strike a solid blow for each stitch, making of his vengeance a mathematical proof of his rage. He would call out Fitzmire that very night, and count the blows, thirty-three to the head, glancing blows would not count.

Naturally Fitzmire was prepared, bringing out to the dark backyard a switchblade. Gravel brought only his math. Fitzmire began to circle, as if this would be a child's fight or an athletic event, Gravel took one step forward, the blade came out and clicked into place, Gravel took the two more steps required to bury his fist in Fitzmire's nose, which broke, the skin flapping and blood spattering. But he didn't fall, nor let loose the knife, which he waved before him as he backed away to recover. Perversely, his own rage now matched Gravel's. He had hated Gravel his entire life. The more Gravel's life persisted without his inclusion, the more he hated it. He had hated Gravel when they were three, when they were five, as they grew, as he grew bigger and more athletic and Gravel remained a solid but shorter man, unremarkable, unremarkable but oblivious to the fortunes nature graced upon Fitzmire, who had first fucked at age twelve, who excelled in three sports, whose family had the money and indulgence to buy him a car at age sixteen, while Gravel still walked everywhere he went.

He too strode directly toward his enemy, a hook to the cheek shaken off and a lunge with the knife in his left followed by a brutal right cross that buckled Gravel's knees. Gravel kept his eyes on the left, managed to grab Fitzmire's wrist with both hands while receiving repeated blows to his head, biting the forearm bloody, the knife dropping, a tumbling brawl of murderminded men, grunting as if pre-Holocene, along the side of Fitzmire's house, tumbling to the street, where they separated, Gravel bent forward, the more athletic Fitzmire aiming a wild kick between Gravel's legs that lifted him off the ground,

balls and perineum in unprecedented pain, Fitzmire leaping
on top of Gravel, cradling his head, driving it into the pavement several times as Gravel's mind surged from its shock to
the mathematical problem he had taken to the fight, realizing
that thirty one more blows were called for, yet he was going to
perhaps die before landing even one more. Fitzmire's position
of advantage was his undoing. He was not on his guard. Gravel had two free hands, one of which clawed into and grabbed
his hair, yanking him hard enough to hurt his neck, while
Gravel's full body powered itself upward to leverage, a terrifying left hook shattering Fitzmire's jaw. Thirty blows were
left. Fitzmire was defeated. Steadily, straddling Fitzmire now,
whose arms were pinned by Gravel's knees as if he were nothing more than an avuncular tickler, Fitzmire's brain was no
longer fully functioning, and Gravel drove his math method-
ically into Fitzmire's face, Fitzmire who was probably clini-
cally dead before ten blows had been struck. Gravel beat him
to a bloody pulp, his hands cut badly by the harder cranial
bones, his knuckles cracking when he pounded the forehead
until it split and caved in—*Nulla ferant talem secla future
virum!*—conscious that he was shortcutting evolution in a way
and that he had but three more punches to throw, entirely
unaware that a stunned crowd had formed, desultorily, shyly,
Fitzmire's parents among them, that police were on their way,
that emotions had been whipping up inside him like furiously
condensed firesmoke at a concrete ceiling...

"He had it coming..."

One after another, bottles of Drewery poured from the
brewery. The card game produced grgles of giggles and the
occasional curse. The slots made their inane simulacra of
happy bells, as if wealth were not stealth.

"You sent your son to me."

"I somehow knew from an early age that I was not a good
man. I shouldn't have married. Knowing your inferiority does
not prevent insane outbursts ignited by resentment..."

"I don't care about your sins. You sent your son to me."

"I came across your book. The name. No author photo.
You were my hero. I had ways of finding out back then, just

before I left the force. I didn't pry. When I found out that it was indeed Tom Gravel, escaped murderer, I shut the tap, though to come clean I think your wife is queer as a spade off—sorry. But I could not resist sending Clay to you. He was, despite all, pleased that I took an interest in his desires. He was easily convinced. No place exceptional accepted him, offered him money."

"And the rest?"

"The...You mean now, the Blackguard events. That is coincidence. I swear to you. I would never have done anything to threaten your existence."

Eddie Vegas was a man who knew men. Rod Strut, pathetic wretch, was telling the truth as far as he could express it.

"Drink your beer. What about my son, then? Why would he use a fake name? He's here as far as you know...but even that's old information. No reason for him to use a fake name, so what do we do? Do we assume they went back to LA? Do we scour LA?"

"The question is why I know he's here? Why did I need to know? And the faggot voice, the guy who called me, he was new. He said to make myself available, *keep* myself available, that probably soon the Fondling son would be arriving. Which is why it seems likely something was going on here."

"I can't accept there's no way to get hold of them. It's a simple fucking thing—I want to find my son. It's got nothing to do with their business. Right," he held up his hand to halt Strut's gash, "they contact you and all that. There's no way for you to send up a flare? What if something went wrong in Brussels?"

"What do you mean?"

"What if you couldn't find them?"

"I never thought about it."

"How would you have contacted them, alerted them?"

Strut was one of those whose concentrations of intense thought were porcine and equine both, the bloat of the boar and the dumb eye of the stud. Vegas couldn't watch. The acne scars assumed a spectrum of changing colors, like a Vegas light bulb extravaganza gone rogue. Even though Vegas intuited

the end of what he was watching he found it difficult to bear.
I'll get us another beer, he said, ambling toward the šank.

Rod Strut bore too much bulk, hide and bone and sin-
ew to be a broken-down machine, so it best be said he resembled a stricken brutish creature, incapable of volition. It
took an army of ants to roll him an inch, two inches, while
another army moved his stumped arm and boneless hand,
it took five entire armies of ants to make of his digits pincers
and nine more to move the hand as it held the wallet—dead
goat—and fifteen armies were lost when the arm and hand
slumped in despair—remember that next war: despair—and
thirty-seven were required to get the hand and wallet back
above table level, maneuvering it over the table, finally letting it drop (wiping out an army or two), and here, seeing
it was a close thing whether he would complete the process
they had started or collapse onto the table, a half-army was
sent ahead to extract the slip of paper with the LA number
on it (here exonerating Strut as he dies of his stroke: he *had*
been told never to divulge the number on pain of death,
which, as it turns out…), seventy-three armies scattering,
perhaps a Russian winter's worth perishing as the majority
fled to survive, as the head came down to the table like a
lead melon.

44

MOJAVE FELIX

Setif scanned the north for mushroom clouds of yore, shouting, "Air-conditioning!" into the coyote country. "Air-conditioning!" She laughed and laughed, doubled up laughing, finally sitting on the ground, thinking of the European girl whose love for he who loved her loved least when he loved most, and she laughed more, chuckling, "Air-conditioning" to the lizard lands before her. What a thing they all have for numbers, she reflected. 72 F in the house, in the hotel room, in the car, but what about outside? Is it 115 yet? They want it to be, all of them. Like accountants at the death camps. It's the numbers that matter. She was hatless under the sun in the desert with a bottle of tap water that was—goodness, what degrees was the water? Certainly not yet 115. So she would live. Thin straps strategically placed between shoulder and neck kept the fabric of her dress from falling off her frame— she was happy with the dress, old as it was, for she had a great desire to feel her biceps, triceps, forearms. She was what Donnie told her was wiry, she had wiry strength and she liked it. Her body was feeling great. She had fucked with Drake perhaps nine times in the few days that were mutually good fucking days, and it had done her much good. I should never go more than a month without fucking, she reckoned. And I should average 17.3 fucks per month. "Air-conditioning!" she shouted, loud again, for the jackrabbits in the ravines.

She had driven north out of Vegas, past a Paiute Indian reservation that was comically square on the map, then turned into the desert where there was a National Wildlife Range called Corn Creek. She drove to the visitor's center, quickly managed to imitate the imitators that survive desert life, and before long was miles up a wash, the land very slowly sloping upwards towards the Sheep Range, one of Nevada's multitude of mini-ranges that did nothing to make the state welcoming to human commerce nor deter the use of the land for military commerce and such. She knew that she was near territory that had killed Donnie's grandfather, for they had gone over the map together that morning after he graciously pretended that her refusing to go into the desert with him was just fine. What nice men she had met. And now she was leaving them, prepared never to see them again—if that has meaning— unsure whether she would ever welcome the opportunity to reconnoiter.

Apparently she had remained still enough that a lizard, while knowing she was there, felt inspired to dash all the way across the wash, which here was about four meters wide (and 115 degrees eff). The body was that of a gray roach, double roach length, but with respectable arms—they were more arms than legs—that kept his torso well off the desert floor, while his tail whisked the air behind.

A gratuitous creak from the sky seemed to have been uttered by a bird of prey that was black matte from her perspective, but may have been commenting on the temerity of the lizard. Currents up there were probably 111 degrees eff. A quick sketch captured the lizard, which, she thought she recalled, had brown stripes on the sides. A fat drop of sweat scumbled the lead. She knew now more than ever what art meant to her, for her plan was to make her way eventually up to Tonopah, making several stops, hundreds of sketches, turn instate to Ely, continuing to seek out silent spaces and animals ungregarious, vistas she expected to differ subtly but distinctly, and from Ely continue northeast into Utah, which instinct told her need not be avoided, just rapidly crossed. She would spend more time in Idaho, drive up to the border, and from there… maybe she would make one call to Drake…no, probably not. From there she would simply decide if it were time to return home or not.

Not far enough above the hawk, probably, three jets passed her, going south if she wasn't too disoriented. That image would be saved for an oil painting. A grotesque à la Dix. A bird of prey with shrieking human skull and the devil birds in blur. She was relieved that she wouldn't be returning to society for some time, especially relieved that she wouldn't be returning to the fringes of Blackguard, to Nordgaard, that creepy storyteller who struck her as the most dangerous man she had ever met, to Drake, who she suspected was in for some surprises, who was naively buoyantly planning to build a casino, to enter a new world just like that while he was whether he knew it or not inheriting one that was not going away. She had wanted to discuss this with Donnie, and had her opening when they discussed the drone attack as first date material. But she had felt an outsider, that she had determined to be an outsider, she already knew that she was not going to make anything of her affair with Drake, and that her feelings for Donnie were common enough, the kind that linger sometimes for decades in the pleasant shades of a nostalgia that could not persist without such. She liked that idea — cultivating nostalgia. It was vague, almost abstract, but Donnie wasn't and nor was her vagina, which wanted Donnie every time she saw him but for that night he met his new lover, a woman she considered perfect for him, sexy, smart, and funny, calm and imperturbable in love, as he could have been had they met alone and met first — but what a stupid thought, that her cunt wanted Donnie, for it wasn't so physical and thinking back if it had been immediate she would have chosen him; now she was grateful to have had the opportunity to place Donnie in a context, even one he resisted, for Hermione was a context if drone strikes were not, and if Donnie belonged somewhere, and perhaps he did not, it was not on the streets of Brussels, where he was a drifter of interest, happy, clever, and utterly inutile. And a man must be utile. Never mind a woman. Need a woman be utile? I do. But my interest is in men, for they are the plague I am forced to adapt to — the ones with the cocks. Cocksure! What a word. Her lust was primarily for Drake, but it was the conversations with Donnie that provided her with gamboling knowledge. "Cocksure air-conditioning!" she averred with menace, reached for her water bottle, emptied half on her head, hoped to see steam rising from her skin as it creamed down her arms. The change in temperature stimulated her nipples, which she studied one at a time, swiveling her head as she moved from one to the other even though she, it must be said, did not really have to. Picasso Tits. She'd probably never hear that again. "But after all, Drake," she said, scanning the wash for movement, for here was the moment of the coyote, "nipples, even if you could keep them in a jar, really played a small role in life, mine maybe more yours than mine, in fact."

No coyotes, no buzzards, no rattlers. No atom bombs, no drones. The desert tries to impress its absences on you, but it is full, dry but ripe. You think them Injuns don't appreciate not having to spend their winters surviving on pine nuts? Denuded. There's another great word, for they are clothed now. And not much interested in selling off their history blanket by blanket. Not one poncho for sale in Vegas, as far as she could tell — so much for that vision of self in Brussels. A black cape would probably be better anyway. Maybe lobster shell forearm armor, pantiled up to the shoulders, capped by vulture skulls.

Here's the scuttlebutt: a frightful face emerged in the sand and rocks near her feet, tiny pieces of bone forming a hideous rictus, one incisor and a top or bottom row, no lips, one dark eye the size of a golf ball and one reddish chip of wood slashing into another eye, bald; this was the type of goblin that chewed fervidly, that simply couldn't be stopped, that terrible little mouth and its mechanical greed, a parasite to denude cities the size of Las Vegas. That's the scuttlebutt. "Tell me the scuttlebutt, little demon." He grinned savagely, innocent of recognizable volition. "Air-conditioning, that's the only way you can be stopped, so you are on your way to cooler climes. Me too. I'd take you with me but then you'd have my shoulder chewed to the bone before we hit Utah, little fucker." She stood and disfigured him out of their shared existence. "Take *that*, litte *fecalith*, right in the bezoar!" She scanned the horizons about. Nothing had changed, except perhaps the temperature. "Air-conditioning!" she called like a mountain climber seeking an echo.

45

CANADIAN WHISKEY, MA TEAMSTER

There is no legitimate reason to suggest that Ma Gravel was the inspiration for the Colombian cartel tactic of flooding the skies with drug planes with the knowledge that if even one made it through they would make enough money to offset the losses and more. She had six trucks she sent to Canada; each would find its own way back to Reno on back roads from North Dakota to Washington State. The liquor mafia from California was responsible for pick up at Reno and self-delivery to their home speakeasies. If anyone resented Ma Gravel for her business sense and refusal to take risks, it was only her wild son Tom, who was what was even then called a ruffian, and a lover of strong drink as well. They fought often over his exclusion from the business until finally when he reached 16 she figured if she didn't give him a job—he wanted to ride shotgun, not drive—he'd sooner or later get mixed up on the California end, or, worse yet, head down to Clark County, where prohibition of local brew— jackass brandy—was a joke, as the law enforcement loved drink even more than bribes. The feds had a hell of a time down there, and that was just fine with Ma Gravel, who liked things quiet in her business, still officially a taxi company. The business further benefitted during the depression, when the routes became legal in 1933 and it became established that mankind prefers liquor to thin soup. She did not care for the influx of miners who spent their savings or earnings on whiskey and gambling, but she was happy to see gambling in-stituted in the state as a clear and rapid step toward a healthy economy. Eventually the mining companies went broke, as did the ranches, but there seemed to always be some way for a feller to make a living, except for Tom, who tended bar at Sam's in Reno once prohibition was repealed. Truly there was nothing for him in Virginia City, and nor did she blame him for being unexcited about the family business. It had seen its best days during wartime, its wealthiest days during prohibition, and would now know competition from all angles as the number of cars and trucks and highway funds increased. The smart move would have been for her to move to Reno and establish her company as the number one taxi/ delivery game in town, which it had the resources for, but she was in her sixties and had no interest in re-locating. Even selling her fleet was a poor option, for too many enterprising men had money and would be buying new cars and trucks. In no time she would be considered quaint, which is probably harmless in direct proportion to financial need, and she had no financial need. But her son did. He impregnated his boss's daughter, a young gal named Adele, of course, and a marriage was the only non-violent resolution. They had a son named Tom, born in 1933, and she had a strong intuition that the boy's only real chance to succeed in life would be if she hung on to her money and put him through college when he came of age. That would mean eighteen years of holding out as her own son presented her with scheme after scheme requiring investment and promising always strangely specific returns that only tended to raise argument against the viability of the schemes. See, if he ran his own bar across the street from Adele's old man, and put in a billiard table, he'd steal a good half his customers and be in the black in three months flat, double her money in one year and three weeks. See, if she could sell three cars, he could buy a used race car and this buddy he met at the bar was a genius with engines and they have these races in California, see, there's nothing says a casino can't be the size of a bar, he'd go in with Adele's old man, his capital so he gets 75% of the return, 50% of which would go to her until he had doubled her money, it couldn't fail, see, now is the perfect time to buy a ranch, several ranches, all the ranchers are going bankrupt, he could buy half the county for nothing, and this is a ranching state, the government isn't going to let ranching disappear, besides, cattle, well, everybody eats beef in good times and bad, see, not a silver or gold mine, but an aluminum mine, that's the future here, the government needs aluminum, he'd get a government contract, he knows a guy who knows of a mine that's far from played out, the guy under-reported for years to stave off bankruptcy and now they aren't taxed, so it's a sure thing, see, with his sales skill and Adele's stitching and she's got this friend good in design, they'll check out the latest fashions in San Francisco and be producing them here cheaper and just in time for Reno to catch up, see mining supplies will be a great business again, but only for those who get started before the boom years return, and it can double as a hardware store, people always need hardware, and Jenkins's is always short of something when I go in there, sometimes they run out of goddamn nails, see, nobody knows everybody like a bartender and a good bartender meets lots of people, makes lots of connections, and they say I'm pretty good looking, keen about politics and history thanks to you, and if I join the party they'll consider me for a seat, but I'll need money for a campaign, but it's worth it cause once I win the first one, there's no limit, there's so few people in this state compared to others, a little guy can go far, I could be in the US Senate in ten years, and there'll be no lacking for money then, I just need to finish high school on the quiet, you don't need to be a college graduate, not out here, it's not like back east, here I'm what they call a self-made man, or will be with a little financial help, see, this hotel is in a perfect place, three casinos within two blocks, only the management was so shabby it's being sold for a loss, and with enough money I could buy it, get a casino license and really turn things around. Why should people have to leave their hotel to gamble?

Usually, Ma could fend these off, confident they would be replaced by a new scheme, or forgotten in the effervesce of verbiage during a three-week drunk. But sometimes she had to confront him directly. See, Ma, donkeys. People forget that—No, Tommy, you're not thinking straight. There's almost no animal you can raise that'll make you money. What about nutria? Tom, nutria need a less variable climate, without the extremes. They will not march up to the Sierras in summer and march down to the lakes and streams in winter. Nor can you find a place that's salubrious for them year round. You'd need— look, anyway, there are nutria breeders all over the world by now. Well, I was just trying to make a point. You did, you made mine. Well, with all the collapse in mining, there's still mines aplenty, only it's no longer giant concerns, it's the little starving guy from back east, willing to give it a try, needing a donkey— Tom, please stop it. How's little Tommy? A bit too much under Adele's governance, if you ask me, a bit, you know, pampered, doesn't get out enough. And she don't like me bringing him into the bar, so I have to try to make time to take him out hunting and fishing and riding. Do you? It's not like I have the time, but I plan on this year taking a full month off and taking him to see the outdoors, go up into the mountains, maybe all the way to San Francisco. You need money for that? I couldn't say no. You just tell me when you've made the arrangements and I'll pay for it. Why not give it to me now while I'm in town. I'll give you a hundred to keep yourself out of trouble, if not get into more, but when you get this trip set up, you let me know.

Of course, she knew the hundred would effectively prevent the trip, keeping Tom in whiskey money. She supposed she loved the boy like a mother should, despite being of a grandmother's age, and she certainly was happy to have him back from the whiskey wars alive, the price perhaps being his overfondness for the drink, though one could never tell: was he sober riding shotgun? He never was for long after returning from a trip. She would get her report from her best driver, Clancey Forthwith, her old pal Rusty's son, as steady a man as could be, nerves of brass balls, Rusty would say, so two nerves, Ma would think. Clancey would report when all cars returned, or if they didn't, and now and again one was seized, he'd be a little late—and of course Tom would still be on a drunk—and, most importantly, Clancey took care of business with the California buyers. He never said much about

Tom, never complained, and she never asked. But she'd heard stories, unsure whether they began with Tom spouting off, like a shootout with Mounties up by the Montana border, one of them shot down, the Mounties ignoring the border, chasing then into Montana, Clancey having to do some fancy driving up to a plateau where they had the high ground and the Mounties were exposed like lame pigeons on the boardwalk, Tom calling out if they wanted to live they had some seconds to clear off and they did. When this might have occurred, Ma had no idea. She liked the story, though; the business had been all too easy for her, she'd like to think there was some action for somebody, a hint of danger, some linger of family drama within the frame of a strange historical period. It wasn't Hector and his bear, but it was as much suffusion of American history: the mountain man phase and prohibition. Now it looked like gambling was going to be another. She dared not tell Tom the real reason she wouldn't ease his entrée into the casino business: it had blood written all over it. Who controlled the whiskey during prohibition? It surely wasn't her. She had put together the trucks and drivers and provided insulation, but the crooks were on both ends, and had she not been such a mutual convenience she surely would have been violently thrust aside. With the casinos it was only a matter of time, if it wasn't happening already. She had heard of illegal gambling down in LA and heard it had become a murder town. How long before the legal gambling was taken over by the same such people?

Finally, she was concerned about the war. A war was coming—she could see that from the early 30s on. The western industrialized world was not going to allow Japan to create a manifestly destined Asian co-prosperity sphere: there were too many China-fevered business men and government officials. The two sorts of demagoguery in Europe, Germany's and Italy's, seemed of different substance, but no doubt one would support the other, which probably meant Italy would support Germany's efforts to smash France, draw England into the war, in the end occupying their colonies and, well, the way things looked in Russia, they would probably be happy if this time everyone would just leave them out of it. Though that mysterious Khan might yet be hankering for Poland.

The Anschluss was fascinating to Ma, as it meant, as far as she was concerned, that the Germans, who clearly wanted back what had been theirs, now had the rudimentary tail of the Hapsburgs and would probably seek the rest of the body. That could mean just about anything—no, but it meant engagement with Italy and almost certainly some kind of action in the Balkans, and worst of all a blind search for the head that was never there. Along with the sedate sudetengrabfest, things were looking pretty bad for Poland, though perhaps better for France, for if they could stomach such a move in Czechoslovakia, surely they could let the Poles come under the thumb of Hitler, and if they could the Khan would probably have to as well. And in that case, though France would look weak and have to negotiate away some good vineyards, war could be avoided until Hitler's enemies held stronger hands, if they ever did. The key was the United States, which was very loudly declaring the lie of isolationism. A sound tactic, she figured, not tipping their hand, but if real war broke out, the US would not let such an opportunity slip away and she wanted Tom at the bar, a dependent wife and child on his hands. After the amazing insanity of "the great war," she had no doubt that this one would be worse if it happened, worse in several unpredictable ways. And one of the best places to wait it out was behind the Sierras, in Reno and Virginia City.

And, of course we now know the war did come and Ma wasn't much surprised by any of the diplomatic turns on the path, particularly the Hitler–Stalin pact and its subsequent violations, and the war did end, with some predictable results— US victory, but many odd surprises. During and after the war Ma was surprised by

The ignobility of France and England

The genius of Hitler

The utter stupidity of Hitler

The whole Jew thing before the war

Japan's obsession with China along with their amazing ability to generate a sprawling Japan that spread all the way to India

The fall of Singapore
The Bataan death march
Mussolini's odd Greek timing
The second Czechocapitulation
The rapidity of the fall of Belgrade
The persistence of irredentism of the Italians
Spain's neutrality (smart fascists?)
Churchill's bombastic bullshit bringing him back to power
France's pathetic showing
The first strafing of refugees
The second strafing of refugees
Mixed message killings in Ukraine, Lithuania...
The German "war machine"
The strange plight of London as if there weren't years of
    warning
The brilliance of French strategy, the rapid Vichylization
The depth of hatred of Slavs by non-Slav Europeans
The attempt by Germany to convince someone that
    Poland attacked them
Hitler's trip to the provincial Styrian city Marburg (Aber-
    deen next?)
The persistent reports of Jewkilling
That apparently Gypsies were *everywhere*
Russia attacking Finland
The Finns winning the Winter War
The exploding of Heydrich
The V1 and V2 rockets–Peenemünde!
Nuking the Japs
Carpet bombing the Krauts
Twisted, mangled peasants she had known of in history,
    but never on such a scale and she was utterly shocked
    by the number who had lived in cities
The Jews were rounded up and put in ghettos just like
    was done with the Injuns
The success of Enigma
The success of Tito
The success of Hoxha (of all people)
The scale of losses during the siege of Leningrad
Germany's dedication

The bizarre things Germany was dedicated to accom-
plishing
The gas vans
The gas factories
The obsession with Jews, its duration and scope
The Salo Republic
The public death of Mussolini
The formulae for death
The complications in Yugoslavia
The very term Ustaši
The very term Chetniks
The Churchill–Tito alliance
The sheer brilliance of Tito
The attack on Pearl Harbor
The German declaration of war on the United States
The shift from island hopping war to Greek fire attack on
Tokyo
The detention of Japanese in Hitler camps in the United
States
The long war in China
The war in China continuing
All that fighting in the desert with names like Benghazi
and Rommel
The number of tanks
The tank battle at Kursk
The Russian victory at Stalingrad
The number of exterminative actions
The race for Trieste
The sudden love the Allies showed the Italians
The bombing of German civilians in cities she had heard
of like Dresden and Hamburg
The importance or not of Danzig
The extermination of life in the Jewish ghetto in Warsaw
The Polish uprising in Warsaw
The pause of the Russians during the extermination of so
many Poles in Warsaw
The image of Eva Braun in Berchtesgaden
Tokyo Rose
The British Troops scurrying off the continent

The British Troops scurrying back

The long delay of the United States landing on the north
    western region of the continent

Allies liberating Paris before Brussels

Thousands of fighters being rendered useless when ships
    are sunk

Ships have landing strips on them

Japanese pilots dive into US ships

Flak replaced dogfight as an aeroplane war term

The scale and variety of the victors' vengeance

The photographs of peasants from France to Bulgaria to
    Russia to Italy to Greece and how they all looked alike

The flight of the allies from Greece

The hospitality of the Egyptians

Ersatz coffee was no surprise but she knew of the differ-
    ence between Parisian and cowboy coffee and she felt
    for them ersatz drinkers

The black market in silk stockings

Orgies during the blackout Bletchley Park

Benjamin Britten's free lunchtime concerts in the Na-
    tional Gallery, London, during the Blitz

The Juden-Häuser Children's evacuations

Vera Lynn

Pathé newsreels

Children held by the feet and swung with force of accel-
    erating headweight, skull into unyielding wall (repeat-
    ed reports)

The rapidity of the occupation of Novi Sad

The concept of lebensraum

British repression in India

Ravines, the widespread use of ravines, the evolution of
    largescale killing without ever abandoning the use of
    the ravine, or in karstal regions any old hole, foibe, all
    over Istria, ravines on every side of the Pripyat Marsh-
    es, Balkan ravines, and no mention of bears through-
    out the six years of perfervid warmaking not one arti-
    cle on bears, or wolves, big cats—no there were a few
    on wolves, in Lithuania, emerging from the forests at

night to nibble the corpses that had yet to be shoveled, bulldozed, toed into the ravines, so okay then, no vultures, even a single death out here, it could be fifty miles away and the buzzards will locate the body for you, will lead you to the body, you'll see the vultures flying, gathering, and at some critical point you'll realize that it is no ordinary death, which makes it astonishing no matter how you look at it, that there was no mention, but even if there were, thirty forty fifty million killed and what?, the vultures, there must have been some real vulture orgies, particularly considering the ravines, in the Balkans, they often simply kicked dozens of dead into a ravine and moved on, which would have meant vultures, and whatever mammalian scavengers, she read in an encyclopedia probably that the other scavengers, maggots and ants and such, that an extraordinary number of them are actually ingested by the larger scavengers, some of which survive the journey but most of which are destroyed by acids, or was it that most of them were immune to acids, or some of them, at any rate at the bottom of a Balkan ravine three hundred slaughtered Bosnians, vultures, something like coyotes probably, maybe even given the chaos starving wolves and bears, and maggots and the survivors great fat colorful flies and shit everywhere and ants, more ants than Germans, Chetniks, Partizans, Ustaši combined in that one ravine, ten different kinds of ants no doubt, feeding, working, alongside each other, avoiding conflict in time of plenty, giant black ants, tiny red ants, red and black ants, funny that with their tripartite bodies they are never of three colors but sometimes two, and certainly different kinds of flies, minor irritants to the larger scavengers, worms, if you turn up a pile of bodies, driving off the vultures, wolves, or bears, or bobcats, ignored the maggots and flies and ants that would be crawling up your arms, underneath you would find every kind of worm and beetle of the region, the dark feeders, those armadillo bugs that seem to be everywhere that curl up into a ball, centipedes, the rapid degeneration of human flesh and bone sinking into the earth and the rapid rise of the dark creatures of fertile riverine earth, the meeting of plenty, not to forget the fish, fish that acquires a taste for human flesh for flesh is flesh, meat is meat, bottomfeeding catfish, which she read probably in an encyclopedia that in Europe in some rivers were enormous, bigger than any in the United States or anywhere in Canada, and trout, and eels, all feeding of flesh, nibbling flesh bits or picking off the strands of the besogged submerged whitening pieces that fray and slowly disintegrate like the dress of a poor woman, and every one of those dead have a skull and every one of those skulls will be polished clean and you have to wonder which creatures finish off that process, something small, perhaps mites, the smallest mites or worms, worms with tiny mouths and teeth like piranhas, scary worms that wait, that rise slowly, inexorably, the skulls seem to know they are coming, the last knowledge of the skulls, that those innocent looking worms with round mouths filled with razor teeth are rising, patient but rising, waiting for the final polishing, a sort of sculpting for in war as in peace nothing is acceptable about a skull with anything at all attached.

46

THE REVENGE OF LANGUIDEIA

If you don't mind my secretary is going to take dictation.

Why would I mind what your secretary does?

She'll be writing down everything we say.

Why? What's her interest in all this?

No, I am asking her to do it.

No, you are not asking her to do it. You run a university—you should have a better grasp of grammar. You may have asked her. But you were not asking her at the moment you said that.

I have asked her and she has agreed. Is that good enough for you, young man?

So what's the question now? Is that good enough or would I mind?

Do you agree to have your words recorded.

Yes, that would be a much better idea—she could take the afternoon off. Simply record this...this whatever it is as if I didn't know.

Oh. What is it that you think this is?

Look: she's writing like an electrified chicken. I guess we can do without the recorder.

She is very skilled at a dying art.

We could perhaps say the same for you.

In what sense?

You tell me.

You—Let's start from the beginning. The rea—

We're past the beginning. That's one of those trite phrases upper echelon bureaucrats use that is virtually never applicable.

Fine. Let us start the *process* at the beginning.

Der Prozess. So it's a trial—or an inquisition.

I simply have some questions for you.

I've noticed that, but I really have yet to detect a pattern.

Let's start, then.

We haven't?

Look, you can be a smartass all you want, but if you don't want to be expelled this time you'll cooperate, and I mean starting right now.

How have I not been cooperating?

Don't play games with me.

Play games with you! I wouldn't even have a drink with you.

Do you know why I had you brought in here?

Probably, but why ask? Just tell me.

Look. Son. We consider you a victim.

Thanks. I agree. I had better things planned for today... Dad.

This is not the first time I've spoken with a victim of... such a sensitive crime.

A sensitive crime—was I pickpocketed?

I know that you know what I'm talking about, but I also understand it may be difficult for you to talk about.

It has been so far.

So you've considered seeking...counsel?

Never. You?

I've been to numerous seminars on the topic.

Of pickpocketing.

You were actually sharing—you were living with Professor Garvin.

No way.

We have records, witnesses—

He was a lot of things, but not a pickpocket.

There is no need to protect him. It's over. He, as you probably know, is missing. You have nothing to fear from him any longer.

Especially if I keep my wallet in my front pocket, right?

If that's the way you wish to put it.

I see no other way.

All right. Fine. Can you tell me, for instance, how this "pickpocketing" came to…how it began. How he approached you.

Like I said, he wasn't a pickpocket.

There were others involved?

In what? Involved in what?

Others "spent time" at the house.

Never that I recall.

Right, he would probably do it while you were away. He of course had your course schedule?

Probably not, but no doubt you did, the course, of course, and in due course, and still do, or do again. But what are you referring to?

I know this is hard for you—

This is not hard for me. Or, well, not Orwell, but: or, well, if I take things at face value.

Is it hard now for you to trust older men? Would you like me to—

Why the fuck would I trust you? And what precisely is it that would make me categorize you as an old man, rather than, say, a pedophile, or pseudo-scholar?

So it was traumatic.

It.

We really need to know as much as you can tell us.

There's hardly time for that.

I see…When was the first time?

The first time what.

When did he…when did he approach you?

Whenever we met and were separated by space. We would both close the gap.

So you came to depend on him.

No. I have been independent since I have been here.

What if I suggested, what do you think when I say the word "denial."

That you claim you're innocent, that you didn't do it.

That's it.

Same it?

What?

You keep bringing it up.

I don't follow.

Do you approach?

Good God no!

Are you offended?

No, son, listen, we're on your side in this. You're the victim, and as soon as we finish this conversation, you'll have ample opportunity to see a counselor.

You are on my side. And I am the victim of this conversation. And I will have a counselor with an ample bosom.

Precisely. Stop that.

Silly. Then why do you press on?

There are certain facts we need to know. To reconstruct an outline. This whole thing has come as a shock to all of us. Imagine his wife.

I don't have to—I've seen her. I know her a little. Horrid.

Of course. You had…let's see…three classes with Professor Garvin. Right, so tell me about your relations with him during the first class, the first workshop.

Primarily, he was the teacher and I was the student.

Primarily. So there was more.

Isn't there always?

No, no there should not be.

Lifeless then.

That, if you'll pardon me, is the sound of despair.

No, but if that's what you want I can produce a despair sound for you.

But you said lifeless.

Yes. Yes, I said lifeless.

You're depressed. That's only natural.

Oddly, I'm rather the opposite: undepressed. Sky high perhaps. This is quite the show.

How do you mean?

I would guess the same way others do, if perhaps tending to arrive at different conclusions.

Are you following me?

No.

You don't know what I'm talking about at all?

Yes, I think I know a great deal about it.

But you said—

I said I'm not following you.

I meant—

I know what you meant.

Listen, son—

No, Dad, not if you continue to call me son.

I'm sorry. I intended no disrespect.

Or, or, or insinuations of intimacy.

Certainly not.

Yet you would like that I trust you.

Yes.

You could perhaps represent, say, a shoulder for me to lean on.

Certainly.

Not that I would know, but this is the language of a sexual predator.

The language Professor Garvin used.

No, the language I used and you felt quite comfortable adopting as a strategy to bring us closer together that I might open up.

I'm afraid you're twisting this around a bit.

This.

This whole thing.

This whole thing.

You know what I mean.

Why don't you just come right out and say it? This investigation?

That's it.

Yes, we're investigating the relations of Professor Garvin with his male students, and we—

I was his best friend, so you, you, you…I…I…I…I can't…

I understand. Some trauma, I'm told, is to be expected—

Can you imagine?

No…but I can listen.

My best professor, and now all this.

But how do you know?

I was there wasn't I?

So he, you and he…

Yes, the two of us…for some time we shared everything.

So—everything?

Well, we ate different food.

Different meals.

Sometimes.

And sometimes you ate the same meals. You shared meals.

Shared, yes. But he ate his and I ate mine. So not everything.

You talked a lot. You were intimate.

Yes, more than, I would think, the average student and professor.

So you know of other cases. We have been told there have been many other cases.

Cases of what?

What?

Precisely.

I'm sorry, I don't follow.

Again with the following. This is difficult for me, all the changing directions.

Where would you like to take it up, then?

With you. With your fear that you are being followed. Do you think Professor Garvin is following you?

I, no, I think Professor Garvin "followed" younger men. He would have no interest in me.

On the contrary. He had great interest in you. He spoke of you with great passion.

Great passion.

Does that make you uncomfortable?

Rather. But let us not get sidetracked.

Look, if you need time to gather yourself. I understand that for a man in your position such a discovery can be, well, to use your word, traumatic.

What discovery?

Something happened that makes you uncomfortable even now. Does it involve Professor Garvin?

What? Yes, this is all about Professor Garvin.

Surely, you have a way out. After all, you were not rector when he was hired.

A way out?

Let's not get ahead of ourselves. What I mean to say is that your secrets are safe with me.

Secrets. Not the slightest cause for discomfort.

What doesn't cause you discomfort?

I can't make a list here and now.

But specifically what did you mean?

I can picture it. I'm not squeamish. Though it would surprise me no end if it were true. You and Professor Garvin. It's absurd. I knew the man. I knew him intimately.

That's what I brought you here to talk about, but we seem to somehow—

Always return to you.

Yes. To reiterate: we are investigating charges that have made—that have been made...charges that have been made, charges of a sensitive nature—

Like pickpocketing...

What? No, I think, I'm beginning to think—

There's a start. And I believe that's really where I can help you.

There was a workshop in which some violence occurred.

Oh that was good.

The workshop.

No, not the—The way you snapped back to a position of authority and regained control of the situation by reverting to a specific event at which both Professor Garvin and I were present.

Thank you. At that workshop there was a...the best term...

Ruckus or brawl.

Yes. What caused this...*ruckus* or "brawl"?

I suppose my anger. I suppose I have a bit of a temper.

Perhaps a certain amount of jealousy was involved?

There always is, there always is. Fine. Now—

No, it's not fine. Jealousy has no place in a workshop.

I agree.

Write it down then. Point of agreement. Basis for taking action: remove jealousy from workshops.

Did you know that the person you assaulted was a homosexual?

No. Did you?

As part of the investigation, and this is of the utmost del-icacy—

Then don't fucking tell me.

Please refrain from using obscenity—

You started it.

No, I merely—

Telling me about a fellow student's—

Fine! Look—

You're screaming at me.

Sorry. I *am* sorry. This issue has us all…none of us are enjoying this.

I am.

What?

I'm enjoying this immensely so far.

Can we come back to that?

Interesting question.

Perhaps you don't know that the inquiry—

Investigation.

Investigation. That the investigation was triggered by an accusation made by the student you were, that you—

Ruckused with.

That student came forward with accusations that unfortu-nately have been backed up by—

His wife.

How do you know that?

You just told me.

I have told no one.

You're a bit thick.

Come again.

Dense.

I've tried very hard to be gentle with you, fair to you.

That's an interesting self-extrapolation, not to sound ob-scene.

As I've said, you're the victim. Had we known then what we know now you would not have been suspended.

And you wouldn't be here now wearing suspenders.

I have to ask you how you came about the information you revealed just now.

Well, first, to go easy on you, I will assume that despite

the predominant lack of clarity that has befogged this interrogation—and it's entirely to your credit, sir, that you haven't the faintest idea how to conduct an interrogation—we need more people like you in the highest echelons of the military—what you are referring to is the fact that this inquiry was generated by Garvin's wife, Languideia Swishpish or whatever her maidenhood long gone is unrecoverable. Am I right?

That's not relevant.

Which.

How the investigation was...instigat—was, what *triggered*—

I'm no psychoanalyst, but you were about to use a very unfortunately loaded term. Instigated.

Well I didn't. The fact is, that—

There has only been one fact established between us here today. I can't get over how fast she is. The only fact is that the abandoned wife of Professor Garvin—

Abandoned? Indeed. Is that his language.

It's all of ours.

In what sense.

English. It's English.

Son—

I warned you about that.

Sorry—young man. Perhaps you don't know as much as you think you know, having only heard from one side, but there's a great deal involved. This whole thing threatens to embroil the entire school in the end in a shameful, embarrassing—

Ruckus?

No!

Shouting.

This could destroy this institution if the investigation is not handled properly, if we don't stay ahead on this thing. And I need you to cooperate fully.

I think I would like your lawyer present.

We are not at that stage yet. This is a preliminary investigation. Nothing you say here today is binding.

Rather inutile then, wouldn't you say?

How is that?

I could tell you what I know about the Gibbon of Marshalltown and Languideia nee Solipschism, how they paid off the state patrol guy at Clear Lake when he came upon them necking, and I could even tell you which motel in Story City—how's that for a ripe town?—they frequent, apparently because the proprietor is deaf and dumb.

What is this gibberish?

Gibbonesque gibberish.

I assure you this is not funny.

And I assure you that humor is not subject to diktat.

Perhaps you aren't aware that this investigation revolves not only around Professor Garvin, but you as well.

So two suns.

What?

Astronomical reference for an astronomical bunglottery.

I fail to follow.

Perhaps for lack of effort.

I assure—I tell you that I am making a very strong effort to contain my feelings here.

Which ones? You've expressed feelings of empathy towards victims.

Frustration and anger at your apparent inability to focus, or perhaps cooperate. I sometimes get the feeling that you are like a cult follower—

And Professor Garvin the cult.

Yes.

Well, put that one to rest. He's gone and I'm still here, so I obviously did not follow him.

I'll put it to you straight: Do you know where he is?

Absolutely not. You ask of me the impossible.

I don't see how it is impossible.

Don't linger in the unknowable, sir, if you wish to obtain facts.

Thanks for your advice. You know nothing of his whereabouts.

That's hardly true. I know a great deal of his whereabouts.

Don't play games with me. Do you know where he is or do you not!

I do not.

Has anyone, anyone at all, spoken to you of this matter?

Besides you?

Obviously.

I'm not sure.

How can you not be sure?

It occurs to me that this matter could mean a wide range of—

I'm talking about the actions of Professor Garvin!

I know a great deal about the actions of Professor Garvin.

And?

And?

And, have you discussed this matter with anyone else?

Yes. I have discussed the actions of Professor Garvin with Professor Garvin and my father.

Oh Christ! Your father knows? Has he…taken any steps?

Oh, my dad, he's always taking steps. Though you know how hot Vegas gets in summer. He drives pretty much everywhere.

What have you told your father?

About?

This, dammit!

Whoa, Doctor. You're on the verge of badgering the victim. So you are afraid my father will spill the beans, is that it?

My primary concerns are the health of our students and the status of our university.

I think I read that brochure in the waiting room.

I don't need your cynicism, young man, but I do need your cooperation.

Right. Gotta get a lid on this thing.

No, I assure—I, no, I intend to get to the bottom of this and do everything it takes to bring to justice and heal all wounds and—

Bring to justice all wounds, and heal all followers and pickpockets. I get that.

You are utterly exasperating. I don't know what Professor Garvin saw in you.

Fascinating admission, sir.

Shit!—don't write that—erase that, Mirna. I mean as a student.

Erase what? From where to where?

Just the curse word.

Curse word. Fuck it.

Would you—Leave that one in. I don't know where we're going with this.

I do.

Would you kindly tell me.

For a second there I honestly thought you were going to call me Mr. Smarty Pants.

Please, tell me where we are going with this.

Precisely nowhere, not that that makes sense, and I'm sorry for my blundering speech, but what I mean to say is we are staying in this room, and yet the story is not, the story is all over campus, all over town, soon to be all over Iowa, and probably the United States, and by that time—I give it two weeks—your buffoonery will have cost you a job, and the poet lariat of the wild somewhatwest will have been thoroughly shamed and discredited, which ought to give her some sense of satisfaction as she was unable to do it with her poetry, which is some of the most elaborately trite and ill-willed, cipheristic claptrap—love that word—I have ever read. And I believe the opinion is widely shared amongst the intimidated initiated as well as the aloof and aloft and away from the stench of this all.

You are insinuating a great deal, young man.

Don't forget I'm a victim.

Of the Stockholm Syndrome.

Hah! That was fucking great—curse stet—the one fucking thing you've said this entire interview that indicated life and mind. Christ, I'll never forget it.

I don't need—

My condescension. Yes, you do. I'll never forget it for another reason, for you are implying, or insinuating, a great deal not only about Professor Garvin, but about myself. I am an adult, as adult as you by law, and, you getting this Mirna?

Mm.

Good, I won't leave without a photocopy. You've opened yourself to a great number of charges that will probably only

be avoided by giving up the Languid Liar. You see, sir, I am
a heterosexual male, who befriended and was befriended
by Professor Garvin, a heterosexual man, and a man who
is innocent of all these charges. You have one pathetic student who hates him and hates me and was suborned by your
queen professor—and I do refer to the female queen in this
case. Garvin is innocent of this charge. I have already seen a
lawyer and taken a polygraph test and passed. They did not
ask me if I knew where he was and I have no interest in revealing whether or not I know that. So you were set up by a
woman scorned, spurned, ditched and of such ego there was
no recourse for her but to seek revenge in a way that would
not tarnish her reputation, would in fact enhance her reputation—a writer husband she discovers plays with boys' balls
like so many baubles, the creep. But of course by then he was
already gone. And had not even, and for this I fault him, slept
with a female student of age, which would cover all of them I
suppose, but who had never so much as flirted for his own no
doubt disturbing reasons that will remain out of reach of this
investigation, quietly entrenched in the bosom of his privacy
where all his essence belongs. I've spoken with a reporter, of
course, and the story is now unstoppable. I made my case and
made it well. It's a story—don't go anywhere with those notes,
Mirna—anyway, you'll have a new boss soon. Not that I am
likely to need them, for the reporter is conducting his own
investigation, parallel to yours, and is at this very moment listening, prying secrets from, taking note of the lies of Languideia the Last, who has no idea she is being sandbagged, for I
have three student witnesses who couldn't have given a shit
either way but were appalled at that which was defined as appalling, and have discussed with said reporter what Languideia let slip in private conversation, naming names, smearing names, mine, Garvin's and I'm not sure of the underage
stooge. A monster, that bitch, and she has created a monster,
Igor, with your unwitting help, with your witless help, your
blind and groping perfervid help, your unimaginative, spineless, indiscriminating, manipulated help.

No, slump silently. There's nothing you can say right
now to save your ass. That will come when and if you get a

chance to prove that you were indeed manipulated, not that, in my opinion, that makes you the least innocenter than the manipulator, each carries with it its own variety of disgust, wouldn't you say? And before I leave this hive of crashlanding inanities, I want to make one more point, which is that had Professor Garvin and I been gay lovers, had Professor Garvin had discrete love affairs with young males, nothing but the drummed up seventeen-year-old would have been anyone's business, and that one only by virtue of law—school rules, rather, not state law.

Mirna, I trust you to type up your notes accurately while I sit here. I'll read them over to be sure nothing of import was left out, though I doubt anything was, but after what you've heard I think you can understand I want to be careful. And then I'll have a copy signed and dated by you and the ex-rector here. And then you will be free for the day, I assume.

Stop whimpering, you ass.

47

SPELUNKING

The air-conditioning was off, the windows open, the heat of the valley was columnar, valley shaped and illimitably high, revisiting upon the dawn. Donnie had slept poorly, dreaming of various amphibious encounters in shallow waters, of remarkable creatures such as large squids lazing or languishing in the still shallows of near shore. People he picked up in the dream, befriended, who also had flights to catch, most the same one, and like him had been to these places before spoke with him of oblique matters of temporal import, and moved on, with him, even as they gathered for an Argentine-style barbecue, indoors, where a room with snakes posed interesting questions, but no venom. He awoke frequently only to re-enter the dream, or so it seemed, the life of the dream as coherent and stubborn as the life of the dreamer. When the light seemed to suddenly pour heat into the valley column, he finally blinked himself awake, touched but mildly by those he left behind, touched effusively by the animate tensility of the woman deeply asleep beside him whom he felt no need to refrain from touching, for he had yet to find her unresponsive in the slightest, whether his touch be sexual, brotherly, avuncular, toddlerian, wrasslish. The sheet had been slept to the floor. He observed her body like a man alone on a bench in a room in a museum, his intimacy his own and inviolable. He was not in a hurry. She lay on her side, so the natural beginning was to slide down the bed, his face even with her scapulae, rest his hand on her side and slide it down to her hi-prise, which made him erect, filled his innards with a replica of the joy of discovery, much like what one feels upon espying a large green lizard on a warm day in a breeze. Before his hand had reached her knee she had moaned and rolled a quarter to her backside, flexing her left, stroked, leg, drawing her right up and caressing that thigh near her groin. Donnie shifted, sliding down and moving over her leg, his face in the mink's fur of her mound, gravidly succumbing to the grace of gravity, his nose finding her clitoris, his tongue beginning to taste the juices as of a peach that excreted from within, from the skin, from, it seemed, the hair itself, which was beginning to slowly rotate as one, the liquid forming in transient densities, addictive elixir, his tongue finding every feel of flesh drawing more liquid, more moaning, more movement, until hands held his head, pressing him against her, his tongue deep inside, orbiting the labia, laving from anus to clitoris, lapping, his teeth closing on the clitoris, the moaning louder, his hands sliding up along the skin as of a mother's suppurating breast, sliding to Hermione's breasts, palpating, swelling, his hands following the heave and pulse of the breasts, the nipples beginning to penetrate finally yielding, his entire face damp with the inquisitive, emotive odor precisely Hermionic adherent like skunk mist that he would wear throughout the long day to come.

Her orgasm clutched him with its thighs, her hands gripping his hair, his own orgasm following from the pain and primitive force of the beast of the coupling. He remained where he was, his head on her hair, until he heard her breathing settling back to deep sleep, when he took up his position again beside her, not touching her, the morning's warm breeze stirring his body's hair and stimulating his brain. This was a start, finally. Who could know what of the lark, the drakelark that was nearing its first anniversary...this woman was the goddess of cynicism, who would regulate his, alter his cynicism and provide him repletion of dereliction, matutinal energies that would strengthen his vision while providing him with armor against the apocalyptical disgust storm that would ever oppose him, energies that would exert properties to empower him to strive as he once did naturally, as a child, before his mind prematurely entered the adult world. These grandiose thoughts obliterated all inanities of rational future planning, leaving him to exist with himself joyfully, thinking only of his coming day, which required him to make his way to the Luxor office—and he recalled Brian and his bombs, that he suffered two years of house arrest for, taking the fall for Brian, happily, delighted to lay this turmoil at the feet of his parents; he felt the same now with Drake and his bizarre insistence on clinging to a plan made in haste, before he had even learned what he had now become upon his inheritance, the inheritance of a global security business, among other activities, and one that Donnie knew Drake would soon find was less scrupulous than Drake Senior had let on.

"Bring in the Blind Venetian," Nordgaard ordered a blond from dreams of the Neolithic, a man of enormity, blonde, rubicund and pitted face, tiny ears, short-sleeve splitting arms, the ass of a woman weight-lifter, and whose body was precisely the same as that of the other guard allowed in the room, a black man, from dreams of the Neolithic—two monoliths, whom, Donnie realized, he theoretically had absolute power over, given Drake's pronouncement that he would be vice-president in charge of whatever he chose. Drake, of course, would be president. Nordgaard would be the silent chief executive, nothing that happened would without his approval. For this, his first meeting at the new Vegas office, his first appearance in Vegas, Nordgaard wore a blue pastel leisure suit that was less comic than Donnie would have thought, perhaps for sleek reptilian motility of his supple body and his longer neck, his ovate head with its eyes ever seeking their brows. And he stood. Short as he was, he stood. Drake invited Donnie to sit behind the boss's desk, while he took up a chair lit by a standing steel lamp, across a short serving table from a chair that was not lit by its lamp, where a man sat with his face perfectly shadowed, as if for a documentary, having been escorted by the lithic blond.

"Earplugs."

The liths immediately opened little plastic bags and stuffed the industrial safety standard earplugs in the absolutely correct orifici.

Nordgaard gave Drake a long impassive look before indicating Donnie with a brief nod.

"I trust him without limit or hesitation."

"Where am I?" came from the dark chair space.

Donnie saw then, dimly, the outlines of a blindfold.

"Safe. Don't ask any more questions like that."

Apparently this would be entirely orchestrated by Nordgaard.

Drake had a yellow legal tablet on his lap, a pen poised. Nordgaard slowly walked toward the blindfolded man, stood waiting for Drake's attention. Drake was oblivious. Donnie wanted to fling a rock at him.

When he finally looked up, Nordgaard said, "Put that away."

"What, sir?"

"Not you. When I address you I will call you 'soldier,'" Nordgaard told him.

Drake took the pad and paper, secluded them in drawers and returned obediently to his seat.

"Right. Soldier. Tell me from the beginning."

"We were in Helmand—"

"I know those details. You're Borm, am I right. Real name, everything?"

"Yes, sir. And that's what they knew me as."

"Fine, soldier. Your assignment that day."

"Our Taliban connection wanted the son of a schismatic targeted, so—"

"A schismatic."

"That's how I understood it, sir. The son of a rival cleric popular in the region."

"Go on."

"Our guys had, say, a thirty-kilometer radius of operations, I had my assignment. I was introduced to the unit as some kind of elite soldier, it wasn't made clear. They were to assume SEAL or whatever. We had a seminar conducted in the morning on social sensitivity to get us near the town where my intelligence alerted me that the target would be in the afternoon and into the evening. But that wasn't good enough, because these guys were trigger-happy. They would have let loose at the first village. I had to assume control or we would never have made the target's village before all hell broke loose. That was problem number one, that I had to guide them and therefore stood out more than we like to. Normally it would be handled such that I was just one of the guys. I had even chosen my stooge, guy called Drippen, who would have worked out perfectly. Had no press been involved, to this day the guys in the unit would have Drippen on their mind and I would have been forgotten, just another—"

"Soldier. You're on the payroll. You are not on trial here. This is a debriefing, the sole purpose being to get on top of the circumstances. I already know that your own behavior has been beyond excellent. The very fact that you're here and not locked up is to your credit. Please continue."

"Thank you, sir. As you know, this recreation began some years ago and has been either ignored by the press, or the press has been assiduously avoided, or bought off one way or another. I believe most or all of the men had some grasp that this was behavior that would not be tolerated outside Afghanistan, and that if press somehow told the story...So, Firpo, the guy who's talking, panicked when we came upon media, which happened just as I spotted and eliminated my target. The media was fired upon, one dead, the other a known entity who could well have been dealt with. It never occurred to me that there might be one more. But there was, apparently frightened, huddled in a hovel that served food. He was also extremely angry. He was able to make the proprietor understand his intentions, to expose the action as murder, and achieved his cooperation. You have seen the pictures, sir?"

"Yes, son, I have. And, yes, I notice you do not appear in any of the photographs."

"The pictures you saw are typical shots secreted away by hundreds, if not thousands, of soldiers. Of course, the brass knows this. Once the photographs were published they had to contain it to one incident. So they pushed hard..."

"And you, soldier?"

"Sir, as soon as the media guy bought it, I knew I had to get out as soon as possible. By the following night I had reached Peshawar and within a week I was back in the States."

"Soldier, from my reports, which accord with your statement, your behavior was precisely what we would expect from one of our men. Exemplary."

"Naturally—"

"You even managed to collect."

"Not to be humble, sir, but my contact, the guy with the money, was also my guide out. I offered him payment, aware of the importance of getting out, which he refused."

"Tell me about the first night."

"The first night, sir?"

"Yes, soldier, the night before you left, the night of the action."

"Yes, sir. We were back at base. We celebrated with beer and whiskey. I waited for someone to show some concern about the media. After some time, Mancuso brought it up. Within five minutes they all looked as if they were already on their way to Leavenworth. I poured a round of shots, laughed, and said, 'Who's gonna talk? Nobody here.' We were sandbagged in a safe zone, in a state of shock, Drippen saw a rifle open a curtain, he saw the barrel and fired. It was a woman. That not only put us on the alert, it sent chills—we came to the corner and all hell broke loose on our left. One teenage fighter ran across the street to the right, that's when the media guy got hit. You understand, sir. Plausible story. Young guys out for an easy day betrayed during a truce. Sure, they had a bit of gruesome fun with the bodies while they were still full of adrenaline. They were all daylight shots, right? So fucking sue us for putting our lives on the line and getting them before they got us. Didn't we find a weapons cache in the house we entered after being shot at from the upstairs?"

"That's very good, soldier. *Very* good. So why did you leave? It worked, didn't it?"

"Absolutely, sir. In ten minutes they were partying more freely than before. They probably even believed nothing was wrong. The place changes every brain that goes there. Mine, too. But each brain is warped to different degrees. There was no way all of them would accept the death of one of our guys, the media guy. We knew the media was there for no reason, that they knew of the truce, so it was either a holiday or a feel good story. You can get to where you can shoot a little fucking foreign-gibberish fucking gnatlike kid in the fucking eye, and maybe you'll have your nightmares years later or maybe you won't. But that dead American guy. And no one said so, but I could see he was not unknown to some of the guys. If it came to it, someone would break. No way to know it would be Firpo specifically, but I wouldn't have ruled him out that night."

"I have received word that he mentioned your name, soldier. How might that have come about?"

"Wasn't—sir, it wasn't legible on my uniform. I was 'Cal' to them and they wouldn't even have remembered that. He was fed my name. But I have absolutely no reason to believe they would be looking for me as anything but an AWOL soldier. There is absolutely nothing to connect me to this organization."

"So Firpo, none of the others if they break, none of them can connect to us."

"Sir, I've been over and over it since it happened. I drifted over from another unit under procedural cover. And at that I see no reason to look elsewhere in the organization for a mistake. If they investigated carefully, Borm would have to come up sooner or later. My guess sooner. Which is why I deemed it appropriate to hightail it outta there."

"I agree, soldier. I agree. So we have nothing to fear, but you do. Tell me, soldier. How many weapons sale operations were you involved in for us?"

"Three, sir. All in the vicinity of Herat, once involving Iranians, but that's all I know."

"What weapons, soldier?"

"RPGs, clusters, mines, sir."

"The source of the weapons?"

"Classified."

"Not in here, soldier."

"Sir, I—"

"NOT...in here, soldier."

"Munitions warehouse near Bagram, sir."

"Means of transfer?"

"Warlord. One of ours. Killed by his own troops, they brought us the weapons and dispersed with some cash."

"Good enough. Are you nervous, soldier?"

"Sir, in truth, I believe it's fifty/fifty I get out of here alive."

"How many people outside our company know who you work for?"

"Sir, you know that, sir."

"Answer the question, soldier."

"No one, sir."

"So you think that might make you expendable. I understand that, soldier. But let me tell you the one quality that absolutely makes for the best fighting man. Or can you guess?"

"Fearlessness, steady nerves, sir, ability to think on your feet."

"That's like, no disrespect intended soldier, but that is like saying that what makes a good sniper is an accurate shooter. No, the foremost quality is loyalty. But I am not going to lecture you on that point. Loyalty is what makes this organization successful. This organization was built by a great, principled man. Were we to kill you on the slightest chance that this horseshit in Afghanistan would damage us we would not be being loyal to a good soldier. No one would ever know, perhaps, no one but ourselves, and our own loyalties would be permanently compromised. I don't expect you to fully understand that. You will be escorted to a safe place, escorted to a safe country where you will live quietly and without money problems. You will return when we can arrange whatever needs to be arranged, up to and including a new identity. I realize that this has its difficulties, but we will be highly alert to your ongoing status and you will memorize an emergency number that will provide some assurance. Before you ask, my answer is between one and three years abroad, though should you wish to rejoin us working out of country, that too can be arranged. Now, go on, and thank you for your excellent work."

"Thank you, sir."

"Boys, same as on the way in, keep the blindfold on til

you're in the air but he knows he's in Vegas so don't overdo it. Make him as comfortable as possible. That's all."

"Scotch, Mister Drake. For, lo, we must celebrate your introduction to your father's business. And you, young Garvin, your discretion was admirable."

Signifiers embedded in the briefest eye contact exchanged discomfort between the two friends.

"Come, let us sit at the grand conference table, for we have much to discuss."

They sat with their Lagavulin, ice cubes in a metal bucket, each poured half a glass by Nordgaard.

"I have told you many tales, lo, and all of them true. Your father has been involved deeply in historical events, horrible events, and he never shirked his responsibilities, always—and for this I loved him, for this he earned my loyalty—always had a grasp of the long view. You no doubt have many questions, and I see by your eyes that you would disapprove of some of our nastier business deals. But lo, this is not a world for yielding to darker powers, nor is it an American utopia, for the empire is always beset by enemies. A conflict is engaged in far across the world, and newspaper articles are written, television reports yield images, and the whole of the story is but a veil of the complexities of life over there. If you are repulsed by what you heard today, know that in this war, an extraordinary few Americans have died, that a fanatical fringe of Islam is being held at bay. Many children have died, yes, and many adult non-combatants, but the alternative would have been far worse, for lo, these are paradoxical people, the poorest of the poor yet warriors to the very core. We have been fighting a delaying action. Naturally we have bombed Pakistani tribal areas, for that is the only way to negotiate with the Taliban. The role of our company is to do at times what no one else can do, what no one else is willing to do. Yet, lo, I assure you that in this particular case you heard today many thousands of lives were saved by the deal our men made secretly with the Taliban. And as for the guns stolen and sold, the warlord in question was of grandiose ideas that amounted to insanity. All the weapons sold will be used against the Taliban and a series of useless slaughters were averted. Yet you drink with the thirst of the shocked. Lo, I say to you, be not judgmental. Our profits are necessary to keep our organization involved, to push events the correct way. This, Drake Junior, is your inheritance. I am here to advise you, but this is what your father planned for you to inherit, an extremely profitable business and a role on the stage of the world, lo. Not for you to build a casino and live a life of superfluity, leisure, indulgence."

Drake's face was formed into a sullen belligerence.

"You know, Nordgaard, that I had many differences with my father—"

"Trifling, trifling. Of no consequence."

"Oh, you're right. Of no consequence compared to what I have heard today. Of no consequence compared to murder for hire in conspiracy with the enemy, of no consequence compared to stealing arms and selling them for profit to the enemy of the enemy and the enemy of his own country."

"I expected this would take some time to sink in, for, lo, there is much for you to learn. Let me just say that the complications exist with or without our organization. We influence events toward more desirable results."

"You don't think much of my plan to build and operate a casino with my inheritance, do you?"

"I did not reach my age in good health by being impatient. You will come to know the folly of your plans, for lo, you are your father's son, and you will learn very quickly that what you envision is far from what you will attain. This is not the city for you. Like in New York, you will make petty enemies who cannot touch you because of our organization. Without our organization, you will be defeated by men who know the business you naively intend to enter into."

"Perhaps you don't understand. With your help, I plan to disband the organization, to offer work at the same pay for any who wish to join the new venture, and to offer the rest generous severance packages. I've given this a lot of thought, and I have thought as my father thought—as my father taught me to think. Everyone will be taken care of. And if we need a small clandestine outfit to care for such as your interrogatee, we will fund that as well. But Blackguard as you know it will be disbanded. As for you, obviously you have a particular place in this and I intend to offer you your choice of retirement, which I am guessing would not interest you, working with me, finding your place here, or even remaining in LA as whatever you design for a job, or to run the vestigial clandestine outfit."

Donnie studied the reactions of Nordgaard, the impassivity, the lack of reactive body language, the pleasance that emanated from him in all its implausibility. He felt for the first time that he was in the presence of an extraordinarily dangerous man. He was not surprised by the response, nor the emptied second glasses of scotch before Drake and him, while Nordgaard had yet to bring his glass to his lips.

"I understand everything, lo, and here is what you must understand. Purchasing land and licensing is no small venture. You have much to learn, and I have contacts who will help you. Lo, at the same time, disbanding an organization such as ours is also a great matter, a matter of time and much planning. You will find that very few if any of our employees will join you. As we differ in our opinions, we must come to a reasonable agreement. As we slowly enact our plans a great deal of money will continue to flow into the organization. That will afford us time. You will proceed as you wish, as will I, and after some months, three to six months, we will have this discussion one last time, and if you have not changed your mind, lo, we will proceed as you have determined. I ask you this one favor: to think it over as you proceed. As I proceed, I will assume that you will not change your mind, so as to be prepared to carry out your wishes. I would take you up on your offer to head up what you referred to as the 'vestigial clandestine outfit,' which would, lo, be fitting for me and a great pleasure, for it would allow me to continue to serve the interests of your father. Now, I propose a toast to a well-reasoned discussion in which all parties are indulged and their wishes respected.

"Lo, to your father and to you, his son, a worthy successor."

The two young friends drank with the lust of relief and

the gusto of incipient binging. Nordgaard drank with deliberation.

"I will return to Los Angeles, lo, and you will hear from me. Please go about your business entirely as you see fit, and contact me at the number if you need my help, if you run into any stubborn difficulties. I will take my leave."

He poured the sincerity of an alien creature into Drake's eyes as he spoke, and when he turned to leave, smiled at Donnie, thinking, What does that boy's father want with me?

"Shall we go down to the cave for some blackjack and drinks?"

"Oh fuck yes."

On the way to the elevator, Drake asked, "Tell me. Do you think 22b is his? Should I have asked him straight out?"

"Why, did you see him again?"

"No, but I keep thinking about you seeing him at some out of the way bar, making no effort to speak to you, no effort to hide. He's so unimposing, I can't imagine the message."

The elevator opened to a man in his fifties with a slim build, reddish hair, and a moustache, accompanied by a woman with a mole the size of a marble that looked as if it had rolled out of her nostril and come to rest above her lip. Their entrance clipped off a nasal depressive sentence she was uttering, and there was the distinct impression that she had made of the man's life a drudgery that he craved.

After some thought, Donnie replied, "No. Somehow I think it's entirely unrelated."

Drake merely nodded. Well, Donnie thought, everybody's hiding something. Doesn't make it important.

Donnie felt as if he needed to shake an incubus off his shoulder. He turned to the man, "You tourists, then?"

"Yes, this is our vacation every two years."

"Midwest?"

"Vermillion, South Dakota."

"Thought so."

The elevator had reached casino level without further aggression.

A brightly lit tunnel lined with expensive, sparsely exhibiting shops of baubular led to the cave of the casino, where the boys sought a blackjack table they would have to themselves and the dealer, finding a ten dollar dealer, an oriental woman with a blackjack dealer's fairly typical, almost sneering, indifference.

Drake had pockets full of ten-dollar chips and split $400 worth between himself and Donnie.

Each pushed one forward.

Cards:

Dealer: nine up.

Donnie: Jack and five.

Drake: five and two.

Donnie draws a four: nineteen.

Drake a nine and three: nineteen.

Dealer has nineteen.

Donnie: "Bizarre start."

Drake draws a postcard from his jacket pocket, and lays it at Donnie's elbow.

Coeur d'Alene: an island, mostly a green, with two sandtraps, rust banks one side, probably wood chips, cedar, an overly involved dock spoiling the entire effect.

Donnie flipped it over:

D,

Dropped the car here. Back to B through Montreal probably. Tell Donnie I like Hermione a lot. I like you a lot, too. I don't suppose I need to explain anything, but right now it's all easy knowing it isn't wrong. Watch out for that false sage old fart "Montagnard," for I suspect he means you no good. Welcome anytime in B as clochard. Don't send money anymore, unless you can't help yourself. We will all think of each other with love and better visions.

PT

Dealer: ace up.

Donnie: ace, deuce.

Drake: five, two again.

"You okay?"

"Expected it in some form. As soon as I saw her at the airport I knew it wasn't going to be great…But you know, a lot of it was…some intense and long stretches. Mostly an absurd, ungainly situation."

The dealer rasped. Donnie held up his hand, calling for patience. He reached around, pulled out his billfold and cracked out two crisp hundreds, tossed them to the suddenly re-impassive dealer.

Donnie indicated hit: four. Seven or seventeen. Hit: queen. Seventeen then. Drake, too, drawing a king.

Dealer had ace, two as well. Three. Eight. Ace. Three. Eighteen.

Donnie: ten, seven.

Drake: jacks.

Dealer: eight, turns up seven. Draws queen.

"Yeah, I wasn't near as excited to see her again as I thought I'd be. We're only right here by the oddest chance. She. Now you know who she reminded me of?"

"Hm."

"That broad on your leg the night we met." Donnie: fours.

Drake: queen, six. Dealer: king up.

"That one—her name was Claire—she meant something to me at one time. Maybe in the end they were neck and neck." "Certainly not tit and tit."

"Tit for twat maybe, though."

"From what I saw."

Donnie: king.

Drake: ace.

Dealer flips a three, draws a king. "Bust."

"Busts—nipple toggle."

"Fuck off, I still don't believe that."

Dealer gets blackjack.

"What do you make of the reference to Nordgaard?"

A waitress arrived, a tray like a pregnancy imagined by Verne appended. Her dress looked more Greek than Egyptian but both men thought the same thing: they could've done a great deal worse.

"Whiskey?"

"Sure, a bottle of something Irish. Bucket of ice." A hundred-dollar bill in a cup.

A waitress who'd seen it before, evinced not the faintest whiff of displeasure.

Donnie: nine, two—double down.

Drake: ace, four.

Dealer: four up.

Donnie draws a two.

Drake: a king and hold.

Dealer nine and seven, busting.

"They spent a lot of time alone together. I gathered he was telling war stories. She seemed to gradually relax while all that was going on. But who knows what she saw, or what she thought."

Donnie: jack, four.

Drake: king, ten.

Dealer: eight showing.

Donnie busts with a queen.

Dealer has seventeen.

Donnie: seven, three, double down when dealer shows two.

Drake: jack, six.

Dealer: five.

Donnie gets his ten; Drake stands; dealer flips king, busts with jack.

Donnie: ten, five.

Drake: queen, nine.

Dealer: seven.

"Obviously he wouldn't have said anything to her. Only thing I gather is that he would rather you ditch the casino idea and run the business."

Donnie draws a five; dealer has an eight, busts on a queen.

"I had a word with him on that back in LA. But I think at that point he figured I'd come out here and find the complications discouraging. We need to talk about options that'll keep everybody happy and leave them choices. I guess the main thing is I have to leave the business in Nordgaard's hands and see if I have enough left, or how to manage it. Fuck if I know anything at all right now. I haven't even properly thought of my folks as dead."

Donnie: queen, ten.

Drake: seven, three.

Dealer: jack up.

Drake busts with a five and eight.

Dealer has seventeen.

Donnie: ace, three.

Drake ten, eight.

Dealer: nine.

"You ever going to tell me what you were running from back that first night?"

"What are you talking about?"

"Don't bullshit me at least." Indicated hit. Six for twenty. Drake indicates hold. Dealer flips another nine. "Something to do with Frot, with your old man's business?"

Drake laughed.

Donnie: ace, five.

Drake: jack, seven.

Dealer: ten.

"Christ, no. fuck it: look, it was a lark. I was involved in a game with some vestigial wop mobsters in Brooklyn, had a game. This Vinnie who ran the fucking game was a cunt. I owed him fifty-grand."

Donnie: four, hold at twenty.

Drake: ace, ten, seventeen.

Dealer: flips a two, draws a two, busts on a jack.

Donnie: blackjack.

Drake: queen, six.

Dealer: six.

Jack busts Drake.

Why didn't you just pay the fucking guy? You had the money. You owed it...such pointless narrative responses were made mad, utter nonsense, by the contingent infinite factor of life. Donnie looked at him with admiration detracted by pity, then with admiration winged by free will, luck, danger, sporadicity, fangs, tits, jealousies, the Degradation—an absolute—within which they roamed.

Donnie: six, seven.

Drake: blackjack.

Dealer: king.

"Well, fuck, Drake. I have to thank you all the more. We sure defeated all the sick unsightly becauses."

Donnie busts on a king.

Donnie: eight, four.

Drake: queen, jack.

Dealer: deuce up.

Donnie draws an eight. Dealer flips an ace, draws a fifth eight.

Donnie: six, four. Will double for dealer has a five.

Drake: ten, jack.

Waitress arrives. Seemed a long time, a real long time. Tullamore Dew, bucket of ice, inflated bill.

Drake looked like he was remembering a specific event involving his father. Odd that his mother was never discussed. Good soldier, no doubt. Donnie thought: maybe there was a very particular reason she was shot as well.

"Fuck, let's just pay up and take the bottle outside."

"Good idea."

"No offense, madame, but if I tip another hundred will you disappear a great deal quicker than you arrived? Leaving the bucket and glasses of course."

Look: she *does* want the money.

Drake faced up the dealer: "Sorry, I'm not an ass, but I hate that unnecessary don't give a shit vibe. We aren't *all* unpleasant."

"That's fine, sir."

Donnie drew a three; dealer turned up a three, drew a seven, busted on a ten.

Donnie won $75, Drake $35. Drake indicated leave the chips to the dealer.

48

MOJAVE KROTALON

In the high desert even the green was yellowing or suffused with an inner gray that imposed itself on the emotional substructure of the viewer. Čćrhččrhččrhččrhččrh: even the mojave green, as the mojave rattlesnake is often called, is rarely that shade. Color exists exiguously in the desert, where it is an extravagance that will lead its bearer to extinction. And this is where Tom Garvin, Tom Gravel, Eddie Vegas supped as a youth on inchoate philosophical verities, veritable vertigoes of verities, none of which, like a desert color, could manage to escape the continuum that gave it a sort of life, so that, as noted before, Eddie never knew an original thought to be new: the desert was infinity, loneliness, the insignificance of man, the contingencies of life, the persistence of life, life, life and bones and parasites and opportunists and madmen and genius in its simulacrum of a vacuum. Still, as a man of dangerously intensified purpose, certain of extremely limited utile action—he dialed the number fewer times each day, each time it rang as long as Vegas listened to it—after a week, Eddie Vegas was able to, through the constrained, temperate and meditative Garvin, to unearth Tommy Gravel, whose love of the desert, whose knowledge of the desert, had been a defining characteristic excised in mid-development; and he was finally able to conquer himself, or perhaps sit himself down and threaten a good talking to, he'd be right back, don't go anywhere, we need you just as you are…But meantime, a mature Tom Gravel took off early one late August morning to visit an old favorite desert spot, a reserve north-northwest of town. (Where, incidentally, though if you know the region not so very coincidentally, Setif Moranus spent her last few hours in the Las Vegas region.)

A little boy in a tree…a little boy like, well, like a monkey in a tree. It was a weekend afternoon, most likely a Sunday, for his father often worked Saturdays. His father, a tall, almost gaunt man, had his mother's triceps gripped firmly and led her directly under the tree he was in. He had not been hiding, but now, sensing secret communication between his parents, he was hiding, remaining as still as, well, a lizard, but also like a monkey with a leopard nearby. His father explained to his mother that he would lose his job and risk jail even if anyone learned that he told her their house was likely bugged. He would not tell her about his work, but he had learned something yesterday that had kept him awake all night. He couldn't get it out of his head. It wasn't during one of the Nevada nuclear tests, but that hardly mattered because in Nevada they did similar things. It was a Pacific test. Several planes were filled with monkeys, had monkeys for passengers but only in the window seats on the left side of the plane. There were hundreds of monkeys. What they wanted to determine was the effect of the blast flash on monkeys looking on. Yes. For that. Each monkey was strapped to his seat, rendered immobile, eyes fixed open, head severely restricted so that he could only look out the window. Their bodies were facing forward, but their heads were turned—that was how they were best able to manage it. They were flown around and around the blast space. After that, Hank Gravel didn't know, but he could not get those monkeys out of his mind.

Tom Gravel, about to drive out to the desert, had that image in his mind. The image was always the same. It was one plane, one very large passenger plane. Every window had a monkey's face looking out. He never dreamed of it, which made it worse. It was the most powerful image from his youth. And there was no linear action to speak of, just the plane in flight. The bomb wasn't even part of the imagery, just the monkeys, monkeys looking out expressionless from every window on the left side of the plane. It was as if the blast flash was an image of monkeys in the windows of a passenger plane, the observer not blinded rather stained with a single image.

For a week he had dialed the number donated by Strut's implosive death, each time getting as many rings as he chose to listen to. Half-hearted efforts to turn up a means of contacting the agency had failed. An interview with a reporter had quickly gone from the assurance that he would have as much luck getting a drink at the bar in Area 51 as he would contacting Blackguard—whom he compared to the Mormon-sealed Howard Hughes—to an impassioned encomium regarding the new Vegas sex museum, which Vegas figured maybe Donnie wouldn't mind taking a look at if he ever found Donnie. Finally one morning he felt the sort of freedom a feller feels once resigned to waiting something out and then it occurred to him that he would lose nothing by setting out early for the desert of his youth. Of course he was wrong about that—some degree of his remaining degree of peace of mind would be eroded—but that didn't make it a bad idea.

Setting off, taking the northwest highway, he developed an inchoate curiosity about the development of the northwest of the city, which had extended many miles since he lived there, near enough to the northwesternmost neighborhood of the city. He was surprised at the utter lack of surprise in the countless miles of new northwest Vegas; the only change was in the expected signs of the expected corporations that lined such highways, no change at all, but for distance, which was rapidly eaten, and a new corporation's promise that their store had EVERYTHING YOU WANT, EVERYTHING YOU NEED. Somehow he felt that grandiose promise might be all too easy to keep.

Yet it wasn't long before he passed from the city to desert, yet to his misfortune the combination of miles of commercial nullity with weeks of forgetting most of his life inevitably led to unwelcome thoughts of his wife, or ex-wife, that abominable blonde arachnoidal creature he had succumbed to, suffered and far too late finally left. EVERYTHING YOU WANT, he thought: she would disdain such a nightmarish "store," yet would be there a week or two after everyone else

had been there, to her scorn. Deep down she would wonder: Everything? Maybe better kitchen knives. But she would
never allow anyone to think she was a mere consumer. Visiting the shop would be an expedition, a poet searching the
last horrific descent of Adam Smith on her horizon and the
way it expressed so perfectly the slaughter of the innocents
of East Timor. Somehow she would even have gotten him to
join her, at least up until a few years ago. She'd had a genius
for such manipulations. Garvin was so used to Languideia
manipulating their every plan he had developed a utilitarian
passivity toward shared events. If he was able to opt out, he
would; if not, he would with unprovocative impassivity accept
her every desire. Often he was in a minefield of her making:
asked his preferences, he could not always refuse to state any,
nor could he predict hers—and he knew that nothing he said
would be accepted without fine-tuning. She would never ask
him if he wanted to go along with her to the new store—she
would find a way to force him to seem to want to join her
on her mission. Every shared event was like that. If he insisted on anything in particular, for instance the restaurant they
were to dine in, she would destroy his will with a dispiriting
argument, forcing him to battle over something he already
cared little about. You choose the restaurant, he might sometimes say. Oh but I always do, this time let's make it your
choice. Fine, the Indian place. But remember last time Cleo
couldn't find anything she liked there. Right. Sushi. Lucy
Provender told me she was there last week and the place has
really gone down. They must be having trouble getting good
frozen fish. She said the shrimp was tasteless. You like the
new Italian place, why not go there. Good idea. Good idea
so we can shitcan this fake discussion, this perverse pretense
that my desires mean anything to you. But dare not, Garvin,
say, Why ask me if we're just going to go on until you choose?
Okay, we'll go to that Indian place, and Cleo can just have a
hamburger on the way, and sit there and read while we eat.
In other words, I dare you to call me a cunt, call me a cunt,
please call me a cunt so I can unloose the vicious wolves that
have grown lean over these months without argument, please

call me a cunt so I can banshee your balls up to your kidneys, call me a cunt so I can parade the disappointments you've delivered me before us, so you can see what a two decade listless puppetshow our marriage has been, your dull stolidity within which your self withers while I live, while I bring light and energy, creativity and novelty to our lives that are dimmed by your mere presence. Normally of course I don't even ask you where you want to go out to eat—first thing, it's too much an effort for you and of course you would rather not go, second it ends like this every time, you naming the least inspiring place which you each and every time should have known better than to suggest, where if you had known your own family, had the energy to think about your own family... You certainly know that Cleo's school supplies have been insufficient and this new store, hideous though it may be, likely has the art pencils she needs and the notebooks we have to drive to that special shop in Des Moines to find, where they are usually sold out anyway. (You fucking selfish pig.)

Miles out of the latest Vegas and, let's say Garvin, was thinking these thoughts as he tended to, in compositions, precursor essays he would later polish with brave deflective cynicism and oblivionismos. This was depressing once for being real, twice for being his life, and thrice for being everlastingly trite. Once the memories infested his brain, he would salvage his peace of mind by focusing on some particular disgrace she perpetrated—this time a poetry contest a couple years ago on which she was the panel, while several lesser poets and academics sat effectively mute. The contest came down to two poems, one by a poet she despised for his refusal to go away, for his insistence on entering contests in which his poems were never assassinated before reaching her eyes, which Garvin was absolutely certain intimidated her for their ability to master what was fraudulent in her own work, for the fluidity of their genuine combinations of the particular and the cosmological, and, worst of all, for being, whether ultimately sad or winsomely expressive of the end times a come, were almost always extremely funny as well, something Languideia could not tolerate in a poem. Doggerel is for dogs, she said several times a year. How much worse that a poem of matchless brilliance was also funny. Laughter was something Languideia could not enjoy unless it was under the control of laboratory conditions she herself designed.

Scott Coffel was the intruder. The other finalist was a woman, he recalled, who had written "The Witherleaf Sestina," a true sestina repetitively strewn with the despair of autumn. Languideia would have despised "The Witherleaf Sestina" had the veins been genocided genealogies. She brought them home to illustrate to Garvin what she was up against, having to yet again dismiss this pretender when it was clear that the sestina was a brilliant display of the form, dizzying, dazzling, a dithyrambostic ode to decay and by virtue of such power an affirmation of thrombosis and golf, or gout, or something like that, something really really good, profound, salubrious, tantalizing, devoid of derision, alliteratively allusive, elusive, all inclusive. Gravel read it, finding it crisp and dull, without soul, a well-crafted piece, yes, but worth nothing, doing nothing that poetry, if it were to continue to take part in human life, must do. He said nothing, of course, waiting to see the superior poem that would be voted down the next day, for the panel already knew Languideia's choice and none had the integrity to challenge her. She slapped Coffel's poem down before him, a cataract of academic abuse delivering it to Garvin. He remembered the phrase "arbitrarily allusive"; Christ, he thought, she was incapable in her own work of the allusive—how could her admirers not see that? What would be taken for the allusive had been moved from her skull by cranes that dumped them into her poems. He wondered if on any level whatsoever she knew she rejected Coffel's poem because it succeeded where she failed?

He did have integrity. Enough to give an honest opinion. But he despised her poetrickery so much by then that he hadn't the integrity not to hope the poem was brilliant. And it was, so much so that he memorized it, something he did rarely after having to sit through Languideia's gushings of such poems as "The Idea of Order at Key West," which, if he had heard it just once, would have led Stevens to withdraw the work from humanity, especially pale Ramon, who gave Languideia post-prandial orgasms before guests who feared her more than anyone ever feared Stalin. Now, turning off the highway, cutting through the little Paiute square of desert to reach his destination, he recited it aloud over the crunch of tires on a place rubber was unwelcome. The poem was called "Midnight Smelting."

> I swerve like a recovering Communist through New
>   York's Southern Tier,
> the dialectical cockfight over but for the memories
> and mea culpas, the mind's lone superego
> crowing in triumph,
> oblivious to the slough of despond along the
>   Susquehanna,
> whose shores Coleridge dreamt of in his sleep
> when he wasn't dreaming of Xanadu.
> He never reached the Southern Tier
> nor broke his bondage to incapacity, never mustered his
>   forces
> for the grand coherent enterprise:
> my hero,
> my comrade in dejection, the apotheosis of
>   underachievement,
> the deepest failure of his age, the electrifying
>   conversationalist
> who bored his friends with talk of pantisocracy on the
>   Susquehanna.

> When I hear thunderstorms in the making
> over this failed society of equals, I pray for a new life:
> my one true job, I've never left it, never been paid, never
>   been passed over.
> When the boys cajole me into midnight smelting
> I keep my phylacteries in the tackle box and my talk of
>   Coleridge
> out of earshot. I lose myself to the heavy water,
> to the rhythms of the working class.

On good days I am a walking Talmud of voices excoriat-
ing materialism,
taking pains to avoid the skunk cabbages and pink-veined
orchids.
On bad days I am at least four decades shabbier
than Eastern Europe, a gray flower of a man who should
have withered
away like the state, a true believer who should have
jumped ship
while he had the chance, a stargazing insomniac habitu-
ated to the Vast,
anonymity exchanged for the higher loneliness of dwarves
and giants.

History jars my confidence in God.
I drive without hope through the Southern Tier
(Thucydides
on the dashboard, the Jew of Malta in the glove
compartment).
I bear witness to economic forces consummating
their hatred in the sky; I see that rain is unavoidable, that
negotiations
have disintegrated into darkness and thunder, that the
lights are going on
all over America, scoundrels having tripped the alarm.

When he had finished he was exhilarated, the car moving
at under ten miles an hour; he was exhilarated, yes, as after a
private listen to a particularly melodic yet disturbing segment
of Mahler. He yearned, now, in fact, specifically, to immediately hear the third movement of the First Symphony—he
braked suddenly and skidded. An upstart coyote had stepped
into his path, right into the road, stopped and stared, taken in
Garvin with a direct challenging look before strutting off into
the desert, occasionally looking back over his shoulder as if to
be sure Gravel understood just what they both were there for.
Garvin's graveled guts yawed violently back to his present
life empty of son. Broadside flashed a row of glaring monkeys,

Garvin galled to a halt at the guest center, bagged bottles of water and disappeared into the first wide wash, where Setif had sat, setting a course away from his life, nothing personal, a different breed of coyote.

> Advancing through the heat's mesquite,
> on paws because he has no feet,
> shaming howls ascourge from deep in throat
> melting the crease from creosote:
> brazen, lying, desert dog: coyote.

The desert was alive with rapid stealth—whiptails scattered at Garvin's heavy tread, rabbits fled. His old man was dead. Perhaps just where Picasso Tits drew her last Mojave creature, Garvin sat and uncapped a water bottle, drank half, poured half on his head. He was facing north, towards his father's desert. In between, short ranges that run northsouth blocked the view subatomic. Some curved, outward arced toward where he sat, again blocking the view. Maybe they had been that way for more than sixty years. He opened another bottle, drank half, monkeys flashed, dumped the rest on his head. A side-splotched lizard scanced toward his fore, glanced his sockets, hindy-leg pranced backing off, little pistolero with no bullet belt holster or gun. Garvin pointed a finger fore his upstrained thumb, but the creature was gone.

Refreshed, he heaved up his bag onto his back, grabbed a stick, broke it down to hiking length and set out east for higher ground and narrower drybeds. Whiptails splashed from his steps, an arthropodal mélange spread desertic disorder oblivious to his presence. He was three rabbits up from his rest, in a wingspan of a wash when he saw in the disorder of desert carpet a short trail near a yucca, and in its shade on closer look a curled mojave rattler. Had he thought "My whole life has been leading up to this" he would not have been wrong. Nor would he have been wrong to move on.

Tom Gravel had seen mojave rattlers before on excursions to the desert with his father, who more than once amazed him by maneuvering one with a stick so he could grab it by the tail. As he grew older he knew he would have to do the same, and he had had his opportunities. The closest he had come was during the week after his father had finally died from his A-bomb cancer. He felt depleted, disgusted, deprived, defiant, inutile, and hated the snake for its easy adoption of a triangle-headed depiction of pure evil. That time the snake was laying on a path in the early morning, way back west on the other side of the highway in Harris Springs Canyon, and coiled before his eyes, turning toward him as he approached, and prematurely springing toward him, falling about a foot short. That was enough to sap Gravel of intent. He flung stones at the reptile until it slowly moved off. He followed until the snake took shelter in the lower, huskish teepee of a yucca.

This time would be different. His father was much longer dead, yet his son was alive. He felt a riot of conflicting, strong emotions, saw dreamstrips of images: the monkeys, Languideia, Donnie, others, even giant bears. He felt what he took to be a spiritual impulse attracting him to the snake. He saw a future in which the head of the snake would be larger than a house.

There was significance to the snake being on higher ground while Eddie Vegas stood transfixed a level down in a dalless ditch. Snapping out of it, moving on, moving past the serpent, he felt within its death range—and he was, for it was more than four feet long and he was just about three feet away and it would strike him high—yet he knew it would remain still, that much of its power derived from watching him and people like him. Several paces further on Vegas hopped from the dry gulch and took two rapid steps back towards the beast, which hunched evil invisible shoulders, seemed to smile, rattled a moment then tried to hypnotize Vegas, opening its mouth, letting out a frightful dehissonance of threat. He wants me to fuck with him, Vegas thought. So he did. Now about five feet away, Vegas thrust his stick forward, meaning to plant it just before the wrapped body. The rattler struck, the stick stuck momentarily, it struck again, it struck again, each time it struck sticking fangs into the stick as if attempting to tug it from Vegas's grasp. The images intensified and included Danny Fitzmire, the pulp of him, the menace of him, the leer of him. He befelt a fanatical fury, yanking the stick back and bringing it down on the snake, gaining no advantage, for the snake unwound and leapt, flopping in the air, landing on its side near Vegas's feet. Vegas quickly swept the fore of the snake with his stick and hopped to the tail, clutching it just above the rattle, squeezing so hard had it been the creature's neck he would have strangled it. But it was the tail, and just as he imagined it would his father the snake snapped at him, writhed to a striking position even as Vegas held it high with his arm extended, and struck so close Vegas jumped back absurdly, still holding the striking snake that was at the same time raising itself to gain striking length, little more of which it needed. Instinctively, Vegas drew the snake back like a whip and lashed the ground, snake head first, and again, and again, more times than he knew, until long after the serpent was dead, until the head was no longer whole.

He sat on the edge of the ditch, his feet touching the desert earth, the monkeys flashed faintly—a belch of sorrow erupted in him, tears came to his head, his pounding forlorn skull he felt he could bash against a rock until it came apart. His stomach was a vacuum and his intestines writhed amongst his brains. A past and a future were clashing like tectonic plates, making of his present a putrid, maggoty dead thing.

He was up and calmly drinking water within a minute, or half an hour, or more, the sun still high, and he strode back to his car suffering no more than the eternal fremescence of thought repulsion. Yet as soon as he did reach his car, as soon as he sat behind the wheel, he knew precisely where he was going. He was going to drop in on the store that had everything he wanted, everything he needed.

49

THE YIELD OF EVERYTHING

The parking lot may have been enormous, but it was dwarfed by the store that on the edge of the desert defied urban comparisons. Was it longer than a city block? Probably. Was it bigger than a federal prison? He ought to have known, but he did not. There were many entrances and exits, lest its shoppers suffer heat stroke on the way from the car to a central point. Monkey fulguration: soon the year would come when the shopper parked his car and was immediately scooped up by a flying egg that delivered him quicker than a pneumatic tube into the department of his choice. But no, Eddie Vegas realized, they decided against such advances long ago. Clusterbombs and softer fenders.

No matter. I probably shouldn't even have mentioned it, exhausted as it is with the flab of sociology and ethicals. What matters here is Eddie's mind. Why stop here, at this place, this place his wife would have contrived to stop at while making clear the very idea was repulsive to her. As we will soon see, the answer is obvious once one allows the oblačeries of mystery to clear like after an especially loud and unexpected petard blows it's no surprise to find once the smoke clears a bloody stump twitching beside the surviving fingers. There's that, which is the main thing, and then, call me banal, the simple lure of the promise of whatever one wants. If it were me, I would stop, go in, and find the two-acre hat section to purchase an exact replica of Donnie's, let's call it rust colored, porkpie.

Eddie Vegas, of course, had no such specific in mind. In fact, he had wandered some quarter mile into the store before he noticed, before he saw anything, and that thing, that first thing he saw was a simple contraption of light wood and mid-range flex metal: an old-fashioned mouse trap. Naturally a person might want a newer model, or even, if one were prone to favoring the perpetuation of life by means of pardon and relocation, a live trap. Catch and release (for aquatic animals see our fishing department). For whatever reason, my guess would be nostalgia, Vegas was quite taken with the mouse traps, and he set one, using a pen from his shirt pocket to spring the trap, which cracked the pen that was made of hard plastic. Sold! If he were buying.

People love animals in many ways. The killing of them is but one manifestation of this love. Killing them with bows and arrows but one manifestation of this manifestation. So sure enough, one mouse trap when set off launched a tooth-pick-sized arrow at the target (if it somehow missed—perhaps a crafty slouching suspicious mouse—a soft wooden wall stood behind to capture the arrow. Evidence of the presence of an animal such as the arrow embedded in the wood evokes and satisfies the love of animals every bit as much as a pierced corpse or a pierced and writhing murine night fiend.

The trap department was nearly as large as some casino floors downtown, though they sold no human traps. The animals targeted ranged in size from mosquitoes to bears. The mosquito vacuum was a particular revelation to Vegas, though its secrets were not revealed—it was simply guaranteed to succeed even outdoors, a circular space with a thirty-foot radius would be cleared and remain mosquito free. Shaped like a small ordinary vacuum cleaner, the machine had three sound options: it could play the music of one's choice, imitate a vacuum cleaner, or be switched to silent mode: tapering toward the front where the mosquitoes were coerced (somehow) into entering a hole, or mouth, that was not quite large enough to eat a baseball, while under its ass end was a grate from which issued mosquito mulch—there were no filters to change; it was self-cleaning; and the batteries that were included were guaranteed to last a year, even if the machine ran all day and night throughout that year.

Garvin was fascinated by a display of Cong line bungee traps that ranged in size from killers of roach to bear. The diabolical mechanism was such that once bait was disturbed a pallet of spikes would catapult to that very spot with extreme violence the eye was not quick enough to follow. Vegas figured these would have a higher success rate than the arrow traps, except when it came to roaches—but as he already knew his thoughts were not typically original, and Cong also offered a combo live/death roach trap on which the bait and spiked catapallet were elevated on stilts like Filipino fishing huts: once the bait was disturbed, at the same time the spikes flung toward vengeance below, on a larger surface, began an upwelling of rapidly inspissate glue that when dried could easily be peeled from its base without ever releasing the roaches that had attempted to make off at the first sign of trouble. Perhaps better, if difficult to fully imagine, were the shrew and mole traps, ingenious devices called Fraggers. They made use of relatively simple robotics, whatever principles of forward motion despite were used by the best World War Two tanks, heat and motion sensors, and elementary spear guns attached by virtually un-breakable fishing line.

"Can I help you?" Vegas was asked as he finally arrived at the array of bear traps, glimpsing an ad that asked "…but are YOU really going to dig the pit?"

"Sorry?" he asked, shuffling along.

"Can I help you find something?"

He looked now. She was an obese, clear-eyed Indian in a store smock, beaming at him, bearing a charming lutrine smile.

"My son."

She chuckled.

"Sorry but that's the one thing we don't have is human traps."

And she chuckled again.

"You Paiute?"

"Ho-Chunk."

"Mm."

They were now standing side by side, marveling at the

exhibit of a stuffed grizzly, a good ten-footer, in the act of being Cong-pronged.

"Anyway," Vegas said, "I want him alive."

"Then I suggest you shop elsewhere."

He subsumed her awkwardness as if they were long married.

"No offense."

"Of course."

They turned to face each other, as polite people do as gruesome display is rendered ordinary by the passing of too little time.

She extended a hand.

"Well, I'm Marie Fire-In-A-Dry-Swamp. If there's anything else I can help you with…"

Folding his left hand over the hand that shook hers, he said, fatefully, "Eddie Vegas."

This time she chuckled like a chorus of otters, eliciting a look of query from Eddie Vegas.

"I'm sorry. It's just the name—"

"I know."

"Twice in one month—or two in once month I should say."

Eddie awoke to a self he had not realized was closeted.

"What?"

"Eddie Vegas."

"Yes, but what do you mean?"

"You're the second in a month I met, the second Eddie Vegas."

"Tell me about the first."

Suddenly she slapped her hand to her yawned mouth like a kid imitating an Indian.

"Your son!"

"Maybe—where—"

"At the Luxor, checking in at the Luxor. We were checking in at the same time. I had a date with a coon trapper I met here, who every time he comes to town—but your son, or maybe your son: I couldn't help but notice the name."

"What he look like."

"Oh gosh—I don't know," she seemed now to be suppressing a rising panic (she was a very empathetic person). "He was young enough to be your son, I remember that much. Taller than you, slim maybe...I'm so sorry, I really don't know, it was just a moment"—now she couldn't look Vegas in the eyes; in fact was looking at her feet as tears welled in her eyes. "I didn't want to stare, and it was, I was with... he...I don't think he was with anyone but how would I..."

But by now Garvin was following extremely well-placed exit signs out of the store at a run.

The traffic flow on the highway was faster than Gravel would have liked—they could pull anyone over at will, laser them with a taser, assuming that's how they work, and if they weren't dead yet, simply shoot them in the head or plug their torsos with six or seven shots. Anything but getting his fingerprints taken. Slow down, assholes. Giant pickup trucks, vans like tanks, or tanks, the rest seventeen sexes of sedans the same. Donnie was at the Luxor. He would soon be at the Luxor. Right lane. Look over there: Red Rock Canyon. Now we turn towards the Stratosphere. What sphere here? More squashed even than oblate. Onto the new migrant trail, get off on whatever, the last one, no, things have changed, just get off, take your time, take the striplights. Each intersection was a five-minute wait. Each block was a five-minute drive. Parking in back, parking lots in the style of the great parking lots of the Comintern. Egyptians didn't have cars. August heat still, taxis, the streets beginning to crowd with oddmentals of high tourism, funges and miniskirts they'll never see again, exhausted children that can see up close the longest walks of their lives. Parents thinking about money. Yesterday was a bit much. Can't they just find a cheap burger joint? Is it safe off the strip? I thought they had cheap buffets. That was the 90s. Limousines shark by as if swimming in private pools, oh hetercercal caudal! swoosh, taxis flipped into Venetian canals. There's the fucking Bellagio. The fucking water show twice before he makes the block: Gravel suspects they never change the orchestration of the jets of water—just the music. Tchaikovsky is licking death's pussy in his grave.

He can't yet see the squatter and squatter pyramid yet.

A strange calm, he thinks, a strange calm has beset something somewhere near him, leaving him to his own devices, barren of devices. He has to piss at least. Savor these moments. Pulling to the side of the highway in Iowa on the way home on summer nights to piss in the ditch beside the road. Donnie up in a tree in the backyard, planes full of monkeys strapped in tight, heads clamped left, eyes forced open, like Górecki's Second diving at him, buzzing around him, they their own tune, in empathic derangery with drumblasts.

Behold the Godchild and the Beetle in the Maze: he, the beetle, does not know that there is but one entrance and exit, the same space. He has been plucked from nature's evolutionary jamboree for the amusement of the Godchild and he is in heat. At the end of the maze he will find a female behind a porous glass wall. He will follow his instincts with ardor through this hell of a labyrinth only to find the center of hell at his proximity to his instinctual goal, to fuck the lady beetle on the other side of the glass. After an hour of false turns yet true directions he will find her there, behind the glass, not behind one of three doors, the lady and the booth-eel and the nuclear blast, no, he will find her, but she will be behind glass he cannot penetrate, cannot penetrate yet cannot stop attempting to penetrate, cannot penetrate, cannot penetrate the super-hymen—for this creator jokery begins with the dissolution of a line between life and death. It's an old trick, trite, like using the abandoned dog running after the car until it dies of a heart attack, except that the beetle never does have a heart attack, never has had a heart attack— no one has ever had the patience to wait out the scene: our godchild, after some distraction returned with renewed malice, has decided to drop the scorpion in on the female side of the partition. The male beetle looks on, by nature deprived of the capacity to experience terror (not an absolute argument against deitism, not in the least), feeling precisely whatever it was he felt before—pterygotic lust? alas, envy the stately peace of the never dithering ephemeropterae!— which, if he were patient, the godchild would find persisting in his attempts to find the breach, never deviating even as the death of the she beetle has been superseded by its devourment, not until at some point thereafter we think hunger stole into the complex, at which point being nearest to edible matter at the wall his behavior did not visibly change; but our godchild is impatient and soon lifts the beetle to his erstwhile goal, where he will be the next victim of the scorpion.

Luckily for Eddie Vegas, his own fate was not extensively analogous to that of the beetle. Donnie as female beetle was, for one thing, beyond an opaque wall, resembling in this particular circumstance more a secret of state than an entrapped female beetle. A secret of state? Just try to get a word out of the desk manager of the Luxor about one of their guests.

"Can you tell me what room Eddie Vegas is in?"

"Can you tell me?"

"No, I just know that he's staying here. He's my son."

"Derek, see if there are any messages from an Eddie Vegas regarding his father, also goes by Eddie Vegas, regarding visits."

"He doesn't know I'm coming."

"Ah, never mind Derek. Well, Mister Vegas, I can only suggest to you that you wait in the lobby and when he arrives—"

"You could simply call his room, couldn't you?"

"Which room would that be?"

"The room he is paying for. The room he is staying in. The room where he receives visits from people such as his father."

"Which room would that be, sir?"

"I don't know."

"There you have it."

"There I have what?"

"The problem. In a nutshell."

"You have a policy against calling rooms if we don't know in which room the visitor is staying?"

"That seems rather obvious at this point."

"So if I were to travel here with friends and we were all to meet at the Luxor where we are renting room, theoretically we could spend a weekend, say, searching for each other."

"Haven't thought this through, have you? You would likely leave messages here at the desk. Connect up immediately."

"No room for surprises."

"Some."

"Look, I really need to find my son. I've been told that he's here. Can you just do the human thing and let me know if he is still here?"

"See? Exactly why there's a policy. Now you don't even know he's here. Let me tell you, if you're going to search for him like this throughout Vegas it's likely he'll be dead of old age before you find him."

"It's likely you'll be dead in a few weeks if you behave like this regularly."

"Derek, call security, I've just been threatened."

"No, you've been insulted, not threatened."

"Derek, hold that call."

"Is there anything else I can do for you, sir—if you turn around you'll see we have a number of people to serve."

Just then, as if things couldn't get worse, Vegas felt a hand in his pocket. Glancing down he saw a midget bellhop slouching to keep his head below the counter, holding a finger to his lips. Reaching into his pocket he found a piece of paper had been slipped in there. The midget quickly lost himself in all things lobby, while Eddie Vegas discretely found a chair. Among a range of chairs, two were taken by men pretending to read newspapers. He drew out the paper and read:

"He checked out about a week ago. Seen him two times since."

50

OIL AND VINEGAR

What dynastic impulse drives families to continue naming their children after the parents? Why, the future, Mister Gitz. At least, Ma Gravel thought, this particular dynasty hasn't embarrassed itself with Roman numerals. The summer that the second to last Tom Gravel was seven years old, Hank Greenberg led the league in doubles, homers, and runs batted in, hitting .340. He won the league's most valuable player award, and as radio rendered geographic proximity as absurd as did living in Nevada, that avid ball player who haunted the sandlots of Reno, Nevada, with a mitt his old man stole from a drunk's kid in Sam's bar and a ball his grandmother gave him money for, could be a fan of the Detroit Tigers. Kids love tigers. And what a hitter Greenberg was: the little Gravel boy would talk about him to anyone who'd listen, which meant primarily a group of adults in Sam's who didn't give a shit who was yammering about what, and his grandmother, who paid close attention, and habitually responded: not bad for a kid from the ghettos of Lublin, or, not bad for a kid from the shores of the Baltic, not bad for the kid who took Kraków by storm, they called him the Tatar Kid…for common interest mattered far less in a relationship than egoless love…From that summer on, little Tom Gravel was known as Hank to his grandma and before long was insisting that his father call him that as well, and his mother, his other grandparents, and finally his teachers and classmates, and he remained Hank long past the time he lost interest in baseball, long past his early acceptance at Stanford at age sixteen, his graduation with degrees in chemistry and biology, his mysterious recruitment and move to Las Vegas, all the way to his grandmother's deathbed: not bad for a kid who survived Dachau, she joked, not bad for a kid who led a rebellion at Sobibór, not bad for a kid who died at Auschwitz—she had in the end done one important thing, she felt, given one boy a good life despite her own ill-fated offspring having conceived him— Hank Gravel, now at 21 years of age a tall, rather gaunt, yet oddly, even clumsily energetic lad with vibrant green eyes of avian movement and Talmudic intelligence. "Never hate anybody, Hank, not even your pa. You know, until about the time you were two years old I didn't even know what a Jew was—I kind of thought of them as someone else's Mormon's, I suppose. I don't know if you're aware of the difficulties of Hank Greenberg's life, because he was a Jew. I read a story on it in a magazine. And if you hate somebody, don't hate their next of kin, Hank. I have some more inkling what you're up to out there in the desert than you might think, and I hope you know it's a tool for hatred you're working on. What they did to the Jews was a modern horror, Hank, but what they did to the Japanese required every bit as much hatred, and per- haps more, or even worse because it was like a big dumb kid playing with ants. And it's modern, too, the same historical epoch...Don't hate your pa, Hank. But don't let him put ya on the skids neither. Never trust him about money. Loan him a little here or there, but don't let him suck your life away.... Two degrees, a bigshot secret job...who can believe the little brat from Treblinka, the Buchenwald buckaroo, the...and, Hank, don't let him visit you—you go up to Reno every month or two—he doesn't mean to be mean, Hank, he just doesn't have much of a heart, don't hate him for it, it's a birth defect...I know what he said about Korea might be hard to forgive, but I made sure he didn't get caught up in World War Two and maybe, maybe it sort of ate at him, though we both know him well enough...tell me you aren't...I know you can't...but this government, Hank, it's maybe not so sane, maybe bomb happy...you're the Plaszów phenom, kid, don't let anybody ruin you...health related, eh, all right, but you watch your own head...and take care of your father, just don't let him move down there, if he does, you move to Indian

Springs or something, you know that guy died, that dwarf hoodlum, Moe Sedway, that's who, "you stupid shitheel, you don't come down to Las Vegas and treat a man like Moe Sedway like *that*, if his pal didn't know me you'd be fucking dead, you understand, Hank, get your pathetic drunken old man outta here, and I mean outta fuckin town," said his best friend from way back, some guy Hank had never heard of, so how many people who had no idea what his old man was talking about had to hear My boy's goin off to college!, Vegas is in an uproar: Hank Gravel, fresh out of the ruins of Gdańsk, is going to Stanford, who would've thought, Hank steered the old man kindly back to their shabby motel, looking over his shoulder for gangsters—he was later to find out that diminutive Moe Sedway was a dangerously violent mob maniac who had killed plenty and here in the late 40s was especially irritable, beset by boils, angina, hemorrhoids, so when he bumped into Tom Gravel and Gravel said watch where you're going you little pissant, right in Moe's own place, it's no wonder there was a scrum, the situation or Tom Gravel's life saved only by some recognition Moe had for this acquaintance of Gravel's, friendship probably forged at Sam's purely by chance, a two hour boozery ending in a phone number mechanically inscribed on a coaster, Sure come on down and visit a real gambling town, giving no thought to actually seeing him there, and of course he wasn't going to put up Gravel and his kid celebrating going off to college, so they ended up in a motel room infested by ants, bedbugs, fleas and roaches, and probably scorpions, all at war with each other, taking breaks to work in concert to remove the humans, neither of whom slept before the long drive back north in July heat, stops to fill the radiator at Indian Springs, Tonopah, awkward silences in the car, Hank wishing to appease an unappeasable drunken fool, yet his silence taken as disgust, which elicited fatherly scorn for the son who already acted better than him, almost never took a drink (a mere 16, he was yet indeed the exception among his age group in Reno), but when your old man's a drunk you either go quick the same way or if provided a different path are likely to take the way out, especially when your most indelible memory of this garrulous drunkard was when at the dinner table Tom was shaking the oil and vinegar dressing and the top came off, the dressing geysering out, and Hank spontaneously laughed, receiving a backhand that bloodied his lip and nearly knocked him off his stool just last summer, a year ago, the old lady shocked, catching her breath and then hissing: Tom! and then looking down at her meatloaf fearfully, as was appropriate if her intention was to eat it, for she was a very poor cook and the butt of many half-drunken jokes and oaths, some of which Hank found himself laughing at despite himself, But goddammit say what you want I always put food on the table, even if, goddammit, there were times it was Adele holding down the steady job and putting the food on the table literally and figuratively, which Hank grasped at a young age and so ate with feigned relish whatever crap she put before him, the worst of it being casserole, which had to be French for mixed shit of numerous vermin, Hank's birthdays the worst for then it was his own responsibility for the gangrenous menu and he hadn't the courage or cruelty to say boiled potatoes, which all goes to argue that a man doesn't become a drunk for no reason, not without a lifetime or several months of bad breaks, or perhaps a ballbusting wife (however ludicrous and clichéd) whose fear of his outbursts manifests as a daily recrimination, and he could be a millionaire they would still eat garbage, add to that his many inspired plans so many fat geese shotgunned before gaining altitude by a tightwad mother who never did have any confidence in him, who never gave him a chance to prove himself, even on liquor runs among dimwitted criminals more like the dalmatian on the firetruck than anything, though a dalmatian with ribs showing, made to do tricks for bits of green steak, ma's handouts serving only to prove the point, sure she gives me a hundred bucks when I'm down and out, she's my mother, but would she ever trust me to make something of myself, maybe if you quit drinking for a year or two, held your job for a couple years, showed her you'd changed, I never once slapped your mother, well, he thinks, so what, you slapped me, sit up here at the bar Tommy, I mean Hank, Christ's sake, shitbird, you may be sixteen but you're still off to college in a week what'll it be, a soda?, good god, I raised a fucking nun, all right, a beer would be nice, whiskey then, two shot glasses, Dad I really don't want— nonsense, time for a father to son, man to man, Hank drank the first as if it were, Dad tossed his down with the glee only an alcoholic knows when he doesn't yet know he'll soon be moving like a boneless phlegmaton making recognizable habitual movements look like high mimery, the second shot Hank lets drool to the tavern floor, before lifting it to his lips, Daddy's eyes dazzled by his own, he'll soon have no idea I'm here, for that matter that he's here, Before long Hank taking over the tending of the bar, stepping over his passed out old man again (and again), that Krakpot from Kraków, while upstairs oblivious mama, the Köndgirl of Königsberg, improvised a dubiously esculent gruel that would perhaps have shortened the Bataan death march, meanwhile to the bar ambles Gusefahrt the ruddy German regular, a bear of a man, gentle though, seasonal customer— south for the summer/north for the winter—sympathetically looking at Hank, pointing to his father, Have mercy for Sam's life is but a finstere Bootsfahrt, ya, tull be better for ye, beer then ya?, beer then, and a whiskey bath, better a bathyscope, Günther thinking from the plural sign SAMS that all who work there must be named Sam, mythical Lotharian Günther Gusefahrt, come north to drink the summer's earnings, could outdrink anyone whoever stepped foot in the bar, even Dixie Doxy, the fat Creole, who but once challenged the Nemski, and finally after long hours of supraswilling in extravagant disemboguery swiveling her head cleared the šank of all contents: ashtrays, bottles, glasses, Runny the Reno dwarf who wound up out cold behind the šank about where Tom was now, coasters, cigarettes, purses, felling numerous barstools as well, so it was said, Hank wasn't there, but knew the combatants and enough of it was likely to be true, besides his old man's tall tales generally were skewed visions of future financial windfalls—hard not to imagine he and Setif's father would have been great friends if not for the generational fac-

tor and the difference that Setif's father had the money to
turn his ventures into catastrophe and spectacular rot—at
some point knowing that his single windfall was that very tavern, for the old man, I mean Sam, Adele's father (her mother
passed on during the war, cancer misdiagnosed as gout, as if
it would have made a difference), had little choice but to
leave the tavern to his son-in-law and daughter, knowing no
provisions could save the bar from mismanagement and his
daughter from penury, having to trust in her inured canni-
ness to maintain Tom's precarious balance of grandiosity and
sousery, and at the time he was upstairs, too, in his own apartment, frying steak to drive off the smell coming from the
neighboring kitchen, his tendency to open the bar he so
loved and where he spent all his better hours with his cronies
playing poker beginning early in the morning and vacating
the joint to watch television which was an extraordinary invention, for he could release his thoughts, which too often
might have ripened into worries and nostalgia, and the machine would swallow them quicker than you could say Kefau-
ver or boiledanginal hemorrhoids, which may well have been
stewing in the neighbor's kitchen, point being the bar was
already more or less in his son-in-law's trembling hands, but
he still kept the books, and lo, would keep the books for some
years after both his daughter and that funge he married per-
ished, even some years into his senility when he was spending
his savings trying to sue the government over infringement
for naming a bar in Area 51 after his bar, which he could
never prove because the place was a secret and everything in
it and about it was a secret, though it all comes out in time,
particularly if some loony with access thinks Reno is a safe
enough distance, spouting off about certain matters too bizarre for the customers of the raunchiest bar, even if the occasional telling detail such as "Sam's Bar" might be of interest to one geezer, the guy was a regular for about a month
before he disappeared, had money too, lodging in the hotel
across the street, Jack A. Naper, how he would go on and on
about his engineering skills, how they were abused, his one
dream in life to be an inventor, and he pulled from his pock-

et what could only be called a gizmo—a two double-wheeled
metal and rubber contraption some three inches high and
long both that one wound with a key that rose like a mast
from the body of the thing, the key winding mechanisms that
turned the wheels such that the vehicle, let's say, wobbled
and moved fore arbitrarily directionwise and at the same time
wheeled two flints against a rough round surface so that it
sparkled as it ambled: sure there was more to the thing, like a
sort of gear and wound strips of metal, but he guarded it with
crabbed zeal fearing theft of patent—the kind of thing he had
to have built himself, proof enough he did have a knack for
invention of a kind, but he spent a great deal more time yack-
ing about apes than he did showing off his gizmo, claiming
the military had after hiring him to a lucrative contract forced
him to devise a contraption that would restrict the movements of monkeys in an airplane such that they would sit
upright in an ordinary seat with their heads precisely 90 degrees left and eyes trained open, including a drip that would
moisten the eyes just so, just so they would not experience
the discomfort of a man buried up to his neck with his eyelids
torn off and staring at the sun, except they would be staring
at a sun, forcibly, eyes suitably, humanely moistened, staring
at a man-made sunburst in the Pacific—truly crazy bullshit,
compelling in its organized narration, bars get these people
all the time, they never have the faintest idea they exist for
the amusement of the other patrons who wink and make, depending on their cultural backgrounds, various gestures suggesting lunacy behind their backs (many of them involving
some sort of forefinger rotation pointing at a brain meant to
represent *that* brain that could easily have designed a mechanical hand that performed that very gesture), and are never terribly surprised nor the least nostalgic when one day they
aren't there and never are again, off perhaps to join Rudolf II,
who Jack A. Naper claims would've made him rich and court
inventor for this very gizmo alone, whoever the fuck Rudolf
II was, Christ in a Can of Spam what a loon, takes all types,
no, actually it doesn't, Ford Snode overrode, contrarian of
the tavern as he was, no, there is actually no need for that

type, they're superfluities that wash up as if this were a beach, he a gelatinous, floating sea diaphane that has no more control over its direction than his gizmo, which he probably designed to follow him around on his midnight desert treks, well anyway, Tom governed, this tavern is like, like, like the first stop before the circus freak show, That it is, that it is, well, he'll miss himself when he's gone, Andy McGreary said, barwit and gambler, who they say makes a couple hundred a week, takes it easy, rarely loses, has a system or something but doesn't overdo it lest he be banned from the casinos, likeable fellow, his defenestration from the Riverside a few years later coming as a complete surprise, that was no suicide, you know Moe Sedway was seen at the casino that same day?, who's Moe Sedway?, poor Andy, you hear they found a safe in his room been pried open or something?, I know a lady who was about twenty feet from the body when it hit, head first she said, that ain't how people jump from buildings—they go feet first—I guarantee he was tossed out, more to that guy than we ever knew, tell you that much, look shitbird, he was my friend, and the last thing he deserved—I ain't saying—then fucking can it, anyway doesn't Sedway use an icepick?, how would you know that, I thought everyone knew that, Right, so he never shot anybody, never blew anybody up...dipshit... What?, that smell, I think it's coming from upstairs—hey Tom, turn the fan on, It's winter, Turn the fan on, open a window, How's your boy doing down at the college?, top of his class, Adele's bursitis?, Also first class, keeps me up nights, You ought to drink more, that's what I do, wife snores like a lumberjack, how does a lumberjack snore?, sneet snort sneet snort, I wake her up shouting Timberrrrr!, cracks her right up, he got a sweetheart?, how would I know, kid doesn't even write asking for money, yeah he knows he wouldn't get none, fuck you and the hearse you rode in in, What's it been, two years?, three and he's already graduating, my ma says he's already got job offers, fucking kid's a genius, got it from—shit's sake, who was that guy?— fuck you and the hearse you're going out in, you crack me up, Gravel, I'll crack you up all right, shit what we need in here's a bouncer but the old man is too cheap, whatta ya need a bouncer for, you got Güntfart over there and if he can't manage have Dixie spread her legs, Don't want all the patrons to run out on me I got a living to make, Hey whatta ya get when ya cross Harry Truman with Mao Tse Tung?, I don't know, a hairy tongue, like we're gonna have in the morning, funny, What do you get when you cross Harry Truman with Ho Chi Minh?, what, Harry Truminh you idiot, fucking hilarious I didn't know you were so Japhappy, me and Mugless DarkArthur, go home before your wife falls asleep and you lose your audience, my wife's been asleep since the day after our honeymoon, continued Johnnie Fresno in this quotidian intarsic dialogue, which, let's face it, in a way served to illustrate that despite the early opening hour, Adele, the day bartender, despite also being the housekeeper of the family apartment, had the easier job, days so dilatory she was known to lean over the bar reading books lent by her mother-in-law, including *War and Peace*, which was a victim of attrition, the cumulate wearing of inane jokes leading her to quit without finding out what happened, though Ma Gravel knew if she ever remembered to ask, which she didn't, you know, son, upstairs spoke Tom Gravel to Hank the day before he caught his train to Frisco, it may be I failed to provide for your education, but your grandma had that taken care of soon as you were born, and in fact, don't take this the wrong way, but if not for her concern over your education maybe she would have funded one of my plans and we'd all be moving to California, but come on in here, I want to show you something, something I was bequeathed, at least I found it among my father's possessions the one time I was shown the few boxes of his post-mortem effects, this here leather case, what's in here I never had it priced, but this here is maybe by now worth as much as four years of college, take a look: the leather case had a gold oval plate — maybe not gold, but golden, and metallic, which in Nevada continues to this day to excite — on which letters in relief spoke: PULVERMACHER'S MEDICAL HYDRO-ELECTRIC CHAINS, and further in smaller caps APPROVED BY THE ACADEMIE OF MEDECINE DE

PARIS, across the Pulvermacher voltaic band logo of facing horseshoes draped with bands: REWARDED BY THE UNIVERSAL EXHIBITION PARIS 1855, 1855! That's almost a hundred years ago and as you'll see this thing's in mint condition, and it was more than that, what Hank saw upon first glimpse was a full treasure chest, two sets of copper and zinc tubes, with two wood and copper handles, 60 links Hank, 60, and the thing's brand new, look at it shine, I tend to it once a month, the red rubber wraps at either end of each battery setting off the copper just right, See what you do is wrap it around the part of your body that's giving you trouble and using vinegar—maybe you can find out how in college—a current gets going and relieves your pain, your rheumatism and whatnot, by which time Hank's stunnery had faded and he realized what he was looking at was a 19th century made genius's quack invention, which was probably worth fifty bucks to a collector, so he was more than happy when he had finished his schooling and been plucked immediately by the government for a job and was visiting his dying grandmother when she told him, Hank, boy, I changed my will now you got a job, for what money I have left, your father will need it more than you will, Good, I'm glad you did, Grandma, I'll be set for life now, there will always be work for someone with my education, and the experience I'm getting would land me a job with any number of enormous companies, then why not take up one of those offers and get out of that poisoned desert, it's not like you think, then tell me what it's like, I can't, you know that, some say our home phones are tapped so they can be sure no one talks, it's top secret stuff, he whispered in her ear I'm involved in health and safety, okay, now don't say nothing, don't answer, I'm sorry to keep going on about it, I'll stop now, just let me say one thing, don't hate your pa, son, I don't, I never have, I—he's okay, he gave me an interesting upbringing, and I believe he does the best he can, go on Hank and say all the right things, but swear to me on this bed on which I will die before I see you again that you will be nice to him and hold nothing against him, I swear, good, that's good, hate is a bad thing, Hank, corrosive and it can ignite, like, well, you can't tell me, just nod your head, Hank, if you're doing right out there, I can't nod my head, look, Grandma, I'll just say one thing and that's all and don't fall into delirium and repeat it, put it right out of your mind, the operation I'm involved in right now is called Operation Nuclear Health, which was a lie but he figured if anyone was listening they would give him a break for saying something to shut the old lady up and nothing about Operation Snorkel or

EG&G	NERVA
Operation Harass	JIOS
Project Pismire	MAD
DUST	SAM
Operation Lusty	Super Kukla
Survival City	Operation Sandstone
Raytheon	BREN Tower
Plutonium Valley	Operation Grubstake
Jasper	Project Mad Sam
Jackass Flats	Project Plowshares
Operation Aphrodite	Project Kempster-Lacroix
Strontium Sandwich	DAFT
E-MAD Building	DAFT
Groom Lake	Operation Stall
Atlas Pulse Power	Project Ornithopter
Project Orion	Password Swordfish
Project Pig Poke	Super Oralloy Bomb
Operation Paperclip	Gracen Atomyd
Project Mime	RBIFF
Horten IX	Project Nutmeg
Bachus site	Operation Ivy
News Nob	Tikaboo Peak
Operation Skylark	Tule Springs bones
Rochester, New York	Sam's Bar
Eastman Kodak	Operation Sideswipe
Project Hornpipe	Gun Turret
Operation Crow Flight	Termite Roads
Project Aquatone	Konrad Schaefer
Railroad Valley	F. Leghorn

Cesium
Page 39
"Them" Crosses
Tepeyac
NPIC
NACA
Monkey euthanasia
Ship of the Desert
Operation Home Run
Operation JackKnife
Project Dempsey-Firpo
Annie Emplacement
Operation Jack Knife
Rapatronics
Red Dog System
Prompt Departure systems
Cosmodrome
Apple-2 Houses
Project Pluto
Door Number 3
Redstone Rocket
Quick Kill system
Operation Roller Coaster
Project 57
Sandia Laboratories
Project End Around
Operation Salmon Downstream
The Ranch
Sage Control
REECO
HAFT
JP-7 fuel
Hughes Aircraft Company
Indoctrination Project
Papoose Lake
Operation Alsos
MKULTRA files
Palomares dirty bomb

Divine Strake
Divine Stake
Divine Strafe
Kiwi TNT
Nerva Test Stand
Teller
Lawrence Radiation Labora-
  tories Livermore
Gas ionization
Pink Cat system
Lockheed
Operation Nose Job
NICAP
Doomtown
X Tunnel
Gate 800
Rochester Radiation Shield
Operation Plumbbob
Operation Morning Light
Project Blue Book
Operation Chrome Dome
Operation Teapot
Krause-Ogle Box
Project Saucer
Project Grudge
Project Dragon Lady
Project Insectothopter
Operation Lusty
Project Sign
Operation Sign
Sign systems
SIGINT
Project Ostrich
Dial-a-Yield
ASUP
Operation Greenhouse
NEST
BEEF

Camp 12
R-MAD Building
VIPER STEAM systems
Neutron Detector Suitcase
GO
Vaporize reptile projects, 1-7
Advanced Development
  Projects
Operation Hardtack II
Mind control program
Tactical Nuclear Artillery
Remote Launch System
CIC
Project Palladium
Drones
DEFSIP
EMF
ERDA
FACA
HAZMAT
Frenchman Flat
Carlyle Group
Project Greenshine Whinny
General Atomics
Dirty bombs
TRIPE
Zinc prostate
Scintillation counters
Project Tripwire
John Wayne as Genghis Khan
Convair
Operation Pinniped
Convex Perception System

Project Lady and the Tiger
Blue Dog System
Depilation and Coloration
  Project
TS/SCI classification
Blytheville Air Force Base
Camp Groan
PHIB
Plan Phuket
Operation Argus
Project Twinkle
St. George, Utah
GST
Project Aquiline
HAZMAT Spill Facility
Bleachers
A-12 Oxcart
Radar absorbing paint
Project Survive
ARPA
ACHR
Operation Black Shield
Camp Mercury
Project Irradiate (MOO)
Project Obliterate
Operation Utah Fallout
Project Stun
Operation Church Door
Stem-Hermes
Operation Tumbler-Snapper
Blast Zone Safety Scheme
Project New Twilight
ABCC, and Climax

Mine, or if there are any others, which we're sure there are not otherwise we would see redaction marks like raccoon tracks all over this manuscript.

51

PHANTASMA GLORIA

Setif's period was late—and light—beginning its four-day trickle on the flight from Montreal back to Brussels. Ah, she thought, there you are; though she always figured a woman knows when she's pregnant and she was sure she was not. For that she was grateful, as her reflections on Drake and Donnie, mostly Drake, would have been befouled by such a durable complication. Jejune, she said out loud before the plane had cleared Canadienne landforms below. BAYnull vs. bNALL. Donnie thought bNALL was pretentious. Jejune. Donnie said he saw the world as, no, the United States and its foulings of the world as, a marasma of intarsic aspect. Setif suspected that the United States only exacerbated a process discernable to the human eye that might actually not even exist, a process the suggestion of which the planet itself would laugh at. Her explanation? Jejune, or in the American nasal sense, BAYnull. Given the condition of inescapable marasmic plight, what is left of the active being but an intarsic scramble, a many faceted chaotic stretch of rational illogicities, fitting what does not, forcing into place what will warp and snap and sometimes pop right to the ceiling. Yet when she had crossed finally into Canada from New York State, she felt a sense of relief that belied the pacific scene and its moments of violence too tightly contained. Passport please. Please!

Drake was a handsome man and slick, yet honest, without excess of ego, generous, existentially mature. Donnie was much of that, less handsome, less slick, more deeply honest, more aware, indecipherable of ego, existentially beyond mature, softer, malleable enough for the long term. Though what in Drake was not desirable in the long term? She could think of nothing. So what had happened? What does she mean by that: what had happened. Nothing had happened, nothing at all. Serendipity ignited a furiously interesting life, and a tragedy more foreign than she could imagine had ended that life. Parents assassinated, or murdered or whatever. Drake then pulled into that life: she could see him with all those strings attached to his back he pulled against that were deathless, that would never stop pulling him. That odd creature Nordgaard, whose tales of outlandish camaraderie…She could not abide the man. The Montagnard. Lo. Something was wrong with what Donnie called the overall, which he said he got from a movie—the overall. That and overalls. She wished she would have had a little notebook just for counting men she saw in overalls. Idaho, Wisconsin. They were probably men who found the overall just fine. Nothing wrong with their overalls. Brussels has the central body of the European Union, yet Drake is CEO of Blackguard Security. A body of brutal men boldly bringing peace to beleaguered victims of the country it billed for its services.

The plane began bucking, benignly lolling about midst turbulence, rivets coming loose. Bucking broncos—why had she never thought of them when she was out west? The plane, after several minutes and a rather redundant mumbling about turbulence from the captain, and all was engine hummery and balance. Catharsis is passé, she thought. Catharsis is kaputt. Something to remember. Perhaps catharsis had always been misunderstood—or a misnomer. At any rate, it no longer existed, of that she was sure. The only international news she could recall that intruded on her while she was in the States was yet another catastrophic drone strike. What is the opposite of catharsis? Deluge? Rain of hellfire?

Drake was an energetic lover when he knew she wanted energy, she tuned him, he licked her clitoris tenderly when she wanted, swallowed her labia whole and wildly tongued when that was what she wanted. He knew when she was on her hands and knees when the slow tease of near complete

withdrawal was what she trembled for and would prolong her
tremble, and how rapid to re-enter; he knew when to pound.
Probably she just knew how to tune him and he was able to
be loyal to her frequency. Either way, he was by far her best
lover yet, perhaps the only acceptable one, the first adult, the
first with whom she was an adult. Yet leaving him was easy,
easier even than when he announced he was leaving Brussels, which was less real to her as his call to confront tragedy
than as the disappearance of a golem, a creature who appears
and disappears at his own delight or fate to whom you owe
nothing, whom it is forbidden to question.

Leaving Drake was a simple matter of rejecting in advance
a foreign quotidian where money was all that could construct
freedom, pursuit was a deconstruction of random distaste-
ful possibilities, pleasure was reliant upon using money to
enjoy events or places utterly detached from the other two
realities she knew: Brussels, and the world of events beyond
her reach, most of which she could not decipher without the
distortions of deranging spectacles through which one must
admit of the supremacy of the United States, where she felt
herself a cipher, where she engrossed herself in the study of
the straw colored hairs of her arms and flexed the muscles
of her thighs because she could not bring herself to trust an
image in a mirror with her corporeality. Worst of all was the
sense that every moment had been subconsciously prognos-
ticated in the very moment she received her invitation, a sort
of scolding of déjà vu for its insipid trickery, a lapse of mind
rather otiose where collapse of mind was ever imminent.

Such musings Setif felt best mused aloft, that in the jet's
hurry she might leave them behind, instinctively assured that
a return to Brussels would be an ordinary event. Her parents
would have no suspicion that she had been absent; her job
at the bar awaited her return; her art studies were already being overtaken by her paintings, which would be unaware of
the imagery that had retained no force of meaning, none of
the devious nature of the succincubus of Brusselian haphaz-
ardry. There were, in fact, no demons in the United States,
she realized, no ghosts and no mythology, the landscape and

cityscape, the farmscape and small townscape all so suffused with the bland connivance of Christianity with Empire that nothing lived unseen. Exterminators did a better business in the vast and clean United States than anywhere, the country with the fewest crannies in the world, the greatest variety of detergents, the most intolerant of ostentatious decay.

Setif raised a hand when a steward lady began a stroll down the aisle toward her.

"Scotch," she said. "In fact, three of them, and a glass with ice."

"We have Famous Grouse, Tullamore Dew—"

"Tullamore Dew! How nice! Yes, please, that's—as they-say behind us and a little south—that's just the thing!"

One for each of us.

She looked past the two sleeping women, both middle-aged, both of a Danish befuddlement that was evident even in their sleep, a perpetual uncertainty regarding how to encounter the pleasantries and simplicities of their existences. Kierkegaard would have to migrate were he alive today. Or write for the masses: *Fear and Trembling, What the Fuck? The Sickness unto Death at 93. Either, Or, What Difference Does it Make.*

And just in time arrived the scotch.

First for Drake. May he build a casino peopled with dwarves! May he be talked out of it and may he walk away with purpose sublime! May he remain Drake! Too trite: may he avoid the jejune!

Donnie! May he wrench that wench from their quietude toward adventure abroad, take the broad abroad! May he part ways with Drake amicably, tenuously…May he speak when Drake is ready to listen!

Ah, Me! May I instill this distilled in myself as two men taught me, a moderate drinker once and still who now has had a taste of the sublimity of debouch, decadence, aimless and indefatigable nonsense! Ah, but Drake, sadly now, pianissimo too—may he find or lose what meaning he finds or seeks in his obsessive gapery at…whatever it is he sees in the interstices, the crannies!, whatever he sees in those films…

52

AMOR AND SHIT

*¡Maligna, la verdad, qué noche tan grande, qué tierra tan
sola! Cuánta sombra de la que hay en mi alma daría por reco-
brarte...*
    That's Pablo Neruda, but I'll get to that. The first time I
had to tell a woman I loved her was the day after she jumped
me on a couch and licked my face, slobbered all over it like
a Newfoundland hound. She never did it again, nor felt need
to, for, like a dog, I had been marked. Other women didn't
have to avoid me, for I was instructed to avoid them. When
the scent wore off there was trouble. I mistook the slavering
for passion. History grinds, history mashes human psyches to
pulps and drupes, passions squirt off into places where like
proud viruses they intensify, transmogrify, the mere human
become an emotional dolt, accepting versions of love at variance with other versions of love, ultimately at variance with
suspected laws of the universe and its inhabitants. Another
woman spewed liters of acidic acrimony from her nethermaw
during orgasm, soaking the bed, which we slept in together
huddled close and damp, for we thought we were enwombed
in the nectar of love. I don't care about that, I don't regret
my bizarre proclamations of love for either woman, nor for
the many others, not even the one that dislocated my jaw
with a single punch I should have seen coming if not for the
delirium I had taken to be love. One wishes to apologize for
committing triteness when speaking of love and its difficulties convincing us that it is something somehow real, when
whatever it isn't, if it were, it would be but rarely glimpsed,
as it so nearly is in Neruda's lines—yet love, being trite, is

adamant, insinuates its mendacity into every life of leisure, every life with a moment to spare from efforts to survive the penalty of life itself. Every character has some notion of love. Tom Gravel the last would call his feelings for his son love. Drake the first would have considered love his sense of the need to protect his wife and son, to educate his son — frogs died for love. Drake the second's mother would have called her acquiescence to and support of her husband love. We think Nordgaard would equate loyalty with love. Clay Strut believed that love was a complex phenomenon, one that required hatred to exist, a Manichean formula, yet that the pursuit of that love was likely as doomed as any epic quest for the good. Drake himself believed that he loved Picasso Tits, the more so in his easy willingness to free her from the pressures of his love, not to say allowing her to leave, but perhaps allowing her to exist free from his importunings. Languideia perhaps had the most poetic vision of love, love as a mystic state wherein words and ideas grew wings, built a nest called soul that grew infinitely, fattening on the salinity from tears of defiant joy. Cleo found love to be Nietzschean as she conceived Nietzscheanism, that is to say as suited her personally, love as the uber-emotion, that which yields the strength to destroy anything in its way: it was love that made her her mother's favorite at the expense of Donnie. Rod Strut defined love as gratitude. I know that love is a senseless notion, because I know the devil not only exists but romps rampant among us — we've seen him many times in this very book — and love and the devil cannot co-exist. Many people have taken Hitler to be the devil, and I understand why they would find life especially difficult knowing what they surely must subconsciously, that Hitler was a bumpkin, a mere devil's acolyte without whom much that was accomplished would have simply required different means. Yet Hitler remains a sign of the devil's greatness, especially as the hapless enemies of the devil derange themselves into loving Hitler despite, they a puppet crowd at the grand puppet show, made of socks and crayons and string by six-year-old brown children in a benighted land, where lives of relentless strife and hunger are relieved only

by floods, cyclones, bombs, overturned ferries, chemical di-
sasters, building collapses and the like...How to explain why
I go on like this in a chapter so simple, that must convey
so little, to invade the bedroom while two characters are at
their most intimate, merely to allow the reader to follow their
progress as lovers—lovers!—and slyly advance the belief in a
subtle character trait that our work hinges on.

For Donnie's erect penis lies in repose within her (her!
Hermione!) spagyrium and I am unable to rid myself of an
obsessive need for her, a true madness that most would indeed call love were it not so preposterous to love across lines
of supposed realities. Preposterous, though? Is it any more
preposterous than to love through glass as we all have some
frequent passerby, or to love someone we have actually been
embraced by, whose legs have crabbed behind our backs
in the first days of attraction, for whom we vibrate our asses in trance like beetles, this latter to sooner or later make
house with us and stop fucking us, become boring enacting
her timeless role as receptacle, guardian of the species, col-
luding with us, pacifying us, passively encouraging our own
enactments of the timeless role as the inutile supernumerary
spermsack with the ego to require illimitable yet paradoxically redundant manifestations of stick up the ass inanities
perpetuated to prevent the simple expedient of adapting to
what we know we are but cannot be or why the fuck are we
so goddamn worried about money?

Hermione in a red dress, always in a red dress, her full
thighs, full lips, full hips, full nates, swelling swollen labia I
imagine sitting on my face, waxing and waning, waxing, swal-
lowing, mouth versus mouth, myself edentate omophagous,
her voracious omniphagous damp—damp, no, *dripping* with
salubricity—nameless...**PRESENCE**,   unborn,   infernal
and eternal, beyond the fathoming ken of human pitimost
griping need, cavernous osculumons, yin and yang, *what I
saw first!*

There he was, on top of her post active coitus yet as I remarked still erect, and she still in coital pleasure now and then
moving, pushing up against him, moaning in mid-sentence.

"I have a plan."

She has no idea I exist and she has a plan; it could only involve their future together, without me.

"That last plan worked out."

"Feels like it still is."

Donnie and I having in common the habit upon meeting a woman who attracts us when we are with a friend of allowing the friend free reign, refusing to compete...

And with her words he pushed a little deeper, their wet mounds meshing. She responds by tightening her leg grip on his calves and arching her back.

"I want us to move to Greece."

She is in a hurry.

I am helpless.

"I wouldn't mind moving to Greece."

"Then it's settled."

"Why not?"

"You should ask why maybe—I mean you and me together should move to Greece."

"Why—other than the obvious reasons."

Her breasts barely slide aside, so well is she aging. Her nipples are a brunette's nipples, almost maroon, and now they are wrinkly and taut, pointing outwards and upwards, the best of all worlds.

"Or how, and what will we do there."

"How, and what will we do there, other than the obvious."

"I can sell this house, I have some savings, and that should come to at least half of what we would need to move there, buy a place, I prefer on an island—"

"Of course on an island. I think I can get whatever we need from Drake, call it a loan to appease ourselves. At this point he would consider a hundred thousand or even more pocket change, nothing that would interfere with his casino plans. And we would..."

"Live there. You could have a library, write anything you please, travel as you need, whatever makes you happy. I think I would like to take up fishing—on a small scale, but with a boat. That would be part of the expense."

"So you feel some need to explain why?"

Ah, at last, his penis is shrinking—he's really picturing Greek islands.

"I'm a lot older than you, but—"

"You're almost the same age as me."

"No, Donnie, I am not."

As if to prove her relative maturity, she rolled him onto his back.

His penis slid out!

Seeing her on top of him does nothing but make me want her more. I'm not jealous, just…exasperated perhaps. I want her and there are her nates, her thighs still spread, her lush hair.

"Don't hurt me. I know it's a cliché but I fucking swear it's true, I never think of age—"

She shut him up with a hard, long dominant kiss.

"Donnie, in five years my tits will look like a forty-year-old woman's tits, I will have wrinkles and I will look like your mother to people because in five years you will not have aged a day—you'll be in your prime. Even now I can see some surprise when people in public figure out we're together. I look significantly older than you."

What an ass! And she's torqueing it up now…The things we could talk about…

"So Greece will slow your aging process?"

"No, nor speed yours. What it will do is provide us a number of great years together, intertwine our lives…and when you, I know you will do this, you will be honest with me, when you begin to lose your feelings, your physical feelings for me, when you fall in love [she can't hear me] with someone else you will tell me, and we will remain close friends always, I will always be able to rely on you, your friendship, some of your companionship…"

"Listen, Hermione, when you said let's go to Greece, that you want us to move to Greece, I immediately thought how nice it would be for us to be in Greece together. I haven't thought at all about anything but how nice it is to be with you here. You came up with a great idea. Why can't we just go through with it without any end plan? I really don't think what you're thinking is going to happen. Of course, there are bronzed fisherboys who will appeal to you, but why should I worry about that?"

How much a relief it is that neither is boring us with talk of how they hardly know each other.

"That's ridiculous."

"Any more ridiculous than your prognosis?"

"Yes, but even if it were not, wouldn't it still be a good idea to agree to remain together? I mean, if not in the same house at least in the same village, or whatever?"

"If I can foresee anything that will alienate me from you it is living with your palpable fear of losing me, so to speak. I'll go to Greece with you, but under the condition that we are going to Greece together because we want to be together, decide that's the best place, visit together, choose the best place for us and simply go."

"No strings attached."

"Do you really think that's what I mean?"

She managed to make herself larger, covering him like a blanket, a blanket of flesh. She has never been so desirable to me. Why her? I can't say, except that the minute she showed up in the bar I've been Majnoon.

Do I want her to fuck it up? — Say yes, say yes. I don't want her to fuck it up, yet without knowing how I could ever have her, be with her, still the thought of never seeing her again is unbearable. (I can't bear it. I will bear it.) Yet it is beyond me in more ways than one to affect their lives. When tortoises fight for the female, the loser is the one that has been nudged onto his back. I am writing this lying on my back.

"No, I guess when you feel so much loved when you love so much it's hard to believe, almost unbearable, as if only by finding doubts…"

"Great, so we'll go. Skip work today, we'll go buy a map of Greece, buy some travel books…"

I have the strength to walk away; and it is truly strength, for I don't believe in resignation. To think that I will never see her again…

53

CRAZY PALAVER

Fallen in love, Donnie strolled Vietville like some outre gonif looking for the bar where he met Hermione on that day of stress, nerves, and tailored musseline erosis, passing the True Hijo, a Mex joint, from which issued the Ka-chang!Ka-chek! of an old fashioned nickels armslut promising Share! Own! Go home prone, and the crazy palaver of matutinal slurpers of that shitlerp two shots cut off feet and who would carry him off? Nix on that, to rios grander, jamais, begin again, listen for a place where no din deems singman rebop sonnet and yahoos unwelcome, come upon a curry shop, good for a stop for samosas from a swarto sikh, spicy? Can I eat them, yeah ya can, who's sayin?, Jammu barracks escapees, salaciously Americanized, perforio diastasians, various monte players forming low knolls, and dice games cast rolls, must be onestreet over, this is two mixed and Mexed, and he no mark, o so bushed, this heat will bury a man, they should install in every street a shower, or up from under, say, lazarus like, some dew veiler, the heat stroking his neck like ben gay, hurry on, turn, nord/soud side street from late forties Idalu-pino Chet Baker Bugsy Siegel Franco Sinatro Meyer Lansky, asbestiform haze as Batistiform sleaze, excruschevy x-ost, Idalupretty—amen— da-da street assuetudes, no!, reagonies of heat, but he'll be there in a se-se-second, atilt, a ton, all-foured: moo, gabioned barbut with some lube-a-yoob can slither under and in to the fanny cool, a drink and a stool, and nostalgialate your saloob.

Finally the heat forced him indoors at a bar called The Desert Rat, a black lady behind the bar. An oval šank, television on the right side this time, and no other dames, no heat-defying Asian businessmen, no 22b, no one but him now and him with a gin and tonic.

He paid for a taxi to the Luxor.

In the elevator Donnie pressed 22. Pure Freud. He exited on that floor and turned right, reached for the handle, saw 22B, froze: It must be the heat. Back to the elevator. One floor up, exit, turn right, reach for the handle of 231, push step in, and before your senses take it in, like a murder scene the dark is darker than the most real dark of star deprived space the dark of ███████████████████████████████████
███
███
███
███
███████ relieved, sweated through, amazed he had only crossed the space of a large hotel suite in those seconds that seemed like seconds only many more, laughing at himself— from whence this notion that something truly dastardly could— 22b, he had dismissed that from his mind, one floor down, 22b, but he hadn't the moments to spare the conundrum for the entire wall before him was *alive*— sorry to use that word—alive before him with life-size live people, Arabs of some kind, seated on screen, all men and boys, all *males*, but for a woman in black from head to toe pouring tea around, exiting left: the camera remained still, as if before him was a play. Of course Drake was there, in the room, somewhere, but why not let it play out, this was new (the entire wall a fucking thin screen, formfit, the latest in monitor technology)...the clarity was remarkable—the men were wearing white and Donnie could see a fly on one man's leg—he held his tea saucer in his right hand, the fly was praying or cleaning or signaling, the man appeared to be in his early twenties, from the shadows the scene was early morning, probably the guy was about Donnie's age and he

needed tea and lots of it to wake up…Next to him, two grand white beards were speaking animatedly—at their age what was time to them? Gradually Donnie realized he could actually match faint voice sounds to moving lips—a bird, that's what started it, a morning bird: if this were his segment he would have a headless chicken dash across the lower portion of the screen…

NOW! The blast was deafening, the second blast was deafening, the light whiter than the black had been black, a flash before a yellow, an orange, a mango of dazzling color accompanied by a crescendo and decrescendo of compressed death symphony grayed the screen, which was now devoid of any human noise (where were the screams?), there—someone is moving, ah, it's Drake (*thank god he survived*, did Donnie just think that?), to the screen in two bounds, pointing, no—*touching*, the screen which was now ash and brown, clearing rather rapidly—morning breeze?—"Look right here, Donnie"…Donnie looked right there and sure enough in seconds, perfectly clear, a forearm, severed bloody end evident, though rather inactive, not spurting blood, no blood even pooling, while the hand was in full splenecdor of spasm, the four fingers gathered and yapping, the thumb playing bottom bird jaw, the hand jawing, Marx brothers stuff, really fucking funny, really, really, Drake had stepped back, was in thrall—then he balleted back to his controls, "Again," almost literally breathlessly, *huffed*, Donnie though, of course, thinking "Of course," don't leap to conclusions, assholes: this is Donnie's best fucking friend and I don't give a shit if I offend by discussing events known somewhat more widely now than then, Daddy Awlaki had been dead a mere five or six weeks, his son two weeks less—his son!, further insulating me from your offense for now that you know you are asking Why, why did they have to kill the kid, too, separately, throwing tantrums, little ineffective ones as you do these days. Why? Why else do humans take it a step further and go after the family? You have a television, right? Watch a mob flick. Some guy will warn, and your wife, your children. Why the fuck do you make me spell it out? I feel like Donnie watching that talking hand for the seventh time now, letting Drake be...

"Shit, Donnie, sorry, a drink, let me turn this off for a minute. Scotch?"

"Please."

"Where—"

"Yemen. Haudramaut."

"That's the southern coastal region, right? Dangerous place for a white man. Who took the film—that's no ordinary—"

"Ice? Maybe gin and tonic would be better, no?"

"No. Not now, not at this temperature. It's about fifty degrees hotter outside. I barely made it and I took a cab."

"Wait—you're getting ahead of me. It's not like I'm not listening, just my mind...You took a cab, you nearly died of heat stroke on the way to the cab."

"No, I started out to walk here and failed to make it, ducked into a tavern for a drink then called a cab. Nordgaard deliver this?"

"No, I lifted it from my old man's office. I looked through a stack, saw this one labeled Yemen Drone, seemed satisfying...I left the rest because I don't really know what Nordgaard needs to do at this point. You know, he may need these things. So I just took one, figuring if he needs it, he'll know I took it so it's safe."

"Can you turn on a light?"

"Sorry."

Light enough from a standing light beside the couch they were both seated on, a vast leather beast, a fucking anaconda wall to wall but for a door-width space, facing the screen-wall, suite turned viewing room, standing bar off to the left, windows right, slatted, shaded, fully deterred,

Fucking impressive, fucking Drake Fondling Junior perfect.

"So, amazing, eh?"

"The film?"

"The film the film."

"I'm not sure amazing does it justice. Who—"

"Be a little patient on that. Let me tell you *when* first—

about two weeks after they killed Awlaki's son.''

Let *that* sink in.

Shortly after the killing of the junior Awlaki, Drake Fondling the father took part in his last field operation, for which he was paid an enormous sum by one faction or another of the United States Department of Defense. That's what we're looking at.

"I know that's some pretty horrific shit, Donnie, and I won't make you watch it again, or watch the full extent of it, the headless dancing lady, the empty outfit with blood for limbs and head like a work of art; but the thing is that's the second camera, the *second*, there were two, and the first one was planted first. That one's got a different set of people, people who arrive shortly after the ones you saw, probably come from a nearby village for some kind of confab, and I'm not going to—I'm going to straight out warn you, in the second one there's a **dwarf**, they killed a fucking dwarf! Just so you're prepared. Your drink ok?"

"No."

'Same?'

"Only more. Fill the fucking glass. In fact, use a bigger glass, I still need the ice cubes. They make me think I'm not an alcoholic yet."

(Believe me, he wasn't an alcoholic yet.)

Lights out, early dawn light on in the Hawdrumout, camera picking up rocky scrub terrain, occasional boot interlopings. Voices:

Is it true boss, you're retiring?

A long pause, breathing, steps forward—down?

Where'd you hear that?

Seems a rumor has spread, more than one guy told me.

I won't lie to you, but yes, this is my last job, then I sell to Frot.

Frot? Everybody hates that son of a bitch. No one will work for him.

Sure they will. He's no different from us, just not quite as careful. Everyone will pursue the same work, same pay.

Don't like it, the retirement is guaranteed.

I won't work for that bastard.

The deal's done. He agreed to my price. The only hang up now is Nordgaard. He and Frot hate each other, so I may have to arrange some sort of independent division for him. You really don't want to work for Frot maybe you can get on with Nordgaard. But look—here, this is where we're going to install the first one. Look, don't repeat a word of this. Word must have come from Frot's side because I've only told my wife and Nordgaard. Other one we put over there, see, get two angles, cover the whole meeting.

You know something, Dwayne? This place is probably about the most dangerous place in the world for an American.

Yemen?

Specifically here, the Hadhramaut.

Then why are we making our escape by chopper in daylight?

No choice—we have to see to aim the cameras. Don't worry, the chopper heads straight to sea and we follow the coast a couple miles out. We're back in Oman before you can say, Jesus Fucking Christ those fucking crazy Arabs scare the fucking shit out of me.

Okay, there's the square, right where Omar said. He'll be collecting the cameras by the way come clean up. I got this zoomed, gimme some of that adhesive.

What if the sun reflects on it and someone sees?

Sun rises at our backs, Dwayne. Camera's covered. Look: perfect.

People are starting to move down there.

Of course, the elders of the other village will be here in an hour. Strike is set for fifteen, twenty minutes after. One missile should get them all. Though they'll surely use at least two.

All of them al Qaeda? What if some wife is serving tea or something?

Dwayne, I'm going to tell you this just because you need to hear it. There's a reason I chose you for this job—you're a natural. But you're a naif. This is an inter-village council over some missing goats. If any of these folks were al Qaeda they wouldn't be in these godforsaken villages unless they were on the run. You're good at what you do, Dwayne, but you have to outgrow your naivete or get out of the business. You're no different from a Frot man.

Why are we doing this?

Government has no ground footage of a drone strike.

Nothing better than live targets. They wanted to do it with the A-bomb, but…Shit, let's get a move on.

The sound of footsteps and then silence. "That's my father's voice."

"Fucking shit."

"I know—I thought he was finished with field work years ago."

"Fucking shit he was selling the business."

"Oh that. I guess. I need to discuss all this with Nordgaard. He may not have known by the sound of it."

"Yeah, right."

"Yeah, maybe not, though they probably at least discussed it."

"Doesn't matter to me. I'm certainly not going to run a security business."

"No, but—Frot was supposed to have killed your parents. Why if they reached a deal? You have no doubt that's your father's voice?"

Drake looked the answer into Donnie. "Then…"

"'Donnie, this is still virgin territory in many ways. Frot was an abstraction to me. Frot killing my parents was an abstraction to me. My parents dead is another story. I'm actually relieved it wasn't Frot. Now I'll work with Nordgaard, find out who's working the case, which feds, and I'll keep on top of it. I suspect Nordgaard will have ideas once he sees this, hears this."

As if he hasn't already.

"This is good news, Donnie."

Donnie realized the camera was still rolling. He watched the occasional figure cross the field of camera vision. There was the lady who served tea.

"Let me fast forward to the bad shit." Fastforwarding: zipping figures, then the arrival, greetings, they all take a seat but one, at the end, now that the camera is back to real time speed. Drake got up, walked to the screen, stood about Arab tall, pointed to the standup Arab. "Look at this guy?" Donnie dwarfed him. "Look! He's a dwarf, Donnie. They fucking took out a dwarf just to get some film of real drone damage. Wait'll you see where he ends up. It took me hours—you have to go back to the other camera—"

"I don't want to see it. Turn the fucking thing off."

"Greece. That's great. I'm happy for you two. Last week I set up an account for you, I have all the documents, you can take them when you leave. I put half a mil in the account. I don't know why not a mil, but, you know, I just wanted to do it and the money part wasn't…maybe you need more, eh? If you're going to Greece."

"I doubt it. Hermione's selling her house. We'll buy something relatively cheap. In some small village on some lesser island, or some lesser part of some bigger island. Here's the thing, Drake: Why don't you come with us?"

"Shit, I knew you'd ask. But you know the answer, too. So let's drop it or we might have to argue. All right?"

"If you accept a meaningful permanent invitation. If you promise to visit within a year. If you—"

"Promise."

54

IT'S LIKE DEATHBED CONVERSATIONS RUN IN THE FUCKING FAMILY

Tom Gravel was never much interested in sports and it's tempting to write that while other kids in other cities had baseball, in Vegas you had mobster antics keeping the kids occupied. The difference would not have been terribly significant, yielding as many dreamers and acolytes, as many lives wasted believing in false probabilities, with a few, like rumors of Psycho Danny Fitzmire joining the Spilotro gang—yeah, I figured that kid for big things, no wait—he got beaten to death, he's dead—rising in the ranks of bank robbers and killers, casino thugunderlings. But the truth is that kids in Vegas played baseball and other sports, but Tom Garvin was never really interested. Sure, he played some ball, he hit some liners, caught some grounders, pissed behind the woodframe dugout. But he was a son of the desert, interested in the strange features of a very particular landscape, who captured and kept horned lizards, non-venomous snakes, scorpions, beetles, ant armies, and so on. He kept count of Coyote sightings, and spent innumerable hours up in the mountains looking for cougars (he never did see one). At school he was a good student of otherwise ordinary disposition with the exception of his innate disgust with bullying, which put him on a course toward extraordinary violence with Psycho Danny Fitzmire. For several years it was limited to Gravel coming upon Fitzmire in the midst of intimidating smaller kids, even banging their heads against school lockers, and Gravel telling him to knock it off with an easy confidence that made the larger Fitzmire suspect that Gravel embodied some secret power that for years caused Fitzmire to acquiesce immediately, saving many kids from beatings. But once they were in high school, Fitzmire was big enough that he no longer feared Gravel nor endowed him with unfamiliar powers, though to be on the safe side, when he finally had had enough of Gravel's interventions—Hey Fitzmire, knock it off; what's it to you; it's I don't like assholes like you picking on smaller kids (here kids note opportunity to flee and scamper off); yeah, fuck you, this time you get it instead, so see ya after school—he jumped Gravel using a lead pipe that grazed Gravel's scalp on the first swipe, but not hard enough to disable him, so Gravel was able to step back and proceed to confront Fitzmire, surprising him with a rapid forward charge aimed at the arm holding the pipe, which Gravel did manage to seize without suffering lumpraising blows to the head for he was inside the arm where his hemi-wrassle style neutralized Fitzmire and he did hurt him about the groin and neck, but, once having the pipe in hand, ended the brawl, for he was not one to press an advantage using a lead pipe. So it ended then and there but for the departing threats of Psycho Danny Fitzmire; You're fucking dead, little rocks, I'll fucking kill you, next time it'll be a knife...

The neighborhood was cohesive to some degree, all ranch houses with big yards and friendships formed, everybody more or less knew what every man did for a living. And while Hank's often long hours prevented any close friendships at least everyone knew he did some secret work for the government, so when Psycho Danny Fitzmire threatened Tom, Hank merely walked over and discussed the matter briefly with his parents, making clear that if Fitzmire didn't lay off immediately he, Hank, would do nothing, wouldn't even call the cops, leaving them to conjure a trouble that would visit the Fitzmire family in some indelible form that was far more frightening, even to Psycho Danny, than any specific threat. It's easy to imagine how pleased Psycho Danny was when he found out Hank was dying of cancer.

Hank Gravel was humility personified, which meant he was widely feared and despised by feckless folk who feigned friendliness, for he spoke little and appeared to need no one or any thing. He married within a year after moving to Vegas. Tom Gravel remembered the first time he heard someone describe his mother as plain. He was in his early teens at a rare block party which his mother had skipped because of a migraine and his father as usual was working the weekend. Snitching olives by the prepubescent hands full, he overheard a description of his father as holier than thou and his mother as plain. Of course, to Tom his mother was anything but plain. She was brown-haired and freckled underfoot to eyeballs, spoke melodically, was extremely intelligent, read omnivorously, and played tennis and golf with girlhood friends, for she had been born and raised in Vegas. She was energetic and Tom thought extremely beautiful—but he had the luxury of experiencing the vivacity of a rather subdued and private woman who in her family life was emotionally engaged at all times. His parents never argued. They discussed. Tom knew his father could not discuss his job; he was told plainly at a very early age that he was working for the government, but as it was connected to the military he could never discuss it, not even with his wife. He suspected that in fact Hank *did* speak about it with his wife, and one day up in a tree he learned that he spoke of at least some of it to his wife. He didn't let on that he was up there, that he had heard— it seemed important to keep secrets, like his father did, and he knew that his persistent nightmares of tortured monkeys, grinning monkeys, monkeys live in death rictus, artificially synchronized monkeys in various landscapes always hiding pain, psychic pain, physical pain, existential pain, empathic pain, soothsayer pain, monkeys that took over his school and committed mass suicide, leaping from the roof that was dreamformed skyscraping, monkeys that sometimes, grinning, flew into volcanos, monkeys overrun by allied forces armlinked in foxholes, grinning, synchronic suicide by pistol, monkeys filling stadiums, monkeys in orchestral pits reaching musical climax revealing themselves skeletal but for the grinning faces, monkeys returning from the atomic desert on fire, monkeys returning from the atomic desert, delivered by skeletal buses, their faces the same as in the plane that started it all, monkeys on evolutionary charts in evolutionary smiles from glee decrescendoing to sufferance, every face on the chart, even erectus onward a monkey smiling, the last one sometimes—this was a frequently repeated dream during the high school years, especially when his father was ill—in a suit and carrying a briefcase, sometimes his father, his father with his head replaced by evil government scientists, his father, voice ape-grotesque, Tommy, go back: he knew that nothing good could come of sharing what he had heard and the resultant terminal albeit occasional terror, for his parents would be burdened somehow, would never lose that burden, that their own secret life would be burdened by a new range of decisions regarding a trustworthy intelligent son who could be trusted, need not be shielded, yet need not be brought to adulthood perverted by the perversions his father faced every day with surface aplomb that went deep underground with the bomb. Even when Hank began to speak quite openly with Tom, without revealing secrets, but slowly revealing distaste for the turn technology had taken, weapons technology in particular, and therefore a deepening disillusionment with the government that paid him, Tom kept his own secret, just the one, but like the secret of the bomb that secret was an infinity.

Tom talked books a great deal with his mother, but rather ironically it was his laconically oriented father he credited with inducing him to fall under the spell of language, with his oft used phrase "Fustian, pleonasmic exornations to the contrary..." and his "I am intoxicated by the (many variants here, such as exquisitry, wizardry, profundity, indubitability, indubiousity, strains of extraneosity, planes of planetary plumocracy, exuberance, protuberance...) of my own verbosity!" And probably just as important, his "Yup yup yo, yup yup yo, make up words as you go," which Tom could not divorce from his earliest memories. The reading was formative as well, for his mother managed to display a genuine interest in what he was reading from an early age, never attempted to guide his reading, and had the gift of knowing absolutely the line between inquiring and prying. Among the unnecessary memories of Gravel's youth remained that strange rather than painful mischaracterization of his mother as plain, which was so wrong. Even long after he had grown up, when she was dead and he was bereft of photos and could but occasionally fairly represent her in memory, he could see that she was an attractive woman, tall, slender, breasts firm, heavy, and freckled (glimpses of her nudity did not disturb Gravel or lead him down mysterious paths), if perhaps her type was ten years ahead of its time, when women carrying signs seemed recently emerged from the soil, as opposed to his wife, who was always tortuously self-choreographed and never off stage (Satan and those early lingorrheal fucks!).

A happy home life, Vegas style, but the grinning monkeys and the leering patient psychopath resting his chin on the top plank of the backyard fence as if wrought there, and even the most private of Las Vegans went public, the last public moment of Hank's life a right cross in the lobby of the Sands, an open party to celebrate the rescue of the town from gangsters by a bizarre creature, who lived out a fantasy life, Karloff of the living dead, by the time Hughes bought the town his toenails were already outgrowing the economy, an odd and festive Let's go from Hank recalled by Tom as Hank knew about the cancer, why wouldn't Laura like anyone else enjoy glimpsing big shots, Laxalt in hushed converse with an animate malignant dwarf who backslapped the champagne glass of Hank's wife, Watch where you're going, bitch, bitch?, Hank knocked the little fuck Steve Wynn cold with a right cross, a silence absolute and brief, maybe he's somebody, the body dragged off, the moment forgotten, Hank suavely plucking a fresh glass of champagne from a floating tray.

Beside his deathbed, Tom was coldly obedient, talk with me, son, don't grieve, spend time with me, tell me how you think, listen to how I think—this country, son, is rich in land, find yourself something to do far out in the land, far from the government, far from power, for insanity reigns, and had I known you would have been born up in the moments among the sheep like that shitbird Laxalt and we would have formed a parallel unknown dynasty of our own, missing nothing, avoiding everything, I can tell you now, Tom, my job was to analyze health risks, and I can tell you my job was finished the moment I understood chemistry—the risks are worth nothing, but insanity is repetition of its spawn, watch that insane John Wayne movie in which he plays Genghis Khan and count the dead, for they all got cancer because it was filmed amidst radioactive dust where we knew there was a second ground zero of radiation and did nothing about it, even if my reports which had to keep me on the job and so were increasingly collaborative, increasingly insane, in that case screamed evacuation, insane Tom, you know you probably know they name the bombs like you name a puppy, one of them was named *Danny Boy* to give you an idea, one of them was named *Climax* to give you a couple ideas — don't give Freud short shrift in your studies, Tom—none were named *Thyroid*, or *Glands*, or *Bloodstream*, but insanity brooks no argument and so there *was* one named *Dead*, believe it or not, Tom, there's nothing you can do about it, but you can't accept, resistance is futile, but never accept it, go about your life, have children for I can tell you that all I know is not nothing, I *know*, Tom, that with you by my side I am dying *happy*, you understand, **happy**, happy because of you, and bless your mother, she would never have been enough, which is only the nature of things, there's only you, Tom... and over the weeks quietus, *pace*, family gatherings at bedside, a minor key sonata laughably impotent, veins of mud, minds of mud, emotions mud, time's movement mud, pursuit and acquiescence mud, intellect mud, unity in mud, the last moment a triumph, an awakening, a right cross in the sands lobby, Tom, listen to this: never mind the karstification of Nevada by mines and bombs, look at the overall: this country has bombed itself more than it has bombed any and all other countries on the planet, nuclear bombed, never forget for it means everything—he was beginning to giggle now, he was laughing now, Tom was laughing, Mom was laughing, When you think about it, it's the funniest goddamn thing, yes, it was uproarious and he was coughing now, but something, he was saying, trying to say something, the coughing, pale mud, to, I heard it, he was saying Range—coughing, a hand up for silence, Ranger…Tom, Laura—coughing, Ranger *Able*, managing in sibilatory salute to life a final sardoniceismic glee, Ranger *Able*, Ranger *Baker*, get…coughing…get this: Ranger *Easy*…coughing decrescendo to death, leaving unsaid:

Ranger Baker 2	Teapot Tesla
Ranger Fox	Teapots Turk
Buster Able	Hornet
Buster Baker	Bee
Buster Charlie	Ess
Buster Dog	Apple 1
Buster Easy	Wasp Prime
Jangle Sugar	HA
Jangle Uncle	Apple 2
Tumbler Snapper Able	Post
TS Baker	MET
TS Charlie	Zucchini
TS Dog	Project 56 1
TS Easy	2
TS Fox	3
TS George	4
TS How	Project 57 1
Upshot-Knothole Grable	Plumbbob Boltzman
UK Nancy	P-Bob Franklin
Dixie	Lassen
Ruth	Wilson
Encore	Priscilla
Badger	Coulomb A
Ray	Diablo
Annie	John
Simon	Kepler
Harry	Stokes
Climax	Saturn
Teapot Wasp	Shasta
Teapot Moth	Doppler

Pascal B
Franklin Prime
Smokey
Galileo
Wheeler
Coulomb B
Laplace
Fizeau
Rainier
Newton
Whitney
Charleston
Hood
Owens
Morgan
Pascal
Project 58 Pascal C
Project 58 Coulomb C
Project 58 A Venus
Project 58 A Uranus
Hardtack II Otero
HT II Bernalillo
HT II Eddy
Luna
Valencia
Mercury
Mars
Colfax
Mora
Hidalgo
Tamalpais
Quay
Lea
Neptune
Hamilton
Logan
Dona Ana
Vesta

Rio Arriba
San Juan
Oberon
Socorro
Wrangell
Rushmore
Caltron
Juno
Ceres
Sanford
De Baca
Chavez
Titania
Humboldt
Evans
Mazama
Santa Fe
Blanca
Ganymede
Nougat Antler
Shrew
Boomer
Chena
Mink
Fisher
Gnome
Mad
Ringtail
Feather
Stoat
Dormouse
Ermine
Agouti
Danny Boy
Dead
Stillwater
Armadillo
Hard Hat

Chinchilla
Codsaw
Cimarron
Platypus
Pampas
Brazos
Hognose
Eel
Hoosic
Chinchilla 2
Dormouse Prime
Passaic
Hudson
Platte
Paca
White
Aardvark
Raccoon
Packrat
Des Moines
Daman I
Haymaker
Marshmallow
Sacramento
Storax Sedan
Little Feller II
Johnnie Boy
Merrimac
Small Boy
Little Feller I
Bobac
Raritan
Wichita
Hyrax
Allegheny
Mississippi
Peba
Wolverine

Apshapa
Roanoke
Tioga
Santee
Gundi
St. Lawrence
Casselman
Bandicoot
Taunton
Double Tracks
Tendrac
Madison
Numbat
Acushi
Manatee
Ferret
Hatchee
Chipmunk
Kaweah
Carmel
Jerboa
Toyah
Gerbil
Ferret Prime
Coypu
Cumberland
Kootanai
Paisano
Gundi Prime
Stones
Harkee
Anacostia
Hutia
Tejon
Clean Slate I
Pleasant
Clean Slate II
Yuba

York
Clean Slate III
Mataco
Kennebec
Niblick Pekan
Satsop
Natches
Ahtanum
Carp
Kohocton
Bilby
Narraguagas
Grunion
Anchovy
Mullet
Shoal
Clearwater
Fore
Mustang
Greys
Barracuda
Tornillo
Eagle
Sardine
Tuna
Bunker
Oconto
Mackerel
Bonefish
Club
Solendon
Klickitat
Handicap
Pike
Hook
Sturgeon
Bogey
Turf

Pipefish
Driver
676
Backswing
Minnow
Fade
Ace
Bitterling
Duffer
Dub
Whetstone Bye
Cormorant
Links
Alva
Player
Trogon
Canvasback
Haddock
Guanay
Spoon
Courser
Auk
Barbel
Par
Turnstone
Salmon
Garden
Forest
Handcar
Crepe
Drill
Mudpack
Cassowary
Parrot
Wool
Hoopoe
Sulky
Cashmere

Alpaca
Tern
Merlin
Wishbone
Seersucker
Wagtail
Suede
Cup
Palanquin
Gum Drop
Muscovy
Tweed
Tee
Buteo
Scaup
Chenille
Organdy
Cambric
Kestrel
Petrel
Diluted Waters
Tiny Tot
Flintlock Pongee
Screamer
Ticking
Bronze
Mauve
Charcoal
Centaur
Moa
Emerson
Longshot
Tomato
Sepia
Buff
Maxwell
Lampblack
Sienna

Dovelike
Reo
Elkhart
Corduroy
Kermet
Plaid II
Rex
Finfoot
Red Hot
Ochre
Traveler
Cinnamon
Clymer
Lime
Izzer
Templar
Purple
Stutz
Duryea
Fenton
Pin Strip
Cyclamen
Chartreuse
Tapestry
Piranha
Dumont
Discus Thrower
Pile Driver
Tan
Puce
Double Play
Kankakee
Vulcan
Halfbeak
Latchkey Saxon
Rovena
Effendi
Derringer

Switch

Newark

Tangerine

Khaki

Simms

Cerese

Ajax

Nash

Agile

Rivet I

Daiquiri

Vigil

Sterling

New Point

Greeley

Absinthe

Sidecar

Bourbon

Rivet II

Ward

Rivet III

Oakland

Mushroom

Persimmon

Fizz

Heilman

Fawn

Chocolate

Mickey

Scotch

Commodore

Umber

Midi Mist

Knickerbocker

Crosstie Vito

Stanley

Gibson

Washer

Russet

Yard

Bordeaux

Lexington

Door Mist

Gilroy

Marvel

Zaza

Lanpher

Cognac

Sazerac

Worth

Cobbler

Polka

Gasbuggy

Stilt

Hupmobile

Staccato

Faultless

Brush

Cabriolet

Mallet

Knox

Torch

Dorsal Fin

Buggy

Stinger

Pommard

Adze

Milk Shake

Bevel

Noor

Throw

Shuffle

Scroll

Boxcar

Hatchet

Crock

Clarksmobile
Wembley
Tub
Rickey
Funnel
Seville
Chateaugay
Bowline Spud
Tanya
Rack
Diana Moon
Noggin
Knife A
Ipecacipecac
Stoddard
Sled
Packard
Aliment
Wineskin
Hudson Seal
Knife C
Welder
Vaat
Hula
Bit
File
Crew
Crewcrew
Knife B
Ming Vase
Tinderbox
Schooner
Tyg
Bayleaf
Scissors
Benham
Shave
Imp

Vise
Auger
Biggin
Nipper
Winch
Cypress
Gourd Amber/Gourd Brown
Valise
Chatty
Barsac
Coffer
Thistle
Blenton
Purse
Torrido
Tapper
Bowlbowl
Mandrel Horehound
Spiderbesider
Hutch
Pliers
Minute Steak
Jorum
Seaweed
Kyackyack
Ildrim
Milrow
Pipkin
Seaweed B
Cruet
Pods
Calabash
Scuttle
Piccalilli
Planer
Diesel Train
Culantro
Tun 4

Grape A
Lovage
Fob Green/Blue/Red
Rulison
Terrine White/Yellow
Grape B
Belen
Labis
Diana Mist
Cumarin
Yannigan Red/Blue/White
Cythus
Arabis Red/Green/Blue
Shaper
Handley
Beebalm
Ajo
Snubber
Hod Green/Red
Hod Blue
Can Green/Red
Jal
Mint Leaf
Diamond Dust
Cornice Yellow/Green
Manzanas
Morrones
Hudson Moon
Flask Green/Yellow/Red
Piton
Arnica Yellow/Violet
Pitonpiton
Emery Penasco
Scree-Acajou/Alhambra/
   Chamois
Truchas-Chacon/Chamisal/
   Rodarte
Abeytas
Tijeras

Carrizozo
Artesia
Corazon
Avens-Andorre/Alkermes/
   Asamite/Cream
Canjilon
Carpetbag
Baneberry
Embudo
Laguna
Camphor
Harebell
Dexter
Grommet Diamond Mine
Chantilly
Apodaca
Bracken
Algodones
Lagoon
Miniata
Barranca
Nama-Amarylis/Mephisto
Baltic
Frijoles-Deming/Espuela/
   Guaje/Petaca
Peternal
Cathay
Cannikin
Diagonal Line
Parnassia
Chaenctis
Hospah
Yerba
Mescalero
Cowles
Dianthus
Sappho
Zinnia

Ocate/Onaja
Longchamps
Tajique
Jicarilla
Misty North
Kara
Monero
Merida
Capitan
Haplopappus
Toggle Diamond Sculls
Atarque
Cebolla/Cuchillo/Solano
Oscuro
Delphinium
Akbar
Arsenate
Canna-Umbrinus/Limogues
Tuloso/Solanum
Flax
Flaxflax
Alumroot
Natoma
Gazook
Miera
Starwort
Mesita
Angus/Velarde
Colmor
Kashan
Rio Blanco X 3
Cabresto
Dido Queen
Almendro
Potrilloo
Portulaca
Silene
Arbor Polygonum

Pajara
Waller
Bernal
Seafoam
Husky Ace
Latir
Elida
Pinedrops-Sloat/Tawny/Bay-
ou
Spar
Hulsea
Sapello
Potrero
Plomo
Jib
Grove
Fallon
Jara
Ming Blade
Bedrock Trumbull
Crestlake-Tansan/Briar
Puye
Portmanteau
Pratt
Escabosa
Estaca
Puddle
Stanyan
Hybla Fair
Temescal
Keel
Portolaportala-Larkin
Teleme
Bilge
Alviso
Stilten
Topgallant
Edam

Mizzen

Obar

Mast

Cabrillo

Camembert

Tybo

Futtock

Dining Car

Anvil Marsh

Leyden

Inlet

Husky Pup

Kasseri

Cheshire

Chiberta

Muenster

Keelson

Fontina

Esrom

Deck

Shallows

Colby

Strait

Pool

Estuary

Rivoli

Mighty Epic

Billet

Banon

Fulcrum Gouda

Asiago

Redmud

Chevre

Ebbtide

Spirit

Sutter

Rudder

Cove/Oarlock

Dofino

Dofino-Lawton

Marsilly

Bulkhead

Crewline

Forefoot

Carnelian

Strake

Flotost

Gruyere

Gruyere-Gradino

Scantling

Scupper

Coulommiers

Cresset Bobstay

Hybla Gold

Sandreef

Seamount

Farallones

Rib

Iceberg

Satz

Karab

Campos

Reblochon

Topmast

Backbeach

Fonduta

Transom

Jackpots

Lowball

Panir

Diablo Hawk

Asco

Draughts

Rummy

Cremino

Cremino-Caerphilly

Quicksilver Emmenthal
Quargel
Quinella
Concentration
Farm
Baccarat
Kloster
Freezeout
Pepato
Chess
Fajy
Burzet
Memory
Offshore
Nessel
Sheepshead
Hearts
Pera
Tinderbox Backgammon
Tarko
Canfield
Huron King
Verdello
Norbo
Bonard
Liptauer
Azul
Tafi
Pyramid
Colwick
Flora
Kash
Riola
Guardian Dutchess
Miners Iron
Dauphin
Pineau
Serpa

Havarti
Islay
Trebbiano
Seco
Aligote
Clairette
Baseball
Vide
Harzer
Niza
Cernada
Praetorian Paliza
Tilci
Tenaja
Jornada
Molbo
Hosta
Monterey
Borrego
Kryddost
Atrisco
Cerro
Rousanne
Akavi
Caboc
Kesti
Gibne
Bouschet
Nebbiolo
Queso
Huron Landing
Frisco
Phalanx Seyval
Manteca
Coalora
Cheedam
Sabado
Cabra

Armada
Laban
Diamond Ace
Turquoise
Jarlsberg
Crowdie
Fahadu
Mini Jade
Chancellor
Tomme/Midnight Zephyr
Branco-Herkimer
Techado
Navata
Fusileer Muggins
Romano
Midas Myth/Milagro
Gorbea
Tortugas
Agrini
Bellow
Orkney
Mundo
Breton
Caprock
Duoo
Normanna
Kappeli
Correo
Dolcetto
Wexford
Grenadier Vermejo
Villita
Sault
Egmont
Cottage
Tierra
Minero
Vaughn

Hermosa
Misty Rain
Towanda
Ville
Maribo
Serena
Cebrero
Chamita
Ponil
Charioteer
Mill Yard
Diamond Beech
Roquefort
Kinibito
Goldstone
Glencoe
Mighty Oak
Mogollon
Jefferson
Panamint
Tajo
Darwin
Cybar
Cornucopia
Galveston
Aleman
Labquark
Abo
Musketeer Belmont
Gascon
Bodie
Hazebrooke-Emerald/Check-
  erberry
Apricot
Tornero
Middle Note
Delamar
Presidio

Hardin
Brie
Mission Ghost
Panchuela
Midland
Tahoka
Lockney
Touchstone Borate
Waco
Abilene
Nightingale
Kernville
Mission Cyber
Schellbourne
Laredo
Alamo
Bullfrog
Kearsarge
Harlingen
Cornerstone Dalhart
Monahans
Kawich
Misty Echo
Disko Elm
Texarkana
Kawich-Red/Black
Palisade X 3
Ingot
Tulia
Amarillo

Comstock
Rhyolite
Aqueduct Hornitos
Muleshoe
Barnwell
Austin
Whiteface-A/B
Ledoux
Metropolis
Bowie
Bullion
Mineral Quarry/Randsburgh
Sundown-A/B
Sculpin Tenabo
Houston
Coso-Bronze/Gray/Silver
Bexar
Montello
Floydada
Hoya
Distant Zenith
Julin Lubbock
Bristol
Junction
Diamond Fortune
Victoria
Galena-Yellow/Orange/
   Green
Hunters Trophy
Divider

55

MIND ENOUGH AND LIME

What's the sound of a six-foot five-inch anthroform pounding on a hotel room door for fifteen minutes compared to shrieking missile strikes? Silence. Like the sequence following the strikes, when the superknocking becomes pertinent insistence. Drake was pissed when he opened the door, sourly took the note from the goon he employed whether he cared or not, and slammed the door before opening it again quickly, to blurt: "Shit, sorry, thanks," before shutting it, leaning back against it in existential disarray, reading, "Please answer your phone— Nordgaard," which was when the phone rang.

"Nordgaard? Sorry, I—"

"No need. We need to meet, but I can't leave LA so here's what you do: tonight, this evening, you need to be at Harris Springs just at sundown. I'll be there, short talk, back to LA, nobody knows I'm gone."

"Right. Where's Harris Springs?"

"Harris Springs Road. Take the northwest highway—95— just after you leave town behind you see Kyle Canyon Road up toward the mountain, head that way, it's west, go about twelve miles, there's a sign on your right, road is on your left, gravel paved. Once you turn you're going straight south, but soon you hit a 90 degree right, once you go right keep going and you'll see a left, a lesser road, recognize it, but don't take it, take the one after the next one, so that's the third left, this one is even narrower, it dips back southeast but quick straightens southward, always southward, with a generally southeastern track once it rounds a foothill. The road curves a lot but generally south and then southeast, take it until you reach the end, where you will see two mesquite trees and you can see you're in a small turnaround, that the road has clearly ended. Got it? It will be easier than it sounds—you can't miss Harris Springs Road, and after that, that left I mentioned will have an indication it's the right one. You won't miss it. Don't tell anyone—I have time for this and this only and have to be back in LA by morning as if I had never left. Figure the light—I want you at the end of that road just before dark."

"Got it, Nordgaard, but, look, give me some leeway on the timing."

"Here's your leeway. Start driving from the strip at 1806, that's six-oh-six civilian time."

After the click, Drake's first thought was This guy's going to be lots of fun to work with.

As luck would have it, I know the spot very well, having fled the fraughts, fates and fatuosities of flailing family fastnesses one hundred-degree night some years back, wife pissed cause I was pissed day after day pissed on gin tonics, Old Rasputin, now vodka if I was going to be driving which I was. I left the old man's 1916 Smith & Wesson .38 at home like a last good idea. Visit venomous Vegas! Bring your family's old demons to meet the new demons, juice up your own demons. Juice up! Keep your head low, lips shut, magma heat, tectonic tremors, and blow! Fling some fucks, and if the kids are asleep break some glass, there was life inside me yet! I took the old man's jeep and drove out of town, figuring maybe to come across a mojave rattler sloughing off the meditations of day— that's a creature I could learn from is what I figured. Harris Springs Road, away from it all, I drove slow and watched for movement of any kind; I drove miles and miles into hidden desert hills—no inhabitants anywhere around; I turned off on a side road, off to my left, drove it to a rise, the road seemed to end there. But no, couldn't be: a few hundred yards below me I saw lights, some kind of desert buggy: that's where I go, down there, never mind the vegetation, never mind the boulders, I took off down there and was just about to the narrow road when a gully sunk before me. I veered left, but the farther along I got, the more that road receded, so I managed a creosote turn and went back to where I first came upon the gulch. It seemed to me I could get up some speed and leap the fucker. That was one of the dumbest ideas I ever had in my life—I only realized I could have killed myself when the thump of success coincided with the realization that my skull dented the metal above my head. It was close. The drop was greater than I had thought and I believe I bounced on a natural embankment at just the right slant to get me on the road I was aiming for. That was a sobering moment, but I had half a bottle of vodka left and had yet to see a snake. I aimed westward, came to what I figured for deep Harris Springs Road, got the hell off that, turned onto a wild, rocky, narrower track that narrowed as I proceeded, narrowed to where branches of some kind of desert trees slapped at the windows, kept narrowing, me plowing forward for it was a track and had to widen at some point, the logic impeccable, the nightmare inevitable, slapping me like those dry branches with its inevitability until finally indeed I found a spot wide enough to turn where in looking over my shoulder I saw the canvas of my old man's jeep that covered the bed was shredded, fucking shredded. And with that I ambled out of the Spring Mountains, found Harris Springs Road, turned right at Kyle Canyon, not so much a defeated man, but one determined to kill off the bottle at home—they'd be gathered around the television, I would walk past them out the patio door. Instead the twelve miles back was one too many. About a mile shy of the highway I thought maybe snakes would like a little more black top, so I took a left northward, passed a power plant, even a few houses, saw a couple of rabbits, pushed on slow, pulled slow on the vodka, failed to note the road going to rock, saw nothing out there in the finality of desert, and after some twenty minutes or two hours, saw I was coming perpendicular to a well-paved road. There was a place to turn around, which may have been a gas station, but this was a few years ago, and as I was pulling back onto the road I saw a cop come up on me. I stopped. He approached the car. You're on reservation land, he said. There was a perfect rectangle of Paiute reservation out northwest of Vegas, six square miles of rectangle, and I guess if you aren't a Paiute you take the main roads and have a reason to. He recognized my lack of guile and sized up the situation short of drink, which he didn't seem to want to notice, even though the bottle, upright on the passenger seat, wasn't buckled in, though he must have thought a lot about the shredded canvas, probably along the order of here's one stupid fucker in trouble when he gets home, for he could only match the last name of the registration with the last name of my identification and I was forced to explain it was my old man's vehicle. I asked him why I never saw mojave rattlers. He said he didn't know, but they spent days hiding out in yuccas. Out there in the desert a man can go many directions, and I was now conversational. I asked, You're Paiute, then? I'm from Michigan, he said, and briskly sent me off with a warning about encroaching on Paiute land and didn't follow me the way cops sometimes do. What the fuck did he want to drive through more desert for?

Drake had more appreciative thoughts on his mind driving up Kyle Canyon Road. In fact, he was thinking more along the lines of what he had been missing holed up in the hotel. The desert was beautiful, the view of the city back over his left shoulder something he'd have to ponder at some length one day, sitting on a hump out in this very region. Maybe he'd bring a folding chair and a cooler with some beer. He'd invite Donnie, and Hermione. A sign on his right seemed to be saying elevation 3000 feet and it took him some time to figure that out, and the simple fact of it was little short of thrilling. Especially when he fairly soon came upon a sign that read 4000 feet. The *valley*, of course: he was *rising*, the road was *rising* toward Mount Charleston. He was experiencing geography and it was good. Now he was eager to find this rock road, to really get into the desert. This was just the kind of wild shit he had to look forward to with Nordgaard running the show, part of the show, whatever it was Nordgaard would be doing.

Nordgaard.

Drake had known Nordgaard pretty much his whole life, but only now was Nordgaard becoming fully human to him.

Nordgaard as shadow, Nordgaard as gargoyle…now Nordgaard as…When it hit him it hit him hard, doubled him up as he pulled off the highway, braking hard, the shoulder one with the desert he instinctively steered too far into. Sometimes, he thought amongst all his thoughts, understanding is like falling from a great height, and you *do* hit the ground — later, you hit the ground, later meaning many things other — but understanding is an intestinal, duodenal, subgut plunge-suck is what it is. He was sobbing now, yowling, willing breath from his skinsack, fleshsack, bonerack, throat-wheezing, rhythm sobbing, emptying his head through his ass, he told himself, shit for brains his old man must have cursed him a hundred thousand times. Now he was dead. Nordgaard was being like a father to him, Nordgaard took care of everything before he arrived, and Nordgaard unbeknownst to Nordgaard had swiped the space for his grief. He would never tell this to Nordgaard, he knew, for who knew what gods Nordgaard played his angles to, nor did he wish Nordgaard to feel anything but Drake's reverence for the man who remained his father's loyal sidekick through innumerable hells — but goddammit Nordgaard was not his father and he better start getting that straight in his slow-bereaving mind.

There, that's better. A short outburst. Look: some of the car still on the shoulder.

Drake wiped his eyes, sucked on a bottle of water, rolled down the windows letting the indigenous desert air slap at the machine-cooled desert air. His skull was thicker now, his eyes taut, his body weightless. His father was dead, his mother was dead. He would understand that better someday, out in the desert, far from a city delineated precisely in hot, crisp high desert air. But now the sun was touching the mountain. Better get a move on.

The foundering, as he named the moment to give it the kind of heft you had to return to, occurred just half a mile short of the Harris Springs Road turn, and the road went like Nordgaard said, and he wasn't worried that Nordgaard was out there expecting him and out there meant a veritable desert maze. Nor need he have worried, for he spotted the third left and prepared to turn even before he saw the slain and bled-out rabbit hanging from a tree branch. Wild. What kind of trees were out here? The darkening desert was fascinating, the greens gathering like some sort of press of wilderness, the farther he drove, the more dense the greens, and he was going so slow if mad mythical creatures ran wild out here there would be little he could do. He turned off the air-conditioning and lowered the windows fully to let them in. Fuck it. He never gave much thought to following in his father's footsteps, never actually expected any need to, but to this extent, a Nordgaard romp, a long creepy crepuscular drive in the desert, having no idea how long and the outgoing always longer than the return, this was communing probably—it was a long, long drive, and his nerves teased him, for he seldom felt real fear, which could have come from either his mother or father, for neither ever showed fear before him, but the road went on, and sure he thought maybe things had taken a turn for the southeast as opposed to more south, but that hump to the left wasn't so big, could that really be the one he was skirting? He didn't see another one, at least not on the left, though there were hills all around, and westways building to mountain, and no creatures, and it was darking fast—did it really matter if he was a couple minutes late? He finally turned his brights on, but no desert manbeast with a torn shirt leaped into the road, if you could call it that. Driving a Mercedes sedan out here, come to think of it—shouldn't Nordgaard have suggested he rent something more rugged?

No, here you had to trust Nordgaard, for if this was as bad as it gets the car would need a wash, maybe, but—look: the road ends in a tiny cul-de-sac, two medium trees.

That was easy.

He got out of the car, rubbed his hands up and down his breasts. This was all to the good. He looked around, he looked around short and long. There were no lights, no noise but birdsquawk, maybe some kind of desert noise that dogs would hear like a symphony but he couldn't be sure he heard at all. Anything was possible with Nordgaard, that was for sure. Nordgaard knew everything a man could know about every kind of terrain at every time of day or night, such as how far the nluk made by the tongue coming unstuck from the roof of the mouth and rapping the gulletgulley behind the teeth would travel. He was just over 600 yards away, a sure shot, but he wanted it direct, he was on his stomach, the shot uphill maybe 23 degrees, his XM21 perfectly still, his finger on the trigger. Drake had taken a step forward, and was thinking, that's odd, a rectangular hole like that out here, when he heard a click, maybe a lizard click (it was a clear nluk) and he looked up, high enough, straight ahead so the shot was low forehead, dead center, death as instant as death can be.

56

THE HAND PLAYED OUT

Next morning, Nordgaard had changed the plates and ditched the car where if it were ever found no questions would be asked, which is all he would want said about that. And when the phone rang as it had done so often lately, he finally answered—Tom Gravel calling, so surprised at getting an answer first ring he nearly hung up.

"This is—"

"Write this down, Gravel: 2213 Los Altos, right across from Elliot's Sprinkler Repair. Got it?"

"Yeah."

"Lose this number." Click.

Gravel dashed out of the hotel room to his car. Meanwhile, Hermione had just left the house, and Donnie, infused with her scent and determined to remain so, was mixing a gin and tonic, which he would take to the balcony along with the cigarettes he had begun smoking with her, when an unusual event occurred: someone knocked at the door. That had yet to happen while he was alone in her house.

"Coming!" he called, thinking how living in a house in a civilization was more like riding a bicycle than was probably healthy. He was going to mix that drink, though.

Pulling in the screen door, then pushing open the wood airstopper, Donnie was faced with 22b with a giant man right behind him, enough to the side he could display a pistol in a way Donnie took to be a gallant attempt at subtlety. "Hello Claude, where'd ya get the galoot?"

"We're coming in."

"Invited."

He held the door til the galoot slapped his paw on it and turned, pointing to the back terrace.

"You know who I am?"

"Yeah. You're the guy who's always there. Water? I'm having a gin and tonic."

"You know why?"

"Probably."

"Your friend doesn't like to pay his gambling debts."

"Two gin and tonics, maybe? Go sit outside and tell the gorilla to put the toy away. It isn't necessary."

"It's not loaded. But he doesn't feel secure without it."

"A tit with a trigger. I'll be right out."

Donnie heard "Whud he mean by that?" too slow for doppler as the visitors edged out the screen door.

Outside, the crooks had taken the chairs facing out, but Donnie thought better of prolonging the meet over trifles.

"So I got a lot more questions than I care to ask, so let's get down to it. My pal Drake owes your boss—Vinnie?"

22b nodded.

"He owes Vinnie 40 grand, right?"

They looked at each other, 22b rolling his eyes over to the goon, the goon huffing, and "40 grand, that's rich."

"Ah, interest, inconvenience, travel costs, right? Here's one question I'll ask. Why not kill him?"

Robinson fielded that one. "You kidding? Kill the son of the head of Blackguard?"

"So you come here intending what? Kidnap or something?"

"Maybe."

"That could get you in as much shit as killing him. That, and I'd probably get shot in the rescue mission. Speaking of which, let me see that gat."

The big feller looked like he'd been told by his boss to eat a turd.

22b gestured to hand it over, and he promptly did so.

It was a .44 magnum, S&W. No bullets. Handing it back barrel first, Donnie said, "Bullets in your pocket, right?"

The galoot patted his right suit pants pocket, looking like he'd just been tossed raw meat.

"Well, look, Claude, we can take care of this real quick. How much is your Vince figuring, I mean how much to make him leave Drake alone and feel satisfied?"

"Vinnie wants two-hundred grand."

"You must have quite the expense account."

"Add salary and interest."

"No, the salary he pays you regardless."

"Hazard pay, plus, like I said, interest."

"I doubt it comes to that, but no matter—I'll pay. I got that much in the bank. We'll go get it. You'll come with me to the bank, I'll give you the money and you'll go back east and we'll all forget about it. I'll break it to Drake when the time is right, so Vinnie can be sure Drake's not going around acting like he pulled a fast one on him. Deal?"

22b wiped the stun off his face and his right hand jerked forward. "Deal."

"I don't have to shake with the galoot, do I?"

22b smirked. The galoot looked like he was beginning to need to know what a galoot was.

Coming through the screen door behind Donnie, 22b said, "I know I don't have to say this, but" while at the front door, open a few inches, about to knock, Tom Gravel heard, "you better not pull anything once we reach the bank." And he knocked, and heard, "Whoever it is, get rid of em," Donnie pulling the door open, Gravel with his right behind his back, having pulled his .38.

"Dad!" Donnie exclaimed. "Hey, it's my dad," Gravel seeing through the screen an unarmed 22b and a goon behind him with a pistol scratching his head, acted fast, pushing the screen with his shoulder, stepping into the room, reaching across to grab Donnie with his left, pulling him behind himself, whipping the gun to face the galoot.

"Drop it now!"

"Look," 22b began.

"Shut up. Drop it."

"Drop it," 22b said, resigned, weary, world weary, fool's errand weary.

The gun bounced off tile.

"Kick it over here."

22b slid the gat to Gravel with his foot, the lopsided piece skidding and scraping. It was a heavy gun.

He picked it up, keeping his eyes on the two hoods, then turned to Donnie, gave him a hasty shove and said, "The Maverick." And they dashed for the car, Gravel because of the perilous circumstances, Donnie because that seemed to be what his old man wanted. They slid rapidly in, neither looking back until they were pulling away from the curb — Gravel caught 22b and muscle coming through the door in the rearview, meaning they had eyeballed his wheels.

"Seat belt."

Donnie complied, but noted, "I don't think they're following us, Dad."

"This is a gambling debt, right? So likely they got two guys in another car. Likely they got an eye on us, and likely the two will be in communication, so it's best if we assume we're being followed."

Donnie shrugged.

The Maverick had emerged at Sahara and Gravel pulled a slow, slaphappy left into angry honking traffic and another left at the next left, back into the same neighborhood, but on Mesquite, which drilled straight up to Charleston, where they would have a broader view of trailing traffic, not to mention any awkward attempts by vehicles attempting to repeat his maneuvers.

"Don't worry, Donnie, I know this town, was born and raised here."

Donnie glanced at his father's thigh, bemused.

"A lot has changed, but you still have the basic grid, and I've had a couple weeks to take note of anything significant, like they got this fucking ring road now…"

"So you turning up here, something to do with you being from here and me being told you were born in Chicago. First question: do I have living grandparents?"

"No. My Dad died of cancer several years before you were born, my ma died in a car wreck here in town about three years before you were born. I was in prison at the time for beating a guy to death."

"With your bare hands."

"You knew?"

Donnie chuckled, "No, fuck no, it's just that seems the natural extension in the lingo. Beat a man to death with his bare hands."

"I made the mistake of my life when—"

"You married mom?"

"No, that eliminates you."

"Anyone else?"

"I have to admit I care nothing for her at this point."

"I can't say the same, but it's probably true enough."

"Not marrying her, but agreeing to the terms of the mar-riage—the children must never know about my real back-ground. It made sense to me at the time because I was an escaped con and—"

"Escaped con? This keeps getting better. Killed a man, on the run, new identity I presume, no statute of limitations…"

"That was the issue. That you would be accessories and all that horseshit."

"What choice did you have?"

"Europe. Once she became a poetry queen and I became known a little it would have been easy. Or get a good lawyer with her family money. I didn't commit premeditated mur-der, just excessively brutal murder, which is kind of a horse-shit distinction, since if I had a gun I would have just shot him a few times and it would have seemed normal, but bul-lets in the face are pretty brutal. Instead I was deemed a sane psychopath and it went rapidly and badly for me."

"Pardon, I'm engrossed, but do all these maneuvers have a purpose?"

Donnie wasn't counting, but there must have been nearly a dozen turns since they left Charleston, all of them tending them westward, which, if they were being followed, would be the best guess.

"Yes. We're already on Durango, which will take us to Blue Diamond, which will take us west out of town and we'll be able to spot a tail with absolute certainty and sooner or later—"

"Okay, but I'm not really in any trouble…"

"Never mind, son, we need time to talk anyway, if you don't mind."

"Hardly, this is like a dream come true."

"I don't expect anything in particular from you, Donnie, just that you understand I know I fucked you, I was a horse-shit father, I made a cowardly deal, and all the more cowardly I stuck with it. There's a purple station wagon on our tail. I noted him before we turned."

"This doesn't seem exactly an obscure route."

"Just worth keeping an eye out. I spotted it first on Charleston. So—"

"You want to start making it up to me, Dad? Can the guilt. I didn't grow up bad. I have a healthy approach to life, a good enough brain, and you ought to meet my girlfriend—"

"I could have *taught* you a lot, Donnie."

"Are you kidding me? You taught me how to *think*."

"How? I hardly ever spoke to you as an adult."

"True enough, at least not about ideas—Mom always interfered is how I remember it."

Gravel laughed. "No doubt there."

"Wait. So what's my real name, if not Garvin?"

"Gravel."

"Gravel?"

"Donnie Gravel. My side of the family is Nevada way back, I mean for this country way back. You got French mountain man in you and some Indian, Blackfoot. Your great-great-grandmother was Blackfoot, married to the first Tom Gravel. He migrated from Oregon territory eventually to Nevada, shot a lawman, died of some disease…"

"After that? All killers, or what?"

"Not til me…This is Blue Diamond. We'll see what that purple wagon does."

"So you're feeling low because you gave me short shrift, is that it?"

"Yes."

He glanced in the mirror. The purple wagon was following, turning west like they had.

"Well, like I said, Dad, you taught me how to think."

"How's that?"

"One time, I was maybe eleven or so, I don't know, I
asked you about God, Christianity. And what did you talk
about? Herodotus."

"Herodotus?"

"You told me that he was considered the father of history, maybe the original historian, yet it was well known that
much of his writings were a crock. Great as he may have been
considering the context, he was unreliable, sometimes wildly
fanciful. But you told me about one particular passage, about
Darius—"

"The sprained ankle."

"The sprained ankle—exactly. He sprained his ankle
getting down off a horse, sprained it bad. And the point you
made was that this detail, this telling detail, Herodotus's use
of this telling detail to describe some medical shenanigans—I
think the tale was a sort of origin myth regarding the establishment of a medical school or a town becoming famous for
its medical knowledge—the detail made it seem true, made
it believable.

"And you proceeded to explain that you knew of nothing
in the New Testament that came close to that simple scene.
So for people to believe in the text made no sense. Parables
are fine and all, but to believe in it, as opposed to learning
from it maybe I thought this or maybe you said it, to believe
in it was an insult to God the Writer or dictater or dictator.
There are a lot of shades of thought in that, and at age eleven
you trusted it wouldn't be wasted on me. And it wasn't. It was
the single best lesson I ever received in my life."

"There could have been—*should* have been—many
more. I don't think I can ever forgive myself for that."

"Bullshit, Dad—this very moment renders all your regrets
utterly obsolete. I survived all your parental crimes intact and
now you're coming clean. What's the problem. I love you
and always have, and criticisms built up over the years aside

you're all I want for a father—unless you turn maudlin and weak, which you never were and which I never want you to be...So tell me about killing a man with your bare hands..."

Grinning monkeys would not be passed to another generation. Donnie's grandfather's story was bad enough as it was. What his dying meant for now was the neighbor psycho released for havoc.

Tom Gravel took a break to fill Donnie in on the escape route. "This highway is the main route to Pahrump. In about fifteen miles, though, we turn left on Tecopa, picking up the Old Spanish Trail."

"Fine, but with so few options out here it wouldn't be all that suspicious if a purple car followed us to Pahrump or along the historic sightseeing trail. Where's it go, Death Valley?"

"Almost. And you're right, but as we near Death Valley we'll have plenty of opportunities to see whether they're following us, the final maneuver being to actually turn off the trail on a road I know that cuts up the valley. If they follow us then we'll know for sure."

By the time Tom Gravel had described the fight with Danny Fitzmire in the detail Donnie requested, went through the legal process, the prison stint—Donnie had a lot of questions about *that* experience: the break out, evading the manhunt—found the anonymous identity expert in Chicago, enrolled in the University of Chicago and was about to meet his wife, they had reached what Gravel recalled he never knew was Harry Wade Road or not, time to turn off the Old Spanish Trail. The purple wagon pulled in at the Tecopa Springs, but after fifteen minutes or so it appeared to be a speck back on the trail, following.

This now was a white rock road that raised clouds of desert and gave away their position from quite a distance if indeed anyone was following, but that would end at blacktop less than thirty miles north, where he would step on it, and disappear on a similar track that would be blocked from view from behind by a butte—they'd be alone in desert and impossible to find before the purple wagon could grasp what happened—the hoods would have to assume they suddenly leadfooted it up and out of the valley after lulling them this far. In country where you could see for dozens and dozens of miles, there was a precise place Gravel knew where they could disappear.

"And it's not radioactive."

"How's the gas?"

"Just over half a tank."

"Wow."

"These old cars had big tanks…anyway, there's gas back there in Tecopa and up ahead if we need it."

Gravel rolled along between forty and fifty miles an hour.

Soon it was Donnie's turn. Describing the last nearly two years to the old man, he realized how bizarre it had all been. Tom had a lot of questions that raised a lot of questions for Donnie about that halfwit Hafbreit, as Gravel called him despite his wife's insistence that he was Iowa's La Follette or something like that—"Christ Donnie, for a woman of words she could say the most stupid fucking things. Iowa's fucking La Follette!" The story was so compelling Gravel missed the turn past the butte, realizing it a good twenty miles late.

"Shit, Donnie, I missed my turn. But never mind. Here the roads split and what we can do is up ahead a ways we go overland to the secondary road, which also runs basically north/south and maybe into a canyon from where we can see for miles—"

"I don't think we're being followed, Dad."

"Neither do I. Fuck it, let's cut over here," pulling the car onto the desert flats, making an easy descent. Gravel nixed familiar grand and fraudulent thoughts, the miscegenatory offspring of vast lands and the urge to write of them.

"So tell me about this Montagnard, then."

Here Gravel had his west and northwest confused, the tale was fascinating, though, so paid little attention as he crossed at an off angle the only other road out there, the rock road, which may not have seen traffic since May anyway, and headed up into Starvation Canyon—"I recognize this place. We go up here, cross a path and there's, I remember there's a shortcut to Furnace Creek where we can get something to eat and drink."

He had no idea how disoriented he had become, his mind peopled with dancing figures in party hats, unfurling noise-makers taunting his ears, a happiness he recalled and knew he would one day have to fight the urge to describe with the inane words that would capture nothing but perhaps something akin to that feeling a human gets pissing outside on a warm summer night. But this was far better than that. It was historic. It was of history. It meant as much and as little as the Battle of Actium.

Onward up the valley of no eats.

At about 2400 feet—up from a low of roughly 250 feet below sea level, Gravel realized that something was obviously not as he remembered, so he took a dubious right on a track that seemed it could turn downward at some point—there's something particularly anti-frontier about retracing your steps, folk just can't manage—and indeed they did descend, tortuously, forced to rise again, by which point they were turned around enough they both knew they were utterly lost on trails not built for cars, not even 4-door Mavericks. All they had were the more or less accurate guesses of the compass directions of a valley that runs more or less south to north and the geography that had so enthused Drake the day before: the meaning of valley. They also had heat, more than 110 fahrenheital degrees of it.

"How much gas, Dad?"

There was a desert pause.

"Shit."

The sound was like the short dash of a whiptail.

"What?"

Donnie leaned over to look for himself: just over half a tank. Just over half a tank. Fucking gauge was broke.

"Here's what we'll do," Dad said, "Once we get turned around, we'll go in neutral down, only down, and that means we have to hit the floor and the highway is just on the other side of that, and we can't be far from Furnace Creek after all this time."

But they were not going to get the car turned around.

Even as they sputtered between rock walls looking for a place to turn around they both knew the tank was empty.

"I think the phrase, Dad, is running on fumes."

"That's one of them."

"All right, let's drink some water, sleep a little, then head down on foot."

"Think so?"

"Meantime I got a deck of cards in the glove compartment."

They slept longer than they should have, heading down on foot too close to sunrise, going at a brisk pace, as if the sun would not rise unbidden — they were like two school kids scurrying in late to class, all their body language suggesting time could be bargained backwards...But the sun did rise, and the sun was not beneficent, nor did it take account of their late start, caring nothing for the emotions of their exhausting day, and as well the sun was unconcerned with their lack of shade, for the sun, stoic, could only express itself in what, if forced into human words, would express one way or the other, simply: this is what I do. And so the men pushed on, finishing a few little bottles of water, what they had left, down below sea level, under the mortiferous mate of the moon, finally collapsed at the edge of Badwater Basin, having seen no point in swaying in the heat like willows on a rock road rarely traveled. Throw in a wrong turn, an impossible fold of terraform, a cold night, another blistering day, if necessary.

Mixed feelings? Such were not in the Gravel bred.

I have them. But thousands of Mexicans perish similarly in less honorific deserts in their old homeland. And when will the description of gore prevent the perpetuations of gore?

So to their final moments at play.

When it was clear that it was going to come to a rapid end, Daddy Gravel pulled out his deck of cards, lifted from the glove box. The desert was so bare here even pebbles were rare, making of them fine gelt. Five card stud. They were two purists.

Tom dealt the last two cards up:

A three of diamonds, a ten of clubs.

Tom Gravel had five stones within reach. In a few minutes he had them in the pot.

"There—bet five." Let us not imagine his thirst, the real sound of those calcified words.

Donnie Gravel's face, crusting, was unperturbed as a skull.

He heaved about like a man with crushed legs, a merman under merciless sun, finally swaying his face like that of a monitor lizard verily hovering the pot, pushing forward nine rocks. We needn't count the seconds it took to move those little stones to the widening pot zone.

"Ten, old man. Bet ten."

Gravel knew a bluff when he saw one. "Take it, Donnie. I drop. Take it," he said.

Izola, July 2, 2015

ZEROGRAM PRESS

WEBSITE:
www.zerogrampress.com
EMAIL:
info@zerogrampress.com

Distributed by Small Press United / Independent Publishers Group
(800) 888-4741 / www.ipgbook.com

*

TITLES

Gabriel Blackwell *Doom Town* 2022
Jen Craig *Panthers and the Museum of Fire* 2020
Steve Erickson *American Stutter* 2022
Hélène Gaudy *A World with No Shore* 2022
Jim Gauer *Novel Explosives* 2016
Greg Gerke *See What I See: Essays* 2021
Rick Harsch *The Manifold Destiny of Eddie Vegas* 2022
Steven Moore *My Back Pages: Reviews and Essays* 2017
    Alexander Theroux: A Fan's Notes 2020
Nicholas John Turner *Hang Him When He Is Not There* 2021